DARK ALLIANCE TRILOGY

THE CHILDREN OF THE GODS SERIES BOOKS 68-70

I. T. LUCAS

My Merman Prince
The Dragon King
My Werewolf Romeo
The Channeler's Companion

The Children of the Gods Series Sets

Books 1-3: Dark Stranger trilogy—Includes a bonus short story: The Fates take a Vacation

Books 4-6: Dark Enemy Trilogy —Includes a bonus short story —The Fates' Post-Wedding Celebration

Books 7-10: Dark Warrior Tetralogy

Books 11-13: Dark Guardian Trilogy

Books 14-16: Dark Angel Trilogy

Books 17-19: Dark Operative Trilogy

Books 20-22: Dark Survivor Trilogy

Books 23-25: Dark Widow Trilogy

Books 26-28: Dark Dream Trilogy

Books 29-31: Dark Prince Trilogy

Books 32-34: Dark Queen Trilogy

Books 35-37: Dark Spy Trilogy

Books 38-40: Dark Overlord Trilogy

Books 41-43: Dark Choices Trilogy

Books 44-46: Dark Secrets Trilogy

Books 47-49: Dark Haven Trilogy

Books 50-52: Dark Power Trilogy

Books 53-55: Dark Memories Trilogy

Books 56-58: Dark Hunter Trilogy

Books 59-61: Dark God Trilogy

Books 62-64: Dark Whispers Trilogy

Books 65-67: Dark Gambit Trilogy

Books 68-70: Dark Alliance Trilogy

MEGA SETS
INCLUDE CHARACTER LISTS

The Children of the Gods: Books 1-6

THE CHILDREN OF THE GODS: BOOKS 6.5-10

PERFECT MATCH BUNDLES
PERFECT MATCH BUNDLE 1

**TRY THE CHILDREN OF THE GODS SERIES ON
AUDIBLE**
2 FREE audiobooks with your new Audible subscription!

KINDRED SOULS

JADE

*J*ade strode into the infirmary and surveyed the cots that had been arranged in two neat rows in the center of the room. Several had been vacated, but many were still occupied.

Immortal Guardians watched over the injured, and for some reason, one of them was sitting on a chair next to her second-in-command's cot and was holding her hand. With his back turned to her, she couldn't see his face, but given the breadth of his shoulders, he wasn't a Kra-ell. The males of her species were much stronger than the immortals, but they were built slimmer.

Besides, no Kra-ell male would have shown Kagra such disrespect.

Mothers held their children's hands when they were small and frightened, but Kagra was a grown female and a warrior, and according to the liberators' doctor, she wasn't dying.

Liberators.

That still remained to be seen.

So far, the god who called himself Tom had done what he'd promised and more, freeing her people without a single unintended casualty, but Jade didn't trust gods, and that included the scions of the progressives who'd fought alongside the Kra-ell in the big rebellion back on the home planet.

Even when their intentions were noble, the gods' patronizing attitude toward the Kra-ell was offensive, and their ingrained belief in their own superiority was infuriating.

Jade had no choice but to accept Tom's help, and she still needed him to catch Igor so she could finally avenge her sons and the other males of her tribe. But once that was done, she wouldn't let the god or his immortal companions rule over her and her people.

Given that Tom was a powerful compeller on a par with Igor, that might not be easy to do, but she'd be damned if she lived another day enslaved to a male or a female, for that matter.

If Jade ever served anyone again, it would be by choice, and she would only serve a worthy Kra-ell ruler like the queen and her children, who Jade had sworn to protect.

Well, she'd only sworn to protect the queen, and she was no longer in the queen's service, but once a vow was made it never expired, and it didn't matter that she wasn't supposed to even know that the royal twins had been onboard the ship heading to Earth.

She'd failed to protect them just as she'd failed to protect her people, but there was no guilt associated with that failure because there had been nothing she could have done to prevent their ship's destruction, and without the mother ship, there was no way for her to locate the other escape pods.

In all likelihood, the twins and most of the other settlers hadn't survived.

Walking over to Kagra's cot, Jade grabbed a stool on the way and placed it next to the immortal's chair. "Does my second-in-command require a dedicated guard?"

It would have been better to conduct this conversation while she was looming over him, but the effect would have been lost if she had wobbled on her feet.

How long had she been awake?

It felt like she hadn't slept for days.

Given the copious quantity of Valstar's blood Jade had gorged on, she should have felt energized, but his blood must have been contaminated by the drug she'd put in his drink, and she could feel its effects. It was only by the Mother's grace that she'd functioned as well as she had and killed four of her sons' murderers. Kagra had dispatched two more, but she'd nearly lost her own life in the process.

Nevertheless, Jade wasn't going to get any sleep until Igor showed up. It was already eleven o'clock in the morning, and she was starting to get worried.

The immortal tilted his head and smiled. "I'm not here to guard your second. I'm checking on the female whose life I saved." He let go of Kagra's hand and offered his hand to Jade. "I'm Phinas."

So he was the one she'd heard about. The Guardian who'd leaped from fifty feet away and smashed his exoskeleton-reinforced fist into Gorven's head, killing him on impact.

From what Jade had been told, it was no small feat to perform such acrobatics with the tremendously heavy suit on.

The immortal was an impressive warrior.

"I'm Jade." Shaking what he'd offered, she dipped her head in respect. "Thank you for saving Kagra. I owe you a life-debt."

He held on to her hand. "You don't owe me anything because I didn't do it for you. But just out of curiosity, what does a life-debt mean?"

She liked his reply. But even though he hadn't saved Kagra for her, she still owed him a life-debt, and once it was offered, it had to be paid. "It means that I will defend you with my life if needed, and anything you ask of me is yours."

He arched a brow with a sly smile lifting one corner of his full lips. "Anything?"

Males.

No matter what species they were, they had only one thing on their minds. Although with how exhausted and dirty Jade was, the evidence of what she'd done crusting over her leathers, Phinas must be either teasing or just not very discriminating about the females he flirted with.

Then again, warriors pumped up from the battle were more lustful than usual.

To answer his question, though, anything meant anything.

Jade held his gaze. "That's what I said."

"What if I ask for your firstborn?"

She winced. "Too late for that. Both my first and second born sons are dead, slaughtered by Igor and his cronies."

The smile died on his lips, and he inclined his head. "My apologies. I didn't know."

"I thought that the Guardians had been briefed about the history of my tribe. Tom knew about my sons even before he got here, and so did Marcel, Sofia's boyfriend."

"I'm not a Guardian," Phinas said.

Was he a medic? That would explain why he was checking up on Kagra. Military medical staff received the same training as warriors, but if he were a medic, the doctor would have introduced him to her. Maybe he was in charge of munitions, or a tech?

"I was told that the one who'd saved Kagra's life wore an exoskeleton suit. Did the techs and medics get to wear them too?"

He smiled. "I'm not a tech or a medic. I'm first and foremost a warrior, but I'm not a Guardian because I'm not part of the Guardian force. I'm part of a group of volunteers." He glanced at one of the Guardians standing watch over the injured. "What do you call me and my men?"

"Kalugal's men," the Guardian said.

"Who is Kalugal?" Jade asked.

When Phinas glanced at the Guardian again, the guy shook his head.

"I'm sorry." Phinas smiled apologetically. "I'm not at liberty to discuss the clan's inner politics with you. You will have to ask Yamanu or Bhathian. They are in charge of this operation."

"I thought Tom was in charge."

Phinas shrugged. "I can't comment on that either. All I can tell you is that Tom is not a Guardian."

"That makes sense." He was a god, but the other Kra-ell in the infirmary didn't know that. She couldn't say it out loud. "He wouldn't be part of the military arm of the clan. That would be left to the descendants."

"That's correct." Phinas flashed her a charming smile. "It's a pleasure to talk to a female who is a warrior herself and knows how those things work."

"I assume that your females are not fighters."

He shook his head. "That's another thing I cannot comment on. All I can say is that I haven't had the pleasure of chatting with a female fighter before." He turned his gaze to Kagra. "Watching her fight was awe-inspiring. I have been trained to fight with swords and daggers, and I recognize skill when I see it. She's incredible."

Pride filled Jade's chest. "Kagra is exceptional. That's why I chose her as my second–in–command. When she wakes up, she will be upset about letting herself get gutted."

Jade turned around to look for the doctor the Guardians had brought along. She found him on the other side of the large room, checking on one of the injured hybrids.

When he felt her gaze and lifted his head, she asked, "Why is Kagra sleeping so much? You said that she's healing well."

He smiled sheepishly. "I gave her sedatives so she'd sleep."

"I thought you were only giving her painkillers."

He put his hand in his coat pocket. "I gave her both. Sleeping will help her heal faster."

2

PHINAS

*P*hinas took the opportunity of Jade talking with Merlin to adjust himself and cross his legs.

From the moment he'd laid eyes on her, he'd been sporting a hard-on that he'd been desperately trying to hide. Despite being exhausted, dirty, and covered in dry blood splotches, the female was so damn hot that she made him as randy as a buck in heat.

It wasn't his style.

Phinas was coolheaded and reserved, and he'd never let females get under his skin.

Perhaps the spike in his libido had been caused by the testosterone still coursing through his blood after the battle, or maybe it was the fault of those damn tight leather pants and sheer mesh shirt of hers, or maybe the turn-on was the sword sheathed in a fancy scabbard and hung low on her hips, her swagger as she'd walked into the infirmary, the palpable power radiating from her, or all of the above.

Regardless of the trigger, though, the result was the same. He'd had trouble stringing two coherent thoughts together, as evidenced by his unfortunate blunder.

He'd heard that the males of Jade's tribe had been slaughtered by her captors, and he should have realized that she could have had a son or sons among them. But that was what happened when his mind was occupied by thoughts of stripping her naked.

He would leave the sword belt and boots on, though.

Jade was tall and slim, and her face was beautiful despite her huge eyes and hard expression. She had no breasts to speak of, but her ass was round and firm, just the way he liked it. However, the disturbing truth was that he was more turned on by her inner power than by her enticing feminine assets, and the fact that she was a ruthless killer only added to her dangerous allure.

That was strange as hell for him and entirely out of character.

Despite having been raised in Navuh's camp among males who believed that women were created to please and serve them and breed, Phinas wasn't a misogynist.

He'd never been one, but he was old, and in days past, women and men had very different roles in society.

Female warriors did not exist in his world, but he'd always believed that being mothers and caretakers was no less important, probably more so, but like other males of the time, he believed that motherhood was a female's ultimate calling and that women weren't suited for jobs that men performed.

Warriors took lives. Women created life and nurtured it.

After he'd been recruited by Kalugal and escaped Navuh's camp, Phinas had traveled to the US, where at the time women had been regarded with a little more respect, but not by much.

It had taken many more years for Western society to realize what had taken him mere weeks.

As soon as Phinas had been able to interact with women who were free to express themselves, he'd realized that they were as smart and as capable as men, just not as physically strong and aggressive, and that was fine. Not every male was born to be a fighter, either.

That being said, he was a dominant male by nature, and he'd never thought he would be attracted to someone like Jade. A female who could hand him his ass.

"Are you going to sit here all day?" Jade asked him. "Aren't you needed somewhere else?"

He arched a brow. "Does it bother you that I'm watching over Kagra?"

What he'd really wanted to ask was whether she was jealous of the attention he was giving her injured second.

"Kagra has the doctor to watch over her." Jade hung her head and let out a breath. "I'm so damn tired, but that's not an excuse. You're not one of my subjects, and what you do with your time is none of my business."

9

"You're not one of my subjects either, but my advice to you is to get some sleep."

"I can't. There is still so much to do, and Kagra is out, so I have no one to assist me. But even if she was fine, I still wouldn't go to sleep. I'm waiting for Igor's capture so I can finally kill him."

As a vicious expression twisted her lips, her fangs made an appearance, and her eyes blazed with red light, but even that wasn't enough to diminish his attraction to her.

On the contrary, he wanted her even more.

"You won't be much good to anyone when you fall flat on your face. You need to sleep for at least a couple of hours to recharge." He waved his hand at the empty cot next to Kagra's. "You can lie down right over here, and I'll wake you up the moment Igor is captured."

"I also need to talk to my daughter." She looked at the cot longingly. "But maybe I should rest for a few minutes before I do that." She pushed to her feet and walked to the other cot.

"How old is she?"

"Drova is sixteen." Jade unbuckled her sword belt. "She's a fine female with a lot of potential, but we don't get along, and I'm about to kill her father, which isn't going to help make things better between us." She put the sword under the cot and lay down with her boots on.

He had a feeling that Jade wouldn't have shared that information if she wasn't so tired, which made her less guarded.

It probably wasn't a secret that Igor was the father of her daughter, but it wasn't the kind of thing a woman told a stranger she'd just met.

The murderer of her sons had forced her to breed with him.

Jade must be forged from titanium alloy.

"Is she close to her father?" Phinas asked.

Jade snorted. "No one is close to Igor. He's a sociopath. But he's still her father." She closed her eyes. "Maybe I should kill him first and talk to her later?"

She turned on her side, giving him a great view of her gorgeous ass. "I'm just going to rest for a few minutes."

"You should rest for longer than that. I'll watch over you," he said with such conviction that she turned around and looked at him.

"Thank you. But that won't be necessary." Jade waved her hand at the Guardians. "I'm sure they can protect me if needed."

He doubted she would rely on them to defend her. Her sword was right there under her cot, reachable in a split second.

"I'm not going anywhere." He crossed his arms over his chest.

"Suit yourself." She turned around again.

Phinas wanted to learn more about Jade, to find out what kind of hellfire had forged such a tough female, but it would have to wait until after she'd exacted revenge for the slaughter of the males of her tribe and the subjugation of its females.

3

KIAN

The last person Kian had expected to walk into the war room at one o'clock in the morning was his mother.

He pushed to his feet, walked over to her, and leaned to kiss her cheek. "Did you have trouble sleeping, Mother?"

A goddess only needed a few hours of sleep, but his mother was an early riser, and she enjoyed walking outside when the sun was just cresting the horizon. Her eyes were too sensitive for the harsh Southern California sun, even in the winter, and she liked being able to forgo the goggle-like sunglasses that she needed to wear other times when getting out of the house.

"I brought you coffee and pastries from the vending machines." She motioned for her butler to come in.

"Good evening, Master Kian." The Odu put the tray with the coffees and the wrapped pastries on the conference table, bowed, and headed out the door.

Kian pulled out a chair for her. "You still haven't told me why you are up and about so late."

She shrugged one delicate shoulder. "I could not sleep, and I did not want to call you in case you were in the midst of directing the battle, and I didn't want to call the house and wake Syssi up either. So I came to see if you were still here and whether the evil Igor was captured." She smiled. "If I

12

had known that you were all alone in here, I would have come to keep you company earlier."

She could've texted him, but she just hadn't wanted to give him a chance to tell her not to come.

After he'd told her about Jade's promise to Toven, Annani probably couldn't contain her curiosity. She wanted to hear what Jade had told Toven about the gods, the Kra-ell, and their home planet.

Kian took one of the paper cups and removed the lid. "Turner and Onegus went home to shower and change and catch a couple of hours of sleep, but they are coming back."

"You should have done the same."

"Until Igor is caught, someone needs to be in the war room at all times. Roni is in the lab, monitoring Igor's bank accounts, and I'm getting updates from the compound."

"How is Toven doing?" she asked.

"He and Mia worked all night to free everyone from Igor's compulsion, and last I heard, they were asleep on the couch in the common room in the human section. William removed everyone's collars, and he's resting as well. The Guardians are taking turns watching the purebloods and the hybrids, and Merlin is taking care of the injured. Did I cover everyone?"

"You didn't mention Marcel and Sofia."

Kian smiled. His mother was well-informed, and she had everyone cataloged in her brain. He could throw at her the name of any clan member, and she would know everything about them, down to their favorite foods and where they had visited on their last vacation.

Remembering that many details about so many people was a truly remarkable ability, but what was even more remarkable was how much she cared about each member of her clan.

"They are also in the human quarters, helping calm people down."

"How is Jade?"

"The last I heard, she took a nap on one of the cots in the infirmary. Her second-in-command was badly injured. Merlin patched her up, and she's going to be fine."

He'd already told her that there were no casualties on their side and that on the Kra-ell side, only Igor's inner circle cronies had been killed by Jade and Kagra, and several purebloods and hybrids were injured.

Annani smoothed the folds of her gown, readjusting it over her knees. "You know what I really want to know. You were too busy before, but this seems like a quiet time, and you can spare a few minutes to tell me what Jade shared with Toven about the gods."

Kian winced. "You're not going to like what I tell you."

"I want to hear it anyway."

"The gods weren't nice people, and those who they sent to Earth were rebels, banished here for their part in a rebellion."

Annani nodded solemnly. "I had a feeling it was something like that. Otherwise, they would not have been abandoned on Earth with no ability to return home or even communicate with their families."

"There is one part that you're going to love, though. You are most likely the granddaughter of the gods' king. Some of the rebels were his own children, and he sent them to Earth along with the others. Given that Ahn, Ekin, and Athor were all leaders of the gods' local community, each in their respective field of authority, they were no doubt royalty."

Annani smiled. "I had a feeling about that as well. My father wore the mantle of leadership with such inborn grace and dignity, but he never called himself king. Nevertheless, my mother insisted that I behave like a princess." She smoothed her skirt again even though it didn't need it. "What was the rebellion about?"

"The Kra-ell. Turns out that the Kra-ell were the gods' first attempt at creating a hybrid creature to serve them. But the old gods were not as progressive as your father and his siblings. They treated the Kra-ell like slaves. The young gods did not approve of the way the Kra-ell were being treated or rather mistreated. First, they demanded better conditions for the Kra-ell, and when that was achieved, they demanded equal rights and access to education, but the king and his council refused." Kian paused to unwrap a pastry. "Jade said that hundreds of generations passed between the stages of the Kra-ell emancipation, so it wasn't like those demands were made one right after the other."

"What happened during the rebellion?" Annani asked.

"The Kra-ell were stronger physically, which was probably by design because they were meant to be laborers, and back then, the gods didn't include susceptibility to mind manipulation in their genetic enhancements, so they couldn't defend themselves by seizing the Kra-ell minds. The gods had superior weapons, and their underground cities were fortified, but the Kra-ell had the numbers. The king mobilized the Odus, who were originally designed to be house servants, and they were converted to be defenders of the gods against the Kra-ell. But even with the Odus, the gods couldn't win, and the casualties on both sides were staggering. The king of the gods and the queen of the Kra-ell negotiated a peace treaty, and part of it was the decommissioning of the Odus." He leaned back and took a sip from his coffee. "In my opinion, the only reason for the king of the gods to agree to decommission the Odus was fear of them being used against him in another rebellion. Otherwise, it makes no sense for the gods to give up their best defensive weapon."

Annani tilted her head. "It might not be their best weapon anymore. Once the rebellion was over, they probably developed something better than the Odus and made sure that it could not fall into the wrong hands, or what they considered rebel hands."

"I agree."

They were probably both right. Kian wasn't much of a politician, but he knew how they operated, especially those who had been in power for too long and had no intentions of losing their seat to another. After the king decommissioned the Odus, most likely with a lot of fanfare and publicity for the consumption of his public, he must have started developing an alternative in secret. There was no way he'd left himself exposed to the possibility of another rebellion.

The next time someone dared to oppose him, he would have had a brutal and efficient response at the ready, one that was entirely under his control.

In fact, with the genetic manipulation mastery of the gods, he'd probably ordered another species to be altered for that purpose—creatures who were as strong as the Kra-ell but susceptible to mind manipulation and easy to destroy.

Was Kian letting his imagination run away from him?

Maybe.

But as it'd been proven time and again, reality was stranger than fiction.

"Was that the full version or a summary of what Jade had told Toven?" Annani asked. "So many questions remain unanswered."

"It was a summary, but Jade's full version was far from complete either. There are many things she probably doesn't know, and her spin is obviously tilted in the Kra-ell's favor. After Igor is apprehended and Jade takes charge of her community, we will ask her to tell us more."

4

TOVEN

"*I*'m worried." Toven ran his fingers through his hair. "Igor should have called by now."

It was almost two o'clock in the afternoon, and it was becoming clear that Igor was onto them. There was still a chance that he was on his way, maybe flying back from Moscow or some other distant location, but the fact that he hadn't tried to call Valstar or anyone else was telling.

That was why Toven had called the meeting. He, William, and the head guardians had assembled in the human quarters' common room, with Kian, Onegus, and Turner participating in the meeting via the tablet propped on the coffee table.

The humans stayed away, giving them the privacy they needed, and Yamanu had encased them in a bubble of silence to make sure no one could listen in on them.

Bhathian nodded. "What really bothers me is that when we turned the compound's communications back on, there weren't any missed calls from him in the logs."

As all eyes turned to William, he rubbed a finger over the bridge of his nose as if he was pushing his glasses up, except he wasn't wearing any. "I don't know what to tell you. I double checked all the transmissions, and everything is working fine. At six o'clock in the morning, we switched on the recorded footage and set it to transmit normal Monday morning activity. He shouldn't have noticed anything amiss unless he spent hours watching and noticed that it was going on a loop."

"Did he try to detonate the explosives?" Kian asked.

William shook his head. "He didn't. Neither did he attempt to detonate the collars. I checked."

"What now?" Toven asked. "Until Igor is caught, we have to keep the purebloods and the hybrids on lockdown. How much longer do we wait?"

"We can't wait," Turner said. "It's true that Igor has only one pureblood and two hybrids with him, but he could use his compulsion power to bring the Russian Army to storm the compound or even their air force to bomb the place, although I doubt he would go that far. I assume that he wants his people back alive."

"I'm not so sure," Kian said. "If he had the entire place rigged, he has no qualms about bombing the compound and killing everyone."

Turner shook his head. "He can't do that. I think the rigging was meant as a last-stand kind of thing, and he didn't intend to implement it unless all hope was lost. According to what Jade told us, it seems that Igor doesn't know where to find more of the surviving Kra-ell, and without his people, he has nothing. He needs the females to keep breeding more Kra-ell, and he even needs some of the males to provide the necessary genetic variety. He would do anything to get his people back, or at least some of them."

Yamanu stretched his long legs in front of him. "I still don't get how he figured out what was going on here. Even if he noticed something was off with what the hidden cameras were transmitting, he couldn't have guessed that a stronger compeller took over his people, because he couldn't possibly have known about Toven. Igor would have assumed that he could just walk back in and compel everyone to his will."

"I'm not sure about that," Toven said. "Jade knew that the gods' king exiled several of his children to Earth, and the king was a powerful compeller. It's not such a huge leap to assume that some of them or their descendants possess the ability. The fact that they couldn't find us didn't mean that we were gone."

"It's also possible that there are strong compellers among the other survivors," Turner said. "Jade didn't mention it, but then she didn't tell us much at all. It's also possible that once Igor suspected something, he gained access to satellite footage of the area. The explosions in the middle of the night would have registered clearly despite the heavy foliage. Yamanu's enormous silencing bubble hid the blasts from the humans in the area, but it could not have hidden them from satellites and other monitoring equipment. If the Russians measure seismic activity in the area, the explosions would have registered on that equipment as well."

"Where is Jade?" Kian asked. "Perhaps she has some ideas."

"Asleep," Bhathian said. "She went to visit her second-in-command in the infirmary and fell asleep on one of the cots. Phinas is watching over her."

"You should wake her up," Turner said. "And you should also interrogate Valstar again. He probably knows Igor better than Jade does."

"I should do that." Toven pushed to his feet. "When I first interrogated him, I asked questions that pertained to catching Igor upon his return. The guy is used to living under a powerful compeller, so he knows all the tricks of how to avoid answering questions unless they are very precisely phrased, and I might not have asked the right ones."

"Are you going to take Mia to him?" Kian asked.

"She's asleep, and I don't need her now that Valstar is no longer under Igor's compulsion." Toven chuckled. "I'm glad that we didn't allow Jade to kill him. He might know a lot of things that she doesn't, and it would be interesting to compare their versions of history."

"By the way," Bhathian said. "Did Igor try to call Safe Haven? He must have suspected that there was a connection."

"All incoming calls are filtered through the translating software," Onegus said. "Even if he tried to get to Emmett, he wouldn't have been able to get any information out of him. Besides, it's the middle of the night there. All he would have gotten was the answering machine."

"True," Turner said. "Leon is on high alert. He will let us know if Igor tries to contact Emmett or Sofia."

5

JADE

*J*ade knew she was dreaming, but it didn't make her anguish any less torturous. For over two decades, she'd been plagued by the nightmare of her people being murdered while she and the other females watched, helpless to do anything to stop the slaughter.

Igor had frozen everyone with one command, making it easy for his cronies to plow through the males of her tribe as if they were stalks of grain. The horror in their eyes was as fresh in her mind today as it had been back then. Unable to move a muscle, the males watched their sons and brothers die moments before their own end had come.

Something had broken inside her that day, and ever since, the only thing keeping her from falling apart was rage and the need for revenge.

Her males hadn't fallen in battle or died in a duel. They had been denied an honorable death and therefore hadn't earned a place in the fields of the brave.

Igor had not only robbed them of their corporeal lives, but he had also destroyed their eternity on the other side of the veil. Back home, only the worst of criminals had been executed without being given the option to fight to win their freedom or die honorably, but the only crime her males had ever committed was having been born male.

Had the Mother shown them mercy and allowed them to enter the fields of the brave? They would have fought if they could. Was it fair to deny them access through no fault of their own?

"Please," Jade begged the deity of her people for the thousandth time. "Please."

"Jade." A hand shook her shoulder. "Wake up."

She bolted up, nearly toppling over the side of the flimsy cot. Nevertheless, her hand shot up to grip the throat of the male standing over her.

"Whoa." He caught her wrist and applied pressure. "It's me, Phinas. Let go."

It took a split second for the memory of him to resurface, and as it did, she released him immediately. "Never do that again," she hissed through elongated fangs.

"Noted." He rubbed his neck. "Were you having a nightmare?"

There was no shame in having nightmares about the slaughter of her people. Being tough didn't mean being heartless or indifferent. "Yes." She reached for the sword under the cot. "How long was I asleep?"

"Almost three hours," Kagra said from behind Phinas.

Jade swallowed a vile curse. "Was Igor caught?"

"No." Phinas moved aside. "I have a feeling he's onto us."

Jade's fangs throbbed with the thirst for Igor's blood. "If he doesn't show up, I will hunt him to the ends of the earth and any other world he might escape to." She buckled the sword belt around her hips. "I will bleed him to death very slowly and very painfully."

Phinas grinned. "I shouldn't say what I'm about to, but I can't help it. You're even hotter when you're vicious."

Males.

Phinas had no sense of self-preservation. She'd had him by the throat only moments ago, and he'd felt the power of her grip. She could've snapped his neck with ease.

The guy was either stupidly reckless or just as stupidly brave.

Nevertheless, his impudence was refreshing.

No one had ever dared speak to her like that, not even Igor.

Except with Igor, it wasn't because he respected or feared her. He just lacked a sense of humor and was too full of himself to engage in any sort of banter or mischief.

Phinas didn't fear her either, but he didn't take himself too seriously, and he had a sense of humor.

Jade glanced down at her blood-encrusted leathers. "Since I'm always vicious, my level of hotness doesn't change."

His grin widened. "I agree. It's a solid ten."

Stifling the urge to roll her eyes, she crouched next to Kagra. "How are you feeling?"

"Mad as hell. As soon as I can stand, I want us to resume training. This would never have happened to you."

"Everyone makes mistakes." Jade put her hand on Kagra's shoulder. "Get well first, and then we will resume training." She turned her head to look at the clan's doctor. "When can she leave?"

He walked over and spoke in a hushed voice. "I stitched her up, but I don't know how fast her inner wounds are healing. Your infirmary doesn't have the equipment to take a look inside of her. You probably have more experience in that than me."

Except for her and Kagra, no one else knew that their liberators were the descendants of gods, so Merlin couldn't talk about it within earshot of the other injured Kra-ell, and she couldn't ask him about it either. It made sense though, that immortals healed faster than them.

Thanks to their enhanced genetics, gods healed so fast that it almost seemed like magic. Their immortal descendants had probably inherited that trait, at least to some degree.

Jade nodded to communicate her understanding. "Kagra should be okay to walk to the bathroom and back, but she needs to rest for another day or two. It doesn't have to be in the infirmary, though. She can convalesce in her room."

"I'd rather keep an eye on her." Merlin looked at Phinas. "But she doesn't need a personal nurse. I'm sure you have better things to do than hang around here."

"I do." Phinas cast Kagra a brief smile before returning his gaze to Jade. "I just wanted to make sure that she was okay."

"I owe you a life—" Kagra started.

Jade snapped her hand faster than she did when she grabbed Phinas's throat and silenced Kagra with a hand on her mouth. "I've already pledged a life-debt to Phinas." She removed her hand. "You don't have to pledge yours as well."

Kagra frowned. "Why did you do that? It's my debt to pay."

"Your life is precious to me, and I'm grateful to Phinas for saving you. Enough said."

Given Kagra's sour expression, there was much more she wanted to say on the subject, but she obeyed Jade's command. "Thank you, Prime." She didn't even try to hide the note of sarcasm in her tone.

"Get some rest." Jade turned to glare at Phinas. "You should have woken me up a long time ago."

"I should have, but I didn't want to. You needed the rest."

She got in his face. "Next time, if there is a next time, I will not trust your promises."

"Ouch."

6

PHINAS

*P*hinas couldn't wipe the stupid grin off his face as he left the infirmary, and it stayed there while he searched for a secluded spot to call Kalugal.

It had been almost comical the way Jade had slapped her hand over Kagra's mouth to stop her from pledging a life-debt to him, and if that wasn't enough, she'd commanded her second to say nothing more on the subject.

Was he kidding himself by thinking that Jade wanted to owe him so he could collect on the debt?

And why the hell did he want her even more after her vicious show of fangs and red eyes?

She'd looked like a sexy demon. Dangerous, deadly, exciting.

Perhaps he had a subconscious death wish? Was that the source of his insane attraction to the Kra-ell leader?

Her commanding personality and palpable aggression weren't the only things that drew him to her, though.

Despite her hard-as-nails attitude, he'd sensed the vulnerability ever-present right under the tough façade. Jade was broken on the inside, and the glue holding the pieces together was her formidable will and her devotion to her people.

He respected that.

He understood that.

He could empathize with that.

Phinas had lost people he'd cared for, and he'd killed people on orders that he should have disobeyed, but his broken pieces were held together by a different bond.

While Jade carried the burden of her losses and her obligations on her shoulders and tried to keep herself from falling apart on her own, Phinas had Kalugal and the promise of better tomorrows helping him hold together the jagged shards of his soul.

When he found a quiet spot between two buildings, he leaned against a wall and pulled out his phone.

"Hello, Phinas," Kalugal answered. "Any news on Igor?"

"As you expected, he didn't show up."

Kalugal chuckled. "When you told me that there were no missed calls from him, I knew that he found out somehow. What are they planning to do next?"

"I don't know. There was a meeting in the human quarters, but I wasn't invited."

Kalugal huffed out a breath. "Kian can be insufferable. He accepted my help with open arms, but he still keeps things close to his chest and doesn't share. Did you manage to befriend the female you saved?"

Phinas grinned. "I did better than that. I befriended the notorious Jade. In her gratitude for saving her second-in-command, she swore a life-debt to me, which means that I can ask anything I want of her, and she's obligated to provide it."

His boss uttered a whistle. "I'm impressed. That's better than anything I was hoping to achieve. You know what I want."

Kalugal wanted information about the Kra-ell, and, if possible, cooperation, but Phinas wanted more than that.

"I do, but I need to wait for an opportune time. As you can imagine, she has her hands full, so it's not like I can sit her down for a chat."

"Naturally. I'll talk with Kian and volunteer your services for the foreseeable future. Once the Guardians leave, you will have her all to yourself."

"They are not going to leave so soon. Not with Igor still at large. Toven has to stay to ensure their safety."

"Right. But they can't stay forever, and they need someone to keep an eye on Jade to ensure that she's not mistreating the humans. You know how important that is to Kian and Annani. Since they can't spare more than one or two Guardians, who will be very unhappy to be stuck in freezing Karelia,

Kian will be very happy when I offer for you to stay for a bit longer. I hope you don't mind."

"I can't say that I'm enjoying the weather out here, but it is beautiful and very serene." He chuckled. "That is when the clan is not blowing things up. But I wouldn't stay just to enjoy the forest and the numerous rivers and lakes. My only motivation is getting close to Jade, and not just because you asked me to do that."

"Other than the life-debt, how friendly did you get with her?"

"Very friendly, and I plan on getting much friendlier still."

Kalugal cleared his throat. "I appreciate your loyalty and your willingness to do anything I ask of you, but you have to know that I would never expect you to get that friendly with a female who repulses you."

A laugh bubbled up Phinas's throat. "Jade is the hottest female I've ever laid eyes on, and I can't wait to lay more than just my gaze on her. She's gorgeous, has a body to kill for, and she's powerful, honorable, and vicious like a viper."

He stopped himself before adding that he'd been hard from the moment she'd walked into the infirmary and sat down next to him. Rufsur had no problem talking like that with Kalugal, but Phinas had always opted to keep a professional distance out of respect for the male who had saved his life in more ways than one.

For a long moment, Kalugal didn't say anything, and then he cleared his throat again. "If you were repulsed by Aliya's occasional need for blood, how are you going to tolerate a female who can't subsist on anything else?"

"I've never said that Aliya's need for blood repulsed me. What made you think that?"

"You stopped seeing her after you took her hunting, so the rumor was that you were disgusted by her being a bloodsucker."

Phinas snorted. "Don't believe all the rumors you hear. That wasn't the reason I disengaged."

"Was it because of Vrog? Since when did you concede a competition to allow a rival to win?"

"Never. I just realized that Aliya wasn't for me. I was attracted to her for many reasons. She's a beautiful girl who is also extremely strong, physically and mentally. But during our hunt together, I got to know her better, and I discovered that emotionally, she's just a girl, young and inexperienced. Vrog loves being a teacher. I don't. I prefer older women who know what they want and how they want it."

7

JADE

ade needed a shower and a change of clothes, not just because hers were filthy but also because they were unsuitable for winter in Karelia and uncomfortable. Except, the worry churning in her gut propelled her toward the human quarters where she'd been told she could find Tom.

She found him walking toward her, looking rested and wearing clean clothes.

Where had he gotten them?

They must have left clothing along with the provisions outside the compound and had gotten them after the dust had settled and everything had been taken care of. She'd seen the Guardians eating field rations, and they couldn't have carried them inside the exoskeletons.

"Good morning." He stopped in front of her. "Did you have a nice nap?"

Was he insinuating that she was a weakling who had taken time to rest while the rest of them had kept working to trap Igor?

"Did you? When I left you earlier, you and your mate were asleep on the couch."

He leaned closer and whispered in her ear. "I only need two to three hours of sleep a night, but my mate needs a little more. What are your sleep requirements?"

Show-off.

The gods prided themselves on how little sleep their bodies needed to keep operating at an optimal level, and she had no doubt that it was one of the first things they had genetically modified. That allowed them to do more each day, either learning or continuing to create miraculous enhancements for themselves.

"I need a little more. What are you going to do about Igor? By now, it's obvious that he knows."

Tom's expression was severe, but he didn't look too worried. "He might still come. The only indication we have to the contrary is that he hasn't called, which seems out of character for him."

"It is. He would have checked with Valstar first thing in the morning. Is it possible that he noticed something was off about the camera feeds?"

"If he watched carefully over an extended period of time, he might have noticed the loop, but even a paranoid guy like him is not likely to do that. He's too busy for that."

"He could have assigned one of the hybrids to do that. What about Veskar? Did Igor try to call him?"

Tom shook his head. "Even if he did, he wouldn't have been able to get any information out of Emmett. All of Safe Haven's communications are routed through a voice translator. It works similarly to the earpieces I showed you."

In all the commotion, she'd forgotten about the devices, but she would need them when the time arrived to end Igor.

"Can I have a pair?"

"With Igor gone, you don't need them, and I don't want you to block my compulsion."

Jade bristled. "You have nothing to fear from me. I owe you, and I will never turn against you unless you go back on your word to me. But what if Igor comes back and manages to overtake the Guardians waiting for him in the tunnel? Are you sure he can't compel you? And even if he can't, you might not be able to compel him either, and he can wrestle control from you over everyone here, including your Guardians. With their unwilling help, he can end even you."

"We all have earpieces." He pulled a pair from his pocket and showed them to her. "But your point is valid. I'll ask William to provide you and Kagra with a pair each."

"Thank you."

"How is Kagra doing?" he asked.

"She's better. She woke up before I left."

"Good." Tom put the earpieces back in his pocket. "I'm on my way to see

Valstar. I might not have asked all the right questions when I interrogated him earlier. Maybe he'll have some valuable insight as to what Igor's next move will be, and he also might know how Igor found out about what happened to his compound."

Her fangs itched as they elongated into her mouth.

"I'll come with you."

"That's not a good idea. I need him calm, which he won't be if you show up with murder in your eyes." He gave her a crooked smile.

"Does it matter if he's calm or not?"

"Compulsion works better if the compelled is not agitated or terrified."

It was one of those 'aha' moments Jade occasionally experienced. "That explains so much. I always wondered why Igor appeared so calm and collected and why he never raised his voice or showed anger. I thought that he just had no feelings whatsoever, but he did it for his compulsion to work better."

Tom shrugged. "Maybe it's the other way around, and his compulsion worked better because he didn't show emotion. Were you terrified of him?"

She nodded. "Compulsion is a terrible weapon in the wrong hands. I would never freeze opponents so I could kill them with ease. It's not only incredibly cruel but also dishonorable."

Tom's eyes softened. "Is that what he did to your people?"

"Yes. And he will pay for it." She took a deep breath. "You might need my input when you question Valstar. I can control myself when I must, and I'm a very good actress. I have a lot of practice."

"I believe you. But I'd rather not have you there."

"Can you at least get me a phone so you can call me?"

"We don't have any spares with us, but we might have spare earpieces, and they are also good for communicating with my people and me." He pulled out his phone and typed on the screen.

Obviously, he didn't trust her with a phone that she could use to communicate with the outside world, but who would she call?

"William says that he can get them ready for you in fifteen minutes. He'll meet you in the common room of the human quarters."

"Thank you." She looked down at her bloodied leathers. "I planned on going to see my people, but fifteen minutes is not long enough for that. Tell William that I'll be there."

She would use the time to shower and change.

Tom typed on his phone some more. "If I have any questions for you while I'm questioning Valstar, I'll contact you via the earpieces."

8

TOVEN

*T*oven entered Valstar's suite of rooms expecting the prisoner to be chained to a chair. Instead, he found him chained to the bed and looking like a corpse.

He wasn't faking it, either. His skin was gray, and there were dark hollows under his eyes and cheekbones. Paired with the bug-like eyes, Valstar wasn't a pretty sight.

"He looks bad," Toven told the Guardian watching Igor's second-in-command. "What's wrong with him?"

"I need to feed," Valstar said, sounding feeble. "Jade drained me multiple times."

"Yeah," the Guardian confirmed. "He's been saying it over and over again, but where am I going to get him blood?"

Good question. The purebloods held in the basement were probably hungry as well.

Toven turned to the prisoner. "How can we feed you? Do you have blood stored in a freezer somewhere?"

Valstar shook his head. "I know that you will not let me hunt, so the only other option is a farm animal. Take me to them."

"I'm not letting you out of this room." He glanced at the Guardian. "Ask for an animal to be brought here."

The Guardian shook his head but tapped his earpiece anyway and communicated the request.

"They are going to ask the humans tending to the animals," he said.

Several long minutes passed until he got a response. "They can bring up a goat."

Valstar licked his lips. "That would do. Have them bring two. I'm starving, and I don't want to drain the animal."

It was strange that a male who had no qualms about slaughtering the males of his kind had compassion for animals, but perhaps it wasn't about that. The Kra-ell didn't kill the animals that provided them with nourishment. It was considered a waste, and in light of what Jade had told him, it made sense. After the gods had infected the animals on their planet with a virus, the Kra-ell had experienced centuries of lack and near starvation. Waste of food would be abhorrent to them, but the culling of excessive mouths who needed to be fed would not.

"Do as he asks." Toven pulled a chair next to the bed.

"Did you catch him?" Valstar asked.

There was no need to elaborate as to who he meant.

"No."

Valstar's big eyes widened even more. "He knows. You need to get everyone out of here."

"We disabled the explosives. He can't detonate them."

"He will come with an army, or he will send a fighter jet to bomb the compound. If he can't take his people back, he would rather destroy them than let them fall into enemy hands."

"Even his own daughter?"

Valstar snorted. "Igor cares only about power. He doesn't care about anyone, including his daughter."

"How about you? Do you care?"

Perhaps it wasn't the most important question to ask the male right now, but Toven was curious. The compulsion he imbued his tone with guaranteed an honest answer.

Valstar closed his eyes and let out a breath. "For too many years, I was only allowed to feel what Igor wanted me to feel, which was nothing. I was to serve him loyally and follow his orders. I don't know who I am anymore, let alone who I care for. But I know that I don't want my daughter and my sons to die today. Nor do I want any of the others to die just because Igor considers them his personal property."

Toven made a mental note to tell Jade what Valstar had said, but he doubted it would change her mind about killing the guy.

"I don't think he would destroy everyone in the compound before exhausting every other alternative first. He is nothing without his people. Besides, there is no reason to panic. Perhaps he's just delayed."

Valstar closed his eyes. "He knows."

"How? There were no missed calls from him, so he didn't even know that the communications were down for half the night, and he didn't try to call you or anyone else."

"That's how I know that he knows." Valstar opened his eyes and turned his head toward Toven. "He didn't have to call to know that the communications were down. He would have discovered that when he tried to access the feed from the surveillance cameras and couldn't get in. I hoped that he would assume a malfunction and try again after they were restored, but the fact that he hasn't called me yet indicates that he knows."

"He can suspect. But he has no way of knowing. He wouldn't attack before finding out what happened."

Valstar shook his head as much as the chains allowed him. "Igor knows several powerful oligarchs, and at least one that I know of has access to the Russian satellite network. As soon as Igor suspected something was wrong, he would have compelled the oligarch to give him access to the network. Last night's explosions would have been clearly visible. His first assumption would have been an attack by the Russian military, but it would have taken him only a few minutes to find out that they were not involved. His next assumption would have been that we had been attacked by other Kra-ell who had somehow found out about us." Valstar's pale grayish skin turned even grayer. "To Igor, the compound falling into the hands of another group of Kra-ell is even worse than it falling to the gods."

Toven should have known that Valstar had guessed who he was.

Jade had taken one look at him and had known right away, but he had still hoped that the story they had spread about being human with enhanced abilities and superior weaponry would hold.

Still, he didn't confirm or deny it. Instead, he asked, "Why is that?"

Valstar closed his eyes. "That would take a long time to explain, and we don't have time. Not if you want to keep everyone alive."

Toven still didn't think that Valstar's panic was justified.

After spending many decades with a powerful compeller, the guy must have figured out every possible trick and loophole to manipulate around the compulsion. He might have convinced himself that the danger was imminent just so he could communicate it to Toven and make him do something hasty.

Except, why would he want them to evacuate the compound? Did he fear for himself and his children, or did he fear for Igor?

9

JADE

"So I just tap here?" Jade asked.

William leaned closer to look at her ear. "You need to push them further in. If the seal is not tight, the compulsion still might reach you."

"Got it."

It was an uncomfortable sensation, but it was well worth it if it protected her from compulsion, whether Igor's or Tom's.

Not that she would wear both of the devices at once in the god's presence. It wasn't what they had agreed on.

She tapped on the earpiece. "Did you manage to isolate the sound waves responsible for compulsion?"

"Not yet. Our doctors are busy with other things, but perhaps my mate will be able to dedicate some time to research this after she's done with the project she's working on now."

"What does she do?"

William opened his mouth, closed it, and opened it again. "I'd better not say. The project she's working on is top secret, and it's very important. That's why she couldn't come with me, and I miss her very much." He pulled out his phone and showed Jade the screen saver. "That's the love of my life. Kaia."

William's mate was a pretty blond girl with big red glasses and smart blue eyes who looked very young, but then it was hard to tell the age of those immortals. In that regard, they were like the gods whose genes they'd inherited.

Even an ancient god could look like a twenty-year-old.

"Your mate is beautiful, and she looks smart."

"She is." William put the phone in his pocket. "The Fates found the perfect mate for me, and I thank them every day for the incredible boon they've bestowed on me." He rubbed the bridge of his nose. "I was a lonely man before Kaia came into my life, and my existence was gray. Now I live in full color."

Something about that statement tugged at her heart.

Jade was lonely, and her world was gray, and not just because there was little sunlight in Karelia in the winter.

Even when she'd had a whole tribe surrounding her, she'd been lonely. Leadership came with a steep cost, and the rewards were probably not worth it, but to refuse the call and not accept the mantle when one was uniquely suited to carry it was dishonorable.

Leadership was the duty of those who were capable and strong enough to provide it.

She tapped again to disconnect. "Should I have Tom try to compel me to make sure that they work?"

"They work." William squared his shoulders. "I had them all tested before loading them on the plane."

She was tempted to ask him where he'd boarded that plane, and she knew he would probably tell her because he wasn't a Guardian, but it was none of her business. If Tom didn't want her to know, she didn't need to.

"Thank you."

"No problem." William handed her another pair. "Let me know if Kagra needs me to show her how to use them."

"I can show her. She doesn't need to bother you."

He nodded. "Very well. I'll see you later."

Jade left one device in her ear, put the other in one of the many pockets of her fatigues, and Kagra's pair in another, and headed to the basement of the office building where her people were held.

The Guardian on duty gave her a nod as he opened the door for her. "Good luck."

She arched a brow. "Did they give you trouble?"

"Not really, but that's only because they couldn't. There's a lot of grumbling going on."

"That's understandable." Jade took a deep breath before walking in.

She surveyed the cots lined up in neat rows and the purebloods sprawled on top of them.

Many of the females that had been captured by Igor years ago were either curled up or staring blankly at the ceiling, no doubt immersed in the grief that they had been compelled to suppress for so long.

Sometimes she'd envied those with weaker minds who had been relieved of their burdens by Igor's compulsion. But the truth was that she didn't want the grief taken away from her, no matter how much it hurt. It was the only way left for her to honor the memory of her sons and the other males.

Those who had been born in the compound, males and females alike, looked either anxious or angry, no doubt wondering what the future held for them.

As no one got up to greet her, Jade realized they must have assumed that she was a prisoner just like them.

"Jade." Borga waved her over. "I'm glad to see that you are alive."

Pavel raised his head and glared at her. "Can you explain why I am here? I cooperated. I did everything that was asked of me."

Borga cast her a quizzical look. "What is he talking about?"

"I'll explain in a moment." Jade scanned the cots for her daughter.

She found Drova lying on a cot near the wall with her knees up, and her head resting on her folded arms. She was staring at the ceiling and ignoring her mother's arrival.

"I need everyone's attention," Jade said.

As more people sat up, Jade assumed a military stance, her legs about two feet apart and her sword hand resting on the hilt.

"I know you are all wondering about the reason for your confinement. Tom released you from Igor's compulsion, and he compelled you all to cooperate, but until Igor is caught, we can't risk someone making contact with him and warning him. Some of you might still be loyal to Igor or hope to gain favor with him by betraying the others."

"Are you close to catching him?" Drova asked.

"Regrettably, no. I don't know how he learned about the compound's liberation, but it would seem that he's aware of what's going on, and he's not coming back."

Drova snorted. "Liberation, my ass. Who are these people, and how did you get them to come here?"

Jade decided to ignore her daughter's impudent attitude and questions for now, and addressed the liberation part first. "For many of you, this is the first time in your lives that you have been free from Igor's compulsion. Tom had to assert his will over you for the time being, but he will remove it once Igor's threat is no longer an issue." She scanned the room searching for the females. "Many of you had their tribes slaughtered by Igor and his henchmen, and to add insult to injury, you were compelled to suppress the memories of loss and grief and forced to breed. Now you are free to think for yourselves, to remember and to mourn."

"Awesome." Drova clapped her hands. "Thank you for that."

Patience. Jade took a deep breath.

"I came here to reassure you that this situation is temporary. As soon as Igor is captured, life in the compound will return to normal, but we will no longer be under Igor's thumb, our traditions will no longer be ignored, and females will no longer be subjugated. The Mother's daughters will once again rise to lead the community."

This time it was Pavel who snorted. "Am I supposed to be happy about that?"

"Females are the natural leaders of our society. What Igor did was an abomination."

Pavel glared at her. "And what you propose is not? Why can't we all be free? Why can't all of us be equal?"

"Someone has to lead," Jade said. "And the Mother of All Life chose her daughters to lead the Kra-ell."

"Says who?" Pavel didn't back down. "I didn't hear the goddess speak to me. Did you?"

Patience.

"Those traditions were passed down from generation to generation, and back on the home planet, the priestesses gave voice to the Mother's wishes. We have none among us, but every Kra-ell female is the Mother's worldly embodiment."

Thankfully, the two priestesses who had accompanied the ship had not been among those Igor had found. To subjugate them would have been a terrible crime and a great offense to the Mother of All Life.

The royal twins had only been acolytes, but since they were royal, they would have carried the same authority.

Regrettably, they were gone. If anyone could have overpowered Igor, it would have been them, and the history of the settlers would have been very different.

Drova chuckled. "I'm a pureblooded Kra-ell female, and according to you I'm a prime, and yet the Mother has never said anything to me. Pavel is right. Our leader should be chosen based on merit, not gender, and not the amount of Kra-ell blood in their veins either. The hybrids have been mistreated for far too long."

There were no hybrids in the basement, but if there were, they would have applauded Drova.

Jade had given the hybrid situation a lot of thought during her years in captivity, and she'd vowed to the Mother that if she ever got free and led her own tribe again, she would treat them better than she had done before.

A good leader learned from her mistakes. She didn't try to excuse them away.

Pavel started clapping, and not surprisingly, most of the males joined him. But when all the young pureblooded females started clapping as well, and even some of the older ones, Jade was taken aback.

Perhaps Pavel and Drova were right, and it was time to toss out gender roles?

They had lived mostly in isolation, apart from the humans, but they watched movies, read books, and were influenced by democratic human societies. Would it be so bad to remove gender from the equation?

It didn't work all that well for humans. Males still dominated most of their societies, and females still had to fight for equal respect.

If the Kra-ell females didn't assert their will, the males would. Igor and his deviants were the perfect examples of that. Jade would never allow herself or the other females to be subjugated again.

When Kra-ell females were in charge, the males were not subjugated. They served because that was their natural inclination. It wasn't a hardship. It was a choice. But Drova and Pavel had never lived in a proper Kra-ell community, so to them, female leadership seemed the same as Igor's, just gender-flipped.

Until they experienced it, no amount of explanation would convince them that it wasn't so.

"This is a new beginning for us, and I can promise you that nothing will be forced upon you, and no member will be subjugated, whether male or female, pureblood or hybrid, Kra-ell or human. We will figure out a system that will be acceptable to all of us as a community."

Jade hadn't expected to add the humans, but once the words had left her mouth, she'd felt the rightness of them. She could practically feel the Mother of All Life nodding her approval.

After all, humans were her children as well, and so were the gods.

Except, the gods had perverted the Mother's gifts with their genetic manipulations and made themselves into something that nature hadn't intended.

10

TOVEN

When the goats were brought in, Toven considered leaving the bedroom but then decided to stay and watch. He'd seen many things throughout his long life, but he'd never seen a vampiric creature drinking blood from a living animal, and he was curious.

"They don't seem nervous," he commented as the Guardian lifted Valstar so he could reach the goat. "Are you thralling them?"

Valstar nodded. "Something like that. If my hands were free, I would have petted the goat while I drank, and it would have calmed them further. It's different when I hunt, but domesticated animals can't be treated the same as wild ones."

"You will have to do without the use of your hands," Toven said.

"You compelled me to refrain from using my physical or mental power on any people in the compound, human, Kra-ell, hybrid, and other, which I took to mean your people. What could I possibly do?"

Toven shrugged. "There are ways to work around compulsion, and I'm sure you know every trick there is."

"You are a wise male." Valstar pulled up until his fangs were within reach of the animal's neck and struck.

The goat didn't even flinch, and the only indication of what was going on was the sucking sound that Valstar made.

It was disturbing but not as bad as Toven had expected. After witnessing the strange feeding a few times, it would probably bother him no more.

A few minutes later, Valstar retracted his fangs and licked the wounds closed.

"Bring the other one," he told the Guardian.

The entire feeding took less time than it would have taken Toven to eat a sandwich, and given that Valstar had been starved, it indicated that the purebloods didn't need a lot of blood to sustain them.

"Thank you," he said after he was done with the second goat. "I hope that wasn't my last meal."

Already he looked better, and the color returned to his face.

"That depends on Jade. I have no vendetta against you."

As the Guardian led the goats out, Valstar leveled his gaze at Toven. "If you let her kill me, you'll regret it. I can tell you things about Igor that she doesn't know." He chuckled. "There is a lot she doesn't know."

The guy was smart, saying the one thing that could convince Toven to keep him alive.

"What do you know that she doesn't?"

"A lot, but now is not the time for questions and answers. Please don't take my warning lightly. If you want to keep your people and mine alive, you need to evacuate the compound. I didn't exaggerate when I told you that Igor could bring an army here. He's probably working on it as we speak, and we are wasting precious time."

"If you want me to believe you, tell me one thing that Jade doesn't know about Igor and that you haven't told me already."

"The account numbers you got from me represent less than half of what he has. The rest is in bitcoin, and only he has access to it. He has several cold wallets in safe storage at different locations, and before you ask, none here that I know of. Even the best hackers in the world can't steal that from him until and unless he is caught and compelled to provide his seed phrases."

Toven didn't know much about cryptocurrency. With all the actual gold he controlled, he found little to be of interest in the so-called digital gold. Valstar's talk about cold wallets and seed phrases was meaningless to him. But now wasn't the time to ask about the particulars. Roni would know much more about it, and the kid could probably get to that money as well.

In any case, it was time to let Kian know that the ruse was up and that they needed to get the money out of the accounts before Igor transferred it somewhere else or even bought more bitcoin with it.

"Thank you for the information." Toven left the bedroom and walked out of Valstar's suite just as the Guardian returned.

Out in the corridor, Toven dialed Kian's number.

"Toven," Kian answered right away. "Any news?"

"I talked with Valstar. He says we need to evacuate as soon as possible. I also suggest we grab the funds before it's too late. Relocating the Kra-ell will not be cheap."

"Hold on a second. I'm calling Roni right now."

A moment later, Roni joined the conversation. "The money is still there, which is surprising. I'm moving it out right now."

"Will Igor be able to trace it?" Kian asked.

"Not once I'm done with it. I'm creating a maze."

"What about the bitcoin?" Toven asked. "Can you hack into that?"

"I can't," Roni said. "But there is enough money in the accounts to provide for the Kra-ell for the next fifty years, and that's after we cover our expenses. If they manage it wisely, it could last them forever. I need to get off the line now. I'll call you once it's done."

"Thank you, Roni," Kian said.

"So what do we do now?" Toven asked. "Do we heed Valstar's warning and get everyone out, or do we keep waiting for Igor to show up? We have earpieces, so I'm not worried about him compelling everyone to obey him, but I am worried about a Russian bomber shelling the compound."

There was a long moment of silence, with neither Kian nor Turner saying anything.

"Did you get Valstar to tell you if he knows or suspects how Igor found out?" Turner asked.

"He said that Igor didn't need to call to find out about the communications going down. He would have known that when he tried to access the surveillance footage, and according to Valstar, he does so often. When he suspected that something was off, he could have used one of his oligarch contacts to check the Russian military's satellite feed, and he would have seen the explosions. Valstar says that he would first assume that the Russian military is behind the attack, but that would be easy to confirm, and his next suspicion would be other Kra-ell, which might prompt him to destroy the compound along with everyone in it to prevent his people from falling into enemy hands."

"Interesting," Turner said. "Then he must assume that there are more powerful compellers among the missing Kra-ell. Did Valstar say anything about it?"

"He said that he knows a lot, so we should keep him alive and since he was under my compulsion when he said that, I assume he didn't lie, but I

41

can't be certain of that. He could have convinced himself that was the truth. We all know that there are ways around compulsion. In any case, though, we've already decided that we can't let Jade kill him for now."

"Didn't you promise her that you would let her do it?" Kian asked.

"I promised to let her kill Valstar after we catch Igor, but we don't have Igor, do we?"

Kian let out a breath. "Regrettably, we don't."

11

JADE

"We should hold elections," Pavel said. "First to choose candidates. Everyone will suggest three names, and the three who get the most votes get to compete. They will need to prepare a platform explaining their ideas for the future, and present them to an assembly, then they will have a debate, and after that, we will vote to choose the winner."

"We need more than just one elected official," Drova said. "We need representatives from each group, and we need a council."

"Why do we need all that?" Morgada asked. "There aren't that many of us, and we can all vote on proposals that each of us will be allowed to bring up for a vote."

Pavel chuckled. "Then nothing will ever get done, and we will spend all of our time arguing and trying to convince each other of this and that. One leader and a small council is the way to go."

Jade listened patiently while her people threw ideas around. It wasn't the time to decide on how their future would look, but her goal had been to calm frayed nerves, and discussing a better future gave the people hope.

The mood in the basement had improved dramatically.

Sitting on her cot, Drova had taken part in the discussion for a few more moments, but then she turned her attention back to Jade. "What are they going to do to Igor once they catch him?"

Jade was grateful for her not referring to Igor as her father.

"They are not going to do anything to him. He's my kill. Tom promised to leave him to me."

She'd expected Drova to protest, but her daughter nodded. "Morgada told me what he did to the males of your tribe." She looked at the female on the cot to her right and then back at Jade. "He killed your sons. My brothers."

It wasn't often that Jade felt tears well in her eyes, and it took a lot to fight them from spilling.

The Kra-ell did not cry. They got revenge.

"He did that to the families of all the females who weren't born in the compound. He froze us with the power of his compulsion, not giving our males a fighting chance. They didn't get to die honorably in battle and enter the fields of the brave. They were slaughtered like cattle while the females watched, frozen in place and unable to help."

Drova swallowed. "I don't believe in all that nonsense about the fields of the brave and the valley of the shamed, but what he did was vile."

"He also put a collar around your neck that was filled with explosives so you couldn't run, and as if that wasn't enough, he rigged this entire compound with explosives as well. The people who came to help us made sure he couldn't detonate them remotely."

Drova nodded. "Yeah, Pavel told us about that too. But you still didn't tell us who are these so-called liberators."

There were no tears in her daughter's eyes, not even a sheen, and Jade couldn't be prouder of her at that moment. Even though Igor was a shitty father, his blood still coursed through Drova's veins, and it must be difficult for her to deal with what Jade intended to do, but she understood, and she accepted.

Drova was a true Kra-ell warrior, even if she didn't know that yet.

"Our liberators are people with special paranormal abilities and advanced technology."

"How did they know about us? Where and how did you find them?"

"It was by sheer luck that I found a former member of my tribe, who had left decades before Igor slaughtered all of my males and enslaved the females. I contacted him in a clever way so Igor wouldn't suspect anything, and I gave him the coordinates of the compound. I hoped he had found other Kra-ell that would be able to help us, but instead, he brought the new friends he'd found among humans."

Jade didn't like lying, but she'd promised not to reveal the immortals' identity. Well, she'd been compelled, but she would have promised if Tom had asked her. Still, those who came from the home planet like she had would have recognized Tom's otherworldly beauty for what it was. No human or Kra-ell was that perfect.

"Maybe they are the descendants of the gods who colonized this planet first," Morgada said. "They had many thousands of years of a head start on us, and they probably enhanced some of the humans like they did us."

Drova gaped at the female. "What are you talking about? What gods?"

Jade lifted her hand to stop Morgada. "There is a lot you don't know about the Kra-ell past, but now is not the time for a history lesson."

"Come on, Jade," Pavel said. "Give us something. You and the other original settlers have kept secrets from us for long enough. Aren't we pure-bloods like you? What are you hiding and why?"

Perhaps Pavel was right, and it was time to tell the young generation about their history, the good and the bad, but perhaps not as much of the bad. She wanted them to feel pride in their heritage, to follow the Mother of All Life's traditions without sneering at their religion like it was something only primitives believed in.

They didn't understand that the belief in the Mother was part of their identity as Kra-ell, and without it, they were just a bunch of aliens squatting on a planet that wasn't theirs. They would have no reason to preserve the purity of their blood so their kind wouldn't disappear, and in time, all that would be left of them would be traces of their genes in their human descendants.

Jade let out a breath. "You already know that we came from another place in the universe. There are many species of humanoids, and no one knows who the progenitor was, but those who call themselves gods claim that title. They were our neighbors back home. They claimed to have made us in their image, and they did the same thing on Earth with humans. That's why humans are compatible with us, and we can produce offspring together."

"I wondered about that," Drova said. "Are the gods still around?"

"I've searched for them, but all I found was mythology. I assumed that they had either left or had been killed by their creations—the humans."

When a barrage of questions was hurled her way, Jade lifted her hand. "That's all for today."

Morgada nodded her approval. "I'm glad that you finally told them something. I never agreed with your edict of secrecy. The young ones need to know, or the knowledge will be lost."

KIAN

"*T*here are three hundred and twenty-seven people living in the compound," Turner said after Toven had joined them via a video call. "And that's not counting our Guardians, Kalugal's men, William, Marcel, Sylvia, and Mia. Getting everyone out and pulling a disappearing act is going to be difficult. Yamanu can shroud them, but not indefinitely. He needs to sleep and replenish his reserves."

"Especially given that at least half of them look alien." Kian swiveled his chair around and picked up his tablet. "One or two can blend in using sunglasses to hide their eyes, but a bunch of tall, willowy people all wearing sunglasses would be noticed."

Onegus chuckled. "We could use the movie set cover. They could look like ogres, and people would still buy it."

"Igor won't," Turner said. "We have four trucks that can carry between thirty to forty people each. It should be enough for the humans, the children of the purebloods and hybrids, and the injured. The rest can head out on foot. I can arrange for more trucks to intercept them on the way and collect the rest."

"Where will we take them?" Toven asked.

"Finland. Igor seems to have connections in Russia, but he probably doesn't have them in Finland. The question is where to take them from there and how." He looked at Kian. "Any ideas?"

Kian shook his head. "I haven't given it much thought because the plan was to leave them where they are and let Jade lead them. The only involvement I had in mind was some loose supervision to make sure that the humans were not mistreated."

"You'll need more trucks for the animals," Toven interjected. "If the Kraell can hunt where we end up taking them, we can let the animals go free. But until we find a place for them to roam and hunt, we need to take the livestock with us so the purebloods, and probably some of the hybrids, have a fresh supply of blood. I don't think we could raid blood banks on the way to feed so many. Igor will have no problem finding us just by following the news about blood supply shortages."

It was a mess Kian didn't want to deal with, but at this point, there was no turning back. He couldn't abandon those people, and he had to finish what he had started. "We need to find them a farm or take them somewhere wild where they can hunt."

"I can find them a place in Finland," Turner said. "But it's not going to be a permanent solution. Igor will find them, and then all we did would be for nothing. He would just take over again. We need to get them as far away from their original location as possible, and we need to do so in a way that won't leave traceable tracks. They will need to be scanned for trackers, and that includes all their clothing and belongings."

When he was a kid, the best way to avoid trackers was to use a waterway, but that wasn't going to solve their problem in today's interconnected, satellite-monitored world. Igor wouldn't follow them by the footprints left in the mud.

However, thinking of water gave Kian an idea.

"We can use the cruise ship. It's still at the shipyard in Stockholm, but it is basically ready to sail. I can tell them to skip the final clean-up and cabin inspections and get it out of there. It will still need time to refuel and resupply, and that will take some time, but the biggest question is whether the captain is done prepping the new crew for the voyage to Long Beach. If all the stars align and the *Aurora* can leave within a day, I can direct it to Helsinki to pick them up."

"I wasn't aware that you found a crew," Turner said.

"It wasn't easy to find what I was looking for. I wanted people with impeccable military and civilian experience who could function well under stress. The core crew we ended up hiring is fully vetted and top-notch. For now, we only have a great captain and a skeleton crew, and that was enough to sail an empty ship to Long Beach, but it's not a fully operable cruise ship yet. That being said, we can have it loaded with food and other supplies for our guests, but the Kra-ell and the others will have to serve themselves."

"Let me remind you again," Toven said. "The Kra-ell can't eat regular food. We will have to bring the animals onboard. The question is whether we take the livestock from here or procure it in Helsinki."

Kian groaned. "I can't believe that I'm allowing our newly remodeled luxury cruise ship to be turned into Noah's ark. But it's going to happen either way and if we get the livestock in Helsinki, it will leave unnecessary breadcrumbs for Igor to follow. We need to take the animals from the compound, but we don't have time to arrange for their transportation. What are we going to do? Run them through the woods?"

"That's an option," Toven said. "At least at the beginning of the exodus before we can get more trucks to pick up the rest of the people and the herd. The problem will be hiding them while they are passing through Karelia. A convoy that size would get noticed."

"We have Yamanu to shroud the convoy while it's passing through," Turner said. "But its passage will leave tracks. That being said, I don't think that a bunch of trucks hauling produce is such a rare occurrence in Karelia. There are many farms in the area, and they must ship produce on a regular basis. However, it might not be the right season. They were probably done harvesting several months ago."

"Animals get shipped all year round." Onegus pulled out his phone. "Let's see what they produce in Karelia." His eyes darted over the screen. "Forestry, iron ore mining, wood processing, paper mills, and trout. Fish seems to be their biggest export industry." He lifted his eyes. "Except for the fish, all those things are not seasonal. There is plenty of reason for trucks to pass through the area year-round."

"I heard that ice fishing was a thing, and that's going on in the winter." Turner cast Kian a sidelong glance. "How soon can your ship get to Helsinki?"

"The voyage will probably take between twelve to sixteen hours, but the *Aurora* still needs to be fueled and loaded with supplies. Those things are solvable but may take some additional time. I just hope that the captain has the crew ready."

"Let's assume thirty-six hours," Turner said. "It will take them four to six hours to get organized, leave the compound, get to the farm where the Guardians stayed overnight, and collect their things. By then, the trucks should arrive. From the farm, it's about a fourteen-hour drive to Helsinki. That's a total of eighteen to twenty hours, which leaves another sixteen to eighteen hours during which they will have to hide until the ship is ready to receive them. I need to find them a place to lay low for half the night and most of the next day." He started typing on his laptop. "It needs to be outside the city, secluded, and big enough to accommodate four hundred guests and the animals, so it needs to be a hotel or a lodge with a large grassy area that is fenced in."

Everything was moving too fast for Kian's liking, and for a moment, he was tempted to halt the action. The Guardians could handle the Russian military provided that the force wasn't overwhelming and provided that they didn't attack from the sky. But even then, it would only be a temporary solution. The attacks would just keep coming.

There was no other way but to evacuate the compound.

He looked at Onegus. "We don't have to bring them all the way to Long Beach. In fact, I'd rather we didn't. We can drop them off somewhere on the way."

The chief lifted a brow. "Where?"

"In Colombia. The *Aurora* needs to make a stop there anyway to get equipped with the armaments I ordered, and the Kra-ell should do just fine in the jungle. It would be the perfect solution for them. They will have plenty of game to hunt, and they might even take care of the drug cartel problem over there." He chuckled. "Talk about killing two birds with one stone."

"Don't you want to keep an eye on them?" Onegus asked. "And what about the humans? Some of them would want to be set free."

Another groan left Kian's throat. "You are right. We can't erase a lifetime of memories, and compulsion needs to be periodically reinforced. They will need to be accessible to Toven."

Onegus nodded. "The good thing about a sea voyage is that it takes a long time. We don't have to decide anything right now. We can consider our options at leisure while they are en route."

13

JADE

When Jade's earpiece vibrated, and a moment later Tom's voice sounded in her ear, she was glad for the distraction.

Her explanation about what she assumed had happened to the gods had been followed by a barrage of questions that she didn't want to answer and dig herself deeper into a pit of lies.

She remembered to tap the device before answering. "Yes, I'm still in the basement."

"We need to evacuate. Get everyone out, have them collect only their most precious and necessary belongings, and assemble in the courtyard in half an hour."

She tensed. "What's going on?"

"Valstar thinks that Igor will get the Russian Army or Air Force involved and bomb the compound."

"I don't think he would do that before he exhausts all other means of retaking it."

The fact that Igor hadn't attempted to activate the explosives the compound was rigged with or the collars proved that he wasn't gung-ho about killing his people. But if he couldn't get them by any other means, she believed he would destroy them rather than let them get taken by humans or other Kra-ell.

"I agree," Tom said. "But he still might show up with a platoon of soldiers equipped with rocket launchers and such, and the casualties will be stagger-ing. We prefer to leave."

"Where will you take us?"

"Let's discuss it on the way. Time is of the essence."

"Got it." She tapped the earpiece closed and addressed her people. "We are moving out. You are to collect only your most necessary belongings and assemble in the front courtyard in half an hour."

It was good that none of them owned much. All of her things would fit in a backpack or in a pillowcase since she didn't own one.

"What happened?" Pavel asked.

"Nothing yet, but Valstar thinks that Igor will show up with the Russian Army. They have weapons we can't defend against or survive."

"Is he still alive?"

"Regrettably, he is."

The door behind her opened, and the Guardian stepped in holding a machine gun. "Let's go, people."

If not for Tom's compulsion, any of the Kra-ell could have wrestled the weapon out of his hands, but even though there was no reason to do that, Jade had to fight the impulse to disarm him.

Showing up with a machine gun wasn't conducive to the spirit of coop-eration, but she could understand why the immortals were wary of her people. They weren't used to interacting with beings who were physically much stronger than them.

As everyone filed out, Jade stood by the door, smiling at the children and murmuring reassuring words.

The little ones didn't understand what was going on, and they were scared. They were about to leave the only home they had known, hopefully for a better one.

When her earpiece vibrated again, she tapped on it. "The purebloods are all out. What about the hybrids and the humans?"

Igor's remaining cronies were held under guard in one of the offices, but she couldn't care less about what happened to them. As far as she was concerned, they could stay chained to the wall and die when the Russians bombarded the place.

"Sofia and Marcel are in charge of assembling the humans," Tom said. "The Guardians are escorting the hybrids. We have only four trucks, so it was decided that the humans, the injured, and the children would ride in them while the rest would follow on foot. We will be intercepted by more trucks on the way."

"Can you tell me where we are going?"

"Helsinki, but don't tell anyone."

"Of course."

"By the way, you'll be glad to know that we have all the money Igor had in his bank and brokerage accounts. Your people will be able to live very comfortably on that."

That was a surprise. Not that the immortals had been able to seize the money, but that they were going to give it to her.

"That's good news. How much was in there?" As the last of her people left the basement, she started up the stairs.

"I don't know, but it's plenty. Regrettably, it's not all of it. Igor kept about half of the money in bitcoin, and we couldn't access that."

Jade's fangs twitched as they elongated. "It's all stolen blood money, and I'm sure that most of it came from my tribe. We had several exceptional enterprises going, and we had big profits."

"I hope to hear all about it on the way."

She might have said too much, but it was ancient history now, so it didn't matter.

"The male who made all that possible was murdered. If Igor wasn't so simpleminded and greedy and exclusively focused on the females, the idiot could have made much more money by leaving that male alive."

14

SOFIA

"Where are we going?" Helmi clutched her childhood teddy bear to her chest.

That thing had slept in her bed since she was three years old, and it hadn't left even to make room for Tomos. It was mended in so many places that there was barely any fake fur left, but Sofia knew better than to make fun of the one-eyed, patched-up wonder.

Instead, she shifted her gaze to Marcel, who shook his head.

She knew where they were heading, but it was supposed to be a secret. They needed to evade Igor, and whatever force he might summon to attack the compound, and given that he could compel anyone in the Russian military to do whatever he would instruct them to do, she wasn't sure how they were going to pull it off.

"Somewhere safe." She wrapped her arm around her cousin's waist. "Did you pack everything?"

Helmi pointed to the pillowcase she'd stuffed with her clothes. "I left my books, and my CDs behind like you told me to. That's all the clothes I had and a few toiletries."

Her father and her aunts had packed their things and handed them over to the Guardians, who had loaded them on the trucks already. They and several others were herding the animals out of the opening that used to be the front gate. The purebloods were going to run until they could rendezvous with more trucks and use their mental powers to get the animals to follow.

"Come on." Sofia led her cousin out of the common room. "We are riding together."

"What about Marcel?"

"He's running with the rest of them."

Helmi frowned. "How is he going to keep up with the Kra-ell? They are so much faster."

As what Helmi had said sank in, Marcel's eyes widened. "I need to call Yamanu." He rushed out the door.

"The liberators will follow behind. They are trained soldiers, so I'm sure they can keep up." It was the best explanation Sofia could come up with.

"I wish I could see Tomos before we leave." Helmi's eyes darted around, looking for her boyfriend.

"You will see him once the other trucks intercept us. Marcel can probably get you permission to ride with Tomos."

When they got to the courtyard, and Helmi saw her boyfriend standing with the other hybrids, she tore out of Sofia's grip and rushed to him.

He opened his arms and caught her as she flung herself at him. Seemingly unperturbed by the other hybrids and purebloods watching the display of affection, he swung her around before crushing her to his chest and kissing her like there was no tomorrow.

Heck, maybe there wasn't, but Sofia smiled nonetheless. The two were so obviously in love, and if the Kra-ell weren't so blinded by their stupid beliefs, they would have realized that as well.

Scanning the gathered crowd, Sofia saw her mother talking to another hybrid female.

Should she approach her?

What was she going to say to her? Should she introduce her to Marcel?

Her musings were interrupted when Valstar entered the courtyard between two Guardians. He was in handcuffs, and his legs were chained as well, so all he could do was shuffle.

Her mother looked at him with a horrified expression on her face, but when she made a move to go to him, the other female put a hand on her shoulder and shook her head.

Did her mother care about her father?

Who knew? She'd never interacted with her only daughter to share her feelings with her.

Joanna was more of a stranger to Sofia than Jade or Kagra, and she barely knew the pureblooded females.

The bleating of sheep and goats interrupted that line of thought. Her father and several of the others herded the animals through the courtyard and out the front, where the humans were boarding the trucks.

Sofia was startled when Marcel suddenly appeared next to her. "You scared me."

"I'm sorry." He leaned to whisper in her ear. "I can't believe no one thought about the Guardians having to keep up appearances and walk at a human speed. Your cousin saved the day."

"What are they going to do?"

"Everyone will have to walk at a rate reasonable for well-trained humans. We can't risk letting the Kra-ell run ahead. If the Russian military shows up, though, we will have no choice but to show our hand. Eventually, we will have to reveal who we are anyway."

"Yeah, I guess it depends on how long your people have to spend with the Kra-ell. The longer it is, the harder it's going to be to keep up appearances."

"It's going to be long." He smiled. "We are about to go on a cruise."

Sofia leaned back and frowned. "We are?"

He nodded and wrapped his arm around her shoulders so he could continue whispering in her ear. "The clan recently acquired a cruise ship and had it renovated at a shipyard in Stockholm. It was supposed to leave for Long Beach in a few days. Kian is dispatching it to the port of Helsinki to pick us up."

She pretended to kiss his cheek to whisper back. "Is he planning on bringing all the Kra-ell to your secret village?"

"I don't think so. He doesn't know what to do with them yet, but thankfully, our hacker was able to grab the money that Igor stole from all the tribes, so they will have enough to settle somewhere else. I heard South America mentioned, but don't say anything to anyone just yet. If there are spies among us, we don't want them to know where we are going."

She nodded. "Maybe we should start spreading rumors about different locations to confuse Igor?"

"That's not a bad idea. So where are we going?"

"Australia. They say it's a wild place. That's perfect for the Kra-ell."

"Or we can say that Jade wants to go back to China," Marcel suggested.

"That's a good one. China is so big."

"Right. One rumor can say Beijing and another Shanghai or some other place." His eyes brightened. "Or Lugu Lake. We have reason to believe that ancient Kra-ell resided there and influenced the local culture. I'll tell you all about it on the way."

15

PHINAS

*W*ith the compound in organized chaos, and people milling all around, it was difficult to find a secluded spot to call Kalugal, and the only place Phinas had found was a bathroom stall in the office building.

It was the middle of the night in California, but the boss wanted updates, and he was probably awake and waiting.

"I don't have much time," he said as soon as Kalugal answered. "Kian is taking the Kra-ell with the humans and the livestock to Helsinki, and from there, they are sailing on the cruise ship he got for the clan. What do you want me to do?"

"What is he doing with the Guardians?"

"Some of them are going back with Bhathian on the amphibian. They are taking the exoskeletons with them and boarding a chartered plane in St. Petersburg to take them home. The rest will be led by Yamanu, who will be instrumental in shrouding the convoy. They will take the light weaponry and accompany the Kra-ell. We are leaving the compound in a few minutes and heading to the farm where we left our camping equipment. We don't have enough trucks for everyone, so most of us are walking. Turner is sending more trucks to collect us on the way, and once we break camp, we will head to Helsinki, where we will spend the night until the ship gets there and is ready to cast off."

"How many Guardians are going with Bhathian, and how many are boarding the ship, and where is the ship heading?"

"Originally, it was supposed to sail to Long Beach, but Kian wants to drop the Kra-ell somewhere on the way, and I wasn't told what the options were. Yamanu asked how many of our men would accompany the ship. He needs to know how many Guardians he will need to take with him. I told him that I would have to ask you."

"Unless some of the men need to go home, take everyone to the ship. The cruise idea plays beautifully into my agenda of befriending the Kra-ell. It will take almost a month for the ship to reach Long Beach, and since there will be more of us than the Guardians, we will form a stronger connection with the Kra-ell. But if the Kra-ell are dropped off on the way, you will continue with the ship back home. I hope the men will have no problem with such a long voyage."

"I don't think they will. I was told that the ship is luxurious."

"Of course, it is, but don't forget that it has no service staff. Everyone will have to pitch in, you and the men included. Make a good impression on our new friends."

It shouldn't have surprised Phinas that Kalugal knew more than even Bhathian and Yamanu about the clan's ship.

"I didn't know that there was no serving staff. Are you sure? Neither Yamanu nor Bhathian mentioned that."

"I'm sure. The ship was supposed to be delivered to the Long Beach port, and Kian hired only a skeleton crew to do that. Nevertheless, I'm sure it will be an enjoyable experience." He chuckled. "Especially for you. Did you have a chance to get even friendlier with the infamous Jade?"

"When? It's a madhouse out here. Everyone is scrambling to evacuate the compound as soon as possible, and that includes the livestock because the Kra-ell need a fresh supply of blood on hand, and they can't get it at sea. Can you imagine a luxury cruise ship with goats and sheep running around?"

Kalugal barked out a laugh. "I can't. Are they bringing the chickens along too?"

Phinas frowned. "How did you know about the chickens? I didn't tell you that."

"Yamanu told Kian about eating the best chicken he ever had. Organic and pasture-raised."

Phinas didn't ask how Kalugal had heard a conversation between

Yamanu and Kian. His boss had his mysterious ways of finding out things he shouldn't have been able to.

"I don't think the chickens are coming. They feed the humans, not the Kra-ell, and the humans can get food at any port."

"I'm glad that they are taking the livestock. Otherwise, the Kra-ell would have to snack on the humans and the immortals, and I wouldn't have been happy about them using my men like blood bags."

Thinking about Jade snacking on him got Phinas hard in an instant, and as he adjusted himself, he realized why Kalugal had said that.

"You did that on purpose," he accused.

"Obviously. I'm curious about your reaction. Was it a turn-on or a turn-off?"

"Definitely a turn-on. Jade can snack on me anytime she wants. I wonder if what I eat makes a difference in how I taste."

Would his blood taste sweet if he ate a lot of sugar? Or tart if he ate berries?

Kalugal groaned. "That was a bit too much information."

Phinas chuckled. "You asked, and I answered. If I have anything more to report, I'll call you again."

"Please do."

16

KIAN

Onegus put the phone down and turned to face Kian and Turner. "They are out of the compound. What's the status with the trucks?"

"ETA about two hours," Turner said. "If the immortals didn't need to moderate their speed, they could have reached the farm on foot and started breaking camp before the trucks arrived."

Kian looked up from his computer screen. "We have no choice. I don't want the Kra-ell or the humans to know who their liberators are. If we offload them somewhere in South America, it would be better if they don't know that immortals exist. If we bring them here on the other hand, which I'm not at all inclined to do, we will obviously have to tell them."

Turner leveled his penetrating stare at Kian and leaned back in his chair. "What are your objections to bringing them to the village?"

"Isn't that obvious?"

"Not at all. You've already allowed three former members of Jade's tribe to join the clan, and the experience was positive. Having this group as allies will shore up our defenses against Navuh's warriors and against other Kra-ell."

Kian returned Turner's stare. The guy was usually the more cautious among them, and his stance on the Kra-ell was out of character. "We have no reason to trust them not to turn on us or betray us when it will serve them to do so. That's one. In addition, Igor will be searching for them, and bringing them here might lead him to us. There must be at least a dozen more reasons that I can't think of right now, but I'm sure they will come to me later. I'm surprised that you are advocating for them."

"I'm not." Turner leaned forward. "I'm just starting a discussion. Do you know the saying about keeping your friends close and your enemies closer? That's why Kalugal volunteered his men not only to join the mission but also to escort the Kra-ell on the cruise."

"It has occurred to me." Kian let out a breath. "Nevertheless, I'm glad he did that because I can't leave all of the Guardians we sent for this mission to babysit this group. I don't like leaving the village without an adequate force to defend it."

"Speaking of Guardians." Onegus swiveled his chair to face Kian. "Yamanu wants Mey to join him on the cruise, and I just got a text from Arwel asking if he and Jin could go as well. Yamanu doesn't want to spend a month without his mate, and the ladies are curious about their relatives."

Kian felt a muscle tic in his jaw. "I don't want to endanger any more females. It's bad enough that Mia and Sofia are going with the ship, and I'm very glad that Sylvia is flying home from Helsinki. I wanted her to go back with the Guardians on the amphibian, but William asked her to stay with him in case he needs her to disable surveillance cameras when the convoy passes through the city and the port."

Turner glanced at him over the screen of his laptop. "Two more females won't really make a difference." He kept on typing. "It would be interesting to get Arwel's opinion on the Kra-ell's feelings. From what I have observed about the three hybrids we know, they are not much different from us. The purebloods front a tough façade, but I wouldn't be surprised if on the inside they are just as vulnerable as the gods, the immortals, and even the humans."

Onegus chuckled. "Except for you, Turner. You are like our Spock. Always the voice of logic."

Turner smirked. "I take that as a compliment."

"It was meant as such. Anyway, I have no problem admitting my feelings, and I can tell you both that I will be very happy to see Toven back in the village. When he's here, I have an added peace of mind knowing that we have such a powerful compeller on our side. If we are ever attacked, I'm sure he would be a great help, freezing our enemies with a verbal command."

"I would like to see him back as well," Turner said. "But we need him and Mia to go with the Kra-ell to keep them in check and to defend them in case Igor shows up with a pirate armada."

"Are pirates still a thing?" Onegus asked.

"Surprisingly, they are." Kian swiveled his laptop around for Onegus to see the article he'd been reading. "*Best Management Practices to Deter Piracy.* They encourage vessels to register their voyages, so the navy knows to protect them. There is also a list of self-protective measures a vessel can take to make itself less of a target for pirates, but they are BS, like rigging the deck with razor wire, rigging firehoses to spray seawater over the side of the ship, and having a pirate alarm. They have other ridiculous suggestions like setting up mannequins posing as armed guards or firing flares at the pirates. Any merchant ship with a valuable cargo that has to sail through pirate-infested waters needs to hire an armed escort, which is what I want to do, but for different reasons." He looked at Turner. "I planned on retrofitting the ship in Colombia with some advanced defensive and offensive weapon systems, but for now the *Aurora* is defenseless. Do you know anyone who provides security to ships crossing the Atlantic?"

Hopefully, the guy knew someone with a navy submarine that could stealthily escort the cruise ship, not only during the Kra-ell voyage, but also during the wedding celebrations that were planned for next month but would probably have to be postponed.

Alena wouldn't be happy, or rather Orion wouldn't be. He was more anxious for them to get married than she was.

"I can make a few inquiries and find us an escort," Turner said. "I'm not sure that Igor would be able to do the same. He doesn't have the contacts I do."

"Don't be so sure," Onegus said. "He can come onboard any Russian naval ship and compel the captain to act as his pirate."

"True." Kian glanced at Turner. "It's not easy to hijack a navy ship, though. Even if the captain severs communications with command, he can't disappear with the ship. Not in the age of satellites. And a rogue ship would be hunted down."

"It can be done," Turner said. "The sea is vast, and vessels disappear all the time. A satellite capable of detecting a small to medium-sized vessel will usually only be able to scan a limited area based on its overhead pass, making it unlikely that the ship it's looking for passes through that exact area at the time it's scanning for it. But regardless, ships communicate with both ground stations and satellites via a dedicated system that tracks their position, heading, course, and more. But for the most part, these trackers can be disabled locally on the ship. It might be more complicated than that to achieve on a Russian navy vessel though. "

This was actually great news. "That means that our cruise ship can disappear, and Igor won't be able to find it."

"He can find out its final destination," Turner asserted. "There is no way to hide the ship from him when it passes through the Panama Canal."

"I'd rather chance it, offload the cargo in Colombia, and bring the ship to its original destination as planned."

Turner shrugged. "Ultimately, it's your decision. I'm just the advisor."

Kian glanced at the timer on his laptop. "We need to tell Leon that they have to evacuate Safe Haven, but I hate dropping the news on him at four in the morning. Igor will probably be busy trying to chase his people, but if he can't find them, he might turn his sights to the only other lead he has. We also need to collect the two hybrids stranded in the area."

"What do you want to do with them?" Onegus asked.

"Lock them in the keep until we figure out what to do with the rest of them. I don't want Igor getting them back."

Onegus smiled. "It's good that we had the foresight to attach a tracker to their car. We know where to find them."

Kian nodded. "Call Leon. We shouldn't waste any time."

"What about the paranormals?" Onegus asked. "What do we do with them?"

"Good question. How many are left in the program?"

"Let me check." Onegus pulled up a file on his laptop. "Nine."

"Tell Eleanor to send them on a vacation. She can claim a family emergency, and with her gone, there will be no one to run the program. We might still catch Igor, so there is no point in making permanent arrangements. I would rather not lose Safe Haven after all we have invested in the place."

Turner chuckled. "If we catch Igor, we can return the Kra-ell to their compound and be done with them, but personally, I prefer them where I can keep an eye on them."

Onegus nodded in agreement. "Speaking of trackers, we have to assume that many of the compound's occupants are implanted with them. They might not all have sophisticated devices like the one we removed from Sofia, but even a simpler version will be just as effective. The only difference is that it will be easier to find."

17

KIAN

*K*ian pulled out his phone. "I hope that William's communication disrupter can help with that. We don't have time to run all three hundred and twenty-seven people and their belongings through an MRI machine and take the trackers out before we let them board the ship."

"Hello, boss." William sounded out of breath. "What can I do for you?"

"Are you walking?"

William chuckled. "Fates forbid. I'm in the van, but there were a lot of things to take care of before leaving. I helped Charlie and Morris move the drone piloting equipment and controls from the van to the amphibian and set them up. We need the drones to provide us with aerial cover on the way to Helsinki, so I left my mods intact. I will trigger the self-destruct circuitry as soon as the drones touch down for the last time. The modifications I installed will be fried, and no one will be able to reverse engineer or realize what exactly was added to the drones. We don't want that technology falling into Igor's or Russian's hands, or for that matter, into the hands of Turner's hired crew."

Regrettably, the military drones were far too large to transport and required a stretch of runway to take off that the cruise ship didn't have, otherwise Kian would have loved to have them on board and use them to defend it.

"Of course. I have a question for you. We have to assume that many of the compound's people have trackers in them. Can your disrupter scramble the signals so they can't be followed?"

"It can, and I activated it before we left the compound, but I will have to turn it off once we reach Helsinki. If suddenly scores of people lose their phone signal across such a major metropolis, too much attention will be drawn, and Igor might be able to figure out where we are heading even without having access to the trackers."

"That's not good." Kian raked his fingers through his hair. "Any suggestions about what can be done in that regard?"

"Not readily. If the location Turner finds for us to spend the night is remote, I can keep the scrambler on until we enter the city the next day."

"Can't you make it so it only affects a small area?"

"We have people in fifteen trucks, and we don't know who has trackers in them. Five more trucks carry livestock. To cover the entire convoy, I'll have to scramble a large area. I can turn it on again once everyone is on board the ship, but I will have to turn it off once the ship casts off. Communication between the ship and port authorities is required, and we want to avoid being blocked or chased because the authorities could not communicate with us. Likewise, a port-assigned pilot will come on board to navigate the ship until it fully clears the port zone, so communication will need to remain available for that duration. But now that I think on it, the Baltic Sea is narrow, and its shipping lanes are concentrated. It makes little sense to scramble signals while we sail through it because the ship will be tracked by many ground stations and passing vessels. Igor will have no problem finding us while we are in the Baltic. Certainly not if he gains access to a Russian, Finnish, or NATO military tracking system. Once we leave the Baltic Sea and enter the North Sea, though, and certainly in the North Atlantic, I can turn the scrambler back on and we can basically disappear."

Kian didn't want William on that ship. Marcel could take over for him, and they needed William back in the village, but that was a discussion for later. "Maybe we should remove the trackers before they board the ship."

Turner held Kian's gaze for a moment. "Even if Merlin works around the clock, it will take several days to do, not to mention the difficulty of getting our hands on an MRI machine first. We can't wait that long. We have to get an MRI on the ship before it leaves the port and do the scanning and removal en route. They can dump the trackers in the water before reaching the North Sea and disappear."

"But Igor will know that his people boarded a ship, and as William just noted, he will have no problem following, either with a Russian naval vessel, a submarine, or virtually. He wants them back and he is not going to give up on them."

"I don't see a way around it unless you want them to hole up in some remote location in Finland and hope that it will take him a while to track the convoy without the help of the trackers, but I don't think it would. He doesn't need to rely solely on the trackers to follow and locate the convoy. There aren't that many roads going through Karelia, and even with Yamanu's shrouding, Igor can find breadcrumbs that will lead him to his people."

"Yeah, in the shape of sheep and goat droppings." William chuckled. "Thankfully, they didn't raise cows in the compound, or those clues would have been bigger and stinkier."

18

PHINAS

*P*hinas scanned the field, searching for Jade among the Guardians that were taking down the tents and packing up the rest of their stuff.

As the only female out there, she was hard to miss, but with her height and striking looks, she would have stood out even in a crowd of women.

Jade was beautiful despite putting zero effort into it. Her long black hair was gathered in a high ponytail, and she was wearing nothing special.

The black tactical pants were loose, providing plenty of pockets to store things. She was probably wearing a thermal layer underneath that was similar to the Henley shirt peeking out from the open collar of her tactical jacket. Absent were the sword and the scabbard, but he was sure she had a full arsenal of daggers and throwing knives hidden in her pants and boots.

One thing was for sure. He would never again startle her by approaching her from behind, and risk a dagger into his gut or a hand crushing his windpipe.

That shouldn't make him want her even more, but Phinas had already established that Jade affected him in strange ways.

It wasn't only the sexual attraction, though. He respected and admired her.

She didn't have to be out there with the men, helping take down the tents. She could've waited in the van where the heater was working, and Toven and Mia were chatting with William and Yamanu.

But maybe that was precisely why she was out there with the Guardians, taking down tents.

Spending more time with Toven meant answering more questions. Regrettably, Phinas hadn't been invited to take part in the history lesson she'd promised Toven, and he'd only heard about it later from Yamanu, who hadn't volunteered to share any details.

Eventually, the information would find its way to Kalugal, as it always did, and his boss would most likely share it with him and Rufsur, but Phinas didn't want to wait.

As soon as he managed to pierce through Jade's formidable protective shields, he would learn as much as he could get her to reveal.

"Hello, beautiful," he said from a few feet away. "You cleaned up nicely, although I have to admit that the other outfit was the stuff of wet dreams."

The see-through mesh shirt and tight leather pants hadn't been practical in the nearly freezing temperature, but it was a hot look.

She looked every inch like the badass she was.

Jade cast him a glance over her shoulder. "When did you have time to dream about me?"

"I've been daydreaming about you since the first moment I laid eyes on you." He helped her fold the tent she'd taken down. "Did you dream about me?"

She looked at him with those huge eyes of hers. "You entered my thoughts once or twice, but I don't daydream about males unless I'm plotting to kill them."

Chuckling, Phinas lifted his hands in the air. "Then I'm very glad that you only thought about me. I don't want to be on your kill list."

Jade put a hand over her chest. "Never. I owe you a life-debt. I'll die to protect you."

She'd said it with such conviction that Phinas had no doubt that she would do just that. His band of adopted brothers would die for him, too, as he would for them, but they had never pledged such a vow to each other.

He dipped his head. "Thank you. I hope you will never have to defend me."

Tilting her head, she regarded him with a frown. "Tell me something, Phinas. Why weren't you put in charge of any of the Kra-ell? Are you second class to the Guardians?"

The female didn't beat around the bush, and she had the tact of a bull in a china shop.

"The Guardians are on active duty, while my men and I had retired a long time ago. We didn't keep up our training as vigilantly as we should have, and that's why we are just assisting and not assuming leadership positions."

She gave him a once-over. "You look in excellent shape to me."

"Thank you. So do you."

"I train daily." She handed him the bag containing the tent.

When he pretended to sag under the weight, a smile tugged at her lips, which had been his intention. The act of pretending to be human had been unnecessary.

The humans and Jade's people were waiting for them in the trucks, and the only ones on the field were the Guardians, Kalugal's men, and Jade.

Immortals were not nearly as strong as the Kra-ell, but they weren't as weak as humans. It was an advantage for the Kra-ell, and supposedly, their females got turned on by fighting their males for dominance.

Jade could overpower him with ease, which was probably a turn-off for her, but she was responding to his flirting, so maybe she was curious about having sex with an immortal.

He would be more than happy to satisfy her curiosity and show her what an immortal male with vast experience and endless stamina could do for her.

She would be glorious. He had no doubt of that.

"I would love to train with you one day." He cast her a suggestive look. "Perhaps later, we could wrestle between the sheets."

He had a feeling that Jade would appreciate his directness, but if he was wrong, his boldness could backfire.

19

JADE

*T*he immortal was so refreshingly bold.

Human females might have considered his approach presumptuous or even rude, but Jade appreciated the directness. Still, she was Kra-ell, and now that she didn't need to obey Igor's rules, she would never again have sex that she didn't initiate. Phinas didn't know the Kra-ell ways, but he would have to learn to regard her with more respect and wait to be invited instead of issuing the invitation first.

The one exception to that was a life-debt.

He could ask anything he wanted, and she would have to deliver. If he asked for sex, though, it would be on her terms.

"Does that line work for you? Or do you just thrall women to wrestle you in bed?" She didn't wait for him to answer as she moved to the next tent.

"Do I look like the kind of guy who has to thrall a woman to get her naked?"

He didn't. He was a fine male specimen, but he was no match for her physically, and that was regrettable.

Jade had never taken a human to her bed or even a hybrid, and the idea of sex with a male she could overpower effortlessly didn't appeal to her. Then again, as a Kra-ell female her duty was to choose the best male to breed with, and immortals had significant advantages over the Kra-ell. If a child resulted from the union, it would be better protected against injury, heal faster, and perhaps possess other abilities that the gods gave to their hybrid descendants with humans but not to the Kra-ell.

She cast him a quick glance. "For a human, you're good-looking, but you need to work on your game. Especially around me."

He cracked a grin. "I don't play games, and neither do you. You're not human, and neither am I. Therefore, human rules of conduct don't apply to us." He took the folded tent from her and stuffed it in its bag.

Jade looked around the campground to see if there was anything left to do, but all the tents were down, and nearly all of the equipment had been taken to the trucks already. "In principle, you are right, but there are nuances you need to learn, and I don't have time to explain them. We need to move out."

Undeterred, Phinas cast her a grin that revealed his slightly elongated fangs. Jade had no doubt that he had done it on purpose to show her that he was attracted to her. "I can't wait to hear all about those nuances. We should resume this conversation as soon as we can." He leaned and pecked her on the cheek. "Until we meet again, beautiful."

Dumbfounded, she watched him collect the two tents, four sleeping bags, and other miscellaneous equipment and carry everything to the truck.

No one had ever taken such familiar liberties with her. Not even her own sons or daughter.

"Jade!" Tom called her over. "You are riding with us."

"Not if I can help it," she muttered under her breath.

She'd managed to avoid walking next to Tom until they were intercepted by the additional trucks, and she'd hopped on one to avoid riding with him on the way to the farm.

Jade hoped her luck would hold and she wouldn't have to ride with him all the way to Helsinki. Being stuck in the command van for so many hours with the compeller, she might be forced to reveal too much.

He would ask a lot of questions, which she would have no choice but to answer, and keeping the few secrets she didn't want him to get out of her would be that much harder.

Casting a quick look at Phinas's back, she considered using him as an excuse.

She could tell Tom that she was interested in the male and that she wanted to ride in the truck with him. It wouldn't even be a lie.

She wanted to continue the silly human-style banter they'd been enjoying.

Phinas amused her, and the smiles she'd given him had been real for a change, not the kind that were meant to intimidate or manipulate.

Heck, she didn't even remember what he'd said that had amused her, and given that Igor and Valstar were still alive, it was a miracle she'd found anything funny or that it could take her mind off revenge for even a few moments.

It had been so long since anything or anyone had managed to distract her from the bottomless pit of grief and rage that had taken permanent residence in her chest.

There had been brief moments of peace when Drova had been born. On occasion, the baby's sweet smiles had managed to loosen the tight vise gripping Jade's dark heart, but it was difficult to enjoy the child when her older brothers hadn't gotten a chance to live and father children of their own. They didn't even get to die an honorable death in battle.

Walking over to the van, Jade peered inside through the open side door. "It looks cramped in here. I'd better ride in one of the trucks." She started to pivot on her heel.

"Stop," Tom commanded. "You're coming with us."

Jade arched a brow. "Why? Are you afraid I'm going to run?"

He'd compelled the other Kra-ell to obey the Guardians who were in charge of them and commanded them not to get farther than fifty feet away from the Guardian they were assigned to.

He hadn't compelled her.

Tom let out a long-suffering sigh. "Do you always assume the worst about people?"

She lifted her other brow. "Shouldn't I?"

"No, you shouldn't. I understand why you do, though." He shook his head. "You are part of this command, so you ride in the command van."

"Yamanu is not in the van, and he's in charge of all the Guardians."

"He is in the lead truck for a good reason." Tom leaned closer. "He can do things that even I can't. He can hide the entire convoy from human eyes, but if there are other vehicles on the road, he has to let them see ours to avoid them crashing into us."

She narrowed her eyes at him. "There is no way Yamanu can do more than you. It doesn't work like that."

"He has more practice. I haven't used such massive shrouding in eons."

"How old are you?"

"Old." He motioned for her to get in.

He was probably younger than she was, but since she hadn't actually lived all those years she'd spent in stasis, perhaps it didn't count. Then again, she'd been through enough torment and anguish to last anyone several life-times, and that was what mattered.

"What position will the van have in the convoy?" she asked as she put her foot on the step.

"One before last."

"Makes sense." She climbed into the cramped interior.

Tom's mate was strapped into a seat with a security belt, and another female who Jade hadn't met yet sat next to her.

William was in the back, immersed in whatever was on the screen of his computer, and a Guardian sat behind the wheel.

"Hi. I'm Sylvia." The woman offered Jade her hand.

She was pretty, but not perfectly beautiful like a goddess, which meant that she was an immortal.

"Hi." Jade shook it. "Handshaking is a human custom."

"Does it bother you?" Sylvia asked.

Jade sat across from her on the bench. "It has been a very long time since I pretended to be human. At first, I found it strange, but I got used to it."

"What do the Kra-ell do for greetings?"

"We nod to acknowledge our superiors. Otherwise, we ignore each other unless we have something to say."

Sylvia stifled a grimace. "That's efficient, just not very friendly."

"We are not friendly people." Jade thought about what she'd said for a moment. "I take that back. We don't express friendliness in the way humans do, but we are tribal people, so bonds of friendship are important to us. In fact, they are crucial for our survival."

Sylvia's expression softened. "That makes much more sense to me."

Jade wasn't friendly, but Kagra definitely was. Did that make Kagra a better leader? Or could Kagra allow herself to be friendly because she wasn't the leader?

Now that they were free, Kagra might want to split and get a tribe of her own, but that was as ill-advised now as it had been all the other times when she'd brought it up before they had been captured. There was strength in numbers, and they needed it now even more than they needed it then.

20

TOVEN

As the van pulled out, Jade leaned back. "What doesn't make sense to me is that Igor didn't show up and didn't arrive with Russian troops in tow, either. There aren't that many paved roads in Karelia, so if any force was coming, we should have crossed paths with it, and if he sent the Russian Air Force to bomb the compound, we would have heard the explosions."

Toven nodded. "I had the same thoughts. William launched one of the small surveillance drones to be our eyes from above, and so far, he has seen no activity. We also have the large military drones we used during the attack circling the entire area at a low altitude overhead, and so far, there has been no troop movement or other military aircraft that we could detect in the area. Perhaps Igor hasn't been able to get organized yet."

"He had plenty of time," Jade said. "He wouldn't want to lose our trail." She looked at William. "Are you running that disrupter of yours?"

He nodded. "Igor can't trace the trackers if that's what you mean, and if he sends humans to track us, they won't see past Yamanu's shrouding. If he comes in person, though, he will have no problem finding a convoy of twenty trucks and a van."

Jade appeared to be focused inwardly for a spell before she raised her eyes to him again. "If Igor doesn't attack us on our way, he must have figured out another way to get what he wants. What worries me is that we are clueless as to what that might be. Underestimating Igor is a mistake typically done only once, if you catch my drift."

"Loud and clear," Toven said. "But you are not telling me anything I don't know. I'm a strong compeller as well, and I have an army of trained immortal warriors with me. Still, I'm moving your people out, and I wouldn't do that if I underestimated Igor."

His answer seemed to satisfy Jade, but only partially. "Perhaps Valstar knows what Igor would do in a situation like this. He should be here in the van with you."

Toven chuckled. "I didn't want to put the two of you in the same vehicle, and I prefer your company to his."

He had many more questions for Jade, and when they arrived at the place that Turner had found for them outside of Helsinki, he would pose the same questions to Valstar.

Toven didn't expect either of them to flat-out lie, but both were strong, and both had lived under Igor's thumb for a long time, so they had plenty of experience withholding information from a compeller.

Given Jade's hard stare, she knew why he wanted her in the van for the next twelve hours. "As much as I detest Valstar, I wouldn't end his miserable life before we've wrung all the information out of him that might help us catch Igor. But after we catch his boss, they are both mine."

Toven dipped his head. "I will keep my promise. Their lives are yours to do with as you please."

"I'm counting on it." She briefly flicked her gaze to Mia before leveling her unnerving eyes on him. "I also might be more pleasing to the eye than Valstar, but I'm sure that's not why you wanted me here."

He smiled. "You whetted my appetite with your brief history account, and I'm curious to learn more. You said that the Kra-ell were not technologically advanced, and yet you embarked on an interstellar voyage across the universe. Were you sent by the gods?"

Jade nodded. "When the gods' king demanded that we start settling on other planets, he also offered to get us there. The ship we arrived in belonged to the gods, but it was a piece of crap vessel that should have been decommissioned ages prior. Instead of the voyage taking two hundred and twenty-three years, it took over seven thousand. I'm surprised any of us survived in the stasis pods and even more surprised that we survived the explosion. I don't know if it was a malfunction, which is possible given how old the ship was when it started the voyage, not to mention how old it was when it arrived at its destination. But I suspect that it was sabotage. I just don't know why or by whose hands."

Toven was still reeling from the seven-thousand-years figure.

The Kra-ell must have left shortly after his parents had been exiled. At the time of Toven's birth, his parents had only been on Earth for a few centuries, but it hadn't been his father's first visit, nor was it Ahn's or Athor's. They had taken part in much earlier expeditions. The difference was that this time, they had been left behind for good.

They had been exiled and banished for their part in the rebellion.

Not that they had told him any of that.

His father hadn't talked about a rebellion or an exile. Most of the other gods who had been born on Earth hadn't even been told that their kind had arrived from somewhere else. Ekin was a little less tight-lipped than Ahn, so he'd let a few things slip, giving Toven the impression that the gods had arrived voluntarily and that, at some point, communications with home had been severed, probably because something terrible had happened back there.

Mortdh, who had been one of the exiles, had thrown hints around for centuries, but he was unhinged, and Toven had dismissed his half-brother's remarks as the rantings of a lunatic.

"How many settlers were on the ship?" Sylvia asked.

When Jade seemed reluctant to answer, Toven added with a touch of compulsion, "I would like to know that as well."

"Twelve hundred, but most didn't make it, and we can safely assume that Igor collected all the survivors and killed off most of the males to even the ratio between males and females."

That was a lot of people.

"How many original purebloods were in the compound?" Toven asked.

"Igor's pod had twenty members, sixteen males, and four females. Of the six purebloaded females he took from my tribe, only three were from the original group, including myself, and the other three were born on Earth. From other tribes, he took fifteen more original purebloaded females."

Toven wrapped his arm around Mia's shoulders. "I assume that you are talking about escape pods?"

Jade nodded. "The stasis pods were ejected from the mother ship before it was destroyed. They had some propulsion capability, and they got dispersed over a very wide area. Most probably ended up in the Arctic Ocean."

That made them extremely difficult to retrieve, if not impossible.

"How did Igor know where to find you and the others?"

She chuckled. "I tried to get him to tell me that for years. I don't know."

William lifted his head. "We found a tracker in Sofia. It's a very sophisti-cated piece of equipment, but since she's a young human, he must have gotten her implanted with it. Perhaps all of the original settlers had implants in them, and Igor either had a stash of them or removed them from himself and his inner-circle buddies."

"I'm not aware of having a tracker in me." Jade grimaced. "Although I wouldn't put it past the gods to trick us and put it in us after we went into stasis."

"How was that done?" Toven asked. "We can only put someone in stasis using our venom."

21

JADE

"It wasn't done with venom, that's for sure." Jade pursed her lips. "We each had an individual pod within the larger escape pod, and the gods hooked us up to all kinds of tubes that were supposed to put us into stasis and keep us healthy during the voyage. I counted to five, and it was lights out for me, as the humans say." She huffed out a breath. "The next time I opened my eyes, seven thousand years had passed. Obviously, I didn't know that right away. I knew that much more time had elapsed than it should have because we were all in pretty bad shape, and we crash-landed with our escape pod creating a crater the size of a stadium. One of our males was able to resurrect the equipment, but we thought that it was still malfunctioning and that the number it displayed was incorrect. When we got out, made it to civilization, and oriented ourselves, it was a shock to discover how advanced humans were, and it confirmed that number. It took us seven thousand years to reach our destination."

Sylvia tilted her head. "Seven thousand exactly?"

"A little longer than that. Why?"

"If it were exactly seven thousand, then it would have been sabotage for sure."

"Well, it was more than that, but I still think that it was done on purpose."

"Do you think it was done by the gods?" Mia asked.

Jade shrugged. "Why send us across the universe? They could have programmed the ship to self-destruct closer to home."

"Because your queen would have known that," Toven said. "By the time your ship arrived at its destination, the queen was long gone, and all your relatives were gone as well, and there was no one to investigate what happened."

"We were supposed to settle in and prepare things for more Kra-ell to arrive, and we were also supposed to provide the exiled gods with labor in payment for the voyage. If the king didn't want the exiled gods to get workers, he could have sent us somewhere else."

Tom lifted a pair of sad eyes at her. "What if your ship wasn't the only one that exploded? What if the king was sending all the Kra-ell on old ships to get rid of them?"

"That wouldn't have been a practical way to get rid of us. Even though the ship was old and it wasn't a great loss, there were only twelve hundred Kra-ell on board. That wasn't enough to tip the head-count scale in the gods' favor."

She'd speculated on that endlessly for years, and one scenario was that someone had found out that the royal twins were on board, and the sabotage had been an assassination. Her guess as to the identity of the assassin was Igor, of course.

But why send an assassin?

Not everyone approved of the queen or of the peace treaty she'd brokered, so it could have been a retaliation. But since the twins had been consecrated to the priesthood, they hadn't been meant to be the next rulers. Besides, they had left, so what was the point of killing them seven thousand years later?

The gods had even less of a motive to assassinate the queen's children, especially since the peace treaty was so tenuous.

Why had they been smuggled on the ship in the first place, though?

Had the queen feared for their lives? Maybe she'd received threats?

If she had, Jade hadn't heard about it.

Throughout their lives, the twins had been kept in seclusion in the Mother's main temple, dedicated from birth to serve the goddess, and no one had known what they looked like.

It was unusual for a male to be dedicated to the priesthood, but the head priestess had made an exception for the prince because twins were extremely rare for the Kra-ell, almost unheard of, and the belief was that they were born sharing a single soul.

There had been rumors about their incredible compulsion powers, but that wasn't surprising. The queen was the most powerful Kra-ell compeller, so it made sense that her children were powerful as well.

Jade had been a junior commander in the Queen's Guard for only five years before drawing the lottery number that had put her on the settlers' ship, but during that time, she'd seen the twins walking the palace garden on several occasions. They'd both been veiled and covered in loose clothing from head to toe, but she'd memorized their bearing and their gait, which she had recognized when they had been escorted to the pod right next to hers.

That had been just one clue, though.

The second clue that those were no ordinary Kra-ell was that their pod had an equal number of males and females, which Jade was sure wasn't the case for any of the other pods. And the last clue was the god technician who had tended to them. The guy was anxious and jumpy, and he couldn't wait to get them and their other pod members hooked up, so he could seal them in.

Jade had only ever shared her suspicions with Kagra, and since Jade didn't have proof that the twins had been aboard the ship, keeping it away from Tom hadn't been difficult. He'd demanded true facts from her, not speculations.

However, she was convinced that Igor knew that the royal twins were onboard, despite never mentioning it. And if the ship had indeed been sabotaged, he was just ruthless enough to have done it.

It was all speculation, though, and no matter how many times Jade turned it over in her head, things just didn't add up. She was either missing pieces of the puzzle or had created a conspiracy theory where there had been none.

Still, if the queen had felt the need to hide her children on the other side of the galaxy, there must have been a reason for that, and Igor might have been sent to end them. He might have caused the explosion to cover his tracks, but he couldn't have been the one who'd made the voyage take so much longer than it had been supposed to.

However much thought Jade had dedicated to the subject, she couldn't find a reason for Igor to delay the ship's arrival for so long.

Someone else must have done that.

"I'm about seven thousand years old," Tom said. "I was born about the time that you embarked on your journey. My parents arrived only a couple of centuries earlier, which from a gods' time perspective is not long, and yet no one ever mentioned a shipment of workers or the Kra-ell. I don't think they knew you were coming."

Jade tilted her head. "Did they say what their mission here was?"

"My parents didn't, but my brother threw hints around." Tom snorted. "He was a nonconformist. I guess you could call him a rebel. The older gods didn't talk about their past or why they left their home."

"It's so weird," Mia said. "Why were they so secretive? And why were the Kra-ell sent here to supposedly help the gods, but no one told the gods that they were coming?"

"I smell a rat." Sylvia leaned her elbow on her knee and her chin on her fist. "A conspiracy. I can understand the gods hiding the fact that they had been exiled for committing treason from their children. It would have cast them in a bad light and could have given their kids rebellious ideas. But if they were expecting the arrival of a ship full of Kra-ell, they would have prepared the younger generation for the guests. If they wanted to keep their past a secret, they might have wanted to prevent the ship from getting to its destination, but I can't see how they could have caused the malfunction that delayed its arrival by thousands of years. They couldn't do that from Earth, and since they had no contact with their home planet, they couldn't have asked their former rebel friends to sabotage it for them either."

Tom cleared his throat. "I'm not sure exactly when all communications were severed." He sighed. "I was one of the first gods born on Earth, and my father wasn't as secretive with me. The other young gods weren't even told that we were extraterrestrials."

His mate lifted her eyes to him. "But if you knew, why didn't you tell the others?"

"Ahn forbade it, and his word was law. No one dared to disobey." He smiled. "Except for my father, that is. Ekin found clever ways of working around Ahn's commands."

"I don't get it," Sylvia said. "Ahn answered to the council, and the council included all the gods of voting age. How could he have forbidden something without securing the council's approval?"

Tom smiled. "The same way Kian sometimes does things without consulting the council. In matters involving the security of the clan, he can make executive decisions without asking for anyone's approval."

Interesting. It seemed that Kian was the one in charge, not Tom.

"Is Kian one of the surviving gods?" Jade asked.

Tom hesitated for a moment before answering. "He's not. He's an immortal."

"So, how come he's in charge?"

Mia avoided her eyes, and Sylvia got busy examining her fingernails.

Tom closed his eyes. "I guess you deserve some information as well, but I need to compel you to keep it to yourself."

Jade widened her eyes, which she knew made her look even more alien than normal. "Who am I going to tell? You've already compelled me to keep your identity and that of your people a secret, and aside from me, only Kagra knows who you are. Do you want me to keep it from Kagra as well?"

"Yes. For now. We still don't know what we are going to do with you and your people, and the less they know about us, the better."

"I disagree. I don't know how many of you there are, but it can't be too many, and there are only a couple of hundred of us, including the hybrids. We should stick together."

The truth was that she hadn't thought along those lines until that moment. When Tom had first approached her, her objective had been to eliminate Igor and his close circle of murderers. Once that was achieved, she'd expected them to leave her at the compound to lead it, and to keep a loose eye on her. Maybe even appoint a liaison. But now that her people were being forced to resettle, joining Tom's clan seemed like the best option.

Even though their hacker had managed to secure the money, it wouldn't be easy to resettle a large group of people who looked different enough to stand out and who were traveling with children and livestock.

22

TOVEN

*J*ade's suggestion had surprised Toven on two accounts.

First, how had she guessed that there were only a few hundred of them?

Secondly, he would have never expected her to relinquish sole authority over the Kra-ell in exchange for security, but perhaps he'd been wrong about her.

Not that what she'd suggested was in the cards. Kian would never agree to invite the Kra-ell to join the clan.

"It's not up to me. As you've observed, I'm not the leader of this community. In fact, I'm a recent addition, and although I've been accepted and welcomed, I'm not even on the council, nor do I hold any official position. I volunteered to help because I'm the strongest compeller the clan has." He tightened his arm around Mia's shoulders. "I was also blessed with a mate who enhances my powers."

Jade gave Mia an appreciative once-over. "That's why you dragged your crippled mate into enemy territory. The gods are not high on my list of good people, but the one quality I've always appreciated about them was their devotion to their mates."

Mia groaned. "I know that I shouldn't expect you to know anything about political correctness, but just for future reference, it's rude to call someone a cripple."

Jade dipped her head. "I meant no offense, but the fact is that you don't have legs. Is there a better way to refer to your condition?"

"Definitely. Disabled or challenged are acceptable terms, but I like it best when people just ignore my legs. Before I started regrowing them, I used prostheses very effectively, and my mobility wasn't restricted. Most people didn't even notice that I had difficulty walking or that my gait was a little stiff. But when I turned immortal and started regrowing my legs, I could no longer wear them because it put pressure on the stumps. It would have impacted the growth."

As Mia had blurted out about turning immortal, Toven tensed, expecting Jade's next question.

She frowned. "What do you mean you turned immortal? You are either born immortal or human. No one can turn immortal." When Mia looked to Toven for help, Jade leveled her eyes at him. "I should have known that the gods would bring their genetic knowhow to Earth. Can you turn anyone immortal?"

It was an odd statement. The gods created humans, so they had to bring their genetic knowhow with them, but Toven had never heard of the gods turning humans into immortals or changing them in any way. They might have done that at some point, hundreds of thousands of years ago, jump-starting the leap from ape-like creatures to homo sapiens by using their own DNA, but from then on, it was just evolution.

"Perhaps the first gods who came to Earth manipulated the genetics of the proto-humans and helped them leap ahead of natural evolution, but the group of gods I was part of did not have advanced genetic abilities. We discovered how to activate Dormants by chance."

Jade looked skeptical. "What's a Dormant?"

"A Dormant is a child of an immortal female with a human male. They are born human but carry the immortal genes, which can be activated with venom."

Jade tilted her head. "What about a child born to an immortal male and a human mother?"

"They don't carry the genes. They are only inherited through the mothers. Even a Dormant mother who hasn't been activated gives her children the genes of immortality."

He could practically see the proverbial wheels spinning in Jade's brain as she processed what he'd just told her.

"So if a child is born to a hybrid female and a human male, she is a carrier of long-lived genes?"

"We don't know whether it works the same for the Kra-ell. Obviously, Marcel hopes that it does."

Jade's eyes widened. "Sofia's mother is a hybrid. Can she turn Kra-ell?"

"A hybrid Kra-ell. But as I said, we don't know if it works. What we do know is that a hybrid Kra-ell's venom can't activate one of our Dormants. Emmett was intimate with one for a long time, but she didn't transition until she took an immortal mate."

In the back of the van, William groaned. "You shouldn't have told her that."

Toven had a feeling that William was right. Looking into Jade's dark eyes, he said, "You can't ever tell anyone about that. Not even Kagra."

She nodded. "If it worked for the children of the males, it would have been huge. It could have given us a new lease on life. But our females don't breed with humans. There is no need and, frankly, no inclination either. We are programmed to seek the best breeders for our offspring, and the natural choice is pureblooded males. As it is, there are not enough of us even for them, and that's after Igor's selective slaughter. I wish there was a way to change our genetics, so we had an equal number of female and male births. That would have solved a lot of problems."

"Perhaps the solution was always in front of you," Sylvia said. "If the Kra-ell females chose human males to father their children, they would have produced hybrids who were capable of transmitting the Kra-ell genes to the next generation, and since those hybrids had half of their DNA from their human fathers, their children could have a more evenly distributed gender birth ratio."

That was an interesting hypothesis.

Vlad, Mey, and Jin were good examples of the kind of offspring a union between an immortal Dormant and a hybrid Kra-ell could produce. It would be interesting to see whether their children would be predominantly male or more evenly gender-distributed.

Jade shook her head. "We can't experiment like that. There are too few pureblooded and hybrid females, and we are having as many children as we can. Our fertility is much better than the gods', but it's a fraction of that of the humans."

23

PHINAS

Karelia's roads were full of potholes and every time the truck hit one, which seemed to happen every couple of minutes, Kagra winced and some of the other injured Kra-ell stifled groans.

By now they were all well enough to sit, with the exception of Kagra, who should have been lying down but had refused to and was paying the price for it.

Phinas got up and walked over to Merlin. "Can't you give Kagra and some of the others more painkillers?"

"I offered." The doctor's lips twisted in a grimace. "They refused. These people are stubborn as oxen. Hell, let me rephrase. I'm sure that they could outdo any ox." Merlin leaned closer to whisper in Phinas's ear. "They consider getting injured a failure, and I think that they are punishing themselves by refusing to take painkillers."

"I suspect that you are right." Phinas glanced around to see if anyone was listening in before leaning closer to Merlin. "Did you bring your sleeping potion? We can knock them out with that."

Merlin shook his head. "I have it, but I'm saving it for an emergency."

"What kind of an emergency are you expecting?"

"It doesn't only work on them. If Igor shows up with an army, the potion might be useful."

"It's not going to do any good against machine guns or rockets."

Merlin pursed his lips. "He's not going to open fire on his people. He wants them back."

"The Kra-ell are resilient, and they heal fast. Igor will assume that most of them will recover, and since he doesn't give a shit about the humans, which includes us because that's what he thinks, it makes perfect sense for him to open fire on the convoy."

Merlin smoothed a hand over his nearly white beard. "You might be right. How come you are not concerned?"

Phinas patted the machine gun slung over his chest. "I'll meet fire with fire."

He and the others had donated their Kevlar vests and hats to protect the children and the humans, and as the exoskeletons had to go back with the amphibian to make room in the trucks, he had no protective gear. But Phinas wasn't worried. It wouldn't be the first time he'd been riddled with bullets. Unless he was hit with a rocket to the head or the heart, he would survive most other injuries.

"Give me the pills and a bottle of water, and I'll convince Kagra to take them."

Merlin pulled a pill bottle out of his pocket, a water canteen from his crate, and handed them to Phinas. "Good luck with that."

"I don't need luck." He tapped his temple. "I'll use cunning and my knowledge of female psychology."

Merlin snorted. "This, I would like to see."

"Watch and learn, my friend." He gave the doctor one last smile before returning to his seat next to Kagra.

Leaning her head against the side of the truck, she had her eyes closed, and her lips pressed together.

"Are you okay?" he asked.

"I'll live," she murmured.

"Yes, you will. And you will fight again."

"You'd better believe it." She didn't even open her eyes.

"It might be sooner than you think. Igor might attack us en route. We expect him to show up with the Russian military and open fire."

She cracked her eyes open. "I don't even have a weapon to fight with."

"You have your fangs and your nails." He took her hand and lifted it to examine her nails. "How hard are they?"

"Hard." She pulled her hand out of his grip. "Are you flirting with me, Phinas?"

"What gave you that impression?"

"That's the second time you've held my hand."

"No offense, but I have my sights set on your boss. Especially since she owes me a life-debt. She said I can ask for anything, and she'll deliver."

Kagra's lips twitched with a smile. "She likes you, so I'm glad you weren't flirting with me. Jade and I decided a long time ago that we would not share males. We are too close to each other for that to work. Usually, females of the same tribe share all the males, but Jade and I divided ours between us. The others could have anyone they wanted, though, and they did."

Phinas lifted his hands. "Do you know the human phrase 'too much information?'"

She smiled again. "I watch a lot of American movies. I know what it means. You don't want to hear about Jade's past sexual exploits."

"Precisely. Let's talk about Igor's imminent attack instead. You are in no shape to fight because you are in too much pain. Your internal organs are most likely healed enough not to tear if you fight, but the pain will make you fear that they will and it will slow you down." He pulled out the container Merlin had given him. "If you can't swallow pills, I can ask the doctor to give you a shot."

"I can swallow." She eyed the container suspiciously. "How big are they, and how many do I need to take?"

"Merlin said that you need six." Phinas opened the container and shook out six small tablets into the palm of his hand. "They are small."

He had a feeling Kagra had very little experience with pills or swallowing any solids, for that matter. She lived on a liquid diet.

She looked at his hand and grimaced. "One isn't big, but six are. Maybe I should take them one at a time?"

"Whatever works for you." He twisted the cap off the water container and handed it to her.

She gagged on each pill, but she didn't give up and took them all.

"Good job." He patted her knee. "You'll start feeling better soon."

A few minutes later, her features smoothed out, and she let out a sigh. "I feel like I do when I drink too much vodka."

Interesting.

"Did you have that reaction before?"

She shook her head. "When Merlin gave me shots for the pain before, I passed out. This just feels like a pleasant buzz." She rubbed a hand over the flat expanse of her stomach. "I'm all warm inside, and I'm a little floaty."

Perhaps it was underhanded of him, but Phinas wasn't going to waste the opportunity to ask Kagra about her boss.

"Did Jade have a favorite?"

Kagra cast him an amused sidelong glance. "Me. I was her favorite."

"I meant from among the males."

"She liked each of them for different reasons, but she didn't favor any one of them over the others."

24

KIAN

"Thank you." Kian took the paper cup from Aliya. "It was very thoughtful of you to bring us breakfast."

She smiled shyly. "I wish I could take credit for the idea, but Syssi texted me and asked if I could do that. Naturally, I was more than happy to help in any way I could." She looked at him expectantly.

"Jade and the others are free, but their captor is at large, so we had to evacuate them from their compound. We are working on a plan to bring them somewhere safe."

She held his gaze, expecting him to elaborate, but he didn't have time to indulge her.

Smart girl that she was, Aliya dipped her head. "Thank you. You have mine and Vrog's eternal gratitude."

"You're welcome, but I'm doing it as part of the clan's humanitarian effort and for security reasons."

"Nevertheless. We are grateful." She turned on her heel and left the room.

Removing the lid, Kian took a sip of coffee and leaned back. The war room didn't have windows, and he missed the view of the village from his office. He loved watching the sunrise and the café filling up with the morning crowd, but it didn't seem like he was going to get a break today.

There was still so much to be done, so much to decide on, and even Turner wasn't as confident as he usually was about the overall plan. They had bits and pieces, things that had to be done, like securing an MRI device in Helsinki and loading it on the *Aurora* and finding a naval security detail for this voyage and the next. After that, he planned to charter the ship for private executive cruises and make back what he'd spent on her.

The original itinerary of the ship was to sail through the Panama Canal and head to a secluded dock in Colombia, where it would be retrofitted with advanced weapon systems that he couldn't get on board in Europe.

Kian had promised Alena a wedding cruise, but there were so many risks involved in having the entire clan, including Annani, on a floating target. The Guardians' combined might and the technological superiority of the clan would be useless against a torpedo, a missile or a bomb.

Any adversary with access to such weapons could fatally injure the ship. The immortals weren't easy to kill, and most would probably survive the initial attack, but their enemies could finish the job by picking off the swimming survivors one at a time at their leisure.

It wasn't very likely that Navuh would find out about the cruise and attack, but Kian couldn't count on that, and he needed to be ready for even the most remote possibility of an ambush at sea. Given that Alena was pregnant and growing larger by the day, he couldn't delay the wedding by much. The ship had to get to Colombia, get fitted with armaments, and arrive at Long Beach more or less on schedule.

The plan was far from perfect, and Turner wanted to bring the Kra-ell to Long Beach, but perhaps they could combine their cerebral prowess and come up with a solution that would satisfy them both.

Putting his cup on the conference table, Kian covered it with the lid to preserve the coffee's temperature. "I have to keep the ship's original itinerary. Since we are heading to Colombia anyway to arm the vessel, we can unload our cargo first, either there or at one of the neighboring countries, and then have it rigged with the weapons we ordered. That would introduce a delay, and the contractor we hired to do the fitting of the weapons systems on board might get antsy, but I'm paying him enough to work around my schedule." He looked at Turner. "What was the name of your friend over there? Stefano? Maybe he can help us settle the Kra-ell somewhere near his place. Do they have jungles nearby?"

"His name is Arturo Sandoval, and I'm sure he'll be more than happy to help settle the Kra-ell and keep an eye on them for you as well. But do you want him to?"

Kian winced. "Good point."

"I see a few problems with that. Until the cruise ship reaches Colombia, it is defenseless and easily found. The longer it is at sea, and the clearer its course, the easier it will be for Igor to come up with a plan of attack. I'm securing an escort, but the submarine I have in mind has a limited range, and it won't be able to follow the ship across the ocean to the Panama Canal without at least two fueling stops, and it most certainly won't be able to follow it through the canal, and we'll need to find a different escort for the Pacific, which will further complicate things. This will present additional challenges, risks, and delays. Also, in case we are proven correct, and Igor sends a military vessel to hunt our ship, I want to control where the battle will take place. If the *Aurora* sustains catastrophic damage, I don't want it to be in the middle of the Pacific where we can't send rescue vessels to retrieve the people in short order."

As usual, Turner's assessment was spot on. "What do you suggest?"

"Let's see." Turner leaned back, braced his elbow on his fist, and stroked his jaw with two fingers. "Even after we get rid of the trackers and dump them in the sea, Igor will know which ship his people are on. If the *Aurora* manages to outrun whoever he sends to follow it and reach the Atlantic, it has a good chance of evading detection. But once in the Panama Canal, it's once again very easy to find. For obvious reasons, the passage cannot be shrouded or thralled, or compelled away. There are just too many people and resources along the way. In addition, there are many operators in that part of the world whom Igor can reach out to and compel to give chase and do damage. All it would take to sink the cruise ship is ramming another big vessel into it."

Kian lifted his hands. "Okay, you win. We have to offload the Kra-ell before the ship reaches the Panama Canal and make it very clear that we don't have any passengers on board. I would much rather avoid getting our newly-remodeled luxury cruise ship that my sister is supposed to get married on damaged or destroyed."

"Right," Onegus said. "We need to bring the Kra-ell to a location that can accommodate a cruise ship, but that's not densely populated or heavily guarded, and it needs to be closer to Helsinki to minimize their time at sea." He turned to his laptop and brought up the world map. "Where can we take close to four hundred people and a large cargo of livestock?"

25

KIAN

*T*urner kept rubbing his chin for a long moment, the faraway look in his eyes one that Kian had seen many times before, while the guy's brain worked out a solution to a difficult problem.

"Our best bet is the southwest coast of Greenland. It meets all three criteria."

Kian brought up a map of Greenland. "Why the southwest coast? The eastern coast of Greenland is closer to Helsinki."

"The eastern seaboard of Greenland doesn't have a dock large enough for a ship that size, and there is no airfield nearby with a runway long enough for the size of the plane that will be required to airlift our passengers out of there. Even the one on the south coast that I'm considering can only accommodate small and midsize aircraft. We will need to charter two narrow-body passenger jets."

"What about the livestock?" Onegus asked. "Can we leave it there?"

"Of course." Turner reached for his coffee cup. "Local farmers would be more than happy to collect however many heads of livestock we leave for them."

"How come you are so familiar with Greenland?" Kian asked.

"It's a long story." Turner took a sip from his coffee cup. "The port I'm thinking of is adjacent to an airfield that was built by the US Air Force." Turner paused to take another sip from his coffee. "The seaport and airport are both tiny, and so is the community that supports both. That will make shrouding and thralling everyone in the vicinity easy, which is crucial for transporting four hundred undocumented travelers and overcoming the typical port-of-entry documentation. It will also make it much easier to circumvent any surveillance."

Kian leaned forward. "The type of aircraft you are talking about can't cross the Atlantic and fly all the way to the western coast of South America. Where do you propose we take the Kra-ell?"

Turner shrugged. "The airliners can layover in some remote airport in Canada to refuel and continue to our airstrip. I don't think they are too big to land there."

"They might not be, but I'd rather not paint a large arrow pointing to our runway. Two approaching jetliners landing in a tower-less airfield will draw a lot of unwanted attention in the crowded Southern California airspace. They should be directed to an active but semi-private airfield that, from time to time, receives jetliner traffic from private parties somewhere out in the boonies. We can bus them from there. But that is beside the point. I am not comfortable with so many Kra-ell in the village. Even with Toven controlling them and ensuring their compliance with our instructions and demands, there are too many of them, and they will change the way we live. In addition, they have their particular nutritional needs, and I'm not ready to have sheep and goats grazing in the village. Then there is the issue of the humans and what to do with them."

"You need to bring the subject to the council and let them decide," Turner said. "You know my opinion."

"This is a security issue, so I don't have to get the council's approval for not accepting the Kra-ell, but I will need it if we decide that it is best to bring them here." Kian flicked his gaze to Onegus. "What do you think?"

"The issues you raised are all valid, and we need to work them out, but think of the alternative. Are we comfortable with such a large group of Kra-ell somewhere where we cannot monitor them? If Jade immediately guessed who Toven was, the other purebloods from the original pods might have guessed it as well, and we can't thrall them to forget what they know. If we don't catch Igor and eliminate him, we can't dismiss the possibility of him tracking them down and taking over again. Only this time, he could get out of Jade everything she already knows about us. In my opinion, those risks far outweigh the difficulties and risks of keeping the Kra-ell right where we can keep an eye on them."

Kian hated to admit it, but Onegus wasn't wrong.

Was he right, though?

The truth was somewhere in the middle, but no matter what was decided, it would require some sort of compromise.

Security was the only thing he wasn't willing to compromise on.

Turner cleared his throat. "Both options are problematic and will require a shift in how we run our security, and they will most likely impact our way of life as well. But of the two, I'd much rather have the Kra-ell closely monitored, routinely compelled to neutralize any threat they might pose, and heavily guarded. These objectives can only be achieved by bringing them to the village."

Kian knew he was in the minority, but he wasn't ready to concede yet. "We can't spare the Guardian manpower to effectively guard them. I could slap security cuffs on the adults, but then I won't be any better than Igor. We are supposed to be their liberators, not their new masters. On the other hand, I don't know these people, I can't anticipate their behavior, and I can't allow them to roam free in our midst. They are simply too powerful."

Turner's lips lifted in a conspiratorial smile. "As we've discussed before, Kalugal is taking great interest in the Kra-ell, and from what we've heard from Toven, his lieutenant fancies Jade. Surprisingly, she hasn't taken his head off yet, so she's not averse to his flirting, either. Maybe there is a match there, and if there is, Kalugal might allow the Kra-ell in his section. Since so many Guardians have moved to the third phase, there are plenty of vacancies in the original part of the village to relocate everyone residing in the second phase, and it can be easily annexed to Kalugal's. All you'll have to do is reinforce the fence surrounding it and open it on Kalugal's side. Once Toven is done with their initial compulsion, Kalugal can keep it up on an ongoing basis, with Toven and Mia providing an occasional deep boost. We even have the adjacent canyon area to provide pasture for the animals. That will save you the need to clear it of weeds every year ahead of the fire season."

Kian grimaced. "I still remember the smell of farm animals, and I don't want it anywhere near my house. But that's a minor consideration that we will find a solution for."

Looking at both Onegus and Turner, Kian addressed the last remaining obstacle, signaling his acceptance of the proposed solution. "What would you suggest we do with the humans? They have decades of memories that can't be erased, and even if that wasn't a problem or could be mitigated with compulsion, many of them are so habituated to serving the Kra-ell that they will be afraid to live on their own."

"Let's cross that bridge when we get to it," Turner said. "We have logistics to figure out."

"True." Kian closed his eyes for a brief moment. "I will need to run this by the council and by my mother."

"Naturally." Turner went back to typing on his laptop. "I'll inform the captain of the course we need him to plot."

Onegus nodded. "I'll notify Yamanu and Toven of the change of plans."

ELEANOR

"We need to evacuate Safe Haven," Leon dropped the bomb Eleanor had been dreading. "It's only temporary until we catch Igor."

When he'd called at five in the morning and asked her and Emmett to come to his office, she'd guessed that was the reason, but she'd hoped it wasn't.

Her gut tied up in knots, she flicked her gaze to Emmett, who looked as if all the blood had left his face.

"How are they going to catch him?" Emmett asked.

"The assumption is that he will want his people back and will follow the trackers implanted in at least some of them. All Toven and the Guardians need is for him to show up. With their earpieces blocking his compulsion and Toven at the ready, they will apprehend him easily."

"I don't understand." Eleanor frowned. "Kian is doing everything he can to get the Kra-ell safely to the ship and evade Igor. How does that mesh with catching him?"

Leon shrugged. "If they make it easy for Igor, he will know that they are setting a trap for him. Besides, Kian is not as worried about him as much as he is about the human forces Igor might compel to help him. We don't want to be forced to fight them, and we don't want to cause an international incident while transporting aliens."

"That's a sticky situation," Emmett said.

"In your opinion, what's more important?" Eleanor asked. "Getting the Kra-ell away from Igor or catching him?"

Leon pursed his lips. "The most important thing is to prevent Igor from getting them back. He can do a lot of damage without them, but he's much less of a threat on his own. If we are lucky, we will lure him out to sea and catch him there."

"I hope the plan works," Emmett murmured. "I really don't want to abandon Safe Haven. It's my baby, my life's achievement, and I love it here."

"I don't want to leave either," Leon said. "We invested a lot of money in the facility, and Ana and I love it here. But it is what it is."

"What do I do with the paranormals?" Eleanor asked.

"They are not immortal, and they don't know anything, so they can stay if they want. But the holidays are coming up, so I'm sure that they would appreciate a vacation back home."

"That will solve the problem for a couple of weeks." Eleanor got up and lifted Cecilia off the windowsill. "What if we can't catch Igor?"

She sat back down and stroked the cat's soft fur. The warmth and the contented purring eased the anxious knot in her gut.

"Then we will come up with a different solution," Leon said. "You will have to resign from the program, and Emmett will have to deliver televised sermons." He shifted his eyes to Emmett. "You can claim some rare autoimmune syndrome that prevents you from interacting with people."

Emmett groaned. "I need to be with the people, to soak up their energy and their adoration. I live for those moments." He let his head drop back and uttered a mournful groan.

Eleanor rolled her eyes. "I think that Leon's idea has merit, and it's certainly better than nothing." She turned to the Guardian. "Can we move the paranormal program somewhere else? We still didn't test whether any of them are Dormants. The ladies are more difficult to test, and regrettably, the Guardians didn't feel any special affinity toward them or toward the men. But since the males are easy to test, we should give them a chance."

"You are right. After they come back from their vacation and this latest crisis is over, I'll ask Kian's permission to start testing the men. But that's a worry for another time. Right now, you need to talk to the paranormals, tell them that you had some sort of a family emergency, and send them on vacation. We need to get out of here."

"What about the two hybrids assigned to Sofia?"

"I have it covered. I sent two Guardians to retrieve them. Kian doesn't want them to join Igor. The fewer people he has around him, the better."

"Where are we taking them?"

"After we remove their trackers, we will take them to the dungeon in the keep."

Emmett let out a dramatic sigh. "I hated being locked up down there. The Kra-ell need sunlight and air."

"It's only temporary," Leon said. "When Kian decides what he wants to do with the Kra-ell, those two will join the rest."

"I have a better idea." Eleanor kept petting the cat. "If Igor wants the two hybrids and calls them to him, we can follow them. Instead of collecting them and taking them to the keep, it's better to leave them where they are and put a couple of Guardians to tail them."

Leon winced. "We are a little short on Guardians at the moment, which is another reason Kian wants us back in the village. Igor might call those two or not. I'll give Onegus a call and tell him what you suggested."

"Are you taking Cecilia with you?"

Leon shifted his gaze to the cat and smiled. "That's another question for Onegus. We will need to take the tracker out of her, and I don't know if he's ready to do that yet."

"There is no more reason to pretend that Sofia is here," Emmett said. "If we take the tracker out, William can take it apart to see where it was made."

27

KIAN

*O*negus put his phone down, lifted the cup of coffee that was probably cold by now, and finished the last of what was in it. "Yamanu wasn't happy about the change of plan. He had his heart set on a month-long vacation with his mate, and now it's shortened to eight days."

"They can still cancel their plans," Kian said. "They didn't leave yet, did they?"

The three were taking a commercial flight to Helsinki, and since no one in their right mind flew to Finland in the winter, getting last-minute tickets hadn't been a problem.

"No, not yet, but Yamanu still wants Mey to come, and Jin and Arwel are going as well. We will soon have twenty-five of the Guardians back, so I don't mind that Arwel is leaving."

"I don't mind that either," Kian muttered under his breath. "What I mind is Mey and Jin on the ship and Mia and Sofia, not to mention Toven. What if Sofia starts transitioning? They have Merlin, and the ship has a clinic, but I planned on outfitting it in Long Beach, so it has no medical equipment in the clinic yet."

"We are getting an MRI," Turner said. "We might as well get the rest of the equipment delivered as well."

Kian arched a brow. "Did you find one for sale in Helsinki?"

"Bridget found a compact MRI in Turku of all places, and it's already making its way to Helsinki. It will get there before the ship docks. I'm sure

Bridget can find everything else that's needed for the clinic locally. I'll let her know to get on it."

Kian hadn't even known that Bridget was assisting Turner, but he should have guessed. The two were a dynamic duo.

"Thanks. And thank Bridget for me as well."

"Sure thing," Turner murmured from behind the screen of his laptop.

"Did you talk with your submariner friend?" Kian asked.

"Not yet." Turner lifted his head. "I'm going to call him once I'm done preparing instructions for him."

"Are you sure he's still in business? You said he retired from the navy over twenty years ago."

Turner smiled. "I know for a fact that he's still taking jobs. I've recommended him to an associate of mine, who used him not too long ago and was very happy with his service. Besides, Nils is never going to quit. He's threatened to do it many times over the years, but he loves what he does too much to let go."

"In case he says no, do you have an alternative?"

"I always do, but it won't be necessary. Nils will come through."

When Kian heard Onegus's phone ping, he turned to the chief with a questioning look.

"It's from Leon. He wants to discuss another option regarding the hybrids. Do you want to call him, or do you want me to do it?"

"I'll call him. I hope we are not too late and the two haven't already disappeared. They could've returned the rental car with the tracker in it and given us the slip."

Onegus shook his head. "That's not likely unless they also found the trackers we put in their backpacks."

"Let's find out." Kian dialed the Guardian's number.

"Hello, boss," Leon answered. "I'll keep it short. Eleanor says that we shouldn't pick up the hybrids. We should follow them instead. If Igor tries to retrieve them, they can lead us to him."

"Good point." Kian rapped his fingers on the tabletop. "Make it so. Put two Guardians on them. They need to have earpieces, tranquilizer darts, and regular guns on them."

Turner lifted his head. "That might not be a good idea. We already know that Igor is super careful and suspicious. If he tells them to come to him, he will do so in a way that will allow him to watch whether they have a tail. If he catches our Guardians, he can compel them to reveal everything they know. It's not worth the risk."

Kian considered it for a moment. "The chances of us catching Igor while he chases his people are slim. We are doing everything we can to keep him from getting to them. Once the dust settles and the Kra-ell are safe, those hybrids might be the only lead we have left."

"We can use Tim," Onegus said. "Jade can describe Igor to him even over the phone, and he can send her pictures of his work in progress. Once he's done, we can use face recognition to find him when he passes through an airport."

"He's too careful to get caught like that." Turner rubbed a spot between his brows as if he was fighting a headache. "He will wear a disguise and the special glasses that elude facial recognition."

"So what do you suggest we do?" Onegus asked.

"I can send a human team to follow the hybrids. If they get caught, they can't tell Igor anything. If we get a good description of him, they can eliminate him for us. As much as I would love to interrogate Igor and learn what he knows, he's too dangerous to capture. The instructions should be kill on sight."

Kian nodded. "I agree, but how do you explain to your human assassins what it takes to kill a Kra-ell?"

"I'll tell them that he's jacked on drugs, super paranoid, and super strong. The only way to take him out is from afar with a small rocket aimed at his head."

Onegus grimaced. "Gruesome, but effective. Just make sure that you instruct them to avoid any collateral damage."

"That might be unavoidable. He will keep the Kra-ell he has close to him."

"I meant innocent bystanders."

"I'll tell them to do their best."

"So, what's the plan?" Leon asked. "Do I send Guardians to watch the hybrids until a human team takes over?"

"Yes. But if they head to the airport before my team arrives, tell the Guardians to follow and verify the flight they are on, but no more. I will have another human team pick up the tail at the destination."

"Got it," Leon said.

"Anything else?" Kian asked.

"The cat. There is no reason to leave the tracker inside of it. Gertrude said that she could take it out, so we are bringing the cat with us, but the question is how to transport the device so William can tinker with it. Supposedly, it doesn't transmit when it's not in a living body, but I don't want to risk it. I can put it inside a thick lead box, but maybe I should ask William what he recommends."

"Do you have a scrambler?" Kian asked.

"I have a small one, but we can't use it on a plane. If you want me to use it, I will have to send it with the Guardians driving the moving van with the equipment from the lab."

Kian lifted his gaze to Turner. "What do you think?"

"Use a scrambler, and don't bring the tracker to the village. If it came from the gods' planet, it could contain technology we are not familiar with that can transmit through lead and could be impervious to the scrambler."

"If so, William's scrambler would have been ineffective, and Igor would have caught up to them by now."

Turner nodded. "You have a point. But since we can't be sure, I suggest caution. Igor discovering the location of the village is much worse than him discovering where his people are."

"You heard the man," Kian told Leon.

"I did. I'll give instructions to the Guardians driving the moving truck to take it with them and leave it at our downtown warehouse."

Kian looked at Turner. "Good enough? Or do you want us to put it in a safe deposit box in a bank?"

"The warehouse is good. William equipped it with so many security features that it's safer than a bank vault."

Kian returned his attention to Leon. "Anything else you need from me?"

"No, that's it. Eleanor is sending the paranormals, the doctor assigned to them, and the kitchen staff on vacation. Emmett is seriously depressed, and the Guardians are packing up all the sensitive equipment from the lab and our offices. I'm waiting for the moving van to get here. I'll send two guys to follow the hybrids, and when they are in position, I'll tell Gertrude to remove the tracker from the cat. It will be interesting to see what they do once it's out."

"Very well. Let me know if there is a problem."

"Will do."

28

CAPTAIN NILS PETERSON

*N*ils poured himself an afternoon tea and headed out to the porch for a smoke.

This time of year the air was brisk and the wind biting, but his wife did not permit smoking inside, so he'd put on a thick sweater, wrapped a scarf around his neck, and pulled on the cap she'd knitted for him last Christmas.

The smoking den he'd set up for himself on the porch overlooked the harbor, and his open man-cave included a comfortable armchair, a side table with a good reading lamp, and most importantly, a high-BTU gas heater to keep him warm and toasty.

When his phone rang, he didn't recognize the number and let the call go to voicemail. In his line of business, getting calls from unknown numbers was the norm rather than the exception, but he never answered before hearing the message first.

A moment later, he checked the mail and heard a voice he hadn't heard in a while.

"It's Turner. I'll call again in five. Pick up the phone."

Over the years, Turner had sent several referrals his way, but they hadn't worked together in at least a decade.

When the phone rang precisely five minutes later, Nils answered with a smile. "Hello, old friend. What a pleasant surprise. How have you been?"

"Very well. I retired a few years ago and now run a private operation. I specialize in hostage retrieval."

"Sounds exciting. How is business?"

"Booming. How is yours?"

"More or less the same. I'm thinking about retiring." Nils took a drag from his cigar. "I'm getting too old for all this crap."

Turner chuckled. "Guys like us don't retire. We get retired."

"That's what I'm afraid of. Against all odds, I managed to stay alive into my sixties and have enough to live on comfortably for what's left of my life. I can do without all the excitement."

"I doubt you can stay away from the sea for more than a week, but you do what's good for you. Before you give retirement a try, though, you need to take the job I'm offering. It might give you the extra cushion to retire comfortably."

His enigmatic friend never bothered with much preamble.

"What's the job?"

"A good friend of mine has a cruise ship that he suspects might get attacked at sea. It will depart Helsinki in about thirty hours and head toward Greenland. I need a heavily armed submarine escort to the Port of Narsaq on its southern coast."

After the long years Nils had known Turner and run clandestine operations for him, he'd thought that he would never be surprised by any request Turner might make, but he should have known better.

A cruise ship? That was new.

"What exactly are you expecting to encounter?"

"Frankly, we are not certain. We believe the aggressor will try to disable and possibly sink the ship to force the passengers off it. While that could be done by attaching detonation devices to the hull, the more likely scenario is an attack with a missile or a torpedo. And because he will need to collect the two hundred or so individuals he is after, I believe we will be dealing with an attacking ship rather than a sub. Therefore, he'll probably get a cruiser-size vessel."

Nils had great respect for the man's mind, but he needed to know what Turner was basing his assumptions on.

"How did you arrive at that conclusion?"

"The aggressor is interested in the passengers and wants them alive. So he will not bomb the ship out of the water and kill all onboard. Taking over by scaling and rappelling would require far more planning and equipment than he has the time or the ability to put together, so that is not an option either. Stealth sabotage would require trained commandos to which he isn't likely to have access. Once he gets the passengers, he also needs to transport them, so we can rule out a sub or a small gunship. It has to be a cruiser."

Tensing, Nils sat up straight. "I am unaware of any such vessel in our neck of the woods that is not flying the Russian flag. Are you proposing that we sink a Russian cruiser? And why would the Russian navy want to attack a civilian cruise ship? What are you not telling me?"

That last one was a question he did not expect an answer for. It was always only the 'need to know,' and even that was kept to a bare minimum. Turner shared only what was absolutely necessary.

"We believe that the aggressor has the means to do just that by way of funds or coercion or both. This will not be a Russian navy sanctioned operation, even if one of its ships is involved."

Well, that changed the picture. If Nils disabled a rogue ship that might have caused an unsanctioned international incident, the Russians wouldn't be too upset. They might even be thankful, as long as no one found out that it had been done by a private operator. They would want to take credit for it.

Stubbing out his cigar, he asked, "When did you say the cruise ship is leaving Helsinki?"

"In about thirty hours."

"There is no way I can get the crew and sub ready for this mission so fast. I need at least forty-eight hours. We are moored in an island far to the west, so we can meet up with the cruise ship when it passes by, but that will leave her exposed for most of the way through the Baltic Sea."

Nils imagined he could hear the well-oiled wheels turning in Turner's head as he considered his input.

"It isn't likely that the ship will be attacked in the Baltic. It's too close to the territorial waters of the surrounding countries, where other navy vessels, not to mention military aircraft of all kinds, are a short hop away. The aggressor will opt to attack as far away from land as possible so that calls for help from the ship will take many hours to be responded to by ships or aircraft arriving at the scene. He will need time to sink the ship, collect those he is interested in from the water, and put a safe distance between himself and any incoming rescue vessels. None of these objectives could be met while in the Baltic."

"I see that you have it all figured out."

"I do, but I needed to know that I can count on your help before making the final arrangements. I will instruct the cruise ship captain to hug the coast all the way to Bergen and make the crossing of the North Sea toward the Shetland Islands there. The proximity to land will provide the cruise ship with some measure of security, but once it leaves the Shetlands behind, we should expect to have at most twenty-four to thirty-six hours before the attack will take place. By that point, anyone responding to a distress call would be many hours away."

Nils considered his options.

A mission so fraught with risks should be planned and thought through with care, not rushed into head-on. An armed altercation with a navy vessel was not the same as stealthily transporting goods and personnel, which was most of what he had been doing for the past decade and a half. He hadn't seen action in so long that he had almost forgotten the rush it used to give him.

He could decline.

Correction, he should decline, but he knew that he wouldn't.

All his talk about retirement and getting tired of the excitement was a lot of bull. The truth was that he was bored with the small-fish operations that kept the lights on. The risks were minimal, but so were the rewards, and the excitement was nil.

Just thinking about a mission of this caliber made his muscles twitch in anticipation. Frankly, he had known that he would say yes to Turner within the first ten seconds of the call.

"Give me a couple of hours to make some calls to make sure I can pull it off for you in time."

"I can't wait that long. If you can't do that, I need to get someone else."

Now Nils tensed for a different reason.

He didn't want Turner to find someone else for this mission. He could already taste it.

"Don't worry. I'll make it happen. Consider it done."

"Excellent. That's what I wanted to hear. What's your price?"

Nils smiled. "I will let you know in a couple of hours, but don't worry. Given our long and successful history of cooperation, I will not take advantage of the tight spot you are in. I'll give you a fair price."

"I'm counting on that. Thank you, Nils."

As soon as Turner ended the call, Nils called Rob Farland, his indispensable second-in-command, and left a message on his secure voicemail. "We are hunting for a big fish, and we need to get on it ASAP. Assemble the crew and have everyone ready in twenty-four hours. I'm taking care of the necessary supplies. "

Supplies were code for munitions.

The line was supposedly secure, but one could never be too careful, and nothing he left in a recorded message could be used to incriminate him.

A couple of moments later, he got a reply. "Aye, aye, captain."

29

JADE

"This is so fancy." Kagra walked over to the bed and sat down.

The wedding venue Tom's people had secured for the night was much nicer than anything Jade had expected, but she'd stayed in some luxury hotels during her travels, and she knew what fancy looked like.

This wasn't it, but it was perfect for their needs.

It was outside of town and had over a hundred guest rooms, rolling hills on one side and the Baltic Sea on the other. Including the Guardians and Phinas's men, nearly four hundred people needed a bed and shower. The staff had been told to vacate the premises so there were no strangers they needed to hide from, and they could use the staff quarters to house more people.

Her and Kagra's room faced the sea, and she loved watching the vast expanse of water and the ice floating in the bay. So far this year, the winter had been mild, so the ice floaters didn't form a solid mass yet. In harsher winters, ice breakers were used to carve out a corridor for ships to sail between the major ports.

Had that been the case, it might have deterred Igor from securing a Russian ship to follow them, but that also could have meant the clan's cruise ship couldn't have gotten from the shipyard in Stockholm to the port of Helsinki.

"Come. Check it out." Kagra patted the mattress. "It's so comfy. I've never stayed in a room this nice. Have you?"

"During my travels, I stayed in nice hotels." She sat next to Kagra. "And I slept on comfortable mattresses."

Their accommodations back in China hadn't been nearly as lavish, and her room in Igor's compound was spartan, but it was sufficient.

Jade wasn't picky. The fact that she had served the queen back in the day and lived on the palace grounds didn't mean that she'd lived like royalty. She'd slept in the barracks with the rest of the guards.

When she'd stayed in fancy hotels, it had been for business, and she'd needed to appear wealthy. Otherwise, she would have opted for more modest accommodations.

Kagra leaned back on her forearms. "Tom's clan must have incredible connections in addition to deep pockets. I don't know how they got us this place on such short notice."

"I told Tom they could use the funds they had taken from Igor to finance our rescue. I owe them enough as it is. I don't want to owe them even more."

"Are you sure they are going to give us what's left after they pay themselves for our liberation?"

Jade shrugged. "Tom has given me his word, but you know how much I trust the promises of a god. To be fair, though, so far he has delivered on every promise, so I'm inclined to believe him."

Kagra toed her boots off. "I'm bone tired and want to go to sleep, but I'm filthy and need to shower. Do you mind if I go first?"

"Go ahead. I managed to shower before we left."

"Thanks." Kagra pushed to her socked feet and lifted her boots off the floor. "Do you want to go to the sauna after we shower? Phinas told me that it's a Finnish tradition to have a bridal sauna. The bride and her girlfriends have a party in the sauna before the wedding."

It shouldn't have bothered her that Kagra had spent twelve hours with Phinas, talking and getting to know him, while Jade had been stuck in the command van and had pretended to sleep for most of it to avoid Tom's never-ending string of questions.

But it did bother her, and that wasn't good.

Jealousy and possessiveness were not only character flaws, but they were also considered a sin in the eyes of the Mother of All Life.

"Did you pump him for information?"

The guilty look on Kagra's face indicated the opposite. "Their doctor gave me pain medication. I didn't want to take it, but Phinas convinced me that I would be better prepared to fight when I wasn't in pain, so I took them, and they made me overly talkative."

Jade glared at her. "There is a reason we avoid them as much as possible. They act like alcohol or *tpaba* on us. What did you tell him?"

"Nothing important. He asked a lot of questions about you."

That shouldn't have pleased Jade as much as it did. "And what did you tell him about me?"

Kagra grinned. "I made you sound like a goddess and the best leader possible for our people. I told him about your selflessness and the risks you took to teach our young the ways of the Mother under Igor's nose. I also told him that you are an incredible fighter and won against all the males of our former tribe."

As Jade winced, Kagra's smile wilted. "It felt good to talk about the old days with someone. But I might have said too much about how we ran our old compound."

"Like what?"

"Like compelling the humans to serve us. Back then, it wasn't a big deal because the Chinese government treated them much worse than we did, but nowadays, it sounds like we were slave owners."

Jade nodded. "I thought about that often during our years of captivity. These people must have felt the same about us as we did about our captors. The only differences between Igor and us were that we didn't slaughter their families, and most of them came to work for us voluntarily. They just didn't know what they were signing up for and that employment was for life."

"Would you have done things differently if given a chance?"

Jade nodded. "I would have been upfront about what was involved in working for us, and I would have compelled those who didn't want to forfeit their freedom to forget what I told them and let them go. I would have probably paid those who chose the security we offered better as well."

"Would you have set free those who wanted to leave?"

Jade shook her head. "The security of my people superseded all other considerations. I couldn't release those who worked for us and bred with our males to tell the world about us."

"Igor released them, and the world is still as ignorant about our existence as it was two decades ago."

"Igor is a much more powerful compeller than I am. Besides, we were no longer there, so there was no risk involved in releasing them. The humans could have told tall stories about us until they were blue in the face, but no one would have believed them without proof."

30

PHINAS

"I'm going to the sauna." Phinas slung a towel over his shoulder. "Either of you want to join me?"

Dandor cast him an incredulous look. "In your underwear, a T-shirt, and barefoot? It's freezing out there."

"It's not like we packed for a vacation. Besides, we are immortals." Phinas thumped his chest. "I bet the Kra-ell don't have a problem with the cold."

Boleck pulled the blanket under his chin. "I heard that the Finns enjoy saunas in the nude. Do they have separate rooms for males and females?"

"I don't know."

Boleck turned on his side. "I'm going to sleep. If there are naked ladies in the sauna, come get me."

"I'm going to sleep as well," Dandor said. "It's four o'clock in the morning, and I want to get some shut-eye before we start hustling again. When are we boarding the ship?"

"When it's ready, which should be this afternoon or evening." Phinas opened the door. "If either of you change your mind, you know where to find me."

As he trudged through the snow to the building where the saunas were located, Phinas hoped that he would find Jade enjoying one of the rooms. According to the brochure, the venue offered different types of saunas, wet, dry, and smoked.

Finnish saunas were the dry heat kind, not steam, and given where

Phinas had grown up, he'd experienced enough dry heat to last him his entire immortal lifetime. Then Navuh had moved the brotherhood to a tropical island, and the humid heat wasn't an improvement, but at least the island was pretty.

Then again, it was freezing cold as Dandor had said, and Phinas's feet were getting numb, so some heat, even the dry kind, would be welcome. But he wasn't going to the sauna to enjoy it. He hoped to meet Jade, but given what he'd learned from Kagra, there was little chance of that.

According to her second, Jade was all work and no play. During the long years of her captivity, the Kra-ell leader had denied herself pleasure as penance for failing to protect her people. Kagra claimed that Jade hadn't been forced to become Igor's prime, and that she'd chosen to do it as additional atonement.

That type of person wouldn't enjoy a sauna in the middle of the night, but hope was a powerful thing, and perhaps fate would smile on him.

As Phinas entered the building, he was immediately enveloped in heat, which was a tremendous relief. The sauna rooms were lined up on both sides of the wide corridor; some of them were small, only big enough for two or three people, while others were large enough to accommodate a small party, and thankfully they all had small windows he could peek through to see whether there was anyone inside.

Most were empty, which wasn't surprising given the hour of the night, but some were occupied, which explained the heat permeating the building. Several Guardians were in one of the larger rooms, enjoying beers in the nude. Their boisterous laughter made him smile, and if he didn't find Jade, he was going to join them and share a couple of beers with them, provided that they had any to spare.

The next several rooms were empty, one had a couple of human females who were wrapped in towels, and the one next to it was where he found Jade and Kagra, both gloriously naked.

They had no breasts to speak of, but their bodies were slender, graceful, and feminine. Their long limbs didn't look overly muscled, but their appearance was deceptive. Phinas had experienced firsthand how powerful Kra-ell females were, and he had only tumbled with an untrained hybrid. Those two were probably twice as strong as Aliya and ten times as lethal.

Should he knock and go in?

Could they sense him standing outside the door and ogling them?

Well, not them. He had eyes only for Jade. Not that Kagra wasn't pleasing to look at, but he wasn't attracted to her.

Jade's inner strength was what drew him to her. Even as relaxed as she appeared now, there was a hard line to her expression, a determination to fight to the very end, to do everything in her power to lead her people to freedom.

He found her formidable will sexy as hell.

Were the Kra-ell females as comfortable with their nudity as their immortal cousins?

There was only one way to find out.

Draping a hand over his eyes, he opened the door. "May I join you, ladies? Or am I not allowed to gaze upon your beautiful naked bodies?"

Jade chuckled. "If you know that our bodies are beautiful, you've already seen them, so you might as well come in."

Grinning, he dropped his hand. "Hallelujah, praise the sweet Fates, and thank you." He went in, closed the door behind him, and sauntered to the bench opposite the two females.

Jade eyed him with an amused smirk lifting the corners of her lush lips. "Are you going to take your shirt and those swimming trunks off? If you're not comfortable getting naked with us, you'll have to leave."

He was glad she'd mistaken his dark gray undershorts for swimming trunks.

"I'm very comfortable with my body." He put the towel on the bench next to him, whipped his shirt over his head, and put it over the towel. Turning around, he gave Kagra and Jade his rearview as he took off the undershorts.

"Very nice," Jade said as he turned to face them with his shaft at half-mast.

It would have been at full mast if Kagra wasn't there. Phinas was proud of his body, but he didn't like to parade it like a show horse.

"Thank you." He gave them a bow before sitting down and crossing his legs to hide his package.

It wasn't that he was embarrassed. As humans and immortals went, he was well endowed, but for all he knew, the Kra-ell might be hung like horses.

Besides, both ladies were sitting with their legs crossed and hiding their feminine treasures, so he could at least try to be a gentleman and do the same instead of flaunting his assets.

31

JADE

"I'd better head to bed." Kagra pretended to rise with effort.

She'd been fine on the way to the sauna.

Jade cast her a glare. "You were the one who insisted on coming here, and now you're leaving?"

Kagra grabbed her underwear and shimmied into them. "I'm recovering from a nearly fatal injury." She took her long-sleeved thermal shirt and pulled it over her head. "Merlin said that I need to rest as much as possible." She turned her back to Phinas and winked at Jade.

"Traitor," Jade mouthed.

"You're welcome," Kagra mouthed back and then turned to Phinas. "See you later, as they say in the movies." She padded out of the room and closed the door behind her.

The female watched way too many American movies. That was not how the Kra-ell behaved when they were prowling for a bed partner. Jade didn't need to create special circumstances to be alone with Phinas, and she didn't need to flirt with him and drop hints like human females did. If she wanted him, all she had to do was issue an invitation, and he could either accept or decline.

Not that there was a chance he would say no to her. The immortal was attracted to her.

Still, sex wasn't the only thing she wanted from Phinas.

She wanted information about the political makeup of the clan and why his people cooperated with Tom's but didn't become one unit with them. She wanted to find out about his boss, the guy named Kalugal, and what role he played in the clan's leadership. Those things couldn't be achieved by a simple invitation to her bed. She needed to play the flirting game that humans engaged in and apparently immortals as well.

Jade needed Phinas to fall for her, and she had no clue how to do that.

Perhaps she should have watched more of those romantic movies Kagra favored, but the truth was that they nauseated her. The female leads in those silly movies were so weak, so pliable, and even the men were mostly spoiled and soft.

Shifting her gaze to Phinas, she saw him watching her intently, but to his credit, his gaze was focused on her face and not her breasts or lower.

Well, her breasts were nonexistent compared to those of human and immortal females. She'd only met two so far. Mia was tiny all over with small breasts to match, but Sylvia had an impressive cleavage.

"Why are you looking at me like that?" she asked.

"Like what?"

"Like you are trying to read my thoughts. I hope it's not one of your paranormal talents."

He smiled. "I have no special talents. I can thrall and shroud, but nothing compared to Yamanu's god-like ability."

"Tom says that even he can't do what Yamanu can. He says that he's out of practice."

Phinas shrugged. "If you're asking whether I can verify that statement, the answer is no. I don't know Tom well. He's a relative newcomer to the clan."

She tilted her head, her long black hair cascading down her front and covering her left breast. "Are you and your men newcomers as well?"

He nodded.

"Why are you collectively called Kalugal's men?"

"Because he's our boss, and we came with him."

Phinas wasn't lying, but he wasn't telling her everything either. He was holding back. Perhaps she needed to flirt with him first to soften him up.

What was she supposed to say? That she found him attractive? Would he consider it too forward? If the immortals were like human males, they didn't like aggressive females, but Jade didn't know what the rules of engagement were.

She really should have paid more attention to those awful movies.

"Your form is pleasing." She gave his body a once-over. "Do you train a lot?"

He was about her height but at least three times as broad and muscular. Not that it mattered. She could still overpower him effortlessly. It was a wonder the gods hadn't improved their descendants' physical strength over the millennia she'd been in stasis.

Given his satisfied grin, it had been the right thing to say.

"I train for about an hour every day. What about you?"

"At least three hours, sometimes more if I'm training someone else."

"Do you enjoy that?"

She tilted her head. "Which part? Training myself or others?"

"Both."

"I enjoy all aspects of training, but teaching the most. It gives me great satisfaction when someone I trained excels."

"What if they best you?"

She laughed. "It hasn't happened yet, but I will feel pride when it does." As a memory of Drova offering her a hand up surfaced, the smile slid off Jade's face. "There was one time when my daughter managed to best me, but that wasn't because of her skill. I was distracted. Still, she did well, and I was proud of her accomplishment."

"Where is she now?"

"In a room with three other pureblooded females and a Guardian posted outside."

"I'm sorry," Phinas said. "I hope she and the others will be allowed more freedom on the ship."

32

PHINAS

*I*t wasn't the strangest conversation Phinas had ever had with a female, but given that they were both naked, it was certainly novel. They were like a couple of buddies hanging out in the sauna and talking shop, with the minor distraction of a raging erection.

Not that there was anything minor about it.

Jade shrugged. "I don't know why they bother. If Drova wasn't compelled to cooperate, she could easily overpower the guard. I trained her well. It's unnecessary to keep her and the others locked up and guarded."

She sounded proud of her daughter, and given who the girl's father was, it wasn't obvious.

Phinas's heart ached for the female and what she'd been through.

He knew what it meant to be forced to breed with the enemy. His mother was a Dormant who'd given Navuh's army eight warriors and four Dormant breeders, each from a different father, and each against her will, and yet she'd loved her children and had done the best she could for them given her circumstances.

His sisters were long gone, and out of his seven brothers, six were still alive and served Navuh.

Phinas had been the odd man out, gifted or maybe cursed with intelligence and compassion the others didn't possess. Perhaps his father had been different.

"We are being vigilant," he said. "You don't want Igor to find you and take over again, do you?"

"Of course not. But if I was in charge of the operation, I would have just posted guards at key access points. Your William disabled all communications, so it's not like any of the Kra-ell or the humans can sneak into an office and call Igor even if they were inclined to." Her eyes widened. "I forgot all about the human descendants away at the university. We will need to collect them. They won't know what happened to their families."

Phinas was surprised that she cared. Kalugal had told him that everyone described Jade as a heartless bitch who didn't give a damn about the humans in her old compound or Igor's.

"I'm sure their families told Yamanu about them. In the meantime, it's unclear where we are taking you, so there is no point in collecting them. On second thought, perhaps we should get to them before Igor does it first. He might do that out of spite."

Jade shook her head. "Igor doesn't do anything out of spite because he's devoid of feelings. He's a calculating bastard who believes that the goal justifies the means."

"What's his goal?"

She shrugged. "In the short term, it was a Kra-ell society that was patriarchal and not matriarchal. In the long run, who knows? He's not the sharing type."

Phinas closed his eyes and leaned his head against the wood panel behind him. He was sitting in a sauna with a gorgeous naked female, both of them sweaty and glistening, and they were talking politics.

It didn't get much more pathetic than that.

How could he turn this tanker in the right direction?

"Did I say something to upset you?" Jade asked. "Or are you tired and want to call it a night?"

He opened his eyes and smiled. "I enjoy talking to you. Hell, I enjoy being with you, and I wouldn't mind calling it a night if we retired to the bedroom together, but I'm out of my element with you. You are unlike any female I've met before, and I don't know how to court you."

"You don't need to court me. I owe you a life-debt, and you can ask anything you want of me."

Phinas flinched. "Let's make one thing clear. I will never use that vow to get you to have sex with me. In fact, I don't plan on ever invoking your vow to demand anything of you. Not even a cup of coffee."

Jade frowned, looking offended. "Why not? Am I so vile that you can't fathom asking anything of me?"

He lifted his hands in the air. "What I said must have been lost in translation. I appreciate your gratitude and am willing to accept a thank you, but nothing more than that. I didn't save Kagra as a favor to you."

"You have to let me repay the debt. If you don't, it will shame me."

"That's nonsense."

Her eyes flickered red. "Don't belittle my beliefs. I owe you a life-debt, and if you don't collect, you will sentence me to forever walk in the valley of the shamed. I've worked very hard to earn my place in the fields of the brave."

Religion was irrational, but it was powerful, and he couldn't change her mind, but he could trick her.

"Does it matter what I ask for?"

She narrowed her huge eyes at him. "Don't make it something insignificant. That would shame me just as much as you not collecting on the debt at all."

Damn it. She wasn't easy to trick.

"Do you know what the Finns like to do after they get all hot and toasty in a sauna?"

She winced. "They like to dunk themselves in ice water."

"You are not a fan."

"I'm not."

"Can you swim?"

She shook her head. "I never tried."

"Then that's what I want as payment. I want you to come with me to the beach, and I'll teach you to swim."

Her huge eyes turned even bigger, and then she blinked. "The water is freezing. Can't you think of something else? I'd much rather escort you to your bedroom and show you how the Kra-ell have sex."

If he wasn't sitting with his legs crossed and cutting the blood supply to his shaft, it would have jumped to attention.

"I'm sharing a room with two other guys, I'm not an exhibitionist, and I'd much rather show you how the immortals make love than learn how the Kra-ell do it. I promise you that you will enjoy it much more than anything you experienced with your purebloods."

33

JADE

*P*hinas's words did something unexpected to Jade. They made her curious, and she'd never been curious about making gentle love.

Love.

It was such a human concept.

The Kra-ell didn't believe in love. There was affection and lust, loyalty and devotion, friendship and camaraderie, but not love. The word was vague and therefore meaningless.

It was also weak.

Love was supposed to be unconditional, and that was what made the concept absurd. Except for lust, which was instinctive because it was necessary for procreation, every emotion worth anything had to be earned. Affection and friendship weren't freely given to the undeserving, and that was even more true for loyalty and devotion, which occupied the top tier on the scale of emotions.

Motherhood was the closest Jade had experienced to feeling love, but that had been fueled by the instinct to nurture and protect the young, which nearly every animal had. It wasn't a choice, and it couldn't be applied to the males who were necessary to the creation of new life.

The only criterion applied should be the kind of offspring they could produce.

Jade had appreciated her sons' fathers, had even admired one of them for his sharp mind, and had enjoyed the rough coupling the males had provided. She mourned their deaths and missed them as much as she'd missed all the other lost members of her tribe, but that was the extent of her feelings for them.

Still, Kagra had enjoyed softer forms of intimacy, and she'd recommended that Jade try them.

Jade had been mildly intrigued, but it hadn't been in the cards until she'd met Phinas.

Kagra had experimented with hybrid males, but Jade had a reputation to uphold, and humans had never been an option.

An immortal male was a different story, though, and Phinas was a natural choice.

He was the commander of Kalugal's men, Tom and the Guardians seemed to respect him, he was intelligent, a good fighter, had a good sense of humor, was good-looking, and most importantly, he could give her immortal offspring. Tom had said that only the immortal mothers transferred their immortal genes to their children, but that was when immortals bred with humans. A union between an immortal male and a pureblooded Kra-ell female might produce different results.

She was long-lived, so perhaps her genes only needed reinforcement from his. After all, they were both related to the gods.

But then, so were humans.

There was the issue of the prohibition on coupling with gods, but Phinas wasn't a god, so technically she wouldn't be breaking any laws by being with him.

Besides, Jade was a long way from home, in distance as well as in time, and she could make her own rules as long as they didn't contradict the Mother's teachings.

Except, the gods back home hadn't allowed unions between gods and Kra-ell either, and a hybrid child was considered an abomination, so maybe Phinas was not allowed to breed with anyone other than immortal females.

Jade had never been clear on the reasons for the strong taboo. Was it just pride and the wish to preserve the purity of their races? Or was there a biological reason?

She believed that it was the former. If both gods and Kra-ell could breed with humans and produce healthy offspring, there was no reason to believe that a union between a god and a Kra-ell would produce an abomination.

Nevertheless, Phinas might believe that.

Thankfully she wasn't in her fertile cycle, so he had nothing to worry about, and by the time she was fertile again, she would find out his people's stance on the subject.

She would also have time to decide whether she wanted to be the first one to put the taboo to the test.

"Ready for your first lesson?" Phinas rose to his feet and offered her a hand up.

With his shaft right in front of her face, she had to pry her eyes from it to lift them to his luminous gaze. When she smiled, exposing her fangs, his shaft twitched and bobbed in excitement.

Was he turned on by her fangs?

Would he welcome her bite?

She hoped so. Drawing blood from a bed partner was a major part of a Kra-ell mating ritual for a reason. It was extremely pleasurable for the taker and the giver and resulted in a powerful climax for both.

"I hope you're not talking about swimming in the icy water," she purred.

Instead of answering her question, he lifted his hand and brushed his fingers over the curve of her cheek. "Your skin is so soft."

Without much thought, she shifted her face into the touch, leaning her cheek against the palm of his hand.

He sucked in a breath, and as she tugged on his hand and pulled him down to the bench, he didn't resist.

She pushed on his chest, guiding him to his back. "The wood must have all burned out. It's getting a little cooler in here." She leaned into him.

"I don't know about that. To me, it feels hotter." His hand closed over the nape of her neck.

Letting him pull her head down, she kissed him.

Phinas parted his lips for her, and as she pushed her tongue into his mouth and flicked it over his, he wrapped his arms around her back and pulled her flat on top of him.

He let her explore him for as long as she pleased, and even though his erection was hard like a steel rod against her belly, he didn't rush her. Caressing her back, he kissed her back softly, unhurriedly.

As he weaved his fingers through her long hair and cupped her bottom, the tenderness of his gentle touch was so different from anything she'd experienced before.

Jade let go of his mouth and trailed a line of kisses down his neck, nipping his salty skin with her sharp fangs but never drawing blood. She followed with her tongue, soothing and healing the small scrapes on contact.

Did Phinas find the implied threat of her fangs as thrilling as a pure-blooded male would?

If the twitch of his shaft was any indication, he did.

Sliding lower down his sweat-slicked body, she licked the skin on his chest, and as she traced the defined lines of his pectorals and his abdominals, she marveled at the sculpted perfection of him.

Phinas was a beautiful specimen, a testament to the perfected genes he had inherited from the gods.

They were manipulative bastards who worshiped perfection, but they knew how to make everything beautiful, including themselves and their offspring.

As Phinas kept himself still, with only his hands moving over her back, Jade wondered whether he was afraid to move lest he spurred her aggression, or whether he was enjoying what she was doing so much that he didn't want her to stop.

His impressive restraint held until she slid further down, and her hardened nipples brushed over his erection. He jerked, and when she settled between his legs and kissed his shaft, he bucked up, nearly toppling them both to the floor.

"Careful." She smiled up at him. "This ledge is very narrow."

"I won't move." He belied his words by gripping her waist. "You're so slim that my fingers touch when my hands encircle your middle."

She stilled. "Does that turn you off?"

A laugh bubbled out of him as he lifted his hips. "Does that look like a turn-off to you?"

"Maybe you haven't been with a female for a while." She curled her hand around his length and moved it up and down. "Males are ruled by their baser needs. A touch in the right place is all that's needed to elicit a response. They are simple creatures."

"They are," he groaned. "But I'm not. You're the hottest female I've ever met. Never doubt that."

She gave him a smile. "I don't have confidence issues, and you don't need to smother me with flattery. I'm just curious about our differences. I've never been with a male who wasn't a pureblooded Kra-ell."

34

PHINAS

$\mathcal{P}$hinas had guessed as much, but hearing Jade confirm it excited him. He liked being the first non-Kra-ell to show her a new way to make love.

No pressure.

If he disappointed her, not only would he bear the shame, but he would also shame all his immortal brethren.

But it was worth it. He was an old immortal, and novelty was his life's spice.

"I'm fascinated by you." He ran his fingers through her long hair, marveling at the silky texture.

"What exactly are you fascinated by?" She flicked her tongue over the tip of his shaft, licking off a drop of precum.

"Everything, but at this moment, I'm fascinated by your tongue. It's long, pointy, and it has a dark triangle at the tip."

Smiling, she stuck her tongue out and wiggled it like a snake. "The tongue is a highly erogenous zone for us, and it's also a status symbol. The darker the triangle, the more royal blood we have in us."

That was an interesting tidbit of information. He'd noticed that the triangle on Kagra's tongue was much lighter. It was just a darker shade of pink.

No wonder Jade had been the leader of her tribe. She was related to the royals.

"How much royal blood do you have in you?"

"Very little. The royals have triangles that are all black. They are much more distinct. Mine is nothing special, but not many settlers had royal blood in them, so out here, it gets more respect than it had back home."

He wanted to know how close Jade had been to the Kra-ell queen, but now he had sex on his mind, and talking could wait for later.

"I find your tongue very sexy, especially when I imagine it around my shaft."

A mischievous grin lifted the corners of her lips. "Like this?" She flicked her tongue out, wrapped it around his shaft, and squeezed.

"Fates, Jade. I must have died and gone to heaven."

Talk about novelty. The things Jade could do with her tongue were the stuff of the most outlandish fantasies. Not that he'd ever fantasized about a tongue like that because he hadn't known that it existed.

Had Jade given this pleasure to the pureblooded males she'd been with?

She'd had no reason to go out of her way to provide pleasure to the males of her tribe who'd been her subordinates, but perhaps Igor had forced her to do that for him.

At the thought, a hiss left Phinas's lips, and his erection deflated.

Letting go of his shaft, Jade looked at him in alarm. "Did I hurt you?"

"No, beautiful, you didn't." He cupped her cheek. "I just let a random thought upset me."

"What was it?"

He wasn't going to mention her servitude to Igor while she was anywhere near his shaft, and perhaps he should never bring it up at all. If she wanted to talk about it, he would listen, but he wouldn't ask.

Jade was a proud female, and she might prefer to bury the past along with the male whose head she was about to chop off.

He forced a smile. "Nothing that should enter this space at this moment."

She nodded. "Shadows of the past have a way of intruding at the most inopportune moments."

Gripping him gently at the base, she flicked her incredible tongue around the top portion of his erection, and as she started moving it up and down, the pleasure was so intense that Phinas knew he had to stop her, or he would shoot his load in seconds.

He could be up and ready for the second round in moments, but this was his first time with Jade, and starting up by filling her mouth with his seed was not the way to go.

Stifling a groan, he cupped her cheek, letting her know he wanted her to stop. "My turn. I promised to show you how immortals make love."

When she unwrapped her tongue, leaving his shaft wet and bereft, he mourned the loss of the sensation.

"And how is that?" Jade asked.

As Phinas folded his arms around her and flipped her under him, he knew he could do that only because she allowed it.

The memory of trying to catch Aliya was still fresh in his mind. She'd handed him his ass and then some, and he'd been attracted to her strength as well, but he'd made the mistake of not seeing the fragile young soul inside the powerful body.

Jade was cut from a very different cloth than the former member of her tribe.

It was like comparing a kitten to a lioness.

Dipping his head, he took her mouth in a kiss that was just a shade on the dominant side to test the waters, and when she responded by wrapping her long arms around him and squeezing his buttocks, he had his answer and got even rougher.

As the flare in Jade's arousal sent a wave of her feminine scent to his nostrils, it was very similar to the scent of the immortal females he'd been with, only more potent.

Maybe the Kra-ell and the immortals weren't so different after all.

Snaking his hand between their bodies, he brushed his fingers over the moist petals guarding her sheath, and as he trailed them over the bundle of nerves at their top, he was happy to discover that Jade's anatomy wasn't different from that of other females he'd been with, human and immortal.

She moaned, her enormous eyes rolling back in her head, and then her hand was between their bodies, covering his and guiding his fingers inside of her.

As he pushed with two fingers and started pumping, she kept her hand over his, her knuckles rubbing against his erection and providing friction that in his heightened state of arousal would make him climax in no time.

He moved his fingers faster, harder, his hips churning and grinding his shaft over Jade's knuckles, and when he dipped his head and grazed his fangs over her nipple, she let out a sound he'd never heard before, and her body shuddered under him.

Her climax snapped Phinas's restraint, and as his seed erupted between their bodies, he sank his fangs into Jade's neck, only dimly aware that she was offering it to him without a fight.

35

JADE

Throughout her adult life, Jade had gotten many bites, and she'd been ready for the venom's aphrodisiac effects and the euphoria that followed, but the Kra-ell had much less venom, only enough to make the bite pleasurable instead of painful.

What she'd experienced after getting bitten by pureblooded Kra-ell males couldn't compare to what she was experiencing now. The rush of pleasure washing over her pulled a string of climaxes from her, leaving her limp and pliant under the heavy weight of Phinas's muscled body.

Jade didn't mind the weight.

She didn't mind being under him instead of on top of him.

She didn't mind anything.

For the first time in longer than she could remember, Jade was at peace, floating on the clouds of euphoria but still tethered to the ground. If her body hadn't been so used to venom, she would have probably blacked out, and the tether would have snapped.

It could have been wonderful to leave her corporeal body for a little while and float in a dream-like state, but it wasn't meant to be.

Not for her.

Her tether was made of duty and responsibility, and she could never let it snap.

Jade opened her eyes and looked into the warmth of Phinas's amber gaze. His eyes, which were normally brown, were illuminated from the inside, turning his irises into twin jewels. His fangs had retracted, though, which was a shame.

He looked feral with them fully elongated.

Sexy. Virile.

"You have beautiful eyes." She lifted her hand and cupped his cheek.

He chuckled. "Thank you. I'm sorry about the poor performance. I promise to do better next time."

"You did fine." She put her hands on his waist, lifted him off her, sat up, and sat him down beside her. "We should hit the showers before we head back to our rooms." She reached for the bucket of water, ladled some, and poured it over the sticky aftermath of their passion.

He took the bucket and the ladle as she passed them to him, but he didn't move to wash himself.

Holding the ladle, he gaped at her. "Fine? That's the worst performance evaluation I've ever gotten. I will forever walk in the valley of the shamed."

Rolling her eyes, she slapped his arm playfully. "Don't make fun of my beliefs."

"I'm not making fun of them. I feel ashamed. I have to make it up to you and turn fine into fabulous. I'm already primed for another round."

Jade glanced at his hardening erection. "That's impressive. It would have taken a Kra-ell pureblood a few moments longer." She shifted her gaze to his eyes. "I enjoyed our interlude very much even though it was different than what I'm used to, and your venom bite was exquisite."

It was odd that he needed reassurance from her.

Hell, it was weird that he was still there, and they were talking.

Kra-ell didn't converse after sex, and the male left as soon as it was over.

Sex the Kra-ell way was a simple affair. All her partners needed to do was overpower her, and nature did the rest. The fight was the foreplay, and being subdued was the primer for climaxing. Everything progressed fast from that moment on, and as soon as it was over, the male was supposed to leave.

Phinas let out a breath. "It's shameful for an immortal male to let the venom do his work for him. I'm glad that I managed to give you at least one orgasm before the bite."

It was so strange to spend time analyzing the sex, but it wasn't unpleasant, and surprisingly, Jade was not counting the moments until Phinas left. She enjoyed his closeness, and she was not in a rush to leave either.

"We are still learning each other in more ways than one, and first times are always awkward. I still remember mine. I was so scared."

He pursed his lips. "I don't believe you. You are not afraid of anything."

"I'm afraid of many things, I just don't let fear rule me. I was scared, the male I chose to invite was as inexperienced as I was, and he was terrified as well. Instead of fighting for dominance, we kind of danced around each other, not knowing what to do."

"How old were you?"

"Twenty. That's the age of consent for the Kra-ell." She smiled at him. "For the males. Females are free to invite males as soon as they believe they are ready, but we were not supposed to invite any male younger than twenty to our beds."

"Interesting. It's seventeen for us, and we live longer. It should have been the other way around."

"Perhaps." She leaned against the back panel and closed her eyes. "I feel languid, and I haven't felt that way for so long." She opened her eyes and slanted him a smile. "It's your doing. You deserve a visit to the fields of the brave just for that. It's one hell of an accomplishment."

Phinas laughed. "I thought it was blasphemy to invoke your religion in such an irreverent way."

"It is for you, not for me."

"Got it." He scooted closer so their thighs and arms were touching and took her hand. "If I am to do better next time, I need more feedback than the dreaded word fine. Obviously, I wasn't too rough, but was I rough enough?"

Jade released a long breath. "I'm not in the habit of analyzing the nuances of pleasure. We are both relaxed after climaxing, we are having a nice, civilized conversation afterward, and I still want to have sex with you again. That should be good enough."

When he smiled, his fangs seemed longer, and his eyes started glowing again. "Do you want to have sex with me now?"

Jade shook her head. "It's almost morning, and I need to catch a few hours of sleep. We will have plenty of opportunities to continue our sexual training on the ship." She let her head fall back against the wood-paneled wall and closed her eyes.

36

PHINAS

*S*exual training.

What a strange way to refer to lovemaking. It might have been a lost-in-translation thing, but when Jade used the term in that fashion, Phinas found it arousing.

Hell, everything she did was sexy to him, except when she used the word fine to describe his performance.

Strangely, though, he wasn't as embarrassed as he should be.

He was Jade's first immortal lover and, as such, a representative of all immortal males. He should have wowed her, left her breathless and panting for more.

He had failed miserably at that, but she'd said he'd satisfied her, and Jade wasn't the type who would say that to stroke a male's ego.

She'd meant it.

But then, she'd also said that she needed to catch up on sleep, but she hadn't shown any indication of wanting to leave, and neither did he.

It felt good being with her, just sitting next to her and talking, and he was too tired to analyze what it meant, only that it wasn't like him. He'd almost never spent the night with a hookup, and if he had, it was because he'd fallen asleep, or it hadn't been safe to leave the lady alone.

"You didn't tell me the rest of the story." He gave Jade's hand a gentle squeeze.

She smiled without opening her eyes. "About my first time?"

"It's the only story you told me, so yeah. The last thing you said was that you didn't fight for dominance and danced around each other instead."

"We circled each other for a few moments, and then he sighed and lowered his arms. He didn't want to fight me, but giving up would have shamed him, and he wouldn't have gotten any other invitations. I didn't want to be responsible for that. So I told him we would pretend to train, and I'd show him a few new moves I'd learned recently. I demonstrated the first move, we practiced it a few times, and when he got better at it, he took over." Jade opened her eyes. "It went smoothly from there. Regrettably, our union did not result in conception. I chose that male because he was smart, not because he was the strongest warrior I knew. I wanted a smart child."

Phinas frowned. "You wanted to get pregnant after your first time?"

"Of course." She looked at him as if his question was dumb. "Every adult Kra-ell female's duty is to produce as many offspring as possible. When we are in our fertile cycle, that's the only reason for breeding. We do it for pleasure only when we are not fertile."

"Are you fertile now?"

She shook her head. "I wouldn't be here if I was."

Her words were like a kick to the gut. "Am I not good enough for you to breed with? You only want pureblooded children?"

She cast him a sidelong glance. "Are you allowed to father a half-breed child?"

"I'm not asking anyone's permission."

"I might not have phrased it correctly." She tapped her long fingers on her bare knee. "Back home, gods and Kra-ell didn't breed, and a mixed offspring was considered an abomination. I don't know whether that's true or they just wanted to preserve the purity of the races, and I also don't know your people's stance on the subject."

"We didn't even know that Kra-ell existed, so we didn't have any rules against producing children with them, but fate put your Vrog in the path of one of the clan females, and they produced a child, who grew up to be a wonderful man. I don't know him personally, but I've heard only good things about him."

Jade's eyes briefly flashed turquoise. "I would like to meet him."

"I wish I could promise you that, but it's not up to me."

Jade sighed. "Your mighty Kian, right?"

"He's not mine, but yeah. He makes the rules."

"I thought he needed to listen to the council."

Phinas chuckled. "I'm not entirely clear on how the clan governs itself and what Kian needs the council's approval on. I think that whenever safety is the issue, he doesn't need to confer with them unless he wants to."

She nodded. "From what Tom told me, I know that Kian does not allow humans into the clan except for some special circumstances."

"That's true."

"So that means he doesn't allow the immortal males to produce children with human females either because their offspring will be human."

"I don't think there is a law about it. It's more of a recommendation. Fortunately, it's not much of a concern. Immortal fertility is very low, and the chances of us getting a female pregnant are almost negligible." He turned to look into her eyes. "So you have nothing to worry about me getting you pregnant even when you are in your fertile cycle. Regardless, I don't like being considered as not good enough to father your child."

She nodded, not bothering to deny it. "It's not about being good enough or not. Before you told me about Vrog's son, I was wary of being the first to risk such an experiment. That's why I would like to meet him. I want to see what combination of Kra-ell and immortal attributes he has."

"As I said, I don't know him, so I can't tell you. I think he's a graphic artist."

She pursed her lips. "That must have come from his mother's side. The gods are into art. The Kra-ell, not as much."

Phinas came from a society that sneered at art, so he wasn't surprised that the Kra-ell didn't appreciate it either.

"I'm curious." He tilted his head. "Was the aversion to mixing gods and Kra-ell a cultural thing, or was it law?"

"The gods were forbidden to take Kra-ell into their beds, and the Kra-ell were forbidden to take gods. Both societies outlawed it."

"Why?"

Jade let out a sigh. "Why are members of one human caste forbidden to marry members of another? Why can't people from different religions get a religious wedding unless one of them converts to the other?"

"I don't know," Phinas said. "I don't understand that."

"The polite explanation is that every group wants to preserve its authentic essence, but the truth is that every group thinks that it's better than the other and doesn't want to dilute what it considers its superior blood."

37

DARLENE

"Welcome back." Darlene hugged Gilbert. "Are you done with everything you set out to do?"

"The house is ready to be rented out, and I have a realtor taking care of that. The building projects are going well, but sales are sluggish. With interest rates going crazy, people can't afford mortgages."

He looked worried, and there were dark circles under his eyes.

"How bad is it?" Eric asked his brother.

"Bad. I got the construction loan before the rate hikes, but the loan has an adjustable rate, so the monthly payments went up a lot, and I'm not selling enough houses to cover the loan payments. I met with the bank manager and the underwriter, and they are willing to extend the loan, but they can't budge on the rate. I will be lucky if I break even on both projects." He raked his fingers through his thinning hair. "It wasn't the best time to leave everything behind and manage things remotely, but it is what it is." He cast a loving glance at Karen. "It's just money, right?"

"Right." Karen nodded. "At least we don't need to worry about going bankrupt. We have everything we need here in the village, and when we transition successfully, we won't need medical insurance either."

"You don't need it now," Eric said. "Bridget and Julian can take care of almost any medical problem."

Gilbert lifted his hands in the air. "We are not destitute yet, and I can still afford medical insurance for my family. However, that's not the case for many Americans. Who can afford premiums of over two grand a month and in addition pay hundreds and sometimes thousands in copays? If I knew I was about to turn immortal, I wouldn't have done the colonoscopy I was charged eighteen hundred dollars copay for."

Karen frowned. "You didn't tell me that you had a colonoscopy. When was that?"

Gilbert blanched. "Remember when I was feeling dizzy, and the doctor said I was anemic?"

"Yeah. She told you to take iron supplements, and you decided to eat more meat instead."

"She wanted me to have a colonoscopy to see if there was any internal bleeding. I didn't want to worry you, so I had it done, and everything was fine. My colon is beautifully clean."

Karen shook her head. "We might not be married on paper, but I'm your partner in sickness and in health. You should have told me."

As the two continued arguing, Darlene ducked into the kitchen, and Eric followed her.

"He should have told her," she said quietly. "I would have been so mad if you pulled something like that on me."

Eric wrapped his arms around her and kissed her forehead. "I promise to always tell you everything. Gilbert is just a stubborn ox, and he thinks men should deal with their problems on their own. Keeping everything inside is part of his oldest-son's syndrome. He always took care of me and our sister and he never complained about anything."

"Speaking of Gabi. When are you going to talk to her about all this? She's not getting any younger either."

"She's thirty-eight, so she has time. I can't deal with Gilbert and Karen's transition and with Gabi at the same time."

"Why? Is she a handful?"

He chuckled. "Gabriella Emerson is more than a handful. She's a whirlwind."

"She sounds exciting. Let's introduce her to Max."

Eric's smile vanished. "No way. Not after what he did with us. That's just gross."

Darlene huffed. "You keep saying that Max's part was marginal, and that he was just the venom donor. Then suddenly, it's a problem to introduce him to your sister?"

"Yeah, it is. I don't want him telling her the details of what the three of us did."

"He wouldn't do that."

Eric arched a brow. "You think? If he falls in love with her, he will tell her everything. Didn't we agree moments ago that there should be no secrets between mates?"

Darlene let out an exasperated breath. "I only suggested introducing them. They might not even like each other."

"They will. Max is a fun guy, and Gabi is a fun girl. Most men can't handle her, but Max will have no problem with her spunk or her big mouth."

Eric was wonderful, but he had a tendency to make contradicting statements. One moment he was against introducing Max and Gabi, and the next, he was stating that they were perfect for each other.

Maybe he just needed to ponder this a little longer and organize his thoughts.

"Let's cut up the watermelon. I promised the boys a treat after dinner."

"Right." Eric opened the fridge and pulled out the twenty-pounder that they had gotten earlier that day. "Do you think it's big enough?" He hefted it in his arms.

She laughed. "I'm sure."

38

ERIC

*W*hen the doorbell rang, Darlene rushed out of the kitchen, but Cheryl beat her to the door.

"I'm sorry I'm late." Kaia hugged her sister. "William called, and we talked for over an hour. I miss him so badly." She smiled apologetically at Darlene as she took off her puffer coat and hung it on a peg next to the door.

"No worries. I saved you a plate."

"Thank you, but I'll just join you for dessert. I snacked while talking." She walked over to the twins and kissed each one on both cheeks.

"When is William coming back?" Darlene asked.

"Hopefully, tomorrow. He's going to escort the Kra-ell to the ship, and Marcel will take over from there. I'm so glad that he's not going with them." Kaia pulled out a chair next to Gilbert. "Welcome back. I missed you too." She leaned over to kiss him on both cheeks. "How are things at home?"

"This is home now." Eric put the bowl with watermelon chunks on the dining table. "The one up north is just a house."

"It's ready to be rented out." Gilbert shifted his gaze to Eric. "You and I need to unload the moving truck. It has been sitting there for over a week."

The Guardians had returned with the truck on Monday and left it in the parking garage. They had shipped out the next day, and Eric was too busy with Darlene and her transition to help move things out.

"No problem. I'm sorry I didn't do it earlier." He looked at his mate. "While Darlene was transitioning, I couldn't think of anything else, and

137

later, I forgot all about the truck." He glanced at Karen. "You should have reminded me."

She waved a dismissive hand. "The entire village was in turmoil about the Guardians and Kalugal's men leaving. Everything in the truck could wait."

As Darlene and Karen chatted about what was in the truck and where it was going, and Kaia and Cheryl fed the little ones watermelon, Eric turned his attention to his brother. "When are you going for it?"

Gilbert winced. "I don't know if I can do it now that the business is teetering. I heard that Kian, Onegus, and Turner have been stuck in the war room for two days, and they are probably going to stay very busy until the mission is over. I can't ask Kian for advice or help, so I can't check out. If I want to save what's left of my so-called fortune, I need to be aware of what's going on."

That was the problem with being a small, independent builder. There was potential for great profits but just as much for catastrophic losses.

"I can look after the business while you are transitioning. We did that before when you and Karen went on vacation."

"It's not the same." Gilbert took a sip of water. "I was always available on the phone and via email to anyone who needed to contact me, and when you didn't know what to do, you called me. Who are you going to call when I'm out?"

"Kian. If something comes up that I can't handle, I'm sure he can spare a moment or two no matter what's going on. Besides, the crisis will be over in a few days. If William is coming back, it can't be too bad out there."

Gilbert stabbed a watermelon chunk with his fork. "Since I need to wait for Toven to return, this discussion is irrelevant." He put the chunk into his mouth.

Eric leaned his elbows on his knees. "You can ask someone else to induce you. Stop pussyfooting around and just go for it. Karen can transition right after you do with the help of a donor's venom. It wasn't that bad with Max. It would have gone even smoother if not for the damn immortal instincts."

The left corner of Gilbert's lips curled up. "Are you still feeling insanely possessive over Darlene? Or did the hormones calm down a little?"

From across the table, Darlene gave him a warning look.

"If anything, they got worse. I want to snarl at any male looking at her." He cast her an air kiss. "She was always beautiful, but now she's stunning."

She was still the same woman he'd fallen in love with, just younger looking, more vibrant, and with stamina to match his.

"Immortality rocks." He smiled at her before returning his gaze to Gilbert. "Darlene says that we shouldn't wait and tell Gabi, but I want you and Karen to transition before we tackle Gabriella. I don't want her to know that you are doing anything potentially dangerous. The freak-out will be epic."

Gilbert winced. "Yeah. Since Mom and Dad died, Gabi can't tolerate any upheaval. That's why I didn't tell Karen about the colonoscopy. I'm used to hiding from Gabi anything that's potentially worrisome or upsetting."

Eric nodded. "Poor Gabriela. Of the three of us, she took it the hardest."

"She was the youngest."

"Imagine how relieved she'll be when she learns that we are practically indestructible. That's the best gift you could ever give her."

Gilbert snorted. "You can stop campaigning. You've already sold me on the idea." He smoothed his fingers over his face as if checking for stubble. "Any suggestion as to who can fulfill Max's role for us?"

"As your inducer?"

"Not for that. I'm not taking any chances. I'm waiting for Toven to return. I meant for Karen."

"I have a couple of candidates, but we will focus on finding a venom donor for Karen after you are safely on the other side. You need to take care of your transition first. You should ask Orion to induce you. He's a demigod, so his venom should be almost as potent as his father's."

"I'll think about it." Gilbert stuffed another chunk of watermelon into his mouth.

39

PHINAS

"*You* look worried." Dandor fell in step with Phinas. "Is there trouble?"

Not the kind that Dandor imagined, but yeah. What had happened last night with Jade bothered Phinas more than it should, but he wasn't about to share it with the guy.

"That's what the meeting is about, and you'll get the update along with everyone else." He opened the door to the conference room where his men had assembled.

As it turned out, the venue wasn't just for weddings. It was also a corporate retreat with two large conference rooms. Right now, one was occupied by the Guardians and the other by Kalugal's men.

Phinas and Yamanu had decided to deliver the news to each group separately.

When Phinas stood in front of the men, they stopped their conversations and turned to face him.

"So here is the situation. As you know, we are boarding the ship in about an hour and a half, but we are not sailing back home as planned. Instead, we are going to Greenland, where we will be picked up by chartered planes and fly home."

He still didn't know where the Kra-ell were going, but he doubted it would be to the village. Kian would never allow them in. He'd asked Yamanu about that, but the head Guardian said it hadn't been decided yet.

"Why the change of plans?" Chad asked.

"The consensus is that Igor will try to get his people back, but he will not know where to find them until William turns off the communication disrupter, which he will have to do when the convoy enters the port. The assumption is that as soon as Igor learns that his people are on a ship, he will get his hands on another vessel and follow. He might compel a merchant ship captain to accidentally ram into ours, and when the ship starts taking in water and we have to abandon ship, he will take part in the rescue and collect his people. That could happen even when we are close to the port. The other possibility is that he will take over a Russian naval vessel, follow us out to sea, and launch a torpedo or missile to disable or sink our ship. The effect will be the same. We will have to abandon ship, and he will collect the survivors. He will assume that his people will survive in the frigid water, and he doesn't care what happens to the humans."

Chad raised his hand. "Who does he think took his people? He can't know that we are not human."

Phinas nodded. "I agree, but no one knows what Igor is thinking or what he will do next. It's all guesswork."

"I'm just thinking what I would do if I were Igor," Chad said. "If he thinks that humans took his people, which he has no reason to doubt because he doesn't know about us, he will for sure try to sink the ship and then take his sweet time to fish the survivors out of the water. That way, he will kill all the humans who will freeze to death and save only the Kra-ell and maybe the hybrids."

"They have kids with them," Dandor said. "The pureblooded kids will probably be okay, but the hybrid kids don't start manifesting Kra-ell characteristics until puberty. They are probably not as resilient yet."

"Igor doesn't care." Phinas let out a breath. "Did Navuh ever care about collateral damage?"

Silence stretched over the room, and the men avoided each other's eyes.

They had all done things they wished they hadn't, following orders they shouldn't have followed. It didn't matter that refusing orders would have resulted in their execution.

Sometimes it was better to die with honor than live with shame.

One of the things he admired most about Jade was that, to her best ability, she lived her life honorably. Not that it had done her any good.

She didn't have peace of mind any more than he had.

Most people only saw the fierce leader, but he'd glimpsed the pain she was hiding, the guilt and the shame for the slaughter she couldn't have prevented.

But what if she could have?

Had Jade known Igor before boarding the mother ship? Had she suspected an attack on her tribe?

Aliya had told him that Jade had been very strict about security, so she must have suspected something, and he doubted that she'd been worried about humans.

With her compulsion ability, she could have handled humans with ease.

Perhaps she feared the gods?

Yamanu had given him a brief summary of what Jade had told Toven about the relationship between the Kra-ell and the gods, and that the original gods had been exiled to Earth as penance for their share in the Kra-ell uprising.

But if those gods had been Kra-ell sympathizers, why would Jade fear them?

She wouldn't.

She must have feared her own people, and since she was a strong compeller, she must have known about Igor and his incredible powers. She could have prepared her people better.

Not that Phinas knew how she could have done that. The clan had discovered only recently that compulsion was carried over sound waves and that it could be blocked with special earpieces.

Jade couldn't have known that twenty-some years ago.

"What are we supposed to do if and when the ship sinks?" Boleck asked.

It took Phinas a split second to return his mind to the present. "Survive, and help as many others as possible, particularly the children. They are the most vulnerable and will die the fastest in cold water. You will have mere moments to get to them and keep them warm. Hopefully, it won't come to that. Kian contracted an armed submarine to follow the ship and protect it. The most likely scenario is that we will enjoy a pleasant ten-day cruise with the Kra-ell, providing us with ample opportunities to befriend them and learn more about them. Kalugal wants us to become allies."

Phinas didn't understand why Kalugal wanted a leg up with the Kra-ell. It didn't matter if the Kra-ell were on friendlier terms with the clan or with Kalugal's faction. In everything security related, they were supposed to fully cooperate. Annani had cemented the accord with compulsion, but it hadn't been necessary. It was in both their peoples' best interest to join forces against Navuh and the Brotherhood.

Before Igor's attack, Jade's tribe had been involved in the communication business, and even though more than two decades had passed, she might still have some connections in China. Perhaps Kalugal had some joint business endeavor in mind? Maybe Kalugal wanted to help his brother with his fashion business there? Although, that didn't make sense either. Lokan was doing that on Navuh's dime, so it wasn't as if he would personally profit from the business's success, and no one wanted to make Navuh richer.

It was difficult to guess what was going on in Kalugal's mind. The guy was so smart that he was usually a hundred steps ahead of everyone around him. He must have a goal in mind that was years in the making for which he would need the Kra-ell.

Dandor snorted. "So that's why you were sweet-talking their leader. I wondered why you went after a female like her."

Phinas bristled at the implied insult, but he forced his fangs to stay dormant. "Jade is beautiful, courageous, and smart. She's most worthy of my attention, and I'm honored to have gained her friendship and trust."

Being a smart male, Dandor lifted his hands in the universal sign for peace. "To each his own. I just like my females a lot softer."

Chad snorted. "That's why you don't get booty calls from clan females. If you want soft, you need to limit yourself to human women."

Dandor looked at Chad with mirth dancing in his eyes. "I wouldn't call it limiting. I have millions of soft, sweet females to choose from. You can have all the immortal and Kra-ell ones. How many are there? Three hundred? Good luck finding the one perfect for you."

40

JADE

*J*ade collected her things and stuffed them in a pillowcase. Back in the day, before Igor had murdered her family and ruined everything she'd worked for, she used to travel with designer luggage filled with designer outfits.

It felt like another lifetime, and it was hard to believe that those things had ever mattered to her.

Nevertheless, she didn't want Phinas to see her carrying a pillowcase stuffed with her meager belongings. The only thing of value on her was the sword strapped to her hips, and even that wasn't anything special. It was a crappy sword that was too heavy for a human to carry, which probably meant that it had been inexpensive.

With the money Igor had stolen from her and the other tribes, he could have afforded the best, but then he most likely hadn't wanted them to have good weapons. It wasn't as if they would ever do battle against the humans using swords and javelins. Those weapons were good only for training, and Igor had wanted his people in good shape.

Kagra slung her own makeshift pack over her shoulder and glared at her. "Are you going to tell me what you and Phinas did last night? Or are you going to keep me in suspense until we get to the ship?"

"First of all, it wasn't last night, it was this morning, and secondly, I don't have to tell you anything." Jade opened the door and took one last look at the room they had occupied for the last fifteen hours. "Come on.

We need to help the humans load the animals on the trucks before it gets dark."

"It's not fair." Kagra pouted. "I tell you everything."

She told her too much.

Kagra was a capable and fearsome warrior, but sometimes she behaved like a young human and mistakenly thought of Jade as a mother figure, or worse, a best friend.

Jade was Kagra's commander first, her friend second, and never her mother. Thankfully, Kagra's mother was alive and well, or as well as any of them could be after what had happened to them.

"We talked." Jade continued down the corridor toward the exit.

Kagra snorted. "I bet you did more than talk. He was devouring you with his eyes, and you were not indifferent to him either. I'm dying to know if the immortals are good sex partners."

"Why?" Jade cast her an amused look. "Did any of them catch your eye?"

"Yamanu looks delicious. I love how tall and broad-shouldered he is, and he's always smiling. That's such a refreshing change from all the males in our compound. The purebloods are too full of themselves, the hybrids are too sour, and the humans are too timid."

"He's taken, and the immortals are exclusive with each other."

"How do you know he's taken?"

"Tom told me that Yamanu's mate is joining us on the cruise." She slanted a glance at Kagra. "It seems that the immortals inherited the gods' unhealthy attachment to their mates. He can't be without her for even a few days. You'll have to choose someone else."

"All you told me about the gods was that they were not to be trusted and that they made themselves look too perfect. So how should I know?"

"Now you do." Jade opened the building's front door. "I need to check on Drova."

"I'll come with you." Kagra moved her pillowcase to her other shoulder. "Why do you refer to their devotion to their mates as unhealthy?"

"It's unnatural, and it makes them weak. A warrior like Yamanu shouldn't be crippled by his inability to stay away from his mate."

"Do you think they tinkered with their genes to create such a strong attachment between mates?"

Jade shrugged. "Who knows? But it fits the pattern. The gods wanted to perfect everything about themselves, so they might have incorporated loyalty and devotion into their genetic makeup instead of leaving it to free will. But the leadership of gods was famous for feeding their population with beautiful propaganda to get them to accept limitations their elite was exempt from. They might have convinced the people that getting their genes altered to ensure fidelity was the right thing to do and took their free will away from them. Unlike what the Eternal King preached to the populous, he had scores of concubines and his official wife and produced numerous offspring. Others in positions of power probably did the same."

"Do you know that for sure, or are you speculating?"

"It wasn't a secret that the Eternal King had many concubines and many children, so he obviously wasn't exclusive with his official wife. On the other hand, I also heard stories about gods who were so strongly bonded to each other that they couldn't stand to be apart. If the stories are true, different genetics is the only explanation."

"Not necessarily. Maybe those who married for love were loyal, and those who had arranged political matings were not."

"Perhaps. I know that the history we were taught was slanted against the gods and meant to make us look great, but I always thought that messing with nature and trying to make everything perfect was wrong. Who knows how many mistakes they've made along the way? They might have left scores of planets populated by monsters."

Kagra snorted. "We are monsters too, and so are the gods, and so are their other creations like the humans. Beauty and ugliness are in the eye of the beholder, and neither defines monsters. Actions do."

"Wise words." Jade clapped her second on her back.

41

MARCEL

"*I*'ll take your things." Marcel took the two stuffed pillowcases from Sofia's father.

The air was cold, around thirty-seven degrees Fahrenheit, but neither Sofia, Helmi, nor Jarmo seemed bothered by the cold. The humans were wrapped in warm puffer jackets, scarves, hats, and gloves, and their cheeks were pinked from the cold, but no one even commented on the weather.

Perhaps because it wasn't raining or snowing, they considered it a nice evening. The sun was setting, though, and at night it got even colder.

Winter in the Scottish Highlands hadn't been any better, but Marcel had spent so many years in sunny Southern California that he'd forgotten what real cold was like. Nevertheless, he was immortal, and he was supposed to be less sensitive to temperature extremes.

Working in the lab had made him go soft.

"Thank you." Jarmo gave him a fond smile. "I'm thankful that the Kra-ell can control the herd. Otherwise, it would have been difficult to load them into the trucks. They didn't enjoy the long journey here."

As he walked away, Helmi scrunched her nose in disgust. "I didn't enjoy cleaning the trucks after them either." She shifted her gaze to Marcel. "Is there any chance that I can ride with Tomos this time?"

"The port is only a couple of hours away, and you have the entire cruise to spend as much time with Tomos as you want. As soon as we are out at sea, he will be free to roam the ship."

Her eyes brightened. "Can we get a cabin together?"

Marcel didn't know what kind of ship Kian had gotten, but if it had enough guest rooms for the entire clan, there was a good chance that Helmi could get her wish.

"I don't see why not." He looked back at the venue's front door. "Should we wait for Isla and Hannele?"

Helmi waved a dismissive hand. "They are not ready yet. We can go." She huffed out a breath. "I just wish I knew where we were going." She cast Marcel a sidelong glance. "Can't you give me a hint?"

"It hasn't been decided yet. The first priority is to get you away from Igor and put you somewhere he cannot find you. Given that he can get his hands on any information he needs, that's not an easy task. Fortunately, this is not our first rodeo, and I'm sure the brains in the war room are working on a solution."

"Rodeo?' Sofia asked. "Isn't that bullfighting?"

"No fighting is involved unless you count the struggle to stay on top of the bull or horse as he's trying to dislodge the rider. It's a skill competition."

"Oh, I get it." Sofia smiled. "So, saying that it's not your first rodeo means that you are skilled at what you do."

"Precisely."

"English." Helmi shook her head. "It has so many idioms. My mother bugged me about watching too many movies, saying that I was wasting my time on nonsense, but that's how I learned to speak it so well." She winked at Sofia. "With your help, of course."

Sofia's cheeks pinked as she smiled at Marcel. "I read a lot of American romance novels to reinforce my knowledge of the language, and I told Helmi the highlights to whet her appetite. When she asked to borrow them, I conditioned loaning her the books on her underlining and checking every word she didn't understand in the dictionary. Before lending her the next book, I tested her to make sure that she did that with the one she finished."

"Did she?"

"So-so." Helmi rotated her hand. "I always rushed to get to the happy ending." She sighed and looked at Marcel. "I want my happy ending with Tomos."

"I wish I could promise you that, but I can't."

"I know."

When they got to the trucks, William waved him over.

"Give me a moment," Marcel said.

"No problem." William waved hello to Sofia and Helmi. "Take two."

148

"I need to go." Marcel helped Sofia and her cousin climb up into the back and handed them Jarmo's bag.

"Are you coming back?" Sofia asked.

"Of course. William probably just needs to tell me something. He doesn't need me in the van."

"Okay."

Helmi jumped back down. "I'm going to look for Tomos." She looked up at Sofia. "You can come if you want."

"Nah, I'll wait for the rest of our family to get here. They won't know which truck to board."

Helmi chuckled. "Are you worried about giving Tomos and me some privacy? He's with all his hybrid buddies. We won't have any privacy anyway."

"In that case, I'll come."

42

KIAN

"Here you go, sweetie." Kian handed Allegra a biscuit.

"Dada." She grabbed it in her chubby hand and pushed it into her mouth.

Since she'd started teething, the chewing biscuits had become her favorite, and she demanded them all the time. If anyone dared to offer her a teething toy, she tossed it away with an expression that was part angry and part offended.

"She should eat her cereal," Syssi said.

"Mama," Allegra said around the biscuit.

She'd started saying mama a couple of weeks ago and learned quite quickly that Syssi would give her anything she wanted when she did.

Kian cast Syssi an amused sidelong glance. "I'll try to sneak her a few spoonfuls."

Finally, getting a full night's sleep had done wonders for Kian's mood, and the precious moments he was enjoying with his wife and daughter were all the sweeter after the long hours he'd been away from them.

He'd been stuck with Turner and Onegus in the war room for what had seemed like an eternity, and they still hadn't finalized their plan.

Kian was starting to think that his idea to transport the Kra-ell on the clan's new cruise ship hadn't been one of his best. That being said, he couldn't think of a viable alternative.

They were operating in the dark, trying to guess what Igor's next move would be, and he didn't like their position. He didn't like that Toven and Mia were planning to remain with the Kra-ell. Hell, he didn't like any of his people being in danger because of the decisions he'd made.

The council supported the move, and so did his mother, but the final decision rested on his shoulders, and it weighed heavily on him.

"Dada." Allegra pointed at the stack of waffles Okidu had put on the table.

He glanced at Syssi. "Can I give her a piece?"

She laughed. "The little manipulator knows who's the weak link. She knew not to ask me."

"I'll give her tiny pieces and follow with the cereal. I played this game with her before, and she knows the rules. She had to eat a spoonful of cereal to get a piece of the waffle."

"Fine." Syssi smiled. "You know that I can't say no to either of you."

Their morning together brought joy to Syssi. A blissful expression of love and contentment was always painted on her face when he was feeding Allegra or playing with her.

Reaching for a waffle, Syssi took a bite and followed it with a sip of her cappuccino. "How are we going to feed the four hundred people on the ship? Cruise ships typically refuel and restock at ports of call along their route, but they might spend a long time at sea. I know that you are planning on them sailing to Greenland, but plans might change in response to Igor's moves."

Kian tore off a small piece and gave it to Allegra. "We are loading the ship up to capacity. It will be carrying both fuel and supplies to last it for weeks. The route we decided on will take much less time, of course, but if we have to throttle up to full speed and sustain it for a duration, the fuel will only last for ten to twelve days. The food is less of an issue. The purebloods subsist on fresh blood, and they bring livestock with them. So that leaves only about three hundred people to feed. The ship can support three times as many passengers and a large service crew to boot, so we have nothing to worry about there."

"That's good." Syssi nibbled on her waffle.

He could sense that something was bothering Syssi, and he'd learned long ago to never dismiss it when she had a bad feeling about something.

"You seem bothered. Are you sensing something I should be aware of?"

As Allegra paused chewing and leveled her intense gaze at her mother, Kian felt the small hairs on the back of his neck tingle. Was she trying to communicate something? Or was she just sensing her mother's unease?

"I am just worried." Syssi let out a breath. "The humans are helpless and untrained, and we have many people on board. What if Turner's assessment proves correct and the ship is attacked? How can we guarantee everyone's safety? Mia is immortal but doesn't have her legs back yet. Can she even swim if the ship sinks?"

Syssi's capacity to always think of the well-being of others was endless. For the umpteenth time, Kian silently blessed the Fates for the boon they had bestowed on him. A boon far greater than what he could have possibly merited, even given his very long life and the many sacrifices he'd made for his people.

Reaching out, he took her hand and kissed it. "We don't even know if anyone will follow them. Igor might be a powerful compeller, but arranging for a vessel that could threaten a cruise ship at a moment's notice might be a tall order even for him. Nevertheless, Turner's plan accounts for that possibility. Our ship will have a fully armed submarine escorting it. If any serious threat materializes, Turner is confident in the sub's ability to handle it."

"I'm sure he's right. It's just that I'm concerned Igor will come up with something no one is expecting." Syssi took another sip of her coffee.

"Dada," came the demanding reminder that it was time to shift his attention back to the most important person at the table.

Smiling, Kian tore another small piece off the waffle and handed it to Allegra, who grabbed it in her drool-covered little hand and stuffed it in her mouth.

43

TURNER

*T*urner stood in front of the vending machine and looked over the selection of coffees.

Was he in the mood for a regular drip, or did he want a cappuccino?

He was well rested, so the coffee wasn't needed as an energy boost, but he was heading to Kian's office, and they had a phone meeting scheduled with the ship's captain and his top officers in about forty minutes, which might take a while.

After choosing a grande-sized drip, he pulled out his phone and called Kian.

"Good morning. I'm getting coffee and pastries at the vending machines. Do you want me to get you anything else?"

"Good morning, Turner." He could hear Allegra's delightful laughter, which explained Kian's lighter-than-usual tone. "I've just finished breakfast with the family, and I'm not hungry, but I can always use more coffee."

"Should I get coffee for Onegus as well?"

"He's not joining us this morning. I'll let him know if there are any changes to the plan after our talk with Captain Olsson."

"Good deal. I'll wait for you in the office."

"I'll be there in fifteen minutes." Kian ended the call.

Turner collected his coffee and pressed the button for another one.

The truth was that he enjoyed working with Kian. The missions he was often called to assist with were on a grand scale, challenging, and of great importance to the clan. He also got to spend more time with Bridget when he stayed in the village, and on occasion she helped him with some of the details, and he enjoyed that as well.

Accepting Kian's offer to work for the clan full-time was tempting.

William's technical wizardry and Roni's incredible hacking talent greatly leveraged how sophisticated and elaborate his plans could get. The impressive resources Kian committed to the critical missions were also a bonus. Turner was always mindful of budgeting, and he never splurged on unnecessary luxuries, but rescue missions required serious funds, and cutting corners meant losing lives. He never had to worry about that with Kian.

When safety was on the line, Kian went all out.

But when all was said and done, Turner didn't like answering to anyone. He was a loner who preferred to be the sole and ultimate arbiter when it came to the missions he was running. Working with others was something he could get behind, but not on a daily basis.

He didn't have to wait long for Kian to arrive.

"Good morning." Kian walked into the conference room, heading straight for the coffee.

"Are we doing a video call?" Turner asked.

"Yes." Kian took a sip from the coffee and put the cup down. "I asked Captain Olsson to get his top officers together so that we can give them an update on where we stand and to get a first-hand update from them. It's also a good opportunity to introduce them to Toven." He walked over to the fridge, took out a couple of water bottles, and threw one Turner's way before sitting next to him. "How much do you think we need to share with them?"

Kian wasn't going to like his answer. The guy's main concern was keeping the immortals' existence a secret, and he didn't like to involve humans in their affairs, but in this case, he would have to relent.

"We must give them all the information they need to do their job. Leaders make better choices when they are cognizant of the ramifications of their decisions. I believe that we need to share our suspicions that the ship might be followed and possibly attacked—potentially catastrophically. That means we also need to share information about the submarine we are sending to protect the ship. Naturally, the crew also needs to know about the detour they'll be making to Greenland, the cargo and passengers manifest, and anything else that affects the voyage." Turner glanced at his watch to see how much time they had left before the call.

Surprisingly, Kian didn't shake his head, and his eyes didn't start blazing either. "Let's get Toven on the line. I want him to compel the crew to secrecy."

"They are human," Turner said. "A simple thrall will do."

"I'm not taking chances with that." Kian pulled out his phone and started typing. "Too much is at stake."

The reply from Toven came in a couple of seconds later. "He is available and waiting for the call."

44

TOVEN

"Good evening, captain," Kian said as the guy came on line. "Thank you for making this conference call possible. Joining us are my two colleagues. Victor Turner, who is right here next to me, and Tom Hartford, who is on the other line, and who will be joining you on the ship with the rest of our guests."

The tablet screen was split in two, half taken by Kian and Turner and half by the captain and his top brass. Toven's own face was framed in a small rectangle on the bottom.

He smiled at the captain. "Your reputation precedes you, Captain Olsson."

In the few minutes before the guy had joined the three-way video call, Kian had given Toven a summary of the captain's resume, and it was impressive.

In person, Captain Johan Olsson was an imposing man. Tall and broad, with piercing blue eyes, a full head of white hair, and a beard to match, he fit the image of a Nordic ship captain to a tee.

"Thank you," the captain said in a deep voice that was pleasantly accented. "Please allow me to introduce my team." He twisted to his right and with a nod of his head acknowledged the officer seated next to him. "This is my executive officer, Lars Lindgren."

"Good morning." Lars dipped his head.

He was a stocky, bald man, seated to the captain's right.

The captain turned to the man sitting to his left. "This is my first officer, Elias Axelsson."

"Good morning, gentlemen." The first officer nodded his greeting.

He had the appearance of a Middle Easterner rather than a Scandinavian. His complexion, hair, and eyes were dark, and there was a calm and confident vitality to him that was reassuring.

The captain pointed at the young officer sitting somewhat apart from the three. "And this is my second officer, Mateo Berg." Olsson pointed to the man sitting on Axelsson's other side.

Berg was the youngest of the four, and he seemed fresh off a navy vessel. He had a military aura about him, and Toven was sure he had served as a naval officer before joining Olsson's crew.

"It's a pleasure to meet you all," Kian said. "Before we continue, I would like Tom to say a few words, and it's important that you listen carefully to what he has to say."

"It is a pleasure to meet you, gentlemen." Toven imbued his voice with strong compulsion. "I would like to stress that you must not share anything of what we are about to discuss here today in any way that could convey meaning or fact with anyone. Not on board the ship and not elsewhere. If you need to communicate any particulars with subordinates on the ship so that tasks can be executed in the best possible way, you will not allude to anything other than the very specific piece of information that is essential for the person to be able to do their job well. Please acknowledge your consent by each raising your right hand straight up."

Given the frowns on all four faces, the crew was puzzled by the odd directive, and as they raised their hands as one, they were visibly startled by their immediate compliance with the command.

"Thank you, Tom," Turner said. "With that out of the way, we can get down to business. The ship should be prepared for close to four hundred passengers and about one hundred and fifty head of livestock. The guests will get their own rooms and meals ready as well as tend to the animals, so there is no need to bring more hands onboard, but someone will need to show the designated leaders where everything is, so they will be able to take over from there."

Lars raised his hand. "We have no physician or nurse on board. Both are required for such a large group of passengers. It's part of the regulations."

"A physician is accompanying the group." Turner lifted a bottle of water and took a quick sip. "We suspect that the ship might be followed at some point of the voyage, possibly by a naval vessel, and it might be fired upon with the intention of disabling it and possibly sinking it. The pursuers' objective is to capture some of the passengers, which they could easily do once all hands abandon the ship and are either in the water or in the lifeboats."

The four men stared at the screen with expressions ranging from 'was that a joke' to 'what the hell is going on here' painted on their faces.

Ignoring their dismayed expressions, Turner pressed on. "Let me assure you that this is only a remote possibility at this point, and we have no concrete intelligence to substantiate it. Nonetheless, we are not taking any chances with the safety and well-being of the passengers, crew, or ship. To that end, we will have a fully armed submarine shadow you all the way from the North Sea to your destination, and it will extend full-force protection against any threats that may materialize during your journey."

Kian signaled Turner to let him interject. "Gentlemen, I know that calling these circumstances odd and unsettling is an understatement. I will, therefore, not hold you bound by your contracts and release any of you who wish to leave. But if any of you wish to do so, I will ask for the resignation right now, so that we have time to plan and adjust accordingly. I have very close friends as well as family among the passengers, and if I doubted our collective ability to deliver them safely to their destination, I would not have authorized this voyage. We have the means and the resources to make this as safe a trip as any other, albeit possibly more memorable. Do any of you wish to resign your commission at this point?"

Kian's interjection was timely and well delivered.

It would have never occurred to Toven to offer the men a way out, but it was a good move despite placing an extraordinary burden on these men's shoulders.

The men exchanged glances and a few sentences in rapid Swedish, and then the captain said, "We are in, but we need to confer with the rest of the crew. I don't expect any of my men to resign, but we need to give them the option."

Kian nodded. "Of course. Please let us know as soon as possible if anyone wishes to leave, as we will need to have Tom speak with them before they disembark. Please also let me know if you need anyone leaving to be replaced or can do without them. Last, I would like to add that given the unique circumstances and the longer duration of the trip, I'm tripling our agreed pay for this voyage for the entire crew."

The captain dipped his head. "I appreciate your generosity, Mr. Kian. But double pay would have sufficed."

Kian smiled. "When you deliver the ship in one piece to its final destination, I'll consider it money well spent."

The captain grinned. "She will be delivered as good as new."

45

KIAN

*K*ian had a feeling that would be Olsson's answer, and not because the guy was greedy for the triple pay.

The man was a proud, decorated ex-naval captain, and the crew he'd assembled was top-notch. Olsson loved what he did, and he took pride in his work. The triple compensation was meant as an acknowledgment of his skill and dedication, not a bribe to convince him to take on a mission that he otherwise might have declined.

"I have no doubt you will," he told the captain. "I knew I had chosen the right crew for the job."

Beside him, Turner tapped his yellow pad impatiently. "Let's continue with the logistics. The submarine will only start shadowing you at the North Sea because it is moored at the west end of the Baltic. You will not have the armed protection while in the Baltic, but our assessment is that it does not present a meaningful increase in risk because the pursuers will not dare attack there. The Baltic is teeming with ships, and the response time to a distress call from a sinking ship would be fast. They will not have enough time to sink the ship and collect the passengers they are after."

Olsson nodded. "The Baltic is swarming with ships from multiple navies, coast guard vessels, commercial fleets, as well as media helicopters and other onlookers."

Turner continued, "That is why we believe the attackers will not engage until our ship is at least twelve to fifteen hours from land and probably closer to twenty-four."

The captain nodded again. "I agree with your assessment. We should hug the coast until we clear out of the Baltic, and we should follow a zigzagging pattern that is hard to predict while monitoring traffic to see if any vessel is following us."

Turner smiled. "It's a pleasure talking to a professional. That's precisely what we need you to do. In order to give the sub enough time to catch up with you and for you to conserve fuel for the ocean crossing, you will need to keep your speed to fifteen knots. Given the rough waters you will be sailing through this time of year, your slow speed should not be suspicious to anyone following the *Aurora*. Once you clear the Baltic Sea, we need you to remain close to the coast until Bergen, at which point you will head to the Shetlands for a crossing of the North Sea and into the North Atlantic. Your speed at this point will be dictated based on the location of the pursuer, if we identify any, and by the position of the sub, as its max speed is slower than yours."

The captain jotted down the instructions and raised his head. "You still didn't tell us our destination, and how long do you expect we will be out at sea."

Kian leaned in to answer. "At this time, there are two possibilities. We might ask you to sail as originally planned, cross the Panama Canal, stop at Colombia for the armaments we ordered, and continue to Long Beach. The other option is first heading to the southwestern coast of Greenland, which is why we are directing you to the Shetland Islands. This is a big detour, but it might be necessary for the safeguarding of our passengers. We will have a final answer for you by the time you need to plot your course upon leaving the Baltic. In either case, you should carry with you the maximum amount of fuel possible and fill your supply stores to the brim so that our hands are not tied due to fuel or food considerations."

"Understood," the captain said.

"Once you do a full assessment of how long you need to get everything ready and accept the passengers and cargo for an immediate departure, please let me know as we need to get ready accordingly. Does anyone have any questions for us at this time?"

The first officer raised his hand.

"Go ahead, Mr. Axelsson," Kian said.

"I assume that you are all aware that the ship broadcasts its location on an ongoing basis. Anyone can see where we are and what our course is at all times. Why would an attacker need to follow us from the Baltic and chase us halfway around the world when they can simply lie in wait for us anywhere along our route and ambush us that way? The sub following from behind will be useless in that situation."

Turner's lips curled in a rare smile. "A great question, sir. That is why, as soon as you clear the busy shipping lanes and leave the Baltic Sea behind, you will disable your AIS system along with your VHF and become a ghost. In fact, you will only use the equipment we will be bringing onboard for communication, and you will only communicate through us."

The captain and his first officer exchanged looks, and then Olsson turned toward the screen. "Going ghost is unconventional, but I've done it before, and for triple pay, I'm willing to do it again. I can always blame it on a malfunction."

Kian nodded. "You have a lot to do, and little time to do it, so I don't want to keep you any longer than necessary. If there are no more questions, I suggest we get busy. I realize that fueling and supplying the ship will be much more expensive due to the time crunch and the circumstances. Feel free to authorize any expenditures that you deem are necessary that will aid in attaining the mission's objectives."

46

TOVEN

*W*hile Turner had been explaining the game plan to Captain Olsson and his team, Toven had received a text from Kian, asking if he could call him after the video call was concluded.

Naturally, his answer had been affirmative even though he knew what Kian wanted to discuss, and he needed more time to think about his position.

Toven still didn't have an answer when the call came a few minutes after the video call ended. "Hello again, Kian."

"It was a good meeting. It confirmed my initial assessment of Captain Olsson and all the good things I've heard about him."

Kian's effort at small talk didn't go unnoticed. He also tried to modulate his gruff tone and sound more amicable. Toven appreciated that, especially given the pressure and time crunch the guy had been operating under these past few days.

Nevertheless, he knew why Kian was trying so hard.

"You have chosen wisely," Toven complimented him. "The captain projected all the right vibes."

"Yes, he did." There was a short pause. "I want to thank you for your invaluable help and contribution to this mission. If it wasn't for Mia and you, there was no way we could have pulled this off, and for that you have my gratitude and that of the entire clan, as well as Annani's and the Kra-ell's."

Although it was clear that this was a preamble to what Kian wanted to get to next, he came across as sincere and earnest.

"I appreciate the sentiment, and I hope to always be here to help the clan. I'm forever in your debt for your unconditional acceptance of my mate, her family, and me into your midst. And as for the mission, it took our collective effort and the hard work of all the teams to make it work. But you know better than most that it is far from complete. It remains to be seen how successful it will prove to be when all is said and done."

Toven was not being self-effacing.

The truth was that others were taking far greater risks and would have died protecting him and his mate, so he truly felt a sense of gratitude.

Modesty aside, though, it was true that no one other than him could have undone Igor's compulsion, and even he had needed Mia's amplification to accomplish that.

Perhaps Annani could have done that on her own, but no one knew how strong of a compeller she was, including Annani herself, and she didn't have as much experience with compulsion as he had.

Besides, she was too important to the clan to risk in any way.

Toven knew that Kian didn't want to risk him either, but his loss wouldn't be as catastrophic for the clan as the loss of their Clan Mother. She was the heart and soul of her people, and without her, they would fall apart.

Kian cleared his throat. "I'm fully aware of the risks ahead, and they are far more serious than what you've had to face until now. That is why I want to ask you and Mia to fly back home from Helsinki with the rest of the group that is not joining the sea voyage. I see no reason to continue exposing Mia and you to more risks. I will feel better knowing that both of you are out of harm's way."

Toven had been expecting that, and he still wasn't clear on what his answer should be.

"Let's think this through together." Unintentionally, Toven assumed a teacher's tone, which some could perceive as condescending, but hopefully, Kian was above such pettiness. "Let's assume that Igor will indeed get a naval vessel to follow the ship, with the intention of firing on it in an attempt to sink her. Is it reasonable to assume that this would be his first and only move, or is it more likely that he will first try to fall back on his compulsion abilities?" He didn't wait for Kian to answer that because he was just thinking out loud. "We know from Jade that he doesn't fight fair. He froze the males of her tribe and slaughtered them where they stood, robbing them of the ability to defend themselves and die honorably in battle. What do you think his most likely first move would be in this case?"

It would be better for Kian to arrive at the conclusion on his own.

"I hate to admit it, but I see your point." Kian sounded resigned. "It should have occurred to me sooner. Igor will first try to compel anyone within hearing range on the ship, and before the disruptor is on, he will try to contact the crew and have them obey his commands. He will start with the bridge, ordering the captain and crew to shut off the engines, drop anchor, and provide access to boarders. I hope that William can come up with a way to install a voice changer on the bridge. But if Igor gets within hearing range, he will attempt to compel the Guardians to drop their weapons, and when that fails because they will be wearing earpieces, he will command his warriors, purebloods and hybrids alike, to attack from within. The Guardians will not stand a chance." Kian's voice carried his growing frustration with the situation. "The only way to prevent it is to keep them chained in their cabins. But that's not a solution either. Eventually, we will have to set them free. We need to make sure that their trail disappears at some point or that Igor is dead. Those are our only two options."

"Since we don't have earpieces for everyone, the only solution is for Mia and me to be onboard. We can counter any compulsion Igor tries to throw at us."

"I don't like it." Kian sounded frustrated. "But I'm grateful for your help. Thank you again, and please give my thanks to Mia as well. I consider you and your mate joining the clan a blessing and a boon. I'm the one who should be grateful, not you."

Toven stifled a chuckle.

Kian wasn't used to thanking anyone so profusely, and he wondered if Syssi had anything to do with it.

"The blessing is mutual, Kian. Besides, in all likelihood we will end up having a grand ol' time in a luxurious cruise liner for a week to ten days on your dime. All in all, it's a good bargain, wouldn't you say?"

Kian chuckled. "It's on the Kra-ell dime, not mine. I will deduct all the expenses from the money we seized from Igor's accounts."

"Perhaps the Fates had a hand in that as well. They didn't want the clan to go bankrupt saving the Kra-ell."

Not that he would have let it happen.

Toven had vast resources, and he'd been sincere when he'd offered to help finance the mission.

His riches meant nothing as long as they sat in gold depositories in Switzerland and elsewhere around the globe.

That being said, he was only willing to support causes where he knew exactly how the money was spent. Human organizations were full of corrupt people. Funneling money there was mostly lining the pockets of the directors, those close to them, and the politicians they needed to bribe with campaign donations.

When helping the clan rescue people or financing the Perfect Match experience for those who couldn't afford but desperately needed it, he knew where every dime went and that none of his fortune was wasted on the undeserving.

That being said, he had no desire to run the show.

Kian was a good and dedicated leader, and Toven had no problem being just a simple clan member. As it was, he felt blessed beyond measure and thanked the Fates daily for his mate, his son, his daughter, his granddaughters, his great-grandson, and their mates. Thanks to them, his zest for life and drive was back.

Toven was finally succeeding in what he'd been miserably failing at for many millennia.

He was making a difference.

47

MARCEL

"Hop in." William waved at the opened door of the command van.

"Am I supposed to ride with you?" Marcel got in and nodded to Yamanu, Toven, Mia, and Sylvia. "I promised Sofia I would ride with her and her family, so I will have to let her know. She's expecting me back."

William looked disappointed. "I thought we would go over the plan on the way."

"I also need to return to my truck," Yamanu said. "I have to keep shrouding the convoy. Besides, I don't trust anyone else with Valstar." He grinned. "I enjoyed chatting with him on the way here."

Marcel couldn't imagine how Yamanu could shroud a convoy that was twenty trucks long and chat at the same time.

Only fifteen of the trucks contained people with trackers; the rest were filled with livestock, but he needed to shroud them all. A convoy that size passing through Helsinki would raise suspicion. Especially since the trucks were an old Russian military make that no one in the Western world used.

"What's the matter?" Yamanu asked him. "Your frown indicates that you have something on your mind. Spit it out."

"Don't you need to focus on the shrouding?"

Yamanu leaned back. "I didn't need much focus when we were crossing Karelia because there was no one around, so I could shroud and chat at the same time. But when we drive through Helsinki, it will require my absolute concentration to take ahold of so many minds at once."

That made sense. Marcel's shrouding ability wasn't great, and the more people were around, the less effective it got. The same went for thralling. The most he could do at once were two people.

"Did Valstar tell you anything useful?" William asked.

"Not really." Yamanu flicked his long hair behind his shoulder. "I can't compel him, so he tried to keep his mouth shut, but I needled him into talking."

William let out a breath. "I'll try to make it fast and go over what we need to cover before the convoy is ready to pull out." He glanced toward the back of the venue, where several humans and Kra-ell were trying to herd the sheep and goats toward the trucks. "Smart animals. They know they are not going to have fun."

"I'd say leave them here," Marcel said. "But I don't want the Kra-ell to use the humans for their blood supply."

"Or us," Yamanu said.

"I'm not going." William sat across from Marcel. "Kian convinced me that I would be more useful back in the village, and the truth is that I didn't even try to argue with him. I'm not really needed on the ship, and I miss Kaia. I want to go home. You will have to operate the disruptor on the ship."

"No problem. I know how to work it." Marcel was glad to have a job to do other than escorting Sofia and her family. "So, what's the plan?"

"I'll have to turn the scrambler off when we pass through the city to get to the port. Yamanu will shroud the convoy, making it look like a regular assortment of cars and vans. Sylvia will disable all the security cameras that we will be passing by, or at least those she can identify, so Igor won't be able to access the feed and see the convoy."

Marcel frowned. "What's the point? He will know where we are heading because of the trackers. I see another issue with this plan. Helsinki is a large metropolis. If Igor can track where we are heading, it will not take him long to identify the port as our destination. How difficult will it be for him to compel the port authorities to disallow anyone from leaving or to send police to board the ship before it casts off or trap us in any number of other ways? I think we should keep killing the signal all the way through the city and the port, and only stop when the ship is ready to cast off and needs open communications with the port authorities. As we arrive at the ship, we will no longer have such a large footprint, and we can modulate the disrupter's bubble to only include a small area. That will allow the port to quickly recover from the momentary loss of communications we cause on our way in."

Yamanu nodded. "Let's bring Kian, Onegus, and Turner into this conversation."

It took all of five minutes to bring the war room up to speed, and the consensus was immediate.

His plan was a go.

"That was a good call," William said after Kian hung up. "The trucks with the animals will back up into the ship's loading docks, and the animals will be transported straight inside. The people will get off and walk in. Naturally, Yamanu will keep shrouding, and Sylvia will take care of the surveillance cameras within line of sight. Port authority and the border agents on duty will all be blind to the fact that we transported passengers and that anyone got on board. All they'll see is cargo being loaded, for which they'll remember checking and approving the bill of lading. The moment everyone is on board, the ship will sail. Everything needs to be done as fast as possible to minimize the time in the port from arrival to casting off. If everything goes according to plan, it should take no more than two hours from the moment we start loading the ship till it can leave. You will need to turn the scrambler off just before the ship sails because communications will have to be restored at that point. Unless Igor is already in Helsinki and somehow guesses our plan and gets his response in motion, he won't be able to stop us in time."

Marcel frowned. "How soon after we sail do I turn the disruptor back on?"

"You'll have to wait until the ship is out of the Baltic Sea and possibly until it reaches the North Sea, but first, you'll have to install a voice changer on the bridge. We can't have Igor contacting the captain and taking over command. I'll reconfigure some of my equipment, but you will have to install it."

"The *Aurora* will hug the coast while it's still in the Baltic," Toven said. "Igor won't dare to do anything when it's so close to shore. Contacting the captain and trying to take over like that would be his best option. I have no doubt that he'll try that."

48

JADE

*A*fter the mandatory hellos to Mia, Sylvia, and everyone else in the van, Jade sat next to the doctor.

Following a full day of rest in the venue, Merlin had asserted that all the injured were doing well enough without him and they no longer needed his supervision.

"Thank you for taking care of our injured and saving Kagra's life," she told him.

Kagra's wounds could have been fatal if Merlin hadn't stitched up her insides. There was only so much that the Kra-ell body could repair, and Kagra's injuries had been too extensive even for her superior healing abilities.

"You're welcome," Merlin said. "She's a trouper."

"She's a Kra-ell warrior." Jade unzipped her jacket. "Are you coming with us on the voyage?"

"I am." He didn't look happy about that. "I'm going to miss my mate and my stepdaughter."

Jade stifled a huff.

Kra-ell didn't form a strong attachment to a singular partner, so going on missions or traveling didn't bother them. Also, they lived in small tribes, so there were many hands to help care for the young and everything else that needed to be done. That was why their way was so much better.

It was a much better system than the gods' and the immortals' exclusive mate bonds.

"All your patients are doing well, so you don't have to come. You can fly back home to your mate and stepdaughter."

His forehead furrowed. "Did nobody tell you I'll be removing the trackers as soon as we board the ship?"

The truth was that she'd forgotten about the trackers. With William scrambling the signals, it hadn't been a concern. Besides, the fact that Sofia had a tracker in her didn't mean that all of them had. Igor might have put it in the girl before he sent her across the ocean on a spying mission.

"I think that only some of us have trackers. Otherwise, why put tracking collars on us? Igor is not the wasteful type. If he had other means to track us by, he wouldn't have spent money on the collars, which needed maintenance and occasional replacements."

Merlin didn't look convinced. "He might have used the collars for intimidation. Also, it's possible that only some of you have the implanted trackers, and he didn't want to explain why some of you had to wear collars and others didn't."

"That actually makes sense." It fit Igor's mode of operation.

He would have done that to avoid questions and speculation.

"How do you think he found your tribe?" Merlin asked.

She'd thought about it after Tom had suggested that the settlers had been implanted with trackers before embarking on the journey to Earth. Still, that hypothesis had a big hole in it.

"I don't think we got them implanted before going into stasis. If all the settlers had trackers in them, Igor would have found all the survivors, but he found only some."

Merlin cast her a sad smile. "The trackers need a live host to transmit. The others are probably dead. It's also possible that some of them malfunctioned after seven thousand years. In fact, I'm surprised that any of them still worked."

He was probably right about the hosts being dead.

The gods made things to last, and since the trackers were inside bodies that were in stasis in protective pods, they could have gone on working forever.

Or not.

She wasn't tech-savvy, and most of what Ragoner had tried to explain to her had gone over her head.

He'd been such a smart male.

Kra-ell didn't get to attend the gods' universities, so all he had known he'd learned on his own. At least the gods hadn't restricted the Kra-ell from accessing their technical knowledge base, so anyone with the brains and the time could teach themselves to build all those marvelous things the gods had used. The hard part had been getting the necessary parts and tooling, some of which were not available for sale to the Kra-ell.

The genetic knowledge was blocked from them in its entirety, though, and Jade couldn't even blame the gods for that. It had been done on the request of the Kra-ell queen, who hadn't wanted her people modified in any way.

She turned to Merlin. "Why didn't you start removing the trackers while we were waiting for the ship to be ready? You could've been done with it by now."

Merlin chuckled. "It's not as easy as pulling out a bad tooth. First, I have to find the tracker, and that takes time. It requires a lot of time when that needs to be done for over three hundred people. Then a small surgery is required to remove the tracker, and even though one is not a big deal, multiplied by three hundred, it is. Still, I would have started on it if I had the right equipment."

"Do you have it on the ship?"

Merlin nodded. "Bridget did the impossible and found us a compact MRI machine. It was delivered and installed in the ship's clinic this afternoon, along with the rest of the medical equipment needed to perform minor operations. I will need the help of your nurse, though."

"Of course. Is Bridget your mate?"

"Bridget is a fellow doctor. My mate's name is Ronja."

"That's a Scandinavian name."

Merlin smiled, his entire face brightening. "It is." He pulled out his phone. "My Ronja is originally from Norway. Let me show you her picture."

Jade glanced at the screen and said what he'd expected her to say. "She's very pretty."

Merlin flicked over to a picture of a young girl with the same blond hair that was nearly white. "That's my stepdaughter, Lisa. Well, not officially, since Ronja and I aren't married yet, but we are planning to have the ceremony soon. In fact, we were hoping to get married on the same ship that is picking us up later today, but we applied too late, and all the nights have already been taken. We will have to wait for the next cruise or do it on land."

"That's why Kian purchased the ship and had it remodeled in the first place," Sylvia said. "His sister is getting married on it. He called the ship the *Aurora*, but we all call it the Love Boat."

"'The Love Boat—'" William started singing softly, and then the others joined in, all except for Toven, who regarded them with the same puzzlement as Jade did.

49

YAMANU

*A*s the convoy entered the port, Yamanu had trouble focusing on shrouding it. Mey was waiting for him on the ship, and his mind kept gravitating toward their reunion.

They had only been apart for four days, but it felt much longer. He couldn't wait to hold Mey in his arms, to kiss her soft lips, to hear her laugh at his corny jokes, to hold her hand, to make love to her. But until everyone was off the trucks and the convoy left the port, he had to banish those thoughts and keep shrouding.

The Guardians would thrall the drivers to forget who their passengers and cargo were and where they had picked them up.

Hopefully, Igor couldn't break through a thrall as easily as he broke through compulsion, but Yamanu had a feeling that there was more to Igor than his people knew about.

Letting his thoughts wander to the snippets of conversation he'd had with Valstar on the way was a good way to take his mind off Mey. Those thoughts were not as consuming or emotionally intense, and he could keep the shroud while pondering the enigma that was Igor.

Why had he chosen a Russian name? To hide his true identity?

It wasn't likely that no one had known him on the ship that had brought the Kra-ell to Earth. His pod members must have known. Valstar had claimed that he didn't, but Yamanu was sure that had been a lie. He had to know his boss's Kra-ell name.

The other option was that, like Emmett, Igor was embarrassed about his name. Perhaps he'd been someone's unwanted child.

Yeah, that was probably it.

Given Igor's immense compulsion power, Yamanu suspected that he was a half-breed. Half god and half Kra-ell. If he were, he was a demigod, which meant that he should be much more handsome than the average Kra-ell.

The Kra-ell were good-looking people, but their features lacked the perfection of the gods and the first-generation hybrid offspring of the gods.

When he'd asked Valstar whether Igor was good-looking, the answer had been affirmative, but it hadn't evoked any unusual reaction, and the guy hadn't elaborated, so Yamanu assumed that Valstar didn't know whether Igor was a half-breed.

If Yamanu's suspicion was correct though, it was possible that Igor had thralling ability in addition to the compulsion. Then again, Kra-ell's compulsion had an element of thralling and shrouding in it anyway.

Yamanu tried to remember what Aliya had said about her visits to the village she'd grown up in. Had she shrouded herself, or had she just hidden in the shadows? She'd only gone at night, so maybe it was the latter.

His musings kept his mind occupied throughout the unloading, but it got more difficult not to think of Mey when he got off the truck. He couldn't go to her yet and had to keep shrouding the convoy until it left the port.

When it was finally done, Yamanu felt like he'd gone through the wringer, but he didn't let the exhaustion slow him down as he rushed into the ship through the cargo bay and took the stairs to the upper decks.

There were way too many of them, and when he finally found his love on the top one, he was out of breath.

"Yamanu!" Mey ran into his arms. "Are you okay?" She leaned back and looked into his eyes. "Why are you panting? Was the shrouding that difficult?"

He grinned. "It was, but only because I couldn't stop thinking about you and about the moment I'd hold you in my arms again." He took her lips in a scorching kiss, ignoring the burn in his lungs.

She broke their kiss first and frowned. "Breathe, my love. You're worrying me. I've never seen you so exhausted after a shroud."

He'd been worse, but he didn't want to tell her that. "It's not the shrouding. This damn ship has way too many decks and too many stairs."

"Why didn't you use the elevator?" Arwel asked.

"There is an elevator?"

Jin laughed. "Don't tell me that you've never been on a cruise ship before."

"The last time I sailed, it was on a sailboat, and it had only one deck and one flight of stairs."

"When was that?" Mey asked.

"A couple of centuries ago. I'm not a fan of boats."

"Then why take this mission?" Arwel asked. "You can still change your mind and go home with Mey. But you have to do it quickly. The captain told us that the *Aurora* is scheduled to leave the port in less than an hour."

"That's good. The sooner we leave, the better. And no, I don't want to take Mey home." He looked into her eyes. "You want to meet your crappy relatives, right?"

She nodded. "But I don't want you to suffer for it."

"I won't. With the help of meditation, I'm sure I can overcome the nausea."

He wasn't sure at all, but he would give it his best shot.

TOVEN

*T*he *Aurora* was small, as cruise ships go, with six passenger decks and three hundred and sixty cabins. Compared to the floating cities moored at the Helsinki port she looked tiny, but she was luxuriously appointed, and she was more than enough for what the clan needed. Hopefully, the cargo bay wouldn't be destroyed by the sheep and goats they had brought on board.

They didn't have time for another remodel before the wedding cruise.

As it was, the event would probably have to be postponed, and given that Alena was rapidly approaching full term, it might be a problem.

His future daughter-in-law couldn't care less, but his son didn't want to wait, and neither did Toven. He hadn't had many reasons to celebrate throughout his long life, and the union between his son and Annani's eldest daughter deserved a grand celebration.

"It is a pleasure to meet you in person, Tom." The captain shook Toven's hand, his eyes roaming his face and body.

Toven was used to the reaction and didn't mind the appraisal. It wasn't sexual, not in Olsson's case, anyway. Humans just needed time to get used to Toven's godly perfection.

He and the captain were about the same height, three inches or so over six feet, but Olsson was stockier. Not that there was an ounce of fat on him. He was just built like a brick wall, and he was groomed to perfection, with his white beard and mustache neatly trimmed and his full head of hair swept back in an elegant style. The only indications that the man was in his late fifties were the laugh lines around his eyes and frown lines on his forehead, as well as the white hair that in his youth had probably been blond.

"I'm sorry," the captain shook his head, "but I don't know your last name, or I would have addressed you properly."

Toven shook his hand firmly. "It's Hartford, but Tom is fine, and the pleasure is all mine, Captain." He put his hand on Mia's shoulder. "This is my fiancée, Mia."

The captain leaned down to offer her his hand. "Welcome aboard the *Aurora*, Miss Mia."

"Thank you, Captain Olsson."

Toven proceeded to introduce Yamanu, Phinas, Merlin, and Marcel as representatives of the passengers. When he got to Jade and Kagra, he wondered what Yamanu was shrouding them as. Olsson's eyes widened momentarily, so Yamanu was probably making them look exceptionally good.

Not that either of them was lacking in any way, but their alien looks would have been too shocking for the captain and his men, and they didn't have time to thrall everyone who needed thralling. The pilot was about to board the ship in mere minutes to get her out of port.

"Welcome aboard, ladies." Olsson shook each of their hands and then turned to Toven. "I'm needed on the bridge. Our first assistant engineer, Mr. Mikael Hedlund, will show Doctor Merlin the clinic, and our chief electrician, Mr. Peter Dahlberg, will show the rest of you where everything is."

"Thank you, Captain."

"I'll come along." Marcel followed the captain, holding a box with William's makeshift voice changer. "I need to check out your communication equipment."

Marcel must have used a thrall because the captain didn't object.

The disrupter was down in the cargo bay, but since they couldn't use it yet anyway, it could stay there until it was needed.

"Do you want to join us on the bridge as well, Mr. Hartford?" the captain asked.

"Not right now. I'm curious to see the rest of the vessel, and please, call me Tom."

The pilot was about to come on board, and Toven didn't want the guy to see that there were passengers on the ship. "Remember what we discussed. The *Aurora* has no passengers. Marcel is part of your crew."

The captain nodded and turned on his heel.

As the engineer left with Merlin, the chief electrician smiled nervously. "Forgive me, but I've never given a ship tour before, so I'm not very good at it, but I'm the only one who is not needed right now."

"That's okay, Mr. Dahlberg." Toven gave him a reassuring smile. "As I said before, we are an informal bunch. We don't need you to show us the cabins or the entertainment areas. We can explore the ship on our own. We only need you to show us where we can get linen and toiletries for the cabins, where we can launder our stuff, where the food is stored, the kitchen, etc. After this first tour, we won't bother you again."

"It's no bother." Dahlberg glanced at Mia's wheelchair. "We need to use the elevator. Follow me."

Marcel's finger hovered over the row of buttons as they entered the spacious elevator. "Which level are the animals stored at?"

"The cargo bay." Dahlberg entered a code on the keypad, and the elevator lurched down. "As the owner requested, we sectioned off part of the bay for the animals. We also got separate crates of feed for the sheep and the goats." He smiled. "I grew up on a farm, so I know that sheep and goats have different nutritional needs. They have plenty of both over there. I just wonder why you are taking them to Greenland."

"These are a special breed," Marcel said.

"Oh, I see." Dahlberg nodded. "This is their breeding season, and gestation is five months. Does or ewes bred in the fall will usually kid or lamb in the spring of the next year. Luckily for you, I knew it was not good to mix the herds during mating season, so I divided the cargo bay into two sections, one for the goats and one for the sheep. The bucks and rams get very aggressive during this time, and a ram can easily kill a buck."

"We wouldn't want that," Kagra said. "We are very fond of these animals. You might say that our lives depend on them."

51

PHINAS

*P*hinas held his breath as their group exited the elevator at the cargo bay. Sofia, her father, and several other humans were tending to the animals. As Dahlberg walked over to show them where everything was, Phinas sidled up to Jade.

"Do they taste good?"

She eyed him from the corner of her eye. "They are not bad, but I prefer the blood of wild animals. It tastes much better."

That shouldn't have excited him, but everything about the Kra-ell leader affected him.

"Which ones are your favorites?"

The corner of her lips kicked up in a lopsided grin. "Those that provide a challenge. I don't like easy prey."

He leaned to whisper in her ear. "Should I play hard to get, then? Do you want me to run so you can give chase?"

She lifted her hand and put a finger on his lips. "Save it for later. We are not alone."

They stood apart from the others, with the bleating of the sheep and goats providing enough background noise to prevent the others from hearing them.

Tonight, he and Jade would resume their sexual training, and he was going to demonstrate what he'd planned to show her the day before.

Yamanu put his hand on Dahlberg's shoulder. "I'm eager to join my mate in our cabin, so the quicker you can complete the tour, the better."

"We will take our leave," Toven said. "I will escort Mia to our cabin, and I'll come down again to get the linens and other necessities."

Mia looked tired, which was not surprising given all that she'd been through lately and the fact that her body was working on regrowing lost limbs.

It was a painful process, and Phinas didn't know how she could handle the pain so well. Evidently, females had a much higher pain tolerance than males.

"Don't worry about it," Kagra said. "I'll get you what you need." She winked at Mia. "We owe you much more than room service."

"Thank you." Mia smiled gratefully. "I appreciate it."

When the two headed toward the elevators, Dahlberg motioned for the rest of them to follow him. "Let's use the stairs. The desalination equipment and waste management are just one level down. I know it's not something you will use, but it's fascinating to see." He glanced at Yamanu, who was emitting impatient vibes. "If that's okay with you."

"Make it quick," the Guardian said.

"I will." The chief electrician opened the door to a staircase and started down the utilitarian stairs. "All modern cruise ships use desalination to turn seawater into drinking water. Pumps on the hull suck the water from the ocean and transfer it to the desalination equipment." He opened the door at the lower deck and ushered them inside.

The clan used desalination equipment to provide water to the village, so Phinas was familiar with how it looked, but Jade eyed the enormous block of equipment with wide eyes.

"How does it take the salt out of the water?" she asked.

"This one uses reverse osmosis." Dahlberg patted the side of the block. "A pump pressurizes the seawater and pushes it through a semi-permeable membrane. Most dissolved salts and organic compounds, including bacteria and suspended solids, can't pass through. What comes out on the other side is mostly clean water. The next step is to mineralize and disinfect it using chlorination, ozonation, silver-ion treatment, and UV radiation. The process is completed with filtration and, finally, heating up the water. Only then can it be used as drinking water." He kept walking and pointed to large water tanks. "This is where the water is stored. From here, it is distributed throughout the ship."

"Fascinating," Yamanu bit out. "Can we get to the food area now? I'm hungry, and I want to know where I can get something to eat."

"Of course." Dahlberg looked disappointed at Yamanu's lack of interest. "The food storage area and the kitchen are two levels up. Would you like to use the elevator or the stairs?"

"The stairs," the Guardian said. "How much food do you have stored?"

"We have enough provisions that should last four hundred passengers two weeks."

As the chief electrician led them up the stairs, Phinas took position behind Jade so he could watch her ass.

Sensing his eyes on her, she exaggerated the sway of her hips, encased in a pair of low-hanging fatigues secured with a wide belt. Her extremely narrow waist was not as prominent in the loose black Henley she was wearing, but he could still trace the contours of her graceful spine through the fabric.

"The *Aurora* has four cold storage rooms," Dahlberg said. "Currently, they contain about eighteen hundred pounds of chicken, seven hundred pounds of fish, five hundred pounds of hamburger meat, and one thousand pounds of hot dogs. That's just the meat."

That was a lot of food, and since the purebloods and some of the hybrids didn't need to eat any of that, they could probably spend a month at sea if needed. The question was whether they had enough fuel.

"How long before the ship needs to refuel?" Phinas asked the chief electrician.

"If we cruise at a moderate speed, we can probably go for nearly a month before we need to refuel, but if we need to speed up, we will go through the reserves much faster." Dahlberg opened the door to another storage room and motioned for them to follow. "Despite the reserves, the protocol is to refuel at every port we stop at so we never run low."

"Got it." Phinas stayed close to Jade as her eyes roamed the contents of the room.

It was stocked with hundreds of wooden crates with a variety of alcoholic beverages. They were stacked one on top of the other and secured with metal bands.

"Four thousand bottles of beer," Dahlberg said. "One thousand bottles of wine and seven hundred bottles of assorted spirits."

Yamanu grinned. "Is there a chance you can hook me up with a few whiskey bottles?"

"It's all yours." The chief electrician waved his hand at the crates. "Just secure the crates after you take what you need. This is a ship, and everything that's not tied down moves."

"Aye, aye, sir." Yamanu clapped the guy on his back. "I'm going to take a few bottles right now."

52

JADE

"Where does the waste go?" Kagra asked after they finished touring the kitchen.

Jade couldn't care less about the food prep areas or the waste processing, but Phinas had seemed very interested in the kitchen tour, which made her wonder if he liked to cook.

Not that she could ever sample what he made, but she was curious.

Fascinated was a better word.

Phinas affected her in unexpected ways. She'd told him that he'd done fine, and he'd taken it as an insult, but the truth was that she couldn't put into words what she'd experienced with him. She'd climaxed from him penetrating her with his fingers, which had never happened to her.

Heck, she'd even licked his shaft and had enjoyed doing so. Another first for her.

The chief electrician cast a cautious look at Yamanu. "Do you want me to take you where it's done?"

"No," Yamanu answered categorically.

Holding two bottles of whiskey under one arm and two bottles of wine under the other, the Guardian seemed impatient to deliver them to his mate and his other companions.

Jade had only seen them in passing, but she'd noticed that the two ladies were of Chinese descent and strikingly beautiful by human standards.

Kagra hadn't been happy to see that Yamanu had a gorgeous mate who he was obviously in love with, but she hadn't been overly disappointed either. Her interest in Yamanu had been nothing but curiosity, which had been sparked by Jade's liaison with Phinas.

Her second had always been a competitive female.

Yamanu nudged Peter Dahlberg with his elbow. "You can tell us all about it while you show us where the linen and the laundry are, and then I'm out of here. After that, if any of the others want to see where the poop goes, you are more than welcome to show them."

"Understood." Peter headed down the corridor. "Housekeeping is on the same level as the kitchens and the food storage."

After showing them the laundry machines, Dahlberg led them through rooms full of housekeeping supplies, and as they each loaded up a cart with what they needed, he talked.

"The ship can't just dump sewage into the ocean, and it has to have a wastewater treatment plant on board. The black water is treated in several steps, mechanically and chemically. First, the coarse stuff gets filtered out, then it goes through biological purification, with microorganisms decomposing the organic matter, and lastly, it runs through filters with extremely fine sieves that sort out all microorganisms. The final step is nitrogen and phosphorus reduction. After that, it can be disposed of into the sea or ocean water, but only if the ship is at least twelve nautical miles from land."

Frowning, Kagra pushed the cart in front of her. "But what do you do with all the stuff filtered out of the water?"

"That's an excellent question." Peter grinned, happy that at least one person was interested in the subject that seemed to fascinate him. "The by-products are dehydrated and dried in a centrifuge, then burned in an incinerator. Once the ship docks, the ashes are disposed of with the remaining waste."

"You mean the garbage?" Kagra asked. "Where we come from, we used to burn it. We need to know what to do with it on the ship."

Most of the waste in the compound had been produced by the humans and the hybrids who needed cooked food. They didn't use a lot of paper or plastic products, and most of the organic stuff had been turned into compost for the vegetable gardens.

Then again, Jade hadn't been involved in any of that, so maybe she was wrong about what was done with the leftovers.

"Food waste can be shredded and thrown overboard if the ship is at least three nautical miles away from land," Peter explained. "Cardboard, metals, and plastics should be collected and brought over to the hydraulic garbage compressor. Glass needs to be fed to the crushing machine and stored in bags. Non-recyclable garbage is burned in incinerators and turned to ash."

"I'm familiar with the process," Yamanu said. "That's what we do with garbage where I come from." He put the bottles in his cart, added a few toiletries, and turned to Jade. "I would like to invite you to our cabin later tonight. My mate and her sister are eager to meet you."

Jade stifled a groan. She had more things to do than she had time, and at some point, she wanted to relax with one of the bottles of fine vodka she'd seen in the liqueur storage room and perhaps invite Phinas over.

She had yet to choose a cabin, and hopefully there were enough left so she could have one to herself and wouldn't have to share with Kagra.

"After we leave the port, I need to deal with my people." She let out a breath. "Except for Valstar and his buddies, all the others need to be released and shown where everything is. I don't know when I will be done."

Yamanu nodded. "Then let's do that tomorrow. Maybe we can meet at the top deck for a swim in the pool."

Peter cleared his throat. "The pool isn't filled with water, but it can be arranged. It will take time, though."

"Don't worry about it." Yamanu clapped him on the back. "We will figure it out on our own. You can go back to your electrical engineering duties." He turned to Jade and Kagra. "Unless the ladies have more questions for you?"

They needed Yamanu to keep shrouding them, and he needed to go.

"We don't," Jade said. "Thank you for the tour, Mr. Dahlberg."

"You are most welcome." He dipped his head.

53

PHINAS

After Jade had declined Yamanu's invitation, Phinas decided it wasn't a good idea to suggest that they meet for drinks in his cabin as he'd planned.

The cabin that he still needed to secure.

He'd put Dandor in charge of allocating rooms to his men, but he hadn't had time to check out the accommodations before meeting with the captain.

"I wonder what the cabins look like." He fell in step with Jade and Kagra, the three of them pushing their loaded carts toward the elevators.

"I hope they are fancy," Kagra said. "I've never been on a cruise ship."

"Neither have I," Jade said. "But I've stayed in nice hotels back in the day when I still traveled for business." She winced. "I also had nice luggage instead of a pillowcase to put my things in."

Phinas regretted not paying more attention to what Aliya had told them about Jade. Now that he thought back to their conversations, he remembered Aliya mentioning the animated movies that Jade had brought for the kids from her travels.

Aliya had also talked about the stories Jade liked to tell the children. He couldn't imagine the hard warrior enjoying doing that. But there was still a lot he didn't know about her, which wasn't surprising, given their short time together. She was always busy with one thing or another, and she'd ridden in the command van that he hadn't been invited into.

Even Merlin had ridden in the van when his patients no longer needed him, and it rankled that Phinas had been left out.

He and his men had volunteered their help, so the least Phinas had expected was to be included in the decision-making.

Kalugal had expected the same, but Kian hadn't invited him to the war room either. After all this time, the clan still regarded them as outsiders.

"Where did you travel to?" he asked Jade as they waited for the elevator.

"I've been all over the world." She had a wistful expression on her beautiful face. "Singapore, South Korea, most of Europe, the United States, Canada, Brazil, Venezuela, and many more. It was mostly for business, but I have to admit that I also did it because I enjoyed it."

"You never took me along," Kagra grumbled.

Jade put a hand on her shoulder. "You were the only one I could trust to hold the fort in my absence."

"I know. But I wish I had seen more of the world. Maybe it would have made captivity easier."

"It made it harder." Jade pressed her lips into a tight line. "I knew what I was missing out on."

As the elevator doors opened and the three of them squeezed in together with their carts, Jade looked at the panel. "Any idea which deck we are on?"

Kagra shook her head. "The Guardians will know."

"Hold the door open while I check." Phinas stepped out and called Dandor. "I'm heading up. Which deck are we on?"

"We are on the fifth deck. I put you in the best cabin at the bow. In ship speak, that's the front. You have a very nice view."

"Thank you. What about the Kra-ell? Which deck are they on?"

"The Guardians put them on decks three and four. I think the purebloods are on the fourth, and the hybrids are on the third. The humans are on decks one and two."

"Who is on deck six?"

"Toven and the Guardians."

"Of course they are." Phinas grimaced. "They think they are at the top of our food chain." He pressed the button for deck four. "Although to be fair, it's their ship. Please arrange for the men to go down in groups and collect what they need. I'll unload my cart and take you and the first group to show you where everything is. After that, you can show the others."

"Yes, boss."

As Phinas stepped inside and the door closed behind him, Jade cast

Kagra a reproachful look. "You should have stayed to help the Guardians organize our people."

"They didn't want my help. I've told you that."

"You should have insisted."

As the door opened, Kagra pushed her cart out, but Jade didn't follow. Instead, she lodged her cart in the door to prevent it from closing. "If it's not too late when I'm done with my duties, I'll come to check out your cabin."

Phinas's heart leaped...

Leaped? What was he, a human teenager?

"It will not be too late for me. I'll be delighted to show you my cabin no matter what time it is. What would you like to drink? Other than blood, that is."

"Vodka with cranberry juice." She pushed her cart out.

Phinas was still smiling long after the elevator door closed and the cabin lurched up.

When he got out of the elevator on deck five, Dandor was waiting for him and took over pushing the cart. "Let me show you your cabin." He sounded excited.

"Aren't they all the same?"

"Most of them are, except for this one, which is why I reserved it for you. It's bigger, and it has a huge balcony. All the cabins have a living room, a bar, and two-bedroom suites. They are very nicely done, but they are small in scale. Nevertheless, I think even Kalugal would approve."

Phinas chuckled. "I wouldn't be sure of that. Kalugal likes everything he owns to be on a grand scale. It would be a luxury yacht if he ever got a boat."

54

KIAN

"They are out of the port," Roni announced as Kian answered the phone.

He already knew that, but Roni was showing off that he could track the *Aurora* in real time. He'd hacked into the navy's system monitoring marine activity and could see her and every vessel surrounding her.

Once Marcel reactivated the scrambler, they would lose the ability to track the ship, but so would everyone else. Thanks to their own satellite network, which William's scrambler was programmed to let through, they could still communicate through their phones and tablets.

"Congratulations, Roni. Thanks for letting me know, and keep me updated if you spot any suspicious activity around the ship."

"Will do, boss." The kid ended the call.

It was too early to determine if any vessel was following the *Aurora*, but Roni might spot something.

"Let's call Yamanu and Toven," Turner said. "If they have nothing of concern to report, I'll take a break to check on a few things in my office."

Kian tilted his head. "I thought you didn't have any pending jobs at the moment."

"I didn't a few days ago, but my office had a couple of inquiries I need to look into."

"Please don't take on any new jobs until this is over. I need you and your international connections."

It seemed as if Turner knew every private operator in every corner of the world. Whenever Kian needed to hire human teams to assist in missions, he was the guy to turn to.

That was the official version.

The unofficial one was that Turner was good at what he did, and neither Onegus nor Kian could match his level of expertise.

"Don't worry," Turner said. "I'm enjoying running this operation too much to let go before seeing it to its happy ending."

That had been a polite way to say that he wouldn't leave a critical mission like this in the hands of amateurs, and as much as it rankled to admit, he was right.

Onegus and Kian might have centuries of experience, but they had never been trained in modern warfare, they didn't have connections to former special operations personnel or their foreign equivalents, and they lacked Turner's computer-like brain.

That being said, even Turner hadn't always thought of all the angles, and several brains working on the same problem were better than one.

"Appreciated." Kian glanced at his watch and calculated the time difference before placing the call.

It was ten o'clock at night in Finland.

"Hello, boss," Yamanu answered.

"How are things going over there?"

"Couldn't be better. The cabin is great, and Mey loves it. She's soaking in the Jacuzzi tub and waiting for me to join her."

Yamanu sounded happy, which Kian was glad about, but he still didn't like that Mey and Jin had joined the cruise.

"What about the Kra-ell?"

"Valstar and the rest of Igor's original group are under guard, and Toven has compelled the hell out of them. They don't dare go to the bathroom without asking permission. We released the rest of the purebloods and hybrids, but we are watching them. Toven's compulsion should prevent them from doing anything they shouldn't, but I prefer to keep an eye on them."

"How is their morale?" Kian asked.

"Some are excited, and others look anxious, but all of them are putting on a brave face. They are trained not to show emotions, but they can't hide from Arwel. He says they don't project much, though, and he has to get close to get a read on them."

"I'm not surprised," Turner said. "Did Arwel sense any anger?"

"Naturally, Valstar and the rest of Igor's circle are angry and anxious. They know that their days are numbered."

"We can't just execute them," Kian said. "Don't let Jade do that either. Everyone deserves a fair trial and a chance to defend themselves."

"Didn't Toven promise Jade Valstar's head?" Yamanu asked.

"Yeah, he did, but only after we caught Igor, and he didn't promise her the heads of the others."

"Got it. Anything else I need to fill you in on?"

There was plenty more, but Kian didn't want to keep the Guardian while his mate waited for him to join her in the Jacuzzi.

"I can get Toven to do that. Have a good night."

"I will. Good day to you."

After ending the call, Kian placed another to Toven.

"Hello, Kian," Toven answered. "We left the port."

"I know. Roni is tracking the ship. How did the meeting with the captain go?"

"As expected, he followed our instructions to the letter, and his crew is doing what we asked as well. After the initial tour, they know to stay out of our way. By the way, the cabin Mia and I are staying in is beautifully done."

Kian smiled even though it wasn't a video call. "Thank you. I had Ingrid design the decor, but I haven't seen the finished product yet. How is the craftsmanship?"

"Excellent."

"I pulled it out of the shipyard before they could do the final detailing, so I assume that not everything is spotless."

Toven chuckled. "Mia says it's as clean as any hotel room we've stayed at, but I don't know if she means it as a compliment." He paused. "She says it is."

"How come I can't hear her?"

"She's out on the balcony, wrapped in a floor-length puffer jacket, a hat, a scarf, and gloves. It's freezing at night, but she enjoys the fresh air."

"What about the food situation? Who is handling the cooking?"

"Sofia's aunts are organizing shifts," Toven said. "We are invited to a midnight feast."

"That's great. I spoke to Yamanu before I called you. He said the Guardians released all the Kra-ell except for Valstar and those remaining from Igor's original crew. It would be a good idea to continue their interrogation tomorrow."

"It is, and I will do that," Toven said. "Merlin is all set up in the clinic and ready to receive his first patients. Who do you want him to start with?"

"It doesn't really matter because we need to check everyone. I assume that all the pureblooded females he captured have trackers in them, so maybe it's a good idea to start with them. Those who were born in the compound probably don't, but who knows."

"It will be interesting to see," Toven said. "If the trackers are from the home planet, they must have been implanted by the gods. According to Jade, the Kra-ell didn't have access to such sophisticated technology. But if that's the case, I wonder where Igor got the one he implanted in Sofia. I doubt their escape pods had equipment that was not necessary for keeping them alive."

"My thoughts exactly," Kian said. "He either took it out of himself, those he trusted, those he killed, or all of the above. I'm waiting for William to return and take apart the one we have to see if it's alien technology. I wouldn't be surprised if he finds a microscopic inscription saying that it was made in China."

JADE

"Who do you want to get checked first?" Kagra asked. "Max said it doesn't matter, and it's up to us."

"Who is Max?"

"A handsome Guardian with a charming smile."

Her second had shifted her focus to a new immortal.

Jade's lips twisted in an involuntary smile. "I see that you found a new candidate to experiment with."

"Maybe." Kagra put her hand on her hip. "We shall see. I haven't asked him if he has been taken yet. So, who goes first?"

"Drova, Morgada, Tomos, and Helmi." Jade started down the corridor, and Kagra fell in step with her. "I'll get Drova and Morgada. You get Tomos and Helmi."

"Why those four?"

"They each represent a different group. Morgada is from our tribe, and I also know her from before we boarded the gods' ship, but she doesn't remember being implanted either.

"Drova is a pureblood who was born in the compound, Tomos is a hybrid, and Helmi is a human who didn't get to study at a university, so there was no reason to implant her, but I want to double-check. Finding out which of them has a tracker will give me valuable insight."

"Why not me?" Kagra asked. "I'm a pureblood who was born on Earth."

"I need you to organize our people, including the humans. I'll get checked first to show them it's not a big deal, and Helmi will go next. We can safely leave the humans for last if she doesn't have a tracker."

"It doesn't really matter." Kagra stopped in front of Morgada and Drova's cabin. "We need to check every person. As long as even one tracker remains, Igor can find us, and Max told me that they can't activate the scrambler until the ship leaves the Baltic Sea."

"The sooner the trackers are out, the better. I don't know how long it takes, but I assume about half an hour to an hour per person. That means between one hundred and fifty hours to three hundred and twenty, and that's with Merlin not taking any breaks, which he can't do. He needs to sleep from time to time."

"Maybe he can teach someone how to do that? How complicated can it be to scan a body for a tracker?"

"I don't know." Jade put her hand on the door handle. "I'll know more after the initial group is scanned. I hope we can do that faster, or we will not get them out before reaching Greenland."

Kagra tilted her head. "Is that where we are going?"

"It's just a stop on the way, and I hope that we catch Igor before we get to the North Sea and can turn around without ever reaching Greenland. That would be the perfect solution and the one I pray for. If we don't catch him, we will sail to Greenland, and from there, they will take us somewhere else. They haven't decided where that would be yet."

"Tell Tom to take us somewhere warm. The jungles of South America would be ideal for us. Plenty of game to hunt and places to hide."

Jade had no desire to live in a jungle. If she had her pick, she would choose a location that was not too far from a major metropolis like her old compound near Beijing. She was a traditionalist in many things, but not when it came to technology.

The Kra-ell had been left in the dust by the gods not only because they'd been tricked into servitude but also because of a much earlier decision.

They'd chosen to cling to their way of life and had looked down their noses at the gods for turning away from nature and trusting their future to genetic manipulation and technology.

That decision had doomed them.

Jade was against tampering with nature and making dramatic genetic changes, but she was all for technology and the conveniences and advantages it offered. It was possible to live traditionally and be technologically advanced at the same time.

"Let's hope we catch him and that he didn't destroy the compound just so we can never take it back. Without Igor, the place is perfect. It's easy to defend, has great hunting grounds, but is still driving distance away from two major cities." Jade tried the door, but it was locked from the inside.

Kagra's lips twisted in a grimace. "I don't want to go back there. You and I got used to the closet-sized rooms and considered them a luxury because others had to share communal spaces, but that's not how I want to live. Just look at this place." She waved a hand around. "This ship's cabins are the nicest rooms I've ever stayed in. Even Igor and Valstar didn't have luxurious accommodations like this."

Their quarters in the old compound in China were much nicer than what Igor had provided them with, but Jade had to admit that they had been spartan compared to the luxury of the ship cabins.

"I would like to have that too, and with the money Tom's people retook from Igor, we can make improvements. But it's not as important as getting our freedom back and being able to protect ourselves. I pray to the Mother that we catch him without him recapturing us. I'd rather die than go back to living under his thumb. And as decent as Tom appears, I don't want to live under his or Kian's thumb either."

56

SOFIA

"I stink." Sofia pulled out of Marcel's arms. "I need a shower."

Helping her father with the animals had been fun. It reminded her of many happy childhood days with him while he tended to the herd.

Even as a young girl, the irony hadn't been lost on her. Most of the time, the herd was in its enclosure, eating hay. But from time to time her father and the other shepherds took the herd to graze in the hunting grounds, and they always headed out with at least one Kra-ell pureblood to guard the animals against predators.

The Kra-ell were the strongest, most dangerous of the predators roaming the hunting grounds, but at the same time, they were the best protection for the herd. The other predators feared them. The Kra-ell didn't kill the animals they fed from, but if a predator dared to attack, they would kill to protect the herd.

"You don't stink." Marcel took her hand. "You smell like sheep and goats."

She crinkled her nose. "I love animals, but I don't like the smell. I hope Helmi got towels and bedding for us." She looked up at him. "I don't even know which cabin we are in. Can you call one of your Guardian buddies and ask?"

"They are not monitoring the human decks. But why would you want to share a cabin with Helmi? You should stay with me."

Her mood lifted in an instant. "Can I? I thought that only Guardians were allowed on deck five."

Sofia had hoped she could stay in the same cabin with Marcel, but he'd been in the meeting with the captain, and she'd been helping her father with the animals, and there had been no one to ask.

"I'm not a Guardian, and I'm staying on deck five. Yamanu and Arwel's mates are also staying with them. They took the two cabins next to Mia and Toven's grand suite."

"Did you get to see it?"

He shook his head. "I was told that each deck has two large cabins and the rest are the same size. Each suite has two bedrooms, though. Even the regular-sized ones."

Sofia was willing to bet that the cabins on the upper decks were fancier than the cabins the humans had been given, but that was fine. The ship belonged to the immortals, the Kra-ell needed to be guarded, and the humans were the least important.

"I can't wait to see your cabin, but let's find Helmi first. I need to tell her that I'm staying with you. Did you ask if it was okay for Tomos to share her cabin?"

Marcel shrugged. "Since the Kra-ell were set free, I figured it wasn't necessary. Tomos can go wherever he wants."

"Isn't he guarded?"

"Toven compelled all of them to behave, so it's not really necessary, but I'm sure Yamanu organized the Guardians to patrol the ship."

She tugged on his hand, guiding him toward the elevators. "Helmi will be so happy to hear that Tomos can stay with her. I hope her mother doesn't have a problem with that."

Marcel halted, pulling her to a stop. "Will your father mind that you're staying with me? I don't want to upset him."

Sofia snorted. "What I told you about my unreasonable father was a made-up story, remember? I've been an adult for a long time, and my father knows that I'm not a virgin."

"There is a difference between knowing hypothetically and having it shoved in his face."

"It's okay." She leaned into Marcel and kissed him on the lips. "You are my fiancé, and he knows that we are working on making me immortal."

Marcel arched a brow. "Are we?"

They'd been using condoms to prevent her from entering transition while her family had been in danger, but now that they were on their way to the village, they could start. They even had a clan doctor with a fully equipped clinic on board, so there was no reason to wait—except for Igor sinking the ship.

"We are." She smiled. "My family is safe. We have a doctor and a clinic, so why wait?"

"We are not out of the woods yet. Igor might try to sink the ship, and I don't want you to be in the middle of transitioning in case that happens. I'm just as anxious as you are for us to start the process, but it would be irresponsible to do it now."

57

JADE

"Do I have to go?" Drova stared at the television. "Do you know that they have all the latest movies?"

Her daughter didn't seem troubled by the prospect of her father catching them or the possibility that they would catch him and end his life. She was enamored with the luxurious cabin, the big-screen television, and all the mindless entertainment she could consume.

Perhaps she was numbing her pain.

After hearing from Morgada more about their tribe's history and what had been lost and stolen, Drova might be distracting herself from dark thoughts by watching silly movies.

Jade had asked to put Drova in the same cabin as Morgada for a reason.

She'd already told the girl about their tribe and what Igor had done to their males, but that was just the tip of the iceberg, and Drova probably had a lot of questions. If she heard them from Jade, she would question whether her mother had put a spin on them to make herself look good, but she would believe Morgada.

Not everything the female would tell her about Jade would be positive, but that would make her stories more believable.

"The movie will still be there when you come back." Jade imbued her tone with command. "Let's go."

"Fine." Drova pushed to her feet and stretched her arms over her head. "I'm so tired. Why do I need to see the doctor tonight? I'm not injured."

"That's not why you need to see the doctor. Tom's people found a tracker implanted in Sofia. All of us probably have one, and I want you to be among the first to get it removed."

Drova's hand lifted to her throat. "Why would we have implanted trackers? We had collars. Sofia lived outside the compound and didn't have a collar. That's why she had an implant."

"That's logical." Jade opened the door. "But then we need to ask ourselves how Igor found our tribe and the others. Trackers that were implanted in the original settlers before would explain that."

"But I was born on Earth."

"That's why you are one of the first to go through the scanner. I chose one representative from each group. Original purebloods, purebloods that were born on Earth, hybrids, and humans that didn't get to leave the compound."

Drova nodded. "Makes sense."

"I'm glad you finally agree."

Her daughter was so much like a human teenager. When Jade had been her age, she'd already been a warrior, training to get a spot on the queen's guard. She never would have dared to talk back or question anything her mother had said.

She'd raised her sons the same way, but she'd been more lenient with Drova, and not by choice. Igor hadn't allowed her to train their daughter for a future position as a Kra-ell leader. He hadn't expected Drova to do anything other than breed and produce strong grandchildren for him.

When they got to the clinic, Helmi and Tomos were already there, and given their solemn expressions, Kagra or Merlin had told them about the trackers. They had brought pillowcases stuffed with all of their belongings so Merlin could put them through the scanner as well.

Jade hadn't brought her things, but she planned on doing so after laundering her clothes.

"The doctor stepped out for a moment," Kagra said. "Who do you want to go first?"

"I'll go." Jade gave Helmi a reassuring smile. "It's a simple procedure. You have nothing to fear."

"I know. Sofia told me."

"Then I assume that all the humans know about the trackers."

Helmi nodded.

"Good. It will save us time explaining."

"Hello." Merlin strode into the clinic. "I grabbed a quick bite." He smiled at Helmi. "Your mother and aunt and several others, whose names I've already forgotten, are cooking a feast in the kitchen. The nurse is with them, so I will start with the scanning first. I don't think she'll be in any shape to assist me with the removal tonight. After the midnight meal, she'll need to go to sleep."

"Perhaps scanning everyone first is a better plan," Jade said. "You can make notes where the trackers are and remove them after all the scanning is done."

The doctor shook his head. "I need the precise location. I will probably need to scan all of you again before I cut the trackers out, but at least I'll know where to look, so I won't have to waste time scanning your entire body again."

"It is what it is." Jade let out a breath. "You can start with me."

"Yes, ma'am." He opened the door to the other room where the machine was.

Even without having any medical knowledge, she had no trouble identifying the donut-shaped contraption with the bench sticking out of it. "I assume that I need to lie down on this." She pointed.

Lifting his hand, he stopped her from taking another step. "First, you need to remove anything made of metal and put it on the chair over there. The device has a powerful magnet inside of it."

Nodding, Jade sat on the chair and removed her boots. Then she unstrapped the sword belt and the knives and put them under the chair. Her spiked bracelets were next.

Merlin eyed her arsenal with an amused expression. "Who did you plan to use all that on?"

"My enemies." She padded to the platform on her socked feet. "What if trackers are hidden in my weapons. If they can't go into the device, how are you going to scan them?"

"How precious are they to you?"

"I don't have an emotional attachment to them. If I can get good replacements, I have no problem throwing the old stuff overboard."

"Good." He gave her a once-over. "Are you sure that is all? Some ladies wear bras with underwire. If you have one of those on, I need you to take it off."

"Do I look like someone who wears a bra? What would I need it for?"

Merlin's eyes never strayed from hers. "My beautiful mate is generously blessed. Since turning immortal, she doesn't need bras, but she wears them anyway. It's always better to make sure."

"I don't."

"Very well. Close your eyes, think happy thoughts, and don't move until I tell you."

"Yes, doctor."

As Jade closed her eyes, she was surprised that she didn't need to frantically search for something happy to think about. Memories of the previous night with Phinas eased her tense muscles, made her heart feel lighter, and brought a smile to her lips. The languid feeling wasn't brought about by the memory of the pleasure he'd given her or the pleasure she'd given back, although that had been very satisfying. It was caused by the memories of their conversation, his silly self-deprecating comments, his humor, and the way he'd regarded her.

When Phinas looked at her, he didn't see a fearsome leader or a female to be conquered or impregnated. He saw the person inside.

He saw her, and he liked what he saw.

58

PHINAS

"Don't you want to stay for the desserts?" Dandor asked as Phinas pushed to his feet and picked up his plate.

"I'm stuffed. But save a piece of cake for me."

"Sure thing, boss. Do you want me to bring it to your cabin?"

"No need. I'll come to yours."

Jade had said she would come to his cabin when she was done with her duties, and Phinas hoped that was still the plan. Dandor wouldn't be too upset if he didn't show up.

Dandor grinned. "We can share a glass of whiskey and watch a game. You can choose any game played over the last five years. I took a couple of bottles from the storage room to my cabin. I checked what they have on their servers, and it's the same as in the village."

"I'll take a rain check." Phinas walked to the dirty dishes bin and put his plate and utensils in.

The humans who had prepared the meal seemed happy to do that, but they probably needed help cleaning up after, and he wanted to offer his men's services.

Striding into the kitchen, he found Sofia's aunt and walked over to her.

His Russian was so-so, but he could manage enough to ask if they needed help.

"Hello, *menya zovut* Phinas." He offered her his hand.

"Isla." She shook it, then turned around and waved over at a girl who looked no older than thirteen.

After the older woman spoke to her in rapid Finnish, the girl nodded and turned to him. "My mom asks if you enjoyed dinner."

Apparently, Isla had determined by his accent that his Russian wasn't good enough.

"Very much. I want to thank her and everyone else who pitched in to prepare this excellent meal." He rubbed his stomach. "It has been a long time since I ate so well."

He hadn't lied. Atzil was an okay cook, but he lacked imagination, and they had been eating the same dishes for years. The alternative was to eat in restaurants or learn how to cook himself, but Phinas didn't like doing either. His repertoire was limited to throwing a frozen pizza into the oven, and he barely even managed that. It either came out undercooked or burned.

Usually, he ate lunch at one of the eateries near Kalugal's office building downtown, and dinner was a sandwich from the café.

Isla smiled, and when the girl translated, her smile grew even wider.

"My mom says she's delighted and appreciates that you came to thank her."

He dipped his head. "I also came to offer the help of my men with the cleanup."

When the girl translated, Isla looked shocked by his offer, and her answer in rapid Finnish took an entire minute.

The girl nodded and turned to him. "My mom says that no help is needed. She and the others are grateful for the help you have provided so far and all the help you will provide in the future. She says that cooking, serving, and cleaning after the meal is the least they can do. They will also take care of the laundry and anything else that needs to be done."

Up until now, he hadn't been sure that the humans appreciated being uprooted. On the voyage through Karelia they'd looked scared, not to mention hungry. There hadn't been time to pack provisions, and all they had on the fourteen-hour journey were the field rations that the clan had brought with them.

"I'm grateful for the offer, but we will take care of the laundry ourselves. The meals, though, will be greatly appreciated. None of us are good in the kitchen."

When the girl translated, Isla bobbed her head and smiled.

"What's your name?" Phinas asked her.

"Lana."

"Nice to meet you, Lana." He offered the girl his hand. "I'm Phinas. If you or your mother or any of the others need help with anything, come find me. I'm on deck five in the first cabin at the front of the ship. Or you can tell any of the Guardians that you are looking for me, and they will let me know."

"Thank you." She pulled her hand out of his grasp. "Do you know where we are going?"

He didn't know whether the humans had been told that they were sailing to Greenland. Besides, their final destination hadn't been decided yet, so he couldn't tell her.

"Maybe you are not going anywhere. If we catch Igor, you can go back to the compound, and those who don't want to can ask to be taken somewhere else."

As Lana translated, Isla nodded and then said something back.

"My mom says they haven't decided what they want to do either. They all want to stay together and don't even mind co-existing with the Kra-ell if they'll get paid for their services, but they don't want to make babies for them. They want to be free to choose who they want to have babies with."

Phinas's fangs twitched as he thought about how terrible it must have been for the women who'd been forced to breed with the Kra-ell to produce hybrids for them.

"Tell your mom that I will personally make sure that this kind of exploitation will never be sanctioned again. I can't guarantee that every male will behave, but I can guarantee that anyone who does that will be severely punished."

"Thank you," Lana said quietly.

59

JADE

The results of the scan were interesting, and as Jade made her way to the fifth deck, she wasn't sure whether it was a reason for celebration or not, but she was excited about sharing the discovery with Phinas.

She took the stairs instead of using the elevator to avoid meeting anyone on her way up and to give herself a few moments to think.

Usually, Kagra was the one with whom she shared everything. On some level, Jade felt as if she was betraying her second by preferring to talk with a male who she'd just met and who wasn't even a Kra-ell. But there was something about Phinas that put her at ease, that made her feel less burdened.

She couldn't put her finger on what it was.

Was it his sarcastic, self-deprecating humor? Or was it that he was an outsider who was also a leader of his people and understood the difficulties she faced?

Or maybe she didn't need to put on a mask with him. She didn't have to front being invincible, untouchable, and above it all. He wasn't one of her subordinates she needed to keep at arm's length.

Most likely, it was all of the above.

No guards were posted on the fifth deck, which indicated that the Guardians put a lot of faith in Tom's compulsion and didn't expect any trouble from the Kra-ell they had freed.

Phinas's cabin was at the front of the ship, which was the nicest cabin on each deck and probably identical to hers. It was such a waste for a single person to occupy such a space, but she appreciated the privacy and didn't want to share the cabin with Kagra or Drova. Her second was too talkative, and Drova would have driven her insane with the television being on all the time.

Jade knocked on the door and waited for Phinas to invite her in, and when he didn't answer, she knocked again, this time louder.

He either wasn't in his cabin or had fallen asleep.

It was after one o'clock at night, so the second option was more likely, but in either case it was disappointing.

Turning around, she started down the corridor and was about to go down the stairs when the elevator door opened, and Phinas walked out. He had a bottle of vodka in one hand and a bottle of cranberry juice in the other.

"I've got what you asked for." He didn't smile, and he sounded as if getting the vodka and juice had been a chore.

"If you're tired, we can do this another time."

"I need to talk to you." He passed by her and kept on walking toward his cabin, expecting her to follow.

What the hell was his problem?

Jade followed more out of curiosity than wanting to be with him. She had no patience with moody males or females, no matter which species.

He opened the door, walked to the sitting area, and put the bottles on the coffee table. "Please, take a seat." He pulled two glasses out of his pockets. "I hope you don't mind." He showed her that they were clean. "I can wash them if it bothers you that I carried them in my pockets."

"That doesn't bother me. What bothers me is your unpleasant mood. I came here to relax, so unless you can shake it off, we should postpone this for another time."

Phinas put the glasses next to the bottles. "I need to talk to you." He opened the vodka, poured it into the two glasses, followed with the cranberry juice, and handed her one of them. "Cheers."

Given his mood, they had no reason to be cheerful. "To catching Igor." She clinked her glass with his and took a long swig. "What do you want to talk about?"

"The humans. No more enforced breeding. If you get to lead them again, you'll have to establish new rules of conduct."

That was what was bothering him in the middle of the night?

"Who told you that the breeding was forced on the humans? Igor is evil, and he's a murderer, but rape was not sanctioned in his compound."

He let out a breath. "Maybe it's a cultural difference that you don't understand, but as a female coerced into breeding with the murderer of her people, you should. If a female feels she has no choice and has to accept the male's advance, that's rape. And if the roles are reversed and the male has no choice but to serve the female, it's also considered rape."

60

PHINAS

*T*he irony wasn't lost on Phinas.

As a former member of the Devout Order of Mortdh Brotherhood, followers of the biggest misogynist to have ever walked the Earth, he had no business lecturing a female about what was consensual sex and what was rape.

But perhaps his past gave him a better insight than most.

Holding the glass between her thumb and forefinger, she eyed him from under lowered lashes. "According to your definition, the entire Kra-ell society perpetrates rape. On the home planet, when a female invited a male to her bed, he felt obligated to accept the invitation because refusing was considered a great offense. Would you consider that coercion?"

He wasn't sure.

There had been times he'd succumbed to a female's advances even when he would have preferred another because he hadn't wanted to hurt her feelings. He could've walked away, and the only consequence would have been a guilty conscience. But he hadn't had to do it.

"I guess it depends on the consequences to the male. What would he suffer other than the anger of the female he scorned?"

She snorted. "He would be shunned by all the other females of his tribe and would never get invited to their beds again. His only choice would be to find another tribe to join, but the chances of that would be slim. The only way he could find a new tribe was if that tribe had lost too many males and needed to replenish its ranks."

"Then it's rape. He has no choice but to accept or live the rest of his life as a hermit."

She lifted her glass in a salute and took a long sip. "That's our culture. You can't apply human standards to Kra-ell society. It doesn't work."

"But it could if you weren't so set in your ways. Your society won't fall apart if the males can politely decline and still get invited by other females."

"Perhaps." She crossed her legs. "It worked fine for hundreds of thousands of years. You have to understand that our society has different values. The tribe was the ultimate entity, not the individual. The females were expected to produce offspring whether they enjoyed motherhood or not. They didn't have options either. We all had to do our share, and everyone knew what their duties were."

Phinas shook his head. "I can't argue with you about how the Kra-ell on your planet should lead their lives, but you are on Earth now, you coexist with humans, and they don't appreciate being coerced to breed with purebloods to produce hybrids. That has to stop."

"Why is it so important to you?"

He briefly closed his eyes. "It's not something that I like to talk about. I didn't choose the circumstances of my birth or the society I grew up in, so I shouldn't feel shamed by it, but I am." He let out a breath. "My mother was forced to breed with humans to produce immortal warriors for our leader. Her life was miserable, and yet she did everything she could to give me and my sisters and brothers as much love as she was allowed. It was a very long time ago, many centuries before I joined the clan, but I never forgot what she suffered and what my sisters had to endure. I couldn't help them back then, and my only option to escape that life was to run away. But I'm no longer forced to live in a society that does that to women, and I'm in a position to make a difference for others."

Jade nodded. "I understand. We all want to do better than our parents. What brought it about tonight, though?"

"I spoke to one of the human females in the kitchen." It would be better if he didn't mention Isla by name. Jade might retaliate against her for opening her mouth. "She said that most humans wouldn't mind returning to the compound and serving the Kra-ell if they were paid decent wages, but only if the enforced breeding stopped. They want none of that. I promised her I would ensure it would never be sanctioned again. If a male disobeyed the rules, he would be severely punished."

Jade glared at him. "It wasn't your promise to make."

"Yes, it was. Kian would demand no less, and if you think he will let you continue running things as they were before, you are gravely mistaken. Do you know what the clan's biggest humanitarian effort is?"

"I didn't know that they had any."

"They save victims of trafficking. If you don't know what that is, it's essentially the kidnapping or manipulating of young women to accompany the traffickers and then forcing them into sex slavery. They also take men and boys, but to a much lesser degree. The clan raids the slavers, frees the victims, and rehabilitates them."

"Are you involved in that?"

Phinas deflated. "I'm not, but I would be if the position was open to me and if I wasn't Kalugal's second-in-command."

"Why isn't the position open to you?"

"It's complicated. Kalugal joined the clan, but more as an affiliate than a member. We live in the same place, but we have our own section, and we don't work on the same things. In case of an attack, though, we will join forces to defend our people."

Her foot swinging back and forth, Jade took another sip from her drink. "Who are you expecting to attack you?"

Had he told her too much?

Yamanu hadn't given him instructions on what was okay to tell Jade and what wasn't, but Phinas saw no harm in telling her about the thousands of immortals Navuh commanded. She needed to know that her Igor was small fry compared to the might of the Brotherhood.

61

JADE

"Who are you expecting to attack you?" Jade regarded Phinas from under lowered lashes, pretending that she wasn't anxious to hear his answer.

She hadn't come to his cabin to pump him for information, but if he was volunteering, she wasn't going to say no.

Her intention had been to relax with a drink, tell him about the trackers, and finish the night in his bed. Perhaps even stay until morning if it didn't feel too weird.

Jade had never spent an entire night with a male, had never felt like it was something that she wanted to try out, and she probably wouldn't enjoy it, but it was liberating to be free of the Kra-ell rules of engagement between the genders and try new things.

For better or worse, Phinas wasn't Kra-ell, and he didn't have the same expectations from her.

But things weren't working out the way she'd planned, and out of the blue, Phinas was criticizing the Kra-ell's way of life and demanding changes as if he was entitled to dictate what she should or shouldn't do with her people.

"My former so-called brothers." Phinas lifted the nearly full glass and emptied it down his throat. "Do you want another one?"

"Please." She handed him hers.

"The clan's immortals are not the only descendants of the gods." He poured vodka into the two glasses and followed up with the cranberry juice. "There is another faction that is much less benevolent. It was founded by a rogue god who pissed on the gods' matriarchal traditions, much like Igor pissed on yours.

"Like you and Igor, his descendants believe that humans should serve their betters, and they want dominion over humanity."

Jade didn't appreciate being lumped together in the same category as Igor. "I don't think that humans should serve us, and I didn't think that back when I was in charge either. We needed their services, and I compensated them for that. A hundred-some years ago in China, providing them with lodging, clothing, and food was considered adequate compensation."

He arched a brow. "Including bearing hybrid children for you? Even the Chinese regime wouldn't have sanctioned that."

Obviously, Phinas didn't know much about China, or he wouldn't have said that.

"You'd be surprised what they sanctioned, but that's a subject for a different time. Please continue."

"Navuh, the son of that rogue god, formed the Brotherhood and a breeding program to provide him with as many immortal warriors as possible. He inherited a few female Dormants from his father, and he prevented them from transitioning by pairing them only with human males. That way, they could bear many more dormant children. If he had let them turn immortal, their fertility would have significantly dropped. The breeding program continues to this day. The boys are induced at puberty, turn immortal, and become warriors. The girls are not turned, and they are forced to continue breeding like their mothers. In time, his army grew to over twenty thousand strong. That's where I grew up, and it wasn't a good place. Females were considered good only for serving males and breeding, and human lives were worth very little."

"What happened to the rogue god? Navuh's father?"

"He attacked the assembly of gods with what we believe was a nuclear weapon, killing nearly all of them and perishing alongside them. No one knows the precise details of what happened because there was no one left alive to tell the story. The entire region was destroyed, and every living thing in a radius of about five hundred miles died."

"At least it was contained. When did that happen?"

"About five thousand years ago."

Two thousand years after their ship had left their home planet, which meant that the incidents were not connected. Their journey was supposed to take a couple of centuries, and no one could have foreseen that they would arrive after the gods were no more.

"Tom survived, and he told me that there were others. How many gods are still around?"

Phinas hesitated. "Three that we know of. They were outside the five-hundred-mile radius. Tom will need to compel you to keep this a secret, and I'm pretty sure that I will be reprimanded for telling you too much."

"Who am I going to tell?" She took a sip from her drink. "How did you escape the son of the rogue god?"

"Navuh is a powerful compeller, perhaps on par with Igor, so even though I was uncomfortable following the orders I was given, I didn't have a choice. Then one day, Kalugal approached me and started a conversation. He was a young commander, but he was Navuh's son, so I was cautious, but I soon discovered we saw eye to eye. He asked for me to be transferred to his unit, releasing me from his father's compulsion. He kept it a secret that he was nearly as strong a compeller as his father. He couldn't command as many minds at once, but he was just as strong one on one." He rubbed a hand over his jaw. "Which makes me think that Navuh is not as strong as Igor. Kalugal couldn't remove the compulsion from Sofia. Then again, he tried to do it over the phone, which is probably not as effective as doing it face to face."

This was all fascinating information but pretty useless to her. Navuh and his followers were not going to help her catch Igor, and given the size of their force, it would be best that they never found out about her and her people.

Nevertheless, Jade wanted to learn more about the new potential threat.

"Did Kalugal fear his father?"

Phinas nodded. "Navuh had many sons, or so we believed. Kalugal feared his father would kill him if he discovered that he had competition. During World War Two, Kalugal got us stationed in Japan. When the Americans dropped a nuclear bomb on Nagasaki and Hiroshima, he used the opportunity to run away with his unit. We were presumed dead."

"Good plan. How did he know that the Americans would drop the bombs?"

"He didn't. He just took advantage of the situation."

Kalugal sounded like a smart and resourceful male, and she would love to meet him and have a conversation with him and with Kian. Those hybrid children of the gods were more interesting than their full-blooded predecessors, and from what she'd heard and witnessed so far, the immortals were not as full of themselves as the gods.

62

PHINAS

hy was he telling Jade about his sordid past? He was supposed to woo her, seduce her, not push her away with sob stories.

"Enough about me." Phinas finished what was left in his glass and poured himself another. "Do you want me to top yours up?"

"Please." She handed him the glass. "Alcohol has only a moderate effect on us. For some reason, we get lightheaded and talk too much when we take human painkillers. I wish I could research the reason for that."

Kagra had said that she felt drunk after taking the painkillers, and she'd become more talkative, but he'd assumed that it was the relief from pain.

"You should ask Merlin. He usually does more research than doctoring."

"I will do that. Speaking of Merlin, he scanned me, Drova, Morgada, Helmi, and Tomos, and the results were very interesting."

Phinas was glad of the change of subject. They hadn't reached an agreement regarding the human females, but he could bring that up another time. Then again, he needed to ensure that the Kra-ell males didn't coerce the human females during the voyage. He'd given Isla his word, and he intended to keep it.

"Was there a reason for choosing these particular people for the first round of scans?"

"There was, and Merlin confirmed my suspicions. Only Morgada and I have tiny trackers like the one that your other doctor took out of Sofia. Tomos and Drova had larger trackers that Merlin said were common and

217

easy to get, and Helmi had none. It confirmed my suspicion that Morgada and I were implanted before boarding the ship. The trackers in Drova and Tomos were obtained on Earth, and Helmi didn't get one because she never left the compound. I bet that other than the students, none of the other humans have trackers. Igor didn't deem them important enough. The other good news is that all four were in the same place on the body. Merlin said it would significantly shorten the time it would take him to scan for them because he knows where to look."

Phinas wasn't sure that was smart. "He needs to conduct a thorough scan on everyone in case there is more than one tracker. If I were a paranoid guy like Igor, I would have implanted everyone in the same way and then hidden additional trackers in random individuals to throw my enemies off."

"You're right. It's precisely the kind of thing Igor would do, and it's bad news for us. Merlin might not be able to take all the trackers out before we leave the Baltic Sea."

"Perhaps that's a good thing. As long as Igor is following us, we have a good chance of catching him."

Jade sighed. "I hope you are right. Everything would be so much simpler if we eliminated him."

"Well, not necessarily. We still didn't solve the issue of coercing human females. I gave my word that it would stop. Promise me that you will have a talk with your people about it. The Kra-ell and the humans should sit together, talk it out, and agree on what is acceptable and what is not."

Jade chuckled. "Do you want to lead the discussion?"

"Sure. But I don't speak Russian or Finnish, and many of your people don't speak English."

"I'll translate for you. After all, you gave your word, not me, so you should give the talk."

Tricky female.

"Fine. I will feel like a fish out of water, but I'm not the type of guy who is afraid of a challenge."

"I guessed as much about you." She leaned over and took his hand. "Out of all the females you could've pursued, I'm probably the most challenging." She tilted her head. "Or maybe you enjoy the exotic and the different?"

"There is some of that."

"Or maybe you like tall, skinny brunettes. What's your type?"

He should tell her about Aliya before someone else mentioned his brief courtship of the girl, and Jade reached the wrong conclusion.

"You are very much my type. I like strong females who know what they want and how they want it." He took another sip from his drink. "For a short while, I was fascinated by Aliya—your former tribe member. She's incredibly strong, smart, and resourceful, and she is also honorable and hard-working, but there were two things she lacked, which were maturity and experience. You have those in spades."

Jade narrowed her eyes at him. "Why are you telling me about her? It's not my business who you had sex with, and it's not your business to inquire about my partners."

Did she think that he was telling her about Aliya as a way to ask her about her past lovers?

He'd already learned all he wanted to know from Kagra.

Jade had never gotten attached to any particular male, and she'd treated the males of her tribe as friends with benefits. Friends wasn't the right word either, but co-workers with benefits didn't sound any better.

"I told you about Aliya so you wouldn't hear it from someone else. I never had sex with her. I was interested in her for a while, and then I got to know her better and realized that she was just a kid. Vrog was a much better choice for her, and she reached the same conclusion."

"Did Aliya pick up several males to breed with? Or is she exclusive with Vrog?"

How she'd said it sounded like exclusivity was a bad word.

Phinas really didn't like Jade's attitudes toward sex. They weren't animals, and sex was about pleasure and intimacy, not just about breeding.

"They are exclusive. They love each other."

Jade shook her head. "Hybrids are too much like humans. Love is an illusion. Devotion, friendship, and loyalty are real because they're earned. The concept of unconditional love with a breeding partner is absurd. It's nothing but lust in a pretty wrapping."

63

JADE

*A*s the word lust left Jade's mouth, something shifted between them, the tension sending a bolt of awareness through her.

She wanted Phinas, but after all his talk about rape and coercion, perhaps it was best to let him make the first move.

His nostrils flared, and his brown eyes turned amber. "What are you thinking about?"

"You."

He narrowed his eyes at her. "What about me?"

"You're confusing me with all this talk about love and exclusivity. Do you want me?"

The glow in his eyes intensified. "You know I do."

"So maybe you should stop talking and start doing." She took her glass and leaned back against the sinfully plush couch pillows.

He arched a brow. "What do you want me to do?"

"Use your imagination." She pretended nonchalance, sipping her cranberry vodka and watching him from under lowered lashes.

"I want to get you naked. Do I have your permission?"

Was he still under the influence of his talk about coercion? Would he ask her permission for every move from now on?

Where was the excitement in that?

"Go ahead." She waved a hand.

"Thank you."

"So polite." She sipped on her drink.

"I'm trying." Sliding off the couch, he turned around, sat on the coffee table, grabbed hold of her boot, and pulled it off.

When a dagger clunked to the floor, he arched a brow. "Do you have more of those on you?"

"You'll have to find out. I suggest caution. I keep my daggers sharp." She leisurely lifted the glass to her lips and took another sip.

"I'll keep that in mind." He lifted her other foot, pulled the top of the boot as far as it would go, and peeked inside. "No daggers here." He pulled it off and tossed it aside.

Her socks were next, and as she wiggled her toes, he watched them with fascination, and the glow in his amber eyes intensified. "You have such elegant toes."

She didn't know that toes could be elegant, but it sounded like a compliment. "Thank you."

"You're welcome. I wasn't sure how you would take it. I'm glad that you considered it a compliment."

Was she wrong to assume that it was?

"What else could it have meant? Am I wrong to think that elegance is a good thing?

"It is, but different cultures have different attitudes toward beauty. Perhaps the Kra-ell consider hobbit feet sexy."

As Jade snorted out a laugh, she was glad that she'd already swallowed the sip of vodka she'd taken, or she would've sprayed him with it.

"I don't think that even hobbits find other hobbit feet sexy. What with all those thick, hairy toes."

His lips curling in a smile, he patted the pockets of her cargo pants. "I wasn't sure you'd get the reference." He pulled out a dagger from one of the pockets. "Why are you carrying so many daggers on you?"

"Where would I put them? The pillowcase?"

"Good point." He leaned over her and unbuckled her belt. "What did you do with the sword?" He curled his fingers under the band and pulled without bothering with the zipper.

"I put it under the bed in my cabin." She lifted her bottom to let him tug them down past her hips.

The moment he exposed her panties, his nostrils flared again, and he closed his eyes as he inhaled. "You smell divine."

She chuckled. "Since the Kra-ell were supposedly created with the help of the gods' genes, I'm part god, and I should smell like one."

He opened his eyes and smiled. "That's not what I meant."

"I know." She took another sip from her vodka. "I'm curious about that godly sexual prowess you boasted about."

"Not godly. Immortal, and it's coming up."

"Same difference."

He pressed a kiss to her mound over her panties, took another sniff, and leaned up. "Lift your arms for me."

"I can't. I'm holding my drink."

He snatched it from her hand and put it on the coffee table. "Lift your arms."

A part of her bristled at the command, but another part, the lazy one enjoying their playfulness, purred like a kitten.

She did as he asked, and his breath caught as he pulled her Henley shirt over her head. "I didn't expect such a nice surprise. No bra."

Her nipples pebbled under his intense gaze. "Why would I wear one?"

"To protect these ripe berries from the cold." He cupped both with his warm palms. "Alternatively, you can hire my services. I will walk behind you and warm them for you." He lifted one palm and closed his lips around the hard peak.

Stifling a moan, she threaded her fingers through his hair. "It would be very awkward to walk around like that, but it would speak of your devotion to me."

He let go of her nipple and lifted his eyes to hers. "Do you want my devotion? Or are you only interested in my body?"

"I'm interested in the whole package, and I shouldn't be."

"Why not?"

"Why not indeed?" She leaned and reached for his shirt. "Lift your arms."

64

PHINAS

𝒶 s Phinas lifted his arms, he wondered if Jade had been holding on to the glass for so long to keep herself from taking over.

He couldn't give her the fight for dominance her kind found so exciting or maybe even needed to get going, but he wished he could.

No, that wasn't true.

A little pretend wrestling could be fun, but he wouldn't have enjoyed scratching, biting, and a real fight. He'd never used his superior strength to subdue a woman, and it didn't appeal to him, even if it turned her on.

Perhaps this was a foolish attempt on both their parts, and despite the mutual attraction, they were sexually incompatible.

It would be a shame since his attraction to her went beyond the physical. Surprisingly, he enjoyed her company more than anyone else's, and that was saying a lot.

Kalugal and Rufsur were like brothers to him, but the truth was that he often felt like the third wheel in their bromance. Still, he would give his life for either of them, and he would also die defending the rest of the men and the clan.

His brothers by blood were a different story. He wouldn't lift a finger to save any of them. If his poor mother could hear him, she would turn in her grave, but she didn't know what monsters they had grown up to be.

Fortunately for her, she hadn't seen them after they'd turned thirteen and had been taken away from the Dormants' enclosure.

She would have been horrified.

As Phinas's shirt hit the floor and Jade put her hands on his chest, the past receded to where it should have stayed, a dark corner of his mind that he didn't visit often.

"You have a beautiful body." She ran her hands down his chest, stopping short of his belt and moving to his arms. "I love how bulky you are."

He chuckled. "Muscular is a better term. Bulky usually means fat."

A smile lifted one corner of her mouth. "Is that one more of those cultural differences you were referring to? Perhaps we should stop talking and let our bodies do it for us. They speak a universal language, and they don't care about our different cultures."

Phinas wished that was true.

"Does it bother you that you are stronger than me?" he asked.

Her hands stilled. "I thought it would, but it doesn't. I'm learning a new way to be intimate with a male. Who knows? Maybe I'll like the gentle style better. The Mother knows I've struggled and fought enough. I long for tranquility."

It was a beautiful sentiment but probably unattainable for Jade.

He doubted she was capable of being tranquil. With the rage simmering just below the surface, and the pain and grief still ravaging her soul, she probably could only find tranquility in her final place of rest.

Phinas could understand that better than most.

Despite how easy and peaceful his life was since running away with Kalugal and the rest of their platoon, he was never at ease, never tranquil, and he suspected that was true for all of them.

They had killed, and there was no coming back from that, no matter the circumstances. Every life he'd taken had cost him a piece of his soul.

Plastering a smile on his face, he looked into Jade's expressive eyes. "Naturally, I hope you'll enjoy this more than anything you've experienced before."

"I admire your confidence. If I do enjoy this, though, don't tell anyone. This is an experiment, and I'm not supposed to enjoy it."

Phinas hoped Jade was just teasing, but he suspected she'd spoken the truth and thought of him as a novelty she wanted to try.

If he didn't care for her, it wouldn't have bothered him, but he did, and he wanted her to be interested in him as a person and not an immortal body to take on a test run.

Then again, hadn't that been precisely what he had promised her? To show her how immortals made love?

"Who would I tell?" he echoed her words.

"Who, indeed." She leaned toward him and kissed him with surprising tenderness.

He let her explore his mouth at her leisure for long moments, but when her long tongue wrapped around his fang, his arousal kicked up a notch, and his patience ran out.

With a groan, he leaned away, wrapped his arms around her narrow waist, and lifted her off the couch. "Tonight, I want to make love to you on a comfortable mattress."

As he shifted her weight so one arm was around her waist and the other under her knees, she wound her arm around his neck. "I will always remember that wood bench fondly. It was our first time."

He groaned. "Please erase it from your memory." He carried her to the bedroom and put her down on the bed. "That one doesn't count. Tonight, is our first real time."

"If you say so." She stretched her arms over her head. "Show me that prowess."

Kicking his boots off, he pushed his fatigues down along with the under-shorts and prowled over to her.

"So amiable," he teased as he got on top of her, letting her bear his weight. "So beautiful." He lowered his head slowly and kissed her.

65

JADE

$\mathcal{P}$hinas's body felt good on top of hers, but Jade's instincts screamed for her to flip them around and pin him down.

That was what she would have done with a Kra-ell male, and if he was strong enough, he wouldn't have let her pin him down for long, and she would have been back under him in a split second. The game would have continued until they both got either exhausted by the struggle, madly turned on, or both.

It couldn't work with Phinas, though. If she pinned him down, he wouldn't be able to get free, and that would be the end of the game. He would feel humiliated, and his arousal would deflate. That was what had happened to the Kra-ell males she'd invited to her bed who couldn't overpower her.

Fighting the instinct, she forced herself to remain still and just experience the pleasure of the closeness.

Closeness.

She hadn't felt that with any male she'd been with.

Kra-ell sex was intense and furious—instinct driven. It didn't leave space for feelings or even thoughts.

The realization that this was more than just sex hit her like a bolt of lightning and disturbed her down to her core.

Phinas's alienness allowed her to transcend convention and regard him as more than a contributor of sperm for conception. She liked him and enjoyed his company, which she'd only experienced before with a handful of Kra-ell females.

To be honest, she'd always considered Kra-ell males inferior, and therefore not worthy of her friendship. She'd cared for the males of her tribe and enjoyed playing sex games with them, but they'd never been her friends.

Phinas was a descendant of the gods and a leader of his men, which made him her equal.

Letting go of her mouth, he lifted his head and looked into her eyes. "Are you with me? You don't seem like you are into this."

"I am more than I should be." She lowered her arms and folded them over his muscular back. "I like you, Phinas. I consider you a friend."

He frowned. "A friend with benefits, I hope."

Jade shook her head. "You don't know what this means to me. It's normal for me to seek the benefits part with a male. It's not normal for me to befriend one. I can only do that because I consider you my equal."

Frowning, he looked at her for a long moment before nodding. "I think I get it. This is one of those cultural differences we will need to work on." He dipped his head and kissed her softly. "Not right now, though. Stop thinking and just let yourself feel."

As he slid down her body and took her nipple in his mouth, sucking on it gently, Jade threaded her fingers in his short hair and closed her eyes.

He spent a few more moments giving equal attention to her other stiff peak. Then he slid further down her body until he was facing her center.

She'd heard about the strange human mating custom of orally pleasuring each other, but since it wasn't conducive to conception, it wasn't something she or the males she'd been with ever tried.

Lodging his broad shoulders between her spread thighs, he lifted her legs. He positioned them over his shoulders, further exposing her to his heated gaze.

She lifted on her forearms, fascinated by what he was about to do.

It was a strange sensation to be gazed upon down there, but it wasn't unpleasant. It sent a zing of pleasure through her that was all about anticipation.

"Ever since I smelled the sweet scent of your desire, I wanted to taste you."

She chuckled. "I doubt there is anything sweet about me."

"Even a prickly pear is sweet on the inside." He lowered his head, and his breath on her sensitive flesh felt like a prelude to pleasure.

She was about to be kissed there for the first time, and her core thrummed with excitement.

He didn't kiss her, though. Instead, he turned his head and dragged his lips along her inner thigh, his fangs scraping the soft skin and adding a touch of danger to his ministrations.

As more moisture gathered in response to his teasing, Phinas inhaled deeply and closed his eyes. "Paradise. That's what you smell like."

He flicked his tongue over her lower lips, and when he flattened it and dragged it upward to where she was the most sensitive, her hips arched off the bed, and as he closed his lips over that nubbin of pleasure, she cried out.

He sucked softly at first and then harder, and when it became too much, he let go and thrust that talented tongue of his inside of her.

Her fingers threaded into his hair, but despite the haze of pleasure, she still had enough presence of mind to let go before she tore out fistfuls of his hair, repaying him with pain for the pleasure he was giving her.

Unable to hold still, Jade arched up, taking more of his tongue inside of her, and as he growled his approval, the vibrations threatened to send her over the edge.

Phinas alternated between thrusting his tongue into her, flicking it over that nubbin, and lapping at her juices while making sounds that belonged to a beast.

When his fangs scraped over her soft flesh, the implied threat snapped the coil inside of her, and she climaxed with a shout.

6 6

PHINAS

*I*t was a thing of beauty to watch Jade fall apart, and Phinas had a feeling that she'd never been pleasured like that before.

He loved being the first to introduce her to the pleasures of the tongue, and he hoped there would be many more opportunities for a repeat performance.

Sucking and licking until her tremors subsided, Phinas wrung every last drop of pleasure out of her, and when the last of them rocked through her, he kissed her petals one more time, put her limp legs down, and came over her.

"Hello, gorgeous." He kissed her, his tongue finding her wicked one and wrapping around it.

She kissed him back, her hands roving over his back gently, almost lovingly.

Where was the ferocious Kra-ell leader who he'd feared would scratch him, bite him? Not that he would mind a bite or two as long as she didn't suck him dry.

In fact, he was looking forward to experiencing it. He wanted her to drink from him.

Would his immortal blood taste good to her?

Would it provide her with more vitality than the blood of animals?

How much would she take?

Would he be able to stop her if she took too much?

As trepidation ignited his arousal, Phinas wondered what was wrong with him. That shouldn't be a turn-on. Besides, he trusted Jade despite barely knowing her.

Above all, she was honorable and would never break his trust if she could help it.

She kissed him back, and as he dragged his shaft through her wetness, the scent of her arousal intensified, and as he eased into her, he found her surprisingly tight for a female who had given birth three times.

He regarded her with concern, searching her face for discomfort, but all he saw in her expression was bliss.

In no time, her sheath stretched to accommodate his girth, and as he seated himself fully inside of her, he had the absurd notion that he had finally found his home.

Resting his forehead against hers, he began to move, rocking into her gently at first, then a little faster when she curled her arms around his neck and lifted her lips to his for a kiss.

Did the Kra-ell enjoy kissing? Or was that a first for her as well?

She seemed to know what she was doing, so maybe it wasn't, but then it didn't require much practice or even imagination to know how to kiss.

As she lifted her hips to meet him halfway, he banded his arms around her slim frame and alternated between shallow, short thrusts and longer, deeper ones. Jade kept the rhythm with him, adjusting to his tempo in perfect harmony.

She was right.

Their bodies knew all the steps to this intimate dance, and their cultural differences didn't matter.

They moved together, faster and faster, their sweat-slicked bodies locked in a tight embrace as if neither of them ever wanted to let go, and as the tension inside of him tightened, he licked her neck and struck with his fangs.

Jade cried out, but not in pain, and as her tight sheath spasmed around his shaft, he erupted inside of her and kept coming for what seemed like forever.

When he stopped shuddering, he retracted his fangs, licked the puncture wounds closed, and lifted his head to look at her.

Her eyes were closed, and her lips were curved up in a relaxed smile he'd never seen on her beautiful face before. The hardness was gone, and she looked almost soft.

"Jade?" he whispered.

She didn't answer, and when he gently pulled out of her, she still didn't move or open her eyes.

She hadn't blacked out the other time, but maybe she had now. He'd pumped her with more venom than he'd ever dared to release into a female, even the few immortals whose beds he'd been invited to.

Worry tightening his chest, he stilled and listened to her heart. Finding the beat strong and steady, he released a relieved breath.

He wouldn't have wanted to harm any female with an excess of venom, but especially Jade.

Over the few days he'd known her, she'd become dear to him.

He cared about her.

After cleaning himself in the bathroom, he brought a couple of wash-cloths and cleaned her as best he could. With that done, he climbed in bed, pulled the blanket over them, and wrapped his arms around her.

"Goodnight, sweetheart." He kissed her forehead and chuckled softly.

If Jade were awake, he wouldn't have dared call her that. The prickly leader didn't want anyone to know that she was sweet on the inside, and she would have taken that as an offense.

YAMANU

*A*lthough the day was cold—check that, the day was freezing— Yamanu leaned against the railing outside the bridge with a big smile plastered on his face.

There should be a law against having so much fun and getting paid for it.

His reunion with Mey had been spectacular. Well, since they were technically still reuniting, it still was.

The ship was much nicer than he'd imagined, and the cabin he and Mey were staying in was fancier than any hotel suite he'd ever stayed in, and he'd been to some nice ones.

The midnight feast the humans had put together for them last night had been the icing on the cake. It had been a long time since he had eaten that well.

Mey and he prepared their meals at home, but neither of them was any good at it. Not that he would ever say that to Mey. She fancied herself a good cook.

Callie's restaurant was amazing, but the waiting line was insane, and it wasn't the same as home-cooked.

As a helicopter passed by a mile or so off the starboard side, Yamanu's happy grin turned into a frown. As instructed, they were keeping close to shore, but no one had considered an air attack. Igor wouldn't send fighter jets to attack them. That would draw too much attention, but he could send a helicopter with a few commandos and a rocket launcher.

Stepping into the bridge, he tapped Olsson's shoulder. "Captain, can I have a word, please?"

Nodding, the captain followed him back outside and closed the hatch behind him.

"Is there a problem?"

"There might be," Yamanu said. "Our working assumption is that the *Aurora* will be followed by an armed vessel, possibly a Russian cruiser, and that we would not be in danger until we are too far from land for the rescuers responding to our distress signal to get to us before the aggressor is done plucking the passengers he is after out of the water."

A short nod from Olsson was an acknowledgment and a signal for him to continue.

"I am not trying to second-guess Kian and Turner, but this close to shore, it wouldn't take much for anyone to put together a band of mercenaries, and either land them on the ship's helipad or have them rappel down on board and attempt to take over the ship. In fact, they could have another helicopter providing cover for them, shooting at the defenders." Yamanu paused and looked questioningly at the captain.

Olsson considered his answer for a spell. "You are correct. As per the instructions we were given, the *Aurora* is only about ten miles offshore. A helicopter taking off from a nearby location could reach us within fifteen to twenty minutes, leaving enough fuel to execute an operation like that and fly back." The captain gestured in the direction of the coast and then pointed ahead to where the ship was heading. "But as they would be uninvited guests, we can make things very difficult for them." The captain's tone and posture hinted at a harnessed excitement at the prospect of such an altercation.

The guy must miss his military days.

"How would you make it difficult for them?" Yamanu asked.

"For a helicopter to land on the helipad, they need us to keep our heading and speed constant, which we obviously won't do. They also need to use their ILS, i.e. Instrument Landing System. If your guy activates the scrambler, they won't be able to use it, and most of their avionics will also be rendered useless. To your concern about a helicopter landing on the ship, I believe we can rule that out."

Yamanu could practically hear the but coming up.

"Having said that, unless the signal scrambler's footprint is larger than I think, it won't be enough to prevent a couple of helicopters from approaching us to weapons' range and launching a shoulder-fired missile directly at the bridge, something that will effectively disable the *Aurora*."

This was not a scenario that Yamanu had considered, and he was certain that neither had Kian or Turner.

"I need to contact my boss and let him know."

Olsson lifted a hand to stop him. "Before you do, I need you to know that our radar will be able to pick up any approaching boat, ship, or aircraft. If they don't identify themselves well in advance, we will know that we are dealing with foes. That should give us a few minutes to take defensive action, which may be all we need."

It was good to know that the bridge would have a forewarning, but if a missile could be launched at the bridge, that wouldn't do them much good.

"If they fire missiles at the ship, what would be their maximum range?"

"For a shoulder-launched missile, it is no more than one kilometer."

"That doesn't sound like much. Are you sure?"

"I'm unaware of any weapons that can be used from a helicopter and have an effective range exceeding that." The captain tilted his head. "Can your scrambler cover a radius of one kilometer around the ship?"

Yamanu nodded. "That is still within its range, so if we identify a threat, we can activate it and render the aircraft's avionics and targeting equipment useless."

"Precisely." The captain offered him a nod.

Yamanu ran his hand over his clean-shaven jaw. "I want to play it safe. I will post armed guards here and on the decks below around the clock, and I will have the device with a trained man on the bridge around the clock so it can be readily activated on a moment's notice."

If the circumstances surrounding this trip were not so extraordinary and unusual, Captain Olsson would have never allowed anyone to presume to do anything aboard his ship without his approval. Given the tightening of the man's lips, Yamanu realized that he should have phrased it as a request and not a statement.

There was no reason to antagonize the man.

"If that meets with your approval, captain."

The tightness eased, and Olsson nodded. "Very well. Make it so."

"Thank you, captain." Yamanu offered Olsson his hand. "It's a pleasure working with you."

"The pleasure is all mine."

68

KIAN

"Good thinking. Keep me updated." Onegus ended the call and turned to Kian and Turner. "I'm surprised that none of us had considered an aerial attack."

"I did," Turner said. "But I dismissed it given how congested the Baltic Sea is and how narrow. The response from shore would be immediate."

Kian opened his water bottle and took a sip. "What will happen if he takes out the bridge?"

Despite Turner's assertion that he'd thought about the possibility of an attack from above, Kian was pretty sure he hadn't. Yamanu's observation and the captain's response had caught them all off guard.

None of them, including Turner, had considered the possibility of Igor trying to take over the ship by blowing up the bridge.

"When the ship signals distress, military jets from the country closest to it will respond within minutes. He's not going to risk that."

"I disagree," Onegus said. "He doesn't care if they blow up the helicopter and its crew. The military jets will destroy the threat and turn around. Until the rescue ships arrive, he can board the ship from another vessel and take over."

Turner smiled victoriously. "Which means that he would have to follow the ship with a naval vessel, which is what we have been discussing all along. It doesn't make sense for him to deploy a helicopter and a ship. He will want to attract as little attention as possible, and he will not attack while the *Aurora* is in the Baltic and staying close to shore."

"I agree." Kian pulled out his phone. "I wonder if Roni has picked up on any vessel following them."

The guy had spent all day hacking into a naval tracking system and working on some program that he claimed would help them to identify a pursuer among the hundreds of vessels crowding the Baltic Sea.

"We are in the war room," he said when Roni answered. "Are you ready to show us what you've been working on?"

"I'll be there in a couple of minutes. I stopped at the café to grab a cup of coffee and a sandwich. Anyone want anything?"

Kian lifted his gaze in an unspoken question to Turner and Onegus, who shook their heads. "We are all good. Thanks. See you here."

"Do you know what he's been working on?" Onegus asked.

"He said he'll explain when he gets here. He said he's designing a program to do the tracking for us."

Several minutes passed until Roni walked in with a cup of coffee in one hand, a paper bag in the other, and a laptop tucked under his arm.

"Good evening, gentlemen." He sat at the conference table, opened his laptop, and turned it toward them so they could see it. "Take a look at the screen. There are literally hundreds of vessels sharing the same shipping lanes in the Baltic right now. Many are heading into or out of existing ports. While most travel up and down the length of the Baltic, a considerable number are crisscrossing it from shore to shore. We are dealing with ferries, ships from several navies in all sizes, fishing boats, yachts, and of course, commercial traffic of goods and commodities."

As Roni paused to take a sip of his coffee, Kian observed the dots in an array of colors filling the entire screen and wondered how they could identify their pursuer in such dense traffic.

"I hacked into NATO's naval surveillance system," Roni said as he unwrapped his sandwich. "So the screen is also showing the whereabouts and movements of naval ships. The civilian systems tracking sea traffic don't show that." Taking a bite of his sandwich, Roni touched the screen and highlighted one of the dots. "This is the *Aurora*. As you can see, there is a huge number of ships that could potentially be our pursuer. When the *Aurora* starts her zigzagging pattern, the number of potentials will naturally decrease, and at some point, only a single vessel will be left that's clearly following her odd course. That will be our pursuer."

Leaning back, Kian looked at the screen. "You can't watch the screen around the clock. You need to assign people to keep watch in shifts and alert us as soon as the pursuer is identified. As soon as we have confirmation, we will need to alert Captain Olsson and our people on the ship as well."

Roni smiled smugly. "Way ahead of you, boss. I wrote an algorithm that monitors the data and continuously eliminates from view any ship that is clearly not a suspect based on its course, heading, and speed over time. It is set up to notify me when only ten possible targets are left and from then on, whenever one more is eliminated. Given the vast number of ships, I don't think we'll have identification by morning, meaning their evening. I estimate that we will need at least another full day before the algorithm narrows the field of possible pursuers down to only ten and then between five to ten hours to narrow it to a single vessel. This will greatly depend on Olsson's heading and course changes at the time."

Smiling, Turner shook his head. "Good work, Roni. I should have thought of that, but given that I don't know much about programming, I probably couldn't have."

Basking in the compliment, Roni squared his shoulders. "Thank you. But with me around, you don't need to know anything about programming."

Onegus cast Turner a glance full of mock horror. "Look what you've done. He was full of himself before. Now he'll get too big for his emperor chair."

When Turner arched a brow, Kian explained, "He's referring to Roni's enormous chair in the lab."

Despite how closely Turner had often worked with them, he'd never visited the lab.

Kian clapped Roni on the back. "I want to know when the count is down to ten, and from that point on, unless it's in the middle of the night, bring the laptop with you and join us here."

"You've got it, boss."

69

JADE

*J*ade woke up in Phinas's arms, calmer and more relaxed than she'd ever felt. Not even as a little girl in her mother's tribe had she felt so safe and cared for.

It was an illusion, a remnant from the euphoric trip Phinas had sent her on, but she wasn't ready to strap herself to the tether of reality yet.

She'd actually managed to sever the tether for once and soar carefree and happy over the clouds. Were the alien landscapes she'd passed over real? Was it another dimension that was only accessible through a venom trip?

The aliens had been friendly, waving and smiling as she passed them by. Did they know who she was?

Maybe what she'd seen were the fields of the brave, and the males waving at her had been her sons? The aliens didn't look like them, but then who said that the soul retained the same shape on the other side?

Perhaps the venom had opened a portal in her brain that allowed her a glimpse of what lay beyond the veil.

As the thought ushered another wave of tranquility and contentment, Jade snuggled closer into Phinas's solid chest and circled her arms around his substantial bulk.

"Muscularity," she murmured. "Not bulkiness."

He opened his eyes and smiled at her. "What are you mumbling under your breath?"

"Nothing important." She kissed his jaw and closed her eyes. "I'm not ready to get up. I feel too good to face the day."

She'd never spent the night with a male, but Phinas's venom had knocked her out, so she could use that as an excuse for enjoying the warmth and connection for a little longer.

Evidently, the venom of an immortal male was much more potent than that of the Kra-ell, and she was still light-headed and a little drunk from it. But what was really priceless was the incredible sense of well-being.

Phinas's venom was a miracle drug.

Jade wished hers had a similar effect on him, but so far, she had refrained from biting Phinas. Like goddesses, immortal females didn't have fangs and venom, so he wasn't used to that and might find it emasculating. It was probably difficult enough for him to deal with her superior strength.

He smoothed his finger over her forehead. "Why are you frowning? You looked so blissed out only moments ago."

"It's nothing." She turned around and presented him with her ass. "Let's go back to sleep."

As his erection prodded her bottom, he groaned, and she smiled.

"Do you think I can sleep like this?" He rubbed himself against her. "You have the most spectacular ass." His hand cupped her breast. "Am I bothering you?"

"Not at all." She covered his hand with hers. "I've never spent the night with a male. They knew they had to leave as soon as we were done."

A breath left him in a whoosh. "This is my cabin, but if you are uncomfortable, I can leave. There is another bedroom."

"I don't want you to leave." She pushed her bottom into his hard length. "I like this. But if anyone asks, it's the venom's fault."

He chuckled. "Who is going to ask?"

"Kagra."

"Tell her to mind her own business."

"That's exactly what I'll do." Jade turned around and cupped Phinas's stubble-covered cheeks. "Kiss me again."

He smiled. "Do you like it when I kiss you?"

"If I didn't like it, I wouldn't have asked for it, now would I?"

"No, ma'am, you wouldn't."

TURBULENT WATERS

1

JADE

*D*awn had broken over the sky hours ago, but Jade was still in bed, reluctant to leave the warmth of Phinas's arms.

It wasn't like her to linger between the sheets when the sun was up, and it wasn't like her to spend a night with a male either, but it had been surprisingly pleasant.

Despite lacking even a shadow of aggression or dominance, their bed play had been unexpectedly satisfying. It had been a very different experience for her, and she suspected it had been just as different for Phinas.

To make it work, both had throttled down their dominant tendencies, but not for the same reasons.

Jade had stifled her aggressive urges to avoid challenging Phinas, who wouldn't have been able to respond with enough physical strength and would have felt humiliated. On his part, Phinas had probably been gentler with her than he would have been with his immortal or human partners to avoid spurring her aggression, which was ironic given that he didn't need to worry about hurting her.

Nevertheless, their joining had been incredible.

Phinas's potent venom had no doubt contributed to the languid sense of satisfaction and well-being she was experiencing, but it would have been just as good even without the venom-induced euphoric trip and string of climaxes.

Unexpectedly, Jade had found emotional respite in Phinas's arms.

Within his embrace, the pain of loss felt less acute, the need for revenge burned less fiercely, and the weight of duty was lighter.

Still, as wonderful as those stolen moments were, it was time to get up and face the world. She needed to check whether Merlin had already extracted some of the trackers from her people, and they had to figure out a way to speed up the removal operation.

The sooner they got rid of those trackers, the sooner they would leave Igor blind in the water.

"I need to get going." She pushed out of Phinas's arms.

"Don't go." He pulled her back. "Stay a little longer."

She let him hold her, enjoying the feel of his large hands as they roved over her back, caressing gently, leisurely.

"I wish I could." She kissed his lips. "But we both have duties to attend to. Besides, I'm hungry, and you are as well. I can hear your stomach rumbling."

He licked his lips. "By now, Isla and her helpers have probably prepared breakfast, and if it's even half as good as dinner was last night, it's going to be a treat." He squeezed her bottom before releasing her.

Jade frowned as it occurred to her that Phinas shouldn't have even known who Isla was, let alone that she was in charge of the kitchen. Isla must have been the one who had approached him to complain about the way humans had been treated in Igor's compound, specifically the breeding with Kra-ell males, and that was what had made him confront her about it last night and sparked their argument.

The thing was, Igor hadn't been terrible to the humans, and he hadn't mistreated them any worse than Jade had done when she'd been in charge of her own compound, so any accusations Isla had voiced were directed at her as well.

Why had she approached Phinas, though?

If Isla wanted help from the liberators, Tom or Yamanu were the more obvious choices.

Perhaps Phinas seemed more approachable?

Jade had to concede that he had a certain charm about him, while Tom seemed standoffish, which was second nature to any god, even one as decent as he was. Yamanu was easygoing and friendly, but his physical size was intimidating.

She needed to have a talk with the woman and see what her problem was. The human hadn't produced any hybrid children, and as far as Jade knew, Isla hadn't accommodated any Kra-ell males either. She wasn't the type they usually preferred. But before she accused the female, she needed to ensure it had been her.

"I didn't know that you were on a first-name basis with my humans. When did you get acquainted with Isla?"

Realizing his mistake, Phinas's eyes widened briefly, but even though it didn't last more than a split second, Jade caught it.

"I met her in the kitchen when I went to thank the cooks for the fabulous meal and to offer my men's help to clean up after dinner."

"That was nice of you. Did Isla accept the offer?"

"Nope. She said that the humans were happy to prepare our meals and clean up after them in gratitude for us freeing them from Igor and protecting them on the voyage."

Jade had her confirmation. It had been Isla who had complained.

"Let's get going. I'll accompany you to the dining hall, but since I don't eat the same food you do, I will not stay."

"Right." He rubbed a hand over his stubble. "When was the last time you fed?" He grimaced. "Don't tell me you haven't had any blood since draining Valstar?"

At the reminder, bile rose in Jade's throat.

She'd never taken such a copious quantity of blood before, but she hadn't had a choice. It had been the only way for her to keep Igor's second-in-command incapacitated while Tom and his Guardians had stormed the compound. Bashing Valstar over the head with a chair might have also done the trick, but not for long. He wouldn't have stayed down, and Jade couldn't risk him activating the explosives that Igor had put under the compound.

When Pavel had arrived with the chains to bind Valstar, she'd left the kid to guard the prisoner and went on a killing spree, eliminating four of her people's murderers. Regrettably, her number one target was still at large, and she wouldn't rest until she'd eliminated him as well.

"I haven't fed since then," she admitted. "I was nauseous for a long time after that, and when I finally felt thirsty again, we were on the move, and I didn't have time."

Phinas cocked his head. "So you don't feel hungry? Only thirsty?"

"It's a combination of both. I can drink water and some other liquids, and that satisfies most of the thirst, but only blood can eliminate it altogether."

A smile lifting one corner of his lips, he tapped his neck. "How about you feed from me? Once you've quenched your thirst, you can join me for coffee while I eat."

As her eyes followed his fingers to the carotid artery he was tapping, her tongue darted over her lips, and she swallowed.

The Kra-ell didn't feed from their partners to satisfy the thirst, but it was a most enjoyable part of the sexual experience that she hadn't dared broach with Phinas yet.

Their relationship was bridging species and cultures, and she was hesitant about introducing blood-sucking into their play. It could easily turn him off, and she couldn't afford to lose him.

She needed Phinas for more than just the pleasures of the flesh or companionship. He was a valuable source of information about the clan and its internal politics.

"We don't use our bed partners as a food source."

"Why not? I'm bigger than the goats and sheep you have in the cargo bay, and I certainly smell better. If they are fine after you get your fill, I will be fine as well."

He might be, but he also might get lightheaded, and that wasn't an option when Igor could strike at the ship at any moment.

It had been fifty-three hours since the clan had taken over the compound, and despite their best efforts to avoid detection, Jade had no doubt that Igor's counterattack was imminent.

He wouldn't let the clan abscond with his people without utilizing every possible weapon in his arsenal, to which there was no limit. He could probably get his hands on a nuclear warhead if he wanted one.

"I'm not going to feed from you." She slid out of bed.

Phinas narrowed his eyes at her. "You said goats and sheep were passable, so your refusal can't be because you prefer their taste to mine."

"I don't prefer it, and I know that your blood will taste exquisite. But the Kra-ell only take a little from their partners to enhance pleasure during intimate moments. We don't feed from them." She padded to the bathroom.

"You didn't take from me even once." He followed her inside. "And you had at least three opportunities."

"I didn't think you'd enjoy it."

"I'm sure I will." His big nude body filling the doorway, Phinas leaned against the doorjamb and gripped his straining erection. "I'm looking forward to it."

His very obvious physical reaction indicated that he was turned on by the prospect of her bite.

Jade smiled. "Tonight, then." She pushed on his chest to clear the doorway and closed the door in his face.

"Is that a promise?" he asked from the other side.

"It is."

2

PHINAS

*T*he promise of Jade's bite put a smile on Phinas's face and pumped even more blood into his erection, but instead of being invited to join her in the shower, he got the door slammed in his face.

It was very disappointing.

The female was comfortable with her nudity, so a desire for privacy couldn't be the reason for her behavior. Perhaps the physical manifestation of his excitement was or Jade was just in a rush to get to her duties. Whatever her reason, it was evident that she didn't want to go another round with him.

Reluctantly, Phinas walked to the cabin's other bedroom and got into the shower.

He shouldn't be surprised. With Jade, everything was about duty and responsibility, and her personal enjoyment was not a priority.

Phinas could respect that, and the truth was that he wasn't all that different. Duty came first for him as well, but since he was supposed to befriend the Kra-ell leader, he was actually doing his job.

Not that it was a hardship, and not that he would have stayed away from Jade if he hadn't been directed to get close to her. She was the hottest female he'd ever been with, and he enjoyed her company more than anyone else's.

It was so strange and unexpected that Phinas was starting to think that the Fates had something to do with it. Except, he didn't believe in the Fates.

He was a loner by nature, and he'd never been particularly close to anyone, but for some inexplicable reason he felt at home with Jade, who wasn't even from the same species and whose culture and belief system were alien to him.

Perhaps it was the luxurious cruise ship?

It created an illusion of a vacation and contributed to a romantic atmosphere.

Or was it the looming danger?

Those intimate moments with Jade were even more precious, given that they didn't know what Igor's next move would be, nor when the attack would come.

Jade was under even more pressure. She'd assumed leadership of the compound's population and was tasked with reorganizing its social structure in a way that would satisfy the three different groups.

Phinas didn't envy her the task. He was okay with leading men into battle, but that was the extent of his leadership skills. Unless it concerned security, he didn't want to tell people how to live their lives and what they were allowed or forbidden to do. That was Kalugal's job, and he was very flexible with his guidelines.

His men were supposed to adhere to common standards of decency, and since joining the clan they were also supposed to follow clan law, but no one policed them to enforce the rules.

Done with the shower, Phinas wrapped a towel around his hips and walked into the cabin's living room.

The sight that greeted him had his erection inflate in an instant.

Jade looked good enough to eat in a pair of his undershorts, a pair of his socks, and nothing else. Bent over, with her magnificent ass in his face, she was picking up clothes off the floor.

Regrettably, he'd already surmised that she wasn't interested in another round of bed play before heading out.

Straightening up, she gave him a sly smile. "I hope you don't mind." She patted her bottom. "I took the liberty of borrowing a pair of your briefs and a pair of socks."

She'd taken them from his duffle bag, but he had no problem with that, except that she hadn't asked in advance. He had no secret items in there, only a stack of clean clothes and a bag of those that needed to be laundered.

"They look better on you than they do on me." He walked into the bedroom and pulled out another pair of shorts for himself.

Using his immortal speed, Phinas put on a pair of jeans and a long-sleeved Henley before returning to the living room. "Do you want to stop by your cabin for a change of clothes?"

Jade waved a hand at his shirt. "If you have another one I can borrow, I can skip stopping by my cabin and go straight down to the cargo bay."

She must be starving if she was so anxious to get there. Or perhaps she wished to avoid explaining to her second-in-command where she'd spent the night.

"It's going to be huge on you." He turned around and pulled a shirt out of his duffle bag.

Shrugging, she took it from him. "We are the same height."

"We are, but I weigh three times as much as you."

Jade cast him an amused smile. "I'm slim, but I'm not light."

He'd noticed that when he'd lifted her last night and carried her to the bedroom. Given her build, he'd expected her weight to be slight and was surprised to find that it was substantial.

Although, given how strong she was, it made sense that she was solidly built.

Evidently, the Kra-ell's body mass was denser than that of humans and immortals.

"Nevertheless, I'm broader."

She pulled the shirt over her head, shimmied into her cargo pants, and tucked it inside them.

"That you are." Her eyes roved over his body.

Jade rolled up the sleeves that were too long, not because her arms were shorter but because her shoulders were narrower. When she was done lacing her boots, Phinas opened the cabin door.

"I'll come with you to the cargo bay, and after you are done feeding, you can join me for coffee in the dining room."

She shook her head. "You have better things to do than watch me eat, but I'll join you for coffee later."

For some reason, Jade didn't want him to see her feed, taking the vein of an animal and sucking its blood.

Did she think it would be a turn-off for him?

Perhaps she'd heard the stupid rumor about his and Aliya's falling out after he'd accompanied the girl on a hunt?

Phinas had told Jade about his short involvement with the young hybrid and had explained why it hadn't worked out between them, but he hadn't mentioned the rumor that had started right after Aliya had chosen Vrog over him. People had assumed he'd gotten turned off after seeing her hunt, but that wasn't the reason.

Should he ask Jade about it or just let it go?

It might be better to wait.

They were still finding their way with each other, and it was going surprisingly well given that they weren't even from the same species. But it was better to be patient and let things evolve between them naturally without pushing for more.

He wrapped his arm around her tiny middle. "What are your plans for the rest of the day?"

She looked at his arm and then lifted her eyes to his. "I have my duties, and you have yours." She looked at his arm again. "I'd rather we didn't display such familiarity in public."

He dropped his arm. "Is it one more of those cultural differences? Or are you embarrassed about being seen with me?"

"It's cultural." Jade started toward the elevators. "The Kra-ell don't hold hands or embrace in public. We don't even shake hands." She pressed the button for the elevator. "Before I was captured, I traveled extensively and spent much time among humans, so I learned to tolerate handshakes, but I'm uncomfortable with casual touching."

Tolerate.

The word was like a knife to Phinas's gut.

Jade had been forced to tolerate so much that he wondered how she'd managed not to fall apart.

Her sons and the other males of her tribe had been slaughtered in front of her eyes, and then she'd been forced to accommodate their murderer sexually and bear him a daughter.

If Toven hadn't promised Jade Igor's kill, Phinas would have taken care of it.

Even though he would be no match for Igor in a hand-to-hand fight, the rage inside him over the evil perpetrated against this amazing female would have given Phinas the strength needed to overcome the much more powerful opponent and tear the guy's throat out with his bare fangs.

As the elevator doors opened, he forced the dark thoughts to a corner of his mind and followed Jade inside. "The truth is that I don't have much to do." It was a waiting game until Igor made his next move, and in the meantime, Phinas and his men were enjoying the clan's luxurious cruise ship. "Dandor wanted to fill the pool with water, but since it's freezing cold and we need to conserve fuel, heating it is out of the question."

Leaning against the wall, Jade cast him an amused smile. "That's a shame. You wanted to teach me how to swim."

"Have you seriously never tried it?"

She shrugged. "I guess it's another cultural difference. The Kra-ell are not great swimmers." She gave him a savage smile. "Back home, there are things in the water that are dangerous even to us."

It occurred to him that amphibian predators were not the only reason for the Kra-ell's reluctance to swim. With how compact their bodies were, they probably couldn't float well.

Then again, even tigers and elephants could swim, so the Kra-ell should be able to manage, and given the current situation, their inability to swim could prove deadly.

"We are on a ship, and we expect an attack. What happens if you find yourself overboard? Will you just sink to the bottom?"

"I can keep myself afloat by treading water."

Phinas frowned. "That's not a good tactic in freezing temperatures." Given their strength, the Kra-ell might be able to keep it up for much longer than humans or even immortals, but eventually the cold would sap their energy. "Can you float on your back?"

"I don't know. I've never tried."

"We have to fill that pool and start training you and your people to flip to your backs to conserve energy. After that, you all need to learn to swim."

She nodded. "You are right. Our humans need to learn that as well. I just hope we have enough time before the attack for everyone to become proficient."

3

JADE

*T*he cruise ship's dining hall was bigger than Jade had expected, but it wasn't full. No purebloods were seated around the tables, which wasn't surprising given that they didn't eat human food, but she'd expected to see at least one or two.

Many of them enjoyed a cup of coffee or tea from time to time and a drink of vodka in the evenings. Besides, mealtime was an excellent opportunity to get to know their liberators and start conversations.

Jade wondered why no one had thought to do that, but she was glad they hadn't.

It wouldn't take her people long to realize that Tom and his guardians were not human.

Several of the hybrids were present, though, and in addition to their nods of greeting, they cast curious looks her way.

"Over here!" One of Phinas's men waved him over.

Given the tight press of his lips, Phinas wasn't enthusiastic about the invitation. Leaning over, he said quietly, "I'd rather be alone with you than join Dandor and Chad."

She would have preferred that as well, but they had appearances to keep up. "Since I'm not eating, you might enjoy their company more. Besides, if the two of us sit separately, rumors will start."

"They will start anyway." He put his hand on the small of her back. "The clan is like a hive, and gossip is everyone's favorite pastime."

Her lips curled in distaste. "I experienced the same in the compound. This deplorable trait seems to transcend cultures and species."

He chuckled. "It would appear so."

"Good morning." Dandor got to his feet and pulled out a chair for her.

The human custom of males rising to their feet when a female joined the table was one of the few Jade would have liked to appropriate for her people, but the seat he offered her was strategically disadvantageous.

"Good morning to you too." She remained standing. "I'd rather not sit with my back to the room. Would you mind switching places with me?"

Dandor had the wall at his back, which was a preferable defensive position.

"No problem." He offered her his seat. "How was your first night aboard the *Aurora*?"

"It was fine." Phinas pretended the question had been directed at him as he pulled out a chair for himself. "I didn't notice the rocking, which was surprising given how choppy the Baltic is this time of year."

Jade stifled a smile.

He hadn't felt the ship rocking because they'd been busy rocking the bed, and after they were done, they'd fallen into such a deep sleep that the boat could have been attacked, and they would have slept through it.

She couldn't speak for him, but she'd slept better than ever. Was it because she'd felt safe in Phinas's arms?

Since he couldn't protect her against a Kra-ell, that didn't make much sense, and yet something about him soothed the storm raging inside of her. Maybe it was his easy charm that had given her such a wonderfully relaxed night, or perhaps it was the fact that he wasn't a Kra-ell and he didn't have any expectations of her. She didn't need to play the role of a leader, she didn't need to play dominance games with him, and she could just be herself.

Did she even know who that self was, though?

Jade had thought she knew, but after her world had come crashing down, a lot of the things she'd considered important had lost meaning, and the only motivation to keep waking up in the morning had been the need for revenge.

"Would you like some coffee?" Phinas asked.

"I would love some."

"I'll get it." Dandor rose to his feet.

As he passed by Yamanu's table, she remembered that the Head

Guardian wanted her to meet his mate and her sister, but Jade hoped he'd forgotten about that.

It wasn't that she minded meeting them and getting the introductions out of the way, but she didn't want to spend more time with them than she had to. Her people needed her, and she didn't have the time or the patience for social calls.

The little free time Jade had, she preferred to spend with Phinas.

Noticing her looking their way, one of the women lifted her hand and waved, her sister flashing Jade a smile that revealed a pair of gleaming canines that could pass for fangs.

She was still focused on that anomaly when Yamanu turned around and waved hello.

"Good morning." He rose to his feet and walked over to their table. "It makes me happy to see the two of you becoming so friendly with one another." He clapped Phinas on the back. "I'm a sucker for romance."

Chad shook his head.

Jade didn't know how to respond to Yamanu's insinuation.

Romance was a human term that was foreign to her. What she and Phinas had were sex and companionship. It wasn't romance, and it wasn't love.

"How can I help you, Yamanu?" Phinas ignored the Guardian's comment.

Yamanu flashed him a toothy smile. "Actually, I came over to invite Jade to our cabin this evening, but since you two seem to have become an item, you are both invited."

Jade lifted her hand. "I can come over to your table right now and be done with the introductions."

The Guardian's expression soured. "Are you declining my invitation again?"

Damn. Had she offended him?

"I'm just trying to be efficient. If all you want is to introduce us, we can save time by doing it right here, right now."

"That's not why I want you to meet my mate and her sister. They will explain when you come over this evening."

Phinas draped his arm over the back of her chair. "We would be delighted to attend a get-together in your cabin. Should I bring a couple of bottles of whiskey?"

The grin returned to Yamanu's face. "I've got the refreshments covered. Just make sure to show up at seven o'clock and have Jade with you."

"We will be there."

4

TOVEN

"*W*ill you be okay by yourself in the cabin?" Toven leaned down and kissed Mia's forehead.

"I'm not going to our cabin. I made plans with Mey and Jin to tour the ship. I'm going to Jin's cabin, and we are going to have coffee and chat and then go on a tour from there."

"When did you make those plans?"

"While you were talking with Yamanu. Is he going with you to see Valstar?"

Toven shook his head. "I'm going alone. Valstar promised me information, and I want to question him at my leisure with no interruptions."

"Have fun." Mia gave him a pat on his rear. "When you are done, call me."

"I will." He kissed her again before returning to the elevator.

When he exited on the Kra-ell level, the two Guardians posted in the hallway were like a double beacon, indicating which cabin Valstar was in.

"Good morning, gentlemen. How is the prisoner behaving so far?"

"He's not giving us any trouble," the Guardian on the left said.

Toven made a mental note to learn the names of all the warriors on board. His memory wasn't the best, and although he memorized faces with ease, he had difficulty remembering names. Perhaps it was the artist in him. He'd always found peace while sketching. It was effortless and calming, while writing stories required focus and effort.

"Is anyone watching him on the inside?" he asked.

The Guardian on the right shook his head. "He has chains on his legs and he's under your compulsion. He's been watching television and has barely moved from the couch."

It could be a convincing act, and Toven wasn't taking any chances. He had a dart gun tucked in the waistband of his pants, which felt odd.

Toven had never needed weapons to protect himself. His mind control ability and superior speed and strength had been enough. For the first time ever, he was facing an opponent who was faster and stronger and who might be resistant to his mind control.

No wonder the gods had sought to enslave the Kra-ell. It was disconcerting to be at a physical disadvantage and to have little or no ability to control their minds either. The only real advantage the gods had over the Kra-ell was their technological superiority and their genetic manipulation ability.

"Please, open the door for me." Toven pulled out his dart gun.

The Guardian eyed the weapon. "It worries me that you don't put much faith in your ability to control him with compulsion."

"It should worry you. Valstar could be pretending to be under my control and just waiting for the right moment to strike."

"Where would he go?" the other Guardian asked as he opened the door. "Overboard?"

Nevertheless, his more cautious friend took a step back and pointed his machine gun at the door.

"You have a visitor," the Guardian announced.

Valstar was seated on the couch, a foot-long chain attached on each end to one of his ankles, but his hands were free, and his back was straight. He didn't look like someone who had given up hope, and he didn't look like he was about to attack either.

The television was on, and a movie was playing, but the sound was turned down low.

"Good morning." Toven walked into the cabin and tucked his gun back into his waistband.

Valstar nodded but didn't repeat the greeting.

It wasn't the Kra-ell way.

"Do you want us inside with you?" the cautious Guardian asked.

"I don't, but thank you for the offer."

The guy nodded and closed the door.

When Toven sat down on the armchair facing the couch, Valstar lifted the remote and clicked the television off. "Did you come to collect?"

"Collect on what?"

"I promised you information. I assume that you are here to collect on my promise."

"I want to ask you some questions."

"Go ahead."

"Did you know Igor before you were assigned to the same pod?" Toven used strong compulsion in his voice to ensure Valstar answered immediately and didn't try to devise a way to circumvent the question.

"I didn't," Valstar said. "None of us knew each other, and we didn't get acquainted before being placed in the pod either, which I found odd."

"Why was it odd?"

As Valstar shifted on the couch, the chain attached to his legs dragged on the hardwood floor. "A lottery was held among young Kra-ell that fit a certain profile, and it was mandatory. Those who had gotten picked were summoned to a processing center, and none of us knew anyone else. That was fine, but since we were supposed to settle on Earth and form a tribe, I expected at least an introduction. There was none. We weren't even given each other's names. To this day, I don't know Igor's Kra-ell name."

"How is that possible? Igor couldn't have chosen the name before waking up and discovering that he'd arrived thousands of years later than he'd been supposed to."

Valstar nodded. "At first, he called himself Ingvar, which I assumed was his Kra-ell name at the time. It wasn't one I'd ever heard before, but it sounded like many other Kra-ell names, so I had no reason to question it. Only later, when he changed it to Igor, I learned that Ingvar was a Scandinavian name from which Igor had been derived."

"Ingvar means gods' warrior in old Norse, so it could have come from an even older name used by the Germanic tribes, but how could Igor have learned of it? Were you briefed about Earth's inhabitants?"

Valstar shook his head. "We knew it was habitable because the gods told us it was. They visited it before us, and the king sent the rebels here, the ones who'd sided with the Kra-ell." Valstar tilted his head and offered Toven a crooked smile. "Are you one of the original exiles, or were you born on Earth?"

5

ELEANOR

*E*leanor nudged Emmett's shoulder. "Wake up. You need to get out of bed."

Groaning, he pulled the blanket over his head and turned on his side.

"It's four in the afternoon. If you keep napping, you won't be able to sleep at night. "

Emmett's excuse for sleeping all day was that he was depressed. He didn't like being back in the village, and despite reassurances that it was probably temporary until they caught Igor, he was acting as if his world had fallen apart and Safe Haven was lost to him forever.

He was such a drama king, and Eleanor was tired of being his cheer lady. She had never been the cheerleader type, and assuming the role for Emmett's sake was exhausting.

Maybe it was the wrong approach, and she should yell at him to snap out of it?

Yeah, that jived much better with her character.

"If you are not out of this bed in one minute, I'm going to leave you and go visit my family by myself."

He lowered the blanket and lifted his head to look at her. "I can't be alone right now."

"Then get up and come with me. Parker is looking forward to seeing you."

"He is?"

259

Her nephew hadn't said anything, but she knew that he liked Emmett, so maybe he could take over the cheerleading role for an hour or so. Besides, Emmett needed an audience to get into his performer persona, which was sure to improve his mood, and even a small family gathering would do. It would help him get out of his head.

"Of course, he is. Vivian told me that he and Ella can't wait to see us."

"We are invited for six." Emmett pulled the blanket back up. "I have two hours until then."

"You need to shower and get dressed." She waved a hand in his direction. "Your beard could use a trim and so could your hair. I can do that for you if you want." Eleanor tried to keep a straight face.

After the one time she'd trimmed his beard and hair for him, Emmett would never let her do it again, and it might convince him to get out of the house and drive to the city for a proper haircut.

"No, thank you. I'd rather do it myself."

That hadn't been her intention. "We can go to the city tomorrow." She patted her hair. "I want to try a Brazilian blowout. I'm tired of how messy my hair gets with even a hint of humidity in the air."

"I love your hair." Emmett flipped the blanket off and swung his legs over the side of the bed. "I don't want you to straighten it."

"Well, tough, because I do." Leaving the door open, Eleanor walked out of the bedroom.

Cecilia lifted her ears and stretched on the windowsill, giving her a questioning look.

"If I feed you again, you'll get fat, and Ana won't let you stay over."

Offended, the cat stretched once again, shifted her pose, and offered Eleanor a view of her butt as she tucked herself into a ball.

Ana had agreed to share her while in the village, and although cats were territorial, Cecilia had no problem calling both houses her own. They had to keep track of who was feeding her and when, because that cat was a glutton and would eat until she blew up.

When Eleanor's phone buzzed in her pocket, she pulled it out and sat on the couch. "What's up, Leon? Do you want me to bring Cecilia over?"

"I'm not calling about the cat. I thought you would want to know that we finally caught the hybrids."

"Hallelujah. I thought that they gave us the slip and were on their way to Igor."

"Yeah, we all did, and I'm glad that I decided to leave two Guardians to watch the Airbnb despite that."

The rental car with the tracker they had planted had been parked in front of the house, but the hybrids hadn't been there since Monday.

"Where were they?"

"I don't know. The Guardians tranquilized them as soon as they got back, loaded them in the car, and are driving them all the way to our downtown warehouse to scan them for implanted trackers. Julian will meet them there so he can remove them if they find any. After that, they will be brought to the dungeon in the keep and questioned. Do you want to attend?"

Leon had gotten to know her well during their time together in Safe Haven, and he knew that she would love that.

"Of course, and I'll bring Emmett along to help interrogate them. What's their ETA?"

"Sometime during the night. We will question them tomorrow morning."

"Good. Vivian invited Emmett and me to dinner, and I would hate to disappoint her. Julian and Ella are invited as well, but if the hybrids are only arriving late at night, Julian doesn't need to leave for the warehouse anytime soon."

6

TOVEN

he cat was out of the bag, or perhaps it had never been inside of it, and Valstar had known from the start that Toven was a god, the same way Jade had known from the first moment she'd seen him.

"What gave me away?"

Valstar smiled. "Did you really think you can pass for a human?"

"Why not? I look human."

"You look like the statues humans erected in honor of their gods. Too perfect, the way all gods are. But even if you managed to make yourself look less exquisite, your incredible compulsion ability would give you away."

"Igor's ability equals or surpasses mine. Is he a god?"

Valstar closed his eyes. "I often wondered if he was a hybrid, part Kra-ell, and part god, but if I had even dared to hint at it, he would have ended me. First of all, it's anathema to the Kra-ell to breed with gods, and vice versa. Secondly, Igor despises the gods, which isn't surprising given how they had used and mistreated the Kra-ell for hundreds of thousands of years, but it is surprising for Igor, who doesn't feel much about anything. They must have done something particularly terrible to him."

"Like produce him and then turn their backs on him. That would make anyone resentful, and especially someone like Igor who is power-hungry."

Valstar shrugged. "Another possibility is that the gods played around with his genes. There were rumors about them conducting secret experiments on Kra-ell. Maybe they gave him his compulsion powers and took away his ability to feel. Maybe they tried to produce the perfect soldier."

It wasn't too big of a leap. Humans had been trying to produce perfect soldiers for decades, and not only via training. The drug experiments were well known, the genetic ones less so.

But who did the gods fight that they needed to create a perfect killing machine?

"What would they have done with such a perfect soldier, though? Wouldn't he pose a threat to his creators?"

Valstar pursed his lips. "Maybe that's why he was sent to Earth. He was a defective specimen who didn't obey his masters."

Toven looked into Valstar's dark eyes. "Perhaps Igor was sent to Earth to kill the gods. You said that the rebels were sent here as punishment. Maybe his job was to eliminate them. Communications with the gods' planet had gone down thousands of years earlier, so no one would have found out about it, and the reputation of the gods' king as a benevolent father and ruler would not have been tarnished."

"The thought crossed my mind," Valstar said. "But I dismissed it. After discovering how much time had elapsed, we made a half-hearted effort to find the gods, but when it became clear that they were relegated to the realm of myths and legends, Igor turned his focus on building a life for us on Earth."

That would have been the logical thing to do, and Igor was ruled by logic, not emotions, so Valstar was probably right.

"When did he start looking for the other survivors?" Toven asked.

"Not right away. The ship was gone, and without it, we couldn't communicate with the other pods. We had to wait until humanity formed global communication networks and finding information became easier."

Toven didn't believe for a second that Igor found the other Kra-ell by looking for clues in the news. The settlers must have been implanted with trackers before ever leaving home, and Igor had waited for human technology to catch up.

"You mean advances in tracking technology. He knew that they were all implanted with trackers, and he also knew how to search for the signal."

"I don't remember being implanted with a tracker, but who knows what the gods did to us. Your guards told me that you are checking everyone from the compound for trackers. What did you find so far?"

Somehow, Valstar was managing to lie to him, which meant that he could resist the compulsion. Either that or he was very skilled at working around it.

He'd been there when the males of other tribes had been slaughtered and their trackers removed to be later implanted in others.

He must be feigning ignorance.

Except, there was no proof Igor had dug out trackers from the bodies of the males he'd killed. The theory was based on the assumption that the settlers had been implanted before boarding the ship to Earth, and the only way Igor could obtain more was by removing them from the dead.

It was a solid assumption, though. Igor had found a way to find some of the Kra-ell, and the only thing that made sense was that he could follow a signal they were emitting.

"All the Kra-ell we checked so far had trackers in them. We gave priority to the purebloods and hybrids, so I don't know what the situation is with the humans. But you must know who has them and who doesn't. You've been with Igor every step of the way."

"Igor didn't share everything with me. I knew that he implanted the Kra-ell who were sent out on missions and the young humans who were sent to study in the university, but the devices were bought from human suppliers, and there was nothing special about them. I didn't know that everyone had them."

"Who did the implanting?"

"We had a human doctor do that."

"Under compulsion, I assume."

Valstar nodded. "Of course. We brought him to the compound blindfolded and then returned him to St. Petersburg after Igor tampered with his memories."

That might be the answer to the inconsistencies. If Igor could thrall in addition to compel, he could erase memories and plant new ones and Valstar might be telling the truth as he knew it.

"Did he compel the doctor to forget what he did? Or did he thrall him?"

Valstar frowned. "Aren't they one and the same?"

The Kra-ell mind manipulation power was a hybrid form of thralling and compulsion, but it was only effective on animals and humans. None of them was as powerful as Igor, who could compel Kra-ell and immortals alike, but not thrall them, or so Toven had believed up until now.

"Let me rephrase. Did Igor command the doctor to forget what he did, or did he reach into his mind and replace his memories of the compound and its occupants with something more mundane?"

Valstar regarded him with a puzzled expression. "Are you suggesting that he hypnotized the doctor to remember a false memory?"

"In so many words, yes."

"I didn't know that Igor could do that. I think that he just commanded the doctor to forget. It worked well enough on humans."

"What about the Kra-ell? Did it work on them as well?"

Toven knew that it had. Igor had commanded the females not to think about the slaughter of the males of their tribes, which was the same as telling them to forget about it. Jade and Kagra were stronger than most, so they had fought off the command.

"It worked on some," Valstar said. "It didn't work on me, in case you were wondering. I wish it had, so I could claim innocence, but regrettably I remember what I did and regret it even though I had no choice."

"There is always a choice." Toven rose to his feet. "You could have plunged that sword into your own heart instead of obeying Igor's command. That would have earned you a place in the hills of the brave or whatever you call it."

"The fields of the brave." Valstar hung his head. "But you are wrong. By taking my own life, I would have condemned myself to forever walk in the valley of the shamed."

"Even if you did it to save others?"

"My action wouldn't have saved them. The others would have obeyed, and those males would have died despite my sacrifice. Besides, I no longer believe in that nonsense. I stopped believing in the Mother a long time ago."

7

KIAN

$\mathcal{K}$ ian folded his newspaper and put it on the kitchen counter. For once, the news didn't hold his interest despite the turmoil that had erupted worldwide. The economy was bad everywhere and getting worse, war was raging in some places and social unrest in others, and he couldn't help but wonder if Navuh had anything to do with the global mess.

When things didn't make sense and the world was spiraling into turmoil, Navuh was Kian's usual suspect. Not that the Brotherhood was the only evil force lighting a fire under the pot and stirring things up, but Kian didn't know who else it could be.

Once the Kra-ell crisis was over, he could clear some bandwidth to dedicate to the issue.

According to Lokan, Navuh was focused on raising an intelligent army and shoring up his finances, but perhaps Lokan wasn't as well informed as he thought.

Navuh was a master of compartmentalization, and he didn't share his plans with all of his sons—either his one remaining son by blood or those he'd adopted. The one possible exception was Losham, whose strategic brilliance made him Navuh's right-hand man.

Perhaps Lokan should get in touch with his adopted brother and try to pump him for information. Navuh didn't credit Losham with the successful strategies he'd come up with, taking the credit for himself, and most members of the Brotherhood believed that Navuh was the mastermind behind everything.

Losham was no doubt bitter about it and wanted someone to know that he deserved credit for his successes. He might want to boast to his half-brother and let a few things slip.

As the thumping and grinding noises of Syssi's cappuccino machine pulled Kian out of his reveries, he felt his shoulders lose their tension and a smile curve up his lips. The sounds were soothing, representing home and good times with his family.

"I don't know how Allegra can sleep through this racket." Syssi walked over to the counter with a cup in each hand. "I hoped she would wake up from the noise."

It was after six in the morning, and Syssi needed to get ready for her workday in the lab, but they both knew that waking Allegra up before she was ready would make the rest of the day miserable.

Their daughter loved sleeping, which most of the time was a blessing, but some mornings it was a problem.

Kian took a sip from the perfect cappuccino his wife had made for him and sighed with pleasure. "You've become a master barista and ruined any other coffee place for me."

Syssi grinned. "Practice makes perfect, and there is no better place than home."

"I couldn't agree more." He leaned over and kissed her cheek. "I'm blessed."

"We are both blessed," Syssi corrected him and then chuckled. "Although I have a feeling that our lives won't be as idyllic when Allegra gets older. You should have seen your daughter with Karen's twins yesterday. They are already fighting over her, and she's basking in the attention. I can just imagine those three sixteen years from now."

Kian frowned. "I really don't want to think about my daughter with boys, and there will be at least four vying for her attention. Ethan and Darius will give Ryan and Evan a run for their money, and if Darius is anything like his father, he's going to win."

"What you mean is that you hope Darius will win." Syssi hid her smile behind her cappuccino cup.

"Why would you think that?"

"Because he's the best candidate. Darius's daddy is a three-quarters god, brilliant, charming, and good-looking. If Darius grows up to be like Kalugal, Allegra would be lucky to snag him."

Kian's good mood took a nosedive. "He'll also be conniving and manipulative. In addition, there is the issue of insanity that runs in Kalugal's bloodline. If Toven and Mia produce a son, he would be a much better match for Allegra."

Toven and Mortdh had different mothers, and the insanity gene had come from Mortdh's mother. Toven's descendants should be perfectly fine.

That being said, Toven's daughter had serious issues, and Kian wasn't at all sure that all of them had been the result of the catastrophic accident she'd been involved in.

Geraldine was lovely and sweet, and she made Shai happy, but she was a little loony.

Syssi shook her head. "I don't know why you are always so suspicious of Kalugal. I know that you like him and enjoy his company, and you trusted him enough to invite him and his men to live in the village. So far, he's been cooperative, and he even volunteered his men to help with the Kra-ell rescue. I don't understand your problem with him."

"I'm sure Kalugal didn't do that out of the goodness of his heart. He has his own agenda."

"Like what?" Syssi lifted the cup to her lips.

"I don't know. Maybe he wants them to become his allies."

"Since Kalugal is part of the clan, his allies are also ours."

"I'm not sure about that. He and his men are a small group, and he might want to increase the number of people under his control."

Syssi put her cup down. "If you were in his position, wouldn't you do the same thing?"

"Probably," he admitted. "I would shore up the number of my supporters and then push for democratic elections. He could potentially replace me as the leader of the clan."

Syssi laughed. "That's never going to happen, and you know that. We are not a democracy, and this is still Annani's clan. Something about Kalugal just rubs you the wrong way. What is it?"

"The list is long." Kian crossed his arms over his chest. "He seems to know everything that's going on, even things that I made an effort to keep a secret. I don't know how he finds out about them. Kalugal, on the other hand, keeps his business shrouded in mystery. But unlike him, I respect his privacy and don't try to find out what it is."

Syssi arched a brow. "He told you what he's been working on. He developed that Instatock app that has teenagers worldwide enthralled." She lifted her cup and took a sip.

"He only told me about it because Jacki insisted that he needed checks and balances, and I applaud her for it. That much power in the hands of Mortdh's grandson is dangerous. Despite his so-called confession, I'm still wary of what Kalugal plans to do with the app. He's not an honest man."

"In what way? Other than being secretive, that is."

"He used insider information to make his fortune."

"Kalugal had no choice. He escaped Navuh with nothing, and he needed to provide for his men."

Kian shook his head. "I could have forgiven him for doing that if he had used his compulsion ability minimally when he just got here, but he continued the practice long after he was no longer struggling to survive."

For a long moment, Syssi didn't say a thing, but Kian knew she was taking her time to formulate a counterargument.

Putting her cup down, she swiveled her stool, so she was facing him, and put her hand on his knee. "You have a tendency to see things in black and white, my love. Kalugal is a light shade of gray. He has done some unsavory things, but given where and how he grew up, he turned out better than anyone could have expected. Also, he's still a young immortal, and he's still finding his way. You should cut him some slack."

Kian opened his mouth to argue, but then Syssi's words sank in, and he realized that she was right. He couldn't compare the way he grew up with the way Kalugal had grown up in Navuh's camp. While Kian had been taught lessons on morality and decency by his mother and rewarded for practicing them in his life, Kalugal had been taught the exact opposite and rewarded for that.

It was a miracle that his cousin had turned out as good as he had, and given how Kalugal could have used his compulsion power, the transgressions he'd committed were minor.

Lifting Syssi's hand, Kian brought it to his lips and kissed her palm. "You are infinitely wise, my love. In less than a minute, you have managed to change my entire perspective on Kalugal."

"Then I should have spoken up earlier." She smiled. "I just hoped you would realize that on your own."

He chuckled. "I'm too stubborn and dense for that."

As Syssi picked up her cup and took another sip, he knew she had more to say.

"Since you see things in a different light now, you might be open to what I'm going to suggest next. You need to invite him to your war room and make him part of the decision-making. After all, he volunteered his men, and he should be included. The same goes for Phinas. When Yamanu and Toven confer with you and your war room team, Phinas should participate."

"Kalugal is not interested in military operations. Since leaving the Brotherhood, he's been solely interested in business. He didn't mention even once that he would like to be included in the decisions regarding this mission. If he had, I would have invited him."

Syssi arched a brow. "Really?"

"Not willingly or happily, but I would have felt obligated. He volunteered his men, his jet, and even offered to help financially. In fact, I expected him to use that as an in, but he never did."

"Maybe he's waiting to be invited."

Kalugal wasn't shy, and when he wanted something, he had no problem asking for it, but Syssi had a point. The decent thing to do would be to offer. If Kalugal didn't want to join, he could decline the invitation.

Hopefully, it would be precisely what Kalugal would do.

Despite his epiphany, Kian still wasn't comfortable with Kalugal being privy to everything that was going on in the war room. Too much information was freely exchanged, and Kalugal might learn more than Kian was comfortable with him knowing.

8

KALUGAL

"I'll be there in half an hour." Kalugal ended the call just as Jacki walked into his home office with Darius draped over her shoulder.

"Who was it?" She bounced lightly on her feet while patting their son's tiny back.

It took forever to feed Darius and just as long to get him to burp, and when he did, it was almost always accompanied by a geyser of clumpy, stinky spit-up. He was the sweetest and most beautiful boy, but he wasn't an easy child to raise.

"Kian." Kalugal smoothed his thumb and forefinger over his short beard. "He wants me to stop by his office before I leave for the city."

"Is there a problem?" Jacki stopped bouncing their son. "Did something happen to our guys?"

"Nothing happened. Kian said that he wanted to discuss plans for the future, and he sounded a lot nicer than usual, which made me suspicious. He must want something."

Usually, he and his cousin engaged in a semi-taunting banter that kept them both on their toes and was quite enjoyable, but this time Kian had been polite, cordial and, most alarmingly, his tone of voice had been warm.

The only times Kalugal had heard Kian use that tone was when talking to his wife or daughter.

"If Kian wanted something, he would have asked for it." Jacki resumed her rocking and bouncing. "Subtlety is not one of his best traits." She chuckled softly. "He's as subtle as a brick."

"True. But he hates asking for favors. Maybe he needs money to finance the Kra-ell exodus."

"You said that Roni managed to snag the evil dude's money, and that there was a lot of it. Kian can finance the operation using that."

"That's true as well." Kalugal pushed to his feet and reached for his son. "I'll burp him."

Jacki shook her head. "You are already dressed for work, and you know what happens when he burps. It's usually accompanied by a geyser."

"I'll put the cloth over my shoulder, and if he shoots over it, I'll change clothes. I want to hold him for a little while before I have to go."

He couldn't leave the house before getting his fix. Otherwise, he wouldn't last the six hours or so that he forced himself to spend in the office each day of the week.

Jacki's eyes softened. "Alright." She handed him their little bundle of joy along with the burping cloth.

Holding his child against his chest and inhaling the sweet baby smell was like a drug Kalugal was getting more and more addicted to each day, and as euphoria washed over him and his eyes nearly rolled back in his head, he couldn't care less about the stinky burps or the cottage-cheese-like projectile.

The love he felt for this tiny being was mind-boggling in its intensity.

Kalugal couldn't comprehend how his own father had been cold and indifferent to him and his brother.

His mother claimed that Navuh cared about him and Lokan, and that he'd been cold to them because he couldn't risk showing them more attention than the other sons he'd claimed as his own but who weren't his by blood.

Kalugal didn't believe her.

Navuh had never shown him even a smidgen of affection, and no one was that good of an actor. His mother wasn't lying to him, but she was lying to herself. Areana saw Navuh through the prism of their mate-bond, with love blinding her to her mate's true nature.

Then again, maybe Navuh was different with her, showing her a side of himself that he didn't show anyone else.

Some men were like that, caring only for their mates and not for their offspring, but Kalugal couldn't understand that either. Wasn't procreation the primary purpose of mating? And weren't fathers supposed to be fiercely protective of their children to ensure their survival?

But as with most everything else in creation, nothing was ever perfect or functioned entirely as intended. People, whether human or immortal, were faulty creatures, with some more broken than others.

As the burp came, it was accompanied by the usual spit-up and Darius's pitiful whimper.

"Poor baby." Jacki massaged his little back. "He's suffering."

Darius was six and a half weeks old, and he hadn't slept for more than two consecutive hours yet. Thankfully, his wife and he were immortals who didn't need much sleep, or they would have been exhausted.

Shamash had turned out to be a pretty good babysitter, but neither Kalugal nor Jacki were comfortable letting him take care of the baby for more than a couple of hours.

"How much longer is this reflux thing going to last?" he asked, more out of frustration than hoping for a different answer than the one Bridget had given them.

According to the doctor, most babies got over reflux at four months, but some suffered from it much longer. The good news was that they all eventually outgrew it.

"I hope it will get better soon." Jacki walked around him and checked his back. "You're good. He didn't get you this time."

"I'm not ready to give him back yet." Kalugal rocked Darius until he fell asleep and only then handed him to Jacki.

"Did you hear from Phinas this morning?" She cradled their baby in her arms, holding him close to her chest.

"Not yet. He said he would call if anything interesting happened, so I guess nothing did."

"No news, good news, right?"

"Perhaps it's the calm before the storm." Kalugal leaned to kiss Jacki on her lips. "I won't be gone for long. If my meeting with Kian drags on for more than an hour, I'll skip the office today and come back home."

Jacki smiled. "I'm so glad that we are rich and can afford for you to stay home as much as you please. I feel sorry for all those parents who can't do that and have to leave their babies in daycare."

"I'm glad that I can afford to do it too, but it's not like all rich parents want to stay home with their babies. Amanda is not exactly destitute, but she leaves her daughter with the babysitter while she's at work."

"That's different. Her babysitter is right there with her at her lab at the university. She gets to see Evie whenever she wants." A smile spread over Jacki's beautiful face. "Maybe we can do that too. We could hire a babysitter to come to your downtown office or take Shamash with us, and we could both work from there. Bridget said that we need to get Darius among humans so he can develop immunity to viruses."

"Not yet. He's too miserable as it is to get a cold or some other human disease on top of that. I'll consider it once he's over the reflux."

She arched a brow. "You will?"

His wife knew him too well. "Probably not. I like knowing that he's safe in the village."

9

KIAN

"Hello, cousin." Kian waved a hand, motioning for Kalugal to come in. "Can I offer you something to drink? The options are bottled water or whiskey, but it's too early for alcohol."

He should have gotten coffee and pastries. The idea was to make Kalugal feel welcome, and Kian was doing his best to look and sound pleasant, but that was probably not enough.

"That's a shame." Kalugal cast him a tight smile as he pulled out a chair next to the conference table. "It has been a while since we enjoyed cigars and whiskey together."

"Indeed. If it weren't so early in the morning, I would invite you for a drink and a cigar on the roof."

"I've heard of your rooftop retreat, and I was hoping to get invited, but I thought I never would."

As always, Syssi was right, and Kalugal had been waiting for more than one invitation from Kian.

"If you don't mind the early hour, we can go up there right now." Kian walked over to his desk to get his whiskey bottle and box of cigars.

"What about the rest of your team? Aren't they supposed to be here with you?"

His cousin was definitely feeling left out.

"Turner and Onegus are in the war room."

"How come you're not with them?"

"Nothing urgent is happening at the moment, and I figured it was a good time to talk with you."

Kalugal cocked a brow. "About what?"

"It occurred to me that you might be interested in joining us in the war room. After all, your men are more than half the force on the ship, and the decisions we make here affect them."

"I appreciate the invitation, but I don't know how much time I can devote to the operation. I don't like leaving the house for too long." He smiled. "First, it was the mate bond, and now it's the baby bond. Whenever I leave the house, I feel like two tethers are pulling me back."

"I know precisely what you mean." Kian sat down next to his cousin. "It's easier for me because Syssi and Allegra are gone most of the day. If they were here, I would have a hard time staying at work."

Kalugal tilted his head. "I don't know how you can tolerate having your mate and daughter away from the protection of the village. It would drive me insane to know they are an hour's drive away and unprotected."

Kian smirked. "Who said they are unprotected? I have the entire place rigged with surveillance cameras and Guardians on standby within a two-minute drive from the lab. My wife, my daughter, my sister, and my niece spend their days in that place. I would never have agreed to that without taking all the necessary precautions to safeguard them."

"Does Syssi know?"

Kian grimaced. "She knows some of it, but she doesn't know the extent of the security measures and the resources I'm dedicating to the security detail. If she had known, she would have quit her job, and she loves it. Besides, I only beefed up what was already in place before Amanda and Syssi decided to take the babies with them to work."

Kalugal eyed him with curiosity mixed with suspicion. "That's more like you. What is not like you is to invite me to your war room or share details about operations and security measures with me. Usually, I need to probe and sweet-talk you into giving me crumbs of information. What happened? Do you need my help financing the Kra-ell relocation project?"

Kian shouldn't be surprised that Kalugal was wary of the sudden change in his attitude.

"I don't need financial help. We seized Igor's money, or rather the money he stole from Jade's tribe and the other tribes he'd robbed." He steepled his fingers. "I just think it's time you took a more active part in what's going on in the village, and this is a good place to start. Your men are on the *Aurora*, and the journey is fraught with peril."

"Oh, now I get it." Kalugal leaned back in his chair and crossed his arms over his chest. "You don't want to assume responsibility for the lives of my men. You want me to take part in the decision-making, so I won't be able to blame you if anything happens to them."

Evidently, the suspicion cut both ways, but Kian knew the blame rested squarely on his shoulders. If he had been more inclusive from the get-go, Kalugal wouldn't be so wary now.

"It's not about that. I've been assuming responsibility for people's lives for so long that it didn't even occur to me. If you're too busy or you don't have the stomach for it, that's fine. I just wanted you to know that the door is open, and you are welcome to join."

Letting out a breath, Kalugal uncrossed his arms. "I need to understand your motives. What brought this change about?"

"Syssi," Kian admitted. "She said that I tend to see things in black and white and that I've been judging you unfairly."

"Judging me? For what?"

"Let's face it, Kalugal. You made your money using insider information. That's dishonest."

"Are you always honest?"

"I try to be. I never take advantage of humans by using mind manipulation. I always try to even out the playing field and use the same resources available to my competitors, meaning smarts and business acumen. But Syssi pointed out something that I was too obtuse to think of myself. I was raised differently than you were and given where you grew up and who your role models were, it's astounding that you got to be as decent as you are." Kian shook his head. "I'm probably botching this speech and offending you left and right while trying to compliment you. What I'm trying to say is that I think you are a good man despite your shady dealings."

Kalugal snorted a laugh. "Diplomacy is not your strong suit, cousin, but your heart is in the right place. I understand what you are trying to convey, and I appreciate it. We each try to do the best we can with what we have, but I don't strive for sainthood, and I admit to quite a bit of shady dealings. That said, I've never ruined anyone financially or otherwise unless they deserved it."

Kian nodded. "Shades of gray."

"The movie? What does that have to do with what we are talking about?"

"Nothing. When Syssi said that I tend to see things in black and white, she described you as slightly gray. I guess that's a fitting description."

Kalugal chuckled. "Despite your sanctimonious disposition, you're not pristine either. There are some gray splotches at your edges."

"I guess you are right." Kian sighed. "All I can say in my defense is that I always try to do my best, but sometimes my best is not good enough."

10

KALUGAL

"Perhaps we should take a break on the roof after all." Kalugal pushed to his feet. "It might be too early for whiskey and cigars, but I want to celebrate this breakthrough in our relationship, and getting invited to your rooftop man-cave is symbolic."

Grinning, Kian got up and walked over to his desk. "I don't have a big selection here, but I have good stuff." He pulled out two cigars and handed one to Kalugal. "Opus-X is unbeatable." A small bottle of whiskey came out of the drawer next. "Royal Salute." Kian showed Kalugal the label. "Perfectly complements the cigars."

"Excellent." Kalugal waited as Kian pulled two glasses out of the same drawer.

The truth was that he didn't care whether the cigar, whiskey, or both were plain or superb. What he cared about was finally getting invited to Kian's roof and enjoying it with his cousin.

They had an odd relationship that had started out on the wrong foot, gotten better over time, and ended up as a tenuous friendship. They liked each other and enjoyed chatting over whiskey and cigars, but they were also suspicious of each other.

It reminded him of one of Jacki's romance novels, subtitled *Enemies to Lovers*. Perhaps his and Kian's relationship was a bromance. They'd started as enemies, with Kian sending a spy to trap him, and him turning the tables on his cousin and taking a Head Guardian hostage. He'd also taken Jacki

279

along with Arwel and had fallen in love with her, so perhaps the Fates had orchestrated that.

Not that Kalugal was a great believer in the Fates, but Kian was, and the Fates provided a convenient excuse.

Somehow, he and Kian had managed to come to an understanding, and they had signed an accord. It should have been smooth sailing from there, but life was not a movie, and nothing ever worked as smoothly and seamlessly as planned.

Kian kept things close to the vest, and so did Kalugal, both for good reasons, but they were family, and despite their very different characters they liked and respected each other.

It would be nice to break the final barrier and demolish the invisible wall between them.

Was he ready for it?

"What are you smirking about?" Kian asked as he opened the office door and stepped into the hallway.

"Our bromance."

"Our what?"

"You heard me." Kalugal followed him up the stairs. "We are an enemies to lovers story just without the sex, therefore a bromance."

Kian shook his head. "We are not lovers, platonic or otherwise, and calling our relationship a bromance is so wrong that I'm starting to regret inviting you over and having this conversation with you."

"You're such a prude." Kalugal kept the banter going.

Teasing his sanctimonious cousin was too much fun to give up just because Kian's conscience had suddenly started troubling him.

When Kian opened the door at the top of the stairs and they stepped out onto the roof, Kalugal regarded the setup. The two foldable outdoor loungers and the small table between them were the kind people took with them to the beach. The sun umbrella shielding the seating arrangement from rain and shine was slightly more upscale, but the entire arrangement was unbecoming of someone of Kian's caliber.

Kalugal clapped his cousin on the back. "Nice man-cave, but it's quite plebeian. I would spruce it up if I were you."

"What's wrong with it?" Kian looked offended. "It's comfortable, and it serves its purpose. I don't need it to impress anyone but me." He put the bottle and two glasses on the table and sat down. "Are you going to join me, or is the furniture not good enough for your royal ass?"

Huffing out a laugh, Kalugal sat down on the other lounger. "I like to surround myself with luxury. Maybe that has to do with how I grew up as well." He cast Kian a sidelong glance. "Being Navuh's son got me the best tutors, but other than that, my living conditions were just as basic as those of other kids."

Kian shook his head. "That excuse will not work for you in this case because I didn't even have the luxury of tutors. My mother and Alena taught me everything they could. Our only so-called riches were the seven Odus my mother got as a wedding present from Khiann. They were a great help, erecting a shelter for us every time we moved, planting a vegetable and medicinal garden, and so on, but it was up to me to hunt and fish and bring game home for the Odus to cook. I did that since I was twelve years old."

Kalugal hadn't known that.

He'd assumed that Annani had thralled humans to give her what she needed and provide her with free labor. She could have also traded her knowledge or used the gold and precious gems she must have taken with her when she ran away.

The goddess was too wise to have run off with nothing.

"Your mother could've easily provided for you and your sister by manip-ulating humans to serve her. Why didn't she do that?"

"Because it wouldn't have been right." Kian unscrewed the cap and poured whiskey into the two glasses. "She did that when she had no other choice, but she always preferred for us to survive by means that didn't involve taking advantage of others. That's the code of conduct she instilled in her children and the rest of the clan."

Kian pulled a cutter out of his pocket, cut off the tip of his cigar, and handed it to Kalugal.

"Thanks." Kalugal chopped off the top and waited for Kian to hand him the lighter. "You shouldn't assume that I didn't learn any morality in my youth because of who my father is. Navuh was never a significant influence because he simply wasn't around. I had excellent tutors, and I also read a lot. One of the only privileges I had growing up as Navuh's son was access to books. Naturally, once I joined the warrior ranks, I was exposed to all the propaganda, and Navuh's presence loomed larger than life, but I was immune to his compulsion, and I wasn't easily impressed either." He smiled. "I'm not the type who succumbs to peer pressure."

"I guess being a conceited bastard has its advantages." Kian finished lighting his cigar and handed him the lighter. "I wondered how you managed to turn out a decent person despite your father's teachings, but I assumed it was the result of your mother's good genes. After all, science has proven that nature trumps nurture."

Kalugal grimaced. "Given my family's history, I would like to believe that we have more free will than being slaves to our genetics. My grandfather was a lunatic and a murderer, and my father is not much better. I don't want that in my future, and even less so in Darius's. I hope to prove that nurture can trump nature."

11

KIAN

"I hope you can prove it too, and not just for the sake of your son."
Kian cast Kalugal a wry smile. "On some level, we are all a little anxious about you showing the first signs of insanity, but I'm not too worried. Lokan shares the same genes, and he has managed to stay sane for over a thousand years, so you have time."

Even Rufsur was on alert, monitoring his boss's behavior with an eye for suspicious signs of megalomania or murderous inclination, and apparently, so was Jacki.

She had mitigated her mate's megalomaniacal plans by convincing him to allow Kian and Annani to monitor him. With the Kra-ell crisis in full bloom, Kian hadn't had time to investigate Kalugal's Instatock application and how it was manipulating young minds to fit Kalugal's agenda. It was one more thing on his to-do list as soon as things returned to normal, or as normal as things ever got for him and his clan.

Leaning back, Kalugal released a puff of smoke. "It's never far from my mind. That's why I agreed to Jacki's suggestion to put checks and balances on myself." He tilted his head toward Kian. "The thing with insanity is that the insane are the last ones to realize that their minds are compromised. Frankly, it's terrifying."

"Indeed. Especially for someone as smart as you." Kian couldn't imagine losing control of his mind or living with the fear of that happening.

"Thank you." Kalugal grinned. "Coming from you, that's a great compliment."

"It's a fact." Kian took a puff from his cigar. "I don't know how you always manage to find out about things I'm trying to keep a secret. When you guessed what my birthday present was, I had the Guardians search the place for listening devices."

Kalugal affected an offended expression. "I would never do such an underhanded thing as planting listening devices around the village. We are allies."

There was also the fact that Annani's compulsion should have prevented him from doing anything of that sort, but there were ways around compulsion, and as a compeller himself, Kalugal probably knew every trick in the book.

"Then how did you find out?"

"You forget that my hobby is archeology and how passionate I am about it. I have a lot of experience piecing together information from mere fragments."

That sounded like a bullshit explanation, and Kian had no problem letting Kalugal know what he thought of it with a not-so-subtle arch of his brow.

His cousin frowned. "Don't give me that face. I told you the truth. I'm very good at solving puzzles, and your people are not as good as you think they are at keeping secrets. I overheard Amanda and Syssi talking about the incredible present you got from Okidu, then in another conversation, someone said something about how wonderful it would be to have more Odus in the village, and the look on Syssi's face was not one of wistfulness but of fear. Those clues were enough for me to figure out what your present from Okidu was."

"Incredible." Kian shook his head. "What about all the other things?"

"I don't know what things you are referring to, but I probably figured them out the same way."

It was a logical explanation, but it was still bullshit.

"I might have been inclined to believe it if you were in the habit of spending your time sitting in the café and listening to gossip, but you are in your downtown office most of the day, and when you come home, you leave your house only to go to a restaurant in town. When do you get to hear all those clues?"

"Jacki fills me in on the village gossip, and sometimes my men also hear things. They spend a lot of time with your clan ladies, and not all of it in bed."

Kian made a mental note to discuss that with Onegus. The Guardians needed to be more careful about what information they let leak.

His relationship with Kalugal was entering a new stage, and he might not wish to continue keeping secrets from his cousin, but leaks needed to be stopped, or they could find their way to other unintended ears.

Then again, security leaks had never been a problem before. Perhaps others weren't as good at piecing clues together, or maybe they didn't have the extra help Kalugal might have gotten from his wife.

"I don't want to sound offensive, but I still don't buy it." Kian tapped the cigar to dislodge a chunk of ash into the ashtray. "Are you using Jacki to spy for you?"

She could see events from the past by touching an object related to them, but she could also see the future. Kian had heard her story about predicting her friend getting into an accident with her new car.

Kalugal shook his head. "If Jacki's had any visions recently, she hasn't told me about them. Her last vision was at the ruins near Lugu Lake."

Kian wasn't sure he believed that, but he'd pushed Kalugal enough, and it was time to change the subject. Besides, he'd forgotten about the ruins and was curious to hear about Kalugal's progress with them.

After the tunnels had collapsed, Kalugal hadn't wanted to endanger lives by continuing the excavation. He'd entered a joint venture with a couple of scientists who'd invented a device that analyzed sediment composition to modify it so it could be used remotely.

"What's new with your investigation over there? Did you manage to alter that contraption to be able to dig its way in?"

"I did, but it got stuck, and my people couldn't retrieve it. They are back to doing it the old-fashioned way, which is taking the whole place apart one stone at a time. I have to find out what's hiding under those ruins. Especially now that we have confirmation that the Kra-ell arrived in escape pods. I'm willing to bet I will find one of those there."

Kian regarded his cousin with an amused smile curling his lips. "Let me guess. You pieced together the information about the Kra-ell ship as well."

"That was easy." Kalugal waved the hand with the cigar. "We suspected that even before Jade told Toven about the pods. But I have no problem admitting that I learned the rest from Phinas, who learned it from Jade."

So that was Kalugal's angle. By volunteering his men and sending Phinas to lead them, he'd hoped to get more information about the gods and the Kra-ell—information that Kian might have chosen not to share with him.

For that, Kian couldn't blame his cousin. They were all eager to solve the mystery of their origins and why a small group of gods had gotten stranded on Earth.

"If there is a pod under those ruins, it couldn't have come from the ship Jade arrived on. It must have belonged to an earlier scouting expedition."

Kalugal looked offended. "I know that, but it doesn't matter which pod I find there. Just think about all the things we could learn from it. The technology alone is worth the effort, but perhaps it also has information stored in its computers that we can retrieve. If Jade's ship managed to survive for thousands of years while traversing the universe, that pod might still be operational."

That got Kian excited. "Perhaps we can find some of the pods Jade and her people arrived on. It will be interesting to compare the technology of the older pod to the newer ones and how much it progressed."

Kalugal eyed him from under lowered lashes. "If you want to get your hands on my pod, or rather get William's hands on it, you will have to share whatever you find. I'm no longer willing to be kept in the dark about whatever you choose to keep to yourself and be forced to scavenge for scraps of information."

Leaning forward, Kian offered Kalugal his hand. "Full cooperation in everything. I want to know everything you are working on, not just Instatock, and I'll share with you everything that we are doing. Are you willing to shake on it?"

Kalugal hesitated. "I keep all my profits. I'm too greedy to share them with the clan."

"I don't need your money, but I want to know what you're working on, and not after the fact. Full transparency."

"If we do that, I also want three seats on your clan's council. For me, Rufsur, and Phinas."

They had discussed creating a special council to supervise Instatock, which was supposed to include Kian, Annani, all current council members, and an equal number of representatives from Kalugal's side. But what Kalugal was asking now was much bigger than that. He wanted to be included in every decision that Kian posed to the council.

"One seat, and I need to have the council approve it first. I suggest that you prepare a speech that will impress them."

"Two seats. If you do the math, my people represent fourteen percent of the village population. Your current council has fourteen members. Even two additional seats are less in percentage than our share in the population."

Kian wondered whether Kalugal had calculated all of that on the spot or had been planning to ask for seats on the council for a while.

"Two it is. Again, it's not solely my decision, and you will have to convince the council to accept two new members. You can choose either Rufsur or Phinas, but in my opinion, Rufsur is a better choice because he's mated to Edna, who is a council member. She'll vote to include him."

"Don't be so sure. Edna does not vote with her heart. She votes with her mind."

"True, but I'm sure you'll deliver a speech that will wow even Edna."

"You can bet on it." Smirking, Kalugal put his hand in Kian's. "To a bright future for all of us." He shook it firmly.

1 2

TOVEN

"*Y*ou're quieter than usual." Mia turned to look at Toven over her shoulder. "Do you want to take a break?"

After leaving Valstar to wallow in his memories and joining Mia and the sisters on their explorations of the ship, Toven's mind had been churning with what he had learned and the questions he still needed to find answers for.

He leaned down and kissed her forehead. "Are you tired, my love? We can take a coffee break and continue later."

"I'm not tired. I'm sitting in a chair and being wheeled around. You're the one doing the pushing."

"I'm fine. I'm just preoccupied with thoughts of my conversation with Valstar. There are still so many questions that I didn't get to ask him."

"What did you talk about?" Jin asked.

"I asked him mostly about Igor and what he knows about him. Turns out that even Valstar doesn't know Igor's Kra-ell name. The settlers were chosen by lottery and weren't introduced to each other. They just loaded them into the pods and sent them on their way."

"That's weird." Mey leaned against a wall. "Didn't they get briefings about where they were supposed to settle? Instructions about what they were supposed to do? How could they have sent all those people across the universe with no guidance?"

"I think I know the answer to that." Mia adjusted the blanket, pulling it a little higher so it didn't drag on the floor, and at the same time scanning the area before lowering her voice. "Jade said they were sent to Earth to serve the gods, so they didn't need instructions. They were supposed to get them once they got to their destination."

Jin looked at Toven. "Did you know about the Kra-ell?"

He shook his head. "The gods who were born on Earth weren't told about them, and that's the biggest hole in that story. If the older gods knew about a ship of Kra-ell workers heading their way, we should have been told to expect them."

"Someone lied." Mey pushed away from the wall and resumed walking. "But who and why is anyone's guess. You should ask Valstar what he thinks about that."

"That's one of the things on my growing list of questions."

"What else did you talk with him about?" Jin asked.

"The trackers. Like Jade, he didn't remember getting implanted, but what threw me off was that he seemed not to know that all the Kra-ell had trackers in them. Valstar only knew about the Kra-ell who got implanted with them before leaving on missions, and the humans who had been sent to study at the university. But if we assume that all the settlers were implanted before boarding the ship, and that Igor cut the sophisticated trackers out of the Kra-ell he murdered, then Valstar must know about it because he went on those missions with Igor. So either our assumption about the trackers is wrong, or Igor made Valstar and everyone else who was there forget about cutting the trackers out of the victims before setting their bodies on fire."

Jin snorted. "Valstar is playing the victim game so you'll feel sorry for him and protect him from Jade. Don't fall for that."

"He can't lie to me, and he's not trying to absolve himself by blaming Igor's compulsion. He's also not faking being sorry for what he did. Given that he was compelled and couldn't disobey the order even if he wanted to, a human court would not have given him the death penalty. They would have given him a lighter sentence. I don't feel right about letting Jade execute him without a trial."

"You gave her your word," Jin said. "If you go back on it, she will never trust you again."

"I know. But now that I've talked to Valstar, I would feel like an accomplice to murder if I let her kill him. I need to talk to her and convince her to allow Valstar a trial."

"You can try it this evening." Mey turned into another hallway, and they all followed. "We invited Jade to our cabin so Jin and I can ask her questions about our parents. You and Mia are welcome to join. Maybe after hearing our story, Jade will be in a more receptive mood."

"She won't," Jin said. "Do you think she feels bad about giving up the children of the hybrids for adoption? She does not."

Mey shook her head. "You haven't exchanged more than one sentence with Jade, and you're already an expert on her character?"

"I don't need to talk to her to know the kind of person she is. It's written all over her face, posture, and salty attitude."

Mey cast her sister a fond smile. "Takes one to know one."

Jin huffed. "I might be salty, but I would never have taken children from their parents and given them up for adoption."

Jade wasn't the cruel and unreasonable female Jin thought she was, but Toven didn't offer his opinion. She wouldn't take his word for it anyway.

"I guess we will find out later this evening." Mey glanced at her watch. "I suggest we end our tour now to prepare for the meeting. I want to jot down my questions."

"Good idea." Mia lifted her eyes to Toven. "Do you want to talk to Valstar again? Maybe you could put together some arguments in his favor before the meeting. Something that would convince Jade to allow him a trial."

"Do you want to come with me?"

Mia shook her head. "Unless you need me there to enhance your compulsion, I'd rather not. Whether willing or not, Valstar is a murderer, and I don't want to be exposed to his bad energy. I'm not as strong as you are."

"You're right. I don't want you to be exposed to it either."

"Go. Come get me when you are done."

"Are you sure?"

Her portable chair wasn't motorized, and its wheels weren't comfortable for her to move over distances longer than getting to the bathroom and back. She needed to be pushed, and it was no trouble for him to take her back to their cabin before seeing Valstar again.

"I'm sure." She took his hand and gave it a loving squeeze. "Mey and Jin will help me."

PHINAS

"I'm surprised at how fast the pool is filling up." Phinas cast a sidelong glance at Karl, the assistant to the chief engineer. "I thought it would take a day or two until I could teach my first swimming lesson. Thankfully, the *Aurora* has plenty of outdoor lighting because the days are so damn short out here."

It was only six in the evening, but it had been dark for over two hours and the cold air was biting even for an immortal, and yet the human didn't seem affected.

Karl wore a coat and a scarf, and his cheeks were ruby, but he wasn't stomping his feet and rubbing his hands like Dandor was doing on Phinas's other side.

The engineer regarded him with a smug expression on his face. "We don't have a shortage of water or depend on the size of the supply pipe. We get as much as we can pump, and we can pump a lot."

"Is that unique to the *Aurora*? Or is it like that on all cruise liners?"

"It's like that on all the new ones. The water needs to be replaced every night."

Phinas arched a brow. "Why so often?"

The assistant engineer leaned over to get closer to Phinas's ear. "Because passengers pee in the pools."

"Gross. But they probably pee in public in-ground pools as well, and I know that they don't change the water in those on a daily basis or even monthly."

"Most pools don't have as many daily users, and their filtration system can handle the contamination."

"Disgusting." Dandor made a face. "I'm never going into a public pool again."

Phinas chuckled. "As if you've never pissed in a pool."

"I didn't. I pissed in the ocean, but that doesn't count."

His phone buzzing with an incoming message put an end to the discussion.

"Excuse me." He pulled the phone out of his pocket.

The message was from Kalugal:

Call me after you find a private spot.

"I have a phone call to make." He offered Karl his hand. "Thank you for helping us with the pool."

"You are most welcome." Karl shook his hand. "But I suggest heating it up. Otherwise, your swimming students will end up with hypothermia."

"We need to conserve fuel, so we can only heat it minimally."

Karl nodded. "You should keep the lessons short and have towels and blankets ready for the students."

"Of course." Phinas left Karl with Dandor and headed to his cabin to make the call.

Five minutes later, he was on the couch with a glass of water in one hand and the phone in the other.

"What's up, boss?"

"You go first. Do you have any juicy tidbits for me? Any conversations you overheard?"

"I know Toven talked with Valstar again, but I haven't heard what he learned from him."

"Keep your ear to the ground. Did anyone mention me in any way?"

"Not today. Why?"

"I just had a fascinating and entirely unexpected talk with Kian. He offered me two seats on the village council, pending the council's approval, of course. One will go to me and the other to Rufsur or you. You can also rotate the position, with each of you serving six months of the year or some other arrangement that works for you."

"Is the position that demanding?"

Kalugal chuckled. "Not at all. Kian rarely remembers to consult his council, and he only does so when it's a major decision that affects the entire clan. I don't think the council meets more than once or twice yearly."

"Then why do you need Rufsur and me to rotate?"

"I don't want to choose one of you over the other. You are both equally dear and important to me, but each brings different qualities to the table."

Phinas rubbed the back of his head. "Did you talk with Rufsur?"

"Not yet. I called you first."

Did that mean that Kalugal believed he was the better man for the job?

Phinas had always been the cool-headed one, while Rufsur had been the fun guy Kalugal liked to go clubbing with. That didn't mean that Rufsur wasn't suited for the job of a councilman, though. Perhaps his charm was precisely what was needed.

"What about Jacki? Did you consider offering the seat to her?"

"I did, but then decided against it. Kian was very gracious by offering me two seats, and I didn't want to repay him by getting him in trouble with his wife. If I offered the seat to Jacki, Syssi might get upset that he didn't offer her a seat as well."

"Maybe he has?"

"But what if he hasn't? I don't want to chance it."

"Then perhaps you should suggest nominating both ladies for the council. I'm saying that not because you are mated to Jacki, and Kian is mated to Syssi, but because the council needs more balance, and I'm not talking about gender. There are three males and three females on the core council. The balance shifts when the Guardians and Onegus are added, but that can't be helped until more females join the force and make it all the way up to Head Guardian. Jacki and Syssi bring more than just their gender to the table. They are both seers, and up until recently, they were both human. I think it's important to consider the impact on humans when making important decisions, and they can authentically represent that side of the equation."

"Bravo." Kalugal clapped. "I'm impressed. The seat goes to you."

"It wasn't my intention to impress you so you'd offer me the seat and not Rufsur. I don't want it, and if you don't want to offer it to Jacki, offer it to him."

"Why not? You seem to have solid opinions about things, and I like how enlightened you are. Frankly, I didn't expect that from you or from Rufsur."

Phinas chuckled. "Now I'm offended. Neither of us is a simpleton, nor are we influenced any longer by what we were fed in Navuh's camps. In fact, neither of us believed in his propaganda even then, which is why you selected us for your unit."

"I know that, and I didn't mean it that way. It's just that all of us are busy with our day-to-day responsibilities, and we seldom stop to think about the big picture."

It was nice of Kalugal to include himself in the 'we,' but he was the consummate big-picture guy, always thinking a few steps ahead of everyone else.

"Usually, you are right, but I'm in a unique position to observe a mini social reform."

"Are you referring to the Kra-ell and the humans they enslaved?"

"Yeah. Jade is a traditionalist, but she's a smart lady, and she listens. She's ready to make changes."

"I'd be most interested to hear about those changes."

"I'll keep you posted."

"Thank you." Kalugal let out a breath. "I'll give the council seat more thought, and I'll consult with Jacki. If she declines, would you be interested?"

"I'll give it some thought as well."

"Excellent. Good day, Phinas."

14

JADE

*J*ade walked into the kitchen and scanned the place for Isla. When she spotted her next to one of the workstations, she strode toward the woman. "Can I have a word with you?"

The human lifted a hand to her chest. "Did something happen?"

"I just want to discuss something with you. Is there a quiet place we can talk?"

Isla's hands started shaking. "What is this about?"

Jade needed to dial down her aggression or the human might faint from fright. She might be less terrified with her brother at her side.

Forcing her shoulders to relax, Jade affected a smile. "It's about our community's future. I want to understand the issues the humans in our community are concerned with."

"Oh." Isla let out a breath. "Perhaps you should talk with Jarmo. I'm not good at things like that."

Jade looked around the busy kitchen. "I disagree. You are good at organization, and people follow your lead, but if you are more comfortable with Jarmo present, I would welcome his input as well."

How was that for diplomacy?

Jade was proud of the polite words she'd chosen to put the woman at ease. She would never have spoken like that to a Kra-ell, and if she had, they wouldn't have taken her seriously. There was no beating around the bush in the Kra-ell culture or being mindful of hurt feelings. It was much better than the nonsensical way humans interacted, but when in Rome and all that. If she wanted to lead a contemporary mixed community, she had to adapt.

Her many years of interacting with humans during her business dealings had taught her a thing or two about their various cultures and accepted speech patterns. She wouldn't need to start from scratch and learn from her mistakes like she'd done back in the day.

"Maybe Sofia and Marcel should join us as well?" Isla asked.

"Since Sofia will most likely choose to live with Marcel, I don't expect them to be part of our community for long, and they shouldn't have a say in how it will be run."

Wording her reply in a way that wouldn't offend or frighten Isla had felt like a tongue-twister, and Jade's patience was starting to wear thin.

Despite her efforts, Isla didn't look happy with her answer, but she knew better than to push for a different one. "Jarmo is down in the animal enclosure. We can go to him." She looked around the kitchen. "I just need to get Helmi to take over for me."

"Very well. I'll meet you down there in ten minutes." That would give her time to calm down.

"Yes, sir."

That was the address that Igor had demanded. 'Yes, mistress,' was the proper way to address a tribe leader, who traditionally was a female. But traditions were changing, and she was attempting to build a community where everyone was comfortable and felt respected.

Besides, it would be odd to be addressed as mistress again. It would also be painful, reminding her of what she'd lost.

"I don't require an honorific. A nod will suffice in most cases, and in others, you can just call me Jade."

Looking surprised, Isla nodded.

Jade used the ten minutes to walk through the deserted corridors of the crew quarters, and when she arrived at the animal enclosure, she was calmer and ready to go through another tongue-twister with Isla and Jarmo, who were already there.

Other than the animals and the two humans, there was no one else in the cargo, which was perfect.

"Let's sit over there." She pointed at the crates separating the goats from the sheep.

"What is it about?" Jarmo asked.

Jade was sure Isla had already told him, but he might have found it unbelievable that she wanted the humans' opinion.

Turning to Isla, Jade got straight to the point. "You told Phinas that the humans wouldn't mind continuing to work for us if they got paid and if the interbreeding stopped. The breeding is essential to us, and if the females are willing, I don't see the problem."

"The females are not willing," Isla said. "They agreed to do it out of fear, and so they would be allowed to marry a human once they had done their duty and produced a hybrid child. Those were Igor's rules, and they were coercive. Our young females didn't have a choice."

Perhaps Isla was projecting her own preferences on the other females of her community.

"You've never produced a hybrid child," Jade pointed out.

Isla nodded. "I was never allowed to marry a human male, but I was still blessed with wonderful children, so I consider it a fair trade. Luckily, I'm plump and short, and the purebloods don't find me attractive."

Jade shifted her eyes to Jarmo. "What about you? Did Joanna force you into her bed?"

"She didn't. I went willingly and more than once. I was young and naive, and I thought that we could be together despite who her father was. But she got tired of playing with the human pretty quickly, or maybe she got what she wanted, which was to get pregnant with a human child and get a rise out of her father."

That wasn't why Joanna had bedded Jarmo, but it was Joanna's story to tell, not Jade's.

"Still, you were willing, and so were many of the females who produced hybrid children for us." She shifted her gaze to Isla. "It would seem that not everyone is against the interbreeding."

Isla's plump lips twisted. "Those who agree do it for something, not because they find the purebloods appealing."

Jarmo cleared his throat.

Isla glared at him. "Besides you, that is, and you were infatuated with a hybrid, not a pureblood."

"Some of the young ladies find the pureblooded males attractive," Jarmo said. "That doesn't mean that they want to get pregnant with a hybrid child, though. They just want the sex."

Jade stifled a chuckle.

As a female, Isla should have been more attuned than her brother to the needs and wants of other women in her community, but she projected her own preferences on others and colored everything through the prism of her own beliefs.

"How do you know that?" Isla frowned at Jarmo.

"I have eyes. I see how they flirt with them and vie for their attention. I don't know how you don't see that."

Isla waved a dismissive hand. "They all want the benefits that come with bedding a pureblood and giving him a child. They are basically whoring themselves out for peanuts."

Jarmo winced. "That's harsh, Isla."

"But true."

Jade lifted her hand to stop the argument. "The women are free to do as they please with their bodies and bed whoever they want. I will prohibit any negative consequences for refusal and will harshly punish any pureblood or hybrid who threatens a woman with retribution for refusing to have sex and/or breed with him. But I will allow incentives for acquiescence. Hybrids are essential to our continuation, and if the ladies are willing to produce them for a price, I see no harm in that."

15

PHINAS

"**R**eady to try the pool?" Phinas whipped his shirt over his head and tossed it on top of one of the lounge chairs.

Dandor's lips curved downward. "Are you nuts? It's freezing."

"I can't tell the Kra-ell to get into the water if my own men are unwilling to get cold."

"What Kra-ell?" Dandor waved his hand around. "There is no one else out here."

"They are coming. I texted Yamanu and asked him to corral a couple of dudes. I want them to see us in the water when they come up here."

Dandor shook his head. "If I knew the things I would have to endure on this mission, I wouldn't have volunteered."

"Liar." Phinas kicked his boots off and unbuckled his belt. "You were chomping at the bit to get out of the village." He pulled down his pants and folded them on top of the shirt.

"We don't have towels or blankets." Dandor crossed his arms over his chest. "You heard Karl. We need those before we get in. I don't know how long our bodies can combat the cold, and I don't want to accidentally go into stasis."

Phinas had never heard about any immortals going into stasis because their bodies couldn't keep generating enough heat to protect them from the cold, but he could imagine an instance where it could happen. Getting buried under an avalanche of snow or frozen inside a block of ice could do that, but getting submerged in cold water that was just a smidgen over freezing temperature should be fine for the hour or so he planned on dedicating to the swimming lesson.

"Stop being such a wuss." Phinas stretched, did a few jumping jacks, and ran in place to get his blood pumping. "The Kra-ell boys are bringing towels and blankets with them."

Letting his chin drop to his chest, Dandor released a resigned sigh. "Fine. But I'm waiting until they get here before I'm plunging into that water."

If Kagra were there, Dandor would have jumped into the pool without a single word of protest, but he had no one to impress.

"No pain, no gain, brother." Phinas cast him a reproachful look before jumping into the pool, feet first.

The shock was nearly paralyzing, but his immortal body was quick to adapt, increasing its inner temperature to compensate.

Floating on his back, he smiled at Dandor. "It's not so bad."

"Right." The guy still stood with his arms crossed over his chest and a pouty expression on his face unworthy of a warrior.

They had gotten soft over the years. Training in a gym and wrestling each other wasn't enough to keep them hard. They didn't push themselves, and after their training sessions they went to their comfortable homes, took showers in their luxurious bathrooms, and dried their bodies with soft towels.

Warriors were forged by surviving in harsh conditions and fighting in real battles.

Still, they had done well against the Kra-ell, even with the added difficulty of trying not to kill any of them.

Flipping to his front, Phinas started doing laps. By the time the two hybrids showed up with a stack of towels and blankets, he'd counted eleven.

They both looked familiar, but Phinas didn't remember their names.

He swam toward the edge of the pool and braced his arms on the concrete. "What are your names?" Not sure they understood English, he pointed to himself. "My name is Phinas."

"I'm Piotr," the one on the left said.

"I'm Tomos." His friend patted his chest.

Now Phinas remembered who he was. He was Sofia's cousin's boyfriend.

"Put the towels and blankets down and strip down to your underwear." He hoped they weren't going commando. "You'll be the first to receive cold water swimming and floating training."

The two exchanged glances, looked at him, and then followed his orders without arguing.

Phinas shifted his gaze to Dandor and lifted a brow. "What are you waiting for?"

"I was hoping the Russians would attack and save me from this torture." With a sigh, he took his clothes off and joined the two hybrids at the pool's edge.

As the three stood there and stared at the water, Phinas laughed. "Come on, boys. It's only cold for the first two seconds, and then it's warmer in the water than outside of it. The pool is not deep enough for a head dive, so jump in feet first."

It was still biting cold, but he and Dandor would survive. The question was whether the hybrids' bodies possessed the same mechanism and would raise their inner temperature.

Uttering a battle cry reminiscent of Tarzan, Tomos jumped in, and his friend followed a split second later.

Their expressions telegraphed the initial shock, but as the seconds ticked off, the two relaxed.

"How are you feeling? Are your bodies regulating the temperature?"

Tomos nodded and translated for Piotr.

"Good. I was worried for a moment."

"What about you? How can you regulate yours?" Tomos asked.

Damn. He'd forgotten that they didn't know their rescuers were immortals.

"Navy SEAL training. Dandor and I trained for a very long time to learn how to do it."

"Oh." Tomos accepted the explanation without batting an eyelid. "So, what do we do now?"

"First, you learn to float on your back." Phinas demonstrated.

It took several tries, a lot of mutual teasing between the young men, and some help from Dandor before they managed to keep themselves afloat.

"How long do we need to do this?" Tomos asked.

"When you can hold yourself for five minutes straight, you can get out."

Phinas swam to the edge of the pool and hoisted himself out.

"Where are you going?" Dandor asked.

"To get Jade." He wrapped a large towel around himself. "I want her to get in the pool as well."

"It's not fair," Dandor whined. "You're leaving us here to freeze."

Reaching under the towel he'd wrapped around his middle, Phinas pulled his wet boxer shorts down. "If you get them to float for five minutes, the three of you will be done for today, and you can get out."

16

TOVEN

*W*hen Toven walked into Valstar's cabin, the guy's face brightened. "I wondered when you'd be back."

Was he so lonely that he was excited to see him? Or was he under the impression that his ploy to play on Toven's heartstrings was working?

Not that he was wrong. Toven would feel much less guilt if Valstar wasn't executed without a trial. The Kra-ell might be savages who lived by the sword, but the gods believed in due process, and despite their murky past, they still had the moral high ground.

Sitting in the same armchair as before, Toven crossed his legs. "I didn't plan on stopping by again today, but I realized that I didn't cover all the issues I wanted to go over with you. I still have many unanswered questions."

"You didn't answer my question either." Valstar tilted his head. "Were you among the original settlers, or were you born on Earth?"

Toven saw no harm in telling the guy the truth. Even if Jade agreed to let Valstar stand trial, Toven doubted the outcome would be any different for him. The guy wasn't going to live long enough to tell anyone.

"I was born on Earth and didn't know that the Kra-ell existed. None of the original settlers mentioned you or the rebellion. The first I heard of it was from Jade."

That wasn't entirely true. Mortdh had thrown a few hints about the gods' dark past, but Toven hadn't paid attention to his brother's ramblings.

"Maybe they were forbidden to mention it," Valstar said. "Exile was probably a diminished sentence for their part in the rebellion, and a stipulation for being allowed to live was not ever mentioning it."

"Perhaps. Or maybe they didn't want the next generation to know that they had been exiled."

"That's possible as well." Valstar nodded. "The gods were a proud people, and they didn't like to acknowledge any wrongdoing."

Hearing the guy talk about the gods in the past tense had a trickle of apprehension slither down Toven's back. It probably didn't mean anything, and the planet of the gods was still out there along with its inhabitants—the gods and the Kra-ell.

"It is probably still as true today as it was then," Valstar added. "People don't change."

"Sometimes they do."

Toven still carried the burden of all of his misdeeds and failures. If he could have shed responsibility, he would have been a happier male. Even now, with a truelove mate at his side and surrounded by a big, loving family, he still suffered from bouts of melancholy whenever he reflected on his long life.

Uncrossing his legs, he leaned forward and looked into Valstar's black eyes. "I didn't come here to talk about me. I came here for answers, and I want you to tell me only the truth. Did you see Igor or anyone else cut the trackers out of the males you slaughtered?"

Valstar's eyes momentarily turned green before going back to black. "I didn't. I was in charge of releasing the humans and searching for any Kra-ell who might be hiding among them. How do you know Igor did that? Did Jade tell you?"

"She didn't, but unless they had active trackers, Igor wouldn't have known where to find the other Kra-ell tribes."

"Maybe they did something to tip their hand?"

"Did he tell you how he found them?" Toven shoved his full power of compulsion into the question.

Valstar shook his head. "He just informed me when he found them and instructed me to conduct reconnaissance and plan the mission. He never told me how he found them."

"Unbelievable." Toven rose to his feet and started pacing. "Was there anyone else he confided in?"

"He didn't confide in anyone, and he used different people for different tasks, forbidding us from sharing what we knew with the others. Don't forget that none of us joined him voluntarily. We were compelled to follow his orders. Some had less of a problem with his agenda than others, and all of us liked having enough females, so no one had to go without, but I doubt everyone was okay with his methods. I wasn't, but I had no choice, and I couldn't confide my displeasure with the others either."

Perhaps Jin was right, and Valstar was playing the victim. He might have even convinced himself of that, and that was how he was able to circumvent Toven's compulsion.

"You were Igor's second-in-command. He wouldn't have chosen you for the position if he didn't believe that you were a hundred percent behind him."

Valstar sighed. "After Igor, I was the most capable and smartest male in our group. That's why he chose me. I learned languages fast, I adapted to human technology quickly, and I was a good administrator. He didn't care about my personal beliefs or whether I agreed with him or not. As long as I did my job well, I got to keep my position." He smiled. "Jade despised him and hated every moment she had to spend with him, and yet he chose her as his prime because she was the best at what she did, which was producing superior offspring. Unfortunately for him, she only gave him one daughter, and he wanted a son. But the moral of the story is that she did exactly what I did. To survive, she gave Igor what he wanted when he wanted it. The only difference was that her job was to spread her legs for him while mine was to kill the competition and make sure that the compound ran smoothly."

17

PHINAS

*P*hinas walked into the dining hall and scanned the tables for Jade, but she wasn't there. She hadn't been in her cabin or Kagra's either, nor had she been at the clinic or any of the other places he'd checked.

He stopped by a table with several hybrids. "Do you know where I can find Jade?"

"She went to the kitchen," one of them said.

Phinas's hackles rose.

The only reason for Jade to go there was to talk to Isla. She must have figured out that Isla had been the one who complained to him about the breeding, which was his fault for blurting out her name this morning, and she'd gone to give her a talking to.

When he turned toward the kitchen, Toven waved him over to his and Mia's table.

"Are you still coming to Yamanu and Mey's cabin after dinner?"

"I hope so." It depended on what was going on in the kitchen and if he and Jade would still be on speaking terms after he confronted her.

"Mia and I are joining as well," Toven said. "I spoke with Valstar earlier and learned a few new things."

That piqued his interest, but he was in a rush to get to the kitchen and protect Isla from Jade. "I would love to hear all about it, but there is something I need to attend to."

Toven nodded. "I will share my findings at the get-together."

"Good deal. See you there." Phinas cast a quick smile at Mia before turning away.

Striding toward the kitchen, he tried to calm down so he could plan his next move, but as he got in there and Isla wasn't to be found, he started to worry in earnest.

Finding Lana, he walked up to her. "Where is your mother?"

"She went down to the animal enclosure to talk to Jarmo."

Phinas released a relieved breath, but then it occurred to him that Isla wouldn't have left the kitchen during the busy dinner time just to go chat with her brother. "Do you know why she went there?"

"Jade wanted to talk to her, and Isla said that they needed to talk with Jarmo."

"Thank you." He forced a smile before turning around.

It was smart of Isla to suggest Jarmo should join. She would at least have him to back her up when Jade attacked.

Impatient to wait for the elevator, Phinas took the stairs down to the animal enclosure.

He walked in as Jade was finishing a sentence.

"—if the ladies are willing to produce them for a price, I see no problem with that."

He'd been right. She was talking with them about the breeding.

Jarmo noticed him first and gave him a tight smile, then Jade turned around and frowned.

"What are you doing here?"

"I was worried about Isla. I came to check that she was alright." He didn't add that he had been worried about what Jade might do to her, but given the red flash of her eyes, she'd guessed it.

"Why?" She put her hands on her hips. "What did you imagine I would do to her?"

"I don't know. You tell me."

If looks could kill, he would be dead.

Jade looked like she was reining in her temper with much difficulty. "We are having a conversation about the future of our community, and it's none of your business."

Tilting his head to look at Isla, he asked, "Are you alright?"

She didn't understand the words, but she understood the tone and gave him the thumbs up.

Did he believe her?

Not really, but it didn't seem as if Jade was abusing her, and Jarmo was there.

Still, he was mad that Jade hadn't told him she was going to talk to Isla and that she hadn't invited him to join after they had discussed the matter this morning.

"If this is about the breedings, then it's very much my business. I was the one who promised Isla that the coercion would stop."

"I'm here to hear it directly from her and from Jarmo, and I don't appreciate you barging in on our private conversation and assuming the worst. Please leave."

Jade was holding her temper at bay and answering him as politely as she could, but Phinas knew that if he stayed even a moment longer, she would explode.

"Fine." He turned around and walked out.

Hovering just outside the entrance for a few moments, he made sure that all Jade did was talk, and when he was certain that Isla and Jarmo were safe, he walked away on silent feet.

18

JADE

*W*hen Jade stepped out of the elevator on her deck, she found Phinas leaning against the wall looking angry.

"Are you waiting for me?" she asked.

"Who else would I be waiting for? We are supposed to be at Mey and Yamanu's cabin in a few minutes, and you stink of animals. Are you planning to shower before we go?"

He was in a foul mood, and she knew why, but he had no right. If anyone should be angry, it was her.

Not only was her conversation with Isla and Jarmo none of his business, but his assumption that she would retaliate against Isla for talking to him was also insulting.

It was true that she was angry at the woman for turning to an outsider instead of talking to her first, but she understood why.

Isla's hands had started shaking when she'd approached her. The woman had been terrified of her, but she didn't know why. She hadn't exchanged more than a few words with her during the past two decades, and those words hadn't been angry.

With a slight arch of her brow, Jade pivoted on her heel and strode toward her cabin.

Uttering a growl, Phinas followed her. "You didn't answer me."

"I'm going to shower and change clothing, so I don't offend your people's delicate sense of smell."

As Jade opened the door to her cabin, she debated whether to close it in Phinas's face or let him come in. It would have been so satisfying to close it, but she was above such petty antics.

"Please, come in," she said in as polite a tone as she could manage. "Sit down and relax while I shower."

He closed his eyes and released a breath. "Why didn't you tell me that you were going to talk to Isla? And don't tell me that it's none of my business because it is. I was the one who brought the issue of the humans wanting a change to your attention."

Again, her knee-jerk reflex was to tell him that he had no right to butt in and that Isla should have come to her first, but she stifled the urge, and not just because she was above that. Phinas was an important asset, and she wasn't going to lose him over a nonsensical human-style childish drama.

"When I figured out that the human you spoke with was Isla, I wanted to hear her complaints first-hand and not through your filter." Heading toward the bedroom, she shrugged off her sweater and carried it into the bathroom to put in the laundry basket.

Phinas followed her inside. "What did you learn?"

She turned her head to look at him over her shoulder. "You should have started with that instead of growling insults at me."

"I just stated the facts. You smell of animals, and it's not pleasant."

"I'm not talking about that." She pulled her shirt over her head and tossed it in the laundry basket. "I'm talking about your insinuation that I might retaliate against my people for speaking up. I admit that I was angry at Isla for coming to you instead of me, but I didn't lash out at her. We just talked."

"What did Isla tell you?"

"More or less the same she told you." Jade removed the rest of her clothing, stepped into the shower, and closed the glass door.

Regrettably, Phinas's eyes didn't blaze with desire upon seeing her naked, which meant that he was still upset over her talk with Isla.

What had he expected? That she would obey his wishes and implement changes without investigating the opinion of the people those changes affected?

Her talk with Isla and Jarmo was just the beginning. She would assemble all the human females and have the same talk with them.

"And?" Phinas leaned against the vanity with his arms crossed over his chest.

"Jarmo had a different perspective on the issue, and so did I." Jade started lathering her body with one of the fragrant soaps lining the shelf. "I agreed to disallow threats of negative consequences for refusal, and I promised that any instance would be severely punished, but I said that I would allow positive incentives. We have no choice. The pureblooded females don't produce enough children to keep our race from dying out."

"Did you address the issue of compulsion? What if the women cannot complain about being threatened because they've been compelled not to?"

"We didn't go into details, but I will address all those issues when I assemble all the adult human females and get their opinions on the matter. With all due respect to Isla and Jarmo, they weren't elected as the humans' representatives, and they have no right to decide for them."

"But you can?"

"If they want to stay under my leadership, the answer is yes. But I'm going to listen and try to devise a system that works for everyone. I don't have any illusions about creating a utopia, though. It's impossible to please everyone, but if I manage to prevent anyone from suffering, I will consider it a job well done."

"That's all I'm asking for."

When she turned the water off and opened the shower door, Phinas handed her a towel. "By the way, I bumped into Tom on the way. He and Mia are going to join us at Yamanu's cabin."

"Great." Jade finished drying off and hung the towel on the hook behind the door. "Anything else?"

"He spoke to Valstar again."

She turned to look at him. "Did he find out anything new about Igor?"

"He did. He said he would tell us at Yamanu's."

19

PHINAS

*P*hinas felt like shit for jumping to conclusions and flying off the handle before giving Jade a chance to explain.

Talk about presumptions.

He'd been sure that she'd berated Isla for confiding in him, but it seemed like they'd had a civilized conversation about their symbiotic coexistence and the future of their community.

But what if Isla and Jarmo had a different take on that conversation?

Jade was intimidating, and they might have said things they hadn't meant just to get her to back off.

He needed to have a talk with them and find out where things really stood.

"I'm ready." Jade zipped up her tight-fitting leather jacket. "Let's go."

"You look good." He put his arm around her.

She didn't brush his hand off until they were at the door. "You know my stance on public displays of affection."

"Yeah, you made it abundantly clear." He dropped his arm.

On the one hand, it was good that Jade didn't beat around the bush and communicated her wishes clearly, but on the other hand it took some getting used to.

He'd always been attracted to strong women, but the ones he'd been with were a little softer around the edges, a little more mindful of his feelings.

The truth was that Jade was mindful as well. She wasn't aggressive with him, and he knew that she held back because of how much stronger she was. She believed that his male ego would suffer if he was overpowered by a female.

Was she right about that?

They wouldn't know until she let loose and had her way with him. The thought had him excited more than it should, and he needed to get rid of the evidence of his excitement before he knocked on Yamanu's door.

Jade eyed him from the corner of her eye and smirked. "You must really like my leather jacket."

"I like everything about you." He gripped the back of her neck and planted a kiss on her lips.

Turning into him, she wound her arms around him and returned the kiss.

When she licked his fang, he groaned into her mouth and cupped her bottom.

"Do you want to get a room?" Toven's voice cut through the haze of desire.

He was wheeling Mia down the corridor, and he wasn't trying to be stealthy about it. If he were an attacker, he would have caught both of them unprepared.

Closing his eyes for a brief moment, Phinas let go of Jade's mouth and turned around. "We have a room, and I plan to get back there as soon as we can."

Given her irritated expression, Jade didn't appreciate getting caught kissing in the corridor, and she didn't appreciate his answer to Toven either.

After nodding hello to Mia, she shifted her hard gaze to Toven. "I heard that you talked with Valstar again and didn't invite me to join you. I think we established already that I'm not going to kill him until we catch Igor."

"It wasn't that kind of an interrogation. I wanted him to feel at ease with me."

"What did you learn?"

"That even Valstar doesn't know Igor's Kra-ell name. I'll tell you more when we get inside. I don't want to have to repeat the story."

She nodded. "As the humans say, all good things come to those who wait. Let's go inside and get it over with."

As Phinas pressed the intercom button, Yamanu threw the door open. "Good evening, ladies and gentlemen. Please come in." He waved his hand in a grand gesture.

"Who said I'm a gentleman?" Phinas murmured.

Jade cast him a wry smile. "And who said that I'm a lady?"

"That's right." He took her hand and gave it a squeeze. "We are both warriors."

"You can be genteel warriors." Yamanu motioned for them to follow him to the sitting area. "I am."

"Hi." Mey got up and offered Jade her hand. "I'm so glad you came. My sister and I have a few questions we would like to ask you."

Yamanu wrapped his arm around his mate's middle and leaned to kiss her temple. "We should get a few drinks in us before we start."

Phinas agreed.

He had a good idea about what the sisters wanted from Jade, and she would need a few drinks to prepare for what was coming.

20

JADE

"Here's your vodka cranberry." Yamanu handed Jade the glass. "Taste it and tell me if I mixed it right."

It was difficult to go wrong with such a simple drink, but she obliged him and took a small sip. "It's perfect, thank you."

Yamanu grinned. "Good quality vodka is the key. The cranberry juice is from concentrate, but that's the best we had on board."

Phinas sipped on the whiskey all the men seemed to prefer. "So, Tom, what new things did you learn from Valstar?"

"He didn't know Igor before boarding the ship. He said he found it odd that no activities had been organized for the settlers to get to know each other, and I agree with him that it's strange." He shifted his eyes to Jade. "After all, you were supposed to build a new community on Earth. How did your queen expect a bunch of strangers to do that once they landed? No command chain was established, no experts were introduced, and you had no bonding activities. If it were an evacuation, I could understand there was no time, but that wasn't the case."

Jade suspected that it had to do with the royal twins who'd been smuggled on board, but since she had no proof of it actually being them, she could hide it from Tom even if he chose to use compulsion, which he wasn't right now.

"It was the first settler ship, so maybe the queen hadn't figured out all the details yet. But since the gods were in charge, they should have thought of that."

Tom tilted his head. "You haven't mentioned that it was a first ship. I was under the impression that they'd been going on for hundreds of years by the time yours was sent."

"Prior to our departure, there had been several scouting expeditions to locations the gods indicated as suitable for us. The scouts were Kra-ell, but the gods provided the ships and programmed their destinations."

"Did your queen receive reports from Earth?" Mia asked.

"Supposedly she did, and the reports were positive, but I doubt that. The allure of coming to Earth was the compatible females our males could breed with, but the scouts must have realized that they weren't really compatible and that the second generation was born human. I'm sure they reported it, and our queen hid that information."

"Why would she do that," Mey asked, "if the idea was to establish a self-sustaining colony, and it wasn't about getting rid of undesirables? From what I've heard so far, the Kra-ell didn't seem to have a problem executing criminals or rebels."

Why did everyone assume that the Kra-ell were savages? They were aggressive, and in the distant past they might indeed have been savage, but so were the humans.

Hell, they still were, despite the gods' attempts to civilize them.

Jade glared at the female. "We only executed the worst of criminals. Those who harmed children or murdered innocent victims. Other transgressors could redeem themselves in several ways."

"Like fighting to the death?" Jin asked. "That's the same as execution."

"It is not when the opponents are equally matched. Can we please change the subject? I don't appreciate having to defend the Kra-ell traditions and way of life to someone who knows nothing about them."

"I might know more than you think." Jin flashed her a smile that revealed a pair of canines that were long enough to be considered fangs.

Jade leaned forward. "Female gods don't have fangs. Did their immortal descendants mutate?"

"They didn't." Mey put a hand on her sister's shoulder. "We suspect that we are hybrids. Part Kra-ell and part immortal. One of the females in your old compound must have been a dormant immortal, and she had us with one of your hybrids."

"What nonsense is that? You couldn't have been born in my compound or fathered by one of my hybrids."

After Mey and Jin exchanged glances, Jin frowned at Jade. "How do you know that we weren't? You gave the children of the hybrids up for adoption when they were babies. We probably looked a lot different back then."

"There was only one girl ever born to a hybrid male and a human female, and she stayed in the compound. I would have never given a girl up for adoption."

"Why not?" Jin asked. "Because you considered girls superior? Not that I disagree, but I admit that it's sexist."

Jade's lips twitched with a smile. Jin reminded her of Kagra. She was gutsy and irreverent.

"Well, there is that. But my reasons were more pragmatic. Humans are not like Kra-ell, and for their community to function properly, they need the ratio of males to females to be nearly equal. Since our males, purebloods as well as hybrids, produce predominately male children, I had no choice but to give the human boys up for adoption. Back then, China had a one-child policy, and since their society was highly patriarchal, families wanted sons who could carry on the family name. There was an abundance of baby girls in orphanages. Baby boys were highly prized and snatched immediately, while baby girls could only hope for adoption by foreigners. At first, it seemed like a reasonable solution, but when I realized that it caused undue suffering to the mothers, I forbade the hybrid males to produce children at all and solved the imbalance problem that way. Human children were fathered only by human males, ensuring an equal gender distribution in their population."

21

PHINAS

*P*hinas observed the sisters, curious to hear their response to Jade's pragmatic and cold solution, but they seemed too stunned to say a thing.

Yamanu was the one to break the silence. "I hate to admit it, but what you did makes sense. Once those boys reached maturity, you couldn't release them, and having too many human males for the number of human females within the compound would have caused unrest. There was already too much competition for their favors from the purebloods and hybrids. You could have abducted more human females for them, but that would have been even worse. On the other hand, though, you created unrest among the hybrids. Having no hope of ever producing offspring was depressing, and they must have disobeyed your orders with women outside the compound." He turned to Mey and Jin. "That's the only explanation for how you were born. One of Jade's hybrids must have had relations with a woman outside the compound, something happened to the mother, and that's how you ended up in an orphanage."

"I doubt that," Jade said. "The hybrids didn't roam free and do whatever they pleased. The only two who had such an opportunity were Vrog and Veskar. Vrog was working in Singapore on my behalf, and Veskar ran off. Vrog was lucky enough to find one of your females and produce a long-lived child, and Veskar might still do that with his mate, but they are the only two exceptions."

"The other hybrids must have found a way to dally with local women." Mey handed Yamanu her glass for a refill. "It's too much of a coincidence that we were given up for adoption in the same area your tribe was located."

Jade cast her an indulgent look. "The Beijing area is enormous. It's possible that the survivors of another pod were located there, and we didn't know about each other."

Phinas put his glass down and turned to face her. "Statistically speaking, Mey's scenario is more likely than yours. The odds of another pod landing in the same area as yours are negligible, but the odds of desperate hybrid males finding a way to procreate is significant."

Jin shook her head. "So why were we given up for adoption? If our father was so desperate for children, wouldn't he want to keep us even if our mother died?"

"Maybe they both died?" Yamanu offered. "Did you lose any of your hybrid males?"

Jade's lips twisted in a grimace. "I lost all of them, but not before Igor's attack. Your father wasn't one of mine."

"Could it have been a pureblood?" Mia asked. "Both of you display Kra-ell characteristics."

"We didn't have them before our transition," Mey said. "But we were born with very special talents." She shifted her gaze to Jade. "Were any of your hybrids able to watch and listen to echoes of past conversations embedded in walls?"

Jade frowned. "I've never heard of anyone with such a talent. Can you do that?"

Mey nodded. "I did it in your old compound. I saw you and Kagra get into a fight. You nearly demolished the storage room."

A smile bloomed on Jade's face. "I remember that fight." Then her smile turned back into a frown. "That's an amazing ability to have. You probably got it from your Dormant mother because no Kra-ell can do that."

Yamanu handed Mey her refilled glass. "None of ours can do that either. Mey and Jin's abilities are one of a kind."

Jade shifted her attention to Jin. "Is your talent the same as your sister's?"

"Mine is better." Jin smiled fondly at Mey. "I can tether a string of my consciousness to anyone I touch and hear and see what they hear and see. I'm the perfect spy."

Jade recoiled. "Did you do that to me?"

"I didn't touch you, did I?"

"And you're not going to."

"I don't tether people just for kicks and giggles. It's draining and often disturbing. I might tune in while the person is on the toilet or when they are having sex. I only keep a tether to loved ones whom I worry about, and I only tune in once in a while to check that they are okay."

Mey put her glass on the table and leaned over to take her sister's hand. "Jin keeps our adoptive parents tethered at all times. They are both healthy, but they are elderly, and they live far away."

"Did you ever use your talent for spying?" Jade asked.

"I did, and it cost me dearly. I'm not going to do it again unless lives are at stake and my tether can help save them."

Arwel, who'd been quiet the entire time, put an arm around his mate's shoulders. "It turned out great, though. Kalugal and Jacki found each other, and Kalugal and his men joined the clan." He shifted his eyes to Phinas. "Aren't you glad that Jin tethered your boss?"

"I am. Moving in with the clan was mostly an improvement."

Yamanu arched a brow. "Mostly? In what way was it not?"

"Privacy, for one thing. Your village is a hive of gossip, and everyone is in everyone else's business."

Letting out a sigh, Mey lifted her glass to her lips and took a sip. "Jin and I thought we had the mystery of our origins figured out, and now we are back to square one."

Next to Phinas, Jade shifted so she was facing Mey. "Your father might have been a descendant of one of the scouts. The scouting missions were a one-way ticket, so to speak. The scouts had to survive wherever they landed and report back using the gods' communication satellites." She looked at Toven. "The Earth satellites must have been destroyed before you were born because you said that your people had lost the ability to communicate with home thousands of years ago."

Toven looked surprised. "I thought that the gods had a ship orbiting Earth and that the ship was the relay, but now that I think back, I remember seeing a depiction of satellites."

"A ship could be a relay, but they probably had satellites too. Otherwise, how did the scouts report to the queen?"

"Makes sense," Mey said. "We suspect that the scouts lived in the area of the Mosuo people and influenced their culture. One of their descendants could have found his way to the Beijing area and met our mother, who just happened to be a Dormant." She smiled. "Apparently, the special affinity immortals and Dormants feel toward each other extends to the Kra-ell. We shouldn't be surprised by that. After all, we originated from the same root species on the same planet."

22

JADE

"We should do what I first suggested," Mey said. "We should start with the orphanage. Yamanu can thrall the bureaucrats to provide us access to our files. We are not that old, so they should still have them."

"How old are you?" Jade asked and regretted it as soon as the words had left her mouth.

She didn't really care how old they were, and asking for their age would only lead to more talking when she wanted to be done and leave.

"I'm twenty-eight," Mey said. "Jin is twenty-four."

They were so young and mated to immortal males who were centuries older. Not that Jade knew for a fact that Yamanu and Arwel were that old, but she had a feeling that they were.

As she listened with half an ear to Jin and Mey come up with several more ideas for investigating their past, none of them promising, Jade glanced at Tom and noted the faraway look in his eyes. He wasn't listening either and seemed preoccupied. Throughout the get-together, Jade had caught him looking at her as if he wanted to ask her something and then changed his mind and looked away.

Maybe he thought she had more secrets to impart about the gods?

The truth was that she'd told him most of what she knew. She could have gone into more detail about the stages of the Kra-ell emancipation, but she doubted he was interested in their side of the story.

322

He wanted to find out more about his people's history, but she could only tell him the Kra-ell's version of it, which wasn't complimentary and probably wasn't accurate either.

When the sisters finally ran out of ideas, Tom rose to his feet. "It's getting late, and Mia and I are tired. Thank you for inviting us and for the lovely evening."

Jade could have kissed him for that.

Pushing to her feet, she murmured her thanks and added a goodnight.

"Goodnight, everyone," Phinas said.

Once they were finally alone in the elevator, Jade sighed in relief. "That was intense."

"It was." Phinas reached for her hand and pulled her to him. "We are alone, so there's no reason for you to brush me off. There is no public here to witness our display of physical affection."

Jade lifted her eyes to the camera, but the truth was that she didn't care if what happened in the elevator was recorded or if someone was monitoring the live feed.

Maybe it was the alcohol's fault.

Yamanu had kept refilling her glass, and Jade had kept drinking long after she should have stopped.

She hadn't appreciated the sisters' accusations even though they were justified. She might not have given them up for adoption, but she'd given up several boys before forbidding the hybrids to father children. She still felt guilty about it, even though it had been the logical thing to do.

She couldn't have risked releasing the women with their babies and everything they'd known about the Kra-ell. Compelling them to keep it a secret would have kept their tongues tied for a while, but not indefinitely, and if they'd started talking about vampiric aliens, they would have been committed to mental institutions.

Besides, even if she could do that, the women had nowhere to go.

They had a life in the compound, they were safe, and at the time, life outside of its walls had been much harsher than inside of them, especially for single mothers.

Leaning into Phinas, she pressed her lips to his and kissed him. The taste of the whiskey he'd drunk wasn't unpleasant, and as it mingled with the taste of the vodka and cranberry in her mouth, it became sweeter. "Mmm," she murmured into his mouth. "You taste good."

His eyes turned into a pair of projectors, and his fangs made an appearance. "You promised to take from me tonight. Are you hungry?"

The elevator door opening delayed her answer for a brief moment. "I seem to be always hungry for you, but not in the way you think."

A smirk lifted one corner of his mouth. "Are you hungry for my hunky body?"

His physique was very appealing, and although he was much bulkier than the slim-built Kra-ell purebloods she was used to, she didn't mind that his body was different or that he looked so much like his godly ancestors, whom she'd despised.

Frankly, her view of them had changed after meeting Tom. He was not terribly conceited, and unlike his ancestors he was an honorable male who stood by his word and kept his promises.

As Jade opened the door to her cabin, Phinas didn't follow her inside. Instead, he stood at her doorway with one hand bracing on the doorjamb and the other on his hip. "You didn't answer me."

She reached for his shirt and tugged him toward her. "You are very handsome, and you know that. So why do you ask?"

He kicked the door closed behind him. "You know that you're beautiful, and you still like it when I tell you that."

"I don't always feel beautiful." She wrapped her arms around him. "But you always make me feel like I am even when you don't say it. I can see it in your eyes and smell it on your skin." She sniffed the spot where his neck met his shoulder. "So male and so virile. It's hard to believe that your fertility is so low."

If he were a Kra-ell pureblood, she would have invited him to her bed based on his smell alone. It was intoxicating to her, which in the Kra-ell culture was believed to indicate that their bodies were well-matched to produce a child.

He lifted her by her bottom and carried her to the bedroom. "Miracles do happen from time to time." He put her down on the bed and sat beside her. "Would you want to have a hybrid child with me, though? I thought that breeding with gods was a big no-no and that a child resulting from such a union was considered an abomination in your world."

"We are not in my world, and you are not a god." She unzipped her jacket, shrugged it off, and put it on the nightstand. "Besides, it's not in the cards. I'm not in my fertile cycle."

"Good. I want to ravish you tonight."

She liked the sound of that.

"I thought that you wanted to be the one to get ravished tonight." Whipping her shirt over her head, she tossed it on top of the jacket and lay back on the bed to unzip her leather pants.

23

PHINAS

he sight of Jade's dark turgid nipples straining toward him had Phinas's mouth water and his fangs punch all the way down over his lower lip.

Without any conscious thought, he shifted his body over hers.

Bracing on his forearms, he looked down at her gorgeous face and the smile that was more than just a lifting of her lush lips. It was in her enormous eyes and the softness of her facial features, and if he didn't know better, he would have thought that she was looking at him lovingly.

Right. The best he could hope for was lust and companionship, and that was enough.

Perhaps Jade was right, and love was an elusive and misleading term, a romanticized expression that described a combination of survival instincts that were hardwired into the human and humanoid psyche.

Spreading her legs, she made room to accommodate his body. "Shouldn't you get undressed?"

"I need to do this first." Tugging off the elastic holding her ponytail, he spread the long, black tresses over the white duvet. "Beautiful."

She chuckled throatily. "You needed to play with my hair?"

"I want to play with all of this." He cupped her cheeks and took her lips in a soft kiss.

Banding her arms around him, she kissed him back, her long tongue pushing into his mouth and doing wicked things to his fangs.

With a groan, he drifted his hand down and palmed her breast, rubbing the stiff nipple in slow, gentle circles.

When Jade arched up and pushed her pants down, he lifted a few inches off her to give her room to maneuver, and when he heard her leathers hit the floor, he let go of her mouth and slid down her body while trailing kisses on her neck, her shoulder, her collarbone, and finally taking a nipple between his lips.

The moan that left her throat was a feral growl he'd only ever heard from her and wouldn't mind hearing for the rest of his life.

As the realization stunned him, he pushed that thought into a corner of his mind to examine later. Right now, his hormones were in charge of his brain, and he wasn't thinking clearly.

Smoothing his hand down her body, he noted the differences between her and every other woman he'd ever been with. She was slim and muscular, her body long and hard, but her skin was silky soft, and she was all female to him.

When his hand reached her center, and he found her bare and moist, he hissed and plunged a finger into her wetness. "I need some of that." He shifted down until he was kneeling on the floor between her spread legs.

Jade didn't object when he lifted her legs over his shoulders and started feasting on her. Sucking and rubbing, he brought her to an orgasm in mere moments, and while she lay languid from her release, he got rid of his clothes and got on top of her.

The moment he was in position, Jade dug her fingers into his buttocks and thrust up with her hips, impaling herself on his length.

They both groaned, and as he started moving, she lifted her hand, clamped it around the back of his neck, and twisted them over, so she was on top of him.

With her eyes blazing red and her fangs on full display, Phinas knew what was coming next and nearly climaxed just from the anticipation. Holding back with an effort, he turned his head sideways and offered her his neck.

The moment her fangs struck his vein, his eyes rolled back in his head, and his shaft spasmed. When he thrust up into her, the wild sound she made had him shoot his load into her welcoming heat, but he wasn't done, not by a long shot.

Hard as if he hadn't released a moment ago, he thrust up into her again and again, and still she drank, the sucking noises and the sensation of pulling bringing him to another orgasm in minutes while pulling one out of her as well.

When her tremors subsided, Jade retracted her fangs, licked the puncture wounds closed, and then lay on top of him, warm, spent, and satiated.

Leisurely caressing her slim back, her rounded bottom, and the silky strands of hair strewn everywhere, Phinas felt himself drifting away on a cloud of bliss.

Was that how Jade felt when he bit her?

Her venom wasn't nearly as strong as his, so he was probably feeling only a fraction of that, but it was still incredible.

She kissed the spot she'd bitten. "I still think I like it better when it's you doing the biting. Your venom is addictive."

He chuckled. "Give me a moment to recuperate, and I'll return the favor. Right now, I'm floating."

She lifted her head and looked down at him. "Do you like the floaty feeling?"

He laughed. "Are you kidding me? This is the best I ever felt." He tightened his arms around her. "How did my blood taste to you?"

"Amazing." She pushed up and kissed him, thrusting her tongue into his mouth.

The coppery taste wasn't as offensive as he'd expected, and thinking of Jade at his throat had him harden again.

He flipped them over and looked down at her. "Are you ready for another round?"

She lifted her hips and rubbed against his erection. "Are you?"

"What does it feel like?"

"It feels like you are. Give it to me, lover boy."

"Just lover." He pushed into her in one long thrust. "It's been a very long time since anyone called me a boy."

A smirk twisted her gorgeous lips. "Give it to me, my immortal lover. Is that better?"

"It still needs work." He pulled out and surged back in.

"Give it to me, lover mine."

"That's perfect."

24

SYSSI

"Ah." Allegra pointed at the spoon in Syssi's hand.

"Yes, I know. It's so yummy." Syssi scooped up more cereal and lifted it to her daughter's mouth.

Pressing her lips closed, her baby girl shook her head. "Ah!" She pointed at the spoon again.

Understanding finally dawning, Syssi asked, "Do you want to hold the spoon?"

"Poon." Allegra nodded.

"Okay." Syssi put it in her little hand.

Smiling her thanks, Allegra gripped it tightly, and with a determined look dipped it in the cereal, but she didn't have the coordination to actually scoop anything up. Undeterred, she lifted the spoon to her mouth and licked whatever cereal had adhered to it.

The sound of the door opening had them both turn to look, and as Kian entered the kitchen, Allegra lifted her spoon triumphantly.

"Dada! Poon!"

"My big girl is eating with a spoon!" He walked up to her and kissed her cheeks despite the cereal smeared all over them. "I'm so proud of you."

"Dada." She dipped the spoon in the cereal and lifted it to her mouth.

"I see. Good job, sweetie." He turned to Syssi. "Will she manage to get any food down like that?"

"I've already fed her mashed carrots and peas. The cereal is her dessert."

Kian chuckled. "I'm surprised that she's not demanding you-know-what."

Allegra loved cookies, but Syssi was trying to limit how many of them she ate a day.

"I'll let her have one later."

"Master! You're home." Okidu rushed into the kitchen as he did every day around the time Kian usually came home for dinner, but lately he'd been disappointed a couple of times when Kian stayed in the war room. "I shall serve dinner expeditiously."

"I'll just wash my hands." Kian went over to the kitchen sink to do that.

"How did your meeting with Kalugal go?" Syssi asked.

"It went well. I offered him two seats on the council. Naturally, it's not final until the council approves the additional seats, but I don't anticipate any objections."

"Oh, wow. I didn't expect that. How did it come to pass?"

It wasn't the first time that Kian had rushed to implement a suggestion she made without thinking it through, and she should have learned her lesson to be more specific.

When she'd suggested that he should talk with Kalugal, she hadn't expected it to go as far as inviting him to join the council.

"As we talked, I realized that Kalugal didn't want to remain an outsider and wished to become an integral part of the clan. We promised each other complete transparency, with him allowing the clan full access to his business dealings and us allowing the same to him, but he keeps his profits and we keep ours. That's the only separation remaining, at least for now. Perhaps the next generation will decide to combine resources." He smiled at Allegra. "Right, sweetheart? When you mate Darius, you will combine us into one big family."

"Kian," Syssi assumed her admonishing tone. "I don't want you to say that even jokingly. Kids are impressionable, and Allegra might grow up thinking she's expected to mate with Darius. I want her to feel free to choose whomever she pleases."

He reached for her hand. "I want my daughter to find love as formidable as ours. Nothing less than a truelove mate will do for our princess. I was just teasing, but if you think my teasing might influence Allegra's future decisions, I'll either never do that again or change the name of her future mate so many times that she would know for sure it wasn't serious."

"Thank you." Syssi squeezed his hand. "Back to Kalugal, though. I'm surprised that both of you made such huge concessions in a few hours of negotiations. Perhaps you went too far too soon?"

Kian frowned. "I thought that was what you wanted me to do."

"That's the end result I was hoping for. I just thought it would take more time and involve a transition period. You know that I don't like rushing into things."

"I know." He leaned over and kissed her cheek. "I, on the other hand, like to move things off my to-do list as quickly as I can."

"I hope it will work out well for all of us." She sighed. "What's new with the Kra-ell situation?"

"Not much. That's why I'm home for dinner. We are waiting for Igor to make his move."

"Did you decide what to do with them?"

"Dada." Allegra held out the spoon to him.

He shifted his gaze to her. "Do you want me to give you the cereal?"

She nodded.

Kian moved to the chair on her other side, took the spoon, and fed their daughter. "I'm waiting to see what will happen with Igor. If we eliminate him, the Kra-ell can return to their compound."

"Didn't Turner advise against leaving them where you can't keep an eye on them?"

"He did, but I don't want them in the village, and I don't know what else to do with them. Along with the humans, there are over three hundred of them. That's a lot of people. If we were talking about one or two, I might have offered them sanctuary here, but I can't bring in a group of people almost equal in size to ours. Even if it wasn't a huge security risk, they would still drastically change the demographics of the village and our way of life. I don't want that. I'm happy with how things are now."

Syssi had a different opinion, but she was afraid to voice it lest Kian rushed to implement it like he had done with Kalugal. She needed to be careful about what she said to him.

25

KIAN

*S*yssi looked like she wanted to add something, but she was hesitating for some reason, and Kian didn't like it. She should feel comfortable saying anything to him, and the idea that he might still intimidate her in some way soured his mood.

He thought they were long past that point.

Then again, Syssi only appeared timid to those who didn't know her because she was soft-spoken and preferred to avoid confrontations. But he knew better. If she wanted to say something or effect a change, she simply waited for an opportune moment when she knew that her suggestions would be received with an open mind.

Except, he didn't understand why she thought now was a bad time to bring up whatever was on her mind. Perhaps she thought he was too busy? Or maybe he'd voiced his position on the Kra-ell too decisively, and she figured out that he needed more time to mull it over before bringing it up?

Kian waited until Okidu served them dinner to ask her.

"You don't seem to agree with my stance on the Kra-ell issue."

"I think we need to evaluate the pros and cons and come up with several alternative solutions. But first, we need to know more about these people. Vrog, Aliya, and Emmett integrated easily into our community, so maybe inviting the Kra-ell to join us wouldn't change things too much. Instead of discussing it with Turner, you should talk with the people who are actually spending time with the Kra-ell and ask their opinions. Also, I'm curious about the humans that came with them and what they want to do once they are free. They already know about aliens, and they can't be thralled to forget them. They can be compelled, but we know that compulsion needs to be reinforced from time to time, so it's actually safer to keep them contained within the village than to let them loose somewhere."

As usual, Syssi distilled the problem to its essence and addressed it both logically and compassionately.

Kian leaned over the table and clasped her hand. "You are so wise, my love."

"Mama," Allegra said in a tone that sounded like confirmation.

Kian smiled at her sweet little face. "Our daughter thinks so too."

"She understands every word we say." Syssi leaned over and kissed Allegra's cheek.

"I believe she does."

Leaning back in her chair, Syssi wound a lock of hair around her finger. "To be frank, I have an ulterior motive, and I'm not thinking only about the Kra-ell plight. I'm thinking about a group of two hundred warrior-like people who can shore up our defenses. If we can trust them, and if they learn to trust us, we will be stronger together. Of course, Igor has to be dealt with first. It would be too dangerous for us to bring them here if he's still around."

"You realize that along with the humans they would outnumber us. Where would we even house them?"

"They would have to be satisfied with living two to a bedroom." She chuckled. "After getting used to the luxury of the cruise ship, it would be an adjustment for them."

"Most of the village homes have only two bedrooms, so that's four to a house. To house three hundred and twenty people, we need eighty houses. We don't have that many available."

"What if you add a bedroom to each of the available ones? The lots can accommodate an addition of even two bedrooms."

"It would take time, and it would be messy, but it's doable. I could move whoever is still living in phase two back to the original village, fence phase two off, and add two bedrooms to each of the houses. Then I could annex phase two to Kalugal's section like Turner suggested and make them Kalugal's headache. Instead of one village, we would have two, and then I only need to worry about security and not about changing the way we live."

Syssi arched a brow. "We were talking about establishing trust. That won't happen if you try to keep them contained."

"It would have to do in the beginning, but we are getting ahead of ourselves. I haven't talked with Yamanu and Toven yet, and even if they are in favor, it's not a decision that I can make without the council's approval. In fact, this requires the unanimous vote of the big assembly."

"Not if you declare it a security issue." Syssi smirked. "You've used that loophole successfully many times before."

His sweet wife had a devious mind, and she wasn't wrong, but he couldn't use that loophole to cram the Kra-ell down his people's throats without earning their resentment, and rightly so.

"It is definitely a security issue, but given the massive impact on our community, not putting it to a vote wouldn't be fair. I would have a rebellion on my hands."

"Dada." Allegra nodded in agreement.

"You see?" He waved a hand at their daughter. "Even the baby agrees that it should be a clan-wide vote."

Syssi regarded Allegra with a smile. "Our daughter is an old sage housed in a baby's body. We'd better heed her advice."

"I'm going to make the calls from my office. Do you want to join and have Okidu watch Allegra?"

Syssi pushed to her feet and pulled a wet wipe from the box. "Perhaps we should let her listen so she can offer us her opinion." She wiped Allegra's cheeks and hands. "Do you want to go to Daddy's office, sweetie?"

"No." Allegra pointed her finger at the television.

Kian laughed. "She knows that Okidu will let her watch as much as she wants."

"Du!" Allegra called.

Okidu dropped the plate he'd been washing into the sink and rushed over. "Yes, Mistress Allegra. How can I serve you?"

"Ah." She pointed at the television.

"Of course." He pulled her out of the highchair and carried her to the couch. "What will it be? *The Wiggles*? Or *Paw Patrol*?"

"We-we." Allegra bounced her bottom on the couch.

"*Wiggles* it is." Okidu clicked the television on.

"Come on." Kian took Syssi's hand. "Let's seize the opportunity that we have a few minutes alone to play footsie in my office."

She laughed. "You're incorrigible."

"But you love me despite that."

"I think I love you because of that. If you are still playful at your advanced age, you'll always be."

When Kian closed his office door behind them, Syssi stretched on her toes and kissed his cheek. "Phone calls first. Footsie later."

Kian grinned. "I've just realized that it's four in the morning over there." Cupping her bottom with both hands and hoisting her up, he flattened her against his chest and straining erection. "Do you think Allegra knew that when she said no?"

Syssi laughed. "I think she knew all along that you wanted to play with Mommy, and she graciously bowed out."

TOVEN

"$\mathcal{I}$ haven't had breakfast yet." Yamanu cradled the cup of coffee Toven had made for him. "I'm good for nothing on an empty stomach."

"It must be important." Toven sat between Yamanu and Arwel on the couch. "Kian texted me an hour ago and asked to speak with the three of us first thing in the morning." He positioned the tablet on the coffee table, so the camera got all three of their faces. "I told him we would be ready for him at six in the morning, so he wouldn't have to wait for us to finish breakfast first."

Mia was still asleep in the bedroom, and he planned to return to her as soon as the phone call was over.

His tablet rang at precisely six in the morning, and as he accepted the call, he was surprised to see Syssi next to Kian instead of Onegus and Turner.

"Good evening," he greeted them.

Arwel nodded.

"It's morning here," Yamanu said. "What's so urgent?"

"There is no real urgency. I need to hear your opinion of the Kra-ell in general and Jade in particular. What kind of people are they?"

"They are people." Yamanu shrugged. "Despite their spartan proclivities, they are just like any other community. Some are nicer than others, some are friendlier, and some are less so, and they are all anxious about their future."

Kian shifted his gaze to Arwel. "What's your take on them?"

"They are guarded and don't show emotions, but that doesn't mean that they don't have them." He smiled. "They are more like the Klingons than the Vulcans, but they are better behaved and not as hot-headed. I'm still not sure about Jade, though. She might have some Ferengi in her. She's a good negotiator."

The names sounded familiar to Toven, but he didn't remember where he'd heard them. Obviously, the Klingons, Vulcans, and Ferengi must be fictional people.

"*Star Trek*," Yamanu whispered in his ear.

"Oh. Now I remember where I heard those names before."

Toven wasn't a fan of the show, but it had become such an integral part of Western culture that most people got the reference even if they'd never watched the show or the movies.

Syssi leaned forward. "What we are trying to find out is whether the Kra-ell are trustworthy and whether bringing them to the village is an option. You've been around them for a while now, and we hoped you could give us an assessment."

Arwel shook his head. "I don't feel comfortable recommending one way or another. Perhaps Edna should run a probe on each individual and find out their motives."

"You should talk with Phinas," Toven said. "He's gotten very close to Jade, and he probably knows her better than any of us."

"Yeah," Yamanu seconded that. "We had a get-together in our cabin last evening, and the two of them seemed very cozy with each other, which is strange since the Kra-ell don't commit to just one partner. I've been watching them, and they really don't form couples. The males hang out with each other, the females do the same, and the young children split their time between their mothers and fathers like children of divorced parents."

"Except for Drova and Pavel," Toven said. "I've seen them sitting together in the dining hall, sipping on coffee and talking quietly. I think they are plotting something."

"Plotting what?" Kian asked.

"Probably a rebellion against Jade." Yamanu chuckled. "Either that or they are just two young people finding comfort in each other's company. By the way, we found out that Mey and Jin were not born in Jade's tribe, and she doesn't think they were fathered by any of her hybrids. The hybrids breed predominantly boys, and there was only one girl born in her compound to a hybrid father and a human mother, and Jade didn't give her up for adoption. She only gave up the boys to prevent gender disparity among her human subjects, which she knew would have led to problems, and when she realized how terribly the mothers suffered as a result, she forbade the hybrids to father children with the humans at all."

"So, who could their father have been?" Syssi asked.

"We speculated about it for hours." Yamanu took a sip from his coffee. "The only logical assumption is that he was a descendant of the scouts, and he made his way from Lugu Lake to the Beijing area. Mey and Jin want to check out the orphanage they were adopted from, and they want me to thrall the people in charge to release the files to them. Do I have permission to do that?"

"Of course, you do." Kian waved a hand. "It's crucial that we find out whether their parents are still alive and whether they have other relatives. We might find more Dormants and more hybrid Kra-ell, but it will have to wait."

"Naturally." Yamanu took another sip from his coffee.

Leaning against Kian's arm, Syssi said, "It's interesting how our view of Jade changes the more we find out about her. She's not the terrible and ruthless person we believed her to be. She seems to have always done what she believed was best for her community. It's a lesson to be learned not to prejudge people before getting to know them."

"I agree," Toven said. "But I think that in Igor's case, the mountain of evidence against him is decisive. I'm not sure about Valstar, though. He and the other males of Igor's pod didn't know Igor before getting on board the ship, and no one appointed him the leader. The moment he and his pod members woke up from stasis, he took over and compelled them to obey him. None of them had a say in it. The bottom line is that I think he and the others deserve a fair trial before we let Jade execute him."

"It's not our call," Kian said. "It's Jade's. If you can persuade her to give Valstar a fair trial, that's great. But if she's adamant about executing him, it's her prerogative."

Toven shook his head. "We are in charge, and if we can stop it, we should. We have a moral obligation."

"No, we don't." Kian regarded him with a hard look. "Unless the Kra-ell become part of our community, accept clan law, and vow to keep our rules, we shouldn't intervene in their affairs."

"But we already did," Toven insisted. "Without us helping to free the compound, Valstar wouldn't be facing his execution."

"It's a difficult call," Syssi said. "We should discuss this with Edna."

It was kicking the can down the road, but Toven was fine with that. His gut instinct was to intervene on Valstar's behalf, but his gut had steered him wrong in the past, so it wasn't all that reliable.

"I have no problem letting Edna decide." Toven put his cup down on the coffee table. "In any case, it's not an urgent matter because we don't have Igor yet, and Valstar enjoys a stay of execution until we do."

2 7

JADE

*O*nce again, Jade woke up with Phinas's body wrapped around hers, but this time they were in her cabin and not his. Not that it made much of a difference.

It felt just as good and just as sinful.

Spending every night with Phinas was a dangerous habit, and she should stop before she got so used to it that she couldn't fall asleep without him.

Except, it was too damn good to give up.

She liked falling asleep in his arms after he left her satiated and languid, and she liked waking up pressed against his big, warm body.

There must be something wrong with her that she was enjoying such an un-Kra-ell connection with a male. He aroused her with such surprising ease and without fighting for dominance that she was starting to suspect that it had something to do with his inherited enhanced genetics.

There had been rumors about the gods manipulating their genes to produce powerful pheromones and increase their libido to compensate for their low fertility. It would have been simpler to change their genetics to increase their fertility, but she had to admit that their solution was more fun. They'd just made themselves constantly horny.

Gently untangling their limbs, she slid away from him, but she didn't get far.

His eyes popping open, he shot an arm around her and pulled her back against his chest. "Where do you think you're going?"

"It's time to get up." She pushed on his pectorals, copping a feel while she was at it.

"Today, you are getting your first swimming lesson, and I don't want to hear any arguments about why you can't make it."

She grimaced. "Not now. I need to see how Merlin is doing with the implant removal. I assigned Morgada to assist the nurse with tending to the patients after the removal, and Pavel to help Merlin with the MRI and the detection. I need to check on their progress."

Phinas frowned at her. "We are running out of time, and your people need to learn to swim or at least float. As soon as we leave the Baltic, Igor will attack, and he might succeed in sinking the ship. I hope it will not happen and that the sub will get him before he gets us, but we need to be prepared."

"Fine. I'll have Kagra arrange our people in shifts. How many can you teach simultaneously, and how long will each lesson take?"

"I can probably fit twenty people in that pool, and the lessons will be forty minutes long. I'm going to run the first one, and then my men will take over. Since you are their leader, you should go first, not Kagra."

Jade stifled a wince. "They don't need me to lend them the courage to get into a pool that's less than two meters deep."

"Perhaps that's true, but you need to get into that pool sometime today."

She wasn't looking forward to her dunking in the freezing water, and the longer she managed to postpone it, the better. Phinas was right about the need to teach her people to float and swim, but it was more important that the others learn first.

If she got lucky, by the time her turn arrived the submarine would take out the Russian cruiser, and she wouldn't have to set foot in that pool.

"I don't have a swimming suit," she tried another evasive tactic.

"Neither do the others. You can go in a bra and panties."

Jade smirked. "I don't have a bra. Do you want me to swim topless? I have no problem with that."

He pulled her tighter against him. "So wear a T-shirt. No one gets to see my woman naked but me."

"I'm not your woman."

He squeezed her bottom. "Yes, you are."

"I'm not."

"You are. You're just too stubborn to admit it. I want you at the pool at four o'clock. That's enough time for you to do everything you had planned for today."

"It will be dark by then."

"So come earlier."

"I can't."

"Then you'll swim in the moonlight. Besides, the top deck has outdoor lighting. Enough with the excuses. If you are not there by four, I will come to get you, and I'll haul you to the pool if I have to carry you over my shoulder."

"You can try," she issued a challenge. "You can't make me."

"I'll find a way. I'll rope you in like a bull in a rodeo, tie you up, and throw you over my shoulder."

She'd heard about the so-called sport. Bulls were stronger than people, but they were dumb. Did he think she would be as easily overpowered as a bull? She was a well-trained warrior.

"Good luck with that. I'm not a bull."

"You're stubborn like one, and you are afraid of water."

"I'm not afraid of it." She pulled out of his arms and got out of bed. "I just don't like it."

Smiling, Phinas patted the spot she'd vacated. "I was just teasing. I know that the formidable Jade is not afraid of anything. Now come back in here and show me how strong you are." He spread his arms, his muscular chest and bulging biceps an invitation she found hard to resist. "Take me, use me. I'm yours."

Damn. How could she say no to that?

How did he manage to get under her armor and obliterate her resolve with such ease?

"You're such a smooth talker." She pounced on him. "Kiss me, lover mine."

2 8

PHINAS

"See you later, gorgeous." Phinas stole a quick kiss from Jade before exiting the elevator on the dining hall level.

"You're so bad," she said when the elevator door was closing, but she did it with a smile.

He blew her an air kiss and headed toward the kitchen.

Jade being occupied in the clinic was the perfect opportunity to check on Isla and see how traumatized she was after her talk with her leader.

He found her chopping carrots while chatting with another woman and sounding perfectly fine, but then she'd had enough time to calm down since yesterday.

Instead of approaching her and risking startling her, he looked for the young interpreter, Lana, and when he spotted her, he waved her over.

"Good morning." She wiped her hands with a dish towel. "How can I help you?"

"I want to speak to your mom, but I don't want to startle her while she is chopping things with a big knife. I don't want her to chop off a finger."

"Don't worry." Lana motioned with her head. "She heard you, and she's coming."

As he turned around, Isla offered him her hand. "*Hei*, Phinas."

"Hello, Isla." He turned to Lana. "I want to ask your mom if she's okay after her talk with Jade."

When Lana translated, Isla smiled, gave him the thumbs up, and said something in Finnish to Lana.

"My mom says that Jade is much more reasonable than she expected her to be. Jade promised the same thing you did, which my mom thanked you for. She knows it was because you talked with Jade."

Phinas didn't deny but didn't confirm either. "What did Jade promise you?"

He waited for Lana to ask and for Isla to answer, which took a while.

"Jade said that the purebloods would be allowed to offer the human women incentives for agreeing to breed with them, but they would not be allowed to threaten them in any way or harm them if they refused. What my mother is worried about is the males using their mind tricks to prevent the women from complaining about being harassed. Jade did not have a solution for that, but she promised to think about it."

She could make the male vow it, but the problem was that those young males grew up under Igor's influence, and they didn't follow the Kra-ell traditions. They might not take their vows seriously.

Nevertheless, he was glad to see that Jade hadn't terrorized the woman for voicing her complaint.

As his phone buzzed with an incoming message, he pulled it out of his pocket. It was from the big boss himself, so he needed to respond quickly.

"Thank you." Phinas patted Lana's shoulder. "I have to make a call." He turned to Isla. "Thank you again for the fabulous meals you and the others prepare for us."

When Lana translated, she smiled. "*Ole hyvä.*"

Out in the hallway, Phinas leaned against the wall and made the call. "Hello, Kian."

"Good morning, Phinas. Thank you for responding so quickly. I want to know your opinion of Jade. I was told that the two of you have gotten very close and that you know her better than any of the others."

A smile lifted Phinas's lips. "She's awesome."

Kian chuckled. "I need details."

"Why?"

"I'm contemplating allowing the Kra-ell and their humans into the village. It's not my idea, and I'm not keen on it because I don't know these people and because of their sheer number. Turner thinks that we should keep a close eye on them, and Syssi thinks it's a good idea to have two hundred or so additional strong warriors to protect the village. What's your take on that?"

The question was unexpected, and Phinas didn't have a ready answer to give. All he could do was think out loud.

"Jade is an honorable person, she cares about her people, and she is open to suggestions." He told Kian about Isla's complaint and Jade's response to it.

"That's a good start," Kian said. "She's willing to adapt."

"Up to a certain point, and I don't think she will accept your invitation. After living so long under Igor's thumb, she craves independence. There is also the issue of hunting. I don't think the Malibu mountains have enough wildlife for so many Kra-ell. They are fine with domesticated animals, but from time to time, they need to hunt. Even Igor allowed that, and he wouldn't have if it wasn't a necessity."

"I don't think it's a major consideration. If lions can live in zoos and be satisfied with steak dinners, the Kra-ell will be satisfied with having access to domesticated animals."

"They might not go hungry or thirsty, but will they be happy?"

"Good point. Do you have another suggestion?"

Phinas closed his eyes for a moment. "How large is the plot around the cabin the clan owns in the mountains? Is it big enough to settle over three hundred people?"

"It might be large enough for very modest accommodations, and by that, I mean dormitory-style sleeping arrangements and communal everything. But to build there, we would need to employ the same camouflaging tactics as in the village, and those are costly to install and need trained operators. Besides, if we allow them to roam the area to hunt, we will not be able to monitor them as closely as we would like. I don't think it's an option, but I'll give it some more thought. What about the other Kra-ell? Did you get to know any of them?"

"Kagra is a fine female. She's an exceptional warrior, has a good sense of humor, and is less rigidly traditional than Jade. I like her. I also interacted with two young hybrid males yesterday when I taught them to swim. They were fun, full of mischief, and up to no good, but no more so than any other young men their age. Bear in mind, though, that I only spent an hour or so with them, so my impression is very superficial."

"Of course. I'm not going to make any decisions based on your testimony alone. I'm collecting information, and I'll probably have Edna probe each of them before making my final decision."

Thralling didn't work on the purebloods, not even Toven's. Phinas didn't know how Edna's probe worked, but if it was related to thralling or shrouding, it might not be effective on the Kra-ell.

"Edna might not be able to penetrate the mental shields of the purebloods."

"Good point," Kian agreed. "Perhaps we will need to do that the mundane way and get Vanessa to do a psychological assessment of them."

29

JADE

*J*ade entered the clinic and nodded at Merlin. "How is the removal of the trackers progressing?"

"It's going well." He motioned for her to follow. "We've removed sixteen trackers." He opened a drawer and pulled out three plastic bags. "I found three different types of trackers." He lifted a bag with a tiny thing that was no larger than a puffy grain of rice. "I suspect that this little fellow is the most sophisticated because I took it out of a pureblood." He lifted another bag with a much larger device. "This is second best. I removed two of them from hybrids." He lifted the third bag. "I assume this one is the least sophisticated one because it's the largest, and I removed this type from three humans."

"Didn't we agree that you would remove the trackers from the purebloods first?"

"We did, but I wanted to test my hypothesis, so I asked for two hybrids and two humans, but three humans showed up, so I figured why not?"

"How is Morgada doing? Is she helpful?"

"Very. We wouldn't have been able to remove as many without her help."

It was still too slow.

"Is there any way we can speed this up? What if we get one more person to help the nurse and another one to help with the machine?"

Merlin smoothed his hand over his white beard. "I can ask Marcel to help me with the scanning. I could use someone capable of replacing me, so

I can concentrate on the removal. It will be crucial when we start removing the trackers from humans. Inga is not experienced enough to perform the extraction or to sew them up, and Morgada is even less so. I'll have to do that."

"What about the Kra-ell? Is Inga good enough to take care of them?"

He smiled sheepishly. "They heal fast, and they don't scar, so I let her sew them up. But I still remove the trackers myself because the little buggers are hard to find and to dig out."

It seemed to her that he could use two operators for the MRI and three nurses.

"Who else can operate the machine? I want you to delegate all the scanning to others."

"I can't. I have to see where the small trackers are hidden. Some are embedded so deep that I almost missed them."

"Then Marcel and whoever else is operating the machine can call you once they locate it, so you can see it and proceed right away to remove it."

He nodded. "That's doable. I'll ask Marcel to find another Guardian who can be taught what to do."

"I'll talk with Sofia," Jade said. "Since Marcel will be spending his days in the clinic, she might want to be the third nurse to be close to him."

Merlin looked around the room and sighed. "I don't know where everyone will work, but we will figure it out."

"What's in the rooms adjacent to the clinic? Maybe we can use one of them."

Merlin shrugged. "I don't know."

"I'll find out."

Jade walked out of the room and opened the door to its right. It was a small storage room filled to the brim with boxes.

If they took everything out, they might be able to get a cot or two to fit there, but that wouldn't solve their problem.

She closed the door and headed the other way, opening the door to the left of the clinic.

It was nearly as large as the main room of the clinic where the MRI machine was, and the only thing inside was a stack of chairs. It was probably meant as a waiting room that no one had bothered to organize.

"We can use the room next door," she told Merlin when she returned. "Do you need beds in there?"

"I need a couple, but we don't have more hospital beds. They will have to be regular beds."

348

"The beds are too big." The ones in her cabin, Kagra's and Phinas's were queen-sized.

"Check the staff quarters," Morgada said from the other room. "The beds in there are single-sized and should fit. If we find something to put under the legs to raise them up, they will do nicely as recovery beds."

"Good idea." Jade pivoted on her heel and headed for the door. "I'll get right on it."

30

KIAN

"Thank you for agreeing to see me at this ungodly hour." Kian took the coffee cup Shai handed him. "And thank you for the coffee. I need it." He took a thankful sip as he sat down.

Despite it still being dark outside and despite all the work Shai had been shouldering while Kian had been dealing with the Kra-ell crisis, his assistant managed to look as fresh and well-groomed as ever.

Still, there was a limit to what Kian could delegate to him.

Since the operation had started, Kian's neglected workload had been stacking higher with every passing hour, and some of the open items on his agenda were becoming urgent. He could no longer postpone addressing them in the hopes of a quick resolution.

Two days had passed since the *Aurora* had left Helsinki, and so far, they hadn't identified a pursuing ship. It might take many more days until Igor made his move.

"I don't think we've ever met at five-thirty in the morning before." Shai put down a stack of files on the conference table. "But we did meet in the war room before." He lifted his eyes to Kian. "I don't know why you choose to do everything from here rather than from your office. It's depressing down here." He looked at the bare walls. "I should order some pictures for the place to liven it up."

"It's partly out of habit and partly out of practical considerations.

Onegus's office and the lab are right here, and it makes it easier for them to come and go as needed without having to trek to the office building."

"Makes sense." Shai set his coffee cup down.

"I wanted to carve out some time to interrogate the two hybrids when they get to the keep, but I will probably have to delegate that to Anandur."

Shai nodded. "Anandur can be very intimidating when he wants to be. Do you think his terrifying monster illusion would work on them?"

Kian chuckled. "It has been so long since he used his red demon to scare his opponents that I'm not sure he can even summon it. But it wouldn't help him with the hybrids. After the experiments we conducted with Vrog and Aliya, we concluded that they can see through shrouds because they don't look substantial to them. The purebloods don't see them at all."

"That's a shame." Shai flipped his laptop open and got ready to take notes.

"Let's start with the most urgent item." Kian pulled the stack of files toward him.

Shai pointed at the file on top. "They are stacked according to urgency and importance. The one on top is naturally the top priority."

As Kian dove into the familiar territory of business dealings and read through the file and Shai's notes, he felt the muscles in his shoulders loosen and the tension in his chest abate.

He hadn't realized how much he'd been bothered by all the things that were falling by the wayside while he was dealing with the crisis. It had been gnawing at his gut and contributing to his disquiet. He didn't have to address all the issues in order to relax, but he at least needed to know what they were and whether anything was on the verge of collapse.

As qualified and reliable as the people managing the various clan businesses were, to stay in line they needed to know that someone was watching over them.

By the time Turner walked in, they'd managed to go over nearly half of the pile.

"Am I too early?" Turner glanced at his watch. "We were supposed to meet at seven-thirty, right?"

Kian was surprised at how fast the time had flown. "That's correct. Onegus should be here at any moment, and Kalugal will join us later." He cast an apologetic look at Shai. "I hoped that two hours would suffice, but I'm afraid we will have to continue either later today or tomorrow at the same hour."

Shai pulled the files toward him. "We've actually gone over most of what

I needed your feedback on. I will send you a summary at the end of the day on where things stand and whether anything else needs your attention."

"Very well. We can address that tomorrow morning."

Shai nodded. "I'm at your disposal at any time you can spare." He put the files under his arm, picked up his laptop, and headed for the door.

"Thank you," Kian called after him.

"My pleasure." Shai tucked the laptop under his arm and reached for the door handle.

Reminded of Syssi's coaching about the power of positive feedback, Kian added, "Great work, Shai. I think that I could retire soon and leave all the day-to-day work in your capable hands."

Shai smiled. "I doubt that, but I appreciate the compliment."

Kian mentally patted himself on the back. He was making progress.

As Shai opened the door, Onegus came in, and as the two exchanged greetings, the sound of pounding footsteps had the three of them look at the doorway.

A moment later, Roni rushed in with his laptop partially open. "You will want to see this," he said as he put the laptop on the conference table, flipped it open all the way, and swiveled the screen toward Kian.

It was the same screen he'd shown them two days ago, and Kian recognized the blue dot representing the *Aurora*, but instead of the myriad of other dots previously littering the screen, there were only two aside from the *Aurora*, and both were flashing red.

Kian suspected that they represented possible pursuers, but he didn't want to make assumptions.

"What am I looking at?" he asked.

Looking cockier than ever, Roni grinned. "Captain Olsson's erratic course was more effective than I expected. The course he chose to follow was ingenious. It was so out of whack that the algorithm had no problem identifying the pursuer. The number of potentials hovered above ten for a while, and then it counted down to this." Roni pointed at the screen.

"There are two pursuers?" Onegus asked. "Or is one of them tailing the other?"

Roni smirked. "It looks like we have two vessels following the *Aurora*. Igor is not taking any chances. He wants his people back."

ONEGUS

*A*s Roni touched the flashing red dot closer to the *Aurora*, an information bubble popped up, and he read it out loud. "The *Marshal Anatolov*, a Parchin class Russian, is an anti-sub naval cruiser commanded by Captain Sergey Gorshekov." Roni glanced at Turner before continuing. "It's a 1972 ship that received a systems' upgrade in 1997. It has been keeping a constant distance of twenty nautical miles from the *Aurora*, and it has been adjusting its course, heading, and speed to match every move Captain Olsson was making. The *Anatolov*'s maximum speed is twenty-four knots. It's slower than the *Aurora*, so I assume it will try to get closer to its target before the *Aurora* clears the Baltic into the North Sea and speeds up. The Russian has to attack before the *Aurora* has a chance to widen the gap between them."

Pointing at the second flashing red dot, Onegus asked the question on everyone's mind. "So, who or what is this?"

"That is the million-dollar question, isn't it?" Roni leaned forward again and touched the dot. "Allow me to introduce the *Grand Helena*, a Mangusta Maxi Open 165. That's a thirty-seven knots maximum speed luxury yacht owned by none other than Anatoli Zebneitski, an international weapons dealer oligarch. Since the *Helena* is keeping a significant distance, whoever is on board can apparently track both the *Marshal Anatolov* and the *Aurora* either with a radar system far more robust than what is typically found on a boat of this size, or they have access to the Russian navy's radar tracking system, which I think is more likely. The *Grand Helena* is trailing the Russian cruiser at a forty nautical miles distance, and it is more sophisticated than the *Marshal Anatolov* in how it is trailing both ships. Because of its far superior speed, her captain does not need to remain in lockstep with either of them. He can make assumptions as to their subsequent heading and correct course as needed. In fact, if not for the algorithm, I might have missed *Helena* tracking them altogether."

"Igor must be on board." Kian said what Onegus was thinking.

Turner nodded. "Based on Jade's account of his attack against her tribe, and based on everything else we've learned about him so far, he appears to be super careful, cunning, sophisticated, and tends to lead from behind. His MO doesn't lend itself to him being personally onboard the cruiser. There could be several reasons for that. First, the ultimate fate of the *Anatolov* might be one he wishes to avoid in person. While he has no reason to suspect that we have an armed sub protecting the *Aurora*, he must have considered that it's only a matter of time before the Russian navy will intervene once it realizes that the *Anatolov* went rogue. As soon as they realize that the cruiser is not where it's supposed to be, the Russian naval command will try to regain control of it, and when they fail to do that, they might decide to disable or even sink it. What's certain is that they will board it, and Igor wouldn't want to be anywhere near when that happens. There is also a chance of navies from neighboring countries coming to the aid of the *Aurora* and attempting to overtake the *Anatolov*."

"Maybe the *Anatolov* is supposed to cruise the Baltic," Onegus suggested. "If I were Igor, I would choose a ship that wouldn't be flagged from the get-go, and since he can access the Russian naval command, he must have known which ship to pick. In my opinion, naval command will not be alerted until the *Anatolov* leaves the Baltic. The further the Russian captain is from Mother Russia when he launches his attack on the *Aurora*, the better his odds of success are."

Turner nodded. "That's possible. But even if Igor doesn't expect the Russian Naval command to go after the *Anatolov* before it leaves the Baltic, he would still prefer not to be onboard. As someone who has existed in the shadows for so long, he would not want to take center stage among a large group of human sailors, in close quarters, and for days on end."

"What I can't figure out," Roni said, "is what the hell does he plan to do with a luxury yacht? Observe? Make sure that the Russian is obeying his commands?"

"It makes perfect sense." Kian got up and started pacing. "He believes that no one will suspect the yacht. It is keeping a significant distance and is not following the two ships in a readily recognizable pattern. But since the yacht is fast enough to close the distance in no time, he can take control of the situation and respond to changing circumstances as the need arises."

"What can he do, though?" Roni asked. "It's not like the yacht is carrying torpedoes that it can fire at the *Aurora* or sink the Russian to hide the evidence."

Kian sat back down. "His presence there is essential, either in person or via a short-range video feed that could not be traced to him. That's why he's following with the yacht. There would have been very little he could have done if he stayed behind in Russia, and it would have been a mistake that a sophisticated player like him wouldn't have made. Don't forget that the chess pieces he's moving are not his people, and he doesn't know how capable they are and what he can entrust them with. That's a lack of control that Igor wouldn't have been able to tolerate. Onboard the trailing yacht, though, he can observe, interject, and improvise as the need arises."

Onegus nodded. "There is one more thing that Igor couldn't delegate. Compelling a captain and likely also his top officers to hunt and sink a ship is one thing, but how will they know who to fish out of the water?"

32

TURNER

*K*ian lifted his gaze from the blinking dot on the screen to glance at Turner. "So what do we do about it? How does that affect our plans?"

"I hate to admit it, but the guy is more than just a powerful compeller, and he impresses me with every move he makes on the proverbial chessboard."

Igor was shrewd, calculated, inventive, and employed guerrilla tactics that kept surprising Turner. In fact, the Kra-ell was starting to undermine Turner's confidence in his ability to always see several steps ahead of his adversaries.

Then again, naval battles were not Turner's field of expertise, and neither were aliens with incredible compulsion abilities. Given those mitigating factors, the fact that he was still outmaneuvering the alien was impressive.

"That does not happen often," Kian said. "Should I be worried?"

Turner arched a brow. "He is certainly keeping me on my toes, but I'm still the better player. I anticipated most of his moves and deployed countermeasures." Turner let his lips tilt up in a smile. "That being said, we were hoping that Igor would take the bait, and he did. He has just handed us a way to finally bag him."

"How so?" Onegus asked.

It was Turner's opportunity to boast a little and lift his esteem in their eyes back to where it should be.

He lifted a finger. "First of all, we anticipated his move with the cruiser and deployed a submarine to counter it. We just got confirmation that our assessment was correct. Igor does not suspect that, and he does not have a contingency for it."

When he raised a second finger, Kian's phone buzzed with an incoming message, and as he read it, he lifted his hand. "Hold on for one second. I need to answer this." He typed up a quick text. "My apologies. My mother asked for an update, and I had to respond."

Turner nodded. "Of course. When the Clan Mother asks a question, it must be answered immediately." He lifted two fingers again. "While Igor probably assumes that we will at some point discover the Russian cruiser following the *Aurora*, he has no reason to think that it will happen before she crosses to the North Sea. In fact, he's banking on her not finding out until it is too late. And he certainly doesn't suspect that we know about the yacht."

Roni tapped his laptop. "It would never occur to him because no one has a program like this."

The kid was overconfident. He was a great hacker, perhaps even one of the best, but he wasn't the only one in the world.

Overconfidence was an issue for Turner as well, but he was aware of it and tried to counterbalance it with an abundance of caution. That was why he added, "Even though it's highly unlikely that Igor suspects we are on to him, I have no doubt that he has a contingency plan for escape in case things go sideways. His capture is not going to be easy, but it's possible."

Kian leaned forward. "I can see the wheels in your mind spinning. What's your plan?"

Turner didn't have one yet, but it was forming in his head as he was speaking. "It's obvious that Igor followed the trackers. With Olsson's erratic course, he wouldn't have been able to narrow his search and zero in on the *Aurora* so quickly otherwise."

Roni cleared his throat. "Not necessarily. The Russian vessel has access to the same networks I hacked into, and if Igor knows which ship his people are on, which he does, he has no problem following the *Aurora* on the screen."

"True," Turner confirmed. "But he knows which ship they are on only because of the trackers. And since he has a fast yacht and knows that his people are on the *Aurora*, he can follow the ship even after Marcel activates the scrambler when it leaves the Baltic. He can catch up to it and maintain a line of sight with it. So even if the *Aurora* disappears from the array, the Russian navy vessel could still follow the yacht to get to it."

"Clever bastard," Kian spat. "He knows we have a scrambler because his people's signals winked out for hours and then returned when they entered the port, and he knows that we will activate it the moment the *Aurora* is out of the Baltic and reaches the open sea. That's why he commandeered the yacht in addition to the Russian cruiser."

"That wasn't his only objective," Turner said. "He plans to use the yacht to fish his people out of the water after the Russian sinks the *Aurora*. He just doesn't know that we have a submarine to protect it."

Kian drummed his fingers on the table. "What if we employ the same tactic? We can split up the Kra-ell and put a few of those who still have trackers in them on another ship and send a small team of Guardians with them. We can equip all of them with earpieces and lure him into a trap while pulling him away from the Aurora. Is that what you have in mind?"

Lacing his fingers, Turner nodded. "I don't have clarity on all the details yet, but here is what I'm thinking." He pulled a pen out of his pocket, flipped his yellow pad to a new page, and started sketching. "We instructed Olsson to hug the coast all the way up to Bergen, from there to cross the North Sea toward the Shetland Islands, and the North Atlantic beyond. There are many ports along the way between the *Aurora*'s current location and Bergen. She can pretend to make a refueling and resupplying stop somewhere en route, and it wouldn't look suspicious because cruise ships typically do that every day or two." He marked several locations along the coastline he'd just sketched. "Depending on what we can find for hire in the area, we can rent a large yacht or a small commercial vessel, and while the *Aurora* will continue on its course toward the North Atlantic, the decoy vessel will sail northward along the coast or southward toward the English Channel, luring Igor away from the *Aurora*."

Roni looked doubtful. "If the Russian cruiser switches to pursuing the decoy, it might sink it because it will be defenseless. Your friend's sub will be too far away, protecting the *Aurora*. Unless we tell Nils ahead of time to follow the Russian, we won't be able to divert him because he can't maintain communications with us while submerged."

"We can tell him to float a buoy," Onegus said. "But that puts him at risk."

Kian looked at them with a deep frown. "I thought that Nils would need to maintain radio silence for security reasons. Are you telling me that he can't communicate with us at all? And what's a buoy?"

"Radio waves don't travel well through salt water," the Chief explained. "Only very low-frequency waves can penetrate through a few hundred feet of seawater, and the transmitters needed to do that are enormous. There are several specialized technologies under development, but nothing that we can get our hands on. Anyway, for Nils to communicate with us, he will have to either surface, raise an antenna above sea level, or float a tethered buoy carrying an antenna, but all three methods will make him vulnerable to detection."

Kian leaned back. "Then we need to decide on a course of action ahead of time. I don't want to risk exposing Nils."

Turner seconded that opinion. "We can't risk Nils, and given that the *Anatolov* is a submarine killer, as soon as they detect him, it will be game over for him."

3 3

KIAN

*O*negus leaned back and crossed his arms over his chest. "The question is whether Igor will send the Russians after the decoy. If the decoy is a yacht, I don't see him dispatching a Russian naval ship to follow it instead of the *Aurora*. Why would he? Taking over a yacht at sea is much easier than taking over a cruise ship, and he can do that with his boat. That way, he will avoid a high-profile incident involving a Russian naval vessel close to shore."

"What about manpower?" Roni asked. "We know that the *Helena* is fast, and we also know that Igor has two purebloods and a hybrid with him. Since the yacht belongs to an oligarch, he might even have some weapons on board, but he's a cautious bastard, and he might still send the Russian cruiser to pursue the smaller craft because he doesn't want to engage in person. He prefers for someone else to do the dirty work for him."

"You forget Igor's strongest weapon," Onegus said. "He doesn't need an army. He's an army of one. He believes that all he has to do is get close enough to the yacht to use a bullhorn and command everyone to stand down."

Exasperated, Roni threw his hands in the air. "How is that different from the cruise ship? If he can get close enough to the *Aurora* to command everyone to freeze, he doesn't need to sink it either."

Onegus cast the kid a smile. "Igor doesn't know who is on the cruise ship and what weapons it has on board. That's why he's being so cautious and has a Russian vessel following it."

Roni shook his head. "I still don't see how a yacht is different except for its size. It can also carry hidden weapons or another powerful compeller."

"It's a probability and perception game." Kian put an end to the back and forth between the two. "That's why we need a small vessel that seems like a lesser challenge, either a rundown yacht that's not too fast or a very small commercial vessel. Anything larger than that is not suitable precisely for the reasons Onegus voiced. If it seems like too much of a challenge, Igor might be wary of going after it with his yacht, and he might send the Russian cruiser to disable or sink it. Also, the speed of his vessel gives him less of an advantage over larger ships, because even if he catches up to them and uses a bullhorn, chances are his voice will not be heard by all onboard. "

Staring at his notes, Turner nodded. "Let's break this newly-hatched tentative plan into bite-size action items. I will make some inquiries about the availability along the route." He turned to Roni. "I will need your help with that. Can you search for suitable vessels using your program?"

"I'll get right on it." Roni typed a note on his laptop.

Shifting his gaze to Kian, Turner continued. "We need to have a video meeting with Olsson and Yamanu and bring them up to speed. Hopefully, the captain can spare a few of his crew to operate the decoy. Yamanu will need to put together a team of Guardians to accompany the Kra-ell we will transfer to the other ship."

Kian nodded. "I want Kalugal to be here when we make the call. I have to check with him when he'll get here and schedule accordingly."

"Do you think Jade should be included in the meeting?" Roni asked. "She knows Igor and might be able to anticipate his moves."

"Jade is still an unknown," Turner said. "I don't want her to get too familiar with our mode of operations. She's a smart lady, and she could use what she learns against us."

It was ironic of Turner to say that after pushing for inviting the Kra-ell to join the village. What did he expect, that they would keep them locked up in an enclosed area with a guard tower and armed Guardians to keep them from leaving?

Hey, maybe that wasn't such a bad idea. Perhaps not the tower and the armed Guardians, but some other form of careful supervision.

Despite what Syssi had said and Yamanu and Toven's positive opinion of Jade, or even Phinas's, it would take a long time for her to prove herself trustworthy enough to be included in their war room discussions, if ever.

"I agree." Kian typed a message to Kalugal. "It's difficult enough for me to include Kalugal and Phinas, whom I've known for a while and trust at least on some level. I'm not going to include a stranger until she has proven herself above and beyond a shadow of a doubt."

"We should supply our Guardians with better weapons," Onegus said. "We didn't have time to get anything fancy to the *Aurora*, and all we have on board are machine guns. Given that Igor's yacht belongs to a weapons dealer, it's safe to assume that it has the most sophisticated weapons one can load on a luxury yacht. If he has a premier shoulder-fired anti-armor system, he can disable or even sink the smaller decoy. The best of them are self-guiding, but I doubt he keeps a weapon of that caliber on board. We should equip the Guardians with hand-held rocket launchers or shoulder-fired missiles so they could fight fire with fire."

Kian looked at Turner. "Can we get our hands on one of those premier self-guiding missiles? That will give us a significant advantage if Igor doesn't have them on board the yacht."

"Not on such short notice," Turner said. "If I'd had a month, I might have been able to procure one. But not in two days."

Onegus nodded in agreement. "I'll put together a list of weapons and munitions that are easily obtained, but I will need you to find a local supplier who can deliver them to the port we'll get the decoy from."

"Maybe you need two decoys," Roni murmured. "If Igor sinks one, the second one can fish our people out of the water."

"That's not a bad idea," Kian said.

When his phone pinged with an incoming message, he glanced at the screen. "Kalugal will get here in forty-five minutes." He lifted his gaze to Onegus. "Schedule a meeting with Yamanu, Toven, and Phinas in an hour and fill them in on what we discussed, so we can get right to it. I'll use the time to brief Kalugal."

3 4

JADE

*J*ade inspected the new clinic room when Tom came in. "I was told I would find you here." He closed the door behind him. "I want to speak with you."

She arched a brow. "About?"

"Please, let's sit down." He pulled out one of the two chairs for her and sat in the other. "It's about Valstar."

She had a feeling it would come to this. Tom had been spending time with the manipulator, and Valstar must have convinced him that he'd been innocent of wrongdoing and that it all had been Igor's fault.

"I hope you don't intend to go back on your word. The moment Igor is captured, both of their heads are mine. One for each of my sons they slaughtered."

Tom winced. "When you put it like that, it's really difficult to come up with an argument against it."

"Then don't." Jade smiled. "Are we done?" She started to rise.

"We are not. Please, just hear me out."

The pleading tone in his voice made her uncomfortable. Gods didn't plead. They issued directives. But Tom wasn't like the gods back home, and he'd helped free her people.

She owed him.

"Fine." She sat back down. "But you are not going to convince me."

"Then at least I'll have a clear conscience for having tried."

"When you put it that way, I have no choice but to hear you out."

"Thank you." As he looked into her eyes, she braced for the compulsion that never came. "Valstar didn't have a choice. He didn't know Igor before boarding the ship, he wasn't in cahoots with him on some grand plan to kill off all the other Kra-ell males and take the females in order to create a new Kra-ell society on Earth that was patriarchal instead of matriarchal. As soon as he and his pod members woke up from stasis, Igor took control of them, and they were enslaved to him the same way you were ever since."

She bared her fangs at him. "I did what I had to in order to survive and to help others, but I've never hidden my hatred for Igor, or that I would kill him the moment I could. In contrast, Valstar and the others were very cozy with him, and not all of them had the excuse of having weak minds."

"Maybe they do? How many aside from you and Kagra were able to resist Igor's compulsion? Not that you could really resist it. All the two of you could do was to remember what he had done to you and why you hated him. The others were unable to do even that. I've seen the grief the other females experienced when I freed them from the compulsion. They couldn't even feel it before that."

Jade shifted on the narrow chair. "It might have been true for most, but not for Valstar. He's smart and cunning, and he's not weak."

"Being smart and cunning doesn't make someone strong. He feels true remorse for what he did, and he wants a better future for his daughter and granddaughter."

"Pfft." She waved a hand in dismissal. "He sent his granddaughter to be captured and possibly tortured for information. Sofia told me how he reacted when she faked a heart condition and pleaded with him to allow Jarmo to come to be at her side during the operation. Valstar refused."

"Did he have a choice? Would Igor have allowed it?"

"He wouldn't," she admitted. "But he might have allowed Valstar to go. If he cared so much about Sofia, he could have suggested it."

Tom nodded. "You have a point. Still, I think Valstar should at least get a fair trial before you execute him."

"Trial by whom? You?"

"The clan has a judge, and she's not a softie by any stretch of the imagination. In fact, she has a special ability that might prove useful, not as evidence for or against Valstar, but perhaps an opinion."

"What is her special talent?"

He smiled. "They call her the alien probe because she has the ability to reach into a person's mind and evaluate their inner core, their intentions.

She can determine whether they are good or evil or somewhere in between. I'm told that Kian uses her ability often, and I'm also told that she's a very strict judge. She's not merciful."

"She's an outsider. If anyone should judge Valstar, it should be the people he harmed. All the females whose families he slaughtered."

Tom shook his head. "They could be witnesses and provide testimonials, but they shouldn't be the judges or even the jury. For the trial to be fair, those need to be impartial people."

"If the judge finds him guilty, will she sentence him to death, though? The gods didn't believe in a death sentence. The worst of their criminals were only sentenced to entombment."

"Personally, I think entombment is a worse punishment than death."

"Perhaps," Jade conceded. "But it's not as satisfying to the families of the murder victims. For over two decades, I've dreamt of taking Valstar and Igor's heads off, along with everyone else who was there that day and either did the killing or stood by and did nothing to prevent it."

Tom's eyes were full of sorrow as he looked at her. "You couldn't prevent it either. Everyone there was a victim in one way or another. The only one who's guilty beyond a shadow of the doubt is Igor, and he's yours to kill."

She let out a breath. "So, what do you expect me to do? Tell you that I'm okay with Valstar standing trial and your judge determining the verdict?"

"I gave you my word that his head is yours, so if you refuse, I'll honor your decision. But I want you to give it some thought. If you want, we can go talk to Valstar together. You know that he can't lie to me, so if he tells us that he's sorry and that he cares about his daughter and granddaughter, it will be the truth, or at least the truth he believes in."

Jade crossed her arms over her chest. "You've just echoed what I was thinking. Valstar might be a pathological liar who believes in his own lies and therefore can lie to you despite being under your compulsion to tell the truth."

"That's possible. Nevertheless, will you do me a favor and give it some more thought?"

When put like that, she had no choice but to agree. She could promise him to think about it, but she wouldn't change her mind.

"For you, I will give it some thought, and I'll even consider talking to the bastard."

"Thank you. I appreciate it."

Jade rose to her feet and offered Tom her hand. "No one can accuse me of being unreasonable. I'm always willing to listen."

He took her hand and smiled. "I have to admit that you impress me."

Well, what do you know?

Should she bask in the praise?

If it were any other god, she would have sneered at the compliment, thinking that it was meant to manipulate her, but Tom had proven to be different, and she took him at face value.

"Thank you. You impress me too."

YAMANU

"This was delectable." Yamanu rose to his feet and offered Mey a hand up. "I wish I could stay for coffee, but I have less than ten minutes to get to the meeting."

Onegus had texted him over half an hour ago with the news about two vessels following the *Aurora*, but he hadn't told Mey what the meeting was about.

There was no reason to worry her. Not yet, anyway.

The consensus was that Igor wouldn't try anything as long as they were in the Baltic, but knowing that he was pursuing them made Yamanu's gut churn with unease.

He didn't like having Mey and Jin on board, but he knew better than to say anything. Both would chew his head off if he suggested that they disembark somewhere on the way. Perhaps he could throw a hint Kian's way and have the boss command it.

Except if Mia stayed, and she had to, Kian couldn't demand that Mey and Jin get off somewhere. Besides, the ship was full of humans and children, and they couldn't leave for the same reasons they couldn't just fly out of Helsinki. They had trackers in their bodies and no passports.

Mey patted her stomach. "I could get used to being served delicious breakfast, lunch, and dinner every day. And to think that you warned me that we would have to make our own food."

"I didn't know that there were such culinary experts on board or that they would volunteer to cook for us."

She leaned closer to whisper in his ear. "I vote for bringing them to the village. Since Callie's is only open for dinner, they can serve breakfast and lunch in her restaurant."

He wrapped his arm around her. "You know what Kian's position on the subject is."

Even though he'd said he was considering allowing the Kra-ell and the humans into the village, Yamanu knew the boss too well to believe that. He might say that to appease Syssi, but he would never allow it.

"He might not allow the Kra-ell, but what about the others?" Mey asked.

They were careful not to refer to the humans as such because they were pretending to be humans themselves. The ruse would be up as soon as the fighting started, and the Guardians, along with Kalugal's men, would have to reveal their superior speed and strength.

"Kian won't allow them in either."

Sighing, Mey leaned her head on his shoulder. "Maybe once this is over, and Igor is no longer a threat, the Kra-ell can go back to their compound, and the others can stay on the ship as its serving crew. Kian is looking for staff, and they are looking for jobs. It could be the perfect solution. The ship is amazing, and living on board is not a hardship." She lifted her head off his shoulder. "Is there a chance that Onegus would allow you to switch positions and become the security detail for the *Aurora*?"

Yamanu laughed. "Only temporarily, and only when I'm escorting the clan's royalty."

"Careful," Mey whispered. "People are looking at us."

His booming laughter must have drawn their attention, or maybe they were looking at his beautiful mate, but in either case, he didn't mind.

"Let them look." Walking Mey out of the dining hall, he tightened his arm around her. "I have to admit that being here is a treat. We are staying in a luxurious cabin, your sister and Arwel are here with us, and so are many of our friends. On top of that, we are being served three gourmet meals a day."

It felt like the honeymoon they'd never gotten to have, provided that they could ignore the looming danger of an attack by the Russian cruiser, the powerful and potentially lethal Kra-ell and hybrids on board, and the worry about the well-being and survival of the humans and the children of both species.

When they reached the elevators, Yamanu turned to Mey and dipped his head to kiss her. "I hope the meeting will not take long. Are you going to be at the cabin?"

"I'll be at Jin's. She wants to go over a few ideas for next year's collection."

"You are supposed to be on vacation."

Mey smiled. "When you are a business owner, you can never unplug."

The sisters weren't making any money yet, but as long as Mey was enjoying it, Yamanu had no problem with her and Jin working long hours and making no profits. But it surely wasn't worth sacrificing personal time for.

"I don't see why not, but I can't talk about it now because I need to go." He leaned and kissed her forehead. "Have fun."

When he got to the cabin they had designated as their war room aboard the *Aurora*, Phinas was already there, pouring himself coffee from a pot.

Since when did Phinas attend their meetings? Not that Yamanu had a problem with that. On the contrary. It was about time.

"Good evening." Phinas lifted the cup. "Do you want some coffee?"

"I'd love some, thanks." Yamanu sat down on the couch and flipped open the tablet, positioning it just so.

"Here you go." Phinas handed him a cup and sat down next to him on the couch.

"Thanks, but you'd better pour one for Toven as well."

"Sure."

Was it his imagination, or did Phinas seem annoyed by the suggestion? Maybe something about the meeting had upset him?

"Did Kian tell you what the meeting is about?" Yamanu asked.

"Onegus filled me in." Phinas rose to his feet. "And half an hour later, Kalugal texted me the same information."

As Phinas poured coffee into the third mug, the door opened, and Toven walked in. "Good evening, gentlemen."

"Here is your coffee." Phinas thrust the cup at him.

"Thank you." Toven regarded him with a puzzled expression. "Did I miss anything? Have you already started the call?"

Had Phinas been offended by Yamanu's request to pour coffee for Toven?

It wasn't likely.

Yamanu had gotten to know Phinas well during the trip to China and on the mission, and the guy wasn't the type who got his feelings hurt over nonsense like who was making coffee for whom.

Phinas had excellent fighting instincts, he was decisive in battle and in

369

his command style, he treated his men with respect, and he was attentive to the humans, which earned him the most points in Yamanu's esteem.

Phinas returned to his spot on the couch. "The call should come in right about now." When the ring sounded, he pressed the green circle on the tablet. "Perfect timing."

"Good evening," Onegus said.

He was seated in his regular spot at the round conference table in the underground war room, with Turner on one side and Kian on the other. Surprisingly though, Kalugal was there as well, seated to Kian's left, opposite Turner.

That was also a first.

The question was what had brought this about. Had Kalugal demanded to be included or had Kian decided that Kalugal needed to be there since his men were on the *Aurora*?

Perhaps that had been Kalugal's plan all along and the reason he had volunteered his men. Maybe he was tired of observing from the sidelines whenever something big was going down, and he'd bought his ticket in by offering his assistance.

"Let's get started," Kian announced without much preamble. "We have both the *Marshal Anatolov* and the *Grand Helena* following the *Aurora*. We assume that Igor is on the *Helena* rather than on the *Anatolov*. It fits his objectives and his mode of operation." He paused to take a drink of water and give the others a chance to jump in and add their comments.

"Why do we assume that Igor is on the *Helena*?" Phinas asked. "Wouldn't he be safer on a Russian warship? It would make more sense for him to be where he can direct the Russian captain and his crew."

36

KALUGAL

*A*s Phinas voiced his unsolicited opinion, Kalugal smiled smugly. His guy was intelligent and confident, and he wasn't intimidated by Turner or Kian.

Unlike Phinas though, Kalugal preferred to sit back and listen first. It had been decades since he'd last participated in any military operation, and he didn't want to appear less capable or brilliant than Turner, which meant that he would probably have to stay quiet throughout this meeting and the ones that followed.

Besides, Kalugal wasn't even ready to formulate an opinion, let alone voice it. Once he was fully briefed on all the details and heard all the arguments behind the assumptions and decisions that had been made so far, he would be in a better position to throw in a few remarks that wouldn't reveal how little he had to contribute in comparison with Turner.

The guy was a hard act to follow, but given enough time, Kalugal was confident that he could outsmart and outmaneuver even the renowned strategist. Except, he didn't have the time or the inclination to immerse himself in military strategizing to such an extent.

He was much more interested in making money and seeing how far he could manipulate humanity through the clever use of social media.

Turner raised his eyes from the screen. "We assume that Igor's plan is for the Russian to sink the *Aurora*. Once that's done, he will need to collect its passengers, or rather just the Kra-ell, load them onto another vessel, and disappear with them before the Russian navy comes after its rogue ship. He doesn't want to be anywhere near the destroyer when that happens."

"Makes sense." Phinas picked up his coffee cup. "That means that he can monitor the Russian cruiser from the yacht and also control the captain, telling him what to do."

"Correct." Turner glanced at his laptop screen. "The *Helena's* top speed is thirty-seven knots, the *Aurora's* is twenty-seven knots, and the *Anatolov's* is twenty-four knots. The yacht's superior speed is an advantage that Igor will make good use of. Once the Russian cruiser hits the *Aurora* she will issue a distress call, and Igor will want to collect his people as quickly as possible and get out of there before the responders arrive. A speedy boat that's faster than any navy vessel in the area is essential for that." Turner shifted his focus to Toven. "If at some point during the battle Igor reveals himself, do you think you can compel him?"

That was something that Kalugal wanted to know as well, but it was anyone's guess.

Toven needed Mia's boost to overcome Igor's compulsion, so he might not be able to compel Igor when pitted against him face to face.

Igor might even be more powerful than Navuh, which would be both remarkable and scary. In Kalugal's opinion, it would be best to kill him and eliminate the threat and not try to capture him, but he wasn't ready to suggest it yet.

"I am not sure," Toven admitted. "I'd rather not base our strategy on the assumption that I can overpower Igor."

Kalugal appreciated the god's honesty.

It was remarkable how little of his prodigious ego Toven injected at times. Growing up on Navuh's teachings, Kalugal had believed that the gods were aloof, arrogant, and condescending. And yet, the three remaining gods on Earth were not that bad.

His mother was loving and kind and never demonstrated the larger-than-life persona he'd associated with the gods.

Annani was not lacking in the diva department, but even though she definitely appeared larger than life, she was never arrogant or condescending. Her palpable power was mitigated by her loving nature and sense of humor. She cared deeply for humans and dedicated her long existence and that of her clan to humanity's advancement.

And then there was Toven. A powerful god who was older than both Annani and Areana, a god who possessed a fortune so vast that his net worth equaled or exceeded that of many of the world's top economies. And yet there he was, comfortable with being a team player and not the one calling the shots.

Perhaps it was Toven's innate nature not to assume the lead. Not everyone was a born leader like Annani or Kian.

"I agree." Kian nodded, echoing Toven's sentiment. "Not necessarily with the part that you can't compel Igor when the need arises, but with your advice not to plan on getting to where it will need to be tested. I would much rather engage with Igor on our terms, at a time and place of our choosing, and where we can have an overwhelming force to ensure the outcome. I don't want to rely on compulsion to apprehend him. We need, however, to make sure that he can't compel any of ours. No one engages with him without earpieces."

"Naturally." Kalugal smoothed his hand over his freshly trimmed beard. "What are your objectives, though? Do you want to capture Igor or do you want to eliminate him?"

"I'm conflicted," Kian admitted. "On the one hand, I want to get out of him whatever we can about the gods' planet, the Kra-ell's mission to Earth, and the fate of the Kra-ell ship and its missing escape pods. But on the other hand, I want to kill him on sight so that the threat is neutralized once and for all."

"Tough call," Kalugal said. "In my opinion, neutralizing the threat is more important. Although, don't get me wrong. I'm just as curious about what we can learn from Igor as you are."

Happy with his cleverly worded remarks, Kalugal sat back and sipped on his coffee. He'd managed to sound smart and involved without actually saying anything.

Maybe he should go into politics. The ability to talk big without actually saying anything seemed to be the most important talent required to win an election.

37

KIAN

*K*ian was surprised that his cousin chose caution over gain, preferring to eliminate the threat rather than learning from Igor about the gods.

Kalugal had gone into archeology in the hopes of finding out more about their ancestors, and yet he was willing to give up on the chance to learn about them in exchange for safety.

Perhaps being a father had rearranged the guy's priorities, or maybe he'd always been cautious. After all, Kalugal had escaped discovery by his father for decades, and he wouldn't have been successful if he hadn't learned how to hide and fly under the radar, so to speak.

If he cared to be honest with himself, Kian had mixed feelings about inviting Kalugal to join their planning session, but he was starting to realize that Kalugal's swagger was misleading. When the stakes were high, Kalugal's approach was careful and levelheaded.

"Personally, I would love for Toven to compel Igor and get him to talk," Onegus said. "But only if we can do that safely. Otherwise, I would rather see him blown to pieces and sunk to the bottom of the ocean with all his knowledge."

Setting down his coffee mug, Toven turned to Kian. "As I said, I do not know if I can compel Igor even under ideal circumstances, but if we manage to capture him without exposing ourselves to too much risk, it's worth a shot. If I fail, Annani might give it a try. I don't know how strong her

374

compulsion ability is, and neither does she, but I have a feeling that she's much more powerful than she realizes. After all, she's Ahn's daughter, and he was the strongest compeller among the Earthbound gods."

Kian's knee-jerk response was a vehement refusal to even consider letting his mother attempt that. "I am not letting Annani anywhere near Igor, not even via a video call. Even if we have him in chains and a muzzle on his mouth, I don't want him to know that Annani exists. It's an unaccept-able risk for her and for the clan."

Phinas nodded in agreement. "I know this is above my pay grade, and I might be overstepping, but I feel I might be remiss if I don't, and this concerns all of us." He paused and looked at Kian.

Kian had no intention of overruling him. Phinas had good instincts, and his opinion was valuable. He had grown to respect the guy during this oper-ation. Yamanu and Bhathian reported that his leadership and fighting skills were exceptional.

Successfully wooing the fearsome Jade was no small achievement either. He was also completely at ease during this meeting, twice now interjecting in a way that could be construed by some to undermine, or at least question, Kian.

That was not the case, of course. Kian welcomed discussion and appre-ciated all points of view, but most people were intimidated by him no matter how hard he tried to appear accommodating.

Not Phinas, though.

The credit was due to Kalugal, no doubt, who must have trained his subordinates to speak their minds freely.

"Go ahead. I might not agree with what you suggest, but I'm always willing to listen."

"Thank you." Phinas dipped his head. "It is true that as long as Igor draws breath, even while in custody, he could somehow get free and pose a threat to the clan or the Kra-ell or both. But the risk can be mitigated." Phinas paused and shifted his gaze to his boss.

Kalugal's nod was almost imperceptible, but it did not escape Kian's notice.

"What do you suggest?" Kian asked.

"When we capture Igor, we can keep him in chains and partially tran-quilized, and while we interrogate him, we can keep all the Kra-ell quaran-tined and guarded. In addition to Guardians with earpieces, we can use Jade and Kagra as backup. They have their own earpieces, and they can be fully armed and in position right behind him. This alone will prompt him to cooperate with no need for compulsion. His life will depend on it, and if he refuses, Jade will cut his head off as she was promised."

The visual Phinas's words painted in Kian's mind was powerful, and given the expressions on Toven and Turner's faces, they liked that image as much as he did.

Even Yamanu, who wasn't particularly bloodthirsty, had a small smile tugging at his lips.

Encouraged by their responses, Phinas continued. "In the unlikely event that Toven could not compel Igor even with Mia's help, we can have the Clan Mother attempt doing so via an audio call. Igor might guess that she's a goddess, but he wouldn't see whose voice it is. This will not pose even an oblique threat to the Clan Mother. On the other hand, we could gain knowledge that otherwise might be forever lost."

38

PHINAS

*S*o far, Kian had seemed semi-agreeable, but as soon as Phinas brought up the Clan Mother, Kian's shields went up and his armor locked in place around him.

"I don't want Igor to know that there are any gods left on Earth even when he's in chains with Jade holding a sword over his head. That is not negotiable."

Toven shook his head. "If I compel him, he will know about the existence of at least one god. He probably already suspects that a god is involved. Who else could have overpowered his compulsion and freed his people?"

"So what if he knows?" Phinas took a quick sip from his coffee and immediately set the cup down. "Igor's days are numbered. We promised Jade his and Valstar's heads, and she is very eager to collect on that promise. We question him and then she offs him."

Turner, who hadn't taken part in the exchange so far, looked up from his notepad, sat back, and tapped the pad with his pen. "We might be able to do that."

"What do you mean by that?" Kian asked.

Phinas wondered what that meant as well.

Was Turner referring to the discussion about Annani or to the previous one about capturing Igor and interrogating him while minimizing the risk?

Seemingly oblivious to the question, Turner picked up his notepad and glanced briefly at what he had written down. "While you were talking, I was thinking, and I came up with a twist on our previous idea. We know that Igor is tracking both the *Aurora* and the *Anatolov*, which means he has access to the Russian Navy's tracking system. We also know that he is tracking his people via the various devices implanted in them."

"Which are getting removed as we speak," Phinas said. "Regrettably, not fast enough."

"Correct," Turner confirmed. "The original plan was to dispose of the trackers in the ocean, shroud the *Aurora* by reactivating the signal disruptor, and basically use the big North Atlantic to pull a disappearing act from anyone tracking and following it. Then we came up with a plan to use a decoy ship, load it with the Kra-ell who still had trackers in them, and have Igor follow them. The problem with that plan was the shortage of earpieces. I assumed that the Guardians who remain on the *Aurora* could lend their earpieces to the Kra-ell, who would transfer to the decoy, but on further thought, I realized that it would have left the *Aurora* unprotected in case Igor decided to follow it instead of the decoy for some reason." He cast a quick glance at Onegus. "There was another problem with that plan that I wasn't aware of until I checked with William. He told me that once the earpieces mold to a specific person's ear, they can't fit securely in someone else's, and the compulsion waves might be able to pass through."

"I didn't know that," Onegus said. "William never mentioned it to me."

Phinas could already guess Turner's solution to the problem. "You want to load the trackers that were already removed onto the decoy vessel and leave those who still have them on the *Aurora*. That way, only Guardians or my men will be on the decoy, and all of them have properly fitting earpieces."

"Correct." Turner cast Phinas an appreciative look. "You're a fast thinker."

It was a nice compliment, especially when it came from someone of Turner's cerebral caliber.

"Thank you." Phinas dipped his head.

"I'm not complimenting you. I'm stating the obvious." Turner swiveled his chair toward Kian. "We need to choose the port where we will make the switch carefully. It needs to be large enough for the *Aurora* to dock, and it has to have a lot of traffic. The port of Copenhagen is perfect for that, but the question is whether we will find a suitable vessel available for rent in its vicinity. Since it needs to be a yacht or commercial vessel large enough to supposedly carry all of the Kra-ell and humans who have had their trackers removed, it might be difficult to find. So far, Roni hasn't found any suitable vessels, so we expanded the search to include ships for sale. The rest of the plan stays the same. Once the *Aurora* is back at sea it will continue as planned, heading toward the Shetland Islands and the North Atlantic, while the decoy vessel, with the trackers and a sufficient force on board, will head northward while still hugging the coast."

"This is a solid idea," Toven interlocked his fingers and set his hands on the table. "But I see several issues with it that need to be addressed. First, can we safely assume that the Russians will continue after the *Aurora* and only Igor will follow the decoy? If the Russian cruiser follows the decoy, the vessel will be defenseless. Second, can we reasonably guess what kinds of weapons Igor has on board the *Helena*? We will need to equip our guys with sufficiently superior firepower. Third, do we know if the *Helena* has a compelled human crew on board and any other collateral targets? We should not plan on shooting at or sinking a vessel with innocents on board. Fourth, Igor seems to have a plan B for every move. Could we reasonably rule out a plan B for this situation, and if not, can we guess what that would be? And lastly, if we miscalculate and get any of these answers wrong, what is our backup plan, and how do we get our guys safely out of there?"

Phinas regarded the god with renewed appreciation. He'd been a warrior most of his life, and he hadn't thought of half of the issues Toven had brought up.

Then again, the god was as ancient as human civilization, and he had seen it all play out in one way or another over and over again.

The weapons and the vessels changed, but people were people no matter what species or culture. They were all motivated by the same things, namely fear and greed.

Turner appeared a little less smug than usual. "We have already come up with answers to most of the issues you've raised, but I have to admit that none of us has thought of the human crew aboard the *Helena*."

39

KALUGAL

*K*alugal stifled a smile. The indomitable Turner had been humbled by Toven's list of issues, and the guy's ego had suffered a blow. Kalugal could think of several solutions to what bothered Toven, but he preferred to leave it to Turner and give him a chance to save his reputation as the guy who thought of every possible angle.

"Let's break for lunch," Kian said, probably thinking along the same lines. "Obviously, we need to spend more time developing the plan." He turned to the camera and addressed Toven. "I hope that by tomorrow morning your time, we will have answers for you."

Toven nodded. "If you need me, call no matter what time it is. We need to act swiftly."

"Same here," Yamanu said with much less enthusiasm.

The Guardian probably couldn't wait to return to his mate and wanted the meeting over.

Kian terminated the call and closed the tablet. "Do you want to get food from the café and bring it here, or should we get some fresh air and eat over there?"

"Let's get out of here." Onegus pushed to his feet.

Kalugal could eat, but he wasn't happy about discussing sensitive issues in public. He knew better than most what could be gleaned from casual eavesdropping.

"Are you sure that's a good idea?" He followed Kian up.

"No, but I'm tired of the basement. We will keep it down."

Kalugal shrugged. "As you wish. You're the boss."

Kian arched a brow. "Do you want to lead this mission? I'll gladly transfer the responsibility to you."

His cousin was just teasing, but even if he wasn't, Kalugal had no wish to take over command. He was only taking part in this and sacrificing time with his wife and son because his men were involved, and he wanted to have a say in the future of the Kra-ell.

"No, thank you. My job is to poke holes in the plans you and Turner come up with, but since Toven is doing that so well, I can sit back and enjoy the show. I'm just an observer."

That was only partially true.

He was glad to finally be included in the war room team, and he was enjoying the company, but those reasons were not important enough to take time away from his family. Given that he had to be there anyway, though, he could at least enjoy himself.

He was finally included in Kian's inner circle.

Turner was his least favorite, even though he was the smartest of the three. He was dry and humorless and despite his vast knowledge, kind of boring. Nevertheless, Kalugal admired him not only for his tactical instincts but also for his superb organizational skills, and most of all for his invaluable worldwide network of military suppliers and subcontractors.

Onegus was a fun guy, but he was also the consummate professional. He knew his stuff and ensured every move was carefully considered from all angles, especially the Guardians'.

Kian was Kalugal's favorite, though, and he found that he enjoyed his cousin's company even more than he enjoyed Rufsur's, which was saying something.

Rufsur was his right-hand man, and until Kalugal had met Jacki, he was the person he'd been the closest to.

Thankfully, Rufsur was happily mated to Edna, or he would have felt neglected. Fates willing, the two would be blessed with a child soon, and then Rufsur's life would be complete. They were working on it, using the potions Merlin had prepared for them before leaving on the Kra-ell mission, and Kalugal was keeping his fingers crossed for them.

Phinas and he had never been that close, but he trusted Phinas just as much as Rufsur.

Still, he liked spending time with Kian more than either of his lieutenants.

It could be the familial connection or the fact that they were equals, or maybe it was the banter they enjoyed over whiskey and cigars, but the affinity was there.

"Igor's yacht is remarkably fast for a vessel of that size," Onegus said as they sat down at the table. "It won't be easy to find a yacht or boat large enough for the number of passengers we will supposedly be carrying, and fast enough to outrun Igor's boat."

"It doesn't need to outrun the *Helena*," Turner said. "In terms of size, any reasonably large yacht or small commercial vessel should do. There is no reason for Igor to think that we set his people up comfortably two-per-cabin. In fact, he would probably assume that we deliberately chose a small craft so he wouldn't suspect that we were using it to sneak his people away."

"What if Roni can't find a boat?" Kalugal asked.

Kian had told him that the kid had hacked into restricted naval systems that gave him access to information about any vessel at any location, but that didn't mean that any of them would be available for rent or even for sale.

Kalugal hadn't known that every ship, whether private or military, was being tracked in real time. Did that include fishing boats, though? Perhaps they could use one of those.

Turner shook his head. "We have a very specific set of pre-qualifiers we are looking for. Roni found several candidates, but they were not offered for hire. I have my people working on it as well. As to the boat's speed, a not-too-swift yacht might actually be an advantage. If our end game is to capture Igor, what better way to lure him closer than to make him think that we cannot outrun him? A boat that is just slightly slower than Igor's will have him speed up right into our trap."

Kalugal liked the way Turner's mind worked. "So, what you're saying is that we need to look for a vessel that can accommodate over two hundred people below deck and that is reasonably fast, but not as fast as Igor's boat. That may prove to be a tall order. Maybe it would be easier to get a couple of smaller vessels and split the people between them. That will further confuse Igor."

"Roni had the same idea," Kian said. "I'm starting to think that maybe we should do that."

As they sat down, Aliya approached their table, and the discussion halted.

"What can I get for you?" she asked.

Kian smiled up at her. "Coffees all around, and some sandwiches and pastries. You know what to get me."

She nodded. "The vegetable wrap. I always save one for you."

"That's so nice of you. But I don't come to the café every day, and I don't want it to go to waste."

"Don't worry, it doesn't. When Jackson restocks the café, Wonder eats your wrap if you didn't get it that day."

"I'm glad."

"Anything else?" She looked at Kalugal.

He cast her a smile. "Whatever you get us is fine."

Did she know that Phinas and Jade were an item? Should he tell her?

Nah. With how fast rumors rushed through the village, she'd hear about it soon enough.

Kalugal looked around at the other patrons. "How secretive are we supposed to be? It's not like we have privacy here. I could shroud us, but the Clan Mother forbade me from using my powers on clan members. If you approve, though, or ask me to do it, I might be able to circumvent her compulsion."

"Don't worry about it." Kian clapped him on the back. "No one here is going to warn Igor about what we are planning for him, and we are not discussing anything else."

"Right." Kalugal leaned closer to Kian. "How important is it for us to catch and question Igor? I still think that blowing him out of the water is the easiest way to get rid of him, while capturing him presents all kinds of risks, both during the operation and after, when he's in our hands." He chuckled. "Are we going to put a muzzle on him, Hannibal Lecter style? Or maybe cutting out his tongue is a safer solution?"

Kian winced. "Very funny."

"What?" Kalugal arched a brow. "Is killing him better?"

"If we can manage to do it safely, I'd rather capture him alive and interrogate him, but he will need to have a tongue for that. Jade and Valstar know a lot, and some of the other original settlers might have additional information, but I have a feeling that Igor was much higher up in the Kra-ell pecking order, and he knows more. Still, we can probably figure out most of it from the others. In other words, I am unwilling to risk anyone's life for what's in Igor's head. If we can capture him without additional risk, I am all for it. Otherwise, I'd rather see him blown to pieces."

"I agree." Onegus started but stopped when Aliya returned with their order.

"He doesn't need a tongue," Kalugal murmured. "He can write his answers."

The others chuckled, but he hadn't said that as a joke. It was a viable solution. Igor needed his tongue to generate the sounds that carried compulsion. Cutting it out would render him harmless, and he could still tell them everything he knew by writing his answers with pen on paper or typing them on a laptop or tablet.

After taking the paper cup marked with his name, Kian leaned back in his chair. "I suggest that we take a break from the planning and let our minds rest."

"I have a great idea." Kalugal unwrapped one of the pastries. "How about we continue the meeting up on your roof? We can drag a couple of chairs up there and smoke your cigars."

Kian grinned. "I like the way you think, cousin. After we finish our coffees and sandwiches, we can move our meeting to the roof."

40

KIAN

"How are the hybrids doing?" Kian asked Onegus.

The topic was related to what they'd been discussing before, but it didn't require any cerebral effort.

Onegus shrugged. "Frankly, I don't know. I didn't check on them this morning. But if they were giving my guys any trouble, I would have heard about it."

Kalugal frowned. "What hybrids?"

Kian unwrapped his sandwich. "Igor sent two hybrids to follow Sofia around, but since we removed the tracker from her body and put it in a cat, they didn't know that she was no longer in Safe Haven and stayed in the area. Then they disappeared for about twenty-four hours, and we were afraid that Igor had retrieved them, but they returned, and our guys got them. They are in the keep right now, and I wanted to pay them a visit later today, but I'm too pressed for time, so I decided to send Anandur instead. I wonder if he'll get anything useful out of them."

"Like what?" Kalugal asked. "What can they know that we don't already?"

"Perhaps Igor contacted them. They were away for a whole day, and they left their car in front of their Airbnb. Maybe they came back to collect their things and go to Igor. The Guardians tranquilized them and loaded them into the van without asking them anything, and they kept tranquilizing them along the way. It's not that anything they can tell us will help with capturing Igor, but I'm curious to know whether he contacted them."

Turner was holding the phone to his ear, but since he wasn't saying anything, Kian assumed that he was listening to a message. When he put the phone down, he asked. "Anything for us?"

Turner nodded. "Nils left me a message. He can meet the *Aurora* at Skagen."

"Where is that?" Kalugal asked.

Turner brought it up on Google maps. "It's the northernmost town and port of Denmark. It's right at the entrance to the North Sea proper. It's a good spot since we don't expect the Russian cruiser to attack before the *Aurora* is a day or so into the North Sea."

Kian frowned. "How many days will it take the *Aurora* to reach Skagen?"

Turner looked at the map. "Taking into consideration a stopover of several hours, probably two days."

Kian released a breath. "That's not too bad."

"Provided that our assumption about the Russian is correct," Onegus said. "If he decides to attack her while she's still in the Baltic, we have no way to protect it."

Kalugal rubbed his jaw between his thumb and forefinger. "She'll be close enough to the coast for rescue to arrive within moments. Our people will have their hands full thralling the rescuers not to see the passengers' peculiarities."

"I'm not worried about that," Kian said. "What worries me are the humans and children on board who will not survive more than a few minutes in the cold water."

"A ship doesn't sink that fast even if it's been hit and takes in water." Turner took a sip of his coffee. "They will have time to load the humans and children onto the lifeboats, and the rescue will arrive quickly enough. So quickly, in fact, that Igor won't have time to get his people. By the time the lifeboats are in the water, the place will be swarming with helicopters. That's why I'm positive he won't make his move until she's out of the Baltic."

He sounded very sure about that, and since Kian didn't have much experience with ships, sinking or afloat, he had to trust the guy's logic.

41

JADE

"*A*re you serious?" Kagra looked at the water as if it was full of poisonous *Pogdas*. "Are we supposed to get in there?"

Jade let out a breath. "I'm as unenthusiastic about it as you are, but Phinas has a point. If the ship goes down, we need to be able to at least float until help arrives."

"We have lifeboats," Drova said. "And if he tells you that there aren't enough of them, it's a lie. I counted, and there were enough seats for every passenger on board. He's just a sadistic bastard."

Pavel pushed his hands into his pockets. "Tomos and Piotr had a swimming lesson earlier today, and they said it wasn't that bad."

"They lied." Drova cast him a baleful look. "They didn't want to be the only suckers who suffered."

"What if the ship capsizes before we can get into the lifeboats?" Jade asked. "People still die at sea despite all the cruise ships having them. Knowing how to swim can save our lives. Besides, the cold is unpleasant, but it's not going to kill us. Our bodies will raise their temperatures."

"That's another thing that bothers me about it." Drova huddled inside her coat. "Phinas and Dandor are human. How come they didn't get hypothermia after spending nearly an hour in this pool?"

Good question.

Jade was proud of her daughter for wondering about it, but she couldn't tell her the truth about the immortals. Not yet, anyway.

"Maybe it's not that cold. The pool is heated. Otherwise, it would have frozen over."

"Hello, everyone." Phinas strode onto the deck. "I wasn't expecting such a large turnout, but I'm glad to see you all here." He smiled at Jade. "Are you planning on swimming fully clothed?"

She glared at him. "We found a solution for the lack of bathing suits."

"I can't wait to see it." He gave her a lascivious look that she hoped Drova didn't notice.

Smiling, she pulled her sweater off, revealing the swath of fabric she'd cut out of one of his black T-shirts and wrapped around her breasts. "They say that necessity is the mother of invention." She pulled her pants down next.

The glow from Phinas's eyes could have illuminated the pool, but thankfully, Drova was busy getting undressed, and Pavel was busy watching Drova.

Jade frowned. Drova was too young to be of interest to an adult Kra-ell male. Even though she was already at her full height and had the hips of a grown female, she was still a child, and she was not ready to have sex yet.

For a moment, Jade considered having a talk with Pavel, but then she reconsidered. Drova was under a lot of stress, and Pavel seemed to make her happy.

Except, Kra-ell didn't do couples.

Or did they?

Whether Jade was willing to admit it or not, she and Phinas were a couple. They had been exclusive with one another, and others regarded them as a couple as well.

Still, Drova and Pavel were probably just friends or rather cohorts. Purebloods didn't flirt or formed exclusive relationships. The two were spending a lot of time together, though, probably plotting a revolution, but it was all good. There were a lot of changes in their future, and she needed to be flexible and listen to what everyone brought to the table.

Turning so she was facing Phinas and blocking him from Drova's view, Jade whispered, "Your blazing gaze should focus elsewhere."

"Damn." He turned to look up at the sky. "Look at all these stars."

"Beautiful, aren't they?" Max walked up to them, wearing a pair of boxer shorts and a towel draped over one shoulder. "I heard there is a pool party going on."

Kagra snorted. "You came even though you didn't have to? Do you enjoy torture?"

He grinned. "It depends on who's inflicting it. I'm willing to suffer if it's you."

"You're crazy." Kagra unzipped her jacket. "Let's just get it over with so I can return to my cabin and soak in a hot tub."

"Can I come with you?" Max dropped the towel.

"In your dreams, hotshot." Kagra shrugged the jacket off, revealing the same makeshift swimming top as Jade's.

Phinas frowned. "Is that my T-shirt?"

"It was." Jade grinned. "We needed a garment large enough to supply fabric for three tops, and your shirt was the only one that fit the bill."

"It was well worth the sacrifice." Phinas whipped his shirt over his head. "I'm going in."

As he pulled his pants off while walking toward the pool and jumped in, Jade stifled a chuckle.

Did he have something to hide?

Without giving herself time to reconsider, she followed him and jumped in as well.

"Dear Mother, it's cold." She wrapped her arms around herself, regretting that they had company.

Right now, Phinas's big warm body would have been a welcome reprieve.

Kagra jumped in next, and Max jumped right after her.

Drova put her foot in the water and pulled it out quickly. "I'm not going in there."

"Come on," Pavel said. "If I can do it, you can do it too." He sat on the edge of the pool and slid inside.

The water barely reached their upper chests, and after the first shock, it wasn't that bad.

"Okay, people," Phinas said. "First lesson is to float on your back. I'll demonstrate on Jade how it's done."

42

KIAN

$\mathcal{T}$urner lifted his eyes to the sky. "It looks like it's going to rain."

"We have an umbrella." Kian put the chair he'd carried from his office next to one of the loungers.

It had been a beautiful sunny day up until about half an hour ago, and then swollen rain clouds had drifted over, hiding the sun. They weren't thick or dark enough to produce rain, but more were drifting over by the minute.

"It's Southern California." Onegus put the chair he'd carried next to the other lounger. "We might get a little drizzle, and then the sky will clear by evening."

"I wouldn't bet on that." Turner sat down on the chair and put his laptop on his knees. "I checked the forecast, and there is a storm heading our way."

After Toven had pointed out all the things he hadn't considered, Turner had gotten into a mood, and all during lunch he'd been either typing on his laptop or jotting notes on his yellow pad.

Not that he was ever cheerful, but now he had his own personal cloud hanging over his head.

"Storm." Kian snorted. "Every rainfall is called a storm in this desert. Where we come from, now, those are storms."

The comment didn't pull a smile out of Turner as he'd expected.

Onegus nodded. "Winters in the Scottish Highlands are brutal, but they are nothing compared to winters in Finland or Northern Russia. I don't envy our people out there." He chuckled. "Phinas decided that the Kra-ell and the humans needed swimming lessons, and he had the pool filled up. Imagine swimming in that freezing water."

"He has to heat it up," Kian said. "Otherwise, the pool water will freeze."

Yamanu had told Kian about Phinas's initiative, and he approved. It was a good idea in case the worst happened and the passengers ended up in the water, but heating up the pool meant an additional expenditure of fuel. If they weren't planning a refueling stop, that would have been a problem.

"He's only heating it up minimally," Onegus said. "He wants the Kra-ell to learn to swim in nearly freezing water, so they won't panic if the *Aurora* gets hit and starts sinking."

"It won't," Turner said. "Nils will sink the Russian before he can fire at the *Aurora*. Besides, the humans will be in the lifeboats. There is no need to torture them by having them take lessons in the freezing pool."

"Nevertheless, I applaud his initiative." Kian pulled four cigars out of his coat pockets and handed out three of them. "Even if the only thing the lessons achieve is entertainment, I'm sure that they all need a way to release the tension."

Onegus took the lighter from Kian and lit his cigar. "Back to our discussion from before. I still think that we should eliminate Igor rather than risk people just for a chance to learn more about our history. But before we rule out capturing him because of the added risks, we need to evaluate them." The Chief looked at Turner.

Leaning forward, Turner placed his hands on the table. "I see several possible scenarios. The most worrisome one involves Igor ordering the Russians to drop the *Aurora* and change directions to follow the smaller vessel. When Nils realizes that, he will need instructions from us, and he will be forced to either surface or float a buoy and break radio silence, risking the sub's discovery. Because of the confusion, he might also fall behind because the vessels will continue on their respective courses while he is surfacing and waiting for our input. Don't forget that the sub is the slowest of the vessels involved. This could lead to him not being where we need him when we need him. We can mitigate that by having the decoy boat progress slowly, but that might raise Igor's suspicion."

Kian didn't understand why that was a problem. "As Roni pointed out, we can still reach Nils, and if he knows the plan ahead of time, he will know what to do. He needs to follow the Russian cruiser no matter which vessel it is following. The yacht will not follow the *Aurora*, and if it does, the force on board can take care of it."

Turner shook his head. "We've just discussed how important it is to safe-guard the *Aurora*. If it is sunk in the North Sea, where rescue will take too long to reach it, everyone on board will be at risk. That's why it's our top priority. Igor might have rocket launchers on board the yacht. A rocket might not be enough to sink a cruise ship, but it can disable it, and he can board it. We also don't have the specialty earpieces for the Kra-ell on board the *Aurora*, and Igor could command them using a bullhorn. They would have no choice but to strike against the remaining Guardians. True, we can lock them up in one of the steel storage spaces before the yacht gets close enough, but the fact remains that whatever we do, without the sub the *Aurora* is vulnerable. The only scenario where we will need Nils to follow the decoy is if Igor follows it along with the Russian cruiser and no vessels follow the *Aurora*. The bottom line is that we can't tell Nils ahead of time who to follow."

43

KALUGAL

Kalugal was puzzled by the exchange and wondered how come the solution hadn't occurred to Turner. "If we can provide air cover to keep the decoy safe, we can tell the submarine captain to stick to the *Aurora*."

Having taken part in WWII and seen first-hand the importance of air superiority, Kalugal thought that should have been crystal clear to everyone. Perhaps the problem was getting the air coverage. Turner's contacts might not be as all-encompassing as he'd led everyone to believe.

Onegus nodded. "If we can contract a military helicopter armed with missiles and a powerful gun, it could work."

As all eyes shifted to Turner, the guy looked absolutely smug. "I have contacts in Europe that have the equipment, aircrew, and armaments." He smiled, his self-assured attitude firmly back in place. "They are going to be costly though, especially on such short notice, but I've contacted two of my best sources earlier today, and I expect to hear back from them this afternoon."

It was both annoying and impressive that the guy had already thought of the solution. Evidently Turner had been waiting for them to catch up, or maybe he'd wanted to show off that he had thought of it first.

After all, he had face to save.

"I like it," Kian said. "Air coverage might prove essential in every scenario, especially if Igor has a plan B, which I suspect he does. I wouldn't be surprised if he thought of the same thing and planned to compel a military vessel or aircraft to join his attack. In case Igor once again pulls the proverbial rabbit out of the hat, having a helicopter on the scene as quickly as possible is vital to the security of our people. The question is how we can pull it off while the ship is progressing. Helicopters have a relatively short range. Will it follow the ship from one refueling station to another?"

Turner put his cigar in the ashtray and started typing on his laptop. "It can be done as long as the decoy follows the coastline but doesn't get too far north. There is a long stretch along the coast of Norway that doesn't have any nearby airports. Frankly, that's more than I planned to use this resource for, but I agree that this approach affords us a better margin of error. I am sending an expanded scope of engagement email as we speak."

"What if we trick him?" Onegus's eyes blazed with an inner light. "Igor's default is compulsion. It is reasonable to assume that this is the first thing he will try to do. When he attempts to compel our men, they could play along, leading him to believe that the decoy is no longer a threat. He will feel confident to board their vessel in order to take control of it, at which point we can take him and his cronies down with tranquilizer darts."

Kian's expression was skeptical. "Igor will not fall for that. As much as I have absolute confidence in the Guardians, and as much as Kalugal's men have proved themselves capable, they are not good enough actors to pull it off and fool him. Besides, he could order our guys to throw their weapons overboard to verify that they are responding to his compulsion. Would they? Of course not. He might order them to bring their passengers on deck, and they couldn't do that either because they will have no passengers. Hell, he could test his compulsion and order them to shoot each other."

Onegus's face fell, but the guy had no ego issues, and he had no problem admitting that his plan had huge holes in it. "Yep. You are correct. I did not think it through."

"Let's continue with the possible scenarios," Turner said. "I agree with Kian that it is not very likely that Igor will order the Russian to follow the decoy. After our tele-meeting with Toven, I asked Roni to do more research about the owner of the yacht Igor had commandeered and to confirm that the oligarch it belongs to is indeed an international weapons dealer. It's safe to assume that the yacht is not only equipped with very un-yacht-like defensive and offensive capabilities but has a security detail onboard, so Igor has additional trained killers with him. He will feel confident about his ability to take over the decoy and will tell the Russian captain to keep trailing the *Aurora*."

"In a way, that's good news," Kian said. "If the *Helena* is run by the Bratva, I have no qualms about blowing it up. I'll let Toven know that he has one less thing to worry about. There are no innocent civilians on board."

Turner lifted his head. "There might be. What about the cook, the maid, the mechanics? They are not all evildoers."

Kian let out an exasperated breath. "Then we will do our best not to blow it up but to disable it instead. But if it's a choice between saving our people and whoever is on board the *Helena*, our people come first."

"Naturally." Turner resumed typing.

The military helicopter idea was solid, but if the yacht was equipped with more than machine guns, it might score a hit before the helicopter arrived, and Kalugal didn't like the odds.

His men comprised the majority of the force on the *Aurora*, and many of them would be on the decoy, including Phinas. He wanted them armed to the teeth so they could protect themselves.

"Is there a way to get shoulder-mounted missiles for our guys?" he asked. "That would buy them time until the helicopter is within range and engages."

"We're already taking care of that," Onegus said. "I made a list of weapons we need, and Turner is getting them from his suppliers. We just need to know which port to deliver them to."

Turner nodded while typing. "I sent another inquiry to my contact. Assuming that he's available and willing to take on the mission, I will run by him what we are dealing with. He is an experienced navy helicopter pilot, and I have no doubt that he will have some suggestions and ideas for us."

4 4

PHINAS

*J*ade adjusted the blanket over her shoulders and lifted the cup of tea Phinas had made her. "I don't even like tea, but I'm chilled all over, and tea seems like a good idea."

He sat next to her on the couch and wrapped his arm around her. "I ramped up the heating. It should get warmer in a few minutes."

She leaned against his side. "Aren't we supposed to conserve fuel?"

"It's less critical with the new plan." He proceeded to tell her about the decoy idea.

Jade looked skeptical. "When I visited Merlin earlier today, he had only sixteen trackers removed. That's not enough to make the decoy attractive enough to lure Igor away from the *Aurora*. He needs to believe that most of the purebloods are on board the decoy to change course and follow it."

"We have two to three days, and Merlin told me that you arranged for two new assistants for him so he could work faster."

"Three." Jade took a sip from the tea. "Marcel promised to find another Guardian who can tackle the scanning."

"Ruvon is good with tech stuff. I can have him stop by the clinic to see whether he can handle the MRI."

"Who is Ruvon? Did I meet him?"

"You've seen him, but you probably don't remember. He's a tall skinny guy, with dark curly hair and smiling brown eyes."

Surprisingly, Jade nodded. "I know who you're talking about. Can you send him over tomorrow?"

"I can, but you should check with Marcel first. Maybe he's already found someone for the job."

"I will, and I'll also check with Pavel. He's a quick study." She sighed. "It would have been so much easier for me if my people and I had phones. It's a pain to track down everyone I need to talk to."

Was this a good opportunity to check with Jade about her thoughts about moving her people into the village?

It was important to find out if Jade would even consider it, but the subject should be broached as a hypothetical because Kian would most likely decide against it. The only reason he was collecting opinions about Jade and the other Kra-ell was to appease Syssi, who wanted them in the village to shore up its defenses. Turner also seemed to be pushing for it, but although Kian respected the guy's opinion, he had no problem overruling it.

He wouldn't overrule Syssi as easily, though, if at all.

In fact, Kian might invite the Kra-ell to the village despite his own objections just to make his mate happy.

Most mated males did everything they could to please their females, and Phinas had no problem with that. Peace and harmony at home were essential to mated bliss, and who did not want that.

Jade lifted her head off his arm. "What are you thinking about?"

"Mated couples."

She arched a brow. "What about them?"

"My boss found the love of his life about a year ago, and they got pregnant right away. They have a little baby boy who is the center of their lives. I've known Kalugal for many decades, but I've never seen him as happy as he is now, and that's despite sleepless nights and a colicky baby who is miserable most of the time and can barely hold any food down. Kalugal and Jacki didn't even leave the house until recently because they were afraid of exposing their baby to viruses. The clan doctor had to convince them that they were doing their son a disservice by overprotecting him. He needs to be exposed to germs so his body will develop immunity to them."

"That's a lovely story. Does it have a point?"

Chuckling, Phinas tightened his arm around her. "The ever pragmatic Jade. Sometimes a story is just a story, and it is not meant as a cautionary tale or encouragement to become more and do heroic things."

"Then it's not a good story." She brought the mug to her lips and took another sip. "If I told you a story about a woman traveling for business and sightseeing while she's at it, you would be bored unless something inter-esting happened to her. She could have met a mysterious man who turned out to be a spy, or she could have been the victim of a terrorist attack and its only survivor, or she might have been running for her life from an assassin. Those are the kinds of things that make a good story."

Phinas smiled. "I heard that you were a good storyteller, but I find that difficult to reconcile with the pragmatic, no-nonsense female who I've grown to like and respect."

He'd almost blurted out that he'd grown to love her, but that would have been a red flag that would have sent her running away. Besides, he wasn't sure that he was in love with her.

Jade was so different from him or anyone else he knew that it might not work out for them in the long term. Right now, they were still enjoying the novelty, but who knew how long it would last.

For a long moment, she regarded him with those huge, unblinking eyes of hers. "I've grown to like and respect you as well. I enjoy your company." She leaned over and smoothed a finger over his lips. "I didn't expect to enjoy our bed play so much. I'm used to rougher games."

"Oh, yeah?" Phinas cupped the back of Jade's neck. "I enjoy your company as well, in bed and outside of it."

He brought their mouths together for a kiss, but Jade didn't respond with her usual fervor, probably because she was still holding the teacup and was afraid it would spill over, but it was also possible that she was uncom-fortable with the direction their conversation had taken.

45

JADE

*J*ade put the teacup down and shrugged the blanket off.

It was either getting much warmer in Phinas's cabin, or it was her response to the kiss and what he'd said as well as what he hadn't said.

She had too little experience with humans and immortals to read them as easily as she read other Kra-ell.

When Phinas had talked about his boss and his mated bliss, his eyes had shone with emotion, and she'd detected wistfulness in his tone. He wanted that for himself, a loving mate and a child to dote on, and she had a feeling he wanted it with her.

Except, she couldn't give him either of those things.

Or could she?

Jade had considered having a child by Phinas, but there were just too many reasons why it was a bad idea, not the least of them that Phinas would want to be part of that child's life, and that was not possible.

They came from different worlds, and their time together was precious but temporary. After Igor was dealt with, they would go their separate ways, and if they had a child together, that child would naturally have to go with her. A hybrid Kra-ell needed to be raised by a Kra-ell mother in a Kra-ell community and learn the Kra-ell way. They couldn't grow up among immortals who weren't as strong or as fast.

Unlike a pureblooded father, Phinas would never be satisfied with just visiting his offspring. He would want to be there every day and witness every milestone.

"What are you thinking about?" Phinas hooked a finger under her chin and turned her head toward him. "I hope it's about sex."

She chuckled. "In a way, it is." She shifted to face him. "You wanted to know why I like to tell stories."

He nodded, even though he hadn't asked that. He just had trouble reconciling her character with storytelling.

"People need something greater than themselves to believe in, heroes to worship, and adventures to crave. Everyday life is mundane, and it's not glamorous. We get up in the morning, work or do our chores, eat, sleep, and repeat the same thing daily. When we hear a story or watch a movie, we identify with the protagonists and live vicariously through them. Suddenly, we feel more important, more heroic, and more glamorous. Stories give meaning to our existence."

He tilted his head. "What about children? Their lives are full of wonder and discovery. The mundane existence is an adult affliction."

"Teaching children through stories is more fun for them and more effective. They might forget dry history lessons, but they will forever remember the fables I've told them." She smiled. "I was telling the children of my tribe stories long before I was captured, and in captivity, I used the fables to circumvent Igor's prohibition to tell them anything about the Kra-ell past or way of life."

He took her hand. "Perhaps you could write children's books."

Jade snorted out a laugh. "If you heard my stories, you wouldn't say that. Mine don't have a happily-ever-after or even a happily-for-now. My stories mimic life and rarely end well. The moral I try to impart is that a life lived well, honorably and courageously, is worth living even if the hero doesn't make it to the end. The journey is what matters."

Phinas grimaced. "Poor children. Why make them face the harsh realities of life at such a young age? They will discover them soon enough when they grow up."

She tilted her head. "You told me that your childhood was terrible. Would hearing happy stories have made you feel better about your life?"

"First of all, my childhood wasn't terrible. I had a loving mother, and life was good in the Dormants' enclosure. It turned bad when I transitioned and was taken away to the war camp. That was miserable. Back then, if anyone told me a happily-ever-after story, I probably would have punched them in the gut."

"See?" She waved a hand. "I was right."

Phinas picked up the blanket and draped it over her shoulder. "When I was a little boy, my mother told me fun stories that never ended badly, and I loved them. I think that those stories helped me through the bad times. They reminded me that there was decency in the world, and that not everyone was cruel. I don't think I would have been the male I am today without them."

It was a sweet sentiment, but he was wrong.

"Didn't your mother tell the same stories to your brothers?"

"She did."

"And yet they didn't turn out like you. They had different fathers and inherited different attributes from them." Jade closed her eyes. "I'm always watching Drova for signs of her father's character. She has some of it, like the bossiness and the condescending attitude, but I think she's good on the inside. I just hope that she stays that way."

"She seems like a good kid." He wrapped his arms around her and pulled her into his lap. "Do you think she suspects that we are together?"

"We are not together. We just happen to spend some time with one another, and I don't think Drova suspects anything."

"You're such a stubborn female." He cupped the back of her neck and took her mouth in a demanding kiss.

When they came up for air, he regarded her with glowing eyes. "One day, you will admit that you are mine."

"Don't hold your breath." She kissed him back to shut him up.

4 6

KIAN

ian was startled awake as the war room door banged open, and William walked in.

Lifting his head off the conference table, he glared at Onegus. "You shouldn't have let me sleep."

"I didn't notice that you'd dozed off."

The guy was not even trying to sound sincere.

"I assume you are all curious and want to hear what I've found out about Sofia's tracker so far." William put his laptop on the table and opened it to display a close-up of a tiny pebble that wasn't really a pebble.

"We definitely are." Kian rose to his feet and walked to the rolling cart Okidu had brought earlier. "But I need some coffee before I can focus enough to understand your technical jargon." He turned to the others. "Anyone?"

The three shook their heads.

Onegus chuckled. "At the rate I've been gulping coffee lately, I'm surprised that it's not going straight through my system and coming out the same color on the other end."

Wincing, William pushed his glasses back on his nose. "You could have spared me that image."

He'd gone back to wearing them in the lab mainly because the glare from the computer irritated his eyes, but also because his mate thought he looked distinguished in them, or something to that effect. Kaia might have said that he looked sexy or hot, but Syssi had used some other adjective when she'd told Kian about it.

When Kian sat back down with his coffee in hand, he took a long grateful sip and waved at William to begin.

"It's alien technology," William stated.

"Are you sure?" Turner asked.

William nodded. "I didn't take it apart because it's a solid-state piece, but I ran a lot of tests on it and put it through various imaging devices. The materials it is made of didn't come from Earth, and neither did the technology. It's inert when not in a living host's body, emitting no signal whatsoever. It uses the body's electricity to work, but the signal it emits is so weak that it barely registers. To compensate, though, it doesn't get any weaker with distance."

Kian frowned. "Did you have it implanted in another animal?"

"I had to. It wouldn't have worked otherwise. Magnus let me borrow Scarlett for a day, and one of my guys drove her around so I could test the signal's strength depending on the distance. He drove all the way to Santa Barbara, and there was no change. I bet we could have flown Scarlett to Scotland, and the signal would have remained the same."

Turner leveled his stare at William. "I hope you didn't implant the tracker in Scarlett in the village or bring her back with it."

"Of course not." William looked offended by the suggestion. "Julian did it in our warehouse downtown, and once we were done with the experiment, he took it out of Scarlett and brought her back to Magnus."

Turner looked as if he was chewing on a lemon. "I'm embarrassed to admit it, but I didn't take that into account, and I should have. We knew that the tracker needed a living host." He looked at Kian. "We can't just take all the trackers that Merlin extracts and give them to the Guardians to put in their pockets when they transfer to the decoy. All trackers of this kind, which I assume are predominantly taken out of the purebloods, will have to be implanted in either the Guardians or the crew."

Onegus flashed him a grin. "Not necessarily. There are plenty of goats and sheep on the *Aurora*. I'm sure the Kra-ell can do without a few of them for a while. We can implant two trackers in each to minimize the number of animals we will need to transfer." He looked at William. "Will that work? Or will it look suspicious that the trackers are moving in pairs? Can he determine where the different signals are coming from when they are so close to one another?"

"He can, and it will look strange, but Igor won't suspect that we removed the trackers from some and implanted them in others, doubling up. Don't forget that he probably thinks that we took his people by force, so he would assume that we chained the purebloods in pairs."

Onegus looked at Kian. "Would that have been your assumption in similar circumstances?"

Kian let out a breath. "That depends on what Igor knows and what he believes."

He'd spent long hours thinking about it, and when he realized that Igor had no reason to believe that a stronger compeller had released his people, he tried to put himself in the guy's shoes and speculate about what had actually happened.

His first thought would have been that they had been taken by other Kra-ell by force. The gaping holes in the compound's wall would have reinforced that suspicion.

The other option was that they had been taken by humans after being drugged, gassed, or incapacitated in some other way and imprisoned.

The one thing that wouldn't have made sense to Igor was the cruise ship they had been loaded onto. It didn't fit either scenario, which was probably why Igor was proceeding with so much caution.

Onegus arched a brow. "Care to elaborate?"

Kian turned to him. "Igor must have investigated what was loaded on the *Aurora* and found out about the MRI and the animals. He's either assuming that we are conducting experiments on his people or suspects that we found the trackers. Chaining the purebloods in twos doesn't fit either scenario."

"What's the solution, then?" Onegus asked.

"Smaller animals, of course." Turner looked at William. "Would gerbils provide enough electricity to power the trackers?"

William removed his glasses and put them on the table. "We know that the tracker worked when it was inside a cat, so I suggest we use a similarly sized animal. If you want, I can get a gerbil and a mouse and test it, but we don't have time. We need to get a hundred and fifty to two hundred cats delivered to the *Aurora* as soon as possible, so Merlin can implant them."

Could the doctor do so many in just a few hours?

The tiny trackers were easier to implant than to remove. Nevertheless, Merlin would have to organize an assembly line to get it done.

Kian groaned. "I can't believe how deep of a hole we've dug for ourselves. It's going from bad to worse. We have sheep and goats on our luxury cruise ship, and now we are going to add cats that will do their business all over the place. I will have to remodel it again."

William pushed to his feet. "I'll drive downtown right now, get a gerbil, and test whether the tracker works in its small body. If it does, it's going to be much easier to get a large number of gerbils to the *Aurora* than cats."

Turner lifted his hand. "We need to check with Merlin about how many of those alien trackers he expects to extract. Perhaps we won't need so many animals after all. The rest of the trackers do not require a living host to operate."

47

SOFIA

"We are cracking today." Sofia bandaged Gordi's thigh. "You are the fifth this morning."

His eyes shone as she tied the bandage and secured it with medical tape. "I like you taking care of me."

She lifted her gaze to him and smiled. "Careful. My boyfriend is in the next room operating the MRI machine."

"I don't mind sharing. Does he?"

Sofia put her hands on her hips and glared at him. "I'm not interested, Gordi. So lay off."

He opened his mouth to say something but thought better of it. Instead, he pulled up his pants and zipped them. "Thank you for the bandaging."

"You're welcome." She waited for him to leave the room before letting out a breath.

It was a difficult transition for everyone involved. Gordi wasn't a bad guy, but he wasn't used to not getting his way with the human females. He was making an effort to adjust to the new rules, though, and that was all she could ask for.

It wasn't easy for her either.

She was still gripped by anxiety whenever she had to deal with pure-blooded males, and since the purebloods were getting their trackers removed first, she'd had to deal with five of them just this morning.

A break would be lovely, but they were all pressed for time.

Merlin had organized a production line type of operation, and they were all working in a synchronized manner. Marcel operated the MRI, and when he found the tracker, he called Merlin to show him where it was. Merlin marked the spot on the body, and then the pureblood was moved to one of the beds in the other room to have the tracker removed. Morgada administered the local anesthetic, Merlin dug out the tracker, Inga sewed the incision up, and Sofia put the bandage around it.

"You look tired," Morgada said. "Take a coffee break. I can bandage the next one."

The Kra-ell could keep working for hours without rest, and so could the immortals, but Sofia was still human, and keeping up was impossible.

"Thanks." She smiled at the female. "I need to get off my feet for five minutes."

"Go." Morgada waved her off.

Isla and her father had set up a refreshments table out in the corridor, with coffee, water, and snacks for the humans and immortals, and Marcel had lined up the chairs they had taken out of the converted waiting room along the corridor on both sides of the snack table.

She poured herself a cup, grabbed a granola bar, and as she sat down with a relieved sigh, Isla walked out of the elevator on the other end of the hallway.

"Hello, my talented niece." She walked over to Sofia and sat down next to her. "You're just the person I wanted to see. What do you think about us organizing a dance party tonight after dinner?"

"Who are us? I'm going to be in the clinic all day, so I can't help organize anything."

Isla waved a hand. "Helmi, Lana, and Hannele are helping me, and I can get more people if I need to. I just wanted your opinion. Do you think the liberators would enjoy a dance when there are not enough ladies for them to dance with?"

Everyone loved dancing and needed some fun time to take their minds off the impending attack.

"You can organize line dancing. That way, no one needs a partner."

"That's a fabulous idea."

Marcel came out of the MRI room and poured himself a cup. "Did I hear you talking about dancing?"

Sofia nodded. "Isla wants to organize a party after dinner tonight, but

there are not enough ladies for couples' dancing, so I suggested line dancing. Do you think your friends would like it?"

"Some of them know the Scottish sword dance. It's kind of like line
dancing, and it's very entertaining, especially when they do it in kilts.
Regrettably, we don't have any here." He sat on Sofia's other side.

"Do you know that dance?"

He winced. "I know a few moves, but I'm clumsy and not well coordi-
nated. I'm not going to perform."

"That's a shame." She smiled. "I would have loved seeing you in a kilt."
She leaned closer and whispered in his ear, "Is it true that the Scots don't
wear anything under them?"

"Not anymore." He wrapped his arm around her. "What about the Kra-
ell? Do they have war dances?"

"I think so. Not that I've ever seen them dancing, but I assume that
they do."

As Boris arrived to have his tracker extracted with Jade escorting him,
Sofia overcame the spike of anxiety and asked, "Do your people have traditional dances?"

Boris shook his head. "We don't."

"Yes, we do," Jade said. "Back home and in my tribe, the males performed
for the females. It was most pleasing, and it got everyone in the mood for
the other kind of dancing." She clapped Boris on the back. "The problem is
that the only ones left who know the steps are Igor's cronies, and they are
all locked up."

Marcel grinned. "Perhaps we could let them out for tonight just to
perform for us and teach the young males the steps. It could be a test of
sorts to see how well they behave."

Jade looked doubtful. "Are you going to post Guardians with tranquilizer
guns to shoot them if they misbehave?"

"I'm sure they are not stupid enough to try anything, but we are not
going to take any chances."

"Learning the steps to the dance is not that important," Jade said. "It's not
worth the risk of letting them out."

"Are you planning to execute them?" Marcel asked.

She shook her head. "Only Valstar and Igor are on my kill list. The
others were not there when my people were slaughtered."

A shiver ran down Sofia's back. Did she care whether Valstar lived or
died?

Perhaps she should talk to him.

Heck, she needed to talk to her mother.

They had been avoiding each other for long enough. Perhaps Valstar's impending demise was reason enough for them to finally talk and maybe go visit him while there was still time.

It might be their last chance.

4 8

JADE

"Are you sure this is a good idea?" Phinas adjusted his holster.

Jade let out a sigh. "Tom assured me that they are under such strong compulsion to obey that they can't go to the bathroom without asking first, and they are the only ones who can teach the young males the dance steps. It would be a shame to lose it."

He arched a brow. "What are your plans for them?"

"They will stand trial, and those they harmed will provide testimony. They weren't among the ones who slaughtered my people, and I don't know if they were involved in the other raids." She stopped in front of the prisoners' cabin.

As the Guardian at the door nodded his greeting and opened the way for them, Phinas put a hand on her shoulder to stop her from going in.

"How have they been behaving?" Phinas reached behind the Guardian and closed the door.

The male shrugged. "Docile as newborn calves. They've been mostly watching television and playing video games. They asked for alcohol, but we didn't give them any. It might mess with the compulsion."

Jade snorted. "If alcohol had any effect on it, I would have been chugging down gallons to get rid of Igor's compulsion. I assure you that it doesn't."

The guy shrugged again. "My apologies, but my orders are not to provide them with alcoholic beverages."

"No apologies are needed. I was just correcting a misconception. Can we go inside now?"

The Guardian put his hand on the handle. "Let me make sure that they are all seated with their hands in their laps before you go in. Toven commanded them to obey my and the other Guardians' orders."

Jade frowned. "Toven?"

The Guardian's eyes widened, and he looked at Phinas as if asking for his help.

"That's Tom's other name," Phinas explained.

"Is it his nickname?"

"You'll have to ask him." Phinas motioned for the Guardian to get on with it.

When the guy ducked inside and closed the door behind him, Jade turned to Phinas. "Why does he have two different names?"

Phinas's lips curved up on one side. "Why do you call yourself Jade? I'm sure that's not your Kra-ell name. Were you given a shameful name like Emmett?"

"I have my reasons, and I'm not ready to share them with you."

"Why not?"

She was saved from having to answer when the Guardian opened the door and motioned for them to enter.

He followed them inside and took a post near the door that offered him a clear line of sight to all six of them.

Three purebloods sat on the couch, another two on armchairs, and the sixth one on a straight-back chair. They were all motionless, and their expressions were schooled to show no emotion, but she could see the trepidation in their eyes.

"Hello." She walked toward the dining table and pulled out two chairs, one for her and the other for Phinas.

He shook his head. "I'll be right here where I can get a clean shot at each one of them." He remained standing next to the Guardian.

It wasn't necessary, but she liked that he wanted to protect her.

Nodding, she put her chair with its back to the balcony doors and sat down facing the six. "I have a proposition for you," she said in Kra-ell. "The humans are organizing a dance tonight, and you are the only males on board who might know the steps to our traditional dances. I thought it would be a good opportunity for you to teach them."

Rodof regarded her with defiance in his eyes. "Why? So the knowledge will not be lost when you execute us?"

"I'm not going to execute you. None of you slaughtered my people, and although I have other grievances with you, none of them justifies an execution. You will stand trial, and those you harmed will testify. If their testimony reveals that you participated in the slaughter of other tribes, though, you will be executed." She gave him a cold smile. "I'm giving you a chance to do something nice for the community, which might earn you an honorable death instead."

Voplach lifted his chained hand and smoothed it over his long braid. "I don't know if I still remember the dance steps or the songs that went with them."

"I do," Mored said and started singing.

As the other five joined him, Jade had to fight the tears stinging the backs of her eyes.

It had been so long since she'd heard the song. Her firstborn son had been gifted with a beautiful, deep voice and perfect pitch. She'd loved hearing him sing.

Choking on the lump in her throat, she pushed to her feet, walked over to the bar, filled a glass with tap water, and took a few sips, slowly regaining her composure.

When the males were done, she clapped her hands. "That was very good. You should practice the other songs and the dance steps and get ready to perform tonight."

The consensus was that Igor and his Russian captain would not attack the *Aurora* as long as it was in the Baltic and close to shore. It might be her people's last opportunity to celebrate their freedom.

As all six turned to look at the Guardian, he nodded. "I allow you to practice singing and dancing in preparation for tonight's performance."

49

SOFIA

Sofia hesitated before ringing the doorbell to her mother's cabin.

She hadn't talked with her in years, and it felt awkward as hell to initiate a conversation with the hybrid female who had given birth to her and then abandoned her to the care of her human father and barely acknowledged her existence.

Joanna shared the cabin with another hybrid female, and she might have guests over as well, so they would not have privacy, but maybe they could go on a walk or find a quiet spot on the top deck. Unless Phinas or his men were conducting a swimming lesson, the place was mostly deserted.

Either way, it needed to be done, and she didn't have much time. She was using her lunch break to do this, and she still needed to grab a bite to eat before returning to the clinic.

Sofia took a deep breath and pressed the ringer.

The door opened a moment later. Her mother narrowed her eyes at her. "Sofia, to what do I owe the pleasure?" She looked pointedly at the bun on top of Sofia's head.

One of the few interactions they'd had involved Joanna commenting on Sofia's chosen hairstyle.

"I need to talk to you. Can I come in?"

Her mother opened the door all the way and waved her in.

"Where is your roommate?" Sofia sat down on the couch.

"Eating lunch in the dining room."

"What about you? Are you not hungry?"

Joanna flashed her a pair of fangs in a mockery of a smile. "I don't eat human food."

"I didn't know that." Sofia snorted. "That just demonstrates how little we have interacted over the years. I don't know anything about you."

"There isn't much to know." Joanna sat across from her on an armchair. "I heard that you got engaged. Congratulations."

"Thank you."

"I also heard that Igor sent you on a mission. Did you bring the so-called liberators?"

"So-called? Did you enjoy having your mind under Igor's control?"

"We were freed from one compeller and right away subjugated by another. I'd rather have my mind controlled by one of ours than by a human."

Sofia stifled the urge to release a relieved breath. If her mother hadn't guessed Toven's true identity, then the others hadn't either. As long as they didn't know who their liberators were, their options after Igor was captured were open.

"I prefer the human, and not because I'm human myself. Tom is a kind man. Igor is a monster who slaughtered the males of several Kra-ell tribes. They weren't given a chance to die honorably in battle. He froze them in place and ordered his cronies to cut off their heads. Valstar was one of those who did the killing."

Joanna's face twisted in a grimace. "I have no love lost for Valstar or Igor, but I don't know whether Tom is a good man or not. No one does what he and his friends did out of the goodness of their hearts. They want something from us, and it might be worse than what Igor wanted."

Sofia knew why they came. Igor was a threat to them, and they needed to eliminate him. But the fact was that they'd mobilized their forces to rescue the people of his compound instead of blowing it to pieces and getting rid of him without risking any of their own.

"What do you think they might want from you?"

Joanna regarded her as if she was mentally impaired. "Isn't that obvious? We are a long-lived alien species. They want to study us to find what makes our lives so much longer than humans and what makes us stronger and faster."

"That's not what they want. If that were the case, you wouldn't be enjoying a comfortable cabin on a luxurious cruise ship. You would be locked down in a cage and transported somewhere to be experimented on."

Joanna nodded. "I wondered about that. I figured that they wanted to study us." She waved a hand around the cabin's living room. "This place is probably full of surveillance cameras and listening devices, and they are recording everything we do and say."

"Did you find any?"

"No," Joanna admitted. "They must be very well hidden."

There was no point in continuing that line of conversation. Sofia had come over to talk about Valstar and not their liberators.

"I think that we should go talk to Valstar. It might be our only chance before Jade executes him. Whether we like it or not, he's our blood. Your father and my grandfather."

Joanna's eyes flashed red. "After I gave birth to a human child, he no longer acknowledged my existence. He doesn't think of me as his daughter, and I have nothing to say to him."

Sofia had known that Joanna and Valstar weren't on the best of terms, but she hadn't known that he had disowned her mother. Perhaps that was why she resented the child that had caused the rift?

"Things that seemed important back in the day seem much less so when one is about to die. He might have changed his mind about it. Also, it's possible that he was ordered by Igor to disown you as a precautionary tale to warn the other females against taking human lovers. You know how important the females were to Igor. He wanted to create a Kra-ell society that was ruled by males, and to do so, he needed to solve the problem of the scarcity of females. That's why he slaughtered the males of the tribes he raided. He also stole their money, but our liberators got some of it back for us."

"I've heard." Joanna grimaced. "I doubt we will get any of it."

This was getting tiresome.

Sofia wasn't the clan's ambassador to her people, and it wasn't her job to defend them. It was Jade's.

"I'm sure we will, but I'm not here to defend the people who saved us. Do you want to accompany me to see Valstar or not?"

Joanna hesitated for a brief moment before nodding. "I'll come with you. He'll probably ask me to leave, but I'll give him one last chance."

50

PHINAS

"The seating will be cramped." Phinas pushed the table further toward the wall. "But that's the best we can do if we want to clear a large enough area in the middle for dancing."

The ship had a club room with a dance floor and a bar, but it could accommodate only up to a hundred people, so it wouldn't work. It also had a theater and several conference rooms, but none of them were suitable. The dance had to be held in the dining hall.

Dandor adjusted the chairs and looked at the work the rest of the men had accomplished so far. "Not everyone will want to dance. We don't have enough ladies." He sighed. "It reminds me of the old days before we moved into the village, and I don't miss those days."

Phinas smiled. "Do you have someone special?"

Dandor grinned. "I have several someones."

That was surprising. Dandor wasn't the best-looking guy, and his charm could also use some work. He was intelligent but not well-read, and his fields of interest were race cars and football. He was also shy and awkward around women, but the clan ladies had no problem initiating, which seemed to work well for him.

Was he really that popular, though? Or was he exaggerating?

Perhaps he was an exceptional lover whose reputation preceded him.

The clan ladies were enjoying Kalugal's men and vice versa, but they weren't forming long-term relationships because none had found their true-love mates. Immortals were naturally promiscuous, and usually remained so even when married. The females didn't want to get addicted to one male's venom, and frequently changing bed partners was the best way to avoid that.

Still, it was odd that no one other than Rufsur and Edna had found each other and bonded. Perhaps it was because suddenly the clan females and Kalugal's men had a selection of potential immortal partners and did not want to commit to one before they sampled all that was available.

At least that was what Phinas had believed before meeting Jade.

He knew better now.

It was like the puzzle pieces had fallen into place, and he knew deep in his gut that she was the one for him. It didn't make sense, and it was probably one-sided, but Phinas wasn't afraid of challenges, even one as formidable as Jade.

It might take a while, and there might be obstacles the size of mountains in his way, but somehow he would make her his.

Regrettably that hadn't happened for his men, and none had found their fated mate among the clan ladies, which was disappointing.

When everything was done and all the tables were pushed away from the center, the dining room still didn't look much different or significantly more festive than it had before. The tables were covered in white table-cloths, and colorful cloth napkins were arranged to look like flowers and tucked inside wine glasses, but those were the only enhancements the humans had come up with from what they could find aboard the ship.

No one would be dressed up either, with the exception of Mey and Jin, who might have brought some evening attire with them, but Phinas doubted that.

Would Jade come up with something inventive like she had done with the swimming tops she'd made from his shirt?

If she used any more of his clothes, he would have to launder the shirt he had on every night and put it on the following day, but he was willing to endure that for her.

Hell, he was willing to endure much more, but for now that was all he could offer her.

When Jade strode into the dining room in her usual garb of cargo pants, a tight-fitting shirt, military boots, and her long black hair gathered in a ponytail, she couldn't have looked more beautiful to him if she had been wearing an evening gown and diamonds.

She was the most stunning female in the room, attracting everyone's attention as if she were the queen of the ball.

He waved her over to his table, and as she smiled at him, his damn heart skipped a bit.

What was he? A teenage boy with his first crush?

Hell, he'd never had the chance to have a teenage crush because his teenage years had been spent in a training camp, and when he was seventeen, he'd been taken to the brothel and lost his virginity to a woman twice his age or more.

He still smiled when he thought back on the clumsy boy he had been. The woman had been kind and patient with him, and he'd fallen in love with her as young men tend to do with the first female they have sex with.

Perhaps that experience had influenced his lifelong preference for mature, experienced women.

When Jade made it to the table, he pushed to his feet and pulled out the chair he'd saved for her, the one that had its back to the wall and faced the dance area and the entrance to the dining room.

"You know me so well." She gave him a brilliant smile as if he had greeted her with flowers. "Thank you for reserving the best seat for me, but I should sit with my people tonight."

"You are sitting with your people. Kagra, Drova, Pavel, and Piotr are going to join us."

He'd arranged it so she would enjoy her evening to the fullest without having to choose between those dear to her.

"What about your people?" Jade asked.

"There are four more seats at the table. Dandor and Chad reserved their spots, and the other two can go to whoever comes first."

51

JADE

$\mathcal{A}$t precisely eight o'clock in the evening, the six members of Igor's pod entered the dining hall. They weren't in chains, but four armed Guardians escorted them.

Murmurs arose all around, mainly from the other purebloods and the hybrids who knew who they were. The humans might not have known the difference between these males and the purebloods who had been born in the compound, but they should have noticed that Igor's inner circle members hadn't worn collars on their necks, while the others had them unless they were going out on missions.

Given that they all had implanted trackers, the tracking devices inside the collars had been redundant, but the collars had also contained explosives. If anyone tried to run, Igor could have activated them remotely. Except, he hadn't attempted that even after he'd realized the compound had been compromised, probably because he believed he could get his people back.

Jade rose to her feet and walked to the center of the room. "Allow me to present tonight's entertainment." She waved her hand at the six males standing in a straight line. "Madbar, Shover, Rodof, Berdogh, Mored, and Voplach will demonstrate several dances from our homeland. Traditionally, males performed these dances to entertain and entice females during festivals, but Igor squashed that custom the same way he did every other time-honored tradition of the Kra-ell. I encourage all the Kra-ell males to form lines behind the performers to learn the steps. Everyone else is welcome to join in singing the songs."

Drova raised her hand. "What if I want to learn the dance moves? Am I not allowed because I'm a female?"

Patience. Jade schooled her features to hide her annoyance.

She'd decided to be flexible and listen to what the people wanted, but it was difficult when her own daughter was challenging tradition.

Perhaps that wasn't a bad thing, though. Her people were at a turning point, and they could create new customs that would take all the positive things from the old ones and improve on them.

There was no reason to prevent females from learning the dance moves or even performing them for the males if they wished. Pragmatically, there was no need for the females to entice the males, but dancing was enjoyable whether it had a purpose or not.

Jade forced a smile. "It's not a question of being allowed or not. Traditionally, the dances are performed by males, but if you want to learn the moves, you are welcome to do so." She switched to English and repeated what she'd just said.

When she was done, Jade turned to the males. "You may begin."

Mored tapped his foot three times on the floor, and on the third tap, the six started singing, their deep male voices reverberating off the walls.

As the sound cut through her heart and reopened old wounds that had never healed and were still bleeding, Jade sat down next to Phinas and kept her expression neutral.

He put his hand on her thigh under the tablecloth. "Are you okay?" he whispered.

"I'm fine. The song evokes bittersweet memories."

"I bet." He gave her thigh a gentle squeeze before removing his hand.

He probably thought that the song reminded her of home, which it had, but the pain he must have felt radiating from her had nothing to do with her missing the place of her birth. She missed her sons, and she missed the males who had fathered them and the other children of her tribe.

Perhaps she wasn't the strong Kra-ell leader she was pretending to be. Or perhaps the many years she'd lived on Earth had changed her. Kra-ell mothers were supposed to be proud of the sons they lost in battle. They were allowed to grieve for them and to seek revenge, but they were not supposed to dream of a world in which their children didn't have to fight at all.

They were also not supposed to choose one male over all others. It wasn't fair, and the right thing was for a female to rotate between the males she had selected for her tribe.

Jade hadn't selected hers, she hadn't even known them before they were put in the same pod, but she'd grown to care for them nonetheless.

What she felt for Phinas, though, wasn't what she'd felt for them. She wanted to be with him and no one else, and that was very un-Kra-ell of her.

It was shameful, disturbing, disquieting, and yet she couldn't bring herself to push him away. Her excuse was that she needed Phinas to get information on the inner workings of the clan, and she would cling to that excuse when challenged, but deep in her soul, she knew that wasn't the real reason she was still with him.

52

PHINAS

*T*he wave of misery that had leaked from Jade when the males had started their performance had been so intense that Phinas had gotten ready to shield her if she burst into tears, but his female was made from titanium alloy, and she'd pushed through the pain.

Her mood had gradually lifted, and now she was smiling, clapping, and stomping her feet to the beat along with him and everyone else who wasn't on the dance floor.

Nearly two hours had passed since the performance had started, and although the males' routine had lasted no more than fifteen minutes, they had spent the rest of the time teaching the steps and the songs that went with them to everyone who wanted to learn, and that included humans, Guardians, and his men.

The purebloods were either good sports or didn't want to go back to the confinement of their cabin.

The Kra-ell language reminded him of the imagined Klingon language, the melody was catching, and the dance moves were aggressive, mimicking fighting, but there was a certain grace to them. They also required agility and flexibility that the humans had a hard time accomplishing, even the young ones.

Still, everyone seemed to be having great fun.

He leaned toward Jade. "Do you want to get up and dance?"

Kagra was on the dance floor with Dandor, Drova, and Pavel, and when

Max had joined their line, he'd gotten between Kagra and Dandor, which hadn't made Dandor happy.

"I'd rather stay here and supply the beat." Jade kept clapping and stomping. "Someone needs to do that."

"There are enough someones." Phinas rose to his feet and offered her a hand up. "Come on. It looks like fun."

"Females are not supposed to participate in these dances. I allowed the others to join if they wish, but I shouldn't."

"Why not?" He waved a hand at the dance floor. "Look at all the ladies enjoying themselves."

Yamanu was there with Mey, and so were Jin and Arwel. Toven had tried to persuade Mia to let him carry her and join the dance in his arms, but she had vehemently refused and was now watching her mate dance and clapping her hands to the beat.

"I'm not a good dancer." Jade lifted her drink and took a sip. "But you go ahead. You look like you're itching to join in."

"Not without you." He leaned to whisper in her ear, "You don't want your people to think that their leader is a dry stick. They need to see you having fun."

When Jade took the bait and took his hand, Phinas stifled a smile. He knew what buttons to push to make her do the things he believed she should.

"Finally!" Kagra said when the two of them joined the line.

She pushed Pavel toward Drova and pulled Jade next to her. "Watch my feet and follow my lead."

Phinas squeezed in on Jade's other side. After watching the steps for two hours, he had the routine memorized, and as he and Jade threaded arms to perform the kicks and flips, they moved in synchronized perfection.

The smile on Jade's face was priceless, and the longer they danced, the wider it got.

Somehow, Max got to the center of the dance floor and waving his hands shouted, "Everyone who knows the sword dance, please come forward. It's our turn to show them how it's done."

Yamanu, Arwel, and some of the other Guardians joined them, and as they started their Scottish sword dance, it took the Kra-ell males mere minutes to follow the complicated footwork. It took the humans a little longer, and some were still fumbling the steps, but it just evoked more laughter and more mirth.

"This is nice," Jade said breathlessly. "All of our people joining to celebrate."

"Isn't that ironic?" Drova said. "The enemies of yesterday are leading today's fun."

Jade's smile vanished, but she didn't respond to her daughter's taunt.

Another hour passed before people started drifting back to their tables to get drinks from the open bar.

"What do you want us to do with the dancers?" Max asked Jade. "Can they be given drinks?"

She nodded. "They earned them. Let them sit at a table and bring them a couple of bottles to share between them. After they are done drinking, take them back to their cabin. Please," she tucked on at the end.

Max grinned as he saluted her. "Yes, ma'am."

"I like him," Kagra said. "Maybe I'll invite him to my bed tonight."

Drova clapped her on the back. "Why maybe? Go for it." She turned to look at Jade. "Right, Mother?"

Jade glared at her. "You are too young to make comments about things like that."

"I'm sixteen, not six."

Jade had told him that the age of consent for males was twenty, but she'd never told him what it was for females. Was it the same?

"You are not having sex until you are at least twenty!"

Apparently, it was the same.

As mother and daughter argued, Phinas hid his smile by turning to Dandor. "Did you enjoy yourself?"

Dandor made a sour face. "I did until a moment ago." He cast a look at Kagra, who got up and headed toward the bar, where Max was collecting bottles for the Kra-ell. "What does Max have that I don't?"

Phinas chuckled. "The question is what he doesn't have that you do, and that's fear of rejection."

"I'm not afraid of anything." Dandor pushed to his feet and headed toward Kagra.

53

ONEGUS

"We have a decoy vessel," Turner said as he put his phone down. "It's an old cruise ship for sale that's currently docked at the port of Copenhagen. As cruise ships go, it's small, with room for one hundred passengers and forty-eight crew. In other words, it's large enough to pass the plausibility test. Our aim is to make it look as if all the pure-bloods and some of the hybrids are on board."

Kian regarded Turner accusingly, pretending dismay, "You bought us another cruise ship, Victor?"

Onegus didn't miss *The Hunt for Red October* reference, and it pulled a chuckle out of him, but Turner didn't even smile, and it wasn't as if he was too young to have seen the movie. The guy was in his forties, so he was a kid when it first came out, but it was a classic, and people watched it years after its release.

At times, Onegus wasn't sure whether Turner was impervious to humor or was just having fun keeping a straight face. If so, he played the part pretty damn convincingly.

"I didn't buy it," Turner said. "I leased the boat for a month at a great price under the pretext that we represent a potential buyer who wants our professional opinion on the ship's condition and value. I should have the paperwork ready for review and approval within a couple of hours, and as soon as we wire the funds and bind insurance coverage, we can get it prepped for departure. We are even getting it fully fueled."

Kian grimaced. "I'm sure they are charging us for the fuel. It's so damn expensive to fill up the tanks on those things."

This time a smile lifted one corner of Turner's lips. "Naturally, but the price for the rental itself is symbolic. They really want to get rid of the old clunker."

Onegus could tell that there was an undertone to the delivery hinting of a 'but' to follow. "What's the catch?"

"There is no catch, but there is a disadvantage that might actually turn out to be an advantage." Turner glanced at his notes. "The ship's maximum speed is fourteen knots. That's a snail's pace compared to Igor's yacht, which can cruise at thirty-seven knots. So outrunning Igor is not in the cards, and neither is choosing the where and when of the battle. It's going to be on his terms, or rather what he thinks are his terms. We are going to outsmart him."

Kian shook his head. "The bastard is always one step ahead of us. We had the element of surprise, superior technology, and greater manpower, and yet Igor is still calling the shots in this cat-and-mouse game we are playing. I can't wait for you to explain how having a slow vessel is an advantage."

A shadow of a smile appeared on Turner's stoic face. "We have a helicopter, so outrunning Igor or choosing the time and location of engagement are not as important as luring him in and encouraging him to engage without raising his suspicions. And that is exactly what we will achieve with this boat. It can accommodate nearly all of his people, which would have been a hard sell with a yacht and would have given him pause. It is also a larger vessel, making it very unlikely that Igor will opt to take it over by forcing his way onboard. He will have to resort to firing on the decoy with the intent of disabling or sinking it."

"How is that an advantage?" Kian asked. "It's exactly what we were trying to avoid, and also the reason we were looking for a smaller vessel and not another cruise ship."

"I know that's counterintuitive, but it might work in our favor. His yacht might be equipped with hand-held rocket launchers, but it's doubtful to have torpedo capability. I assume he will have to slow down to align his yacht with the cruise ship for the kill shot, telegraphing his intent and timing. This will give our pilot an advantage by allowing him to approach Igor's yacht from the rear while Igor's attention is focused on the ship in front of him."

Kian regarded Turner with a doubtful expression on his face. "Since the trackers will move to another cruise ship, and Igor will assume that his people are on the decoy, he will command the Russian to leave the *Aurora* and follow it instead. That's good because we can get the Kra-ell safely away. But I'm worried about the risk to our people on board the decoy."

Turner's smug smile reminded Onegus of a cat that just ate a mouse. "He will not command the *Anatolov* to leave the *Aurora* and follow the decoy for two reasons. The decoy will hug the coast, so launching a torpedo at it to sink it doesn't make sense any more than launching it at the *Aurora* before it's in the open sea. If we could remove all the trackers before reaching Copenhagen and transfer all of them to the decoy, he might have commanded the Russian to stand down because it was no longer needed. But since we can't remove them all in time, and some will remain on board the *Aurora* before Marcel can activate the signal scrambler, Igor will not allow them to get away. If he can't get them back, he'd rather kill them along with the people who took them. He can't let them fall into the hands of other Kra-ell or humans who will experiment on them. Thinking that the decoy has most of his people, he will go after it with the yacht and command the Russian to sink the larger cruise ship."

"Brilliant," Kian murmured.

"Thank you." Turner leaned back and crossed his arms over his chest. "Turning circumstances from disadvantageous into advantageous is very satisfying to me."

Onegus narrowed his eyes at the strategist. "You weren't looking for a yacht and settled on an old boat instead. You were actually looking for this type of vessel when you finalized your plan."

"Correct."

"Why didn't you tell us?" Kian asked.

Onegus snorted. "So you'd call him brilliant."

Turner's ego had taken several blows during the planning of this mission, and he needed to get it back to where it had been before, with everyone admiring him and calling him a strategic genius.

"I don't need ego boosters," Turner said. "I wasn't sure I'd be able to find the kind of vessel I was looking for, and I didn't want to get you two excited for nothing."

5 4

KIAN

*A*t first glance Turner's plan seemed brilliant, but the more Kian thought about it, the more his confidence in it wavered. A lot was based on assumptions and guesswork trying to anticipate Igor's moves, but the guy had been proven difficult to predict.

If the decoy hugged the coast, he would not choose to sink the vessel for the same reason he hadn't told the Russian cruiser to attack the *Aurora* yet. Rescue helicopters would arrive too quickly for him to collect his people.

On the other hand, he couldn't board the decoy and compel its passengers as long as the decoy was moving. Given his Kra-ell super strength, he could potentially leap onboard along with a couple of his cronies, provided that the vessels were matched in speed and course and provided that the decoy vessel's deck was not too high. But without knowing the force he'd meet onboard, that would not be wise, and Igor was not the kind of guy who made unwise decisions.

"I don't think Igor will attempt to sink the decoy. At least not initially." Kian proceeded to explain his reasoning. "Sinking the decoy vessel so close to shore would not give him enough time to do what he needs to do and would expose him to the risk of being shot at by the Norwegian Navy or Air Force. His likely initial move would therefore be to try and compel whoever is on board. If successful, and he should have no reason to suspect that he won't be, he could board the vessel at his leisure and assume command."

Turner tilted his head. "I agree that it would be his most likely first move. But if we are planning on luring him in and disabling his yacht, does it really matter what happens when he realizes that he cannot compel the crew?"

Turner's question was clearly rhetorical, but Onegus answered it anyway, "The effective range for him to compel everyone onboard the decoy, and especially those on the bridge, is limited. He needs to be close enough for the sound waves of his voice to reach them. My guess is that he will attempt to get within one hundred meters of the boat to do so, or even closer if the sea is rough or the weather stormy."

Kian drummed his fingers on the table. "Why do we need to wait for Igor to make his move, though? We can have the helicopter fire at him long before that and be done with it. We just need to lure him far enough up the coast of Norway, where there is barely any population so there are no witnesses." As the wheels in his mind kept spinning, he continued drumming his fingers. "I assume that Igor will issue a distress call, but even if he does, we can collect him and his cohorts from the yacht before the search and rescue parties arrive at the scene. Grabbing four people is not as time-consuming as grabbing nearly two hundred. I also suggest that we have the helicopter fire on the yacht as soon as it is safe to do so. I want us to choose the time and location."

"We don't know what weapons Igor has on board," Turner said. "If he has shoulder-mounted missiles as we suspect, he can shoot at the helicopter. Those rockets are not accurate, and it's hard to hit a moving target with them, but he might get lucky, and we can't risk that. The helicopter is equipped with superior guided missiles that are not going to miss, and our best bet is to keep Igor focused on the decoy while the helicopter approaches from his aft and fires a killing shot."

Kian groaned. "There are too many ifs for my liking."

"Nothing is ever guaranteed," Onegus said. "But we can improve our odds by not waiting for events to unfold and force the outcome we want. Igor either gets close to try and compel, and we launch a missile at him first, or he doesn't, and we fake a mechanical issue slowing the decoy to a crawl. That will lure him closer, and then we fire. It's great if we hit him, but not necessary. The idea is to keep him focused on the ship in front of him while missing the danger from behind."

Kian found a gaping hole in Onegus's logic. "How? Until he's ready to attack, he won't get close enough to be in range even if the decoy vessel slows down to a crawl. In fact, being as careful and paranoid as he's proved

429

himself to be, he will probably suspect a trap and be more likely to keep his distance."

Onegus smirked. "We make him get in range. We transfer the disruptor to the decoy, and we activate it when the boat is not in Igor's line of sight yet. He will freak out and have no choice but to get closer to investigate. Even if he suspects it's a trap, he won't turn around and abandon the pursuit. He's too invested by now. And even if he does, we can still get him with the helicopter."

Turner shook his head. "Again, we can't risk the helicopter like that. Without a proper distraction, Igor will see it coming and shoot at it."

"What if the decoy just stops?" Kian asked. "It can pretend a malfunction. After all, it's an old clunker. It can even signal an SOS, claiming loss of power. Losing the signals from the trackers at the same time the ship breaks down may prove odd enough for him to want to get closer to investigate."

"I love it," Onegus said. "He'll probably think that his people tried to overpower their captors, and we killed them all, and that's why the trackers stopped transmitting."

"No, he won't." Turner let out a sigh. "Don't forget that we are also transferring some of the human-made trackers on board the decoy, and they would have continued transmitting even after their hosts were dead. I believe Kian's prior assumption that Igor will get closer on his own accord is correct. His aim will be to compel everyone on board."

Kian felt smug for a brief moment, but the truth was that he hadn't suggested anything that hadn't been discussed before in one way or another.

In fact, all the different scenarios and possibilities were scrambled in his head, and he needed a few quiet moments alone to sort it all out. But perhaps Turner's analytical brain had already done that.

Leaning back, Kian looked at the strategist. "So, what's our next step, Victor?"

"I need to make a few phone calls. Can we continue in half an hour?"

It seemed that Turner also needed time to organize his thoughts.

"No problem." Kian pushed to his feet. "I could use a walk in the fresh air and a cup of good coffee." He looked at Onegus. "Do you want to join me at the café?"

The Chief shook his head. "I have a few things I need to go over as well."

Kian nodded. "I'll see you both in half an hour."

SOFIA

$\mathcal{A}$s Sofia walked out of the elevator with her mother, she was surprised to find Toven standing outside Valstar's cabin.

"I hope you don't mind me butting in." He pushed away from the wall. "After you asked me for permission to see Valstar, it occurred to me that you might need my help to get truthful answers from him. He can't lie to me. "

Joanna snorted. "He can still manipulate you. My father is very smart."

"Your English is very good." Toven regarded her briefly. "Your daughter must have inherited her talent for languages from you." He smiled. "She definitely didn't inherit it from Jarmo."

If Toven hoped to get some response from Joanna by bringing up Jarmo's name, he would be disappointed. Joanna had never cared for him, and she hadn't expected to get pregnant. Then again, she had engaged with him while in her fertile cycle, so maybe she had?

But why? What had she tried to prove?

"We both got the talent from Valstar," her mother said. "Can we go in now? I want to be done with this."

"What do you want to achieve by speaking with your father?"

Joanna closed her eyes and let out a sigh. "I want to make my peace with him before he dies. He might not want me there, though. He has a better relationship with Sofia than he has with me, which is ironic given that our falling out was because of her."

Sofia's ire ignited as if Joanna had thrown a match into a vat of gasoline.

"It's not my fault that you wanted to piss off your father by taking a human to your bed. I'm the result of your actions. And even if you didn't have me, what kind of a relationship did you expect to have with the pureblood who fathered you? In his eyes, you are an inferior. Not only because you're a hybrid but because you are a female. Back on the home planet, where females ruled, that would have been an advantage, but not in Igor's camp."

She'd wanted to say that for so long to get back at her mother for all the years of neglect, but up until now Joanna had never admitted the reason for her indifference.

The truth was that the purebloods didn't interact much with the children they produced with human females, so Valstar's and Joanna's lack of a relationship wasn't unusual. But the hybrids were more accepting of their children.

Many of the hybrid males didn't want to produce human offspring, using protection to ensure that they didn't procreate with the humans they took to their beds, and there had been very few children born to them. Aside from Sofia, all the others were males, and they had some sort of relationship with their fathers. The hybrid males who had sons couldn't get too close to them without undermining their position in the Kra-ell society, but none pretended that their children didn't exist, like Joanna had done.

"I can't argue with that," her mother said. "I hope things will be different under Jade's rule, and the purebloods will treat the hybrids better. As Sofia pointed out, we didn't choose to be born. The choice belongs to our parents, and they should take responsibility for the results of their actions." She looked at Toven. "Can we please go in?"

That was as close to an apology as Sofia could expect. It wasn't enough to douse the fire burning inside her, but it sufficed to smother it to a mere smolder.

"Yes, of course." Toven rang the bell.

A Guardian opened the door and motioned for them to come in. "He's ready for you."

"Good afternoon." Valstar smiled at them. "What a special treat it is to get a visit from my daughter and granddaughter. Please, sit down."

He looked no worse for wear, but his attitude was unrecognizable. It was disconcerting to hear Valstar talk like a human grandfather.

Had Toven compelled him before their arrival?

"How are they treating you?" Joanna asked in Russian.

"As well as can be expected for a prisoner awaiting his execution."

Toven pulled out a chair from the dining table and brought it over. "I spoke with Jade and asked her to consider allowing you to stand trial."

Valstar's eyes flickered green with hope. "Who will be the judge?"

"It remains to be decided, and Jade hasn't given me her answer yet."

Valstar dipped his head. "Thank you for doing this for me."

"You're welcome. Now I want you to answer Joanna's and Sofia's questions truthfully. Don't lie to them, and don't try to manipulate them."

Sofia could feel the compulsion even though it hadn't been directed at her, and given Joanna's shiver, she'd felt it too.

Looking like a new male, Valstar cast them a bright smile. "What do you want to know?"

"Did you ever care for me?" Joanna asked.

"Of course, I care. You are my daughter. But it's not the Kra-ell way to show emotions. You're half human, so your need for coddling is greater than that of a pureblooded child, and your mother supplied that in excess. You were always rebellious and did not show proper respect to your elders like the other hybrid children did. Then you took a human lover, which you did for the sole purpose of getting a rise out of me. When you got pregnant, and none of the pureblooded or hybrid males claimed your child, making it obvious that the child was fathered by a human, I had to beg Igor not to punish you. He wanted to whip you in front of the entire community to scare the other females from taking humans to their beds."

Joanna's eyes widened. "He wanted to whip me while I was carrying a child?"

"You disobeyed the rules, and you should have been punished. You escaped punishment thanks to my intervention. I told Igor that you were mentally unstable and incapable of proper Kra-ell behavior."

Her mother's shoulders stiffened. "That could have cost me my life. If Igor thought I was defective, he could have executed me."

Valstar shook his head. "I knew that he would never execute a female. You were too valuable, and your womb could still produce other children regardless of your mental instability."

"That was smart," Sofia said. "You found a way to manipulate Igor."

"Regrettably, to a minimal extent." Valstar sighed. "I did what I could."

"What about me?" Sofia asked. "Did you care for me?"

"Naturally. How do you think you got to spend nearly eight years in the university? I convinced Igor that we needed a linguist and suggested you. I told him that as my granddaughter, you had an exceptional talent for languages."

"Thank you. I loved the university. But when you trained me for the mission, you didn't act as if you even liked me, and when I told you that I had a heart problem, you were dismissive."

Valstar nodded. "As I said before, the Kra-ell don't show emotions, but that wasn't the only reason I didn't express my concern when you told me about your fake heart problem. Igor had all the phones tapped, and he often listened to my conversations. I suspected that you were lying, but I couldn't confront you about it without undermining us both."

5 6

KIAN

*W*hen Kian returned from his coffee break, Onegus nodded in greeting, and Turner swiveled his chair around and looked at him. "Did William get back to you about the gerbils?"

Kian had forgotten about that. Since nothing major had been happening the day before and they had just been waiting for Turner to find a decoy vessel, he'd used the time to catch up on work and spend time with his family.

"He did." Kian pulled out a chair and sat down. "The trackers work even when implanted in gerbils."

"Good." Turner swiveled his chair back to face the table and tapped his pen on his yellow pad. "I've already spoken with Captain Olsson and told him about the refueling stop in Copenhagen. I've also spoken with Merlin, and he said that all the purebloods he's scanned so far had the alien trackers. I asked him to scan several of the hybrids to check what kind of trackers they had, and all those he tested had human-made ones that don't require a living host to operate. After doing some math, though, I figured that Igor must have more of those alien trackers than the number of purebloods, so Merlin might find more of them among the hybrids he hasn't checked yet. It's also possible that Igor is keeping the alien trackers for the purebloooded children to be implanted when they reach maturity and for those yet to be born."

Kian lifted his hand to stop Turner from continuing. "I'm very interested in hearing that math."

Turner flipped to the previous page on his yellow pad. "I asked Yamanu to sit down with Jade and go over the number of purebloods in her community and who came from where. There were eighty-seven adult purebloods in the compound, of which seventy-eight are on board the *Aurora*. Fifty of them are females, but only twelve were born in the compound. The other forty came from other tribes. Out of the forty, four came from Igor's pod, and twenty-five came from other pods. The remaining eleven were born in the other tribes. If we assume that most pods contained four females and sixteen males, then to obtain the twenty-five females, Igor had killed ninety-six original settler males and extracted their trackers. Since only fifty-three purebloods were born in his compound, and eleven Earth-born females came from other tribes, Igor still had about thirty-two alien trackers to spare. The question is what he did with them. We know that he put one in Sofia, but the two hybrids that were assigned to her had simple trackers in them. My bet is that he saved the rest for the pureblooded children and special missions like the one he sent Sofia on."

"Makes sense," Onegus said. "So, given that fascinating math exercise, how many gerbils do we need?"

"Merlin said that he can extract trackers from about sixty of the purebloods, so sixty gerbils, or maybe a little more just in case some don't make it. I don't know how resilient gerbils are."

"What about the kids?" Onegus asked. "He might have implanted them already. Would there have been a reason for him to wait until they were fully grown?"

"It's irrelevant whether they do or don't. Merlin can extract about sixty trackers by the time the ship docks in Copenhagen and no more. It doesn't matter who he extracts them from."

"Right." Onegus nodded. "We need to get the gerbils to Merlin by tomorrow afternoon." He cast an amused sidelong glance at Kian. "You should be happy that we don't need to get sixty cats. The gerbils don't take a lot of space and can be kept in a cage."

"Cages," Turner corrected. "They can't be all clustered in the same spot. The Guardians will have to distribute them around the ship."

"Can you take care of that as well?" Onegus asked. "Or should I do that?"

Kian wondered how one went about getting sixty gerbils in Copenhagen, but he was confident in Turner's ability to do so.

"I'll have my secretary arrange that." Turner flipped to the most recent page on his yellow pad. "It might be a good idea to get Mey and Jin off the *Aurora* while she's docking in Copenhagen. I wish we could have gotten the humans and the children off as well, but we can't. The adults still have trackers in them, and we won't have time to remove them. We also don't have time to prepare fake passports, even for the children. Copenhagen's international airport is modern and sophisticated, and we won't be able to smuggle people out through it on a commercial flight or even on a chartered plane. There are too many security cameras and fail-safes."

"Mey and Jin will refuse to leave." Onegus turned to Kian. "Not unless you order them to disembark. Since it's a security issue, you can use it as an excuse. "

"Not really. If I don't order Mia to leave, then I can't order them. And in any case, I wouldn't do that. I'm not risking getting in trouble with Jin."

Onegus chuckled, thinking it had been a joke, but Kian was serious. That girl's talent was scary, and with her contrary character, the Fates knew what she was capable of when feeling slighted.

"Mia can also disembark," Turner said. "And even Toven. His compulsion over the Kra-ell will hold until the *Aurora* arrives at Greenland. He and Mia can fly there and wait for the ship to arrive, and if they do that, Mey and Jin might choose to accompany them."

"I'll talk with him." Kian swiveled his chair to face Turner. "The next thing we need to figure out is what to do once we get Igor and his men, either dead or alive. Even if the decoy remains intact after the confrontation, it can't catch up to the *Aurora*, so we have to fly our men out of Norway, either to meet up with the others in Greenland or back home."

"By the way, the decoy's name is the *Seafarer*." Turner flipped through his yellow pad until he found what he was looking for. "The helicopter is capable of transporting twelve fully armed soldiers. Assuming that it is still operational and didn't get hit, it can fly them to a nearby airfield in two trips. I can arrange a chartered plane to pick them up from there, but it will be much easier to arrange a flight to Greenland than to fly them all the way back to Los Angeles. We've already made arrangements to pick everyone up from Greenland, but I still need to supply them with a final destination." He looked at Kian. "Did you decide where we are taking the Kra-ell and their humans?"

"It depends on whether we catch Igor. If we do, I'll put the Kra-ell inclusion in the village up for a vote. But since I need the big assembly's unanimous approval, it will have to wait until the Guardians are back."

"We need to put them somewhere in the meantime," Onegus said. "We don't have enough space in the keep, and we rented out all the apartments in the building across from it. Any ideas?"

Kian shook his head. "Not yet, but I will come up with something."

"What about our fake campsite?" Turner asked. "It's already fenced off and equipped with William's security system. We already have twenty-seven mobile homes parked there, but there is enough room to double the number. It will not be comfortable, and they will be cramped for a few days, but it will give us some breathing room until we find a different solution."

The campsite had been built close to the tunnel entrance leading to the village to explain the extra traffic on the road. Housing over three hundred people in there would attract too much attention, but it could work as a temporary solution.

PHINAS

When Onegus and Kian finished explaining their newest plan, Yamanu looked at Phinas. "I don't have enough Guardians I can assign to the decoy. I will need some of your men, but I will lead the mission. I can leave Arwel in charge."

Phinas shook his head. "I'm going to the decoy with my men. Your Guardians are much better at babysitting the Kra-ell than my men and I are, so they need to stay on the *Aurora*."

Phinas had thirty men with him, and Yamanu had only sixteen Guardians, including Arwel, who was technically on vacation. Together with the two of them, their force was forty-eight warriors strong—too small to secure the Kra-ell on board the *Aurora* and to go after Igor, but it would have to do. He would capture the bastard for Jade and bring him hogtied to her so she could chop off his head while he was immobilized.

There was no greater gift he could give her.

Yamanu flashed him a toothy smile. "Thank you for the offer, but I insist on having Guardians on board the *Seafarer*. You can contribute half of yours, and I'll contribute half of mine."

That was reasonable, except for the fact that it would be difficult for him to choose who would go and who would stay, and those that stayed would have to assist the remaining Guardians babysitting the Kra-ell.

"Fine, but I lead the mission. I'll transfer command of my remaining men to you."

Nodding, Yamanu turned to the tablet to get the Chief's approval.

"That's fine with me," Onegus said. "In fact, that was what I wanted to suggest." He looked at Phinas. "You seem confident in your ability to face Igor and capture or eliminate him, and so far, you've done exceptionally well on this mission. That being said, it has been many years since you've led men into battle. Are you sure that you can handle the task?"

"I'm sure. For better or worse, the training I received was hardwired into me. My instincts and response times are still excellent."

Phinas was also a fast thinker and a decent strategist, but he didn't want to toot his own horn. Actions spoke louder than words, and he would prove his worth by delivering Igor to Jade.

Onegus nodded. "Agreed. You lead the mission with half of your force and half of Yamanu's. Max will lead the Guardians, but he will answer to you."

Phinas nodded.

"Let's move to the next item." Onegus shifted his focus to Toven. "Since we are docking at Copenhagen, you and Mia can get off and either fly home or to Greenland to meet up with the *Aurora* when she arrives."

"Why would we want to do that?"

Kian leaned forward. "Because you have a Russian cruiser on your ass. Don't you want to get your mate out of harm's way?"

"She won't go unless I do, and I don't feel comfortable abandoning these people. My compulsion will hold until they get to Greenland, but I prefer to stay on the *Aurora* in case the unexpected happens. Especially since half of the force is transferring to the decoy."

"He has a point," Turner said.

Kian let out a breath. "Then I guess I shouldn't suggest the same to Jin and Mey."

"Probably not," Yamanu said. "But I'll give it a try. Arwel can go back with them as well. He's not on official duty on the *Aurora*, and if I'm not leaving to lead the force on the *Seafarer*, he doesn't need to stay."

"I'm putting him back on official duty," Onegus said. "You need him."

Yamanu nodded. "That I do."

"Next." Onegus glanced at his notes. "As soon as the Aurora docks in Copenhagen, you will receive a crate that will be marked as live lobsters. But instead of lobsters, it will be packed with sixty-five gerbils for Merlin to implant the alien trackers in. Get it to him as soon as possible. I've already spoken to him about arranging an assembly line for that purpose. Once all the gerbils are implanted, they will be put back in the same crate and transferred to the *Seafarer* along with other provisions for the voyage. We will do the same with the other supply crates, except the other ones will be empty when they leave for the *Seafarer*. We want Igor to think that we smuggled his people out in them, so they will be making the rounds for most of the day. Any questions about that?"

"What about food for the gerbils?" Yamanu asked.

"There will be food for them in the crate," Turner said. "They will be delivered in individual small cages, and the food will be inside. When you take them out of the crate on the decoy, spread them throughout the ship in a way that you would've spread out people."

Yamanu still looked worried about the critters. "Won't they be making a racket, chirping and scratching, or whatever other noises gerbils make?"

Turner returned to typing on his laptop when he gave Yamanu the answer. "They will still be sedated after the operation when they are put back in their cages and transferred in the crate to the *Seafarer*. Any other questions?"

Phinas lifted his hand. "What do I tell Jade?"

"You can tell her our plan," Kian said.

"She'll want to be aboard the decoy and help capture Igor."

Kian nodded. "I bet she will, but she's needed on the *Aurora*. Her people cannot lose their leader, and given her vendetta, I don't think she should be on the decoy. She might be more of a liability than an asset."

Marcel raised his hand. "Do I need to be on the decoy to activate the scrambler?"

"You can show someone else how to do it," Kian said. "I prefer for you to stay on the *Aurora*."

Marcel looked relieved. "I can show Max how to do it."

"Or you can show my tech guy," Phinas offered.

"Show both of them." Onegus solved the problem.

"We are going to arrive a day late to Greenland." Toven leaned toward the tablet. "Did you change the charter plane's schedule?"

"There's no need," Onegus said. "Since the *Aurora* is refueling at Copenhagen, it no longer needs to conserve fuel, and she can go faster and still arrive on time."

"Awesome." Yamanu grinned. "I just hope we don't get hit. I would hate to miss that flight."

5 8

JADE

When Phinas finished explaining the plan, Jade pushed to her feet and started pacing the length of the cabin. "I want to go with you. I can leave Kagra in charge."

How could they deny her the satisfaction of catching Igor and ending him on the spot? She wasn't one of their soft females who they coddled and protected. She was a capable warrior, stronger, faster, and better trained than the Guardians and Phinas's men.

He looked at her helplessly. "I know that, and I told Kian that you would want to be there when we catch Igor, but he said that you are too important to lose. Your people need you."

She stopped and glared at him. "Does that imply that you are dispensable?"

"Yeah, I am."

The conviction and acceptance in his tone made her angry, but then wasn't she also guilty of regarding males as dispensable?

It was the Kra-ell way for males to fight and die honorably in battle. Reaching old age was considered a failure for a warrior. When she was younger, Jade had accepted the Mother's doctrines without question. But it had been a very long time since she'd attended a sermon, and without the high priestesses drumming it into her head, she'd pondered the validity of those teachings over the years.

Perhaps the priestesses were not the mouthpieces of the Mother, and maybe tradition should not be followed blindly.

After her sons were murdered, her doubts had doubled. It wasn't only her anger about the way they had died, it was about the way she still missed them. She would have missed them just as much if they had fallen in battle while performing heroic acts of bravery, but perhaps she wouldn't have been as bitter and consumed by the need for vengeance.

Jade was a Kra-ell warrior herself, and dying in battle was how she'd always expected her corporeal life to end and her afterlife to begin in the idyllic fields of the brave.

She would never have tried to shield her sons from battle and rob them of the opportunity to earn their place as well. But it wouldn't have been easy, and pride in their bravery would have never compensated for their loss. She wasn't like the soft human females who dreamt of attending their sons' weddings and holding their grandchildren in their arms, but after spending most of her life on Earth, she could understand them better.

"You are not dispensable, Phinas."

He smiled. "Are you going to miss me?"

Of course, she was, but she wasn't going to admit it. "Don't flatter yourself."

He kept on smiling. "Admit it. You'll miss me when I'm gone."

"Fine. I admit it." She plopped on the couch next to him. "But don't you dare breathe a word of it to anyone. I have a reputation to uphold."

"I know. The Kra-ell way." He wrapped his arm around her shoulders and pulled her toward him. "We had all kinds of traditions where I grew up, and none of them were worth preserving. Perhaps you should rethink yours as well. I don't think that the Kra-ell's tribe-style family is natural. I think it was a solution to a problem and that the Kra-ell are not so different from the gods and the humans in that regard."

"You're projecting your values onto us."

He rubbed his hand up and down her arm. "And yet, here you are, cozying up to an immortal and totally uninterested in the pureblooded males of your species."

"It's the novelty." She put her head on his shoulder. "And it's the fact that you are an outsider, and I don't need to keep up the leader persona with you. I can relax and be myself. Being with you is like a sanctuary, but it doesn't mean that I'm in love with you. I'm not capable of that. But I admit that I like you a lot."

Was it true, though?

Could she still think that when the thought of not having him sleeping next to her depressed her?

How would she go back to sleeping alone? And why did it bother her so much that he wouldn't always be there?

Perhaps she should establish a new tradition of the extended Kra-ell family all sleeping together in one huge bed, with those who wanted to engage in sexual activities using a different room and returning once they were done.

Dipping his head, he kissed the top of her head. "I like you a lot too, and I promise to bring Igor to you, hopefully still alive. I'll drop him at your feet, so you can finally get your revenge and chop off his head."

She lifted her head and smiled at him. "You say the sweetest things."

5 9

TOVEN

"*I* need to get to the clinic." Mia wheeled her chair to the door. "They should be getting the shipment of gerbils any minute now."

Toven put a hand on her shoulder. "Are you sure that you can handle the little critters? What if they bite you?"

She smiled. "I'm an immortal now, so I will heal fast. I have a way with animals and a gentle touch. I can make it easier for them. Besides, it will be fun to work with people for a change."

Toven crouched next to her wheelchair. "I thought I was the only company you needed."

When he wasn't busy planning the mission, they were working together in silent harmony. Mia worked on illustrations for her next children's book, and when she needed a break, she sketched environments for Perfect Match adventures.

He worked on a science fiction dystopian romance that was very loosely based on their shared virtual adventure.

Toven found that he enjoyed writing science fiction and exploring the different possibilities of where humanity could be in five hundred years or more. With his perspective on history, his predictions were probably more accurate than most, but probably not as good as the ones produced by artificial intelligence. The computer could process nearly endless pieces of information and base its predictions on all of the history stored in its database, which was infinitely more than Toven could store in his head.

Mia cupped his cheek. "I love working side by side with you. I wouldn't trade it for anything in the world, but from time to time, I crave the company of other people." She leaned to kiss him on the lips. "I also love animals."

"I would like you to reconsider getting off and taking a flight to Greenland."

She shook her head. "We talked about it. If you are staying, I'm staying with you. There are children and pregnant women on board. Leaving while they have to stay would be cowardly on my part."

"You are one of the bravest people I know, but you have restricted mobility, and they don't. That's why I'm worried about you."

She smiled indulgently. "I'm still an immortal who will not get hypothermia if the ship sinks and we can't get into the lifeboats for some reason. That can't be said about the humans and the children. I'm in less danger than they are."

There was one more thing he could try. "If you agree to fly to Greenland, Mey and Jin might consider that as well. If you don't, they won't either."

"They are not going to consider it even if I do." She patted her stumps. "As you've pointed out, I'm the one with mobility issues. They are not. My departure will not influence their decision to stay."

Letting out a sigh, he pushed to his feet. "I'll take you to the clinic." He opened the door and wheeled her chair out into the corridor.

She turned to look at him over her shoulder. "What are your plans for today?"

"I'll be supervising the Kra-ell and making sure that none try to leave the ship. We locked up those who are still loyal to Igor, and we keep an eye on the others."

She was quiet on the way to the elevator and then turned her head to look at him again. "How come you are not joining the team on the decoy? Not that I want you to, but I assumed that we were needed to compel Igor. I understand why I can't be included, but what about you?"

When the elevator door opened, he wheeled her inside and pressed the button for the level the clinic was on. "Everyone on the decoy will have earpieces. If they capture Igor, they will tranquilize him and keep him that way until they get him to Greenland for me to interrogate, so there is no reason for me to be there. Though frankly, I don't think Igor will be captured alive. They will most likely have to kill him."

"What makes you think that?"

"It's just a hunch. If Igor can't escape, he'll choose death over captivity. He will fight to the death."

6 0

JADE

*J*ade stood at the entrance to the ship's loading dock and waited for Phinas to come back to her.

Everything was ready. The gerbils had been implanted with the gods-made trackers, each member of the decoy team was carrying two human-made trackers in his pocket, the crates were being loaded on forklifts, and it was time to say goodbye to Phinas.

Neither the *Anatolov* nor the *Helena* had followed the *Aurora* into the port, and both were keeping their distance from the harbor, which was good news for the team leaving for the decoy.

Nevertheless, they were maintaining a low profile and keeping up the charade. Large crates had been loaded onto the *Aurora* and were now being offloaded to be driven across the harbor to the decoy. The Guardians and Phinas's men would follow on foot. If Igor had informers in the port, they would report the transfer of the crates, and he would assume that his people had been transported inside them.

Watching Phinas with his men, she felt tears prickling the back of her eyes, which made her angry, and the anger burned through the moisture.

She wasn't some weak human female, watching her lover leave for war and anxious for him to return to her unharmed.

Except, that was precisely what she felt.

Would she let him kiss her in front of everyone like the humans did in the movies?

Yes, she would.

None of her people were there, so only the Guardians and Phinas's men would see them kissing, and they wouldn't make a big deal out of it.

She couldn't let him go without showing him how much she cared about him.

What if he didn't come back?

She would never forgive herself for sending him off, thinking that he was only a temporary distraction and that she would forget him in no time. She couldn't say the words, but she could show him by kissing the living daylights out of him as the humans liked to say. She wasn't sure what the phrase meant and what was the significance of daylights, living or dead, but it was supposed to indicate a particularly passionate kiss.

He would get what she was trying to communicate.

As he turned around and strode toward her, she forced a smile. "Ready to go?"

He tilted his head. "You look worried. Don't be. This is not my first rodeo, and I know what I'm doing."

"I know." She closed the distance between them and wound her arms around his neck. "Don't get killed. It would really piss me off."

Getting over the initial shock of her initiating a public display of affection, Phinas grinned and wrapped his arms around her. "Don't worry. I'll come back as promised, with Igor bound in chains with a pretty bow on top."

She wanted to kill Igor, but more than that, she wanted Phinas to come back in one piece. "Don't take unnecessary risks to take him alive. Just blow him out of the water if you can."

As he looked into her eyes, his grin turned into a frown. "You really mean it."

"I do."

"You'll give up the satisfaction of chopping off Igor's head just to get me back."

"Yes. I owe you a life debt. I'm not allowed to accompany you to protect you, but I can sacrifice killing Igor myself to keep you safe. Knowing that he's dead will have to satisfy my need for revenge."

With a smile tugging on his lips, he pulled her closer against his chest. "I know it's not about the life debt. Admit it, you love me."

"The Kra-ell don't feel love, but you have my respect and friendship in addition to the life debt."

"Right." He smirked. "I'll play along for now, and I won't take unnecessary risks to get the bastard alive. The safety of my men and the Guardians comes first. But if I can get him for you, I will."

"Thank you." She pulled his head toward hers and kissed him hard.

When his hand closed on her bottom, she felt her cheeks warming, but she didn't do anything to stop him and kept on ravishing his mouth.

"Save it for later," Yamanu said behind Phinas. "You need to get going."

Phinas didn't let go of her right away, and she didn't let go of him until they were both out of air.

"Get back to me," she whispered.

"I will. I promise."

61

PHINAS

Saying goodbye to Jade had been oddly difficult. They were not parting ways for an extended time, not unless something went terribly wrong.

Phinas was heading out to a potential battle on board the decoy, and Jade was on the *Aurora*, which had been shadowed for days by a Russian navy cruiser that they surmised would attempt to sink them at some point. They were both heading into danger, but that was only partially responsible for making the separation so hard.

Somewhere along the way, during the several short days they had shared, he'd gotten accustomed to spending his nights with Jade and waking by her side in the morning. They had both been busy during the days, but he could find her whenever he pleased, and he'd done it several times each day, and so had she.

It was as if they couldn't stay apart for too long without an invisible cord getting pulled too taut and forcing them to seek each other.

Not having her near was a lack he was constantly aware of, and Phinas felt like something was missing even while attending the command meetings to which he'd been invited as of late.

He hadn't admitted the extent of his feelings to her, and she hadn't either, but his guess was that she felt the same way.

The parting kiss she'd given him was proof of that. For Jade to do that in public was a sign of a significant change in the way she viewed herself and their relationship.

What was at play was not entirely clear to him yet, but when he came back, hopefully with Igor in chains, he intended to explore it together with Jade. They both needed to get over their reluctance to open up and share their feelings with each other.

It had been almost two days since the *Seafarer* and the *Aurora* cleared the Baltic and sailed along the coast of Norway toward Bergen, and a couple of hours since the *Aurora* changed its heading, sailing toward the Shetland Islands on its way to the North Atlantic.

Phinas was still staring in the direction the *Aurora* sailed, but she was long gone from sight. Max walked over to him. "We are on in five."

"Captain's quarters?" He fell in step with the Guardian.

Max nodded. "If you can call them that. Berg is on the bridge, and he let us use his quarters for the call. Don't get excited. They are just as bad as the rest of this ship."

Compared to the *Aurora*, the *Seafarer* was a rusty old bucket that seemed to cut through the waves with effort. It was manned by volunteers from Captain Olsson's crew, and led by Second Officer Mateo Berg, who was its acting captain.

When they entered the captain's quarters, Phinas saw what Max had meant. The place needed a major remodel, and if not that, at least a good scrubbing and a coat of paint.

They sat at the small table, and Max put the tablet in front of them and made the call.

"Good evening." Max lifted the tablet and turned it in a circle to show the room to the other team members. "Phinas and Max reporting from the lovely *Seafarer*."

"Good morning, gentlemen," Kian said.

The screen was split, showing Kian, Kalugal, Turner, and Onegus on the left side and Toven, Yamanu, and Marcel on the right side.

"I am pleased to share that our assumption was proven correct. The *Helena* has maintained its course and is now following you, while the *Anatolov* changed course and is now shadowing the *Aurora*. If both vessels maintain current speeds and heading, the *Helena*, which we assume has Igor on board, will get in position to fire at the *Seafarer* within ten hours, but that doesn't mean it will do so right away. He might keep following you up the coast until he's comfortable to launch the attack, which could take a day or two."

On board the *Aurora*, Toven leaned forward. "What about the Russians?"

Kian shared his screen so they could all see what he was looking at. "As you can see, the Russian cruiser, represented by this red dot, is mirroring the *Aurora*'s heading and did not pick up speed to close the distance between the ships as of yet."

Phinas calculated the timeline. "It's almost noon here. It will be dark by the time Igor catches up to us. I don't think he will attack at night."

Turner leaned in. "I agree. Igor will prefer daylight for better aim and assessment of the damage when he hits the *Seafarer*. He will also prefer it because it will be a little warmer, giving the Kra-ell, who are not good swimmers, more time to float before hypothermia gets the better of them. They can't regulate their body heat indefinitely. He will also have an easier time fishing them out of the water."

"I assume that someone is monitoring the tracking feed twenty-four-seven," Yamanu said. "We need to know right away if there is any change in the Russians' cruiser speed or heading."

"Of course," Kian said. "We arranged for the war room to be manned around the clock until this crisis is over. Have someone on your side available to respond to a call at all times as well. Once the *Anatolov* or the *Helena* pick up speed, we will have very little time to coordinate our moves."

Kalugal lifted his hand to get their attention. "Also, please make sure to have life vests distributed and handed to all hands onboard and double-check on the lifeboats, first-aid kits, and emergency rations. If events go south and we end up with people in the water, remember that at these temps, the humans will only last for minutes, the children possibly less. Go over the emergency plan with your men and with the passengers and make sure to communicate calm and confidence. I'm sure there are a lot of frayed nerves on the *Aurora*."

Phinas was surprised by Kalugal's concern. The guy was typically myopic when it came to humans. It seemed that Jacki was rubbing off on him.

Perhaps her influence was also responsible for the new energy between Kian and Kalugal. Syssi definitely had something to do with Kian's change of attitude and his proposal to offer Kalugal two seats on the council.

However, it still remained to be seen if the council would approve the move.

"How far is the helicopter?" Toven asked. "And how fast can it respond in case Igor surprises us and attacks at night?"

"The helicopter is fully equipped for night missions, so that won't be a problem," Turner reassured the god. "It's currently at a small airstrip to the north of the *Seafarer*'s current position, about twenty-two miles east. A flight plan for the next leg was already filed, and they will soon take off to keep up with the boats' northbound progress. The plan is to land close to the shoreline by early morning. This will make the flight to intercept a quick affair. Depending on how late in the morning Igor decides to make his move, the helicopter will be about fifteen to twenty minutes away. We will have enough warning before Igor gets within weapons range."

Phinas was disappointed that Kian had abandoned his quest to attack first, for the simple reason that they couldn't determine beyond a shadow of a doubt that the *Helena* had Igor on board and intended to fire on them. In case they had all been mistaken about the yacht and its crew's intentions, Kian didn't want to be the aggressor.

It was probably a mistake that would cost them, but he could understand Kian's reluctance.

"Let's make sure everyone has their earpieces fully charged and within reach," Turner said. "I want everyone to wear them starting at dawn. From now until this is over, you should all carry your sidearms at all times as well."

Phinas wondered if these instructions had been meant for his team's ears. He doubted Turner would have repeated such basic instructions to the Guardians.

Onegus took over from Turner. "As soon as we are done here, have a couple of guys that have experience with shoulder-fired rockets on deck with the missiles ready. Launching a missile at the *Helena* will further focus Igor's attention on you, helping the pilot sneak in, and will keep Igor in a defensive mode, which might give us just the time we need in case the helicopter is not yet on the scene."

The Guardians, as an active and heavily trained force, practiced with shoulder-fired missiles as part of their weapons training, while the last time Kalugal's men used that type of weapon it was called a bazooka and probably looked nothing like its contemporary grandchild.

Turner had been able to get four shoulder-launched missiles delivered onboard the *Seafarer* before they'd left the port, but Phinas hadn't seen them yet. They had been delivered in unmarked crates.

"Any questions?" Kian asked.

When there were none, he saluted them with two fingers. "Be safe and good hunting to all!"

62

KIAN

*K*ian rubbed the sleep out of his eyes.

It had been less than two hours since he'd gotten in bed to get some shuteye, but anxiety had made it impossible to rest, urging him to check his phone every so often for updates about new developments.

Telling himself that he would have received a call if anything had happened didn't help.

With a sigh he got out of bed, got dressed, and headed to his home office.

After a few minutes of rapid texting exchanges with the two teams in the North Sea and his war room, he was reassured that there were no new developments.

So far, the morning and afternoon out in the North Sea had passed without incident. Igor's yacht maintained a ten-kilometer distance from the *Seafarer*, and the Russians maintained their heading and speed as well.

Evidently, Turner's assessment that Igor would wait to attack until the decoy was further up north was correct, and so was his assumption that the Russian was waiting for the *Aurora* to get further away from land before making his move.

Kian suspected that very few had gotten a good night's sleep on board either the *Aurora* or the *Seafarer*, and that was probably true for many in the village as well.

Everyone seemed to be collectively holding their breath, part in anticipation and part in worry.

Regrettably, his people were well acquainted with danger and crisis. So much of their time and resources were spent to avoid detection by Navuh and humans. Kian had lost count of how many times he had to shepherd the clan through one crisis or another throughout the many centuries he'd been leading it. At first, it had been a simple matter of protecting his family, but as the clan grew and his mother's mission to continue the gods' work of enlightening humanity had caught momentum, Navuh had realized that Annani had survived and was meddling in what he considered his affairs, and the real battle had begun.

There had been so many close calls that Kian suspected the Fates had a hand in protecting the clan, but this crisis felt different.

They were dealing with a large group of people from a different species who had fought the gods and had persevered despite the gods' technological and genetic advantage. If he allowed them to join the village or even settle nearby, and they became adversarial for some reason, they would pose a serious threat.

The Kra-ell negated most of the advantages immortals relied upon for their survival. They were faster and stronger than the Guardians, and they were immune to mind tricks. And now, Jade and Kagra knew about the clan's existence and had a measure of its capabilities.

They had no real reason to go against the clan, but they harbored old resentments against the gods, which the Kra-ell could easily project onto the gods' immortal descendants.

The flip side of the problem was that they could be a huge asset as allies —a secret weapon he could deploy against the superior military power of the Brotherhood. Not that a couple of hundred Kra-ell would make much of a difference if Navuh attacked full force, but Navuh wouldn't dare do that on American soil, and the force he would be comfortable deploying against the clan on its home turf wouldn't be more than two or three hundred strong.

The Kra-ell would be indispensable against a force that size.

Except, the two hundred or so Kra-ell came with the complication of excess baggage that couldn't be discarded. The large group of humans who had lived with them in the compound was completely dependent on the aliens. Most of the humans, if not all, had been born in the compound, and they would be lost out in the world. Surprisingly, those who Arwel and Yamanu had talked to didn't mind staying with the Kra-ell as long as they were fairly compensated for their services and not coerced into breeding hybrids for them.

Perhaps it was just fear of the unknown, and with the clan's help they could sever their ties to the Kra-ell. But the problem was that their knowledge of the aliens couldn't be erased by thralling, and compelling them to keep quiet about it was not a permanent solution. Compulsion faded over time and had to be periodically reinforced.

In a way, the humans were more of a problem than the Kra-ell, and Kian didn't know what to do with them yet, but their issue had to be addressed as well.

And there was Igor, an adversary who was not only a terrifyingly powerful compeller but also ruthless, cunning, and resourceful. Now that he could potentially learn of the clan's existence, the neutralization or elimination of this threat was critical.

63

JADE

*J*ade pressed the ringer button for Yamanu's cabin and took a step back as she waited for the door to open. She knew he wasn't there, but she hadn't come for him.

She was there to borrow his mate's phone.

After all, Mey was part Kra-ell. They might not be friends, but they were on friendly terms.

As Mey opened the door, her eyes widened momentarily. "Good evening, Jade. Yamanu is not here."

"I know. I didn't come to see him." Damn, she hated asking for favors. "I came to ask to borrow your phone. I want to talk to Phinas, and I know you have a secure connection that Igor can't track. If you need to ask Yamanu's permission to let me make the call, that's okay. I will wait out here for your answer."

A smile lifted Mey's full lips, and she opened the door wider. "Please, come in."

"Thank you." Jade followed her inside.

"Take a seat." Mey waved her hand at the couch. "Do you have Phinas's number?"

"I hoped you had it."

"I don't, but I can get it from Yamanu. Anyway, I need to check with him whether you can call Phinas, but not because it is you who is requesting to make the call. I need to ask him if anyone is allowed to call the people on the decoy. I'll text him."

Evidently, Mey had no military training.

They were in the middle of a crisis, about to face a dangerous enemy, and Jade was an unconfirmed ally at this point. If the roles were reversed, she wouldn't have allowed Mey to make the call unsupervised, or maybe not at all.

Mey sent the text and shifted her eyes to Jade. "Can I offer you something to drink while we wait?"

"No, thank you." Jade could use some water, but she didn't want to inconvenience the female.

"A glass of water, maybe?" Mey asked.

Jade tilted her head. "How did you know that I was thinking about water?"

Had the female read her mind? If Mey could hear echoes of past conversations that had been embedded in the walls, she might be able to also read minds.

Mey chuckled. "I didn't read your mind. I can't, and not just because you are a pureblooded Kra-ell."

"So, how did you know?"

"You licked your lips. Besides, I also get thirsty when I'm anxious."

"I'm not anxious." Jade squared her shoulders.

Mey arched a brow. "So, what's the urgency to speak to Phinas?"

Lifting her chin, Jade briefly closed her eyes. "I don't know what's going on with me. I've never felt like this before."

"Let me guess." Mey sat down next to her on the couch. "The longer you are away from Phinas, the worse the pain here gets." She patted her chest. "You are going crazy, and you figured that talking with him is the only thing that would help."

The female claimed to not be able to read minds, and yet she'd nailed it, describing precisely what Jade was feeling.

"How are you doing that?"

Mey smiled. "I know what you feel because it's the same for me. It gets easier after a while, and the longer you are with your mate, the longer you can tolerate being away from him. I can be away from Yamanu for two to three days now, but at the beginning, a separation of even a few hours was too difficult."

"What are you talking about? Love? I'm Kra-ell. I don't do love."

The woman cast her an indulgent look. "I'm talking about the bond, which is stronger than love. For some, it forms before the couple realizes that they are in love."

"The Kra-ell don't bond. We don't work the same as the gods, and we are physically incapable of forming bonds. It would have been disastrous to our society. Phinas might be experiencing what you're describing, but I shouldn't."

"And yet you are." Mey lifted her phone and looked at the screen. "Yamanu says that you can talk to Phinas, but I should make the call and hand you the phone." She lifted her eyes to Jade. "I'm sorry. I didn't expect him to ask that."

"It is exactly what I would have done if the roles were reversed. You just don't have the military training and experience that Yamanu has."

Mey smirked. "You'd be surprised, but that's not something I can talk about."

Her curiosity was piqued, but as Mey made the call, the cryptic comment was forgotten, and all Jade cared about was hearing Phinas's voice.

64

PHINAS

*O*ver forty hours had passed since the decoy had left the harbor, and as night had fallen, the anxious energy on the *Seafarer* had subsided.

Igor wasn't likely to attack at night because of the visibility. Shoulder-fired rockets were not a precise weapon, and the yacht most likely didn't carry the kind that was self-guiding. Those were premier weapons, and the oligarch who owned the yacht had no reason to have one of those on board.

But the problem with should haves and could haves was that they were just educated guesses, and those were not always correct.

Phinas groaned. "I could kill for a bottle of Snake Venom."

"No booze allowed on missions." Dandor pulled a pack of cigarettes out of his pocket. "But smoking is okay." He tapped the bottom of the pack to push one cigarette out and offered it to Phinas.

"No, thanks, but you can go ahead. It doesn't bother me."

They were on the decoy's top deck, sitting on loungers while huddled in their puffer jackets and keeping their gloved hands inside their pockets for warmth. If it weren't so damn cold, Phinas might have indulged, but it wasn't worth taking his gloves off for a smoke.

Neither of them was a regular smoker, not since their days in the Brotherhood. Back then, they'd used to smoke while on missions, and Dandor remembered the tradition.

It evoked memories of camaraderie, and for a brief moment, Phinas was tempted to light up, but smoking before a battle was one of those traditions that were better abandoned.

Jade had a bunch of them that she should shed, but he understood why she was clinging to them. It was because Igor had pissed on the Kra-ell customs, turning them on their heads.

Perhaps once she had her revenge, she could reexamine her beliefs. She was a smart female, rational and pragmatic, and adhering to religious doctrines did not suit an independent thinker like her.

In Phinas's humble opinion, religion was propaganda, a way to control the population and give people a false sense of control over the chaos of life.

Fates, he missed that stubborn, magnificent female.

Phinas chuckled at his own hypocrisy. Why was he invoking the Fates? He had grown up with Mortdh's teachings shoved down his throat, and he'd detested that even as a teenager. He'd never been a devout follower of Mortdh, and when he had joined the clan, he hadn't adopted their belief system either. But invoking the Fates felt better than invoking Mortdh, so there was that.

When his phone rang, he fumbled to pull it out of his pocket and frowned at the name on the screen.

Why was Mey calling him?

Touching the screen with his gloved hand produced no result, so he pulled it off with his teeth and was finally able to accept the call.

"Good evening, Mey. How are things on the *Aurora*?"

"As well as can be expected from a bunch of people stressed out of their minds, but thank you for asking. How are the gerbils?"

"The gerbils?" He chuckled. "That's who you want to check on?"

"I know the men are all right."

"The gerbils are fine. They are enjoying a cruise in shitty little cabins, but since they are just small critters, they think that they are in a huge palace."

Mey laughed. "Is it that bad?"

"After spending time on the *Aurora*, yeah. It is. Not where I would choose to spend my honeymoon, not even if I was given a ride for free."

"Speaking of honeymoons, someone is waiting impatiently to talk to you."

Phinas's heartbeat accelerated. He'd wanted to call one of his guys and tell them to find Jade and give her the phone, but he'd thought she would be angry if he did that. Public displays of affection and all that. But here she was, doing it herself.

"Hi," she said. "How are you doing?"

"Missing you. Do you miss me?"

She hesitated for a moment. "Yes."

"Is Mey standing right next to you?"

"Yes. I'm still not trusted enough to make outside calls without supervision."

He needed to have a talk with Yamanu about that. If they wanted Jade as an ally, they needed to start treating her as one.

"I'm sorry. I'll have a word with the boss about it."

"It's okay. I would have done the same if I were in Yamanu's position. You and your people are heading into a dangerous confrontation, and keeping security tight is of the utmost importance."

He smiled. "Did I tell you already how much I enjoy chatting with a female warrior?"

She chuckled. "How many females do you usually chat with?"

"Not many," he admitted. "I'm not the chatty sort."

"You could have fooled me."

"I'm like that only with you, gorgeous."

This time the silence lasted even longer. "How are you holding up?"

Phinas stifled a snort.

Evidently, Jade had reached her limit of mushy, personal talk.

"Everyone is antsy. Igor is keeping a steady distance from us, and it's nerve-wracking to wait for him to make his move. I liked Kian's plan much better, but he changed his mind about luring Igor to get closer and attacking the yacht first."

"I'm with you on that. You and your friends are basically sitting ducks, waiting for Igor to launch a rocket at your ship. What if people get hurt?"

"They'll heal. We are immortals, and we've all gotten injured at one time or another. It's not a big deal."

"It is if he can blow up the bridge or hit an area where your people are. There is only so much that our bodies can heal. If the injuries are too massive, we die."

"Don't worry. I promised to come back to you in one piece, and I always deliver on my promises."

65

KIAN

*S*yssi's light footsteps pulled Kian out of his reverie.

"Good morning, love." He pushed to his feet. "Did I wake you?" He gathered her in a hug, savoring her warmth.

"You didn't." She lifted her face for a kiss. "Or maybe you did. My subconscious mind must have sensed your absence from our bed and woken me up to check in on you."

He kissed the tip of her nose. "I'm fine. You can go back to sleep."

Syssi shook her head. "I want to keep you company, but first, I need some coffee. I'll make us cappuccinos." She pulled out of his arms.

"Let me make us some tea. It's four in the morning, and I want you to go back to sleep."

Yawning, she nodded.

Kian took Syssi's hand, led her to the kitchen, and sat her down on a barstool.

"Any updates?" she asked.

"Not really. Everyone is waiting for Igor to make his move."

While waiting for the water to boil, Kian pulled out the box of assorted teas and a bag of cookies from the pantry and put them on the counter next to Syssi.

She took a cookie and nibbled on it for a brief moment. "You need to decide how you are going to deal with Igor once you catch him. Toven promised his life to Jade, and she wants to execute him on the spot. But since you want to interrogate him, you'll have to persuade her to wait." She adjusted her night robe over her knees. "I'm curious whether he had anything to do with the Kra-ell interstellar ship's sabotage."

"I doubt it." Kian pulled out two cups from the top cabinet and put them on the table. "I don't think anyone would have wanted to delay the ship's arrival for thousands of years and then make it explode." He poured hot water into the cups.

"On the contrary." Syssi dunked a teabag in the water. "If he was a fugitive, he might have wanted to arrive on Earth long after whoever was looking for him was dead, and to prevent anyone on board from discovering who he really was, he did something to make it explode, but only after the escape pods were safely deployed."

That was a very plausible scenario that Kian hadn't considered before.

Smiling, he leaned to take her lips in a quick kiss. "Did I already tell you how brilliant you are?"

"Many times. It's just something that occurred to me during the night when I couldn't fall asleep because you weren't in bed with me."

More than sleep had been sacrificed on the altar of this crisis. Intimacy with his wife had been sacrificed as well.

"I'm sorry." He sat on the stool next to hers and swiveled it toward her. "Soon, things will go back to normal, and we will spend a lot of time in bed together." He leaned to kiss the spot on her neck he liked to bite.

She shivered. "Don't tease me. It's not fair."

"It's not a tease. It's a promise." He leaned away and dunked a teabag in the fast-cooling water. "We still have two potentially major battles on our hands, but I believe they will both go down soon."

Holding the warm cup in her palms and breathing in the aroma of the tea, Syssi closed her eyes and sighed. "That's why you need to decide now what to do with him once you catch him."

"It's not a foregone conclusion that we will catch him. We might kill him, or he might escape."

"You'll catch him."

The small hairs on the back of Kian's neck tingled. "Are you simply thinking ahead, or do you have a feeling?"

When Syssi 'had a feeling,' Kian knew better than to second-guess her.

"I didn't have a vision if that is what you are asking, and it's not a feeling or a premonition either. It's a logical assumption and calculated probability. I know you, and I know how competent our Guardians are. Igor will be caught alive, and you'd better decide now what to do with him and what bribe you can offer Jade to agree to give him a stay of execution."

If it wasn't a premonition, all possibilities were still open, and he didn't need to deal with that until it became relevant.

"I don't have the bandwidth to deal with that now. I'll decide on that when and if we catch him."

66

ONEGUS

"About damn time." Onegus rubbed his hands.

It was just his luck that it was his turn to sit in the war room when things were finally starting to progress toward resolution.

Nearly forty-eight hours had passed since the decoy had left the Copenhagen harbor and about forty hours since it had started up the Norwegian coast while the *Aurora* continued to the North Atlantic. Everyone had been getting antsier in anticipation of the confrontation.

Kian, Turner, and Kalugal had left about two hours ago to shower and change clothes, but they would have to drop everything and rush back.

Imagining Kalugal walking in with a towel wrapped around him made Onegus's lips twitch, but this was not the time to amuse himself. He needed to act fast.

The first order of business was to call the pilot. "This is McLean. The *Helena* has increased its speed and is heading toward the *Seafarer* at thirty-seven knots. It will be in weapons range in under an hour." He gave the pilot the estimated coordinates.

"Got it. I'm taking off and will be there in under twenty minutes. I'll find a spot to land and wait for your signal."

"Roger that." Onegus terminated the call.

The next went to Phinas. He would have preferred to talk to Max, but Phinas was in charge of the mission, and he was the one Onegus needed to call.

467

Phinas answered immediately. "Are we on?"

Onegus repeated the information.

"Finally." The guy let out a breath. "I'll get everyone in position."

"Don't forget to double-check that everyone's earpieces are secure in place and well fitting."

"I've already done that, but I'll do it again. From now on, the earpieces stay in."

"Excellent. I'll keep you posted."

The last call was to Kian.

"Talk to me." The boss's gruff voice was laced with urgency.

"The *Helena* started increasing its speed about seven minutes ago, and if it maintains current speed, it will reach the *Seafarer* in a little under an hour. I've already notified the helicopter pilot, and he'll be in position in about twenty minutes. I also spoke with Phinas, and our guys are getting in position and checking their earpieces."

"Very well. Did you notify Turner and Kalugal?"

"Not yet."

"I'll do it. Call Yamanu to let him know and keep monitoring the situation."

"Yes, boss."

"I'm on my way. I'll be there in ten minutes."

Unless Kian had one of the golf carts parked in front of his house, he would have to run to get to the underground war room in such a short time.

Taking a quick look at Roni's laptop and the two flashing red dots following the two blue ones, Onegus placed a call to Yamanu.

"Good morning, chief. What's up?"

The *Aurora* command team was using one of the cabins as their war room, but with Phinas gone, only Yamanu and Toven remained.

"Is Toven with you?" Onegus asked.

"He's right here. Do you want to talk to him?"

"I need you both. Just activate the speakerphone."

"Done."

"Igor is making his move," Onegus said without much preamble. "The *Helena* picked up speed a few minutes ago and is heading toward the decoy. The ETA is a little under an hour, and the helicopter will be there with plenty of time to spare. There is no indication that the Russians changed their speed or heading as of this time."

His update was received with a silent pause as the gravity of the news sank in. For better or worse, it was finally happening, and the confrontation they had all been waiting for was about to unfold in less than an hour, or rather one part of the confrontation. It still remained to be seen if the Russian captain would engage.

If he did, Nils would take care of that problem.

"Thank you for letting us know," Toven said. "We will keep everyone here on high alert from now on. I'll get Mia up here in case you need our help with Igor, his men, or both."

Onegus doubted that Toven would be able to do that remotely, even with Mia's help, but he kept his opinion to himself. After all, Toven probably suspected the same.

"Thank you. I will keep you updated."

As Onegus ended the call, Kian arrived, and less than a minute later, Turner and Kalugal walked in, neither wearing a towel nor a bathrobe.

Roni was the last one to arrive. "I'm taking over monitoring the ships."

"Be my guest." Onegus turned the kid's laptop toward him. "This application is your baby, your brilliant invention."

Roni sighed. "It is brilliant. I just wish it had more market potential."

Kalugal moved to the chair next to Roni and looked at the screen. "Your invention has plenty of market potential. I bet we can sell it to navies around the world."

"We?" Roni arched a brow. "Are we partners now?"

"If you want to make money from this application, then we are."

67

KIAN

*W*hen the *Helena* started to slow down to match the *Seafarer*'s speed, Kian signaled Onegus and Turner. "Let's put the main players on."

Regrettably, the live broadcast would be audio only because they hadn't thought to send the surveillance drones with the decoy team.

Turner put the pilot on speaker for a live update from the helicopter, and Onegus put Phinas and Max on speaker as well.

Later, they would switch communications to the earpieces, but for now they could still use their phones.

"The captain is aware of the *Helena*'s approach," Phinas said. "He's maintaining steady heading and speed, pretending that he didn't notice the fast-approaching yacht. He is also aware of the helicopter's ETA. We put two guys on the observation deck with strong binoculars that transmit information straight to Max's phone. We can see what's happening on the yacht's front decks, and the moment we see activity that indicates they are preparing to launch an attack, we will shoot first. Other than Max and me, the rest of the team is out of sight and hidden from anyone on the *Helena* trying to see what we are up to."

Max took it from there. "I have four Guardians with shoulder-fired rockets in position and ready to engage, but they won't be visible from the yacht because they are behind the waterslide and hiding under a tarp. As soon as the yacht is within range, and provided that our guys on the observation deck report signs of aggression from the *Helena*, we will fire two missiles simultaneously at her."

Max followed the finalized battle plan that was a compromise between all the various iterations they had come up with before. The *Seafarer* team would not attack until they were certain that Igor intended to shoot at them, but as soon as his intentions to launch a rocket at them became clear, they would give him hell first.

Hopefully, Igor didn't have superior rockets like self-guided missiles on board the yacht, and having two incoming missiles would get his full attention and give the helicopter pilot a chance to shoot its missile and get away before Igor could shoot back.

Kian's objective was to avoid, or at least minimize, casualties on all sides. The only death that was acceptable to him and wouldn't weigh on his conscience was Igor's.

"The *Helena* is now five minutes from weapons range," Roni said from his station in front of the laptop.

"Time to switch to the earpieces," Onegus said.

Kian ended the call and activated his earpiece.

The others did the same.

"We are in the air," the pilot reported. "ETA is seven minutes."

"The *Helena* will be in weapons range in one minute," Roni updated.

"The *Helena* is now in weapons range." Roni was starting to lose his calm, and his announcement had come out a squawk.

"No sign of activity on the Helena yet," Phinas said. "We are holding fire for now."

"We are one minute out," came the pilot's garbled voice.

"Hold on," Max said. "There is activity on board the *Helena*. It looks like they are wheeling in something. Now they are removing the cover. Fuck! It's a damn missile battery. Fire!" Max gave the command.

68

PHINAS

*A*s soon as Max issued the fire command, the whoosh of the missiles exiting the launching tubes sounded.

The sound was filtered through the specialty earpieces and was a little off, but it was still the most satisfying sound Phinas had heard in a long time.

The *Helena* was still a far-off blob to the naked eye, even for an immortal, but the Guardians had telescopic scopes, and their aim was true.

"The *Helena* is changing its heading," Max said. "It is trying to avoid getting hit."

Clearly, someone on board the yacht had noticed the approaching missiles and was attempting evasive maneuvers while those in charge of the missile battery were still fumbling with it. Those kinds of missiles were self-guided, and once fired they would hit their target even if those operating them had a shitty aim.

The *Seafarer*'s first missile missed the target. The second didn't.

"We have a hit," Max said. "Damage is minimal. The missile only grazed the side of the boat."

Max cursed under his breath. "It's up to the helicopter now."

Phinas held his breath as a race against time ensued. Who would manage the first shot? The *Helena* or the helicopter?

If the missiles launched at the same time, they were all fucked. Both vessels would start taking in water. The *Seafarer* had life rafts, and probably the *Helena* had them as well, but it would be a major shit show if the crews of both fought their way to the ladder that the helicopter would drop to collect their team.

"We are in range," the helicopter pilot announced. "Locking target. Missile fired."

Phinas didn't dare take a breath, clutching his binoculars as if his life depended on it.

Why hadn't the *Helena* deployed its missiles yet? A battery could fire them all at once and do so much damage to the *Seafarer* that they might not survive.

Was the battery defective? Its operators inexperienced? Or were the Fates looking out for them?

"Why aren't they firing?" Max asked.

"They must have a malfunction." Phinas kept his binoculars trained on the *Helena*. "Someone just rushed in with a handheld rocket launcher. He's getting ready to fire. Missile away."

As a clear white plume rose from the front deck of the *Helena*, a flash of light was seen a split second before a loud boom sounded.

"Yes!" Max pumped his fist in the air. "We have a hit."

"Hit confirmed," the helicopter pilot announced.

Phinas let out half a breath as his eyes locked on the incoming missile.

The captain had initiated evasive maneuvers as soon as the *Helena* had deployed the missile, but the *Seafarer* was large and slow to turn.

Phinas braced for impact...that never came.

As the missile missed the *Seafarer* by mere meters and splashed into the water without detonating, a cheer arose from all team members on board.

Max pulled him into a brief bro hug. "Thank the merciful Fates."

Another loud explosion drew all eyes to the *Helena*.

The helicopter's guided missile must have caused serious structural damage, and the yacht caught fire. When it reached the fuel tank, or maybe the munitions onboard, it caused a major explosion.

The *Helena* was sinking fast.

"There was a big explosion on the yacht," Max updated the war rooms in the village and on board the *Aurora*. "The *Helena* is sinking, and people are jumping overboard."

"What do you want me to do?" the captain asked on the com.

"Please bring the *Seafarer* about to collect the survivors," Kian said. "But stay on the bridge and do not assist our men. The same goes for your crew. Everyone stays at their stations."

The crew was equipped with specialty earpieces like the rest of them, but they were human, and they needed to stay out of the fray.

"We are circling above to provide coverage and assistance as needed," the pilot announced.

As their team came out of hiding and assembled to get instructions, Max pulled out his tranquilizer gun. "Switch your weapons from firearms to tranquilizer guns and check your earpieces."

Phinas could barely contain the grin that threatened to split his face.

After the many days of cat and mouse with the guy, he had grown larger than life in all of their minds, but they had defeated him, and if he was still alive, he was in the water and at their mercy.

It wasn't over yet, and Igor might still pull the proverbial rabbit out of his hat, but Phinas doubted that. He was moments away from bagging the guy, and he couldn't wait to deliver Igor to Jade with a red bow tied around his neck.

69

JADE

Jade alternated between pacing in front of the cabin designated as the *Aurora*'s war room and sitting on the floor right next to the door. It was pathetic, and it made her feel like a beggar, but she was beyond caring.

She hadn't stooped so low as eavesdropping with her ear to the door, mostly because the ship's doors were so thick and the fit so precise that even with her Kra-ell hearing, it was impossible to discern what was being said inside. But if Toven or Yamanu stepped out for even a moment, she would badger them for information about the battle until they gave her something.

They had been in there for hours, and even though no one had told her a thing, she knew in her gut that the battle had begun.

Closing her eyes, she prayed to the Mother not for Phinas to emerge victorious or perform exceptional acts of bravery, and definitely not to die as a hero and forever find peace in the fields of the brave.

She prayed for him to come back to her alive and well.

To pray for his life bordered on blasphemy, but she no longer blindly believed in the sermons she'd heard as a young female, and she could not suffer another loss.

The Mother forgive her, but she couldn't lose anyone else she cared about.

When the door opened, and Toven stepped out, she jumped to her feet. "Tell me what's going on."

He smiled. "Everyone on the *Seafarer* is okay. No one got hurt."

Her hand landed on her chest. "Thank the Mother. Did Igor fire on them?"

"He tried. They had a missile battery on board the *Helena*, but the Fates must have smiled upon our men, and the battery malfunctioned. They managed to fire one handheld rocket, but it missed."

"What about the other side?"

Phinas had told her the plan, but she didn't know which parts of it had been implemented and which had been discarded. It had gone through so many changes and back and forth that she'd lost track of the final plan.

"The helicopter got a good shot, causing a fire that must have ignited the fuel tank or the munitions on board, the yacht exploded and sank. People were seen jumping into the water right after the explosion, but we don't know yet who the survivors are and if Igor is among them."

"Do we even have proof that he was on board?"

Toven shook his head. "We don't."

At this point she would be satisfied with a confirmation of his demise, but until she saw him or his dead body, she wouldn't have a moment's rest. Even if the other survivors claimed that he'd been there, she wouldn't believe them.

"You need to keep looking. If he's not among the dead or the living, we are back to square one, and all of this insane effort was for nothing. He could have compelled those on board the *Helena* to follow his commands and to claim that he was there when it exploded. I wouldn't put it past him to plant explosives on the yacht just in case it was overpowered and detonate them to throw us off his tail."

Toven smiled. "It's a bit of a stretch, but at this point, I would believe anything when it comes to Igor. He's a cunning bastard."

"When will we know?"

"They are fishing the survivors out of the water as we speak. Let's pray that he's one of them just so we can end him ourselves and know for sure that he's no longer a threat."

Jade bared her fangs. "We are not going to kill him. I am. He's my kill, not yours."

"If we catch him alive, he's yours. But perhaps you could wait a few days to have your revenge, so we can get some information out of him first."

The fire in her gut ignited. "Unless you are a stronger compeller than he is, he's not going to tell you anything unless you promise to spare his life, but it's not yours to spare. It's mine, and I'm not going to spare it in exchange for information or anything else."

PHINAS

"*N*ine people in the water," the helicopter pilot reported. "They are clinging to debris, but they are not going to last long in the freezing water. Do you want me to drop the ladder?"

"Do not engage," Phinas replied. "And don't get any closer. We will get there in a few minutes."

"They might not have those minutes," the pilot argued.

The guy's good intentions might cost him and his crew their lives if they got within earshot of Igor.

"I repeat. Do not engage and keep your current altitude. Don't get any closer to the survivors. They are all extremely dangerous criminals, and some of them are highly-trained commandos."

"Roger that."

They were about to shoot tranquilizer darts at the survivors, and although he didn't owe the hired pilot an explanation, it was always good to have people cooperate willingly and not grudgingly.

Max lifted the binoculars to his eyes. "Is it possible that's the entire crew, including Igor and his three compadres? How many people are needed to operate a yacht this size?"

Max's words were delivered by the machine voice, sounding exactly the same as everyone else's on board, but even though Phinas was used to that by now and despite the excellent quality of the computerized voice, it was still jarring.

"I don't know," he admitted. He had never gone on a naval mission, let alone had been part of a crew. "I've been on very few sea voyages and only as a passenger."

"There couldn't have been just nine people operating a vessel this size. Even if the others were killed, where are their bodies?" Max lowered his binoculars. "Aren't bodies supposed to float?"

It was a rhetorical question, but Phinas answered anyway. "They are."

"You said that the Kra-ell bodies are dense. So Igor and his guys could have sunk all the way to the bottom of the ocean."

"Their bodies are denser than ours, but they will still float when dead. Besides, they are not that easily killed."

Or so he hoped.

According to Jade, the Kra-ell didn't enter stasis when severely injured like the immortals did. They'd had to be put into stasis artificially and placed in life-sustaining pods to traverse the universe in a spaceship.

If Igor had been killed in the explosion, but his body wasn't found, they would have no proof of his demise, and Phinas would have no trophy to bring to Jade.

That would be very disappointing.

Lifting the binoculars again, he scanned the ocean where the *Helena* had been. All that remained of her was a field of scattered smoldering debris. The rest had sunk. It was possible that Igor's body, or whatever was left of it, was trapped in the parts that were on their way to the bottom.

It was also possible that he hadn't been on board at all and had been puppeteering the crew from afar.

When the *Seafarer* neared the field of debris, the survivors became clearer through the binoculars, and Phinas released a relieved breath. The four Kra-ell were easy to identify thanks to their long black hair, and when the ship got even closer, he could even see their alert, glowing red eyes.

The humans were in much worse shape, and if they didn't get to them soon, they would lose their hold on the debris and drown.

The helicopter was still circling at a low altitude overhead, but Phinas couldn't allow it to go lower before the Kra-ell were apprehended and muzzled. Besides, the humans were in a bad state and wouldn't be able to climb the rope ladder. It was a difficult feat even for trained combat soldiers who were not suffering from hypothermia.

Hopefully, the noise of its engines and rotor would be enough to disperse the sound waves of Igor's compulsion.

Phinas lowered the binoculars, put them aside, and tapped his earpiece.

"Three minutes until we are in range. Lower the lifeboats at the back. The rest come to me, but stay away from the railing."

After the Kra-ell were hit with the tranquilizer darts, the men in the lifeboats would have mere seconds to fish them out of the water. If they didn't get to them in time, the males would drown, and that was unacceptable.

Four lifeboats with two men each should be enough to get the Kra-ell and the humans.

As the rest of his men and Guardians rushed over, he turned to Max. "You and I take out two?"

Grinning, Max nodded.

"Boleck and Dandor will take the other two."

They were the best snipers on board, probably better than him and Max.

"It's time to go hunting." Phinas motioned for Boleck and Dandor to come forward. "The Kra-ell do not succumb to hypothermia as quickly as the humans, and they are still in full command of their bodies. Expect them to be armed and open fire the moment they have a shot. Take cover and shoot only the Kra-ell. By now, the humans are too numb to pose a threat."

When the men nodded, Max took over. "The humans will be pulled out first. I need five of you to get a human each and treat them for hypothermia. You know what to do. The rest of you will help us deal with the Kra-ell."

Phinas didn't know what the treatment for hypothermia was, and neither did his men, but evidently the Guardians had gone through medic training.

"Don't shoot more than two darts if both hit target," he reminded Max and the two snipers.

From experience, they knew that one dart might not be enough to knock out a Kra-ell, and sometimes a second one was needed, but four could be deadly. They wanted to catch Igor alive, although for different reasons.

Kian wanted to interrogate him, but all Phinas wanted was to deliver him to Jade.

He didn't know why Kian thought that Igor would have more information about the gods than the other original settlers on board the *Aurora*, who were more than happy to answer Toven's questions, even without him having to resort to compulsion.

But Phinas didn't care about that.

All he cared about was delivering Igor to Jade. Other females might be thrilled with expensive jewelry or luxury vacations, but there was no gift his female would appreciate more than Igor's head on the proverbial platter.

He and Max and the two snipers took positions behind the lifesavers attached to the railing at even intervals and took aim, each at the Kra-ell closest to them.

When the captain slowed the *Seafarer*, and it started turning sideways as planned, Phinas tapped his earpiece. "Fire at will."

All four darts hit their targets almost simultaneously, but three of the Kra-ell had to be shot with another dose before going limp in the water and starting to sink.

The rafts arrived in the nick of time, and only one Guardian had to dive into the water to fish out the Kra-ell who'd been hard to get to with the raft because of the debris. Somehow, the humans were still conscious and clinging to the flotsam when the men got to them, and they were pulled into the rafts and wrapped in blankets right away.

Phinas allowed himself a brief moment to exchange high-fives with Max before they gave Yamanu an update while walking over to where the winch operators were pulling up the first human.

He was wrapped in several blankets and held by a harness, but he was awake, and the hard look in his eyes reinforced Phinas's assumption that the five humans were employees of the oligarch, a weapons dealer with ties to the Bratva.

"I got him." A Guardian released the man from the harness and threw him over his shoulder before running with him to where they'd prepared a treatment area.

The static noise in Phinas's earpiece preceded the helicopter pilot's machine-translated voice. "Do you need me to evacuate anyone to the hospital?"

Given that the humans were still conscious, Phinas didn't think that they needed more medical attention than they were getting from the Guardians.

Besides, these weren't innocent civilians. They were most likely members of the Bratva and dangerous as hell.

"That's a negative, captain. How are you doing on the fuel?"

"I have enough for another round, and then I need to head back to refuel."

"Then do it now and come back with a full tank. You know the plan."

The helicopter was to shuttle them and the Kra-ell to a nearby airfield where a plane would wait for them to take them to Greenland.

"Roger that."

He and Max waited impatiently until the last human was pulled up and rushed away, and the Kra-ell's turn finally arrived.

They were still unconscious and bound in titanium chains, and as they were hoisted up one by one, they were laid out on the deck and covered in blankets.

"How long before they wake up?" Max asked, although his guess was as good as Phinas's.

"Not long. Minutes probably for the one who was shot with one dart, and longer for the others."

"That's the hybrid." Max pointed at the one who looked more human. "He's been shot with only one dart."

"Then maybe they will all wake up at the same time."

They hadn't gagged them on purpose. Igor would reveal himself readily enough as soon as he tried to compel them to release him and his men.

Phinas couldn't wait to find out which one it was. He hadn't asked Jade for a description because he didn't want her to think about the bastard even more than she already did, and Sofia's description could have described nearly all of the adult Kra-ell males.

Tall, slim, with long black hair. The one feature that distinguished Igor from the others was the look in his eyes that had given Sofia the creeps. She'd told Phinas that he would know it when he saw it.

The first one to stir was a pureblood, and as soon as he opened his eyes and they became focused, Phinas knew who he was.

"Release my men and me immediately," he said in heavily accented English.

Phinas grinned. "Hello, Igor. It's my distinct pleasure to finally make your acquaintance. Jade is looking forward to seeing you again."

Those probably were not the words Kian would have chosen or would have wanted Phinas to say, but they achieved the desired effect, dimming some of the bravado in Igor's eyes.

Even paralyzed and in captivity, he still didn't appear beaten or subdued by any stretch, but maybe he was starting to realize that he'd underestimated what and who he'd gone up against.

Phinas put his hand on Max's arm, stopping him from tapping his earpiece. "Allow me."

The Guardian nodded.

The moment they had all been waiting for had finally arrived, and once

Phinas said the words, everyone on board the *Aurora* and in the village could take a collective breath, at least for now. They still had the Russian destroyer to deal with.

Phinas tapped his earpiece. "We got him."

PERFECT STORM

1

JADE

"This is unacceptable," Jade murmured under her breath as she stared at the cabin's closed door, willing it to open.

The *Helena* had exploded nearly half an hour ago, and the survivors must have been fished out of the water by now. Still, no one had bothered to notify her whether Igor had been among them.

She was relegated to pacing in front of the closed door of the war room and waiting like a beggar for Yamanu or Tom to give her an update.

Her agitation was growing by the minute.

At least they had deigned to tell her that Phinas had been unharmed, so some of the agonizing aches in her chest had been assuaged, but not the emotional upheaval she'd gone through while he was away.

Phinas's absence and the worry for him had pulled the proverbial rug from under her feet, destabilizing her foundation and shaking up her belief system. Cracks had appeared in both before, but Mey's suggestion that they'd bonded had turned the small fissures into deep chasms.

It shouldn't be possible for a Kra-ell to bond with anyone, not one of her own people, and certainly not with a member of a different species.

And yet, what Mey had said explained so much.

The irrational need to be with Phinas at all times, the struggle to leave him in the morning so she could do her job and not see him until the evening, and the fact that she'd experienced what humans would call a panic attack when he'd left on the *Seafarer* to lure Igor away from the *Aurora*.

That had never happened before, and Jade had been through more adversity than one person should ever endure in a lifetime.

And yet, she found herself agonizing about being apart from Phinas for a couple of days. The fifty-two hours and seventeen minutes had felt like an eternity, but not because she'd been so worried about him.

The truth was that she cared about him more deeply than she was willing to admit.

Hell, she'd prayed to the Mother to keep him safe, and she had even been willing to sacrifice the one thing that had kept her from falling apart during her years in captivity.

Avenging her sons and all the other males of her tribe had been her number one goal, and plotting how to do it had occupied most of her thoughts. But instead of praying for victory and for the butcher of her people to be delivered to her so she could finally end him, Jade had prayed for Phinas to return unharmed.

She was a disgrace to everything the Kra-ell held dear, and she should step down as the leader of Igor's former compound. The people should select someone who better embodied the Kra-ell way.

The door banged open, startling Jade from her self-disparaging thoughts. As she saw Yamanu's hulking body filling the doorway with a huge grin spread over his face, her heart leaped with hope.

"Well?" she asked.

"We got him." He reached for her and pulled her into a crushing embrace, lifting her off her feet and slapping her back with his giant paw.

"Put the lady down, Yamanu," Tom said from behind him. "You're making her uncomfortable."

Tom or Toven. She didn't know which name the god preferred, but she liked Toven better. Tom was too plain of a name for a being like him.

"Sorry." Yamanu put her back down on her feet. "I'm just so excited it's finally over. I can't imagine how thrilled you must be."

It wasn't over until Igor's head was no longer attached to his neck, but it was a big step in the right direction. Hopefully, Phinas was keeping Igor sedated and not taking any chances.

Toven cleared his throat. "We are not in the clear yet. We still have the Russian cruiser on our tail, but we can talk about that inside instead of making a spectacle of ourselves in the corridor."

So that was it?

They'd given her the news, and now the two of them were going to disappear back into the cabin, and she would be left to guess the rest of what had happened?

As Yamanu stepped back in, Toven kept the door open. "Are you coming?"

She arched a brow. "Am I invited?"

"Yes, you are, and with Kian's blessing. He wants to talk to you."

That was a surprise. The immortals' leader hadn't wanted her to be part of the planning, but maybe he was okay with her being there for the celebration.

"Am I going to see him this time?" She walked into the cabin and looked around. "Or am I going to just hear his voice again?"

A tablet was propped up on the dining table, but that didn't mean that Kian had approved visual communication. When she'd told Toven and Yamanu about the history of the conflict between the Kra-ell and the gods, the tablet had been there, and Kian had listened in, but the screen had been blank.

Toven glanced at Yamanu. "He didn't give us instructions one way or another."

Yamanu shrugged. "If he doesn't want Jade to see him, he can deactivate the camera on his side."

When the door opened again, Jade pivoted on her heel to see who had come in without ringing the bell. The soundproofing in this ship was so damn good that sometimes it was difficult to hear when someone was knocking, and most opted to use the doorbells each cabin was equipped with.

"Champagne and three glasses as requested." The Guardian put the items on the table and gave her the thumbs up. "You must be over the moon. Your people don't need to run anymore."

"The Russian cruiser is still on our tail." She eyed the champagne. "And we are still on the run."

Carbonated drinks did a number on the Kra-ell digestive system, and there was no way she could drink that. Should she pretend and just wet her lips? Or should she tell Toven that she couldn't tolerate his choice of celebratory beverage?

Usually, Jade was the direct type who didn't tiptoe around anyone's preferences, but she was in a precarious position, dependent on Toven and Kian's good graces. Insulting them even indirectly wouldn't be wise.

But then being dishonest wasn't wise either.

As the god handed her a glass and reached for the champagne, Jade put it back on the table. "I can't drink that."

He put the bottle down. "What can you drink?"

"Vodka with cranberry juice or some other tart-tasting beverage."

"I'm on it." The Guardian headed to the door. "I'll be back in a few minutes."

"We can wait for his return to celebrate." Toven pulled out a chair for her.

Jade wanted to tell him that she wasn't a human female and that he shouldn't do that, but it wasn't in the same category as her inability to tolerate carbonated drinks. It was a cultural difference that Toven was unaware of. To her, the gesture was insulting, but to him, it was the polite thing to do. It was a trivial matter that wasn't worth alienating her allies for.

She might mention it in passing some other time, but right now it was more important to her to hear details about Igor's capture and what they were doing with him.

The original plan regarding the decoy ship had been for the crew to return the *Seafarer* to Copenhagen and for the Guardians and their prisoners to be flown to Greenland, where they would wait for the *Aurora* to arrive, but Kian kept changing plans for various reasons, so maybe that had changed as well.

In any case, it would take the *Aurora* about five days to reach Greenland, and Jade didn't know how she would survive so long without Phinas. Just thinking about it made her heart ache and her throat close up.

Her anger flared.

She was a Kra-ell warrior, a veteran of hardship and suffering. She shouldn't be agonizing about missing her boyfriend.

Damn. Since when did a Kra-ell pureblooded female have a boyfriend?

Shaking her head to dispel the annoying thoughts, Jade asked, "So, how was Igor captured, and are they sure it's him? It's not like they had a picture of him, and we all look alike to your people."

Toven arched a brow. "What makes you think that?"

"Phinas said that out of the three humanoid species on Earth, the Kra-ell are the most androgynous and that it's difficult to tell us apart. We all have the same coloring, are all about the same height and body build, and most of us wear our hair long."

Yamanu snorted. "He must have been teasing you. I can assure you that you look nothing like Pavel or even Kagra to me." He leaned closer. "If I weren't a happily mated male, I would have found you attractive."

It was an odd way to phrase a compliment, but she wasn't the type who sought them or even enjoyed positive comments about her looks unless they came from Phinas.

As the door opened again, the Guardian from before entered with a bottle of vodka in one hand and a bottle of cranberry juice in another. "Good?" he asked.

"Perfect. Thank you." She took the two bottles from him and twisted off the caps. "Let's toast this victory."

After the guy left, she mixed herself a drink in one of the champagne glasses, ignoring the disapproving look from Toven.

Gods were such snobs. Even the nice progressive ones.

Toven uncorked the other bottle and poured the bubbly for Yamanu and himself.

"Let's put the others on the line." Yamanu leaned over to the tablet.

As the screen filled up with a strikingly handsome face, Jade didn't need to be told who it belonged to. If she saw Kian on the street, she would have immediately suspected that he was a god. Humans were never that perfect, not even with the help of plastic surgery.

"Kian, I presume."

He dipped his head. "The formidable Jade. It is a pleasure to finally talk to you face to face."

She hadn't been the one who'd refused to show her face, but Jade kept her mouth shut and forced a pleasant smile.

Kian obviously wanted something from her, and she had a good idea what that was. Negotiations were about to start, and she needed to put her diplomat hat on and act the part.

"The pleasure is all mine, Kian."

2

KIAN

*J*ade looked precisely as Kian had imagined—an alien beauty who radiated power. Her large eyes were intelligent, and they regarded him with curiosity, assessing him the way he was assessing her.

If not for the eyes, she could have passed for a human of Asian descent, but only on casual inspection. Her cheekbones were pronounced, her forehead a little too broad, and her nose too small for her face. And yet, everything somehow came together in perfect harmony.

He could definitely understand Phinas's attraction to her.

It wasn't just about her alien beauty, though. Jade radiated the kind of power and intensity that only true leaders possessed, and as her black eyes bored into his, Kian knew that he was facing an equal. She wouldn't be intimidated by him or the might of the clan he represented.

As Kalugal leaned over so his face was in view of the camera, Kian leaned away to make room for him. "Let me introduce my companions. To my right is Kalugal, Phinas's boss."

"Delighted to meet you, Jade," Kalugal said.

She dipped her head. "Well met, Kalugal."

"To my left is our Chief Guardian, Onegus."

"Hello." Onegus flashed her one of his super charming smiles, but all he got in return was the same slight head incline she'd given Kalugal.

Jade was either not overly impressed with either of them, or she had a great poker face.

"On Kalugal's left is Victor Turner, and he's responsible not only for coming up with the strategy to entrap and capture Igor but also for procuring all the vessels, munitions, and other equipment that made this mission a success. We couldn't have done it without him."

This time Jade's large eyes registered interest. "You must be very well connected, Mr. Turner. What's your position in the clan?"

Turner regarded her with the same interest she was showing him. "I have no official position, but I lend my expertise whenever needed. I'm in the business of hostage retrieval, which is independent of the clan."

Jade dipped her head lower than she'd done for Kalugal and Onegus. "Your chosen occupation speaks well of your character. Saving hostages and returning them to their families is a profession worthy of a warrior."

Turner cracked a rare smile. "Perhaps, but my motives are not purely altruistic. I'm the best at what I do, and people are willing to pay me exceptionally well for my services."

The bright smile Jade returned to him was genuine. "There is nothing wrong with getting proper compensation corresponding to your ability and its scarcity. I might have started my life in the military, but upon arriving on Earth, I discovered that I had an entrepreneurial spirit. I enjoyed making money and providing for my tribe."

Kian liked the female more by the minute, and even Turner seemed taken with her.

"We have that in common," Turner said. "I learned my craft serving as a strategist for special ops. When I retired, I started my hostage retrieval business."

"I like her," Kalugal whispered in Kian's ear. "She reminds me of you."

Shifting her eyes to Kalugal, she tilted her head. "What is your position in the clan?"

"Right now, I don't have one, but Kian has offered me a seat on the council, and if the council approves my nomination, I might become a councilman soon. Right now, I'm just a wealthy businessman, and my main interest is new technology."

She didn't seem surprised, and Kian suspected that Phinas had told her about his boss more than he'd told her about the rest of them.

"Thank you for volunteering your men, Kalugal, and thank you for helping them escape Navuh, the clan's archenemy. Phinas speaks very highly of you."

So he was right, and Phinas had told Jade about his and Kalugal's past. Had he told her that the tyrant was Kalugal's father, though?

"Now that the introductions are over let's make a toast." Yamanu lifted his champagne glass. "To freedom and a better future for all of us."

"Shouldn't Phinas join the toast?" Jade asked. "After all, it is his victory that we are celebrating."

"Indeed," Kian said. "But he has his hands full at the moment. Phinas will call as soon as he gets everyone on board the chartered plane."

Jade looked like she wanted to say something but stopped and turned to Yamanu. "I like your toast. I will also drink to freedom and a better future for our people. May we all enjoy many years of peace and prosperity."

3

PHINAS

"I sedated the three purebloods with a dose that could knock out an elephant," Aiden reported. "And as you've requested, I went light on the hybrid so you could interrogate him on the way to Greenland."

"Thanks." Phinas clapped him on the back.

He wanted nothing more than to keep Igor awake for just long enough to beat the crap out of him until even his mother couldn't recognize the bloody pulp, but even bound and gagged, and despite the earpieces they all wore, the guy was too dangerous to leave conscious.

Perhaps they'd made him into a bigger threat than he really was, but Phinas wasn't taking chances just because he wanted the satisfaction of beating the crap out of the maggot that had abused Jade for over two decades.

And then there was the fact that Jade wasn't the type of female who would tolerate anyone avenging her while she was more than capable of doing so herself.

"What do you want to do with the humans?" Max asked. "We can ask the helicopter pilot to deliver them to the nearest police station and save Berg's crew the trouble of having to deal with them on their way back to Copenhagen. I have no doubt that the crew can handle them, but why burden them with the scum? They barely have enough hands to run the ship, let alone deal with five surly prisoners."

"You are right. What the police do with them is of no concern to us.

Their boss is going to find them and release them anyway, and then he'll probably execute them for letting his precious yacht get taken and blown to pieces."

Max snorted. "Even oligarchs carry insurance, and he would get his money back. Besides, he was the one who Igor contacted and compelled to allow him the use of the yacht, so he can't blame his men for what happened to his precious *Helena*, which I found out was named after his daughter." The Guardian smiled. "That's kind of sweet, and it makes me less eager to kill the fucker."

"The oligarch is not our problem." Phinas headed inside the ship.

"He's everyone's problem." Max fell in step with him. "When I was a kid, I dreamt about becoming a vigilante and killing the bad people who made life miserable for everyone else."

Phinas cast him a sidelong glance. "What happened to that dream?"

"I'm living it." Max put his hand on his chest. "That's why I became a Guardian. I don't get to kill whoever I want, but I do my part in eradicating evil. Rescuing trafficking victims is my contribution to the greater good." He put his arm around Phinas as if they were best buddies. "You and your men should join our humanitarian effort at least part-time. It's very gratifying. Saving damsels in real distress will make you feel better about yourself."

Phinas had enough skeletons in his proverbial closet to fill a department store, but the good deeds of tomorrow could not erase the misdeeds of yesterday.

"I'll think about it, but unlike you, my time is not free to do with as I please. I have a boss who decides what I do and when."

Max shrugged. "I have a boss too. Onegus tells me what to do and assigns me to missions, but if I'm not happy and want a change of pace, all I have to do is ask. I can also resign, but I have no intention of doing that. I love being a Guardian."

Phinas envied the guy.

Max had chosen to be a Guardian; he was good at it and still enjoyed doing it after who knew how long.

Phinas was also good at his job, perhaps even exceptional, but he hadn't chosen it. He didn't love it and didn't hate it either, but he would have loved to explore other options.

That wasn't going to happen.

Kalugal had saved him from the nightmare of serving in the Brotherhood, and he owed him his life. He would serve Kalugal until he was no longer needed and Kalugal dismissed him.

Looking at the blank expressions on the humans' faces, he turned to Max. "What kind of story did you plant in their heads?"

Toven had made quick work of releasing the humans from Igor's compulsion over the phone, and Max had taken it from there, thralling them to forget the details of what had happened to them and replacing those memories with others that were more plausible and didn't hint at an alien with incredible compulsion ability.

"Nothing overly exciting. The story is that Igor wanted to test the missile battery they had on board, and the thing malfunctioned, blowing up in his face, killing him and his men, and blowing a hole in the deck. Then a fire started, and as the men realized that the yacht was about to blow, they jumped into the water and swam away as quickly as they could." Max smiled. "The closer a story is to the truth, the more believable it is."

The men had suffered minor burns, which Aiden had treated, and hypothermia, which the other Guardians with medic training were still treating, but remarkably that was the extent of their injuries, and no one had died.

When questioned, the humans had told Max that there had been no cooks or maids on board and that they had subsisted on frozen meals.

Phinas wondered what Igor and the two other purebloods had done for food. Had they fed on the humans? Or had they brought bagged blood with them?

Kian should be happy that there had been no civilian casualties or any casualties at all, but Phinas was disappointed. The humans they'd saved were professional killers, and getting rid of them would have been a service to humanity.

But they weren't his or the clan's problem, and he had no business appointing himself their judge and executioner. Besides, Max and his Guardian buddies would not stand for that.

The important thing was that Phinas had the ones he'd come for, and the sense of satisfaction was incredible, mainly because he knew how happy it would make Jade.

Well, happy might not be the right word.

Satisfied wasn't right either.

Jade was keeping so much grief and anger bottled up inside of her that once her vengeance was complete and grief flooded the void created by the departure of rage, she would fall apart.

Hopefully, he would be there to catch her. The question was whether she would allow it.

4

JADE

"I used a little more cranberry juice and a little less vodka this time." Yamanu handed Jade another glass. "Tell me if you like it."

It was her fourth, and she was starting to feel a little tipsy, which she suspected was Yamanu's intention. They wanted to make her more amenable before asking her to postpone killing Igor so Toven could interrogate him.

"Thank you." She took a small sip. "It's good. It's still a little too heavy on the alcohol, but that's fine. I don't get drunk easily." Even when her head was spinning and her balance was off, her mind worked just fine.

It was both a blessing and a curse.

There had been so many times she'd wished alcohol would do for her what it did for others. Regrettably, it didn't muddle her thinking, nor did it numb the pain, and she could never get a vacation from her own head. The effects were only physical, and she didn't like them.

"We don't get drunk easily either." Yamanu leaned back against the couch cushions. "This crap doesn't even tickle me."

She lifted her glass. "You're welcome to some of my poison."

He eyed the half empty vodka bottle. "I think I'll take you up on your offer. If we finish the vodka, we can always get more."

Ignoring Toven's sour expression, Yamanu mixed himself a drink in his champagne glass.

"So, what now?" Jade put hers down on the table. "Do we continue removing the trackers? Or do we tell Merlin to stop?"

The three of them looked at the four males crowding the small screen.

"He can definitely slow down now that he has more time," Kian said. "I assume that your people want the trackers out." He cast her a questioning look.

What was he implying? That she wanted the trackers to stay so she could keep tabs on her people?

A good leader didn't need to monitor her people with technology. Their vows of loyalty should suffice to keep them from running off or betraying her trust in other ways. The only one who'd broken his vow to her was Veskar, but she had a feeling that the clever male had found a way around the vow, convincing himself that by leaving he was doing her and the tribe a favor.

The problem was that those who'd been born in Igor's compound didn't believe in the power of vows, and neither did the humans.

Nevertheless, she wouldn't employ any of Igor's tactics to keep her people in line. She'd find a way to reinstall the old beliefs that had kept the Kra-ell society functioning for hundreds of thousands of years.

"We have no need of trackers. I would appreciate it if Merlin continued the removal. It's no longer an emergency or a necessity, so his services might not be offered freely, but I will gladly pay him to finish the job."

It was also a hint, reminding Kian that he had the money Igor had stolen from her tribe and the others, and that he should at some point transfer the funds to them.

"You don't need to pay Merlin for his services," Kian said. "He volunteered for this mission, and he's doing it to help your people."

She dipped her head. "He has my thanks, and I'll thank him in person as soon as I see him."

"I'm sure he will appreciate it," Kian said. "The next and perhaps most important item we have to discuss is whether you want to return to your compound. With Igor gone, you and your people are no longer in danger there."

She'd thought about it at length, and there were many more negatives than positives to returning to the compound.

The only positive was that the humans might be comfortable there, but she wasn't even sure about that. Igor hadn't tormented them as he had the Kra-ell, but she doubted they had fond memories of the place.

Karelia was beautiful, and the forests were filled with wildlife, which was perfect for the Kra-ell, but the harsh winters were miserably cold and dark.

The planet the Kra-ell shared with the gods was warm and humid, and even though their sun wasn't as bright as Earth's and its hues were red and purple instead of yellow, there was light for approximately the same time as the absence of it. Anumati's axis had much less of a tilt than Earth's, so the daytime in winter was almost the same as in summer.

Still, Karelia's harsh weather wasn't as much of a problem as the memories of living under Igor's rule. The compound had his imprint all over it, and it would be a constant reminder of what she'd suffered.

"I'd rather not." Jade lifted her glass and took a long sip before putting it back down. "A fresh start in a new place is preferable."

Kian nodded. "I understand. Too many bad memories, eh?"

"That too. I also don't know who Igor compelled to shield the compound from human eyes, and what other directives he implanted in the local authorities' minds. It might not be safe for us to return there even with Igor gone."

"I agree," Turner said. "Where would you like to go?"

She smiled. "Somewhere warmer. Do you know of a deserted tropical island we can inhabit?"

Kian chuckled. "I know just the one, but regrettably, it belongs to our enemies."

"You mean the Doomers and their leader Navuh? Perhaps we can launch an offensive and conquer it?"

The force she commanded was laughable in comparison to the might of the Brotherhood, and Jade hadn't said it seriously, but she was curious to see how Kalugal would respond to it.

"How much did Phinas tell you about his past?" Kian asked.

"He only told me the highlights, but I understand that the island is home to thousands of immortal warriors, and it's ruled by Kalugal's father."

"Correct," Kalugal said. "And that's why conquering it is not on the table."

5

KIAN

"That's a shame." Jade smiled behind her glass of cranberry vodka. "Perhaps we can find a similar island somewhere else."

Turner shook his head. "Purchasing an island that size and keeping it hidden from the world was doable when Navuh took possession of it. In today's internet connected world, it's much more difficult."

Perhaps even impossible.

Kian hadn't explored the option because he had no desire to live on an island, but he'd often wondered how Navuh was managing to keep it hidden. It probably involved a lot of compulsion work on his part and was reinforced with hefty bribes to human leaders in the area.

Jade leaned closer to the tablet so her face took up the entire screen. "There aren't that many of us, including the humans. A group so small could fit in a gated community in the middle of a city, and no one would be any the wiser. We could also get a very small island somewhere, one of those that rich people buy to build a castle on. The problem with such a small landmass is that it might not be enough to contain the wildlife needed to sustain us."

As Turner and Jade kept exploring the island idea, Kian stifled a groan.

Up until now he'd still entertained the option of returning the Kra-ell to their old compound, but now that was off the table. Even if Jade could be convinced to go back there, he wouldn't do that because the issues she'd raised were valid.

With Igor gone, the Kra-ell and the humans of their community were safe from him but not from the humans on the outside, who might have been compromised by Igor and problematic to control without him.

Humans couldn't be allowed to find out about the aliens living amongst them.

Once a single Kra-ell or immortal was captured and brought to the authorities, the hunt would begin, and even their immortality and super abilities wouldn't protect them from the sheer numbers that humans could throw at them.

No wonder the gods had been concerned with the rapidly expanding human population. Their method of solving the problem had been terrible, but they must have felt that they had no choice. They had either caused the flood or had known it was coming and hadn't warned humanity to seek higher ground.

Ironically, the gods' end hadn't been caused by the humans they had feared, but by one of their own.

Still, it made sense for Igor and the other Kra-ell to assume that the gods who had settled on Earth had been obliterated by the humans they'd created.

When there was a lull in the conversation, Kian refocused his gaze on Jade and realized she was waiting for him to answer her.

"I'm sorry. What was the question?"

"I asked Turner what you are planning to do with the trackers you remove from my people, and he said it's up to you."

"The simple trackers can be trashed, but we will probably want to keep the sophisticated ones and analyze them. We have the one we took out of Sophia, but William didn't want to take it apart because of its solid state and it would have destroyed it. If we have many more, he won't have to be so careful."

Kian expected her to object and demand that the trackers be returned to her people for safekeeping, but she surprised him by nodding. "I don't have a problem with that as long as William shares his findings with me. I would also like to have a few for safekeeping in case William can't decipher them, and I decide to launch an investigation of my own."

Translation—Jade wanted to have the alien trackers in case the findings weren't shared with her. It was an opportunity to create more goodwill and get something in return from her.

"I see no problem with that. By the time the removal is done, we will have plenty of them to divide between us."

Jade swished the alcohol in her glass for a moment. "What I want to find out is how Igor monitored the signals. He had to have the signal receiver with him on the yacht, and unless it could fit inside his pocket, it's now in pieces at the bottom of the sea. How are we going to find the other survivors without it?"

"Are you interested in finding their bodies to give them a proper Kra-ell passing ceremony?" Toven asked.

"If they are dead, yes. But maybe some are alive."

"Other than those Igor found, the others probably didn't make it." Kian didn't know how to phrase it more gently, but thankfully Jade wasn't the kind of female who needed coddling. She was a straight shooter just like him. "The alien trackers need a living host to transmit a signal, and since Igor didn't find them, we have to assume that the hosts are no longer alive."

6

JADE

*K*ian was probably right, and the same had occurred to Jade, but she wasn't willing to give up hope yet.

There could be other explanations.

Perhaps Igor had access to a receiver that could follow only a small portion of the Kra-ell settlers, but that was grasping at straws.

Perhaps the other pods were under water, and that's why the signal couldn't travel far. After all, that's the explanation Phinas had given her for why they couldn't communicate with the submarine following them. Something about radio signals not traveling well in salt water. But given how advanced the gods' technology was, that was a weak straw as well.

"There could be another explanation," Turner said. "The others might still be in stasis, and perhaps the trackers are not designed to transmit when the host's body is in that state. I can ask Bridget what happens to the body's electrical activity during stasis. Perhaps it's not enough to energize the trackers."

Hope surged in Jade's chest. Perhaps the twins were alive after all.

How would she find them, though?

If Igor hadn't found them despite having access to the monitoring equipment and knowing how to identify the signal, how would she manage what he couldn't?

What if he had found the twins and killed them?

At the thought, a shiver of dread slithered down her spine. That wasn't a far-fetched scenario if Igor was an assassin who'd been sent to eliminate the twins. But what about the other settlers? Why hadn't he gone after them? Surely he wanted their females.

The new generation of purebloods born in the compound was predominantly male, and without a continuous influx of pureblooded females, the gender disparity would have only grown.

But if the twins were still alive, her only chance of finding them was with the help of the clan. From what she'd seen so far, they had access to technology she didn't, and Turner had resources in the human world that she wouldn't even know where to start looking for.

Except, she would have to tell them about the twins, and she couldn't trust them with that information.

They seemed like good people, and they'd helped her against Igor, but it was only because their interests had aligned. Her email to Safe Haven had exposed the clan and they had been forced to eliminate the threat.

Kian shook his head. "That doesn't make sense. The trackers were most likely meant for precisely the kind of disastrous scenario as the ship exploding and the escape pods getting scattered all over. It was done to locate survivors. The trackers must operate even when the hosts are in stasis, but if the hosts are dead, there's no sense in wasting resources on finding them. It's more crucial to get to the survivors as quickly as possible."

Turner pursed his lips. "You've got a point. Although it depends on what the purpose of the trackers was. Maybe they were meant as a general means to track the settlers and not as an emergency beacon. In that case, it makes sense that the trackers were activated only when the host was awake. Don't forget that they had to travel hundreds of years to get to their destination. The chances of malfunctions increase the longer a device is used."

"You might be right as well." Kian leveled his eyes at Jade. "The only one who has the answers is Igor."

Here it comes.

Kian was about to ask her not to execute Igor on the spot and to allow them time to interrogate him.

"I know what you're about to suggest, and if I thought that we could learn something useful from him, I would be willing to wait. But I know Igor, and he's not going to tell you anything. Why would he? He knows he's a dead man either way."

"Tom might be able to compel him," Kian said. "It's worth a try."

"I don't think he can, but I'm willing to give him a chance. One day."

She would have preferred to chop off Igor's head the moment she stepped off the ship, but there was also satisfaction in letting him think about his impending death. Besides, it was good to show Kian that she was reasonable and would make a good ally.

Kalugal cleared his throat. "One day might not be practical. As soon as the *Aurora* docks in Greenland, you will board the planes and get out of there. I know there is no rush now, but the flights were scheduled, and the pilots can't wait around for Toven to be done interrogating Igor. That means he has to be loaded onto one of the planes, and Toven can question him on the way."

Jade narrowed her eyes at him. "Why would you risk getting him on a plane? The prudent thing to do is interrogate him in Greenland, kill him, and dispose of the body."

"We came up with an interesting idea," Kalugal said. "We can ask Merlin to tamper with Igor's vocal cords so he can no longer generate the special sound waves to produce compulsion. That will render him nearly harmless."

"How do you know that tampering with his vocal cords will do that?"

Kalugal shrugged. "It makes sense since compulsion works only when the voice is heard. But since Igor can heal pretty fast, maybe it's better to remove them completely, which will take him much longer to regenerate, and he'll be dead before that. Even when mute, he can still tell us what we want to know by writing the answers either with pen and paper or on a keyboard."

The idea was intriguing for the simple reason that seeing Igor helpless and desperate would be immensely satisfying. The problem was that removing his vocal cords would not make him any more susceptible to compulsion than he was with them intact.

"The problem with your idea is that he still can't be compelled to cooperate. He might try to bargain for his life with information, but you can't promise him a stay of execution in exchange for what he can tell you, and I know that you won't lie."

Kian chuckled and tilted his head toward Kalugal. "He might, but I won't."

Kalugal didn't look offended. "Then leave him to me."

"That means bringing him to you," Jade said. "I'd rather be done with him in Greenland."

Kalugal cast Kian a sidelong glance before turning back to her. "We have one more person who might be able to compel Igor, so maybe bringing him with you is not such a bad idea. Once you kill him, the door is closed, and I believe in leaving doors open."

He must have meant his mother, the goddess. Should she tell him that Phinas had told her about Annani? Or was it supposed to be a secret?

Jade closed her eyes. "Let me think about it. We have four more days until we reach Greenland. That should be enough." She rose to her feet. "If we are done celebrating here, I would like to share the good news with my people and celebrate with them."

"Of course." Kian gave her a slight nod. "We can talk more tomorrow after you've had some rest."

"Before I go, is there any news from the *Anatolov*? Is it still keeping the same distance from us?"

"It is," Turner said. "But not for long. You have nothing to worry about, though. As soon as it tries to close the distance or make any aggressive move, our submarine will take it out."

7

PHINAS

*A*s the plane finished its ascent, Phinas unbuckled his seatbelt and walked over to the chained hybrid. Assuming his most intimidating expression, he leaned toward him. "How did Igor know that the compound was compromised?"

The guy looked at him with a blank expression, but the brief flare of red in his eyes gave him away. He'd understood the question and was just playing dumb.

"Maybe he doesn't understand English." Max walked over and leaned against the seat.

"He understands."

"How do you know?"

"Kra-ell eyes give away their emotions. Red can mean either aggression or desire."

Max chuckled. "So, he either wants to punch you or boink you." He leaned closer. "What's your name, buddy?"

The hybrid didn't even turn his head to glance at the Guardian.

Max crossed his arms over his chest. "Igor must have compelled him to keep his mouth shut."

"Maybe. Or perhaps he thinks he's a dead man either way." Phinas trained his gaze on the hybrid. "If you cooperate, we might let you live. If you don't, I'll let Jade deal with you."

The guy's eyes blazed blue for a moment. "She's alive?"

It should have occurred to Phinas that Igor and his men had believed that they were on a rescue mission to save their people from an enemy.

They had no reason to believe that the people had left voluntarily, especially given the powerful compulsion they had been under to defend the compound at all costs.

"Very much so, and so are most of your people. We came to liberate the compound and brought along a powerful compeller who freed your people from Igor's compulsion. They were all very happy to leave."

That wasn't entirely true, but mostly.

"So no one died?"

"The only ones who are no longer breathing are Igor's men who participated in the slaughter of Jade's tribe. She and Kagra dispatched them."

He'd killed one, but only because Kagra had been in trouble, and he'd jumped in to save her. It wasn't worth mentioning.

The guy frowned. "I don't know what you're talking about."

Of course not. The hybrid was born in the compound and didn't know how and why the females had gotten there. He might not even know that it wasn't natural for a Kra-ell community to have that many females.

"How did Igor find out about the compound?" Phinas tried again.

"I can't tell you."

"You can't, or you won't?"

"I can't. Where is your compeller?"

Phinas let out a breath. "He's not here." He looked up at Max. "Let's put him under. He's useless to us."

"Aiden!" Max called. "Get over here. Put him to sleep."

The Guardian ambled toward them. "We can't keep them sedated forever. I mean, it's okay for the duration of the flight and to get them into the hotel, but we can't do it for five days until the ship gets to Greenland. They will need to relieve themselves, and if we don't let them stay awake long enough to do that, we will have a mess to clean up."

Max grimaced. "How do they do it in hospitals?"

"They put a catheter in sedated people and feed them intravenously, but I don't know how to do either. I just know how to stick them with a needle." He pulled a syringe out of his pocket and stuck it in the guy's thigh through his clothes.

"We will worry about it when we get there." Phinas let out a sigh and pushed up to his feet. "I'm going to the bathroom. Keep an eye on him."

Max grinned. "Are you going to call your girlfriend?"

"She's not my girlfriend."

"Right. So you're not calling Jade?"

"Nope. I'm calling Mey."

"Same thing." Max waved him off. "Tell her to say hi to Kagra for me and ask her if she misses me."

Phinas shook his head. "Find your own way to call Kagra. Maybe Jin will do you a favor."

He walked into the tiny bathroom, closed the door behind him, and called Mey.

"Hi, Phinas," she answered in a cheerful voice. "How are things on the *Seafarer*?"

"Good, but we are no longer on the ship. We are on the plane on our way to Greenland. Can I ask you for a favor?"

"Of course. I'll go find her."

He smiled. "How did you know what I was going to ask?"

"What other reason do you have to call me?"

"I'm sorry to keep bothering you like this."

"It's not a bother. I'm happy to help two people so obviously in love."

If Jade had heard Mey, she would have jumped overboard.

"We are not in love. We are friends with benefits."

She laughed. "Keep telling yourself that. I'll call you when I find her."

"Thank you. You're the best."

"I know, right?"

8

JADE

"*L*et's make another toast!" Kagra poured vodka into Jade and Morgada's glasses. "To our freedom!"

Morgada followed. "To Igor's head rolling off into the ocean."

"To a new beginning." Jade lifted her glass with an unsteady hand and poured the vodka down her throat.

It burned, the same way the six that had come before it had burned, but she didn't care even though her vision was swimming, and she was the closest to passing out from drinking than she'd ever been before.

The cranberry juice had run out, and none of them was in a state to go looking for more. Instead, they were downing the vodka straight.

She and Kagra had gone from cabin to cabin, sharing the good news of Igor's capture with their people. Tomos and Boris had offered to inform the humans, and Jade had accepted their offer even though she should have done it herself. She just didn't have the energy to continue repeating the same story.

Jade was exhausted from the worry for Phinas, the fear that Igor would pull an unexpected move and gain the upper hand, the lack of sleep, and now nausea and a headache from imbibing too much alcohol, but despite it all, she felt better than she had in years.

After decades of hopelessness, and losing time and again, winning for a change felt incredibly good. The only thing that could have made these moments better was having Phinas there and culminating the celebrations in his bed.

As the doorbell rang, the three of them turned to look at it, but only Morgada was sober enough to get up and let their visitor inside.

When she opened the door, and Mey walked in, Jade welcomed her with a grin. "Did you come to join our celebration?" She lifted the bottle of vodka. "There is plenty left, but only because it's the second bottle. We finished the first bottle and all the cranberry juice, so you'll have to drink it straight up."

"I'll pass." Mey walked over to the couch and sat next to Jade. "Phinas wants to talk to you. Do you want to call him from here or somewhere more private?"

"That depends." She put her hand on Mey's arm. "Do you still have to be there when I use your phone? Because if I can call him in private, there are some things I want to say to him that are not for your ears." She gave Mey what she hoped was a meaningful look.

The female laughed. "If you weren't about to pass out, I would take the chance and let you take my phone to the bedroom, but I need it back, and I don't want to have to pry it from your fingers."

"Then come into the bedroom in fifteen minutes to get it."

Mey hesitated for a moment. "I wish I could, but I can't. There is too much personal information on it, some of it classified, so I have to come with you, but I'll do my best not to listen." She pulled a pair of earbuds from her pocket.

Jade eyed the devices with a frown. "Those are not the specialty earpieces."

"They are just regular earbuds that I use to listen to podcasts while I exercise."

With Mey's enhanced hearing, those wouldn't do much to keep Jade's conversation with Phinas private unless the female blasted music.

Jade let out a breath and rose to her feet with effort. "I don't know why you are all so worried. I have absolutely no one to call except Phinas." She started toward the bedroom on unsteady legs. "Aside from him, everyone I care about is on this ship."

Mey followed her to the bedroom. "It's not about that. All of our calls are recorded. No one is listening, but if anything happens, and there is reason to suspect something isn't kosher, the Guardians can and will listen to the recording. It's just that there is too much information on this device that I'm not at liberty to share."

Jade looked over her shoulder at the female. "If it was up to you, would you trust me with it?"

Mey took in a deep breath and nodded. "I would. I don't think you are the kind of person who would ever repay kindness with betrayal. You are honorable."

"Thank you." Jade dropped her bottom on the bed. "That's exactly right. Can I have the phone now?"

"Let me dial Phinas for you."

"Okay." Jade lay down on the bed and groaned. "I'm getting a headache."

"Do you want me to get you a couple of Motrin? I'm sure Merlin has them in his clinic."

Jade laughed. "Haven't you heard what Motrin does to Kra-ell?"

"No." Mey regarded her with a frown. "What does it do?"

"It affects us like alcohol affects humans."

9

_____

PHINAS

*W*hile waiting for Mey to find Jade, Phinas had to vacate the bathroom twice to let others use it, and when the call finally came in, he was outside the bathroom, leaning against the opposite wall.

"Hello, my brave warrior," Jade slurred her words. "Are you delivering my prize bull hogtied with a red bow around his neck?"

Phinas chuckled. "I still need to find a red bow, but affirmative on all the rest. By the sound of it, you either celebrated with too much alcohol or someone snuck a Motrin or two into your drink."

"No Motrin, but too much vodka. Don't get fooled by my impaired mouth, though. Even though my head is swimming, my mind works perfectly fine."

He stifled a snort. "I have no doubt. Where are you now?"

As the bathroom door opened, he waited until Vortek stepped out to duck inside and shut the door behind him.

"In my cabin. Kagra and Morgada are in the living room, and Mey is with me in the bedroom. She is sitting on a chair pretending she can't hear me, but I know she can. But maybe she can't hear you, so we can have one-way phone sex. Where are you?"

Jade was definitely drunk, and she was saying stuff she wouldn't have said when sober. Not that she was shy or even concerned with decorum, but she was never that carefree.

"I'm on the plane, hiding in the bathroom so I can have some privacy."

"Goodie. Do you want sexy-talk? I heard that humans are into that. I never tried it before."

"I would love to, but not while you are using Mey's phone and not while I'm in a stinky bathroom."

Vortek had left toxic fumes behind him.

Jade groaned. "Why did you tell me that? It's gross, and now I want to puke. Get out of there."

"I'll survive. I need a private spot so I can tell you how much I miss you."

"I miss you too, but it makes me very uncomfortable, so let's talk about something else. What did you do with your prisoners?"

Had she meant that missing him was making her uncomfortable or that he was talking to her from a stinky bathroom?

"We're keeping them sedated. I left the hybrid semi-sedated so I could interrogate him, but he's under Igor's compulsion not to reveal anything."

"Maybe you should put Tom on the phone with him."

Evidently Jade was right about her mind staying clear despite the alcohol's effect. She'd remembered to call Toven by his fake name.

"I thought about doing that, but it can wait for when we meet in Greenland. The guy probably doesn't know much, and even if he does, none of it is urgent."

"True. I wonder if he knows which officials Igor compelled to ignore our compound."

Phinas's gut clenched. Did Jade plan to return to Karelia?

"Why do you need to know that? Do you want to go back?"

She sighed. "Kian and your boss asked me the same question. I said no, and Kian looked disappointed. I think he would prefer for us to go back there, and I don't want to repay his kindness by placing more burden on him. So, I reexamined my decision, trying to find solutions for the issues that prevent us from going back. One of those issues is that I don't know which of the local officials is under Igor's compulsion and what they are compelled to do. If Porgut knows who they are, Tom can release them from Igor's compulsion, and I can use mine to compel them to do what I tell them. I'm not nearly as strong as Igor or Tom, but I'm strong enough to compel most humans."

Toven could make the hybrid talk, and if Porgut didn't know the answers, the two purebloods probably did. But Jade said that the compelled officials were just one of the issues.

"What were your other reasons for not wanting to go back?"

She sighed. "The weather and too many bad memories. There is hardly any sunlight in the winter, and that's not healthy for Kra-ell. But those are not life-and-death issues. Security is."

Phinas closed his eyes. "You should not compromise on your new location. This is an opportunity for a fresh start, and it shouldn't be diminished by practical considerations. You are making so many positive changes in the way your people live and interact. If you go back to the compound, they will fall back on old habits, and everything will revert to how it was when Igor was in charge. You don't want that."

Was he being a selfish bastard for pushing her to relocate?

Maybe.

But his gut was telling him that she shouldn't return to the old compound. Then again, his gut was informed by his preferences, and he didn't want Jade to be on the other side of the world from him.

"Yeah, you're right. But I'm too nauseous to think right now. My head is swimming."

"It's not your head," he heard Mey say. "It's the ship. The ocean is getting turbulent."

Phinas clutched the phone to his ear. "What does she mean by turbulent? What's going on?"

"It's raining," Mey said. "And the wind is picking up. I should check what's happening."

"Yeah, and when you find out, call me, please."

"Will do," Mey said. "I need the phone back."

"I have to go." Jade groaned. "I wish I hadn't had so much to drink. I'm going with Mey to find out what the deal is with this bad weather. No one said anything about a storm."

Mey chuckled. "Try not to puke on me."

10

TOVEN

*W*hen Toven entered Valstar's cabin, the television was playing without sound, and the guy was staring at it with unfocused eyes. Given his pallor, he'd probably heard about Igor's capture, but Toven was curious about what terrified him.

He should be much more worried about Jade than about Igor.

"Hello, Valstar." Toven sat across from him on one of the armchairs. "You don't look so good."

"The ship is swaying, and the guards told me there is a storm. Is this vessel safe?"

So that was what the formidable Valstar was scared of. Apparently, phobias affected Kra-ell in the same way they did humans and immortals.

The truth was that Toven had been a little worried himself, mostly because of Mia and the humans on board, so he'd read up on the subject to reassure himself that they weren't going to sink even if the weather got worse.

"The storm is not that bad, but even if it was, modern cruise ships are very safe, and it's extremely rare for them to get into real trouble that requires evacuation."

"What about the *Titanic*?"

Toven chuckled. "That was a very long time ago, and it collided with an iceberg. This ship and others like it have equipment that detects obstacles long in advance so they can avoid them."

Valstar didn't look convinced. "We are in a floating bucket. If the waves get really big, what will prevent it from tipping so low that it starts taking in water and sinking?"

"The ship is made from heavy steel, and everything in it makes it even heavier. It can easily roll through rough waters or rogue waves. The worst that can happen is that it will tilt to one side, but even that's unlikely. The ship's center of gravity is designed to keep her steady even in hurricanes, and the storm we are experiencing is nowhere near as violent as that. Ships also have several ballast tanks, and the water inside of them can be pumped to either side of the ship to help keep her balanced."

"So why is it rocking so badly?"

Toven chuckled. "It would have been much worse without the stabilizing. Anyway, you shouldn't worry about the weather. If you want to worry about something, it should be the Russian destroyer on our tail, or that we caught Igor, although neither represents a clear and present danger to us."

Valstar's shoulders stiffened, but given that his expression changed only marginally, he'd already known about Igor's capture.

"Why didn't you order your men to kill him on the spot?"

"I promised Jade his head, and I'm not one to go back on my promise."

That got Valstar's attention. "What about me? You promised her my head as well."

"I did, but I pleaded your case with her, and she promised to give it some thought. I told her that you should be given a fair trial."

Valstar sighed. "You're just postponing my execution."

"Would you rather die today than tomorrow?"

The male shrugged. "I don't know. Sometimes I think that ending it all is preferable. I hate being alone in this cabin, chained like a dog, and I hate not knowing when and how my end will come."

"Well, if you don't want to wait for a trial, let me know, and I can arrange your execution."

"I might take you up on your offer. At least I would be able to choose the when and how."

Toven nodded. Having even a tiny bit of control over one's destiny was comforting, and Valstar wasn't enough of a monster to be denied that. He had done monstrous things, but he hadn't chosen to do so. He'd been as much of a victim as the ones he'd killed.

"If you're keeping Igor alive because you want to get information out of him, that's a mistake." Valstar shifted his position, and as his chains made a clanking sound, he winced. "He won't talk even if you torture him."

"What makes you say that? The guy has always relied on his compulsion ability to get anything he wanted. He has never been tortured, and he might sing after the first squeeze."

Valstar shook his head. "He's tough, and he had military training that was superior to the rest of us. Perhaps he served in one of the queen's special units."

That was a new piece of information, and Toven jumped right on it. "What did the queen do with her special units?"

"I don't know." Valstar lifted a hand to rub the back of his neck. "What are special ops units for?"

"Good point." Toven made a mental note to ask Turner about it. He had a general idea, but it was based mainly on books he'd read and movies he'd seen. "Infiltrations, espionage, retrieval of captured operatives." He frowned. "Why would the queen send a special operator on a settler ship?"

"I often wondered the same thing," Valstar admitted. "But Igor is like a vault. He doesn't reveal anything he doesn't have to or want to."

11

YAMANU

"I'll talk with the captain." Yamanu kissed Mey's cheek and cast Jade a sidelong glance. She wasn't looking good, and he was worried about her barfing in their cabin. "Perhaps you should escort Jade back to her cabin and put her in bed."

"I'm not going anywhere." Jade plopped down on the couch. "I want to know what's going on with the weather and how bad it's going to get, but since I don't think I can make it across the deck to the bridge, I'll wait here for you to return and tell me what you learned. If we are in danger, I need to let my people know so they can take the necessary precautions."

While Mey's lips twitched with amusement, Yamanu turned his face away from Jade so she couldn't see his expression.

It wasn't nice to make fun of the Kra-ell's water phobia, but the weather wasn't bad enough to justify safety drills.

"What kind of precautions?" Mey asked.

"To start with, we need to get life vests on the children. Maybe even go to the lifeboats and wait there in case we need to board them." Jade's speech was slurred, but her eyes were completely lucid.

"I'll make coffee." Mey cast him an amused glance as she walked over to the cabin's kitchenette.

Trying to keep a straight face, Yamanu headed for the door. "The situation doesn't call for such extreme measures, but I'll call Mey as soon as I know anything."

"Thank you." Jade put a hand on her forehead as she slumped against the couch cushions.

When Yamanu stepped through the sliding doors onto the top deck, the rain pelted him with cold droplets, but even though it seemed as if the temperature was freezing, it wasn't. The rain didn't turn into sleet, but the wind was making it miserably cold, and as he made his way toward the bridge, he kept his hands in the pockets of his coat and cursed himself for not putting on a hat or at least wrapping a scarf around his neck.

Pulling the door open, he was quick about getting in and closing it behind him. "Good evening, gentlemen." He strode toward the captain. "How is the weather looking?"

"It could be worse," the captain said.

The guy looked like he hadn't slept in days, which was probably spot on since nearly half his crew had gone to the *Seafarer*, and he was severely understaffed.

Once Berg had delivered the decoy back to Copenhagen, he, his crew members, and the Guardians accompanying them would fly to Greenland to meet up with the *Aurora*. The ship would continue its journey south with its whole crew on board, while all the passengers would leave on the planes Turner had chartered.

The question was where the Kra-ell and the humans would land. That had yet to be decided, and there was little time left.

"I'm glad it's not too bad." Yamanu rubbed his hands to warm them up. "Perhaps it's a good idea to speed up a little and get away from the Russian trailing us."

The captain shook his head. "I have to slow her down to avoid the storm." He pulled up a weather map on the screen. "Here is the storm's center." He pointed. "And here is the *Aurora*." He pointed at a spot east of it. "If I want to avoid sailing right into the storm, I have to slow her down to sixteen knots."

"That's a shame. I thought the storm was behind us."

The captain turned to look at him. "Why is the Russian still on our tail? He should have either attacked or gone back. The *Parchin* is mainly used to patrol the Baltic. It's not a blue-water vessel, and it can't keep following us across the North Atlantic. What's more, the Russian naval command will have realized by now that they have a rogue ship on their hands, and the *Anatolov's* captain must be aware of that."

Perhaps Captain Sergey Gorshekov was waiting for Igor's command?

It was likely that Igor had compelled him to follow the *Aurora* and wait for his instructions. The captain would keep following them until told otherwise by Igor or taken over by the Russian navy. Turner's instructions to Nils were to attack only if the Russian made an aggressive move or sped up to close the distance between him and the *Aurora*.

Maybe now that they were being forced to slow down, they would force the confrontation, and Nils would disable the Russian cruiser.

Yamanu would have preferred a resolution that didn't involve unnecessary loss of life, and if the Russian was hit hard enough, sailors would die. It would be preferable to run, but the Fates might have other plans, and they were not always merciful.

"Thank you for the update, captain. I will inform the command center back home."

Olsson responded with a slight nod and went back to his monitoring equipment.

Sticking his hands back in his coat pockets, Yamanu made his way across the deck and through the sliding doors inside. Once out of the rain, he pulled out his phone and called Toven.

"I'm heading to the war room to call Kian and the gang. Do you want to join?"

"Of course," the god said. "Is it about the storm? Is it getting worse?"

"Not unless Olsson sails right into it, which he might have to if Kian wants to avoid confrontation with the Russian. Meet me in the war room, and I'll explain the situation."

"I'll be there in a moment."

"See you there." Yamanu ended the call and made another to his mate.

"Well?" Mey answered. "Are we sinking any time soon?"

"We are not. Tell Jade that the captain is slowing the ship down to avoid the worst of the storm. This is probably as bad as it's going to get."

"That's good news. Are you on your way back?"

"Not yet. I'm heading to the war room to talk to Kian and the others about our tail."

"What about him?"

"He should have made his move already, and since he hasn't, he must be waiting for a command from Igor, which isn't going to come. At least, that's what I'm hoping for. It would be a shame for those Russian sailors to die for no good reason."

12

KIAN

*A*s Kian listened to Yamanu's update about the storm, he glanced at Turner to see the guy's expression, but what he found was not what he'd been hoping for.

When Turner had answers at the ready, he looked smug, and when the gears in his mind were spinning, working out a solution, he had a faraway look in his eyes. Now he just looked indifferent.

"We need to force the Russian to either engage or disengage," Onegus said. "We can't allow him to continue trailing the *Aurora*. If the Russian navy intercepts him, they will want to know why he was trailing us, and they might want to investigate. If we want to keep the ship, we can't allow even a speck of suspicion to be attached to her."

Kian grimaced. "I really don't want to have to tell my sister that her wedding on board a cruise ship is not happening. She has her heart set on it."

Yamanu chuckled. "The one who has his heart set on it is you. Alena couldn't care less where and when she gets married."

Toven smiled. Onegus nodded in agreement.

Turner ignored the entire exchange and turned to Roni. "We need to find out whether the Russian navy is diverting vessels to go after the *Anatolov*. Can your program do that?"

Roni pursed his lips. "The one I designed to identify ships pursuing the

Aurora is not going to be helpful for that. I need to write a new program with new parameters."

"Why do we need a program?" Onegus asked. "We are only interested in Russian navy vessels, and there can't be too many of them in the North Atlantic."

Roni cast him a condescending look. "Do you want to click on each dot to check whether it's a Russian navy ship or a fishing boat? I assure you that would take more time than it will take me to write a simple program that will keep monitoring their movements on autopilot." He pushed to his feet. "It shouldn't take me more than fifteen minutes."

Tucking his laptop under his arm, he walked out of the room.

Kian drummed his fingers on the table. "While Roni is working on the program, let's discuss how to stop the *Anatolov*'s captain."

Onegus turned to Kalugal, who hadn't taken part in the conversation yet. "Can Phinas force Igor to compel the captain to disengage?"

"Phinas will do whatever we ask of him, but I doubt Igor will do that even under torture and the threat of death. He knows he's a dead man, and he doesn't care about anyone other than himself."

Onegus nodded. "That's what we all assume. But what if we are wrong? I say it's worth a try." He looked at Turner. "What do you think?"

"At the moment, Igor is sedated, and I prefer him to remain that way and not endanger our people. I was thinking of getting Roni to hack into the *Anatolov*'s communication system, and hook Toven in, posing as Igor." He looked at Toven. "Do you think you can remove Igor's compulsion remotely and impose your own?"

Toven shook his head. "I can give it a try, but I wouldn't base our decision on the assumption that I would succeed. The humans on the yacht were easy enough to release from Igor's compulsion, but then he most likely didn't have to compel them as deeply and with as much power as he needed to force the captain of the *Anatolov* to do his bidding."

Kian had run through the same logic loop, arriving at the same conclusion. Neither Toven nor Igor himself could be used to divert the *Anatolov* away from the *Aurora*. Their only options were to outrun him, which could be done if Olsson was willing to brave the storm, or to wait for the Russian captain to make his move, which was no doubt imminent.

That was what they had prepared for, and Nils would take the *Anatolov* out.

The first option risked the *Aurora*'s passengers because of the storm and because the submarine couldn't keep up. The second option meant dealing with the Russian navy and potentially having to sell the cruise ship and get a new one.

Perhaps that wasn't such a bad idea. He could sell the ship to Jade, and she could turn it into their new compound. With the money, he could get a larger ship that didn't need remodeling, but there was no way it would be ready in time for Alena's wedding. Maybe he should sell it right after the wedding cruise?

"I have it." Roni strode into the war room as if he owned the place. "Two Russian ships changed course in the last twenty-four hours, and they are on an intercept course with the *Anatolov*." He pointed at a dot. "This one will only catch up to it tomorrow morning at about ten o'clock." He pointed at the other dot. "But this one will get there sooner. ETA six and a half hours."

"What kind of ship is it?" Turner asked.

Kian cocked a brow. "Does it matter? It's not as if we are going to engage with it. We have only two options. The *Aurora* takes a risk and speeds up into the storm, or we wait for the *Anatolov* to make its move and for Nils to take it out. After that, we will have to deal with the Russian navy."

13

TOVEN

*T*oven got up and poured himself vodka from the bottle Jade had left behind. "It's a perfect storm. We have a real storm, a Russian destroyer on our tail with torpedoes ready to launch, a submarine on the Russian's tail, ready to take it out before he's in range to fire a torpedo at us, and the Russian navy closing in on their rogue destroyer. Perhaps our best bet is to hazard the storm full speed ahead and get away from the rest."

"Olsson is not going to like it," Yamanu said. "And given our passengers, I agree with him. Besides, storms are unpredictable, and this one could still get worse."

Turner leaned back. "If the Russian doesn't make his move within the next two hours, he's not going to. Maybe it's worth increasing the speed just for a short time to force his hand. I just hope that Nils is monitoring the situation closely."

"I'm sure he is," Onegus said. "He's using a periscope to get visual confirmation."

"Is he dancing with the gray lady?" Toven asked.

Onegus regarded him with a puzzled expression. "Is being stuck on a ship getting to you?"

Toven laughed. "It's an expression used on submarines. I wondered how the sub's captain was monitoring the situation while maintaining radio silence, so I read up on it. Standing watch at the periscope is called dancing with the gray lady, I guess because it's a metal cylinder that can be raised, lowered, and rotated. It's kind of a dance."

"I've never heard that expression, but I'll take your word for it."

Toven crossed his legs and interlaced his fingers. "I wondered how he could raise the periscope without being detected. Apparently, the material it's made from reflects the water around it, so it's not visible even at short range. Modern periscopes are equipped with high-resolution optics and sensors, thermal imaging, lowlight imaging, image intensified cameras, and low observables technology—whatever that is."

Onegus cast him a condescending smile. "You are talking about the level of equipment on nuclear submarines. Nils probably has something much simpler." He glanced at Turner. "Am I right?"

"Probably. He has an old submarine that was decommissioned by the Norwegian navy decades ago. He's done some upgrades, but I don't have the details. What I do know is that he's a responsible guy, and he wouldn't have undertaken a mission he's not equipped to handle. He knew that he would have to monitor the tail closely, and I'm sure he has the proper equipment. What he's not going to do is follow the *Aurora* all the way to Greenland, and the same goes for the *Anatolov*. I say let's end it. When the *Aurora* speeds up, he will have two choices, either chase it or turn around, and we will have our answer."

"Can he even catch up?" Kian asked. "You said that he's slower."

"He is, and the submarine is even slower, so we will lose both by having her speed away. The thing is, she can't maintain that speed without burning through her fuel before reaching Greenland, and a boat without fuel is a boat that can easily sink even in a mild storm. She needs to keep moving to stay balanced. The Russian knows that all he needs to do is keep going, and eventually he would find her stranded and defenseless, or an even worse scenario, sinking fast."

Yamanu nodded. "I'm not a sailor, but thanks to the internet, I found out that engine failure is more dangerous for a cruise ship than I assumed. I thought that it wasn't a big deal since it could just float until help arrived, but that's not the case. Still, cruise ships have several engines, and it's very rare for all of them to fail at the same time."

Kian lifted his hand. "Bottom line, can Nils keep up if the *Aurora* speeds up?"

"Not in stealth mode," Turner said. "But as soon as he detects that the Russian is increasing speed, he will switch to diesel, chase him, and fire a torpedo at him before the *Anatolov* is in range of the *Aurora*."

"Good." Kian tapped his palm on the table. "Let Olsson know that if the Russian doesn't make his move in the next couple of hours, we will need him to put on a short burst of speed to force the *Anatolov* captain's hand."

14

KIAN

With another crisis looming close, going to his mother's for lunch might not be the most prudent way Kian could utilize his time, but he'd been summoned, and wiggling out of it was not an option. His mother expected to be obeyed, and despite her diva personality, she rarely did that for frivolous reasons.

Besides, if he was needed, the war room was only minutes away.

Oridu opened the door and bowed. "Master Kian. The Clan Mother is expecting you."

"Thank you." Kian rushed by the butler, bee-lining for the dining table and kissing his mother on her offered cheek before taking a seat next to her.

He'd expected Alena and Orion to be there as well, but there were only two place settings on the table.

"It's just the two of us?"

"Yes." She patted his hand. "I know that you are pressed for time, but I need you to tell me about our interests in the North Sea, and having more people over would have meant more questions that you would not have the time to answer." She waved at her butler. "We are ready to eat. Please serve lunch, Oridu."

He bowed. "Right away, Clan Mother."

"Thank you." She reached for the water pitcher and filled Kian's glass. "How are things between you and your cousin?"

Annani had been overjoyed when he'd told her about the talk he'd had with Kalugal and the agreement they had reached, but she'd been skeptical about the implementation, hence the question.

"Good. He's participating in most of the war room meetings, but not all, and he's contributing as much as he can. He's rusty on strategy, but he's smart enough to improvise."

"Why is he not present at all the meetings?"

Kian smiled. "He can't stay away from Darius for too long, or at least that's the excuse he gives me. Making money is still Kalugal's first priority after his family. His men and the Kra-ell are a distant third."

Annani wagged her finger at him. "You are doing it again. You are letting yourself think less of your cousin because you are judging him based on your standards. Kalugal is not the leader of this community, and he does not carry the same responsibility as you."

"True." Kian unfurled the cloth napkin and draped it over his slacks. "I need your advice on the Kra-ell issue."

That was the best way to divert the conversation to another topic. His mother loved it when he asked her advice.

Annani smiled brightly. "I am delighted that you seek my input. Usually, I have to insist that you listen to what I have to say."

"I value your opinion, Mother. I don't always need it, though."

She looked down her nose at him. "Well, let us get right to the subject of the Kra-ell, lest we spoil each other's moods. What do you need my advice on?"

As Oridu brought the appetizer plates, Kian took a moment to reply. "As you know, we captured Igor, so the Kra-ell are no longer in danger. I asked Jade if she wanted to return to the compound, and she replied that she preferred a fresh start."

"That is understandable. If I were in her position, I would not want to live where I was enslaved, even with my slaver gone."

That was a succinct way to put it.

"Jade is also concerned about the officials who Igor compelled to shield the compound or just ignore it. I agree that it might not be safe for them to go back there. Turner and Syssi are both pushing for inviting them and the humans who shared their lives with them to the village. Turner wants to keep a close eye on them, and Syssi wants the added security of having an additional legion of capable warriors protecting our community. I'm not too keen on the idea, mainly because there are too many of them, which is problematic on several fronts."

His mother nodded. "It would be difficult to hide all the traffic going in and out of the tunnel."

"Indeed. They would double the population of the village, which would put a strain on everything, but mostly security and hiding the village from the humans and the Brotherhood. The Kra-ell also have over a hundred humans with them. They lived with these aliens all of their lives and can't be thralled to forget them. You know how I feel about humans in the village." He groaned. "But compared to how I feel about over two hundred Kra-ell, that's the lesser problem."

15

ANNANI

"It is indeed a conundrum." Annani leaned closer to Kian and put her hand over his. "You know what I say about handling big problems."

He nodded. "Break them up into small chunks and address each piece separately. Except, I don't see how I can do that with the Kra-ell problem unless you are suggesting that I break them up into smaller groups and settle each one in a different location."

Annani smiled. "That is one possible solution, but that is not what I meant. Let us start with the problem of Igor. What do you plan to do with him?"

"I want to interrogate him, but if Toven can't compel him, we probably won't be able to get anything out of him. Jade gave us one day to do that, but I think I can convince her to give us more time. She's surprisingly reasonable."

"Why surprisingly?"

Kian reached for a breadstick. "My preconceived idea of her came from Stella, and she got her impression from what Vrog had told her about Jade. Once it was formed in my mind, it got stuck there. I was pleasantly surprised to find out that Jade is very different in person."

What surprised Annani was the note of admiration in Kian's tone. "You like her."

He nodded. "She's tough, brave, and she does the best she can for her people. I don't know if I could have endured what she's been through and remained sane. She saw her sons murdered in front of her eyes, and then she was forced to become their killer's breeder."

As Kian's fangs elongated and his eyes blazed with inner light, Annani patted his hand. "Calm down, my son. There was nothing you could have done to help her."

With a sigh, he put his hand on top of hers and nodded. "I can't imagine the suffering she's endured. But that's neither here nor there. Before the tragedy that befell her, she was a strict but fair leader, which even Emmett admits, and her subjects were loyal to her. She'd never been cruel for the sake of cruelty or for the sake of aggrandizing herself. She tried to do what was right, and she made mistakes, to which she readily admits. She's willing to adapt and make changes, so all members of her community are treated with respect, including the humans, and she wants everyone to be reasonably comfortable coexisting."

"Are you sure she is not feeding you what you want to hear?"

He chuckled. "It's possible, but by all accounts, she's an honorable person. Besides, my gut tells me that she means what she says, and I feel real affinity toward her. I can see a lot of myself in her, and since I know that I'm far from perfect, I'm more forgiving of her mistakes."

Annani had a feeling that Kian's compassion for what Jade had gone through was coloring his impression of her, but she'd reserved judgment for when she met the female in person.

"So, Jade's chunk of the bigger problem is settled. You respect and like her, so you will have no problem working with her."

"I think so. That's a very astute observation, Mother. Thank you."

Annani nodded. "Let us move to the next problem. The over two hundred Kra-ell. What are your misgivings about them?"

"I don't know them. I like Vrog and Aliya. I like Emmett less, but I don't hate him. But all of them are hybrids, and their human part makes them more palatable to me. If all the purebloods were like Jade, I would probably like them as well, but we know that they are not. Many of them were born in the compound and grew up on Igor's philosophy, which embraced all the militant Kra-ell tendencies but rejected the honorable tradition that served to mitigate their innate aggression. Still, if there were only a few of them, that wouldn't be a problem."

Annani nodded. "So it is less about the people themselves and whether they are purebloods, hybrids, or human, and more about their sheer number and what it would do to life in the village."

"Precisely. It's also a matter of security. I would have to put cuffs on all of them, and given that they were just liberated from a tyrant that had most of them wearing collars, that would not go well with them."

"I agree. Although it could be mitigated. Jade could explain that it is a temporary measure until both sides feel secure living together."

"It would still cause resentment."

"That is true. Let us look at it from another angle. Where else can you settle them?"

"I don't know. Turner keeps saying that we need to keep an eye on them, and that means that I would need to put them somewhere nearby. I don't have enough space in the keep, and even if I did, I don't want to have to guard them from now until forever. Besides, they need to hunt, and other than humans, there is no game in downtown Los Angeles."

Annani was taken aback. "Do they feed from humans?"

"They don't. Taking a little blood during sex is part of their bed play, but for food they prefer animals."

"Thank the merciful Fates. If they planned to feed from my children, I would never allow them anywhere near my people."

16

KIAN

"That's actually what I wanted to ask you. How do you feel about the Kra-ell and the humans joining the village?"

His mother's gut feelings were usually spot on, and they had saved her life and later those of her descendants on multiple occasions. Sometimes her decisions had seemed erratic or emotional, but in hindsight, they had been proven not only correct but also timely.

Annani let out a sigh. "I am not thrilled about it, but that is a natural response. We all cling to the familiar and want to preserve our way of life. If their inclusion would improve life in the village, it would be a good thing. Let us discuss the advantages and disadvantages of their inclusion. What are the advantages of having them here?"

"You mean provided that we can trust them?"

Annani nodded. "Obviously, that is essential. But if they are trustworthy and dependable, they will provide added security."

"I agree. They are incredibly strong, well-trained, and fierce warriors. I would sleep better at night knowing that I had a large force defending the village. They would also provide diversity, but that could be just as detrimental as it could be beneficial. In the long run, though, their higher birth rate and propensity to produce males predominantly could be a big problem."

"What if they mate with clan members?" Annani asked. "Vlad is a delightful young man, and a village full of Vlads and Vladettes does not seem so bad. Maybe the Kra-ell and the immortals are each other's answer to survival. Their genetics would increase our birth rates, and our genetics would even out their gender disparity."

Annani was the quintessential optimist.

"What if it doesn't work like that? I don't know much about genetics, but it could work the other way around, and we might end up with a village of mostly Vlads. He is a sweetheart of a guy, but I don't want our sons to live in harems, or tribal units, as the Kra-ell refer to them."

"Neither do I." Annani sighed. "Maybe we should not think of inviting them to the village as a final solution but as a transitional period until a better solution presents itself. We might need to keep our communities separate but close, and to do so, you will need to find a new location that can accommodate both of our clans."

"I don't want to move. We've just completed phase three, and I love our new home."

"I know, my son." Annani leaned closer to him and kissed his cheek. "The village is lovely, and its location is perfect. It is remote and well-hidden while still close to a major metropolis. But a community is made out of people, not buildings, and you can create an even better one somewhere else that is just as lovely and checks all the boxes. There is no rush either. You can house the Kra-ell and their humans in the village for several years without worrying about overpopulation, and in the meantime, you can build a new place." She smiled. "You should consult with Sari before selecting a new location. Perhaps she can suggest an arrangement that will allow her the autonomy she needs while at the same time being close to the rest of her family."

"Like what? Three separate villages? One for us, one for Sari's people, and one for the Kra-ell?"

"Why not? I think it is a brilliant idea."

Kian chuckled. "Jade asked me if we could find her an island like the one Navuh has. Maybe I should look into that. Do you think we can buy Catalina Island?"

"I do not see why not. How many people live there?"

"Not that many. Probably under five thousand."

Annani waved a hand. "There you go. Give them incentive to leave, buy their businesses and homes, and take over the island. It's only an hour away by boat."

It was a crazy idea, but his mother was thinking outside the box. Catalina Island was small, but given that they needed space for less than a thousand people, including Sari's part of the clan and everyone in Annani's sanctuary, it was big enough.

"We should have a family meeting," Annani said. "Put all of our heads together."

"I was hoping to finalize a decision and bring it in front of the council, and once they approve it, to bring it to the large assembly for a clan-wide vote. But since I don't seem to be capable of solving this puzzle, a family meeting might be a good idea. What I need to decide now, though, is where to fly the Kra-ell from Greenland. I can't keep them there until we make up our minds."

Annani pursed her lips. "Why not? Instead of flying them back, they could cruise back on the ship. That will give you a couple of weeks to solve this puzzle and make arrangements for receiving them."

"The idea has occurred to me, but there are several logistical issues involved that I don't want to bore you with." He rose to his feet. "I should return to the war room." He leaned in and kissed her cheek. "Thank you for lunch and for the advice."

"Any time. It was my pleasure." She held on to his hand. "I am always here for you."

"I know." He leaned again and kissed her forehead. "I love you, Mother."

As he made his way back to the war room, Kian tried to analyze the uneasy feeling his conversation with Annani had left him with. She hadn't offered him a solution, and perhaps he'd hoped she would, and she hadn't even indicated her preference.

His subconscious mind was processing the input and not liking the results.

Letting his thoughts wander often crystallized things for him, but he needed some quiet time for that, which he wouldn't have in the war room, and stopping at the café at this time of day wasn't a good idea either. The place was teeming with people, and just walking by it forced him to smile and wave back at everyone who smiled and waved at him.

Suddenly it dawned on him that his unwillingness to welcome the Kra-ell into the clan was a kind of racism. He didn't want their genetics to mix with his immortals. The Kra-ell were long-lived, not immortal, and it was still unknown how long Vlad or other hybrids produced by immortal mothers and Kra-ell fathers would live.

Since the immortality gene was passed on by the mother, chances were that the hybrids would be immortal as well, but it wasn't a given.

Longevity wasn't the only problem either. The Kra-ell's alien looks made it more difficult for them to blend in with humans. In the long run, Annani's clan would veer so far off the source that its members could no longer call themselves the descendants of the gods.

Whose descendants would they be? Half gods, half demons?

Kian stifled a chuckle. With their nearly perfect features, immortals embodied the image of the gods, while the Kra-ell, with their large black eyes that turned red on occasion, embodied the image of demons.

Perhaps that was why the gods and the Kra-ell had both prohibited the breeding of hybrids. Neither people wanted to blend their genetics.

On the other hand, there were also benefits to blending the two species. For the immortals, the benefits would be stronger offspring with a better fertility ratio. For the Kra-ell, the benefits would be longer life spans and better gender distribution.

The only example they had was Vlad, who was stronger than the average immortal and looked a little strange but could still pass for a human. It remained to be seen whether he and Wendy would produce a daughter. Vlad's longevity was also in question.

Perhaps Bridget should conduct a few experiments on him. The Kra-ell didn't heal as fast as immortals did, so Vlad's healing rate might be a good indicator of whose longevity genes he'd inherited.

17

PHINAS

*P*hinas opened the door to the prisoner's room and walked in.

The two beds hadn't been designed for double occupancy, but the Kra-ell were long and slim, so stuffing them two per bed wasn't too bad.

They were also sedated.

Besides, they could sleep in hell as far as he was concerned.

"What are you doing here?" Max waved him away. "I got them. Go, call your girl."

Jade wasn't a girl. She was a powerhouse of a female, but Phinas didn't comment on Max's choice of words. The Guardian's heart was in the right place.

Then again, perhaps he should warn him not to call Jade or Kagra girls and risk their wrath.

Or maybe not.

Max and Dandor were competing for Kagra's attention, and so far, no clear winner had emerged. Kagra was happy to flirt with them both but hadn't invited either to her bed. Naturally, Phinas was rooting for Dandor, so giving Max pointers for how to act around Kagra could be considered a betrayal.

Dandor would surely think that.

"Thanks." He clapped the Guardian on the back. "Make sure that Aiden checks on the Kra-ell every thirty minutes or so. We want to keep them sedated enough to be barely conscious, but if we don't want to put them in diapers, they need to be able to relieve themselves."

Maybe getting adult-sized diapers wasn't such a bad idea. He should send someone to a local supermarket as soon as the stores opened.

Max smirked. "I'm way ahead of you, buddy. Aiden gave me a list of what he needed to keep them fully sedated, and I sent Sal to get the supplies from the local clinic."

Since it was too late for the clinic to be open, Phinas assumed that the supplies would be taken without permission. He had no doubt that the Guardian would leave money for what he took, but the question was whether the clinic could do without the medical supplies he was about to take.

"I hope they have supplies to spare. This town is so small that they probably don't stock much."

The fact that the tiny port town had a hotel with nine vacant rooms for their party of twenty-seven was a small miracle. They had to book three people per room, with one of them sleeping on a rolling cot, but it was better than sleeping on the floor.

"We don't need much." Max waved a hand. "Mainly catheters and feeding solutions."

"I thought that Aiden didn't know how to insert a catheter."

"He talked with Merlin and watched a YouTube video. He's confident that he can manage the catheters and the intravenous feeding. It's not like he needs to be super gentle." Max grinned evilly as he mimed jabbing a tube where it needed to go.

Phinas cringed. "Please. I could have done without that visual. You have a sadistic streak."

Max's grin got broader. "No mercy for the bad guys."

Forcing a smile, Phinas walked away.

There was a time when he'd been considered a bad guy and for good reason. A male like Max wouldn't have shown him mercy, and perhaps he would have been right.

Even though Phinas had been following orders, that wasn't good enough of an excuse, and he deserved punishment for all the bad things he'd done. If he'd refused to carry out orders, he would have been executed, and he'd been too weak to choose the lives of strangers over his own, but he often wondered if he should have chosen death over a life of guilt.

When judgment time came, he wasn't going to the fields of the brave, or any of the other imagined good places.

He was going to hell.

Perhaps he should take Max up on his suggestion and join the clan's humanitarian effort part-time. Maybe rescuing trafficking victims would ease his conscience a little. It might even keep his soul from ending up in the worst part of hell.

Talk about being melodramatic.

As villains went, Phinas was way down at the bottom. There were so many much worse than him that he surely didn't belong in the deepest chasms of hell.

Not even a cold-blooded murderer like Igor qualified for that special place, and for that matter, neither did Navuh. They were bad, but there were much worse monsters than them among the humans.

Except, Phinas had a feeling that every villain thought he wasn't the worst. It's like the people in this little town who thought that their climate was moderate compared to the northern parts of Greenland, and the hotel front desk clerk thought that she was running the Ritz, with how haughty her attitude had been toward them.

Not that it mattered what she thought about the large group of big males staying at her hotel. What she would remember after they were gone was a bunch of middle-aged tourists.

Passing by her desk, he smiled and waved and got a tight, nervous smile in return.

The hotel had two old-fashioned telephone booths in its lobby that no longer had phones in them, but they were nonetheless perfect for conducting a private conversation.

Phinas got inside, closed the glass door behind him, and sat on the chair. The only person he could call and ask to find Jade for him was Mey, and he hoped that she was still okay with being the go-to person between them.

"Hi, Phinas," she answered in a cheerful voice. "How are things in Greenland?"

"Good. The bad guys are sedated and in Max's care. Can I ask you for a favor?"

"Of course. I'll go find her."

He smiled. "How did you know what I was going to ask?"

As if he had any other reason to call her.

"It's easy to guess. I'll call you when I find her."

"Thank you. You're the best, and I owe you. When we get back, I'm inviting you and Yamanu to a fancy dinner in town."

"I hope it will be a double date with you and Jade."

"That would be nice, but Jade doesn't eat food. We can go to a bar, though. Evidently she likes to drink."

Mey laughed. "That she does."

18

JADE

*A*t first, Jade didn't understand where the buzzing sound was coming from, but as the cobwebs of sleep lifted, she realized that it was the doorbell.

Despite the anxiety over the swaying of the ship and the impending attack, she'd somehow fallen asleep on the couch.

Perhaps she'd slept through the attack?

With a groan, Jade pushed to her feet and shuffled toward the door as quickly as the noodles that her legs had turned into could carry her.

"I'm never going to touch alcohol again," she grumbled as she opened the door. "Are we under attack?"

"Not as far as I know." Mey lifted her phone. "Phinas called. I told him that I'd find you and call him back." She looked Jade over. "You look even worse now than you did three hours ago. Did you keep drinking?"

"No, but I fell asleep on the couch." Jade took a step back and motioned for Mey to come in. "Can I offer you coffee?"

"No, thanks."

"Are you sure?" Jade walked over to the kitchenette and popped a pod in the coffee maker. "I'm going to make some for myself."

"Well, in that case, why not? I'll have some."

"Any news about the *Anatolov*?" Jade put a mug under the spout and waited for the coffee to brew.

"No change so far. Our hacker is monitoring the cruiser, and it is still keeping a forty-mile distance from us, but that will change soon."

"Why?" Jade removed the mug, put another pod inside the machine, and another mug under the spout.

"Kian's instructions were to wait a couple of hours to give him time to make his move, and if he doesn't, to increase speed for a little while to force him to react. The two hours are almost up."

"Oh." Jade looked at the floor as if she could gauge the speed from the way it was swaying under her feet, or was it her head that was swaying?

"Then perhaps I shouldn't call Phinas at a time like this."

Mey shrugged. "The sub will take care of the Russian. Nothing is going to happen to the *Aurora*."

Jade removed the second mug from the platform under the coffee maker and brought both to the coffee table. "You seem very confident in the submarine captain's ability. Has he proven himself before?"

"Not to me personally." Mey reached for the mug and took a sip. "But I'm sure he proved himself to Turner. Otherwise, he wouldn't have recruited him for this job."

Jade was about to ask about Turner and his connection to the clan, but Mey lifted her phone. "Phinas is waiting. He'll get worried if we don't call him soon. He'll think you've passed out from too much drinking."

"Yeah, though he shouldn't." The protest sounded weak even to her own ears.

Jade liked that Phinas was concerned about her and had called for the second time today. He'd even told her that he missed her, and no one had ever told her that before. Not even her sons when she'd been away on business trips.

Had she been a bad mother?

By human standards, probably, but she'd been a perfect Kra-ell mother.

As pain gripped her insides, Jade hid her face behind the coffee mug and took several long sips.

"Hi," Mey said into the receiver. "I'm in Jade's cabin. Here she is." She handed her the phone.

Jade put the mug down and took the device. "Hello," she said in a neutral tone.

"Hello to you, gorgeous. How are things on the *Aurora*?"

"We are in a storm, or rather at the edges of it. The ship is swaying, and I have a hangover. Other than that, Captain Olsson is about to accelerate to force the *Anatolov* to make its move. That's all I have to report. How about you? Is Igor still sedated?"

Phinas chuckled. "As romantic conversations go, ours sucks. To answer your question, Igor and his three companions are all sedated, and I know about the plan to force the *Anatolov* to either play or leave the game."

"If you want a romantic partner, you should find a different female." The brave words had zero intent behind them.

If Phinas so much as looked at another female, she was dead meat.

Damn, where had that come from?

Jealousy was one of the worst sins a Kra-ell could commit.

"You are the perfect female for me. You might not be romantic, but you're hotter than the deepest inferno in hell."

That shouldn't please her as much as it did, especially given that Mey was privy to the entire conversation and was smirking behind her coffee mug.

"I don't know whether you're trying to flatter or insult me, but I'll take it as a compliment."

"It was meant as a compliment."

"Good. Can you do me a favor?"

"For you, anything."

"Tomorrow morning, search for a secluded spot for Igor's execution. I promised Kian I'd give him one day to interrogate Igor in Greenland, but given the storm, I don't think we will arrive early enough for a full day of interrogation before we need to fly out. We will probably only have a couple of hours."

There was a moment of silence on the other side of the line, and Mey regarded her with a somber expression on her gentle face.

"What? Would you want to wait to avenge the murders of your children?"

Eyes blazing, Mey bared her tiny fangs. "No."

"That's what I thought." Jade returned to Phinas. "Are you still there?"

"Didn't you tell Kian that you need to confer with your people about it?"

She didn't remember promising that. "I told him that I needed to think about it. I did, and that is what I want to do."

"Perhaps you should sober up first and think about it logically instead of emotionally. It doesn't matter when you kill Igor, as long as you get to kill him in the end. If he has useful information, isn't it worth a slight delay of his execution?"

Jade uttered a long-suffering sigh. "If Toven can make Igor talk, he can get what he needs out of him in a couple of hours. If he can't, Igor will not tell us anything, and there will be no reason to delay his execution."

19

ELEANOR

*V*ivian leaned closer to Eleanor and hugged her tightly. "I'm happy and sad. I don't want you to leave, but I'm happy for you."

"I feel the same." Eleanor held her sister-in-law in an awkward embrace.

She'd never been much of a hugger, but Vivian was, and so were her children.

"Will you come to say goodbye to Parker before you leave?"

Eleanor chuckled. "I'll try to hold off leaving until he comes back from school. Emmett is all packed and bouncing off the walls with excitement. He was so depressed when he thought that we could never return to Safe Haven. It's his baby, and he really loves the place."

With Igor captured and his cronies either dead or imprisoned, it was safe to go back. They were flying along with Anastasia, Leon, and three Guardians. The secret project Marcel was working on would have to wait until he returned, and Onegus would probably assign more Guardians to the place once the project resumed.

"What about you? Do you love it there?" Vivian asked.

"I like my autonomy and being in charge of the paranormal program."

She also liked Emmett better when he was happy than when he was depressed and dragging her down with him, and he was happiest in Safe Haven.

Vivian tilted her head, her long blond hair cascading in perfect waves down one side. "Is that all? The flip side of autonomy is loneliness."

Eleanor smoothed her hand over her frizzy mane and cursed her genes. When she'd transitioned, she'd hoped to emerge prettier, with lovely, manageable hair that looked effortlessly styled without her having to work on it. But that hadn't happened. She looked younger than she had before her transition, for which she was grateful, but she wasn't any prettier than she was in her twenties, and unless she used a flat iron on her hair, it was a frizzy mess.

Oh, well. Beauty wasn't everything. There were many beautiful women in the world, but only a handful or two of compellers. Besides, she had plenty of other great qualities. She was intelligent, tenacious, and good at managing people, even without resorting to compulsion.

"I'm not lonely. Leon and Anastasia became good friends, and I enjoy spending time with my paranormals. I also like running the paranormal workshops in the new retreats."

Vivian nodded her approval. "Did you pick up any new prospects for your paranormal program?"

"Not from the one retreat we've run so far, but there are a couple that the Echelon system flagged that look promising. With the Kra-ell crisis going on, I couldn't ask Onegus to send Guardians to investigate them, and Kian doesn't want me to do it myself, so it will have to wait until the rest of the Guardians return home."

Vivian winced. "If they come with the Kra-ell, they might be busy policing them. This crisis is far from over."

"I haven't heard about any such plans. Did Magnus tell you that?"

Vivian assumed a sheepish expression. "I shouldn't have said anything. I thought you knew."

"Don't worry about it. I'm sure Leon will tell us about it on the way to Safe Haven. If Kian plans to bring the Kra-ell here, he needs to tell everyone so they can prepare. In fact, he should ask the council's permission before he brings a bunch of strangers into the village."

Vivian laughed. "Not too long ago, you were the stranger."

"It seems like it was eons ago. I'm a proud member of the clan now." And if anyone dared to dispute her claim, she would challenge them to a fistfight.

Vivian nodded. "Yes, you are. Now, tell me about those prospects. Who are they, and why were they flagged by Echelon?"

Eleanor lifted her empty teacup. "I'll need another cup of tea for that."

"With pleasure." Vivian lifted the porcelain teapot and poured more tea into Eleanor's cup.

"One is a psychic, and the other is a gambler. The psychic is a female, and the reason she's believable is that she doesn't charge money for her predictions. The gambler's winning streak is uncanny, but the casinos can't pin anything on him. He just seems too lucky. After the big casinos banned him, he started circling the smaller ones and wised up. He leaves after his first win not to draw their attention."

20

CAPTAIN NILS

"Captain to control," Rob Farland sounded at the com.

"On my way," Nils responded.

Finally.

He'd been worried that his infallible instincts had failed him.

Nils had chosen to move ahead of the *Aurora* and the Russian cruiser shadowing it, plotting a course that should have put him in their path over two hours ago, but weather wasn't always predictable, and a storm had started out of nowhere near the coast of Iceland. It didn't affect the submarine, but it did affect the ships cruising above.

Captain Olsson must have decided to slow down to avoid heading right into the storm, and he was crawling ahead with the Russian behind him.

The *Aurora* had only passed them twenty-one minutes ago, and Farland must have spotted the *Anatolov*, which was why he was summoning Nils to control.

Passing through several bulkheads and two decks to get there, he exchanged smiles with his men instead of the salutes that would have been required if this was a navy vessel. Everyone on board had served in one navy or another and had spent years following strict protocols, but this was a private boat, and Nils encouraged familiarity. It kept his crew loyal and motivated.

Well, the money was good too, but they were operating in a shady area of private military subcontractors and had to keep a low profile, which was not how most of his men had imagined their retirement years.

"What have you got for me, Rob?"

"Take a look." His XO moved aside so he could take over the periscope.

"The *Anatolov* is exactly where you said he would be."

"Only two hours late."

Nils looked through the periscope at the almost indistinguishable dot on the horizon that was barely visible even in the periscope's magnified optical view. "Did they change course or speed since you found them?"

"They slowed down to adjust to the *Aurora*'s lower speed, and they kept shadowing her while keeping the same distance they did before. They don't appear to be in a hurry to engage."

Moving over to the navigation control, Nils noted their position relative to the closest land. "They will be making their move soon. We are over a day's time from any land, and they can't keep it up for long. The *Anatolov* is not meant for the Atlantic, and its navy command is probably getting ready to retrieve its rogue ship. I still don't understand how the hell a Russian captain can take control of a cruiser without anyone on board raising hell or contacting command."

Farland shrugged. "The *Anatolov* was stationed in the Baltic, and its job was probably to monitor that entire area. That's why no one suspected anything until he got out to the North Sea. The Russian navy command has no doubt tried to contact him and order him to turn around, and when he didn't respond, they sent ships after him. It's probably a matter of hours before they get here, and when they do, we don't want to be anywhere near the cruiser."

Nils nodded. "If he doesn't make his move in the next hour or so, we will have to get out of here."

The situation was bizarre, and Turner's explanation didn't make much sense.

He'd said something about an oligarch taking control of the *Anatolov*, but with all due respect to those mafiosi, they wouldn't take on the entire Russian navy. Then again, maybe they could. Corruption was rampant all over the world and in all countries, and the Russians didn't even try to hide it. Maybe someone higher up in the Russian power ladder was chasing after someone on the *Aurora* and was using a third party to do the dirty work for him.

"We are approaching torpedo range," Rob said. "Should we switch to electric now or wait until we are closer?"

At their current speed, any sonar operator listening in would be alerted to their presence, and they didn't want the *Anatolov* to know they were within range. In all likelihood, it would ignore them and continue after the *Aurora*, but it could also turn around to investigate.

Nils was not taking any chances. "Switch to electric and take us down to 50 meters."

21

KIAN

$\mathcal{K}$ ian walked into the war room and took a seat next to Turner. "Any news about the storm?"

"It's getting worse. Olsson was wise to slow down and let it blow over instead of heading right into it. He will probably need to slow it down even more or head in a different direction."

Since there was nothing for him to do but wait, Kian flipped his laptop open and started an idle search on the global map application.

If he were to choose a new location for the clan, where would be the ideal place?

In days past, being close to Hollywood had been important because of the influence the clan could gain through scripting movies to push their agenda of human rights and equal opportunity for all. But times had changed, and everything could be done remotely. He could move the entire clan to Alaska and build several sanctuaries around Annani's, and still manage most of the clan's business and social agenda objectives without having to fly over to Los Angeles.

The war on trafficking, however, was waged in large urban areas, and it had become such an integral part of the clan's makeup that abandoning it was out of the question.

Besides, he liked being close to nice restaurants and shopping venues, even if he didn't indulge in either often. It was the ability to do so that made him feel less closed off in his hidden village.

"What are you working on?" Onegus asked.

"Nothing concrete. The Clan Mother had a few interesting ideas regarding the relocation of the Kra-ell and our future, with or without them. One of those ideas was to move once again to a new location that was larger and could accommodate several communities. That way, the Kra-ell can have their own place, we can retain our exclusivity, and Sari might consider joining as well since we can offer her people a separate area that will allow her to retain her autonomy."

Turner chuckled from behind his screen. "History moves in cyclic ways. The gods divided the humans under their rule, and each god or goddess ruled over a city-state. The cities were largely autonomous, but they joined forces to defend each other, and every major decision had to be agreed on by the assembly of all gods. You are basically talking about recreating that system."

"I didn't get that far, but yeah, that can work. It's always good to use an existing model rather than to try to reinvent the wheel."

Onegus shook his head. "I don't want to move. I love the village, but it's already too secluded for my taste. I don't want to move somewhere even more remote." He cast Kian a sidelong glance. "I hope you're not thinking of Safe Haven. It's a nice place to visit, but not to live full time. It's too damn cold and secluded."

"Don't worry. I have no intention of moving to the Oregon Coast. I have a daughter to raise, and I want her to hang out with humans her age." He winced. "Correction. I don't want her to ever leave the house, but I'm sure she'll want to be around other young people."

Onegus let out a breath. "Thank the merciful Fates. You scared me for a moment. I thought that the real Kian had been abducted by aliens and replaced by a clone."

Turner chuckled behind his screen. "I don't envy Allegra or the young males who will want to court her."

Ignoring him, Kian arched a brow. "Do you have any other ideas for where we can live comfortably, safely, and also independently of the Kra-ell while keeping a close eye on them, and at the same time not being more than forty-five minutes away from downtown Los Angeles?"

"We should stay right here." The chief leaned back in his chair. "Maybe we can get another piece of land or two on the adjacent mountains, build two more villages and connect them with underground tunnels like we did with the keep and the office buildings on the other side of the street."

"Too risky," Turner said under his breath. "In my opinion, it's better to hide in plain sight than to truly hide." He slid his laptop aside. "You're a developer, Kian. Right now, you are building hotels and office buildings, but you can easily get into building gated communities. Some would be sold to humans, while a few would be dedicated to us, the Kra-ell, and Sari's people. It will be a major headache to design a security system for them and to keep them connected, but it's doable."

Kian shook his head. "The village is much easier to defend than a gated community in the middle of suburbia."

"Not true." Turner crossed his arms over his chest. "Even the Doomers are not stupid enough to draw the attention of humans. We will be safer surrounded by them."

Despite his strategic acumen, Turner hadn't spent centuries hiding from the Doomers and ensuring his people's safety.

"That's precisely what we did with the keep, and it wasn't good enough. Our people are much safer in the village, not to mention happier."

Turner was about to offer another rebuttal when Roni ran into the room.

"Guys, the *Anatolov* is closing the distance. He's only thirty-six miles away from the *Aurora* now." He put his laptop on the desk.

"Did he increase his speed?" Kian asked.

"I can't tell from looking at the screen, but I can tell that he's closer to the *Aurora* now than he was twenty minutes ago."

"Maybe it is not intentional." Onegus leaned closer to the screen. "Because of the storm, Olsson has slowed down the *Aurora* significantly. The Russian might be keeping the same speed without realizing that he's getting closer."

Turner shook his head. "He knows the *Aurora*'s speed. This is intentional. I just hope that Nils is keeping a close watch on the *Anatolov* and noticed what Roni just did."

"I'm calling Olsson." Onegus pulled out his phone.

Kian did the same. "I'll call Yamanu and Toven."

22

CAPTAIN NILS

*A*natoly lifted his head from the sonar station. "The *Anatolov* has increased its speed."

Nils walked over to him. "By how much?"

Anatoly pursed his lips. "About four knots faster, give or take twenty percent."

To remain hidden, they were using passive sonar when not in periscope depth, which wasn't as good as sending an active ping and calculating precisely where the *Anatolov* was relative to the submarine, but that couldn't be helped.

The *Anatolov* was a sub-destroyer, and if she discovered them, it was game over.

Not that they were easy to detect, even if the Russian suspected something and sent a sonar ping to locate them. Nils had spent a small fortune to cover the submarine in anechoic tiles. The synthetic polymer tiles contained thousands of tiny voids to absorb the sound waves of active sonar, reducing and distorting the return signal, which limited its effective range. They also attenuated the sounds emitted by the sub, reducing the range it could be detected by passive sonar.

Thankfully, the *Anatolov* hadn't been built for stealth, and it was easy to detect. Since the *Aurora* had passed them by about thirty-six minutes ago, they had been carefully monitoring the *Anatolov*'s progress, waiting for it to increase speed.

In order to get within the five-mile torpedo range, it had to speed up significantly, and since it had been maintaining a large distance from the *Aurora*, they would have plenty of advance notice to take the Anatolov out before the vessel got close enough to fire at the cruise ship.

"How long until the cruiser is within torpedo range?" Nils asked.

Anatoly arched a brow. "Of the *Aurora* or us?"

Was he joking? It was sometimes hard to tell with the guy. He had a warped sense of humor that no one but him found funny.

"The *Aurora*, of course. Hopefully, the *Anatolov* still doesn't know about us."

"If both ships keep current speed, she'll be within torpedo speed within forty-two minutes."

"Ready torpedo," Nils said. "If he keeps speeding ahead, let him pass us and fire when he's two miles away."

"Aye, aye, captain," Rob acknowledged.

Time slowed to a crawl as Nils and the rest of the crew waited for the *Anatolov* to get within range.

"We were just pinged," Anatoly announced. "They are changing course."

That was impossible. How the hell had the Russian detected them? And why was he abandoning his pursuit of the *Aurora* to go after them?

"Change course to one-six-one and increase speed. Let's see if he follows."

Nils half listened to the acknowledgment repeating his order as he plotted his next move.

The Russian cruiser was old, but it was faster, and it was designed to hunt and kill subs. They had to get away but, at the same time, lure her away from the civilian cruise ship.

"He's adjusting his heading and speed," Anatoly said. "He's in pursuit. He'll be within firing range in two minutes." The guy smirked. "Of us, not the *Aurora*."

That wasn't funny. They were in mortal danger, and if they failed, it wouldn't just cost them their lives. They would doom a ship full of civilians. As soon as the *Anatolov* was done with them, she would turn around and go after the *Aurora*. Hopefully, Olsson would be smart and speed into the storm to avoid the Russian. It could survive the storm, but it wouldn't survive a torpedo.

Nils turned to Rob. "Plot a new firing solution and fire as soon as he's in range."

"Aye, captain," Rob replied. "Torpedo away," he stated, matter-of-fact.

Right now, the Russian was giving his crew a similar command, and Nils was not waiting.

"Change course to two-five-zero and dive to one hundred meters."

It was crucial to move unexpectedly and erratically to avoid the torpedo the Russians would be firing at them any second now.

Every hand on both boats, his and the Russian's, was counting down the seconds as the torpedo made its way to its target. One crew praying for a direct hit, while the other was praying for a miss.

"It's a direct hit!" Anatoly said at the same time as the torpedo found its prey and exploded.

"They are still in pursuit," Anatoly said.

The Russian was crippled but not killed, and they were going to even the score.

"Torpedo in the water," Anatoly announced.

"Release countermeasures and take us down to one hundred and twenty-five."

His command was followed as soon as the words left his mouth.

His crew knew what they were about, and in moments like this, he blessed the stars for each one of them.

"We will survive this and live another day," Nils said.

Every hand on board grabbed hold of something as the sub tilted sharply downward in rapid descent, and the countermeasures were deployed to guide the torpedo away from the sub's hull.

"Second torpedo armed and ready, captain," Rob said.

"Fire as soon as we level off, Rob. As soon as the torpedo clears, go back to diesel and change course again back to one-six-one and climb to fifty meters."

With the Russian ready for the torpedo, he would deploy countermeasures the same way Nils had, but his objective was not hitting the cruiser but rather distracting its crew and giving him a small window of opportunity to increase his distance from them beyond torpedo range.

Normally the cruiser would be able to outrun and kill them, but they'd been hit, so hopefully that was no longer the case. The sub was easily detectable to radar when running on diesel power, but it no longer mattered. As soon as they were a safe distance away, he would go back to stealth to avoid detection by the Russian navy, which was no doubt closing in on its runaway ship.

With the cruiser disabled, the *Aurora* was no longer in danger, and Nils's only objective was to disengage while still in one piece.

The sonar pings of the approaching torpedo were getting closer together, and as the sounds got louder, Nils and all hands on board held their breath.

This time the explosion was both heard and felt, the two sensations arriving at the same instant, indicative of how close the torpedo was before it was eliminated. The boat was violently thrown about by the concussion wave. But the torpedo did not hit the hull, and that was all that mattered.

Nils caught Rob's eye and nodded. They had upgraded their weaponry and were carrying some cutting-edge tech on board, but when it came to their countermeasures, it was Rob who insisted they upgrade to Rafael Technologies' Shade system. This Israeli defensive tech had just saved their lives. Shade came at a steep cost, but it brought new dimensions to countermeasure deployment and capabilities. Nils had resisted approving the added expenditure required for a long time, but in the end, Rob had convinced him.

He owed the guy a fat cigar and a promotion.

As soon as the sub settled, Rob announced, "Torpedo away."

The helmsman repeated the new bearing while changing course and depth.

The sub tilted sharply again in the opposite direction, making a rapid ascent to fifty meters.

Nils didn't wait to see if the second torpedo hit the target or the countermeasures.

With the *Anatolov*'s crew busy maneuvering out of the incoming torpedo's path and deploying its countermeasures, Nils rapidly increased his distance from the Russian ship.

"The Russians are not in pursuit, captain," Rob announced.

They were not in the clear yet, but the worst was behind them.

"Maintain heading and course at full speed and take us to periscope depth. I want to scope the extent of damage the cruiser sustained and share the good news with Turner. The *Aurora* is no longer in danger."

23

KIAN

"I have a message from Nils," Turner said.

If Nils was sending messages, he was no longer maintaining radio silence, which hopefully meant that the *Anatolov* was no longer a threat. The other option was that either the *Aurora* or the submarine had been hit, with the submarine being the more likely one. If the *Aurora* had been hit, they would have heard about it already.

As usual, Turner's expressionless face revealed nothing.

All eyes were on him as he read the message aloud, "The lady got away without a scratch. The naughty boy got spanked twice for wrecking daddy's car, and he's crying for his mommy, but mommy won't be home in time to comfort him. He might need the lady to comfort him instead."

As Kian tried to decipher the strange message, Turner looked at Roni. "Check the location of the approaching Russian navy ships. How far away are they?"

Roni shook his head. "It will take them hours to reach him."

Kian scratched his head. "Is that some pre-agreed coded message language?"

Turner cracked a smile. "Nothing as fancy as that. It's just a way to say things without actually saying them. The *Anatolov* got hit twice, it's sinking, and it needs the *Aurora* to turn around and rescue the sailors."

Now that Turner had interpreted the message, the meaning had become clear, but Kian didn't like the idea of having the *Aurora* turn around.

"What about rescue helicopters?" Kian asked. "Can they make it to them in time?"

"They are too far out," Onegus said. "A military helicopter's range is long, and it might make it to them, but it will not have enough fuel for the return flight. We have to tell Olsson to turn around."

Kian didn't like it one bit. "What if they can still fire a torpedo at the *Aurora?* They are under compulsion, so we can't count on them acting logically and not shooting at their rescuer. Besides, they must have lifeboats or rafts. They should be fine for a few hours until the Russian navy ships arrive."

"Probably." Turner tapped his pen on his yellow pad. "But we should get to them before their comrades do. Igor might have compelled them to say that the *Aurora* was carrying dangerous chemical or biological weapons. I don't need to tell you what will happen if the Russian naval command follows up on that intel."

"Why would they believe him?" Onegus asked. "Where did he get the information from? Why didn't he report to command that he was pursuing a potentially dangerous cargo? No one will buy that story."

Turner leveled his gaze at the chief. "If one person tells a crazy story, they might deem him mad. But when the *Anatolov's* entire command tells the same story, the Russians will take it seriously and chase after the *Aurora.* Toven needs to release them from the compulsion and thrall them to remember a different scenario before the two navy ships arrive."

He had a point, but Kian didn't want to risk it. "I will only approve it if Nils can verify that the *Anatolov* is no longer capable of shooting a torpedo at the *Aurora.* But even then, they can still shoot at the rescuers."

"We don't have a choice." Turner typed on his laptop. "In Toven's words, it's a perfect storm."

"We should have thought of this before." Kian groaned. "This scenario would have played out even if the *Anatolov* wasn't sinking."

Turner lifted his eyes to him. "The *Aurora* was supposed to be farther away by now, which might have deterred the Russians from going after it and referring the intel to the Canadian and American navies. It would have been much easier to deal with them."

Kian assumed Turner's connections would have helped with those navies.

"I'm waiting for a return message from Nils." Turner closed his laptop. "In the meantime, we should tell Olsson to turn around."

When Onegus looked at Kian for approval, he nodded. "Tell him to send out a distress call. He saw an explosion and turned around to investigate. That alone should convince the Russians that the *Aurora* is not a smuggler ship. It wouldn't have turned around to help its pursuer. They will assume that the captain has gone mad, and his crew believed his story. Captains are gods on their vessels. Their word is the law."

When Turner's computer pinged, everyone's eyes shifted to him.

"Nils says that they are deploying inflatables and abandoning ship. In his estimate, the *Anatolov* will sink in less than half an hour." He lifted his head. "He didn't say it in those exact words, but that's my interpretation."

Kian would have loved to hear the wording Nils had chosen to convey that meaning, but it could wait for later.

"It must have been one hell of a hit," Roni said. "Why isn't Nils just calling you instead of sending you weird messages? You have a secure clan phone."

Turner cast him a smile. "Nils doesn't know what security measures I employ. We are using a secure channel to leave each other messages that can't be traced to either of us. And even if someone can trace them, they are worded in a way that's not incriminating Nils. It's safer for him this way."

Kian rubbed a hand over his chin. "What kind of a scenario can Toven plant in the crew's heads that could possibly explain away the captain and his crew going rogue?"

Turner pursed his lips. "Not much can be done to exonerate them. Perhaps a story of receiving false commands from the secret service or something of that nature. The important thing is that the Russians don't figure out that the *Anatolov* was trailing the *Aurora* and why. If the captain and his officers all tell the same story, and it's even remotely plausible, they might be believed. It should be scripted in a way that would seem like a malicious cyber hack."

"I like that," Roni said. "We can incriminate the North Koreans. They are known for their malicious hacking."

Onegus frowned. "Why would the North Koreans mess with the Russians? Aren't they allies?"

Roni waved a dismissive hand. "Who cares? Everyone knows that the North Korean leader is insane. It's not a story that's going to be hard to sell. Give me a few minutes, and I'll have a script ready for Toven with all the right hacker terminology."

2 4

TOVEN

*B*y the time the *Aurora* arrived at the approximate coordinates that Onegus had provided Olsson, there was no trace of the *Anatolov* or the survivors, but perhaps they were still too far away, even for Toven's eyes.

The pouring rain and the wind weren't helping either.

Lifting the binoculars, he scanned the dark water and located the rafts by their beacon lights.

The captain must have done the same from the bridge because the ship made a slight adjustment in course and headed right toward them.

The skill of the captain or his navigator was admirable. Despite the bad weather, the wind and the rain, he aligned the *Aurora*'s starboard with the group of three rafts in one go, providing some protection for the rafts from the gale winds and rain.

Was that the entire crew?

Or had some perished?

The senseless loss of life shouldn't bother him after all this time, but since Mia had restarted his heart, all the old emotions that he'd tamped down, the compassion and sorrow that had made life so difficult for him, had returned.

That was the flip side of being capable of feeling love again, and for that, he was willing to suffer the less desirable emotions that he'd worked so hard to get rid of.

Toven's empathy and compassion were the reasons he could have never assumed a leadership role. That wasn't what he was destined for. He just felt too much to make decisions that could result in the loss of life.

After this mission was over, he wouldn't volunteer again unless the clan's survival was on the line.

"I found you a megaphone," Yamanu said from behind him.

The Guardian's long hair was wet and braided into at least two dozen thin dreadlocks which were gathered with an elastic to keep them away from his face.

The guy smiled. "Mey was stressed, so I let her braid my hair. It always relaxes her." He extended his tongue and caught a few droplets of rain.

"Thank you." Toven took the megaphone and leaned over the railing.

Switching to Russian, he said, *"Bros'te oruzhiye v vodu*—drop your weapons into the water. *My zdes, chtoby pomoch*—we are here to help."

The sailors obeyed immediately, the sound of their handguns hitting the water confirming that the compulsion worked.

"That was easy," Yamanu murmured from behind him. "The Guardians are securing the shell doors. Tell the sailors to get closer. When we open them, they should jump in one at a time."

"I'll explain and join you. Don't open the doors until I'm there."

"They are human. We can handle them."

"I want to be there in case Igor compelled them to attempt a last-ditch suicide attack."

"Got it." Yamanu saluted him before turning on his heel and marching away.

Toven translated the instructions, asked the sailors to raise their hands in confirmation that they understood, and hurried down to the cargo bay.

The place was prepared to receive the rescued sailors, with piles of towels and blankets at the ready, water bottles, snacks, and several bottles of vodka.

Toven smiled. "Who brought the vodka?"

One of Kalugal's men lifted his hand. "This is to warm them up from the inside."

Standing next to him, Merlin shrugged. "Nothing wrong with that. Just don't give it to anyone who's bleeding."

The guy saluted. "Yes, doctor."

The rest of the ship's passengers were in their cabins with the lights out, which wasn't a big deal since most were asleep. Once the Soviet ships arrived, they would be told that the *Aurora* had only crew on board and was being delivered to its owners in the US. If they demanded to search the ship, he would have to thrall them to believe that they didn't see a thing. Especially the livestock in the adjacent cargo bay.

Hopefully, the animals were asleep and wouldn't bleat.

"Let's do this." Yamanu turned the wheel, unlocking the watertight door.

As the Guardian next to him pulled it open, wind-driven rain pelted all of those standing near the door, and then the first sailor jumped in.

"*Pridi s mirom*—come in peace," Toven said as one of Kalugal's men handed the sailor a towel and a blanket. He should have said, *my prishli s mirom*—we come in peace, but he phrased his welcome as a command on purpose and imbued it with compulsion.

The men would just assume that his command of the language wasn't good.

He repeated the same greeting with every new sailor who either jumped or was hoisted by his friends and pulled in by the Guardians.

When everyone was inside, he asked for the captain.

"He's dead," one of the officers spat in Russian. "We weren't hit hard enough to sink, but the dog sabotaged the ship and put a bullet in his own head."

The poor guy had probably been compelled to do that once his objective was achieved or he failed. It was a miracle that the rest of the crew had somehow survived.

Or maybe it wasn't a miracle but Captain Sergey Gorshekov's last act of defiance and bravery. He'd obeyed the compulsion almost to the letter, but he'd found a loophole to save his crew.

25

KIAN

$\mathcal{K}$ ian waited until every member of his family was seated around the dinner table before pushing to his feet and raising his wine glass.

"As you all know, Igor is in our custody, and the Russian vessel pursuing our ship is gone. Let's toast our victory."

It was one hell of a mission. It had cost a fortune, had been nerve-wracking, and it wasn't over yet, but after all that stress and hard work, they all deserved to celebrate their victory.

After the toasting was done, Kalugal leaned back with his wine glass. "What happened to the Russian sailors? Did any of them survive?"

Kian was surprised that Kalugal cared, but perhaps it was just curiosity. His cousin hadn't been in the war room when the *Anatolov* had gone down, and Kian hadn't told him any details yet, saving himself the trouble of having to repeat the story to every member of his family.

"Other than the captain, all the sailors were picked up by our people and delivered to the Russian navy. Captain Sergey Gorshekov sank his ship and shot himself in the head, most likely following Igor's compulsion, but Toven theorizes that he did everything he could not to fire on the *Aurora* and to save his crew. The compulsion probably hadn't specified the exact timing and conditions needed for the *Anatolov* to fire a torpedo at the cruise ship, and the captain used that as a loophole, dragging it out as long as he could. It's not clear whether he chose to attack the submarine as a way to draw its fire and prevent him from firing on the civilian ship or whether that was part of Igor's instructions. One of the officers told Toven that the damage the *Anatolov* had sustained from the torpedoes wouldn't have been enough to sink it, but it would have been dead in the water. We assume that Igor's compulsion included the destruction of the evidence. As soon as the mission was complete or as soon as it became clear that it wasn't going to be achieved, the captain was compelled to sink the ship and kill everyone on board, including himself. He found another loophole, doing it in a way that allowed his men time to escape the sinking ship." Kian lifted his glass again. "Captain Sergey Gorshekov died a hero."

Kalugal raised his glass as well. "In the words of the formidable Jade, may he forever walk in the fields of the brave."

Given everyone's nods, they had all heard the expression by now and knew what it meant.

If the Kra-ell joined his community, would it become part of the vernacular like 'Thank the merciful Fates'?

Syssi sighed. "It's a shame no one will know about the captain's bravery."

Kian hadn't asked Toven about what story he had planted in the sailors' heads, but hopefully he'd painted the captain in a better light than a madman who wanted to kill himself and his crew.

"An unsung hero," Amanda murmured. "The world is full of them."

When a long silence stretched across the table, Andrew put his glass down and turned to Kian. "What are you planning to do with Igor? I heard that Jade gave you one day to interrogate him. Do you need me to fly out to Greenland and assist with my truth detecting?"

It hadn't occurred to Kian for the simple reason that he hadn't figured out yet how to get Igor to talk.

"If Toven can compel him, he can force the truth out of him. And if he can't, Igor is not going to tell us anything, so there will be nothing for you to confirm."

Andrew glanced at Annani. "Perhaps the Clan Mother can give it a shot. With or without Mia's enhancing powers."

That was another thing that Kian hadn't thought of, and for another simple reason. He wasn't letting his mother anywhere near the compeller.

"That's not on the table."

His mother gave him a reproachful look. "This is my decision, Kian. Not yours. I want to find out who sent Igor and for what purpose. If Toven cannot force that information out of him, then I will surely give it a try."

Toven had spoken to Valstar, and according to the guy, Igor had some military background. Valstar suspected that he'd served in one of the queen's special units.

Perhaps he'd been sent on the settler ship to spy on the gods they'd been supposed to serve, or maybe to do something worse, like trying to take over their community.

Could it be that Igor was more powerful than Annani's father had been?

That was unlikely and, although interesting, irrelevant. The queen was long dead, and so were most of the gods.

"Igor is dangerous, and he might have been sent to do damage to the gods, but they were long gone by the time he got here. He saw an opportunity for a power grab and took it. The guy is a sociopath with no regard for anyone's life, and you are not flying to Greenland to talk to him."

She arched a brow. "If I want to fly to Greenland, I will."

He wouldn't argue with her in front of everyone, but there was no way she was doing that.

"Why not bring him here?" Kalugal smiled sweetly at Annani as if he was conspiring with her. "Did anyone run my idea by Bridget or Merlin?"

"What idea?" Amanda asked.

26

KALUGAL

*K*alugal shouldn't feel disappointed that Kian hadn't told anyone about his brilliant idea to render Igor mute by removing his vocal cords, but he couldn't help it.

It was a stroke of genius if he said so himself.

Then again, perhaps he shouldn't have suggested it. He was also a compeller, and giving others ideas for how to disable him was not wise. He and Kian were buddy-buddy now, but no one had a crystal ball to see the future, and things might change between them.

Oh, wait. That wasn't true. Both of them had crystal balls. Syssi and Jacki were seers of sorts, but their visions and predictions were so sporadic and unpredictable that they weren't of any real utility.

He stifled a chuckle. Unpredictable prediction—that was an oxymoron.

Amanda was still looking at him expectantly. "Well? I'm waiting to hear your idea."

"It might not work," he prefaced. "That's why I wanted the doctors' opinions, but evidently, Kian hadn't thought it was worth pursuing."

"There was no time," his cousin said.

There had certainly been enough time for a simple phone call. Kian had probably forgotten about it mere minutes after he'd suggested it.

Kalugal smiled graciously at his cousins. "I could have called the doctors myself, so I can't really blame you for forgetting when it didn't occur to me to do it." He turned to Amanda. "Since compulsion requires vocalization,

568

disabling Igor's ability to speak should render him harmless, or as harmless as any other super-strong Kra-ell male."

Amanda frowned. "That's an interesting idea. I assume that you are suggesting taking out his vocal cords?"

Kalugal nodded. "The Kra-ell heal faster than humans, but not as fast as we do. He might be able to regrow them, but it will take time."

"Given the power of his compulsion, he might be part god," Kian said. "In which case, he will regrow them almost as fast as it would take us to remove them."

Annani stiffened. "I do not like the idea of maiming a person even if he is about to be executed. Naturally, I do not condone executions either, but I cannot intervene."

Kian cast her a sidelong glance. "You wanted to get information out of him. I will be much less reluctant to let you near him if I know he can't compel you and anyone who's with you, but removing his vocal cords does not guarantee that. Firstly because he might regrow them too fast, and secondly, he might be able to compel without using his voice. We don't know how compulsion works. Sound waves are just the vehicle by which the compulsion is delivered. If he's part god, he might piggyback them on top of thralling."

"I do not think it can be done like that." Annani flicked her fingers against her wine glass. "At least I've never tried it, but then I am not a fan of compulsion." She cast Kalugal an apologetic look. "No offense, my dear nephew, but I do not think that compulsion should be used for any reason other than to save lives or as a party trick with the full consent of the participants. I am a firm believer in free will."

He dipped his head. "I agree wholeheartedly. Compulsion is a slimy trick, and I never use it unless I have no other choice."

Kian snorted. "Since you decide when it is okay to use it, and you don't limit its usage to life and death situations, that doesn't require much restraint from you. You use it when it benefits you."

Evidently, their new cooperation agreement didn't extend to mutual courtesy. The repartee continued, which was fine by him. He enjoyed it too much to give it up.

He looked down his nose at Kian. "Morality is not absolute, and everyone has a different interpretation of what is morally right or wrong."

Amanda lifted her hand to stop their banter. "I have a better idea, but it might not work if his body rejects implants like ours do. We know that the Kra-ell bodies don't do that because they all had those implants, but if Igor is half god, then his body would. If he's not half god, though, we can implant a voice box over his vocal cords and change the pitch and frequency of the sound waves he emits. If we do that, we will have to test the procedure's effectiveness somehow." She turned to Andrew. "Your lie-detecting services would be required to verify whether Igor is trying to use compulsion and failing or just pretending to do so to fool us."

Andrew shook his head. "I don't like any of these ideas. They involve too many ifs. The best thing would be to build a special cell for him. It shouldn't be too difficult to construct a soundproof room and have Igor speak into a microphone. His voice will be converted to a machine voice the same way the earpieces do, and we know that works because the technology has been proven effective."

Leaning back, Kian gave Andrew a smile. "That's a great idea except for two things. We don't have time to build a soundproof room and test it before Jade loses her patience and demands Igor's head. Secondly, Toven or Annani won't be able to compel him to answer their questions if their voices have to travel through wiring to the loudspeakers in that soundproof room. It would be the same as them trying to compel him via phone or tablet. We know that is much less effective."

Andrew's face fell. "You make a good point."

Kalugal was glad that his idea wasn't the only one to get rebuffed. "We should discuss it with the doctors. Perhaps Merlin can put a mechanical device on his vocal cords and attach it somehow to his spine so his body can't reject it." He cast Annani an apologetic glance. "I know that it sounds barbaric, but so does chopping off his head, which we promised to allow Jade as soon as we are done with him."

"He is a very bad man," Syssi said. "I'm usually compassionate and forgiving, but I feel no compassion for that monster. Do whatever you want with him to get him to talk, and then let Jade kill him. She's waited long enough to avenge her sons."

27

ANNANI

*A*nnani had never heard Syssi sound so vehement, and it was shocking coming from her gentle daughter-in-law.

Had living with Kian's sharp edges hardened Syssi? Or had being a mother changed her, making her empathize with Jade's terrible loss?

Letting out a sigh, Annani reached over and patted her arm. "Fate will teach Igor to do better, my dear Syssi. If not in this life, then in the next."

Syssi's eyes blazed with inner light as she returned her gaze, which Annani had never seen them do before, either. "I am not as forgiving as you are, Clan Mother. I want Jade to get her revenge, justice to be served, and to have one less monster walking the Earth and spreading more death and misery."

Annani smiled. "I am not forgiving, but I've lived long enough to know that revenge does not soothe the soul of those who were wronged. It only breeds more bloodshed and misery."

Syssi looked like she was biting her tongue not to answer, which was a wise choice. Not because she would have angered Annani but because she would have worked herself into a fit of anger that was not conducive to anything.

"You are all overthinking this," Dalhu said.

Since he rarely expressed his opinion, everyone hushed and turned to look at him.

"What do you suggest we do with Igor?" Orion asked.

"Igor needs to die, not only because Jade was promised his head but also because he's too dangerous alive, not just to the Kra-ell or us, but to humanity at large. We don't need another Navuh."

Kalugal let out a sigh. "One is more than enough."

Dalhu cast a tentative look at Allegra, who was sitting on the floor with Phoenix and playing with a toy bus. Seeing that the girls were immersed in their role-play game, he lowered his voice and leaned forward. "That being said, before his head is separated from his body, he must be interrogated and forced to talk using any means available to us, whether compulsion or torture. We can mitigate the danger by having him in chains and the Guardians wearing earpieces. It wouldn't take more than a day or two to be done with him, and then he can be executed." He turned to Kian. "If you need help with the interrogation, I can fly to Greenland for a couple of days and lend the Guardians a hand."

It was the longest speech Annani had heard Dalhu deliver in a while. It was also a reminder that the talented artist used to be a ruthless killer and that he did not have any qualms about getting his hands dirty once again for the clan.

He had decapitated Carol's tormentor, and she had no doubt he would have gladly done so to Igor, but he respected Jade's right to do it herself.

Kian smiled at Amanda's mate. "I think the Guardians can manage, but you seem eager to release some pent-up energy." He turned to Andrew. "The three of us can go together. Can you take time off work?"

"Sure. I haven't taken time off in a while."

Syssi did not look happy, but she did not say anything. They had been mated long enough for her to withstand Kian's absence for a couple of days.

"Do you have a place to stay there?" Amanda asked. "From what I under-stand, it's a tiny town with a small hotel that barely has enough rooms for our men and their prisoners."

"True." Kian leaned back in his chair. "It's not the best location to conduct the interrogation. The question is, where can we take him?"

"Only the keep," Andrew said. "You already have a dungeon with rein-forced cells, and no one will hear him scream down there."

Syssi winced. "Please. Don't say things like that next to Allegra and Phoenix. You can never know what they pick up while we think they are busy playing and not paying attention to what the grownups are talking about."

"What about Safe Haven?" Nathalie asked. "The lab you built for William is underground. You could convert it into a temporary jail. You can also use the lair Emmett has under his cottage."

Kian regarded her with a frown. "That's actually a good idea. I was wracking my brain what to do with the Kra-ell until we decided where we wanted them. Safe Haven has enough room providing that they are not running a retreat right now." He pulled out his phone and then cast an apologetic glance at Annani. "Do you mind if I make the call here?"

Family dinners were for spending time with loved ones and not with phones. Usually, Annani did not approve of phone calls or texts or browsing the internet at the dinner table, but these were not normal circumstances.

She nodded. "Give my regards to Emmett."

"Thank you, Mother. I'll make it quick."

28

KIAN

"We have a retreat scheduled for this weekend," Emmett said. "But we are not booked to capacity. In fact, we have sold only half of the spots. People just don't want to be on the Oregon coast in the winter. I might combine this group with the next retreat, but I'll have to offer them a refund or a significant discount for canceling it so close to the start date. If you want to bring the Kra-ell to Safe Haven, you must tell me now."

"Can I give you my answer in a couple of hours? I'm having a family meeting to decide what to do with them."

Emmett was silent for a long moment before answering. "We can make a home for them in Safe Haven. The property is big enough, and it's in the middle of nowhere, with nature all around us, so hunting will not be a problem. But we don't have sufficient lodging for them even when we are not running a retreat. There is also the problem of the Safe Haven community. I can compel them to keep the Kra-ell presence a secret, but you conditioned my return on me never compelling them again."

Kian had a feeling that Emmett liked the idea of leading the new Kra-ell community along with his human one. When he was still a member of Jade's tribe, he'd been relegated to a second-class citizen, and this was his chance to return the favor, so to speak.

"Naturally, I will rescind that contingency. I like your idea, but you might not have thought it through. Jade is the new unofficial leader of those

Kra-ell, and she will not want to answer to you or anyone else. I'm sure you don't want your former mistress to take over Safe Haven. It is your baby."

"I have no wish to lead these Kra-ell or become part of their community and answer to Jade again. I'm only offering them a temporary sanctuary. If we come to an agreement of mutual coexistence, I would consider it becoming a permanent solution. I just hope you wouldn't force me to accept them."

It seemed like Kian had been wrong about the guy's motives, and he was surprised that Emmett was willing to compromise his location to offer sanctuary to the Kra-ell without asking for anything in return. Perhaps he missed his people more than he was willing to admit.

"I will never force your community to accept people they don't get along with and don't want to coexist with."

The clan owned half of Safe Haven, but Kian respected the right of their community to either accept or reject the newcomers.

"I appreciate that," Emmett said. "I'm just not sure how to go about it."

"A permanent solution will be based on a mutual agreement between all parties, and by that, I mean a majority vote of all members." There was no way to get a unanimous vote on something like that, and a decisive majority of over seventy-five percent should be good enough.

"If the Kra-ell accept Jade as their leader, they will vote the way she tells them."

If that was so, Kian would have to insist on a democratic vote. "Jade is in the process of adapting her leadership style and making it more inclusive. I will convince her to let her people vote freely. Maybe anonymous voting is preferable in this situation."

The big assembly voted by a show of hands, but his people didn't fear repercussions if their vote didn't align with his or even Annani's.

"Good luck persuading Jade to go for it." Emmett let out a sigh. "But we are getting ahead of ourselves. Housing the Kra-ell in Safe Haven, even temporarily, is not a foregone conclusion. You still need to discuss it with your people."

Kian suspected that Emmett was having second thoughts about his offer, and Jade wasn't going to like Safe Haven either. Compared to Karelia, it had balmy weather, but she wanted to settle in the tropics.

"I'll run it by all the usual suspects and let you know."

"Don't wait too long. If it's happening, I need to get Riley to start contacting people about rescheduling their retreat."

"Worst case scenario, you can do that at the last minute and claim a malfunction like a pipe bursting and flooding the lodge. I'll refund their money and pay for their next retreat. I doubt many will have a problem with that. These retreats are costly."

Emmett sighed. "You obviously don't have personal experience dealing with customers. If you did, you wouldn't be saying that. Some people are a pain in the rear, especially when I can't compel them into a more coopera- tive mood, but I love having them here anyway. I must be a masochist."

That was a big hint, and if need be, Kian would allow Emmett a one- time exception to compel problematic customers to accept the deal, but it was premature. "You are a narcissist who loves to perform for a crowd of adoring fans, and you are willing to suffer the occasional pain in your back- side for the privilege of being worshiped by everyone else."

Emmett snorted. "I didn't know that you knew me so well. I'm flattered that you were paying attention."

"It was hard not to." The guy had loved to sit in the café and collect admirers for his sermons. "Thank you for offering Jade and her people a sanctuary. That's very generous of you, especially given your history with Jade."

"They are my people too, but I'm not sure I want them in my life again. It's perfect as it is."

"I can understand that. I'll call you later today."

29

KIAN

*K*ian ended the call and looked at his dinner companions. "What do you think?"

They had all listened in, so there was no need to repeat what had been said.

"I think it's a wonderful idea," Alena said. "I was concerned that you would invite the Kra-ell to join the village."

"That was on the agenda until I talked with Emmett, but I like his idea better."

The security measures around the place would have to be modified to keep the Kra-ell within a certain perimeter and not just to keep intruders out, but that shouldn't be too complicated since William and his crew had installed state-of-the-art surveillance in and around Safe Haven.

The more Kian thought about the idea, the more he liked it.

"I do not like it," Annani said. "We have enough room in the village. Why not bring them here?"

Kian frowned. They had discussed the issue earlier today, and Annani had seemed ambivalent about where the Kra-ell should settle.

"Do you prefer for them to come here?" Amanda asked.

"Yes." Annani leaned back in her chair. "I want to learn about these people and would rather do it from the comfort of the village." She turned to look at Kian. "If I asked to visit Safe Haven, you would have a fit. Am I right?"

He had no problem with her visiting Safe Haven. It was much safer than most places she traveled to, but he didn't want to publicly contradict his mother. However, he could make it sound like he had changed his mind.

"I took Syssi and Allegra for a visit even before William made the place super secure for the lab we've built. At the moment, we don't have enough Guardians there, but once we do, I might consider taking you for a visit. The place is not fancy, though. You might not like it."

"I do not care about that, but it is not going to be the same as having the Kra-ell here in the village, accessible to me whenever I wish to explore their culture. I find the differences between them fascinating, and I want to learn more about life on the home planet."

That was actually a very good reason not to invite the Kra-ell to the village. They were too strong, and they were immune to thralling and shrouding. Compulsion worked on them, which was the only reason he was even considering it, but it wasn't foolproof.

"I will present both options to the council, and if the council decides that the village is preferable, I will call for the big assembly and put it up for a vote. This is too big and too impactful on our future for us to decide on for everyone."

"There is a third option," Alena said. "You could split them up. The humans and some of the more human-looking hybrids could remain on the *Aurora*, and the purebloods could either join the village or the Safe Haven community. That way, we don't overcrowd one location with so many new people. In fact, you should cancel the planes that are supposed to pick them up from Greenland and have them sail here. That will give us enough time to get organized to receive them."

Kian had considered the idea as well, but there were some logistical considerations. The *Aurora* would need to restock on provisions for those who didn't subsist on blood and to get the quantities needed for the three-week trip would require the ship to dock in one of the big ports in Canada to restock. They also had to arrange transportation for the Guardians, who were needed back home, and Kalugal's men, whom he no doubt needed back in the office.

The problem was that some of the men would have to stay behind to guard the Kra-ell and provide thralling and shrouding as required, and Kian wasn't keen on that.

"That's not such a great idea," Andrew said. "We will need to prepare passports and crew visas for everyone on board, and that's one hell of a task given that we are talking about over three hundred people that would need those done before they arrive at Long Beach."

Syssi folded her napkin on top of her plate. "If we managed to smuggle them into the ship with supply trucks, we can smuggle them out the same way. I don't think the port of Long Beach has more security in place than the port of Helsinki."

"You'd be surprised." Andrew puffed out his chest. "The Europeans have nothing on us. The Finns don't have a problem with foreign nationals trying to get into their country illegally, smuggle drugs, or plot terrorist attacks, at least not as big of a problem as we do. They are lucky to be on the periphery of Europe, so they don't attract as many foreigners with malicious intent."

Orion chuckled. "They only have to worry about their friendly neighbors the Russians, but that's not a big deal, right?"

30

SYSSI

*S*yssi didn't know whether Andrew had been exaggerating the security measures in Long Beach, but a glance at Kian's expression made it clear to her that he wasn't interested in that solution.

He turned to Alena. "We might be able to smuggle them in, but the question is whether we want them together with their livestock on the *Aurora* for so long. I can just imagine how bad the ship will smell, and we might never get the stink out. Your wedding cruise might be compromised."

"I'm fine with a small wedding." Smiling, Alena reached for Orion's hand. "We can have a ceremony only with our siblings and their families and my children."

Orion leaned over and kissed her cheek. "The entire clan is your family, my love. Every person you don't invite will be offended, and rightfully so."

"That's a very good point." She turned to Amanda. "It seems that it's back to the village square. We can have a lovely wedding with a big tent in case it rains and with the Odus preparing a feast under Callie and Gerard's supervision."

Amanda nodded. "I can make it happen."

Alena didn't look overly disappointed to have her wedding in the village instead of on the cruise ship, but they hadn't gone to all the trouble of getting a ship and remodeling it to give up on the idea because of a herd of sheep and goats doing their business in the cargo bay. If need be, the Kra-ell could be put to work and scrub it clean until no smell remained. After all, it was their responsibility to clean up after their meals.

But if they wanted to keep the wedding cruise dream alive, the option of inviting the Kra-ell and their humans to the village was problematic. They couldn't leave them alone in the village while everyone else went on the cruise.

"What are you frowning about?" Kian asked.

Syssi sighed. "I'm not ready to give up on the wedding cruise idea, but if we still want to make it happen, we can't invite the Kra-ell to the village. We can't leave them alone here while we are all gone."

"My men can stay behind to guard them." Kalugal turned to Kian. "Or do you still not trust me with the village security?"

Syssi stifled a chuckle. Kalugal knew how to push Kian's buttons, and he didn't miss a single opportunity to do so. The thing was, they both enjoyed the banter.

It was one big game to them, in which each of them was trying to get the upper hand with snarky remarks that would leave the other one speechless. Perhaps it was natural for two type A males to always compete even when they genuinely liked each other.

Didn't brothers do that?

As always, thinking about the brother she'd lost triggered a wave of sadness that Syssi had learned not to fight but to let wash over her.

It was easier now that she had Allegra.

One look at her daughter playing with her cousin on the floor was enough to banish sad thoughts and keep them at bay.

Leaning back, Kian cast his cousin a smile. "Given that we've just renewed our vows, I'm still in the trusting stage of our honeymoon."

Amanda snorted, and Syssi chuckled behind her hand.

Kian had told her about Kalugal teasing him by calling their relationship a bromance, an enemies-to-lovers story between two cousins. She thought it was funny, but Kian had been annoyed, and she would have never expected him to use it and expand on it.

"Then it's settled." Kalugal lifted his wine glass. "Let's make a toast to our bromance."

"Not so fast." Kian lifted his hand. "I'm sure your men are all looking forward to the cruise and celebrating seven weddings with their new extended family. Leaving your men behind in the village while the rest of us party goes against the spirit of full cooperation, transparency, and integration we both agreed on. It will be construed as discriminatory and offensive."

"Seven?" Kalugal ignored the rest of Kian's words. "Who else is getting married?"

"We have a long list," Amanda said. "We will need to launch several cruises to cover everyone, but so far, for this maiden voyage, the first seven couples are Alena and Orion, Dalhu and me, Wendy and Vlad, Callie and Brundar, Wonder and Anandur, Aliya and Vrog, and either Richard and Stella or Bridget and Turner. Both couples say that they can wait for the next round."

"Two or three cruises should cover it," Syssi said. "At least for now. I expect more couples will want a wedding cruise." She took Kian's hand. "Perhaps we can renew our vows."

The smoldering look he gave her was bone-melting. "I renew my vows to you every morning when I wake up next to you in bed and every night when I hold you in my arms."

"Bravo." Kalugal clapped his hands. "That should go right into a romance novel."

Jacki elbowed him playfully. "You should take notes."

"Ouch." Kalugal assumed an offended expression. "Am I not romantic enough for you?"

Syssi leaned over and kissed her husband. If they weren't surrounded by immortals with excellent hearing, she would have whispered, *Way to go. You won this one.*

31

KIAN

ian didn't want to leave Kalugal's men in charge of the village while the clan was celebrating, especially since Kalugal would be on the cruise ship along with Rufsur. That would leave Phinas in charge—the guy who was currently dating Jade.

As bad ideas went, this one was up there with the worst of them, but Kian had been smart enough to use a different argument against them watching over the Kra-ell, one that didn't paint him as paranoid but rather as someone who cared about Kalugal's men's full integration in the clan.

Kian stifled a smile. He was learning to think like a politician, but he hadn't decided yet whether that was a good or a bad thing. It certainly was helpful, but he had no love lost for smooth-talking manipulators who only cared about money and power, and he didn't want to be grouped together with them.

Truth be told, he cared about money too, but only as a means to provide for his clan and to finance the clan's humanitarian and social activities. He didn't care about power or what people thought about him, and if there was someone else capable and willing to take over from him, he would gladly step down and transfer the baton to the new person.

The problem was that there were no volunteers, and his people were happy to leave the management of the clan businesses and security to him while complaining that he was overcautious at best and paranoid at worst.

Kian could live with that.

He was tasked with keeping everyone in the village safe, and he'd rather be called paranoid than let even one clan member get hurt on his watch.

Well, that might be the wrong term. A watch implied a defined time frame, while his watch was indefinite.

Glancing at his precious daughter playing with her cousin on the carpet, he didn't wish her the burden of responsibility he carried. Hopefully, when the time came for him to step down, she would no longer have to worry about deadly enemies and keeping everyone safe.

Would she even want to take over from him?

He had a feeling that she would. Allegra was a born leader.

But if she didn't, perhaps the clan would vote someone else into the position. After all, the job was never meant to be hereditary, but since he and Sari had been groomed from childhood to become the future leaders of the clan, they had assumed the positions, and no one had opposed them.

The thing was, he should plan for one day stepping down and make it a habit to work more with the council. If a future elected leader wasn't Annani's direct descendant, Kian would feel better knowing that the council held that person accountable.

"Cruising over here will give me enough time to bring the issue to the big assembly's vote," he said. "But the same objective can be achieved with much less headache by temporarily housing the Kra-ell in Safe Haven. If Emmett cancels the upcoming retreat, very little preparation will be needed for him to host the Kra-ell."

"I was hoping to include the Kra-ell in the village for added security," Syssi said. "If we bring them to Safe Haven and then decide to move them somewhere else, the place will once again get compromised, and we can't do that to Emmett. He was so broken up about having to evacuate when Igor was still at large."

Kian frowned at her. "I don't understand how inviting them to the village is better."

"We will bring them here the way we do with everyone else. They will not know where they are or how they got there."

"They are not like everyone else." It occurred to Kian that the same was true about Vrog and Aliya. "They are stronger, faster, and they need to hunt. If we let them hunt in the area, they will realize where they are. They can scale these mountains with ease."

Vrog and Emmett didn't hunt often, and even Aliya did it only once in a while, but the purebloods would need to do so more frequently.

"Right." Syssi pushed a strand of hair behind her ear. "So, I guess inviting them to live with us in the village is off the table."

"It's not. If they can subsist on blood from domesticated animals and go hunting only occasionally somewhere else, like near our mountain cabin, then the village is an option. I will have William make location cuffs for all of them, so we can monitor their location at all times, but I doubt Jade will be willing to accept that for the dubious pleasure of sharing our village." He picked up a glass of water and took a sip. "We love the village, but to them, it's just a location, and if it means less freedom, they will prefer to go somewhere else. If I were in her shoes, I would choose Safe Haven and negotiate as much autonomy as possible."

Amanda nodded. "Me too. There is another factor that none of you have considered. Their humans comprise a population that genetically is too small to safely reproduce. They will need to bring new members into their community. How is that going to work? Are we going to allow the Kra-ell to kidnap more humans?"

Kian groaned. "That's why I wanted to return them to their compound with a Guardian or two as liaisons. Marcel would have no doubt volunteered, and perhaps Phinas as well."

Amanda cast him an incredulous look. "The fact that we won't be there to witness the kidnapping doesn't mean that we are not responsible for letting them continue. It does not absolve you or the rest of us from making sure that the Kra-ell don't kidnap any more humans."

"So what do you suggest we do? Let the humans go?"

"Of course not." Amanda crossed her arms over her chest. "What I was trying to convey is that Safe Haven is a great solution for the humans as well. They can become part of the Safe Haven community, and the young ones can find love among retreat attendees. The attendees who decide to stay and join the community will do so voluntarily. It's like we do with Dormants. After the rules of the game are explained to them, and they are told about the aliens, they will be given a choice to leave after getting their memories thralled away."

Kian nodded. "That's a good solution. I'll present it to Jade and the council, and if both are in favor, I will put it up for a vote in the big assembly."

"Why do you need the big assembly to approve?" Annani asked. "Safe Haven is an auxiliary location, and the Kra-ell living there will not affect the clan."

"I agree with the Clan Mother," Kalugal said. "And I also have an idea that might be a bit outlandish. What if we get one of those enormous cruise ships that can house thousands of passengers? We can have a floating village with enough space for every member of the clan, the Kra-ell, and a bunch of humans to serve us all. Naturally, we will have large, luxurious apartments instead of the thousands of small cabins, and we will have several restaurants, so there will be a nice selection of menus. A buffet that's open twenty-four-seven, offices, clinic, in short, the works." His eyes sparkled as he looked at Kian. "What do you think, cousin?"

"As lovely as that sounds, I prefer solid land for my permanent living quarters."

32

TOVEN

"$\mathcal{W}$e should go to sleep." Yamanu stretched his arms over his head. "Mey is probably wondering where I am."

Toven nodded. "I should check on Mia as well." She was probably asleep. Otherwise, she would have texted him to ask how things had gone with the Russian ship that had arrived to collect the rescued sailors. "I'm surprised we didn't get a visit from Jade yet. It's not like her to let others take care of things."

The sailors had been collected over an hour ago, and everything had gone smoothly. The Russians hadn't asked to search the ship, and no thralling or compulsion had been needed to convince them that the *Aurora* had no passengers and was on its way to its owners in the United States. Toven and Yamanu had gotten a few curious looks, but no one had questioned their claim that they were part of Captain Olsson's crew.

The captain of the other ship had thanked Olsson and Toven for keeping their men safe and warm, they had shaken hands, and that was the end of the story.

"We didn't give her much choice." Yamanu took a sip from his coffee. "We told her to stay in her cabin and not come out until we tell her it's okay, which we should have done as soon as the Russian ship was far enough for us to turn the lights back on."

On the couch, Merlin turned on his side and kept snoring.

It wasn't loud, and it didn't bother Toven. It just made him curious about the differences between the gods and their immortal descendants. Gods were too perfectly made to have an obstruction that caused snoring, but apparently, immortals weren't as perfect.

"What do you want to do with the good doctor? Should we leave him here to sleep or carry him to his cabin?"

Yamanu cast an amused look at Merlin. "He can sleep here. I'm not carrying him and putting him to bed like some damn princess."

"He did well earlier." Toven refilled his glass with more whiskey. "I wasn't sure about him staying with the sailors who he'd patched up and transferring them to the care of their doctor, but that was a good call. It made our rescue story more believable."

Yamanu chuckled. "You didn't even have to work hard on planting a good story in their heads. They all believed that their captain had gone mad."

Toven's smile wilted. "It's a damn shame that no one will ever know how remarkable that man was and what he accomplished. These men wouldn't be alive now if not for his strong will and smarts."

Yamanu put his coffee cup down and lifted the whiskey glass that had only a few drops left in it. "To Captain Sergey Gorshekov. He will forever live in our immortal minds and be remembered with respect and admiration."

"To Captain Gorshekov." Toven emptied his glass and reached for the bottle for another refill. "I embellished the story a little to make his intentions seem less malevolent but not so much as to make it unbelievable. The best option was to make them unaware that their captain wasn't following navy command orders and was on a suicide mission. I just hate that his family will be told the same story, and think he abandoned them."

"It is what it is." Yamanu put the empty glass down.

As the Guardian's phone pinged with an incoming message, he pulled it out of his pocket. "Kian's asking me to get the two of you in our war room and call him after we wake up. Should I call him back?"

"Yeah." Merlin turned around and lowered his feet to the floor. "Right after I make myself a coffee."

"I'm calling him now. You can make yourself a coffee while we talk."

When Merlin waved a hand instead of answering, Yamanu placed the call and propped his phone against the half-empty whiskey bottle.

"Good morning," Kian's gruff voice came through. "What are you doing awake?"

"We never went to sleep. Toven, Merlin, and I came up here to celebrate the successful conclusion of the sailor rescue operation, and Merlin fell asleep on the couch, but he's awake now."

"Good. I'm glad to have the three of you together, and I'll try to make it short so you can catch some sleep. I want to discuss with you a few options regarding Igor, and where to take the Kra-ell and their humans."

"Shouldn't we get Jade in here?" Toven asked.

"Not yet. I want to run the options by you first and then tell her what we decide are the best."

"Go ahead." Merlin sat down with a fresh cup of coffee in his hands.

"Actually, the first idea has to do with you. What do you think about damaging or removing Igor's vocal cords to prevent him from using his compulsion ability?"

Merlin frowned. "Damaging them probably wouldn't be enough because we don't know how compulsion works. I suspect that it piggybacks on sound waves, and it doesn't matter what those sound waves are. I would have to remove his vocal cords altogether. But since we have William's earpieces, why bother?"

"Because not everyone on the ship has them, and shit happens. I want to neutralize him. But before you do that, I want you to test how fast he heals. We suspect that he's a hybrid, half god and half Kra-ell, so if he heals as fast as we do, it will confirm that. Also, he would probably regrow his vocal cords in a matter of days, so we need to keep checking their status."

"He doesn't have days," Toven said. "Jade agreed to give me one day to interrogate him. If I can compel him, one day will suffice for what we need to get out of him, and if he can't be compelled, then we shouldn't waste any more energy on him and let Jade have him. Taking out his vocal cords will just waste time I could use to learn more."

33

KIAN

*K*ian hoped to get Jade to agree to more than just one day. If they could get Igor to talk and reveal a thread of information that she was interested in, she might be tempted to let him live for a few more days. But if she did not agree to extend her stay of execution, Kian wasn't going to push the issue and start their relationship by going back on Toven's word.

"I agree with Toven regarding the vocal cords," Merlin said. "Nevertheless, I would still like to test whether Igor is part god, and that would take no time at all. One small cut will do the trick. If he's part god, we might have a bargaining chip in case compulsion doesn't work. As part god, he is not exclusively Jade's to punish, and he falls under our jurisdiction as well. We can offer him entombment instead of beheading in exchange for information."

Merlin was a smart guy. Neither Kian nor Turner had thought of that loophole.

"That's a good point, but I don't think we will win points with Jade by using this as an excuse to rob her of her right to revenge."

Frowning, Toven leaned back in his armchair. "Let's first see if I can compel the scumbag, and if I can't, we will take it from there."

"Agreed." That wasn't the only thing Kian needed to discuss with them, and the three looked like they were running out of steam. "Let me bring you up to speed about the options for the Kra-ell relocation I discussed with my mother and the rest of the family over dinner."

When he was done, Toven nodded. "I like the Safe Haven idea the best. It solves nearly all the problems associated with integrating the Kra-ell into our community."

"Jade is not going to like Safe Haven," Yamanu said. "Hell, I don't like the place. It's cold and dreary, and the free-love community gives me the creeps."

Kian laughed. "You haven't been there since we stormed the place to free Eleanor and get Peter back."

"That was enough. I wouldn't want to live there full-time. Visiting is a different story."

"Do you prefer for them to join the village?"

Yamanu shrugged. "Why not? It will shake things up a little. When Kalugal and his men joined us, people were wary of them, but it turned out pretty good. We have extra help defending the place, and the clan ladies enjoy plenty of immortal shagging and venom bites that they didn't get to experience before. If we can coexist in perfect harmony with our former enemies, we should be able to do so with the Kra-ell. They might have fought the gods back in the day, but if what Jade told us is true, then they had been right to rebel. Navuh, on the other hand, fights us for the simple reason that he hates Annani and that her assistance to humans interferes with his world domination ambitions."

Was he the only one bothered by the fact that the Kra-ell were a different species?

"One major difference works in favor of Kalugal's men. The former Doomers are genetically the same as us, a combination of human and god genetics, and it's easy to forget that they weren't always on our side. The Kra-ell are fundamentally different. They don't look like us or eat the same things we do, and they produce four males for every female."

"So? I say let's celebrate the differences."

Yamanu was the quintessential optimist.

"Let's decide on two or three options that we are comfortable with and present them to Jade," Toven said. "She and her people need to have a say in this too."

Kian preferred for the choice to be his and the clan's. If Jade didn't like it, they could negotiate a compromise. "What about the cruise ship option? Do any of you think it's a good idea?"

"It might be for the humans," Merlin said. "They like it here, and it can provide them with jobs. I don't think the Kra-ell are comfortable living on a ship. In fact, most of them are water phobic. They tolerate it, but it's not a long-term solution for them."

"We can't separate them unless they want it." Kian groaned. "Every time I think I have a solution figured out, another thing comes to mind that puts it in question. In my opinion, Safe Haven is the best solution. Let's do our best to sell it to Jade." He trained his gaze on Yamanu. "Don't share your opinion of the place with her."

The Guardian shrugged. "I'll keep my mouth shut, but once she sees the place, she will refuse to stay there."

"We can tell her that it's the best we can do for her," Kian said. "Even if I was willing to accept the Kra-ell, which I'm not, what about the humans? Are you comfortable with them living in the village with us?"

Yamanu grinned. "I'd be thrilled. I vote for opening a big dining hall and paying them to prepare three meals a day for the entire population of the village. Talk about a symbiotic coexistence. The humans enjoy preparing meals for us, and we enjoy eating them."

Had the Guardian been joking?

Sometimes it was hard to tell with Yamanu. Hopefully, when it came time for the council to vote, he would take it more seriously and vote with his brain rather than his stomach.

34

JADE

*J*ade tossed and turned in the overly comfortable bed, exhaustion weighing heavily but sleep eluding her.

She was agitated and hungover and missed having Phinas with her in bed, which made her even more agitated.

If he were there, he would have wrapped his arms around her and said something that would have made her smile, soothing her frayed nerves and making her feel like she wasn't alone and that the entire world was not set against her. Until he'd entered her life, Kagra had been the only one who had stood by her side and made her feel like the two of them were united against the world.

Now Phinas was added, but as much more than Kagra was, and that was disturbing.

She'd known Kagra since she'd been born.

And yet Phinas was her antidote to loneliness, the balm to the simmering anger inside her, and the companion she'd never known she needed. And that was all in addition to the physical bliss he so masterfully provided.

Jade had sought to drown her yearning for him in alcohol, but all she'd gotten for her efforts was a headache and an upset stomach.

If only she had a phone, she could call him and find solace in his voice, but she was still considered a risk, and the immortals refused to even let her talk to him in private.

With a groan, Jade grabbed a pillow and hugged it to her roiling stomach.

Yamanu was supposed to tell her and the others who were confined to their cabins when it was okay to turn on the lights and step outside their doors. He must have fallen asleep, or thought that everyone was still sleeping, and therefore didn't bother to let them know that the Russian ship was gone and it was okay to turn on the lights and roam about the ship.

The windows and doors of the cabins didn't have shutters, and the curtains weren't completely opaque, but perhaps she could turn on the television to check what time it was. Could the light from the TV be seen from outside the ship, though?

Did it matter? Was the Russian vessel that had collected the sailors still within sight?

So far north, the sun didn't rise until nearly noon, so if she wanted to venture out of her cabin and check, she had to do it in the dark.

So be it.

She was done fighting for sleep that wouldn't come.

Ten minutes later, Jade was out in the dark corridor, finding her way to the stairs by keeping her hand on the wall. Her night vision was excellent, but no light filtered into the hallway, and she had to rely on her other senses and memory to guide her in the right direction.

When she reached the stairs, things got better. One of the upper floors must have had some illumination because the stairwell wasn't as utterly dark as the hallway outside her cabin.

Her destination was the cabin the immortals had designated as their war room and the bridge if they weren't there. Whoever was at the helm could tell her whether the Russians were gone and whether it was okay to let everyone know that they could leave their cabins.

The humans needed to start working on breakfast, and she needed to find a phone and call Phinas before she went crazy.

Was Mey right about the bond? Or had her words planted the idea in Jade's head, and she was having a psychosomatic reaction to them? It wasn't possible for her to form a bond with an immortal unless she had some godly blood in her, which she couldn't have.

She was purely Kra-ell through and through.

Still, the gods and the Kra-ell were related species who had probably sprouted from the same root. At some point in their natural evolution, they had diverged, or as the legends suggested, the gods had been genetically altered.

The bottom line was that the Kra-ell might have recessive genes that could make them susceptible to bonding, and the trigger was intermixing. Since that had been strictly forbidden by both cultures, it wasn't a well-known fact.

It was all speculation, but that was the only thing that could explain her reaction to Phinas and her intense need to be with him.

How the hell was she going to survive three more days without him? Or was it four because of the delay?

And what was she going to do once they were reunited?

They couldn't stay together. Her people would never accept a leader who chose one male instead of forming a family tribe, and that male wasn't even one of them.

Mother of All Life, what a mess she'd gotten herself into.

The right thing to do was to be strong and sever the connection to Phinas no matter the cost to her.

She had an obligation to her people to carry on the Kra-ell tradition and keep them from becoming extinct. Her own needs and wishes were secondary.

35

TOVEN

*T*oven wasn't surprised when the doorbell rang.

"I was wondering when Jade would show up." He rose to his feet. "I bet she didn't sleep either." He opened the door for her. "Good morning."

The female looked almost as bad as she had the night of the attack on Igor's compound. There were dark circles under her eyes, and her skin was pale and lacked its normal vibrancy.

"I've had better." She strode into the cabin and glared at Yamanu. "You said you would let me know when it was okay to leave the cabin. The lights are off everywhere except on this deck."

Yamanu winced. "I thought everyone was still asleep."

"Yeah, well. I wasn't." She walked over to the kitchenette and poured herself coffee. "Did the Russians give you any trouble?" She walked over to the couch and sat next to Merlin.

"Not at all." Toven returned to his armchair. "They were thankful for our help." He continued to tell her about the Russian captain's last act of bravery.

Jade nodded. "May he forever walk in the fields of the brave. I know how difficult it is to resist Igor's compulsion, even in a small way, and I'm not human. The captain must have had a powerful mind."

"Speaking of Igor's ability." Toven crossed his legs. "We decided not to tamper with his vocal cords. Since you are giving us just one day to interrogate him, that would be a waste of time." He didn't add that Igor might be able to regrow them.

They didn't know that for sure, and until Merlin tested his healing speed, it was just speculation.

Jade narrowed her eyes at him. "Is that another attempt to convince me to let him live more than one day after we arrive in Greenland?"

"It is," Yamanu admitted. "If Toven can't compel him, there are other ways to get him to talk, but they all take time. We can starve him or torture him until he sings just to stop the pain. You say that he's a sociopath, so it's not like he wants to protect someone by withholding information. He would keep his mouth shut out of spite, as a fuck-you to you and to us. But since he's a selfish bastard who cares only about himself, he will tell us whatever we want to know in exchange for food and comfort, even if he knows that he's about to die anyway."

"I doubt that." Jade pushed a strand of hair away from her face. "I'm too tired to think right now." She looked at Yamanu. "First, let's see how Toven manages with Mia's help, and if that doesn't work, we will take it from there."

Yamanu nodded. "I just want you to think about it. Don't you want to see him suffer? It's much more satisfying than just one swipe of the sword to end him. I can arrange a front-row seat for you and anyone else who needs to see him getting beaten into a pulp."

The smile she gave him was chilling. "I like the way you think, and I promise to give it serious consideration. Is there a chance that in the spirit of our mutual understanding and cooperation, you could give me a phone that I can use without someone monitoring what I say? I would like to talk to Phinas in private."

The Guardian winced. "We don't have any spare phones, and I can't give you mine."

"You can have mine," Merlin said. "I've already talked with Ronja, and I don't need to call anyone else, but I have a lot of personal information on this device that I would like to keep private." He smiled apologetically. "It's not about you. I wouldn't want Toven or Yamanu scrawling through my notes, either. But I think William can block everything except my contact list remotely." He pulled out the device. "He should still be awake."

Jade seemed to perk up as Merlin typed a message to William. "How long can I keep it?"

Merlin lifted his head. "First, let's check that William can block all that other stuff. If he can, you can keep it for a couple of hours. I'm going to my cabin for a little shut-eye, so when you're done, just come over and ring the bell."

"If you're going to be asleep, I don't want to wake you up."

"Two hours should be enough for me, and I'm sure you can make good use of the time talking to your gentleman caller."

She hadn't heard that expression in ages. "Phinas is not my gentleman caller."

Merlin waved a hand in dismissal. "I don't like the term boyfriend because Phinas is not a boy. And I don't like the term lover because it implies an illicit affair."

"Mate is a good one." Yamanu cast her a meaningful look.

"Oh, look at that." Merlin lifted his phone. "It's already done." He handed the phone to Jade. "You can call and message everyone on my contact list, but nothing else."

Jade took the device with both hands and dipped her head. "Thank you, Merlin. Your kindness is greatly appreciated, and I vow to repay it."

36

PHINAS

"*M*erlin?" Phinas answered the phone sleepily.

"It's me," Jade said. "Merlin was kind enough to let me borrow his phone."

"Hi." Smiling, Phinas sat up and glanced at the other two beds in the room, which were thankfully empty. His roommates must have woken up early and left him to sleep.

"You sound sleepy. Did I wake you up?"

He'd been up late, talking with Kalugal and getting updates about the *Aurora* and the rescue of the Russian sailors.

"It's the best wake-up call. Hearing your voice first thing in the morning will make the rest of my day better. I miss you so badly that it hurts."

There was a long moment of silence, and when Jade finally spoke, it wasn't to say the words he'd been hoping for. "I need your advice."

Swallowing his disappointment, he switched the phone to his other ear. "Of course. What can I help you with?"

"Toven and Yamanu are putting pressure on me to let Igor stay alive longer so they can force information out of him in case Toven can't compel him. I don't think taking him with us on the plane is smart. I don't know what they hope to learn from him, and I want to be done with him. When we arrive wherever you are taking us, I want my people to have a fresh start without Igor and Valstar's executions hanging over our heads. I want to do it in Greenland."

"Was there a question somewhere in there that I've missed?"

She let out a breath. "It's coming. I still don't know where you plan to take us, and I don't want to piss Kian off by refusing to give him those extra days and have him get rid of us in some remote location and wash his hands of us. As much as I crave revenge, I can't think just about what I want. My people need me to look after their interests. I need access to our money, and I need help settling my people. When it was just my pod-mates and me, it was difficult to adjust to the new world we found ourselves in, but there were only twenty of us, and with our combined skills, we managed just fine. Now I have over three hundred people to care for, and I can't do that without your clan's help."

It was on the tip of his tongue to say that it wasn't his clan, but with the latest developments Kalugal had told him about, that was about to change. Two seats on the council and complete transparency were the beginning of full integration.

He also knew the possible options for settling the Kra-ell, but he wasn't supposed to tell Jade about them until the council voted on one of them.

"Kian will not retaliate against you if you refuse to let him have more time to interrogate Igor, but it would be a good move on your part to allow it and have Kian owe you a favor. He knows how much this means to you and the magnitude of your sacrifice if you agree to wait with the beheading."

"Good point. But it is a huge sacrifice, and it might bite him and me in the ass. I really want to close that chapter of my life."

Phinas could empathize, but he knew that chapter would never close, not even with Igor and Valstar's deaths. Jade could never get back what had been taken from her, and she could never forget and start a new life.

There was no point in smashing her hopes, though. She would figure it out on her own.

"Shouldn't you talk with your people about Igor and Valstar's fate?"

"It's not up to them. They could have the heads of the others if they wronged them. I've seen these two kill my males, and I have the right and obligation to avenge them."

"True, but given the other factors that affect all of them, perhaps you shouldn't carry the weight of this decision solely on your shoulders. Let it be decided by the majority."

"No. That's my burden to carry."

Stubborn female.

"I see you've made up your mind, so what exactly do you need my advice on?"

She let out a breath. "You helped me crystallize my thoughts."

He hadn't said much, but maybe she'd just needed a sounding board.

"I'm glad that I was able to help. What did you decide to do?"

"I'll wait to see whether Toven can compel Igor and decide then. Kian asked me if I wanted to go back to the compound. I told him that I didn't, but if he's planning to send us somewhere worse or wash his hands of us, perhaps I should accept that offer. If he gives us our money back, I can manage."

Perhaps that was what she'd been trying to find out. Whether she could trust Kian to make good on his promise to return the funds to her.

"I don't doubt even for a moment that you'll get the money. But you've just said that you want a fresh start, and that's not going to happen in that compound. Even after you kill Igor, you'll see his fingertips on every surface and his shadow in every corner."

"What are my alternatives?"

Phinas closed his eyes and let out a breath. "If I tell you, you have to promise to keep it to yourself. Nothing has been decided yet, but there are several options that Kian is going to bring to the clan council for a vote."

3 7

JADE

*J*ade's heart rate accelerated. "How do you know what Kian plans?"

"Kalugal told me. They are meeting with the council tomorrow."

The purpose of her call hadn't been to get Phinas to reveal things. Heck, it hadn't been to ask his advice either. She'd just wanted to hear his voice and quiet the unease churning in her stomach.

But then he'd said that he missed her so badly that it hurt, echoing what she was feeling, and she'd had to change the subject before she'd admitted to missing him as well.

Their story didn't have a happy ending. There was no future for them. And after Greenland, they probably would go their separate ways.

Except, he just offered her a secret that he wasn't supposed to share with her, which meant—

What?

That he loved her?

Phinas was loyal to his boss, and if he was willing to betray Kalugal's trust for her, what else could it mean?

"What are the options?"

"There are several. One is inviting you to join the village, which Kian is not too keen on, but others are in favor of. The second is Safe Haven, which the clan outfitted with state-of-the-art security. The third is a mountain property that the clan owns, but it has no lodging ready to receive you, and the fourth is to use either of the two first options as a temporary solution until a suitable location is found. Kalugal also had the crazy idea of getting one of those huge cruise ships that can host thousands of passengers and have everyone move there, but no one else was in favor of that."

"The Kra-ell and water don't mix well together, so the ship is definitely a no-go. We are not seafarers. We are hunters. What are the pros and cons of the other two options?"

Kian was only considering inviting them to the village or Emmett's location because he still thought of them as a threat for some reason and wanted to control them. They would probably have very restricted mobility, if any. It would be like Igor's compound all over again, just without Igor.

"The village is where my men and I live too, and it's beautiful. It's located in Southern California near a major metropolis, but it's extremely well hidden. I don't even know its precise location because we use special self-driving vehicles to get there, and their windows turn opaque several miles before the hidden entrance to the tunnel leading to it. I could probably find it if I put my mind to it, but I prefer not to know so no one can torture it out of me. There are two problems with that location, though. Your people would almost double the village's population, making it more difficult to keep it hidden. The other problem is that the mountains surrounding it might not have enough hunting game for your people. One of the suggested solutions was to organize weekly trips to where there was game. The rest of the time, you and the other purebloods would have to make do with domesticated animals or refrigerated blood."

"That's doable. We don't need to hunt every day. What's Emmett's place like?"

"It's very secluded, has plenty of wildlife, and is located on the Oregon Coast. It's a beautiful location, and the winters are mild compared to what you are used to in Karelia, but it still gets quite cold there, and I know you prefer a warmer climate."

"And the third option? Where is the mountain property that the clan owns?"

"It's also in Southern California, and in the winter it snows there, but there is plenty of game, very few humans around, and it's an hour's drive from the edges of the metropolis, where you can go shopping for clothes and other necessities. Emmett's place is an hour and a half drive from the nearest small town, but you can order what you need online and get it delivered."

It wasn't like she and the other purebloods enjoyed shopping, so that was not a problem.

They could pass for humans if they wore dark sunglasses to conceal their large eyes and baggy clothes to hide their too-narrow middles, but that still left the fangs that didn't retract all the way like the immortals' and the dark triangle some of them had on their tongues. Both were easily explained away, but it was still better to minimize their exposure to humans.

"All three options sound good. Which one do you think they'll vote for?"

"Emmett's place."

"Because they don't want us in their village?"

"It's more about the humans than it is about you. In fact, the humans are the biggest problem. Perhaps the solution is to settle the humans in Emmett's place and the Kra-ell in the village. Kian is much more likely to agree to that."

"Many of the humans don't know how to live independently of us, and others are in relationships with our hybrids. Besides, we need them to thwart extinction."

"Then Safe Haven is probably the best solution for all of you, but it's up to the council. They might decide that having you in the village is a better solution because of the added security. With you and your people helping us defend the place, we will all sleep better at night."

It was good to hear that at least some of the immortals considered the Kra-ell a beneficial ally and not a threat or a burden.

"Do you think they will let us choose?"

"I don't know. The council is also voting tomorrow to approve or deny Kalugal the two seats that Kian offered him. If they agree and we join the council, I can probably convince Kalugal to vote for your preferred choice."

"Which one do you prefer?"

"It depends. For me, the best option would be for you to come live in the village, so I don't have to leave Kalugal and the rest of my friends. But I think that Emmett's place is the best for your people given your mixed population. It checks all of the boxes."

Jade's mouth suddenly felt dry. "You would abandon the male who saved you from the tyrant to be with me?"

"In a heartbeat."

38

PHINAS

*H*e'd said it, he meant it, and he wouldn't take it back even if he could.

When a long moment passed, and all he could hear were Jade's ragged breaths, Phinas asked, "Are you okay?"

"Yes. I don't know. I don't know what to say."

He understood that the concept of fated mates and bonding was foreign to her, and given that they had known each other for only days, her response was understandable, but Jade wasn't like other females. She wasn't afraid of anything, not even her own feelings, and it was time she stopped lying to herself.

He was tired of dancing around the issue and letting her put up shields to keep him out.

"I know you, Jade. And you are not a coward. You feel the same about me, and it's about bloody time you stop fighting your feelings and hiding behind the bullshit of the Kra-ell do this and don't do that. The only thing that matters is what you feel and want."

"I want you," she blurted. "There, I said it. But it has never been about what I want or what I need. I have a duty to lead my people. What kind of a Kra-ell leader would I be if I spat on my people's entire way of life and chose to be with only one male? A male who isn't even one of my own?"

"The kind of leader who thinks for herself and doesn't blindly follow

605

customs and doctrines created out of necessity and not because they were true or morally right."

"I bet Igor thought the same thing when he decided that the Kra-ell needed to be led by males, not females. If everyone decided for themselves what was right and what was wrong, society couldn't function. If I selfishly choose to be exclusive with you, I will have to step down, but there is no one else to lead them."

"Don't give me that crap, Jade."

She hissed. "You don't get to talk to me like that, Phinas."

"You're right." He ran his fingers through his hair. "I apologize, and it's not going to happen again. I'm just so frustrated with you. I know that you are the one for me, and you know that I'm the one for you. To make us happen, I'm willing to give up a position that I worked very hard to climb to, and you are not willing to do a single thing. You can't even admit your feelings for me."

"I just did! I told you that I want you."

"I need more than that. What are you willing to sacrifice to be with me?"

She let out a breath. "I was willing to sacrifice the thing that kept me going ever since I lost everything that mattered to me. When you left on the *Seafarer*, I prayed to the Mother of All Life to keep you alive and to bring you back to me in one piece. I didn't pray for victory, and I didn't pray for Igor's capture. I was willing to give up the dream of avenging my sons and slicing Igor's head off just so you wouldn't get hurt."

That shut him up.

For Jade, that was the ultimate sacrifice, and Phinas felt humbled. The sacrifice he was willing to make for her paled in comparison to the one she'd been willing to make for him.

"I love you, Jade. I know that you can't bring yourself to say it back, but the prayer you offered to your deity on my behalf was as good as a declaration of love." He closed his eyes. "And please, for the love of the Fates and the Mother of All Life, don't tell me that the Kra-ell can't feel love because we both know that it's not true. You loved your sons, you still love them and mourn their loss every day, and you love your daughter. You also love me."

39

JADE

Tears stung the backs of Jade's eyes, and her throat clogged with a lump, producing a familiar choking sensation.

Most of the time, she managed to swallow the grief and pain that threatened to overwhelm her and rob her of reason, and when it became too much, she usually burned through it with a vigorous run or a vicious practice fight.

The Kra-ell did not cry, and to let the tears flow would be humiliating, but there was nowhere to run, no one to practice fighting with, and also no one to see her lose it.

She would never allow anyone to see her crying.

Even if what Phinas had said rang true, she couldn't allow herself to feel love. She was held together by duty and obligation, by the Kra-ell tradition and adherence to the teaching of the Mother of All Life, and if she accepted that even part of it wasn't true, her house of cards would collapse and scatter on the wind, and there would be nothing left of her.

"Jade? Are you there? Talk to me, sweetheart."

Sweetheart? Did he just call her sweetheart? Was he delusional?

"There is nothing sweet-hearted about me, Phinas."

He chuckled. "My bad. Should I call you iron heart?"

Despite the lump lodged in her throat, her lips twitched with a smile. "Yeah. That's much better."

He sighed. "I shouldn't have had this conversation with you over the phone. I know that it's difficult for you to acknowledge your feelings. You've been disassociating from them your entire life, and when they manage to penetrate that iron shield you've built around your heart, you don't know how to handle them. But you are strong and brave, and you can conquer the whole world if you set your mind to it, and you can conquer your own fears as well. If you let me, I will be there to help you every step of the way."

How could he possibly know her so well? How could he penetrate her shields and see the places in her soul that she was afraid to look at?

"How did you become so smart?"

He laughed. "I was born that way. Seriously, though, I'm not that smart or that insightful. I just see you, Jade. I see all of you and admire every facet of you. Don't think for a moment that anything I said was meant as a criticism. You are the strongest, bravest person I know, and I'm in awe of you."

That was the nicest thing anyone had ever said to her, but instead of making her happy, it just wrung more tears out of her.

"You're too nice to me, Phinas."

"Are you crying? Did I just make you cry?"

"I'm not crying," she lied.

"Oh, so you must have caught a cold. Come on, Jade."

"Fine. But if you tell anyone, I'll have to kill you."

He laughed. "You can't. You owe me a life debt. You are sworn to protect me. Does that vow expire once you save my life, or is it a life-long commitment?"

"It's a life-long commitment."

"Then you have a perfect excuse for choosing me over your pureblooded males. You have to be with me because of your vow. How else are you going to protect me?"

He was just teasing, trying to make her laugh, but there was something to it. A life debt didn't require the one giving the vow to be with the person they vowed to protect at all times, but the holder of the vow had the right to call upon it anytime. If Phinas demanded her protection, she couldn't deny the request.

"Do you have enemies that want to see you dead?"

"Plenty. The entire Brotherhood and even my own blood brothers would kill me on sight. I need your protection twenty-four-seven."

Was he still teasing, or was he in real danger from his own brothers?

"Seriously. Are they after you?"

"They think that I'm dead, and no one is actively looking for me, but if I encounter them by chance, they will try to kill me."

"Then you indeed require my protection."

"Will that be a good enough excuse to appease your people? They all know that you gave me the life-debt vow for saving Kagra."

"Yeah. Kagra herself has spread the story. Only in her version, I robbed her of vowing it herself."

The truth is that Jade didn't know what had possessed her to offer Phinas a life debt for saving her second-in-command. A simple thank you and a promise to repay the favor would have been enough. Maybe it had been the exhaustion or perhaps the feeling of freedom that had prompted her to be so generous, giving Phinas the most sacred of vows, but she didn't regret doing that. If anyone deserved it from her, it was him.

"I'm glad it was you and not Kagra," Phinas said. "So, would the excuse work?"

She sighed. "I don't know. If my people want me to lead them, they might accept the vow as a viable excuse for my unorthodox behavior. But if anyone wants my position, they will use it as proof that I'm not suitable to be their leader."

"Don't they have to challenge you to a duel to prove their worth?"

"In certain circumstances, yes. In others, no. It depends on what the challenge is based on."

"Perhaps it's something that you should bring up in the big meeting you're planning. There are many changes in your people's future, and it's better to let them know in advance that their mistress will no longer be choosing to procreate with any of them."

She chuckled. "You sound very sure of yourself. I didn't promise you exclusivity yet."

"You don't have to promise me anything. We have bonded, and it will be physically impossible for you to feel attraction toward any other male. In fact, you'll be repulsed by any who attempt to seduce you."

MARCEL

arcel cleaned up the MRI machine with a disinfectant wipe, threw it in the trash bin, and glanced at Merlin, who was looking at the printout of the last patient for the day.

They'd opened the clinic a little later than usual because breakfast had been delayed, but they'd caught up to their planned quota by the end of the day. Nevertheless, it was an easy pace compared to what it had been before Igor was caught.

They were removing the remaining trackers at a slower rate, and work at the clinic had become less hectic, so Sofia wouldn't be as exhausted at the end of the day.

They were both eager to start working on her transition, and now that the ship was safe and there was no one chasing them or threatening them in any way, perhaps they could.

But what if she started transitioning on the ship? Or on the flight back home?

He walked up to Merlin and leaned against his desk. "Can I ask you something?"

"Sure." Merlin lifted his head and looked at him. "What's bothering you?"

"If Sofia and I start working on her transition, and it starts while we are still on the ship, can you take care of her with the equipment you have in the clinic?"

Merlin grinned. "I can, and I will be more than happy to assist her and welcome her to immortality. That being said, she might not transition right away. She might make it to the village beforehand. We have four or five days before we make it back, and some Dormants transition within that time frame, while others take longer."

"What if she starts transitioning but is still not past the first stage when we get to Greenland? How are we going to transport her?"

Merlin gave him a one-shoulder shrug. "The same way injured Guardians are transported. We load her up with the gurney, and I take portable equipment with me to monitor her. It's not as good as the stuff I have here, but it should do. As long as I have the medications she might need on the way, we are good."

That was reassuring. "One last question. What if she starts transitioning on the flight back home? It's a seven-hour flight."

Merlin smiled indulgently. "I can take emergency supplies with me. But if you are so worried, wait until you get back to the village. Another week or so won't make much of a difference."

"True. I will leave it up to Sofia. I just wanted to have all the scenarios covered before I talked with her."

Merlin put the printout into the file and rose to his feet. "Whatever you two decide is fine with me. I'll take out this one last bugger for today and head to the dining hall for dinner."

As Merlin ducked into the surgery room, Marcel stepped out of the clinic and walked over to the recovery room where Sofia worked.

Knocking lightly on the door, he opened it a crack and stuck his head inside. "Do you have a minute?"

"I'm almost done." She leaned over the cloth partition to look at him. "Is Merlin doing another one?"

He nodded. "The last for the day, but he just got started, so you have time for a short break. Do you want me to make you coffee?"

"Yes, please."

As he headed to the snack table and popped a pod into the coffeemaker, Marcel second-guessed his decision to have the conversation in the hallway where everyone could hear them while Sofia was on a short break.

The correct way to do it was to wait until they were in their cabin and discuss it over a glass of wine or, even better, in bed. It was a simple matter of condom or no condom.

Yeah, as if that was romantic.

He needed to go to the storage area and get a good bottle of wine. After dinner, they would head to their cabin, and he would open it and pour Sofia

611

a glass, maybe also offer her a foot massage to put her in a relaxed mood. He should start talking about the transition only when she was in the right mood for such an intimate conversation.

Except, she might want to visit her family or friends, or they might drop by as they had done nearly every evening since boarding the ship.

Perhaps he should start now and suggest that they continue later in their cabin so she would know not to make plans with her father, aunts, cousins or friends.

Marcel loved seeing how happy Sofia was with her extended family and friends, and he was glad she wouldn't have to live without them. But he was also a selfish guy who wanted her all to himself from time to time, or rather all of the time.

"Possessiveness is a personality flaw," he murmured under his breath. "It got you in trouble before."

With all the commotion, Sofia had forgotten about his upcoming meeting with Edna and his impending confession, but he hadn't, and now that the time was getting closer, he was becoming anxious. Hopefully, Edna would not choose entombment as his punishment. Even if it was only for a week, he couldn't stand the thought of being away from Sofia for so long.

Nevertheless, he would do that so he could put the past where it belonged and start a new life with her.

41

SOFIA

Sofia finished bandaging Dugmon and handed him a lollipop. "I found these in the storage. I remember the doctor who came to give us vaccines had those for the kids to make the jabs sweeter. I thought that it was nice of him."

Dugmon took the pop and removed the wrapping. "The hybrid kids didn't get vaccines. We don't get sick."

"Lucky you." She patted his shoulder. "You can remove the bandage in three to four hours. The incision will be healed by then."

He nodded. "Thank you."

"You're welcome."

It was a new trend among the Kra-ell to try being more polite, and Sofia was glad for it. They were preparing to venture into the world and needed to adjust to how most people interacted. They knew from the movies they'd watched that in most cultures grunting or nodding heads was not a substitute for actually saying the words.

She was also becoming more comfortable around the hybrid and the pureblooded males. After Jade's speech, they were all on their best behavior. On the other hand, it could have been Marcel's presence that stopped them from flirting and making suggestive comments.

He might not be as physically strong as them, but he was one of the others, and they still didn't know who and what the others were, so they were being careful.

Stepping outside, she found Marcel sitting on one of the chairs next to the snack table, with a coffee cup in each hand.

"Hello, handsome." She sat down next to him and took the cup he handed her. "Are you done for the day?"

"Yeah. I cleaned the machine and covered it."

She took a sip from the cup and sighed. "You make the best coffee. Just the way I like it."

Marcel grinned. "Of course." He wrapped an arm around her shoulders and leaned to plant a peck on her lips. "It's my job to look after you."

That was so sweet, but he was taking that job too seriously. All she had to do was mention in passing something she needed or wanted, and he would do everything to get it for her.

"Oh yeah? So what's my job? To be looked after?"

"What's wrong with that?"

"Nothing." She leaned over to return the peck on his lips. "I like taking care of you too."

"That's what mated couples do. We take care of each other." His expression sobered. "I talked with Merlin earlier about your transition. He said that he has everything you'll need here in the clinic, meaning that we can start working on it if you like."

She nodded. "You must have read my mind. I was just thinking about that this morning." She lowered her voice and leaned closer. "The danger is gone, so there is no reason to keep using condoms. I will be really glad to feel you without barriers."

Marcel's eyes shone with inner light, and she knew that if he opened his mouth, she would see his fangs elongating.

"I can't wait either." He closed his eyes, and when he opened them, the glow was gone. "On the other hand, one more week won't make much of a difference, and it will be much safer for you to start transitioning in the village. Another bonus is that you will be less anxious. I'm not a doctor, but supposedly humans are healthier when they are not stressed, and you need to be in perfect health for the induction to work."

"I don't know about that. There will be so much to do before we even get there. It hasn't been decided yet where everyone is going, but wherever it is, I will need to help my family settle. On the other hand, if I transition and become immortal even before we end this voyage, it will give people hope that the children of the hybrids can become long-lived like them."

His lips curved in a barely-there smile. "You forget that only the children of the hybrid females can transition, and you are the only one."

"I didn't forget. But things are different for the Kra-ell in so many ways that it could be different in that regard as well. I think we should test it, at least on the male children of the hybrid males, because it's easier and doesn't involve sex."

"Are you hoping that your cousin Helmi can transition?"

"I wish." She sighed. "But Helmi is fully human. Her father is human as well."

"I'm sorry."

"There's nothing to be sorry about. It's just the way it is, and Tomos loves her anyway."

"He's going to outlive her."

"He knows that." Sofia cupped Marcel's cheek. "Do you remember what you said when no one thought I could be anything other than human?"

He nodded. "I said I would take whatever time you could give me."

"That's how Tomos feels."

42

KIAN

$\mathcal{K}$ian entered the large subterranean assembly hall and turned on the lights.

He was so glad Amanda's ostentatious chairs had been left in the keep. When it was time to decide on the theme for the new assembly hall in the village, his instructions to Ingrid had been to make it functional, comfortable, and contemporary.

The result was a little stark and reminded him of an elegant movie theater. Perhaps he shouldn't have built it at all and changed the voting to virtual. In part, it already was, with Sari's people assembling in Scotland and those residing in Annani's sanctuary assembling in Alaska, but old traditions were hard to give up, especially ones that were so fundamental to how the clan governed itself.

There was no substitute for the energy created by the clan physically congregating in one place to vote on important issues. There was something magical about it that couldn't be replicated in a virtual assembly.

Taking one last look, he turned the lights off and continued to the council's conference room. It was much smaller, and the oblong table had been originally designed to accommodate twelve seats, but they could make room for two more. However, if the Kra-ell joined the clan, and in time demanded a seat on the council, he would have to commission a new table.

As if that was the only concern. Perhaps he shouldn't even offer the option to the council's vote. Safe Haven was the best solution for the Kra-ell, at least temporarily, and that was what he would push for.

The door opened, and Shai came in with his laptop tucked under his arm. "Today is the big day." He walked over to the recording station situated in the corner.

"Big day because I'm going to put Kalugal's inclusion up to the vote or because of the Kra-ell?"

"Both." Shai sat down and connected his laptop to the recording equipment.

It wasn't necessary for his assistant to be there for that, and his time would have been better utilized in the office, but it was one more tradition that Kian didn't feel right about ending. Having a person dedicated to recording and archiving formal council meetings added formality and weight to the decision-making process.

When Shai finished his prep, he pushed to his feet and walked over to the bar fridge. "I expect this meeting to be lengthy." He pulled out several bottles of water and brought them to the table.

Kian helped distribute them while Shai went for more. "I don't think so. Kalugal's inclusion in the council will not meet with any objections, and I don't expect much pushback about taking the Kra-ell to Safe Haven. Most of the clan members haven't even visited the place and have no emotional connection to it. They won't mind if we settle the Kra-ell there."

"I assume that you will station Guardians dedicated to keeping an eye on them in Safe Haven."

"Of course."

"In addition to the ones guarding the research?"

Kaia claimed that she didn't need the human bioinformaticians team's assistance and that she could continue deciphering Okidu's journals on her own. Kian didn't have a problem with that. He wasn't in a rush to have the journals translated, and it was safer to keep the work in the village. The fewer people who had access to it, the better.

"The Fates provided us with the best in-house bioinformatician, so I don't think I will continue the research in Safe Haven. But since we made such a huge investment in building the facility, I might use it for something else. I just don't know what yet."

Shai shrugged. "It can be our escape contingency. If we need to evacuate the village for some reason, we will have a second command center ready."

"The place is already set up with incredible security measures. They will just need some tweaking for the Kra-ell because they are designed to keep undesirables out and not to keep people from leaving Safe Haven."

Shai tilted his head. "Are you planning to keep them imprisoned there?"

"Imprisoned is a harsh word. I prefer contained. It will not be much different from how they lived before."

Given his sour expression, Shai didn't like his answer. "What are you going to do with the human students that are still in the universities and don't know what happened to their families?"

The truth was that Kian had forgotten about them, but the plan had been to wait until the Kra-ell future was settled before contacting them and bringing them in. It wasn't as if they could be notified over the phone. Someone had to go and personally pick them up one by one.

Kian pulled out a chair at the head of the table and sat down. "We will address the issue once we have the Kra-ell settled. We will have to send people to collect them."

"And do what? Throw them into the same confined area as the rest of their families? What if they want to continue their studies?"

That was a good point, but it wasn't like Shai to be so contrary. "What do you suggest we do?"

"First of all, they need to know that their families are okay and that they shouldn't go back to the compound. Yamanu can have a couple of Guardians loan their family members their phones and provide them a script that will not get flagged by Echelon or any other systems listening in on calls. Then we need to establish a protocol similar to what Igor has done. The students will come to visit, get their compulsion reinforced, and go back to continue their studies."

Kian groaned. "I hate that I'm being put in a position where I have to continue Igor's methods, and I don't see how I can do things differently without risking our people."

Shai cracked a smile. "There is one more option. Find Jade a place that's not anywhere near us and give her complete autonomy over her people. She did well without having to resort to compulsion. Vows were enough to keep her people obedient."

"That's the power of religion." Kian leaned back in the chair. "The problem is that once religion is abandoned, it's very difficult to bring it back and use it to control people. It's not going to work for Jade with the young generation of Kra-ell who were born in the compound under Igor's rule. Religion can be replaced with ideology, but it takes a lot of time and concentrated effort until it takes root deep enough to compel blind adherence."

"That's true."

When Bridget walked in, Shai rose to his feet. "Good afternoon, doctor."

"Good afternoon." She pulled a chair next to Kian and pulled out her tablet. "Where is everyone?"

"On their way. You are a little early."

They didn't have assigned places around the conference table, but Bridget was usually one of the first to arrive, so she often sat next to him. Edna would probably arrive next and take the seat to his right.

Pushing a thick lock of her flaming red hair behind her ear, she glanced at the door. "How is Kalugal? Is he nervous about addressing the council?"

"If he is, he didn't confide in me. But knowing my cousin, he's assuming that it's just a formality and the seats are his."

"He isn't wrong. With you recommending him, I don't see any council members opposing his inclusion."

"I hope that if they do approve, it is because they believe that it's a good move for the clan. I need to know that I can depend on the council to stop me when I make a wrong decision."

43

KALUGAL

*K*alugal nodded and smiled until his face hurt, and he did his best to conduct lively conversations to charm the council members until the session officially began and his case was brought up for a vote.

Except for Amanda all the council members were already there, either in person or via teleconference with the *Aurora*, but they couldn't start until she arrived.

Kalugal had known that the head Guardians were part of the council, but he'd thought that they only voted on security issues. Perhaps he was still considered a security risk and that was why the six had been included?

He was on friendly terms with Yamanu, Bhathian, Anandur, and Brundar. However, Arwel might still hold a grudge against him, and Kri was an unknown factor.

Out of the core council members the one he didn't know well was Brandon, the media specialist. Edna would vote in his favor, and so would Amanda. William and Bridget were a good bet but not a sure thing, and Onegus was a maybe.

Kian cast Kalugal an apologetic glance. "Amanda is always late. I should have asked Shai to tell her that the meeting was fifteen minutes earlier so maybe she would have gotten here on time."

"That's fine." Kalugal twisted the cap off his water bottle and took a sip.

"It looks like no one is overly upset about the delay. They must have expected it."

The council members were discussing the Kra-ell situation and debating the different options for their resettlement. It seemed that Kian hadn't been secretive about what he was going to suggest, and they all knew what was on the table. Perhaps Amanda's tardiness was a good thing, allowing them to debate the issue unofficially and get a feel for what the others were thinking.

As for himself, Kalugal's only misgiving was his choice of attire.

Expecting an official council meeting, he'd put on a nice conservative suit, but he was the only one wearing a tie and a jacket. Even the dapper Brandon was dressed in a pair of gray slacks and a black cashmere turtleneck. He'd arrived with a smart black leather jacket on, but it was now draped on the back of his chair.

Was wearing leather still okay in Hollywood? Or was the jacket made from vegan leather?

It looked real enough.

Onegus and Kian were dressed similarly in slacks and sweaters, and William had a thin colorful shirt on and slacks that didn't match it. Bhathian, Anandur, and Brundar were all in jeans, T-shirts, and leather jackets.

Theirs were no doubt the real thing.

Kalugal wondered whether Kian's shoes and belt were leather. The guy was vegan, so it would have made sense for him to avoid real leather. But it was hypocritical for all the meat-eaters to avoid it on moral grounds.

Amanda walked through the open door with a coffee cup. "Sorry I'm late. I would have brought all of you coffee, but I was already running late, and Kian would have been upset." She slanted him a look.

He shook his head at her and pushed to his feet.

"We have two items on the agenda today. One is the expansion of the council from twelve members to fourteen, with the two additional seats going to Kalugal and another representative from his section of the village. The second item on our agenda is the Kra-ell relocation and choosing the best option for the clan."

Amanda lifted her hand. "Shouldn't it be the best option for the Kra-ell?"

"Our responsibility is first and foremost to the clan. We will discuss the various options and choose the one or perhaps two that best serve our interests. We will let the Kra-ell choose from the options we agree are beneficial to the clan."

It was a good answer, and Kalugal approved. Should he give Kian a nod?

Inconspicuously glancing at the other council members, he saw some nod in approval and added his nod as well.

Kian turned to him. "I'll let Kalugal present his case, and then you will vote twice. Once for a seat for him, and the second time for the additional seat he's requesting."

Sneaky bastard.

Kian hadn't told him there would be two separate votes, and he hadn't prepared two separate pitches, but he could improvise. In days past he could have relied on his compulsion ability to sway people's minds in favorable ways, but he reminded himself that he didn't need compulsion to win people over. He was charming, smart, and likable.

Rising to his feet, Kalugal offered Kian his hand. "Thank you for allowing me to present my case to the council."

"You're welcome." Kian shook his hand briefly before sitting back down.

Kalugal smiled at the council members assembled around the table and the two participating via tablet, making brief eye contact with each person before moving to the next.

"I know you are all busy, and I promise not to take long."

"Take as long as you need," Bridget said.

Did that mean she wasn't in favor? The female was hard to read, but she'd been very helpful with Jacki's transition and pregnancy and then delivering Darius. She'd also been very patient, answering their numerous questions and assuaging their concerns.

Kalugal nodded and then turned to address the council members as a group. "It has been a year since my people and I moved into the village, and both sides were suspicious at first. We didn't know whether we could trust each other, and many clan members resented the inclusion of former Doomers in their community." He smiled. "Especially the males. The ladies were more welcoming."

That got him a few smiles and a couple of chuckles.

He continued, "Over time, things got better, mutual trust grew, and the culmination of our integration into the clan was the joined mission to save the Kra-ell from their oppressor. My men worked seamlessly with the Guardians to bring this mission to its successful conclusion, and I joined Kian, Turner, and Onegus in the war room. I admit that my military skills are rusty, and my contribution was limited, but I was honored to be included in the decision-making. It was an excellent litmus test, and we all passed it with flying colors."

He clapped his hands, and the others joined but without much enthusiasm. Perhaps he wasn't communicating what he felt in the right way, and he needed to come up with a more personal angle.

"Jacki and I feel blessed to have such a thriving and supportive community to raise our son in, and we can't imagine ourselves living elsewhere. My men are happy here as well. I didn't run a survey, asking each of them individually how they felt about life in the village, but I didn't have to. If anyone was unhappy, they would have voiced their displeasure. But I haven't heard any dissatisfied comments or even reminiscing about the days before we moved into the village. The bottom line is that we are here to stay, and the next step in our full integration into the clan is fair representation in the council. Given the number of my people relative to the number of clan members in the village, we should be awarded two and a half seats, but since Darius can't speak yet, I can't ask for the half seat to be given to him, so I'm asking only for two."

It was a lame joke, but it was cute, and he got some smiles.

Amanda chuckled. "He'll be sitting on this council before you know it."

Kalugal shrugged. "Perhaps he won't be interested in politics or a leadership position. He might choose to be an artist."

"Will you be okay with that?" Edna asked.

"I will be proud of my son no matter what path he chooses, as long as he's passionate about it and works hard to excel at it."

44

KIAN

*K*ian clapped his hands. "Well said, cousin."

Hopefully Kalugal had meant it, and it hadn't been a ploy to win over the council members. If it was, the guy had much better people skills than Kian and an awareness of what would convince them.

"Thank you." Kalugal dipped his head. "We all want our children to be happy and fulfilled, and we can't expect them to be replicas of us."

"Well said again. I will be proud of my Allegra no matter what path she chooses, but given her personality, she will want to lead. She is very much like her daddy."

Well, she was much more than that, but he wasn't going to spend the next hour telling everyone why his daughter was the pinnacle of creation and that there would never be another child born to the clan more suitable to lead it. Well, unless Syssi and he were blessed with another child, but he doubted that anyone could ever outshine Allegra. Even his mother said she was unique, and Annani didn't say things like that lightly.

She wasn't the type of grandmother who waxed poetic about her grandchildren.

Rising to his feet, he smiled at Kalugal. "Do you want to stay for the vote? Or do you prefer to wait outside?"

There was no doubt in Kian's mind about what option Kalugal would choose.

"I'll stay."

"Of course." He turned to the assembled council members. "Kalugal is asking for two seats. Let's vote first on one seat, and if that's approved, we will vote on the second." When everyone nodded their agreement, he continued. "All in favor of Kalugal joining the council as its thirteenth member, raise your hands."

Kian raised his and was soon followed by the others. Brandon was the last one to raise his hand, and he seemed to raise it only because everyone else had done so.

He would have to talk to the media specialist later and ask him about his reservations regarding Kalugal's seat on the council.

Turning to Kalugal, Kian offered him his hand. "Congratulations, cousin, and welcome to the council."

"Thank you." Kalugal shook his hand while smiling at the other council members. "Thank you all for your welcome and your vote of confidence. I promise to do my duty and attend all future meetings."

After he and Kalugal had sat back down, Kian turned to his people. "Now, let's vote on the second seat. All in favor, raise your hands."

Kian lifted his, but only four other hands joined him this time. Edna, Onegus, Yamanu, and Bhathian.

Those who voted in favor had been exposed to Kalugal and his men lately and had first-hand experience working with them. That included William, though, but for some reason, he wasn't in favor of granting them one more seat.

"You can put your hands down." Kian turned to Bridget. "I respect your decision, and I'm not going to try to convince you to change your mind, but just out of curiosity. Why are you opposed to granting Kalugal another seat?"

She turned her gaze to Kalugal. "I have nothing against you or your men. You've all proven yourself as a good fit for our community. But I don't like rushing into things. I suggest doing this in two stages. First, you join the council, and if that works out well, we will reconvene in one year and vote on adding one more seat."

Kalugal nodded graciously. "That's reasonable. Perhaps it will give me time and better insight into who I want to award the seat to. I can't decide between Rufsur and Phinas, so I was thinking about dividing it between them, with one serving half a year and the other the other half."

Lifting a brow, Bridget glanced at Edna. "Is that even allowed?"

"I'm not sure. I'll have to check the records." She looked at Kian. "Do you remember a time when that was done?"

He shook his head. "Never, but I don't see why that would be a problem. When the time comes to award Kalugal another seat, we can vote on that as well. Let's move to the next item on the agenda, and that's what to do with the Kra-ell."

"What are the options?" Edna asked. "I've heard that the village is one and Safe Haven is another. Are there more?"

Anandur lifted his hand. "What about returning them to their compound? Why was that idea scrapped?"

Kian hadn't fully discarded it yet, and the truth was that he preferred a solution that didn't involve keeping an eye on them on the other side of the globe and allocating Guardians from the clan's small force to the task. There was a big difference between having people stationed at Safe Haven, which was only two hours away by plane and another hour by car, than in Karelia, which was more than a day's travel away, and in a foreign country that wasn't on friendly terms with the US.

"Jade prefers to have a fresh start, and we prefer to have them where we can watch them. I don't need to tell you what the dangers of rogue aliens roaming free are. If they are discovered, a global hunt will start, and we will be dealing with a heightened risk we can all do without. Besides, these Kra-ell represent a fraction of everyone that was on that ship. The others might be dead or still in their stasis pods, and leaving them where they are represents the same danger. If any of those pods are discovered, it wouldn't matter whether their occupants are dead or alive. A hunt would ensue, and we must do everything we can to prevent that."

"How are we going to find them?" William asked. "The trackers don't transmit unless the bodies hosting them are alive."

"I don't know yet," Kian admitted. "But now that we have Igor in our hands, I hope to find out how he located the pods of those who were awake and why it took him nearly a century to go after them."

45

YAMANU

$\mathcal{I}$t was the first time Kian had mentioned his interest in finding the other pods, and Yamanu wondered what Turner's take on that was. Perhaps he had been the one who had brought it to Kian's attention?

So far, none of them had considered the possibility that the pods could be discovered by humans. After all, if they hadn't been found by now, they probably never would be.

Most likely, they had landed in the ocean where they would stay unless someone actively looked for them and tried to fish them out. But to do that, they would need a signal or some kind of unique emission to guide them toward the pods.

As far as he knew, satellites could only see up to a depth of thirty feet, while the average depth of oceans was about twelve thousand feet. Good luck finding anything that had sunk to the bottom.

But that wasn't a discussion for the council to have, and he felt odd about discussing the future of the Kra-ell without Turner and Toven present.

So what if they didn't have seats on the council?

Kian should have invited them to join the meeting as temporary councilmen or advisors. By now, they knew much more about the Kra-ell situation than most of the council members, including Anandur, Brundar, and Kri, who'd probably gotten updates from Onegus. But since they hadn't been part of the mission, they hadn't interacted with the Kra-ell.

"I don't know why it has taken Igor so long to go after the settlers he could find," Onegus said. "Perhaps the idea to do so didn't occur to him before. He might have been busy building his stronghold and accumulating wealth and influence. He might have even tried breeding with human females and found them either lacking or their offspring even more so since they couldn't produce hybrid Kra-ell children. Then he got the brilliant idea to obtain more Kra-ell females by finding the other pods and killing their males."

Kian nodded. "That's possible. Hopefully, we will know more when Toven arrives in Greenland and gets him to talk."

Bhathian crossed his massive arms over his even more massive chest. "Make sure that Toven doesn't approach him without his earpieces. It would be really bad if Igor is the stronger compeller and takes control of Toven."

As the discussion veered toward the safety precautions that everyone dealing with Igor should take, Yamanu glanced at Arwel, who hadn't said a word so far. The guy either didn't have anything to add on the subject or was preoccupied with shielding his mind from the emotions of all the humans on board.

Yamanu loved the guy, but he would have preferred to have Toven there or even Phinas.

"Has anyone considered the campground?" Kri asked. "It's not big enough to house over three hundred people as it is, but we can get more mobile homes in there. It has an excellent security system, and the greenery surrounding it has grown dense enough to hide what's happening inside. Not having to travel far will make it easy on the Guardian force."

"We considered that," Kian said. "But only as a temporary solution until a permanent one can be found. We can't build homes there, and we can't expect the Kra-ell and the humans to live in mobile homes forever. Besides, we can't fit enough of those in the area we have to house them comfortably."

"Why not?" Kri shifted to face Kian. "Many humans live in mobile homes, and from what I've heard, the living conditions they had in Karelia were very basic. Their expectations are probably modest."

Kian shook his head. "As I said, it can barely function as a temporary solution, and it would take a major effort to get so many additional mobile homes there on short notice. Right now, we don't even have enough connections to water and sewage facilities."

"At least give them the option," Kri insisted. "From what I heard so far about Jade, she will not want to be under anyone's jurisdiction, which would be the case in the village and in Safe Haven. The campground is the only place we can offer her that can belong exclusively to their group."

Letting out a breath, Kian nodded. "I'll offer it as one of the options. Our mountain cabin area was also suggested, but it has no infrastructure, and it will be difficult to conceal such a large population there. My first choice is Safe Haven." He lifted his hand to stop further discussion. "Who's in favor?"

Yamanu lifted his hand, but Arwel didn't. In the conference room, five more hands joined Kian's.

"Good. We have enough votes for that. Who is in favor of offering the Kra-ell the option of joining our village?"

Yamanu wasn't sure he wanted that, and when Arwel lifted his hand, he arched a brow at his friend.

Arwel shrugged. "They don't emit many emotions, which means that they don't bother me, and they are strong warriors. I wouldn't mind having them fight by our side in case Navuh finds us and decides to attack in force. Kian said that we need to think about what's best for the clan, and I believe that together with them, we will be stronger. Also, let's not forget the other pods, which I assume we will start actively seeking once we get Igor to reveal how he found the ones he did. For obvious reasons, we will need the Kra-ell to join the effort."

Kian nodded. "Those are excellent points." He lifted his hand. "Who's in favor?"

Yamanu joined him, and so did four more council members. Brandon, Anandur, Brundar, and Kri didn't.

"Good," Kian said. "I can offer them this option as well. Is there a point to voting on the less desirable options?"

Edna lifted her hand. "We should vote on them in case Kri is right, and Jade doesn't accept the two we think are best. As I see it, we have the option of using the mobile site or the cabin area as a temporary solution and an entirely different location as a permanent solution. The Kra-ell have sufficient funds to purchase a gated community if they please, and as long as it's not too far away for our Guardians to monitor and William outfits it with proper security measures, it could be a viable solution that Jade would prefer."

Kian nodded. "Very well. Let's put that to a vote as well."

46

JADE

*J*ade listened with half an ear to Kian's explanations about the advantages and disadvantages of each of the options his council had approved.

She should have paid more attention, but with Phinas's words from earlier that morning running on repeat in her head, it was difficult to concentrate.

You don't have to promise me anything. We have bonded, and it will be physically impossible for you to feel attraction toward any other male. In fact, you'll be repulsed by any who attempt to seduce you.

She'd returned the phone to Merlin and hadn't asked for it again. If Phinas had wanted to talk to her, he knew how to reach her, but evidently he wanted her to ponder them without putting more pressure on her, which she appreciated. But with that song playing in the background, it had been difficult to concentrate on anything else, including the list of options she'd just been given.

"Thank you for the invitation to join your village and for the other offers, but I can't give you an answer before I run them by my people."

She should have written them down.

Kian nodded. "Of course. Take your time and discuss it with your people, all three groups, but I need an answer no later than this evening. I need time to make all the necessary arrangements so whatever option you choose, it will be ready for you. You can also choose a combination of the

630

options. The humans can settle in one place while the purebloods and hybrids settle in another. I suspect the humans will be most comfortable in Safe Haven. They can join the community that's already there and work in the lodge. Emmett and his mate can ensure that they keep your existence secret, and it will also solve the problem of their community obtaining new genetic material. They will be free to find partners among the community members and visitors to the retreats."

Jade had to admit that it was the best solution for the humans. They would be taken care of and protected in a supportive environment, and they would enjoy some freedom without being overwhelmed by it.

"I agree, and that's why I think Safe Haven is a good option for us as well. We need humans to breed with. Without them, we will go extinct."

"You can also decide to go back to your old compound. It's not an option I prefer, but we can make it work."

Obviously, Kian had no intention of just letting them go, and Jade understood his reasons perfectly well. But his reasons were not hers, and she needed to choose what was best for her people.

Jade nodded. "I don't think anyone wants to go back, but I'll bring up this option as well."

"You have a lot to think about and not much time. I suggest that you assemble your people as soon as possible and discuss the options with them."

She sighed. "No pressure."

"One more thing before I go." She glanced at Toven and Yamanu before shifting her eyes back to Kian. "I can't present the options to my people without telling them the truth about who their rescuers are."

Other than her, Kagra, and Sofia, no one knew that their rescuers were not human. Valstar had guessed who Toven was, but he had no contact with the others, so he couldn't tell them. Besides, he'd only guessed the god's identity. He didn't know that the others were the immortal descendants of the gods.

"If they choose Safe Haven or one of the other options, it's not necessary to tell them about us, but if they decide to join the village, they need to know who their new neighbors are."

She cracked a smile. "I can't present them with the village option without telling them who its current residents are."

"That's true." Kian turned his eyes to Toven. "Once they decide where they want to settle, and if it's not the village, can you erase the humans' and hybrids' memories and compel the purebloods to secrecy?"

Toven nodded. "The humans will be easy, the hybrids manageable, and the purebloods a pain in the rear, but Mia and I can do that."

"Excellent. Let me know as soon as the decision is made."

"I will." Jade dipped her head. "Thank you again. I know that you are looking after your own people's interests, but I also know that you genuinely care about mine, and I'm grateful."

"You're welcome. Good day, Jade." Kian terminated the call.

"I should go." Jade pushed to her feet and turned to the beautiful god and almost equally beautiful immortal. "Do either of you have some sage words of advice for me?"

Both Toven and Yamanu were perfect male specimens, and yet she felt not a lick of attraction for either of them.

Was Phinas right, and it was the bond's doing? Would she be repulsed if a male approached her?

The Kra-ell knew better than to initiate anything with her, and the immortals knew about her and Phinas, so none of them even looked at her with covetous eyes. As for her, she'd been asking herself the same question throughout the day, examining her feelings toward the males she'd interacted with. Apart from annoyance, none stirred even one nerve in her, but then she hadn't been interested in anyone since the massacre of her tribe. She'd had no choice but to tolerate Igor, but thankfully she wasn't the only female he used to satisfy his urges, and he'd called upon her mainly in her fertile cycle.

Hating to even think about it, she quickly shoved the thought deep into the crevice in her mind along with all the other things she couldn't deal with.

Turning her thoughts to Phinas and the passion they had shared helped clear her head, and as she smiled at the memories, she realized that he was the only male to stir her passion and make her feel alive in over two decades.

47

TOVEN

"Do you want me to come with you?" Toven asked. "Your people might not believe you, and I can provide proof."

Jade shook her head. "It's not going to be difficult to convince them. Many probably already suspect who you are as it is. The only reason no one has challenged you is that I pretended you were just a paranormally talented human, and they took my word for it." She smiled sadly. "I have a reputation for being honest and direct, which will be tarnished once I admit to hiding the truth from them."

"You had no choice," Yamanu said. "We forced you to do it, literally. Toven compelled you, and they know it's impossible to fight compulsion."

"I hope that will be enough. What about the various options? Which one do you think I should take?"

"Safe Haven," Yamanu said. "It's headed by Emmett, who is one of yours, and the humans will be comfortable there because the resort is run by a community of humans. They adhere to a free-love philosophy, probably due to Emmett's influence, but they are very accepting of others, and they rarely leave the place, so keeping them from talking about the aliens living among them will not be a problem."

"Is that so?" Jade turned to Toven. "What do you think? Is Safe Haven as good as it sounds?"

"I vote for the village," Toven said.

He hadn't consciously arrived at that conclusion up until that moment. Perhaps the many suggestions had had to marinate for a while in his subconscious before his mind could spit up the correct answer, but now that it had, Toven had no doubt that it was the way to go.

Yamanu regarded him with a puzzled expression. "What makes you say that?"

"In the long run, it's the best option." Toven looked into Jade's huge eyes. "You can stay in Safe Haven until the village is ready to receive you, but once it is, leave the humans and some of the hybrids who can pass for humans there. You don't need them for breeding. Your people can mate with clan members and produce long-lived or immortal offspring. Not only that, you are proof that the Kra-ell beliefs about love and relationships are wrong, or rather misguided. If you and Phinas could bond, so could others."

Jade's eyes became even bigger. "How do you know that Phinas and I have bonded?"

He smiled. "You were so desperate to call him this morning that you practically begged us for a phone that you could use in private. Other than the obsession that comes with a new bond, I can't imagine anything capable of reducing the formidable Jade to begging."

Glaring at him, she crossed her arms over her chest. "I didn't beg. I asked. Phinas and I enjoy each other's company, that's all. It doesn't make sense that we somehow bonded despite it not being possible for Kra-ell. Even among the gods, bonding between mates was rare. Most of them had multiple partners same as my people, with the only difference being that they had one official mate and scores of paramours, while my people made having multiple partners official. Our way is more honest."

"You've just proven what I was trying to say. The gods and the Kra-ell are not fundamentally different. Both have the ability to bond with one person or to have non-committed relationships with several. It's the same for humans. Some are committed to one person for life, others never feel bound by their commitment, and some cultures still condone and even encourage males to take several wives. A small minority enjoys polyamorous relationships as a personal choice."

Jade looked down her nose at him. "The Kra-ell are committed to the tribe instead of committing to one person. The tribe unit is like a group marriage. The males vow their loyalty to their mistress or mistresses, but it's more about their commitment to the tribe than about their personal relationship with the female or females heading their tribe. The human equivalent would be a harem, but I don't like using the term because it implies sexual subjugation and exploitation, and that's untrue of our tribal system."

"No, it's not." Toven smiled indulgently. "The Kra-ell religion established rules of conduct that made it seem like a fair system, and I respect that. Whoever came up with that solution was brilliant. I just don't understand why the gods didn't do anything to help your people. With their genetic manipulation mastery, they should have been able to even out the gender disparity."

"Maybe they did." Jade smiled evilly. "Maybe the legends are right, and the gods were originally the same as the Kra-ell, but they found a way to change their genetics. The bond between mates might have been one of their modifications."

The addiction between exclusive mates had been most likely genetically created, but the bond between fated mates couldn't have been.

"A genetic manipulation would have affected everyone, and it wouldn't have left finding one's truelove to chance. The gods didn't engineer each person individually but rather introduced global enhancements that changed everyone. If they could have created the bonding mechanisms artificially, they would have done it for everyone. In my opinion, the ability to bond to one special person is innate and predates all genetic manipulations. Therefore, both the gods and the Kra-ell are capable of it."

For a long moment Jade just stared at him, and he thought that he'd managed to convince her, but then she shook her head. "If it was possible for the Kra-ell, some must have found that one special person and the bond was formed. Since the bond prevents the lovers from having any other partners, it would have been difficult to hide."

She made a good point, and he didn't have an answer. "Perhaps it is even rarer for the Kra-ell than for the gods, and you are one of the lucky ones."

"Lucky." She snorted. "More like cursed."

At least she was no longer denying it.

Jade swallowed audibly and plopped on the couch. "Why me? Why do I need to be the odd one who bonds with an immortal?"

"Fate." Toven sat next to her and patted her shoulder, remembering too late that Jade didn't like casual touching. Thankfully she was too distraught to notice, and he continued, "Your people look up to you, and that's why the Fates chose you to be the first, the trailblazer so to speak. Once your people see that it's possible, they will open their hearts to the possibility of finding love and companionship with a single partner."

"We can't." Jade groaned. "There aren't enough females for all the males, and it's unfair to them. Even if the tribe system was only invented to solve this problem and was not innate to our people, it was the best solution, and it still is as long as four males are born to every female."

Toven shook his head. "I'm not a geneticist, but my father was a scientist, and he taught me to think scientifically. The gender disparity probably started as a mutation, and the social system that was established to solve the problem propagated it instead of solving it."

"How?" Yamanu asked. "I mean, what could have caused the original mutation, and how could it have corrected itself if they had developed a different social system? Evolution takes a very long time."

"The Kra-ell are an ancient race, by order of magnitude older than humans. Evolution had enough time to adjust their biology to their way of life." Toven paused to collect his thoughts. "All I'm saying is speculation because I don't know how it really happened. But here is a plausible scenario. The gender disparity created the tribal system and the taboo on forming couple relationships. The same system also encouraged the males to fight and kill each other off to cull their numbers and to promote the survival of the fittest. I wouldn't be surprised if the incredible physical strength is the result of hundreds of thousands of generations allowing only the strongest males to father offspring. The system worked, and it was reinforced by their religion, so no one challenged it. Because of the culling, there weren't four males competing for every female, but maybe just two, which was more manageable. Then a forward-thinking, progressive queen came to power and sought to end the bloodshed. She disallowed tribal wars and duels to the death, inadvertently upending a system that had prevented their society from falling apart and bringing about the unrest that ended up in a rebellion."

"That's not what happened." Jade shook her head vehemently. "The rebellion wasn't the result of an overpopulation of males. The unrest resulted from the gods exploiting the Kra-ell, and the rebellion was against the gods, not against their own queen. It also didn't happen all at once. I told you the history of the conflict. It spanned many generations and many queens."

Toven had given it a lot of thought, and even though he didn't doubt that there was some truth to the claim, he'd lived through enough to know that history was more of a fable than a record of actual events.

"You know that history is not reliable and that it's either entirely fabricated or twisted to portray one faction as virtuous and the other as villainous, depending on who's writing it. When the unrest started, the original queen might have resorted to a tactic that was successfully used by many rulers throughout history. She blamed others for what ailed her people and diverted their anger elsewhere, and her successors followed in her footsteps."

48

JADE

*J*ade stood in the back of the dining hall, watching her people taking seats around the tables. The humans no longer looked at her with fear in their eyes, for which she gave herself a pat on the back, the hybrids looked at her with respect, which was surprising since she hadn't made any effort to earn it, and the purebloods regarded her with wariness, which she didn't understand either.

Since taking command of their community, she hadn't acted with the arrogance she'd wielded like a weapon during her days of glory in her own compound, and she'd tried to be attuned to their concerns.

The young ones didn't know what to expect, and the old ones were probably dealing with years of suppressed grief that had finally been allowed to surface when Toven had freed them from Igor's compulsion.

Igor hadn't been able to compel her to ignore her own grief, and it had always been there, manifesting mostly as anger and a need for revenge. She needed to deal with it properly, but she didn't have the luxury of doing it now or in the near future.

She had people to lead, Igor to kill, and a clan of immortals to negotiate terms with.

Breakfast was long over, the dining hall had been cleaned and prepared for the meeting, and Kagra, Drova, and Pavel were in charge of corralling everyone to attend. The problem was that Jade still didn't have a speech ready despite trying to write one late into the night.

Her mind had kept wandering to what Toven had told her, and it was still doing that even though she'd run out of time and would have to improvise the most important speech of her career as a leader.

Toven was an old and smart god, and she couldn't dismiss his speculations as groundless or fanciful because she'd entertained similar thoughts, just not as well formulated and thought out. But then, she wasn't a scientist, and her thinking process was based on her military and business experience.

Toven might have twisted things to fit his agenda, and since he was smart, he could do that quite convincingly. But why would he?

She could see the mutual benefits of coexisting with the immortals, but she also imagined that incorporating a large group of purebloods into their small community would make many of them unhappy.

Was it about the money?

Her people wouldn't come as paupers who would strain the clan's resources. They were like a rich bride with a hefty dowry. She might not be as beautiful or charming as the groom would have hoped, but he still wanted her because of what she could bring to the marriage.

Kian had made it sound as if the immortals were mostly interested in the added military strength the Kra-ell would bring to their village, but since the clan wasn't in any imminent danger from their enemies, that couldn't be the main motivation behind the invitation.

Still, Toven had sounded sincere when he speculated about the Kra-ell and the gods being more similar than not, and that the Kra-ell could form bonds with one special person the same as the gods.

Jade doubted that her people were ready to hear that the tribal family unit had been a solution to a problem and not innate to their species. Then again, with Igor doing away with their religion and traditions, perhaps it would be easier to convince them of that than it would have been before they had experienced his version of Kra-ell patriarchy.

There was so much she needed to tell her people that it was difficult to decide where to start. Perhaps she should open with telling them who their rescuers were.

Should she admit her feelings for Phinas?

Nah, that would immediately disqualify her as their leader, and someone else would be chosen. She wouldn't have minded if there was anyone capable of leading them at this turning point in their lives, but she knew every person, and there was no one she would entrust with the future of their people.

Perhaps she could present it as a case study. As their leader, she had taken it upon herself to test the possibility of inter-species mating, and so far, the results had exceeded expectations. She could tell them about Vrog's son with an immortal female and how everyone said he was an exceptional young male.

What did they mean by exceptional, though? Was he a strong warrior? Handsome? Charming? She should have asked Toven and Yamanu about him, but it was too late now. She would have to improvise.

Kagra walked up to her. "Everyone is here except the six dancers."

Jade's lips twitched with a smile. Ever since the dance they had performed, their collective name was changed from Igor's cronies to the dancers.

"Did you do a head count?" Jade asked.

"Not yet. I'll do it right now."

"Make sure that all the humans are here too."

"Of course."

Jade still had to deal with the six, though, as well as with Valstar. She'd promised Toven to think about letting Igor's second stand trial. Toven insisted that she needed to give Valstar a chance to explain himself, but she was reluctant to do so.

The male was smart and a master manipulator. He might be able to lie despite Toven's compulsion by making himself believe in his own lies. It wasn't even that difficult to do. No one thought of themselves as evil, probably not even Igor, and convincing himself that he'd been a victim shouldn't be a problem for him.

"Everyone is here," Kagra said. "Are you ready to start?"

Jade swept her gaze over the faces of her people, noting the expectant expressions on some, the tight-lipped on others, the fearful and the hopeful.

"I am. Please close the doors and make sure that no one leaves before I'm done."

"Yes, ma'am."

49

PHINAS

" He doesn't look good." Phinas lifted Igor's hand and checked his pulse. "Maybe the solution you're feeding him is not suitable for Kra-ell?"

His skin color was grayish and looked dry, and his fingertips were an even darker shade of gray.

Aiden shrugged. "I'm doing precisely what Merlin told me to do. Besides, what do you care if he dies? He's a dead man anyway."

"His death belongs to Jade. I promised to deliver him alive with a red bow tied around his neck to mark the spot for her sword."

Aiden's lips curled in a smile. "You've really got it bad for her, don't you?"

There was no point in trying to deny it or make light of what he was feeling for Jade. He didn't care if others thought he was insane for falling for the Kra-ell leader or if they pitied him for fate pairing him with the wrong female.

She might not be ready to admit that they had bonded, but he was going to tell that to anyone who cared to listen.

"She's my truelove mate, and we've bonded, but she refuses to accept it."

"Wow." Aiden lifted his hands and smoothed his long bangs back with both. "Just thinking how complicated this must be for you gives me a headache."

"It's not complicated at all."

"If you say so." Aiden dropped his hands down and pulled out his phone.

"I'll send a picture of him to Merlin. Maybe Igor needs a blood transfusion instead of the nutrients in a regular IV drip."

"I'm not giving him any of mine." Phinas clapped Aiden on the back and stepped out of the room.

"Where are you going?" Max asked as he passed by his open door.

"For a walk."

"Do you want company?"

"No, thanks. I need time to think."

The Guardian lifted his hand with a thumbs up. "Good luck."

"With what?"

"Not with what, but with whom. Jade, of course. You were moping about like a lovesick puppy the whole day yesterday."

Max was a good guy, but he was a lot to handle. He was like the nosy girlfriend in movies who was too nice to get mad at but also too annoying to tolerate for more than a few minutes.

Dudes were supposed to mind their own business and only offer advice if asked. If they wanted to help, the most they should offer was a drink.

"See you later." Phinas lifted his coat collar and opened the outside door. "Damn, it's cold out here."

It wasn't just the northern latitude or the time of year. The rain had finally stopped after two days of constant deluge, and now only the wind remained, chilling him to the bone.

Then again, the chill was coming from the inside as well as from the outside.

The realization that he had found his truelove mate should make him feel elated. Instead, he had a sinking feeling that he'd blown it with Jade. He'd thought they'd made progress, and she'd accepted that they had bonded, but then she hadn't called him the entire day.

He could have called, but he'd wanted to give her time to process what had been said between them, and apparently, she had decided to distance herself from him.

It wasn't that he doubted she wanted him. It was that Jade always put her people first, and if she got it in her head that they would not accept her choice of an exclusive relationship with a male who wasn't a pureblood or even a hybrid, she would give him up in a heartbeat.

On the one hand, her self-sacrificing attitude was admirable, but on the other hand, it was irritating because it was uncalled for. Her people were lucky to have her as their leader, and if they couldn't see that, they didn't deserve her. She shouldn't give up her own happiness for theirs.

With a groan, he pulled his phone out of his pocket, yanked his glove off his hand, and called Mey.

"Hello, Phinas," she answered with a cheerful tone. "How are things in Greenland?"

"Boring. I'm in charge of keeping four unconscious Kra-ell from dying just so Jade can kill them at her leisure. Am I the best boyfriend ever, or what?"

Mey laughed. "To each her own. I'm sure Jade appreciates your dedication."

"I wish. Can I bother you once again with finding her? I need to talk to her."

"It's not a bother, but right now is not a good time. She's in the middle of a meeting with her people to discuss their settlement options. Kian wants an answer as soon as possible, so it needs to be decided today."

It shouldn't feel like a kick to the gut that she hadn't called to ask his advice. After all, he'd already given her his opinion on the various options. And yet he knew he would have called her if the situation was reversed.

"Can you do me a favor and ask her to call me once the meeting is over?"

"Sure thing. I expect that she will tell either Yamanu or Toven what was decided, and I'll ask both to tell her to come to see me."

"Thank you. I appreciate it."

"Anytime. I'm happy to help. "

50

JADE

*J*ade lifted her hand to get everyone to hush.

"As you all know, Igor was captured and taken to Greenland to await our arrival. I'm giving Tom one day to interrogate him. After that, I will execute him for the crime of murdering the males of my tribe and probably many of yours as well."

She scanned the older pureblooded females, noting their nods of agreement.

"What about Valstar?" Joanna asked.

Jade doubted it was a daughter's concern for her father that had prompted her to ask about his fate.

"I haven't decided yet whether I'll execute him along with Igor or let him stand trial for his crimes. The six remaining male members of Igor's pod didn't take part in the slaughter of my people, so I will leave their fate in the hands of those they wronged. They will stand trial and be given a chance to defend themselves."

Once again, she scanned the faces of the pureblooded females and was surprised by them nodding in agreement. Had none of their males been killed by those six?

Or did these females not feel the need for revenge as acutely as she did?

Jade had been observing them, and it seemed that their spirits had been quashed for too long under Igor's rule, and they couldn't bounce back to being the proud Kra-ell females they had been before the subjugation.

She wished there was something she could do for them, but she wasn't skilled in offering counsel and encouragement. She wasn't that kind of a leader.

"I'm sure all of you are wondering where we are heading after arriving at Greenland, and what the future holds for us."

Several pureblooded females, the older ones who'd been among the original settlers, tapped the tables with their palms. It was the customary way of agreeing with what was said, but since no meeting had even been held or issues discussed in Igor's camp, this custom had been forgotten. To disagree, they would tap the floor with one foot.

Jade smiled. "I'm glad to see that not all of our ways have been forgotten. Now that we are free, I hope the elders will teach the young ones, so our traditions won't die out."

"Are we free?" Drova asked. "Because it seems to me that these paranormally talented humans with their strong compeller hold all the cards."

That was her cue to reveal the truth. "Our rescuers are not human. They are the immortal descendants of the gods."

The older purebloods hissed and tapped their feet while the younger ones frowned. Except for the fables that she'd told the children, they hadn't been taught the history of the conflict and didn't know that the gods preceded them on Earth.

"Where are the gods?" Morgada asked. "Why didn't they search for survivors after our ship exploded? Are we supposed to serve them after they abandoned us?"

"Most of the Earth gods are gone, and Tom claims that they didn't even know that we were coming. We were told a lie. No one was expecting us, and I suspect that the ship's thousands of years' delay was not a malfunction but sabotage."

"Why?" Morgada asked. "What purpose could it have served?"

It had to do with the twins, Jade was sure of that, but she wasn't clear on the reasons yet. If Toven managed to compel Igor, she would ask him to command him to answer her questions, and the first one would be whether he was sent to kill the royals. But maybe it wasn't such a good idea. Even if she asked it in Kra-ell, Igor might choose to answer in Russian or English just to get back at her, and it was crucial to keep the twins' existence a secret.

Tom and Kian and the other immortals seemed to be decent people, but their obligation was to keep their families and friends safe. The twins would pose too much of a threat to them which they would try to eliminate.

The immortals had been afraid of Igor's compulsion ability, and rightfully so. The twins were doubly dangerous because there were two of them. They might not be as powerful as Igor, but with their powers combined, who knew what they could do?

"I don't know why it was sabotaged. Maybe it was Igor's doing."

"Why would he do that?" Drova asked. "In what way could it have benefited him? And more importantly, how long did you know who they were and kept it from us?"

"I'll start with your last question. I recognized Tom as a god right away, and he told me that his companions were immortal but not gods. I was compelled to keep it a secret from everyone except Kagra. Now that joining their settlement is one of the options for us, I was permitted to tell you about them. As for the first part of your question, your guess is as good as mine. Maybe Igor wanted to arrive on Earth after everyone we knew back home was dead. If he was an escaped criminal, that would make sense."

She'd just pulled that argument out of her ass, but now that she thought of it, it really made sense, and not just if Igor was an escaped criminal. If he was sent to kill the twins, he would have preferred to do that after their mother was no longer the queen.

But what if the queen herself wanted them dead?

A chill ran through Jade. There must have been a good reason for them having always been veiled, even in the private palace gardens where only the queen, the head priestess, and the queen's family were allowed. The priestesses wore similar veils, but they took them off when there were no worshipers around. The twins never did.

Maybe they were deformed?

It was common practice to dedicate females who were born with abnormalities to priesthood and males to serve as temple guards and perform other duties. The twins' only known abnormality was being born at the same time, but what if there were more?

No, that couldn't be the reason. She'd only gotten a quick glimpse at the two settlers she suspected were the twins before they lay down in their pod, but if they'd had abnormalities, she would have noticed them. They could have worn makeup to hide them, but if makeup could do that, they wouldn't have needed to veil themselves at all times.

Perhaps the explanation was much simpler than that.

The queen had known that she would need to smuggle them off the planet one day, and she planned in advance, making sure that no one would recognize them.

"Why were we lied to about serving the gods?" Morgada asked, pulling Jade out of her reveries. "It wasn't essential to tell us that. We were selected by a lottery, and no one asked us if we wanted to settle on Earth. It wouldn't have made a difference to us. Why tell us that serving the gods on Earth was the queen's way to pay for the voyage?"

Those were all valid questions for which Jade had no answers.

"Again. I don't know. Maybe none of us was supposed to make it, and the ship was supposed to explode before the escape pods were launched."

"Are you saying that the gods planned it?" Pavel asked. "That they didn't tell their settlers on Earth to expect our arrival because they knew we would never get here?"

"I don't know why the gods would want to get rid of a bunch of Kra-ell." Unless they wanted the twins dead. "At this point, all we can do is speculate. I hope we will learn more from Igor, provided that Tom can compel him."

Pavel raised his hand. "Will you share with us what you find?"

"Of course." Not if it was about the twins. "Let's leave the past where it belongs for now. We need to discuss the future and decide where we want to settle."

51

PHINAS

*W*hen Phinas's phone rang twenty minutes into the walk, his heart leaped, but when he pulled it out of his pocket, it sank back to where it had been floating for the past twenty-eight hours.

Pulling off his glove, he accepted the call. "Hello, boss. What are you doing up so late?"

"Darius is fussy as usual, and I don't want Jacki to wake up. I'm sitting in his room, waiting for the next time he cries, so I can be there right away to take care of him."

Kalugal had turned into a dadzilla, and it was adorable. Maybe he was compensating for his own fatherless childhood. Then again, all the immortals in the village had grown up without fathers, and yet those who had been blessed with children of their own hadn't turned into dadzillas like his boss.

Maybe knowing who his father was and being exposed to him without getting the love and guidance children naturally expected from their fathers was worse than not having a father at all.

As a boy, Phinas had often wondered who his father had been, but once he'd understood how things worked in the Dormant enclosure and who the men brought in to breed with the Dormants were, he'd stopped wondering and started hating. Eventually, he'd stopped thinking about it at all.

Later, when he realized how different he was from his brothers and the other trainees in the camp, he wondered whether his father had been different as well. He had made up all kinds of scenarios in his mind about how his father had been tricked into breeding with his mother and imagining that he was a decent, intelligent guy.

He was well aware that the real male who'd fathered him had been just as nasty as all the others who had used the Dormants for their pleasure, but he had the benefit of the doubt. He could pretend that the male who'd contributed his genetic material to his was a good guy.

Kalugal didn't have that luxury. He knew who his father was, and he knew the kind of genes he'd gotten from him.

"Doesn't it disturb the baby that you are talking right next to him?"

"It doesn't. I've noticed that he sleeps more peacefully when he hears my voice in the background. I'm thinking about taking him with me to the office."

It took a very confident male to ignore people's expectations from fathers, and Kalugal was precisely the kind of male who would lead by example.

"Go for it. I think it would be good for both of you. Jacki needs a breather."

"She does." Kalugal sighed. "A baby is a lot of work, but he's worth it. The love we feel for him is just indescribable, and it is priceless."

"I believe you, but I'm sure you didn't call me in the middle of the night to talk about fatherhood."

Kalugal chuckled. "Frankly, my mind is always on Darius, and I'm running our business with diminished capacity. Fortunately, I'm so brilliant that even a fraction of my ability is more than enough."

He'd said that teasingly, but he meant it. Kalugal's ego was the size of the solar system or maybe the galaxy.

The guy had big ambitions.

"Your modesty astounds me."

"As it should, my friend, as it should. I petitioned the council yesterday, and they approved my seat."

"Congratulations."

"I didn't get the two I wanted, and that's disappointing. They want to see how having me on the council will work out before granting us another seat. I'm not happy about it, and I don't think it's fair, especially since Kian was willing to give us two seats, but it is what it is. They said a year, but I'm not going to wait that long. I'll petition them again in three months, and by then they will be eating out of my hand."

Phinas had no doubt that, given the chance Kalugal would succeed in turning all the council members into his fans. He'd always been charming, and he'd become even more so since marrying Jacki and moving into the village. Kalugal no longer suffered from the bouts of melancholy he'd often been afflicted with before.

Not that he'd ever admitted to being depressed. He used to call those his contemplative periods.

Phinas found a bench and sat down. "The problem with your plan to charm the council is that they don't meet often. The next three months might pass without a single meeting."

"Right." Kalugal sighed. "You are always so pragmatic."

"Sorry to burst your bubble, but someone has to anchor you in reality."

"I know. That's why I need you back here. I need both of my devils to balance my shoulders."

"Devils?"

"Well, yeah. It's supposed to be an angel on one shoulder and a devil on the other, but since neither you nor Rufsur is an angel, I think of you as different colored devils. You are blue, and Rufsur is red."

"I'm glad that you at least painted me in angelic colors."

"Blue is for reason, and red is for passion."

"I see. Although lately, my reason's faltering, and my emotions are all over the place." Phinas stretched his legs in front of him and crossed them at the ankles.

"Jade trouble?"

"I don't know. I haven't spoken to her since yesterday morning, and I feel like my intestines are being pulled out of my body. I need to be with her or at least hear her voice, but apparently, she doesn't feel the same about me."

Kalugal was silent for a long moment. "You've bonded with her."

"It would seem so. And I think she's bonded with me, but she's stubborn and refuses to accept it."

"How is that even possible? She's not immortal."

"Apparently, Kra-ell and gods are not all that different genetically, and the Kra-ell have the ability to bond, if not with each other, then at least with immortals."

"Don't tell that to Eleanor and Emmett. I don't think they have bonded."

"Right. I forgot about them. Maybe it has to do with the venom? The Kra-ell's venom is not as potent as ours. And it's not just the hybrids' problem. The purebloods' venom is weak as well. That might explain why the Kra-ell didn't bond with each other. The tribal family system can't explain the utter lack of reported cases of bonded couples, and it's not like it would be easy to hide. A bonded pair couldn't want to be with anyone other than the bonded partner, and that would have gotten noticed in a society that encourages variety and does not accept exclusivity."

Kalugal sighed. "Neither of us is a geneticist, and I have to admit that I haven't explored the subject nearly as thoroughly as I should. The new developments in gene editing have opened opportunities that were unimaginable before. It can change human society the way it changed the gods, but I digress. What I was trying to say before this long preamble was that we don't know enough about the bond and how it works, and the Kra-ell might have the ability to bond with more than one partner."

Phinas felt his body swell with aggression and his fangs elongate. "I hope that's not the case. I'm not sharing Jade with anyone."

"Of course not." Kalugal chuckled. "It just occurred to me that maybe the duels between the Kra-ell males over females had started that way. You sounded as if you would tear apart any other male Jade might bond with."

"Not going to happen. I will keep her so busy that she will not have a chance to bond with anyone else. Besides, the addiction will set in at some point, and then I will not have to worry about it ever again."

52

JADE

"What happened to the gods?" Pavel asked. "Did they go home?"

Jade stifled a groan. She should have expected this. She'd asked the same questions and had gotten most of the answers from Phinas, who'd been much less reserved about sharing the gods' history with her than Toven and Yamanu.

"They didn't go home. One god killed most of the others and died along with them, or so the story goes. No one is sure what actually happened, but the result was that the gods were gone. That's why we only found legends about them but not the gods themselves. We are on our own here, with no way to communicate with our people back home, provided that they are still there and didn't annihilate each other, and we need to do the best with what we have. Can we please move on?"

Drova raised her hand. "You said that these people are the immortal descendants of the gods. Does that mean that they are hybrids?"

"Yes. They are part human and part god. They don't have the same problem we do with their second-generation offspring. Their hybrid females produce hybrid children. There is more to it, but I don't want to get into that right now. That's a discussion we will have later once we decide where we want to settle."

"Only the females?" Helmi asked without raising her hand. "What about their male hybrids?"

"If the mother is human and the father is hybrid, the children are born human." Jade lifted a hand. "I will not answer any more questions about the gods, their immortal descendants, or how their genetics work. This meeting is about the options Tom's people offer us." She paused and added, "Please hold your questions until I've listed them all. Otherwise, we will not be done before dinner, let alone lunchtime."

She proceeded to explain the various options, the advantages and disadvantages of each, and she even went into explaining how they could choose a combination of them by dividing their community.

"Any questions?" Jade asked when she was done.

Drova lifted her hand. "What do you think is our best option?"

Jade had made a conscious effort not to inject her personal preferences into her speech, mostly because she didn't have clarity yet. Toven's speech about immortals and Kra-ell breeding to produce a stronger long-lived next generation had hit a chord with her, but after giving it more thought, she'd found a number of problems with his suggestion.

"I'm conflicted," Jade admitted. "On the one hand, I want to keep our community united and settle everyone in one place, but on the other hand, I realize that what's best for the Kra-ell among us is not necessarily what's best for the humans and the other way around. Right now, there are no humans in the village, and their leader is very strict about keeping it that way for security reasons, so I don't know how comfortable the humans among us will be there."

According to Phinas, there were a few humans in the village, but they were all confirmed Dormants awaiting transition, so she could bundle them up with the immortals.

She wasn't ready to tell her people about the potential for long-lived children produced by unions between hybrid males and immortal females. The younger purebloods who'd been born in the compound and hadn't grown up on Kra-ell traditions would have no problem mating with immortal females, and the older males were all from Igor's pod, and they didn't matter because their days were numbered. They might get a trial, but she doubted they would be exonerated.

The question was how the immortal males would react to outsiders mating with their females. The good news was that most of them were related and forbidden to each other, so it wasn't as if the Kra-ell males would be stealing potential mates from the clan males. The clan males would also have access to the Kra-ell females, but not every male was as secure in his masculinity as Phinas, and they might have a problem with the Kra-ell females' superior strength. On the females' side, they might not be attracted to males who were physically weaker than them and who couldn't offer them a fight for dominance that most pureblooded females considered a form of foreplay and couldn't get aroused without.

Isla raised a hesitant hand. "I have a question."

Jade nodded. "Go ahead."

"Will the immortal males expect us to breed with them?"

"No. All clan members, whether male or female, are discouraged from having long-term relationships with humans. They have sex with humans, though, and the immortal females welcome pregnancies, but the human fathers are never part of their lives. As for the males, they have no reason to produce children with human females because their children are born human."

Isla smiled. "Then I vote for the village. It sounds like a much nicer place than Safe Haven."

Helmi didn't seem to agree with her mother. "It might be a nicer place, but not better. You've heard what Jade said about the security there. If we settle in the village, it will be exactly like it was in the compound. We will be prisoners there. We will have more freedom in Safe Haven."

"There wouldn't be much difference, at least not at the beginning." Jade leaned against the table at her back and crossed her arms over her chest. "Our mobility will be restricted whether we move into the village or Safe Haven. It will take time for both camps to build trust, and since we are their guests, we will have to abide by their rules. But after a transition period, I believe we will be granted the same freedoms as the clan members. We need to hide our existence as much as they do so our interests align."

"What are they getting out of it?" Pavel asked. "No one is that altruistic, especially when it comes to inviting strangers into their fold."

"They get strong warriors to defend their village and a capable work-force for whatever projects they can use us for."

Pavel didn't look happy. "We are finally free of Igor, and I don't want to become anyone's slave again. Not yours and not the immortals'."

Jade intended to grant her new tribe members more liberties and choices than she'd done in her original tribe, but that didn't mean that people could choose to be idle or do whatever they pleased without regard for others. Once they got settled, she would assign each member of her community tasks according to their abilities.

She narrowed her eyes at him. "Are you challenging my leadership?"

"Not yet." Pavel's eyes were full of challenge. "Right now, you are the most qualified person to lead this community. What I meant was that I didn't want to become a slave to the descendants of the gods. I don't want Tom or anyone else to compel me and subjugate my will. I want to choose what I do and why."

"They will use compulsion on us, but not to force us to serve them. The compulsion would be to never rise against them or betray their existence to humans or to their enemies. It will only be about security."

"Are you sure? What's to prevent Tom from compelling us to do whatever?"

She smiled. "If that was their mode of operation, we wouldn't be meeting here and voting on the best place to settle in. Tom would have compelled us to follow his commands the same way Igor did. But Tom and his relatives are not like Igor. They are giving us a choice. We might choose to settle somewhere else entirely or go back to our old compound, and they will respect our wishes. Their council voted and approved those options as well."

Pavel nodded. "To sum up, we need to decide whether we should go back to the old place, find a new place and start from scratch, or join the immortals either in their village or one of the three other locations they control."

"Correct." Jade pushed away from the table. "We will vote with a show of hands. Let's start with the least desirable choice. Whoever thinks that going back to our old compound is our best choice, raise your hands."

Surprisingly, many of the humans were for it, and some purebloods and hybrids as well, but it wasn't the majority. Nevertheless, they needed to count the number of hands for each option and compare the results.

"Kagra, please count the hands and note the result." Jade motioned for Drova to come over. "I want you to count as well. We want to make sure that the counts are accurate."

Drova regarded her with a frown. "Did you ever put anything up for a vote before?"

"No, this is my first time. I've gained a new perspective during my years of captivity, and I intend to run things differently from the way I ran them before." She put her hand on her daughter's shoulder. "Igor got one thing right. We are on our own here, and we make our own rules. We are no longer bound by our traditions and our religion. But unlike Igor, I don't intend to discard them in their entirety. We will keep the good and modify the not-so-good to serve our needs."

PHINAS

*N*early three hours had passed since Phinas had called Mey, and he was starting to think that Jade was ghosting him, but then as he was paying for his coffee in the town's only coffee shop, his phone rang, and this time the caller was Mey.

"Hello," he said into a receiver as he collected his credit card from the cashier.

"It's me," Jade said.

He smiled at the cashier, took his coffee, and sat down in the corner of the shop.

"How are you?" He started with a bland question that didn't convey any of his thoughts or emotions.

The people in the coffee shop/bakery probably didn't speak English, but most people on the western side of Europe could probably understand it. Nevertheless, it was too damn cold outside, and he wanted to sit his ass in a chair and drink hot coffee to warm himself from the inside.

He might still have what it took to be a warrior, but outside of battle, he'd become a creature of comfort, and he wasn't going to apologize for it.

"Exhausted." Jade sighed. "Everyone had questions, and the meeting took forever. The hardest part was summoning patience and answering everyone without tearing their heads off."

The ice in Phinas's gut was starting to melt, and it wasn't because of the coffee.

Jade wasn't telling him that she loved him and that she couldn't live without him, but she talked to him like she would to a confidant, a friend, and not someone she was trying to distance herself from.

Perhaps she'd been too busy to call him or maybe she'd expected him to call.

"What did they decide? Or rather, what did you decide?"

"It was a tie between Safe Haven and the village, with humans mostly voting for Safe Haven and the Kra-ell mostly voting for the village. About a quarter of the purebloods voted on settling in the jungles of South America, some of the young ones voted for the camping grounds, and some voted for the mountain cabin, but they were in a minority, as were the ones who wanted to go back to the compound. I gave everyone a couple of hours to mull it over and discuss it among themselves, and we will have another meeting after lunch to vote on whether the majority is in favor of splitting our community. If the majority agrees that's the best course of action, we will need another round of voting to choose the best options for the split."

Phinas was glad that the most popular choices brought her closer to him. It would have been a real pain if they decided to go back to the compound or settle somewhere in South America. He knew that he would follow her wherever she went, but it would be nice to be able to visit his friends in the village more than once every few months.

"What is your preference?"

"Along the same lines as the votes went. The village for the Kra-ell, Safe Haven for the humans, with a few exceptions to accommodate couples like Tomos and Helmi. Perhaps some of the older humans would prefer the peaceful life in the village as well. If we are to rely on livestock for sustenance, I would like to have Jarmo in charge of that."

Phinas chuckled. "I hear you. I would like to have Isla and some of her helpers cook meals in the village, but my wishes are irrelevant. Although I'm surprised that you are willing to split your people. When we last talked, you said that your community can't survive without the humans."

"I had a long talk with Kian and then with Toven and Yamanu. Toven brought up some compelling arguments neither of us considered before, and it got me thinking, but the solution didn't crystallize in my mind until this morning."

"Enlighten me. Why do you want to split them up like that? I thought that you needed the humans to keep your people from going extinct?"

"Not if we move into the village and form relationships with immortals."

Phinas was surprised that Jade was open to Kra-ell and immortals producing hybrid children. "Our fertility rate is even lower than yours, but I agree that's a good solution. You'll have more genetic variety, and so will we. The only problem I can see with that is reluctance on both sides to intermingle and produce hybrid offspring."

There was also the issue of different traditions and other cultural differences. Many would not want to deal with that.

"They will have us as an example of a mixed couple, and they will have Vlad as an example of the offspring of such a union. You said that he's well liked in their community, so even if we are the only couple, there still might be children produced from mixed encounters. Those children might inherit better genetics, from us in regards to better fertility and strength, and from you in regards to longer lifespans and better gender distribution." She chuckled. "I'm usually not an optimist. But I'm allowing myself to hope for a better future for our people."

Everything she'd said was music to his ears, and for the first time in his life, Phinas experienced what it meant for a heart to soar.

He felt buoyant.

"I love you." He couldn't think of anything else to say despite having so much that he wanted to convey. He simply didn't have the words.

Jade chuckled nervously. "If you expect me to say it back to you, you'll be disappointed. However, I'm ready to admit that we have bonded. I just can't deny it any longer. I miss you with every fiber of my being, and I can't wait to hold you in my arms. I don't think I can ever let you go again."

"That's good enough for me. Did accepting our bond have anything to do with your decision to move into the village?"

"It did. Toven helped me realize that if you and I have bonded, so could other Kra-ell. We must have similar genetics to the gods, and the bonding with the one we are destined to be with must be a recessive gene that is rarely expressed. Otherwise, there would have been truelove matches among the Kra-ell as well."

"There might be another explanation for that. The venom of immortal males is much more potent than the venom of Kra-ell males, and since it's a crucial component in the bonding process, it's possible that only immortal males can induce it."

There was a long moment of silence as Jade processed the information. "Fate seems to disfavor Kra-ell males. The gender birth ratio prevents them from having mates of their own, and they also can't bond with immortal females."

"I might be wrong about that. The reason it occurred to me is that

Emmett and Eleanor are in a committed, loving relationship, but they don't seem to have bonded."

"Maybe they have, and you are not aware of it? I wouldn't have known we bonded if we weren't forced to separate. I would have never expected being away from you to be so difficult."

"Is that the only indication?"

"To me, it is more than enough. I had several partners throughout my life, and when I established a tribal family unit with my pod members, I grew to care for all of them, both males and females. But I never missed them when I traveled abroad." She was quiet for a moment. "Frankly, I never enjoyed the squabbles and posturing the males engaged in to get my attention or that of the other females. I always thought that it was demeaning and wished there was a better way. I even implemented a scheduled rotation so no one would feel neglected, but they didn't like it. Evidently, it's part of the male psyche to compete and show off to get the female's attention. They weren't happy with the schedule."

Phinas didn't like her mentioning her past lovers, but it wasn't so bad when she talked about them in such a dispassionate manner. She'd regarded it as her duty to bear children for the tribe and to look after her males' well-being, but she hadn't loved them or even craved them sexually.

On the one hand, it gladdened him that he was the first she really wanted, but on the other hand, he was saddened that she'd experienced mostly meh sex before.

"My poor iron heart. It sounds like you had no fun until you met me."

Jade snorted. "I had fun, just not often."

A growl rose in his throat. "Please, can you just agree with me? I'm okay with you lying to me and telling me that you didn't enjoy any of the males you've been with."

There was a long moment of silence before Jade answered. "It was so long ago that I hardly remember whether it was good or so-so, which makes me think that it was so-so or I would have remembered it. What I do remember, and quite vividly, is our last bed play, so that tells you something."

Phinas let out an exaggerated relieved breath. "Thank you. My ego is saved."

"I didn't lie, Phinas. I never truly enjoyed intimacy before I met you."

54

KIAN

"Good evening, Jade." Kian examined her expression for clues, but it revealed very little.

She looked just as stressed and tired as the day before, so the results of the vote were neither disappointing nor satisfactory.

"Good morning, Kian." She shifted her gaze to his right. "Hello, Onegus. Where is the third leg of your triad?"

Turner hadn't been in their last video meeting either, but she hadn't noticed his absence, and they were no longer in the war room but in his office. "Now that we have Igor, the Russians are dealt with, and all the arrangements have been made, Turner's expertise is no longer needed, and he's free to return to his own office and accept new rescue jobs."

She nodded. "That's a very admirable business. Do you know if he's hiring?"

"Are you looking for a job?"

"I don't want to be idle, and from what Phinas tells me, there isn't much to do in your village."

His gut clenched, but he forced a smile. "So that's where the vote went? The majority wanted to join our village?"

"Not exactly. We decided to split up. Most of the humans will go to Safe Haven, but some want to join us in the village if that's possible. Mostly it's the older ones who don't want to change their lives too significantly, and Isla's two daughters. One is in a relationship with a hybrid male, and the other one is still a teenager and wants to stay with her mother. They are also asking if it will be possible to visit each other. Isla and Jarmo's sister, Hannele, wants to go to Safe Haven, but she also wants to be able to visit her brother and sister and her nieces, or for them to visit her, and the same goes for the others."

Kian was starting to develop a headache. "I don't think it can work because of security. It will have to be either all the humans in one place or all of them in the other. We can't allow them to shuffle from one location to the other."

Jade tilted her head. "I don't see why. All the humans will be under compulsion to keep our existence a secret as well as yours, and as long as their permanent residence is in one of the two locations controlled by the clan, your compellers can periodically reinforce the compulsion. The risk of them revealing anything they're not supposed to while traveling from place to place is nonexistent. Igor sent humans to study in universities, and they had to return to the compound once a month for him to reinforce the compulsion. The system worked, and the compound's location remained a secret. If it worked for him, it would work for you."

He couldn't argue with her logic, but he still didn't like the idea of humans in the village, and even less so humans traveling back and forth between Safe Haven and the village.

"The travel arrangements would be a nightmare. The distance between the two locations is about twelve hours by car or five hours using a commercial airliner and driving to and from the respective airports."

"I will cover their travel expenses and any associated security costs, so that shouldn't be a concern either."

Onegus leaned toward Kian. "I heard that Isla is an exceptional cook, and she knows how to run a big kitchen. We can use her in the village. I wouldn't mind a buffet that serves breakfast, lunch, and dinner. Neither Cassandra nor I have the time or inclination to cook, and I'm tired of eating restaurant fare."

You too, Brutus? That was what Kian wanted to say. Instead, he tackled the problem from another angle. "I can deal with having the older humans here. My problem is the teenager. She will be isolated here."

Jade took a deep breath. "We have forty-five Kra-ell children of varying ages with us, and twenty-five human children. Lana will have other kids close to her age in either community, but perhaps she will prefer to be with other human children. Perhaps I can convince Isla to let Lana stay with Hannele."

"How old is Lana?" Onegus asked.

"Thirteen."

"We have three kids around that age in the village. One is immortal and two are Dormants. They are a little older than her, but I'm sure they will happily include her in their little group." He looked at Kian. "Lana grew up with aliens, and she will have to be compelled anyway. Besides, if it doesn't work out or the big assembly votes against the Kra-ell inclusion, we can find a different solution. None of this is final until everyone casts their votes."

Kian closed his eyes for a brief moment and then returned his gaze to Jade. "Did you tell the humans about the restrictions they will face in the village?"

"I touched on it briefly, but I didn't go into details. For some reason, the humans have got the impression that they would have more freedom in Safe Haven, but that's not really true. They won't be allowed to leave the area, not in the beginning, but at least they will have contact with other humans. Between the Safe Haven community members and visitors to the retreat, they will have ample opportunity to increase their small genetic pool."

"That's true." Kian rapped his fingers on his desk.

Everything said so far seemed reasonable, but his gut was rebelling against the imminent monumental changes to life in his village.

"When are you going to have a final answer for us? I don't want my people to get excited about this plan, and then your assembly votes against it. Shouldn't you put it up for a vote before our arrival?"

Things were never that simple when so many moving parts were involved, and each of those parts was a person with their own set of beliefs and preferences.

"We decided that it would be better to let the two groups intermingle for a while before a final decision is made. At this time, most clan members haven't been exposed to your people, not even to the three hybrids who have been part of our community for a while now. They need to spend some time with the purebloods to realize that they are not as different from them as they appear."

She chuckled. "I can just imagine the conversations in your village. Has Kian lost his mind? Why is he inviting bloodsuckers to live in our community? What if they want to suck our blood?" She bared her fangs and hissed.

As pretty as she was, Jade looked terrifying with her fangs bared and her eyes blazing red. Then again, he didn't look any less scary with his fangs on full display and dripping venom, and yet Syssi fell in love with him despite his vampiric appearance.

"Please refrain from doing that in the village," Onegus said. "You might scare some people."

"Why? Your males have fangs. Is a female with fangs scarier than a male?"

Onegus smiled. "Generally, no, but you are not just anyone. You're Jade. The one and only."

"Thank you." She returned his smile. "I hope that you meant that as a compliment."

"Let's put it this way. In a battle, I'd rather fight with you than against you."

55

TOVEN

*W*hen the call ended, Jade turned to Toven. "I have a favor to ask."
"Go ahead."

"My people would like you to tell them about the history of the gods and what happened to them. They have a lot of questions I couldn't answer, some because I didn't know, and some because I wasn't sure whether it was okay to tell them what I learned from Phinas and what I guessed from reading between the lines."

"I should have expected that, but you should have asked Kian first. I'm a newcomer to the clan, and there is a lot I don't know yet about their history. Our paths diverged right after the disaster. I didn't even know that anyone other than me had survived."

Her eyes softened. "It must have been awful to think you were the only one left. Finding out that Annani had survived and created a whole clan of immortals must have been incredible."

"It was." He arched a brow. "Should I ask who told you about Annani?"

"Isn't it obvious?"

Phinas talked too much.

Toven pinned Jade with a hard stare. "Add her name and existence to all the things you are not allowed to disclose to anyone who doesn't already know about them."

"Naturally." Jade grimaced. "I wouldn't have told anyone about the goddess even without the compulsion. I know how important it is to keep her existence a secret. Your enemies are powerful and ruthless."

"I appreciate that, but I prefer to err on the side of caution." He let out a breath. "For many years, I tried to do what Annani has done, but where she has succeeded, I failed. Perhaps it was because I was doing it wrong or perhaps because I didn't have the help she did. But before I gave up and let ennui set in, I was busy pursuing the lofty goal of bringing civilization to the primitives."

"How did you find out that Annani survived?"

He smiled. "That's a long and convoluted story with a simple ending. The gist is that I fathered two immortal children whom I didn't know about, and one of them is my spitting image. When he was found by the clan, Annani immediately recognized him as my son, and they started looking for me."

"How did they find you?"

"They didn't. We found each other by chance, or what is more likely, by fate. I'll tell you more about it in the village." He leaned back. "By the way, Kian's mate is a seer, and she foresaw your people. Have you heard about the Perfect Match Virtual Adventures Studios?"

Jade frowned. "I might have seen an advertisement on the internet for the service. What does it have to do with Kian's mate or with us?"

"Syssi owns a large chunk of the company, and she designed a made-up adventure starring aliens called the Krall, who are tall and slim, drink blood, and produce way more males than females. She was sure that it was a product of her imagination, but here you are."

"When was that?"

"A few years back. It was long before we found Emmett or Vrog and learned that the Kra-ell are real. She foresaw your arrival."

Jade strengthened, her shoulders tensing. "What else did she foresee?"

"Her visions are sporadic and most often useless. We might have never discovered you, and she would have never known that her imaginary Krall are real people."

Jade's shoulders still didn't lose their tension. "What did she see about the Krall? Did more of us come?"

"Did you expect more?"

She shrugged. "If none came in the seven thousand years it took us to get here, then probably none are coming. And that's what worries me. There should have been more ships sent with more settlers. Something must have happened back home. It's not like anyone I cared for is still alive, but I worry about my people."

"Perhaps losing contact with your ship was the reason the program was stopped," Toven suggested.

"But you lost contact as well, and it happened around the same time. Maybe a natural disaster destroyed the gods and the Kra-ell."

"It's possible. But I suspect that they just wanted to forget about the rebels they had sent to Earth."

"Yeah, it might be." Jade let out a breath. "There is no way for us to find out what happened there."

Toven wasn't sure about that. With how fast technology was moving forward, they would one day find the place they'd come from. "Does the planet of the gods have a name?"

"We call it Anumati."

"Does it mean anything?"

She nodded. "Loosely translated, it means we are the children of the Mother."

"What do the gods call it?"

She chuckled. "The same thing, but it means something else in their language. Again, loosely translated, it means we are omnipotent. Isn't that fitting?"

"It's fitting only when filtered through the prism of your beliefs."

"Perhaps." She averted her eyes, maybe because she knew he was right or because she didn't want him to see that he'd angered her. "Are you going to speak with my people?"

So it was the second one.

"I'd rather leave it to Kian when they get to the village. I'm not much of a public speaker."

"They already know you, and they are curious about you."

They wanted to ask about the gods, and he didn't want to talk about them. There was still too much pain and guilt involved. It didn't matter that logically he knew that he couldn't have stopped Mortdh, but the niggling feeling that perhaps he could have done something refused to go away. Maybe if he'd been a better brother, Mortdh would have been less psychotic. Perhaps he would have hesitated to drop the bomb because someone he cared about was in the assembly, namely Toven and Ekin.

"Toven?" Jade prompted.

He wasn't surprised she knew his real name.

If Phinas had told her about Annani, he had told her that as well.

Toven let out a breath. "I'll make a deal with you. If you come with me to speak to Valstar, I'll speak with your people, but I can't promise I'll answer all their questions. In fact, I will probably answer only a few and tell them that the rest will have to wait until we get to the village."

Her lips twisted in a grimace. "If that's what it takes, I'll talk to Valstar."

5 6

JADE

*T*he last place Jade wanted to be was Valstar's cabin, facing the male she was about to execute.

Having to sit across from the sniveling manipulator was its own kind of torture, and Jade was tempted to just agree to the trial so she could be done with it. She'd spent over two decades interacting with him while dreaming of the day she would make him shorter by a head, but this was different.

Jade didn't want to hear him groveling and making himself appear like one more of Igor's victims. Just a settler like her who had been forced to do unthinkable things.

She listened to his explanations with half an ear while her mind wandered to Phinas and their conversation from earlier that day. Why did it feel as if she'd capitulated? Like she'd chosen the easy way out instead of standing her ground and sticking to her decisions?

Was she weakening?

Yeah, she was.

Now that it was almost over, and Igor was about to meet his end, she felt like a deflated balloon. Plotting vengeance and stoking the fire inside of her was all she'd known for so long that she didn't know what to do with herself once that objective was met.

Joining an established village with all the comforts ready for her people's use was another capitulation. She should have convinced them that a fresh start somewhere else was the best option, that building their lives from the ground up was the way to go. But she was tired, and the immortals' village sounded like a vacation in paradise.

Especially since it would be with Phinas.

"Give me another chance," Valstar pleaded. "I will serve you well, better than I served Igor because I'd be doing it willingly. I have experience running a large community. I can be helpful."

Was he delusional?

"I'm done here." She pushed to her feet and turned to Toven. "If you want him to stand trial, be my guest. It won't change the outcome."

Toven didn't move from the armchair. "What if it does? Will you abide by the court's decision?"

She let out a breath. "If your judge finds him innocent, I will lose faith in your system, and I will not abide by her ruling. Assuming that she will use human crime terminology, finds him guilty only of being an accessory to murder, and sentences him to entombment rather than a beheading, I might be willing to consider that as an option, but don't take it as a promise. It's a maybe."

The coward hadn't even asked for a duel to the death. Not that she would have granted it, but at least he would have preserved his honor.

Except he didn't have any.

Valstar's panicked expression was priceless. "I'm not a god. I can't go into stasis without a life pod to sustain me. I will die."

She shrugged. "Then choose beheading. At least it's a quick death." She walked to the door, opened it, and looked at Toven. "Are you coming?"

With a sigh, he rose to his feet. "Let's agree not to decide until Edna probes him. She will see straight to his soul and find the truth. She might give you a different perspective."

"She will see that I was a victim just like you."

"I doubt it." Jade walked out of the cabin. "How much are you willing to bet that your judge will see exactly what I see? A rotten soul that should never be reborn."

Toven closed the door behind him. "I've lived for a very long time, and I know people. If Valstar was lying in there, he's the best actor who has ever lived or he's a sociopath like Igor."

"He's worse. Igor will not beg for his life like a coward."

"Don't be so sure." Toven fell in step with her. "He will certainly try to bargain for it."

"He has nothing I want."

If Igor knew where the twins were, he would have found them already and killed them. Whether he was an assassin sent to end them or an agent for the queen meant to protect them, he would have gotten rid of the twins so he wouldn't have to bow to them. The queen was long dead, and there would have been no one to hold him accountable. Knowing what their fate had been would have given her closure, but it wasn't worth bargaining with Igor.

"When do you want me to meet up with your people?" Toven asked.

Jade was surprised he was still going to do that after the way she'd brushed off Valstar's pleading his case.

"After dinner tonight." She stopped and looked at him. "I know that you are disappointed I didn't soften up my position regarding Valstar, and I appreciate that you are still willing to speak with my people despite that."

"I promised to do that in exchange for you meeting Valstar. You fulfilled your part, and I'll fulfill mine." He smiled. "I keep my promises, Jade, and just like you, I try not to overpromise. Don't expect me to tell them much."

"I don't. As long as you show up and answer a few questions, I'll consider it a promise fulfilled."

57

PHINAS

*P*hinas stood on the dock, ignoring the drizzling rain and freezing cold. It was getting dark, and the *Aurora* was just a speck on the horizon, but even if it started raining in earnest, he wouldn't move from that spot until it docked.

The tether inside of him hummed with anticipation, the pain worsening instead of abating as Jade got nearer.

He had a plan, and if anyone tried to stop him, they would regret it. As soon as the ship opened its shell doors, he would leap inside, and if he found Jade waiting for him there, he would pick her up, rush her to his cabin or hers, and make love to her all night.

Knowing her, she would want to see Igor, and a small part of him wanted to present his trophy to her as a mating present, but a much bigger part of him needed to get naked with her, and he wasn't referring to the one throbbing in his boxer briefs despite the cold.

Max had thankfully volunteered to guard Igor and the other three, or he would be there teasing Phinas mercilessly about his reunion with Jade. The guy had a warped sense of humor, which Phinas enjoyed most of the time, but he was too strung out to tolerate it right now.

Several of his men had made it to the dock and were waiting along with him, but they knew him well enough to know to leave him alone and keep their distance.

Patting his pocket, he checked that the box with the necklace he'd bought for Jade was there. It had been an impulse buy, and now he wasn't sure about giving it to her. She wasn't the type of woman who appreciated jewelry.

Hell, she wasn't a woman at all. She was a Kra-ell female with different traditions and a strange culture, and giving her a necklace might offend her.

There were still so many things he didn't know about her, but thank the Fates and the Mother of All Life and every other power out there, they would have plenty of time to explore their differences in the village.

It took another hour for the ship to finally dock, and as soon as the doors opened, he didn't even wait for the plank to be fully extended and leaped across the remaining ten feet or so.

Yamanu and Toven were there with several Guardians and a few of his men, and he knew that he was being rude by ignoring them as his eyes darted around, looking for his mate.

"Where is she?"

Toven chuckled. "She's on her way. A couple of the hybrids got into a squabble, and she had to deal with them."

"I'll meet her halfway."

Phinas ran inside, ignoring the snorts of laughter from the Guardians.

When he saw her striding toward him, he gave a burst of speed. Stopping himself at the last moment from tackling her, he grabbed her by the waist, lifted her to his chest, and smashed his lips over hers.

Wrapping her arms around his neck and her legs around his middle, she kissed him with such force that his lips tingled, and his neck felt like it was going to snap, but he didn't care and kept kissing her.

When they finally came up for air, they were both panting.

"I don't care if the ship catches fire, or we are under attack. I'm taking you to bed." He hoisted her higher and started running.

Jade laughed. "Put me down." She got free of his arms with little effort, halting him with a hand to his chest. "I still have appearances to keep up."

Damn. She probably wanted to see Igor first.

"What do you want to do? Do you want me to take you to Igor?"

The smile melted off her face. "He can wait." She took his hand. "Right now, I want you, just without giving everyone on this ship a show. Can you do that?"

"I can do anything you want as long as it leads us to a bed, but a supply closet would do at a pinch."

"Hmm, sounds fun, but perhaps we'll try the closet some other time."

5 8

JADE

*J*ade had never had sex in a supply closet, but she'd fought with Kagra in a supply room, and they'd made quite a mess.

Grasping Phinas's chin, she leaned in and feathered her lips over his. "Your cabin or mine?"

"Mine." Phinas gripped the back of her neck. "Let's use the elevator, so no one stops us on the way." He pulled her in for another quick kiss and then took her hand and ran toward the elevator.

Standing next to each other with their fingers entwined, they both stared at the numbers on the display, urging them to change faster and praying that no one called the elevator on one of the other floors.

The Mother must have answered Jade's prayers, and she sent a silent apology for bothering her with such a frivolous request.

As soon as Phinas kicked the door to his cabin closed, she yanked his coat down his arms and his sweater over his head, desperately needing to touch his naked skin. She missed his hard, muscled body, the solid bulk of him, the warmth, and as she ran her hands over his chest, her sex squeezed with need.

"Jade," he whispered her name as if it was a prayer.

Lifting her into his arms, he waited until she wrapped her legs around his hips, and as he carried her to the bedroom, she kissed down his neck and scraped her fangs along the strong column.

He laid her on the bed, and as she whipped her shirt over her head, his eyes roved over her naked breasts, and his fangs punched down over his lower lip.

"Perfect," he hissed through his fangs.

Catching one foot, he pulled down her boot, tossed it behind him, and then did the same with the other. Her socks were next, and as he lifted her foot and kissed her toes one at a time, she squirmed and giggled like a child.

"It tickles." She popped the button on her leathers and unzipped them.

The faster they got naked, the sooner he could be inside her and relieve the ache that had settled there in his absence.

"I know." He kissed the arch of her foot and then tugged her pants down her hips.

When they hit the floor behind him, and all that covered her body was a pair of simple panties, he sucked in a breath.

"You are so beautiful, my iron heart."

A grin spread over her face. "I love it when you call me that. Now get naked and come here before I tackle you to the ground and ride you like you've never been ridden before."

He arched a brow. "Is that supposed to be a threat?"

"No, it's a promise. Now give me what I want." Her eyes roamed over his magnificent torso, going down to the impressive bulge, testing the strength of his zipper.

Smiling with his fangs on full display and his eyes glowing, he was magnificent. His male beauty was rugged and perfect in its imperfection. He wasn't like the gods, who were so beautiful that they looked airbrushed, unreal, and to her, unappealing.

"Do you like what you see?" He kicked his boots off, unbuckled his belt, unbuttoned his jeans, and pushed them down his hips with deliberate slowness.

"You're such a tease." Jade licked her lips, knowing what the sight of her tongue did to him.

"Look who's talking." He shoved down his jeans along with the boxer shorts, and his erection sprang free.

His manhood wasn't longer than the pureblooded males, but it was definitely thicker, and he knew how to use it just the right way to please her.

His smirk was all male satisfaction as he prowled on the bed and put one big hand on her stomach.

"Mine."

The possessive tone and gesture should have annoyed her, but she was too needy to care, and right now, everything he did and said was a turn-on.

"Prove it," she hissed at him, immediately regretting the words.

This wasn't a Kra-ell foreplay, and Phinas couldn't overpower her, but it didn't seem like her blunder had affected him.

As he settled between her legs and drew a nipple into his mouth, his massive erection was hot and heavy between her legs, a promise of pleasure mingled with a little pain just the way she liked it.

He paid attention to both nipples, licking and sucking and pinching. It took all of her resolve not to flip them over and ride him like she'd threatened.

Her growls, however, betrayed her hunger.

"Patience," he murmured against her nipple. "I'm just as desperate for you."

She arched up, rubbing her mound against his arousal. "We have all night to play around. Right now, we both need to sate our hunger. I need you inside of me."

"Is that so?" He reached between their bodies and slid a finger inside of her. "You're so wet for me, my iron heart."

"Did you expect anything else?" She gripped his butt and lifted hers to position her entrance at the tip of his manhood.

59

PHINAS

*P*hinas gripped his shaft in his fist, positioning himself at her entrance. "Do you want this?"

Her eyes blazing purple with desire, Jade bared her fangs. "You know I do."

He nudged just the head inside of her. It wasn't their first time together, but they'd been apart for several days, and Jade was built long and narrow, while he was both long and thick. If he slammed into her like she wanted, it wouldn't be comfortable, and he didn't want to cause her pain even though he suspected she craved it.

Besides, there was always the chance that pain would unleash the tigress in her, and she would attack him, which he didn't have a problem with, but she might. He couldn't overpower her, and it might be a turn-off for her.

As Jade lifted her hips, trying to get more of him inside her, he gripped her hip and gazed down at where their bodies were joined. "Patience, sweetheart."

"I'm not a sweetheart." She rolled her hips, impaling herself on a couple more inches.

"My bad, my ferocious iron heart." He clamped his hands over the back of her thighs, spreading her wide as he pressed in a little further.

"Yes." She groaned. "Stop teasing and give me everything. I'm not some fragile human you need to be careful with."

He dipped his head and kissed her. "Maybe not, but you're precious to me, and I want to take care of you."

She softened under him, her taut muscles going lax. "It's my job to protect you. Not the other way around."

"We can protect each other." He pushed the rest of the way in.

She gasped and arched her back. "You can take care of me like that all night long."

"I intend to." He pulled back and thrust in again, going as far as her body allowed, which was deeper than any other female he'd been with. "You're perfect for me."

He'd hoped she would echo his words, but he should have known better. Jade expressed herself with her body, not her words. As her hands drifted up his back and cupped his head, her touch was gentle and loving, and when she lifted her head and kissed him, her lips were soft against his.

He wanted to take it slow and savor the moment, the connection, to feel their bond hum in satisfaction, but when she gripped his buttocks and squeezed hard, his restraint broke, and he withdrew only to ram back into her.

Going fast and hard, he twisted his hips and ground against the seat of her pleasure with every thrust.

Jade growled and moaned, her fingertips digging painfully into the flesh of his buttocks and intensifying the ecstasy of their joining.

He tightened his hold of her. "I will never give you up."

Her answer was a pained groan, and then she gripped the nape of his neck, lifted her head, and bit into his vein.

Fire and ecstasy mingled as pain turned to pleasure, and as she sucked his blood, her sheath clenched around his shaft, and seed exploded out of him along with a bellow that must have shaken the ship.

When her tremors subsided, she pulled out her fangs, licked the puncture wounds closed, and wrapped her arms around him. "Thank you."

Was she thanking him for one of the best orgasms he'd ever had? And he hadn't even bitten her yet.

Still panting like a locomotive, he lifted off her just enough to brace his weight on his forearms. "Why are you thanking me?"

"For the gift of your blood and your seed." She smiled, her fangs retracting into her gums. "You nourished me and perhaps gifted me with a child."

Phinas wished he could, but he didn't want her to have false hope.

"I don't know about that." He dipped his head and kissed her lightly. "The chances of that happening are less than slim. But you are welcome for the blood. It's yours whenever you please. I don't mind becoming your exclusive source."

"Don't make promises you will regret later. I might get addicted to your blood. It tastes better than anything I've ever had."

Why did that make him feel like thumping his chest and grunting 'mine?'

His shaft swelled inside her, eliciting a delightful purr from Jade.

"Please do." He kissed the side of her neck. "I'm an immortal, and my body will replenish whatever you take within minutes, not hours or days. It's like having a personal juice bar that never runs out of juice."

She arched up and swiveled her hips. "Speaking of never running out of juice. You haven't bitten me yet, and I crave your venom bite."

He suddenly found himself on his back with Jade straddling him, still impaled on his erection. "I promised you a ride, big boy."

Somehow when she called him a boy, he didn't mind, especially when it was prefaced with big.

"I'm yours, beautiful." He gripped her hips to keep her in place and punched his hips up.

"Tsk, tsk." She took his hands and pinned them to the bed by his sides. "You're not taking over. It's my turn to be in charge."

60

JADE

"Whatever is your pleasure, my iron heart." Despite his words, Phinas's eyes blazed with defiance, but he didn't try to fight her to get free, and given how his shaft swelled and throbbed inside of her, he hadn't gotten turned off by her show of dominance either. "I'm yours."

He kept saying that, no doubt hoping that she would say the same thing back to him, but even though it was true to the core of her being, the words couldn't pass her lips.

But, Mother of All Life, how she wished she could tell him that she couldn't imagine a future without him, and that she was his for as long as he wanted her, and since they had bonded, it would be for as long as she lived.

It should have saddened her to think that he would outlive her, but she was too hyped up on the blood she'd taken from him, buzzing with energy and arousal, and something else she couldn't define. It was as if the tether tying her to him was happy that they were finally together and was singing a merry tune inside her heart, making it buoyant.

But her heart wasn't the only organ affected by his incredibly potent blood. Her sex had contracted around his swollen shaft, the need so intense that it bordered on pain.

Perhaps she'd taken too much of his immortal blood and was now suffering a sort of intoxication?

It had been much more than she'd taken the other time, almost as much as she would have taken from an animal to satisfy her thirst, and the energy boost was incredible.

Leaning down, she took his lips in a teasing kiss, flicking her long tongue around his fangs, which she knew drove him up the wall.

Releasing a frustrated groan, he bucked under her, and despite her superior strength she couldn't hold him down because she didn't have sufficient weight for that.

The male weighed at least twice as much as she did.

"Drinking from you is incredible." She lifted herself, bracing on her outstretched arms. "You're like an energy drink." She swiveled her hips in a corkscrew motion, then lifted off him and slammed back down.

"You are welcome to imbibe on my vein whenever. I love your fangs at my neck, and I love knowing that I'm providing for you." He grinned. "As long as you are with me, you will never go hungry or thirsty."

Letting go of his wrists, she put her hands on his chest. "That's a bonus I hadn't considered when I decided you were the one for me."

His eyes blazed. "Is it official, then?"

She nodded and lifted off him before slamming down again. "It's official between you and me."

Phinas didn't like her answer, and in a move that took her by surprise, he flipped them around and pinned her arms by her sides. "That's not good enough." He pulled his hips back and thrust inside of her again. "I want everyone to know that you are mine, and I'm yours. I don't want to be your dirty little secret." He punctuated his words by retracting and surging in again.

She could've gotten free with ease, but she let him hold her down, pretending that she couldn't.

It pleased her to have his large, heavy body on top of hers, and the angle of penetration was more pleasurable as well. There was something to be said for the missionary position, as humans called it.

"You're not my dirty little secret. You are my everything, but for now, it will have to remain between us."

He stilled on top of her. "Your everything? What about your people? Your daughter?"

No matter what species, males were so damn literal.

"They are my other everything. Would you shut up already and do your duty by me?"

Amusement sparkling in his eyes, he lifted his hips and held himself suspended on top of her with just the tip at her entrance. "My duty? As what? Your mate? Your plaything?"

It was a Kra-ell expression, and it didn't belong between her and Phinas. Male Kra-ell had a duty to answer their mistress's summons and service her. Immortal and human males did it just for the pleasure of it or to procreate.

Yanking her wrists out of his hold, she wrapped her arms around his torso. "It's one of those cultural differences we need to work out. I expect to be pleasured when I'm in the mood or in my fertile cycle."

"Oh, sweetheart. You'll be pleasured so often and so thoroughly that you will never even think to ask for more." He smiled. "I have satisfaction guaranteed practically stamped on my ass."

61

TOVEN

*P*avel pulled on the brig's bars with all his strength. "They will hold. Who did you build this jail for?"

Toven chuckled. "I didn't even know that the ship had one. It wasn't on the tour we were given when we got here."

Toven had been thinking about where to interrogate Igor, and although Yamanu could shroud the hotel, Toven didn't like the idea of doing it in a place that was surrounded by humans. Igor was an unknown factor, and once Merlin administered the antidote or whatever it was that would wake him up, Toven preferred not to do it in a cheap hotel room with walls that a Kra-ell could burst through even while chained.

After all, chains had to be attached to something.

The brig was perfect for that, but he needed to make sure that it would withstand the strength of a Kra-ell pureblood.

"I found it by chance." Merlin stuck his hands in his pockets. "I got lost looking for the booze storage, and when I noticed the steel door, I tried to open it, but it was locked. I was intrigued, so I asked Karl, and he said that it led to a corridor where the brig and the morgue were located." Merlin snorted. "How convenient."

Pavel seemed to agree.

"How is Drova taking it?" Merlin asked. "It must be difficult for her, knowing that her mother is about to execute her father."

Pavel's smile wilted. "She is doing what humans call dissociation. She pretends like Igor isn't her father." He grimaced. "All of us who were born in the compound are either the children or grandchildren of Igor's pod buddies. It's not easy for any of us."

That hadn't occurred to Toven, but it should have. The Kra-ell fronted a tough and unemotional attitude, but inside, they were like any other humanoid or animal for that matter.

Apes, monkeys, and dogs mourned lost companions and often couldn't be consoled, and he was sure it was true of other animals as well. Those who were too limited to understand death and loss were the lucky ones.

Toven had often thought about the chains of love that connected beings of all kinds to each other. He knew better than most how meaningless life was in an emotional vacuum.

As someone who had lost everyone and had roamed the Earth alone, he knew firsthand that the loss of connection to others meant the loss of the will to live. He'd been tethered to life by the thin thread of wanting to continue the gods' work and bring civilization to humans so they would live better lives, but after his failures, he hadn't had even that.

What had saved him were the fleeting connections to human females and the stories of love he'd written to immortalize them.

The Kra-ell had each other, and they were united by their survival, but many had lost so much, and now that he'd released their memories and their ability to grieve, many might sink into a deep depression.

All of the captured females had lost all of the male members of their families, and some of those who'd been born in the compound had recently lost a parent or a grandparent to Jade's and Kagra's swords.

The rest of Igor's male pod members were awaiting trial, but given Jade's attitude toward Valstar, Toven doubted any of those males would be found innocent or pardoned. Many more would lose their fathers and grand-fathers.

The whole lot of them would need to get counseling when they got to the village, but as far as he knew, Vanessa was the clan's only therapist, and she had her hands full with the rescued trafficking victims.

He should have brought it up with Kian, but with all the battle plans, the human aspect had been ignored. Well, the Kra-ell aspect, but that was semantics.

They'd been primarily concerned with the humans of Igor's compound, but the truth was that the humans were the least damaged of the three groups.

If any of the Kra-ell asked him to compel them to forget again, he would be inclined to comply with their requests even though it wasn't the best way to deal with grief. He doubted Kian would bring a bunch of therapists for the Kra-ell and then have them thralled to forget their alien patients.

Merlin patted the young Kra-ell's back. "If you need to talk to someone, my door is open. I'm always willing to lend an ear or offer advice if you want it from a guy who most people think is a little crazy."

"Are you crazy?"

Merlin chuckled. "Of course not, but then crazy people never think they are."

"We should go." Toven locked the brig and put the key in his pocket. "It's getting late, and if I can't compel Igor to obey me, I want to transfer him here tonight."

Merlin nodded. "I'm at your disposal."

"So am I," Pavel said. "If you need a strong pureblood to muscle Igor down, I'm your male."

"I appreciate the offer, but without the special earpieces to protect you from Igor's compulsion, you will be more of a liability than a help."

Pavel's face fell. "Can't you compel me to ignore his compulsion?"

"If Igor is a weaker compeller than I am, it might work, but I don't think that's the case."

Pavel regarded him with curiosity in his big eyes. "How strong are the gods? Are they stronger than their hybrid offspring?"

"Physically, there isn't much of a difference. I can run faster and see farther, but not by much. The big difference is in mental abilities. Immortals can't thrall each other, only humans, but I can thrall immortals and humans and do that on a larger scale."

Pavel's grin returned. "But you can't thrall me, right?"

"No, I can't."

"So that puts me on a par with the gods."

"It does," Toven admitted. "What I find curious is that the purebloods can't thrall or shroud."

Pavel shrugged. "I don't get what's the difference between compulsion and thralling."

"They have a lot in common," Merlin said. "But they use different delivery systems. Compulsion is carried on voice waves, and although it's powerful, it doesn't feel integral. On some level, you always know it didn't originate from your own will. Thralling, on the other hand, is mind-to-mind communicating, and you won't be able to tell that the thoughts and memories were not yours."

"So thralling is more powerful." Pavel turned to Toven. "It's a shame you can't use thralling on Igor."

"Indeed. One-on-one thralling might be more useful, but compulsion affects anyone within hearing distance. Both have their uses."

When Pavel still looked confused, Merlin wrapped an arm around his shoulders and led him toward the exit. "I'll try to explain it better. When someone compels you to do something, you know that you have been compelled, and you do it even if you don't want to. When someone thralls you, you don't know that it wasn't your decision to do whatever they wanted you to do. You think that you are doing it of your own free will."

"I don't get it. So how did Igor make all those settler females forget what he had done to their males? Can he thrall?"

"He might be able to," Toven said. "But he relied on compulsion to force them to avoid thinking about their losses, which was nearly as effective as thralling them to forget them."

Merlin shook his head. "Let me explain it better. If someone compels you to forget one thing and remember another, you might do that, but it will feel odd. You will always feel as if you have forgotten something important. Thralling, on the other hand, will achieve the same thing but feel more natural. You might dream about the things you were thralled to forget, but when you are conscious, and something reminds you of the thing you forgot, you'll get a headache if you try to remember it."

"I'm getting a headache now." Pavel lifted a hand to rub his temple. "This is all very confusing." He looked over his shoulder at Toven. "But I'm still volunteering to stand guard outside the door."

There was no need, but the guy looked eager to help, and Toven didn't have the heart to deny him. "Thank you. I'll speak with Yamanu about the security procedures and let you know."

62

SOFIA

*S*ofia hopped on top of one of the crates and sat down with her knees pulled up like she used to do as a child. "I'm glad you decided to come with me to the village."

Her father patted the flank of the sheep he was checking on. "Where else would I go? You are my only daughter. I'm just glad that I'm allowed to join you in the immortals' village." He walked over to her and hopped onto the crate next to her. "How are things going with Marcel? Are you still in love?"

She cast him a sidelong glance. "What does it look like?"

"I don't know. I barely get to see you. You were so busy in the clinic, helping with removal of the trackers, and when I saw you, you looked tired and stressed."

"Marcel is wonderful. He's not the storybook boyfriend who knows all the right things to say at the right time, but he loves me, and he's obsessed with taking care of me. Don't get me wrong, it's nice, but I want him to ease up a bit. I'm not some fragile doll that needs constant protection."

"To him, you do." He glanced at the entrance to the animal enclosure and lowered his voice. "When you turn immortal, he will be less worried about you. Did you start working on it?"

Sofia chuckled. "Not yet."

It was as if her father was asking her whether she and Marcel were working on making a baby. It wasn't the kind of conversation fathers and daughters usually had, but since her mother had been practically absent, her father had assumed both roles. Her aunts had helped a lot, but he was the one she'd turned to with everything. Well, except for when she needed help with using tampons. Had it been Isla or Hannele who had explained to her what to do?

She didn't remember.

"Why not?" her father asked. "The danger is over, the future has been decided on, and you are happy with Marcel."

"I'd rather wait for us to get settled in the village. Marcel says that the body needs to be in optimal health to start transitioning, and it's common knowledge that stress and anxiety have a negative impact on health."

Sighing, her father wrapped his arm around her shoulders. "You're afraid that it's not going to happen. That's why you keep postponing it. As long as you don't try, the possibility exists. When you try and fail, the hope is gone. It's like when you were afraid of taking tests even though you were beyond ready. You were terrified of failing."

He knew her so well.

Sofia nodded. "I think that the same is true for Marcel. He suggested that we start working on it, but he took it back right away with the optimal health explanation. And since I was afraid too, I didn't argue the point." She turned to look into her father's kind eyes. "Do you think we should just go for it?"

Jarmo shook his head. "There's no rush, and you can just spend the time enjoying each other. But if the uncertainty creates tension for the two of you, then maybe you shouldn't wait." He smiled. "I heard that meditation and yoga are good for relaxation. Perhaps now that you are not so busy in the clinic, you can try both as a way to release stress. Soaking in a bathtub is also known to be relaxing."

She leaned her head on his shoulder. "Talking to you is relaxing. Perhaps listening to your voice reminds my subconscious of all the nighttime stories you told me, and that's why I automatically relax."

"Well, that can be another good relaxation technique. I can come over to your cabin every night and read you a bedtime story. Except, I don't think your boyfriend will be too thrilled about my visits."

She wasn't sure about that.

Marcel would do anything to make her happy, even if it was letting her father tell her a bedtime story.

Lifting her head off his shoulder, she kissed his cheek. "You need to write down the stories you told me as a child so you won't forget them. One day, Marcel and I will have children of our own, and when you come over to tell them bedtime stories, you won't have to make them up on the spot like you did for me."

He chuckled. "Half the fun was neither of us knowing how the story would end."

"That's true. I always tried to get the ending out of you, and when you said that you didn't know, I thought you just wanted to keep me in suspense. In a way, your stories imitated life. We don't know how our story will end either."

"I do." He smiled. "And they lived happily ever after."

"How can you know that?"

"What other ending could a love story have?"

6 3

TOVEN

$\mathcal{M}$ax opened the hotel room door and motioned for Merlin and Toven to go in. "We put the four of them together. I just hope Aiden didn't mess up things and turn them into vegetables."

The medic flipped him the bird.

As a panicked expression twisted Merlin's lips, and he rushed into the room to examine the medic's work, Toven cast Max a reproachful look. "Why did you say that?"

"I like messing with Merlin, but they really don't look so good."

The medic crossed his arms over his chest. "I followed Merlin's instructions to the letter."

A moment later, the doctor let out a breath. "Everything looks okay, and they are breathing fine."

The medic cast Max a smug look. "I told you that you had nothing to worry about."

Max shook his head. "If Igor dies before Phinas can deliver him to Jade, he will blame me. He left me in charge."

Merlin pulled out his stethoscope. "Which one is Igor?"

Aiden pointed to the cot under the window.

Toven walked over and looked down at the pureblood. Was he a pureblood, though?

He looked Kra-ell, and although he was handsome, he didn't have the perfect skin and symmetrical features of a god or even an immortal. If he was a hybrid, he hadn't inherited his physical attributes from his god parent.

After Merlin checked the male's vitals, he pulled out a syringe from one pocket and a large vial from another. "How conscious do you want him?"

"Only semi-conscious. Are you sure you can dial it so precisely?"

"I believe so, and if he gives us any trouble, I can incapacitate him with my sleeping serum until the new dose of tranquilizer takes effect." He shook the vial. "I tested it on Pavel, and it worked. The kid was a very good sport about it. I left him to sleep it off in the clinic."

Max arched a brow. "What did you promise him in return?"

"Nothing much. I just told him some funny stories from my colorful past that made him laugh."

"Pavel is thirty-two years old, so I don't think he appreciates being called a kid." Max finished wrapping Igor in chains. "But a good laugh is worth its weight in gold. We all need more of that." He secured the lock. "Check your earpieces, please."

"I have them in." Merlin moved his long hair to show that he had them in his ears. "Thirty-two is a baby immortal and a teenage pureblood. To me, Pavel is a kid, and he doesn't mind me calling him that."

It seemed that the doctor had taken a liking to the young pureblood.

Max checked to ensure that the fit was as perfect as it should be and then looked at Toven. "Just in case, you should put yours in as well."

"I know. I wouldn't risk rousing him without them. If he can compel me, he can command me to unchain him, and none of you would be able to stop me."

Max arched a brow. "If you say so, your Highness."

Ignoring the Guardian's impudence, Toven pulled the earpieces out of his pocket and stuck them in his ears. "Please, go ahead, Merlin."

Without much preamble, the doctor stuck the needle in Igor's neck and depressed the syringe. "That should do it."

"How long until he wakes up?" Toven asked.

"Right about now."

Igor gasped and opened a pair of unfocused eyes. "*Kto ty?*"

"He asked who you are," Aiden said as if Toven needed the translation.

"*Skazhite mne vashe imya,*" Toven commanded. "Tell me your name."

Igor tried to focus his eyes. "*Kto ty?*" he repeated.

"*Vo-pervykh, skazhi mne svoye imya!*" Toven repeated, using the full force of his compulsion. "First, tell me your name."

"Igor."

Hope surged in Toven's chest. Perhaps he could compel Igor after all. "Tell me where you came from," he commanded in Russian.

"No," Igor answered in English, his eyes focusing on Toven with a knowing look.

"Fuck," Max murmured under his breath.

"Put him back under," Toven said, but Aiden was already injecting the liquid bag with the sedative.

Igor made a feeble tug on the chains binding him, and his eyes closed.

They waited a few moments longer until Merlin confirmed that he was out.

"Now, the other test, please," Toven told Merlin.

The doctor pulled a stopwatch from his pocket and handed it to Max. "Start the timer the moment I make the cut, please."

Nodding, Max took the watch. "Ready when you are, doc."

Merlin pulled a small box from his pocket and opened it to reveal a surgical knife that was no bigger than a pair of nail clippers.

Igor's wrists were shackled to the chains around his torso, but Merlin didn't make a fuss about having to bend close to the prisoner. "On my mark." He positioned the knife on Igor's palm. "Now!"

Blood welled where Merlin had made the cut, but the cut itself disappeared in three and a half seconds.

Merlin lifted his head and looked at Toven. "That's way too fast for a Kra-ell, or even an immortal. He's definitely part god."

Toven nodded. "He doesn't look like a god, but there is no other explanation for his rapid healing."

"How fast do you heal?" Aiden asked.

"A little faster than that, but not by much." Toven let out a breath. "Make arrangements to transfer the prisoners to the ship. Igor goes into the brig. The other three can be put in a cabin like the rest of Igor's pod-mates. Just not together with them. I don't want anyone filling them in on what happened."

"Aye, aye, captain." Max saluted. "I'll gladly get out of this hotel and spend the rest of the night in the comfort of my old cabin." He sighed. "I'm going to miss the *Aurora*. She's a classy lady and a comfortable lay."

Toven shook his head. "You're something, Max."

"Yeah, I know." The Guardian smirked. "I'm one of a kind."

"Thank the Fates for that," Aiden murmured under his breath.

64

KIAN

"I can't compel Igor." Toven delivered the news Kian didn't want to hear.

"I was afraid of that." Kian got up, walked over to the bar, and poured himself a shot of whiskey.

"I'm going to try again tomorrow with Mia," Toven said. "But if that doesn't work, we are out of options. One day will not be enough to break him the old-fashioned way."

"Take Arwel with you when you go to see him with Mia. I'm curious what he'll make of the guy."

"I will." Toven sighed. "I'm afraid that Igor's immunity to my compulsion is not the only bad news."

Kian stopped his pacing. "Don't tell me that he can compel you."

"I had the earpieces in, so I don't know that he can, but I doubt it. It's common for compellers to be immune to compulsion by others."

"Annani can override most. I thought that being a god, you would also have the ability."

"We can still have her try to compel Igor remotely. What's the worst that could happen? If she can't, at least we tried."

"Talk to me again after you try to compel him with Mia enhancing your powers. If the two of you together fail as well, I'll talk to my mother."

The only reason he agreed to it was that Toven might do that anyway.

The god didn't answer to Kian, and there was nothing stopping him from calling Annani and asking her to give it a try.

"Thank you. She would be peeved if you didn't."

Kian chuckled. "Yeah, and that's putting it mildly. So, what's the other bad news?"

"Igor definitely has godly genes in him. The cut healed in less than four seconds. That's how fast Orion and Geraldine heal, and I guess you and your siblings as well. The curious thing is that he doesn't look like a god. He looks fully Kra-ell. I talked with Kagra, and she said that he hunted and used animal blood like all the other purebloods, and she'd never seen him eating regular food. If he's half god, he should be able to tolerate grains and dairy and all the other good stuff."

"Maybe he can, but since he didn't want anyone to know that he's not really a pureblood, he hid it well. He's probably like Emmett, who can tolerate some nearly raw meat but needs to supplement it with blood." Kian groaned. "I really hope you'll be able to compel Igor to talk with Mia's help. I need to know what and who he is. He's such an enigma."

"I'm very curious myself," Toven said. "Before I called you, I was wracking my brain trying to come up with something that we could offer Jade in exchange for giving him a longer stay of execution. I'm not a proponent of torture, but starving him would have the same effect. The problem with that is the time it would take. He can last weeks if not months without food."

"Perhaps we can offer her the freedom to come and go as she pleases." Kian resumed his pacing. "I'm not really worried about her betraying our trust, and I'm willing to give her one of our special vehicles. After being imprisoned for so long, I bet that will appeal to her."

"That's a good idea, but I don't think it's going to be enough. She's really hankering to behead both Igor and Valstar. I did my best to convince her to let Valstar stand trial together with Igor's other pod members, and she even agreed, but then she told me in front of him that no matter what the verdict was, she was going to execute him. So, what's the point of having him stand trial?"

"Time." Kian plopped down on the couch. "The more time passes and the more freedom Jade has, the less angry she will be, and perhaps her need for revenge will subside. Not that I care either way. If the bastard deserves to die, then he dies."

"That's the thing," Toven said. "I'm not sure that he does. He was a tool in Igor's hands. If I compelled you to kill Anandur or Brundar, you would have no choice but to do it even though it would break you. Under those circumstances, would Edna find you guilty of murder?"

"She wouldn't, but I might want her to. The problem is that we don't know whether Valstar would have acted differently without the compulsion."

"We don't. But the possibility casts a shadow of doubt, and no judge would agree to a death penalty unless a premeditated murder has been proven beyond a reasonable doubt."

65

JADE

*J*ade snuggled closer to Phinas.

He was so warm, and she wasn't thinking just about the heat his big body was emitting. His soul was warm, and it thawed the ice in hers.

Being with him brought to the surface soft feelings she'd suppressed for so long that it was like discovering for the first time that she could feel anything other than duty, loyalty, hatred, and rage.

The thing was, Igor wasn't the only one to blame for her emotional handicap. The Kra-ell way didn't allow for soft feelings like love and kindness, and those had been beaten out of her at such a young age that she'd forgotten ever experiencing them. But she had. She'd loved her mother, and she'd loved her father and the other males in her mother's tribe who had been as much her fathers as the one who'd contributed his genetic material to hers.

Except, love and kindness had been beaten out of them as well, and they hadn't returned her love, not overtly anyway. There had been small acts of kindness that she still remembered to this day, although sometimes she wasn't sure whether she'd lived them or dreamt them.

From time to time, she even considered that none of her memories were real and that they had been implanted in her mind during the long voyage. Perhaps she wasn't who she thought she was, and neither were the others.

It was a terrifying thought, and usually, she tried to get rid of it as soon as it flitted through her mind, but it had a nasty habit of coming back when her mental shields were down.

"Good morning, my iron heart." Phinas planted a soft kiss on her forehead while his hand smoothed down her back and cupped her bottom. "What are you thinking about?"

"That I don't want to get up." She put her hand on his chest. "And that you are like my own personal furnace. How come you are so much warmer than me?"

"I'm bigger." He pulled her closer, his impressive erection pressing against her belly.

She chuckled. "Indeed." Trailing her hand down his muscular chest, she gripped that throbbing, velvety length and gave it a gentle squeeze. "Is this for me?"

"Always." He was on top of her in an instant, cupping her cheeks in his large hands and looking at her with so much warmth in his eyes that the ice covering her heart melted a little further. "You are so beautiful. I could look at your face for days and not get tired of looking."

She smiled and tilted her head up to catch his lips in a quick kiss. "Hold that thought. I need to use the bathroom and shower, and so do you."

They'd played so many times last night that she didn't want to think about what was covering them and the state of the bedding. They probably should change the sheets.

For a brief moment, Phinas looked disappointed, but then mischief sparked in his eyes. "We can play in the shower or the closet if you prefer a darker, drier place."

Jade liked to see Phinas playful like that. Despite his sunshiny disposition, he harbored darkness deep inside of him, and he'd allowed her glimpses of it, but she had a feeling that it was just the tip of the iceberg.

Perhaps that was why they were such kindred souls. They had both gone through hell and survived to find solace in each other's arms.

Phinas called it love, and maybe it was time she called what was in her heart by its proper name, but her past and what had been drilled into her head still had too strong of a hold over her. Maybe she needed to practice saying that damn word in front of the mirror while no one was there to hear her.

Wrapping her arms around Phinas's broad back, she palmed his buttocks and squeezed hard. "We could try both and see which one we like better."

Phinas grinned. "I like the way you think, my sexy mate."

Rolling her eyes, Jade pushed on his chest. "Is that word going to be in every other sentence from now on?"

"Which one? Sexy or mate?"

"You know which one." She gave him a stronger push, forcing him to let her go. "I'm going to use the toilet." She got out of bed and headed toward the bathroom. "If you need to use it too, go to the other bedroom."

"Always so pragmatic, my iron-hearted mate." Phinas swung his legs over the side of the bed and got up.

She stopped with her hand on the door handle. "If you say mate one more time today, I'm going to punch you."

6 6

PHINAS

*S*tifling a laugh, Phinas followed Jade's magnificent ass to the bathroom. "If the moratorium on the word mate is just for today, I can abide by your wishes, my iron-hearted beauty. But I can't make any promises about tomorrow."

She turned around and put her hands on her hips, looking formidable even in the nude. "Tomorrow, you can say it two times, and only when we are alone."

His lips twitching, he arched a brow. "What about the day after? Can I say it three times?"

Jade's eyes traveled over his body, and when they reached his prominent erection, she licked her lips. "I can't think with you looking at me like that."

He gripped his shaft. "Are you referring to him or to me?"

"Him?" She arched a brow. "Does he have eyes?"

"He has one, and it's just for you."

Jade burst out laughing, and it was the most beautiful sound Phinas had ever heard, and given that he'd heard Annani laugh, that was saying something.

It wasn't a musical sound like the goddess's. It was throaty and coarse, but it was wholehearted, and it was the first time he'd heard Jade really laugh.

Unable to help himself, he closed the distance between them in one long step and plucked her into his arms. "I love you." He smashed his lips over hers.

Winding her long legs around his hips, she kissed him back.

When he put her down next to the toilet, she smiled a little shyly and made a circular motion with her hand. "I can't do my business with you watching. Go to the other bathroom."

She would get used to the familiarity, but they had the rest of their very long lives to work on it, and for now, he could accommodate her.

Turning his back, Phinas waggled his butt cheeks, hoping to get another laugh out of her, but he only got a sigh. Then again, it might have been a sigh of relief at finally emptying her bladder.

"I love your laugh." He walked over to the vanity and reached for the toothbrush. "I want to hear it more often."

She flushed the toilet and joined him at the other sink. "You are the only one who can make me laugh." She pulled the other toothbrush from the cup and squeezed toothpaste over it.

It hadn't been the first time Jade had slept in his cabin, and he'd gotten her a toothbrush from the supply room before leaving. He liked the mornings of them standing next to each other and brushing their teeth in the nude.

Jade finished brushing first and rinsed out her mouth. "I used to laugh back in the day, not a lot, but enough. I haven't laughed this hard in a very long time."

Phinas's heart squeezed at the thought that she hadn't laughed since her world came crashing down. Once they left the haven of his cabin, she would come face to face with the one responsible for her pain, and he doubted she would be in the mood for jokes after that.

Dropping his toothbrush in the cup, he turned to her and engulfed her in his arms. "I promise to make you laugh at least once a day."

Amusement dancing in her dark eyes, she cupped his cheek. "I'll make you a deal. Every time you make me laugh, you can say the forbidden word one more time that day."

"Which word?" He pretended ignorance. "Mate?"

Affecting an angry expression, she playfully punched his chest. "Yeah, that one. You've reached your quota for today, and I told you that I'd punch you if you said it again."

"Yeah, but I made you laugh."

"True." She patted the spot she punched. "I take it back."

"Oh, no, you don't. Now you have to pay." He lifted her and carried her over to the shower.

"Start the water while I take care of my bladder."

"Is that how I'm going to pay for punching you?"

"Not even close." He flushed the toilet and sauntered over to the sink to wash his hands.

Jade got the water running and stood under the spray. With her tiny waist, enormous eyes, and her long wet hair forming a black curtain over her silky skin, she looked like a nymph, otherworldly and magical.

Getting under the spray with her, he cupped the back of her head and kissed the tip of her tiny nose. "I'll take your real name as payment. The Kra-ell name you were given by your mother. Or are the fathers in charge of that?"

"No, it was my mother, and she gave me a very unbecoming name for a Kra-ell girl. I was teased mercilessly for it and got into more fights than I care to remember."

"Wasn't she happy about giving birth to you? I thought that girls were highly prized."

"They were, and that's why my mother called me precious. My Kra-ell name is Je-kara, and I hate it passionately. I wanted a warrior name like Gi-bera or A-zuma."

"I love it. Can I call you Je-kara?"

Her lips twisted in distaste. "Please, don't."

"Then I'll have to use that other word that you don't like."

She smiled. "You know the rules for that one."

"Then laugh for me." He tickled her waist. "I need to say it."

A small laugh left her lips. "That wasn't fair." She removed his hands from her waist. "The deal is that you need to do or say something that amuses me."

Tilting his head back, he let the water pelt his face as he thought of another funny thing to say, but he felt too raw and too emotional to come up with anything amusing.

"I want to have ten children with you. Five girls and five boys."

"That's not funny. You can't give me that even if you really want to have that many kids."

He'd said it as a poorly conceived joke, but she sounded as if she really wanted that.

Sitting on the bench, he pulled her into his lap. "Maybe I can. Your fertility is better than mine, and Merlin has a potion that is supposed to improve it."

Jade smiled sadly. "You didn't think it through, Phinas. Any children we have will not be immortal, only long-lived, and the same goes for me. I have less than nine hundred years left, give or take a couple of centuries, while you have eternity. Do you really want me as your mate?"

Talk about dissociation. The thought hadn't occurred to him even once.

"The Fates chose for us to bond and mate, and they didn't do it to be cruel. A truelove mate is rare and precious, and only a few are blessed with one. The immortals believe that the Fates reward those who have suffered greatly or sacrificed a lot for others with that once-in-a-lifetime boon. If that's true, then I know no one more deserving of a truelove mate than you."

Jade swallowed. "You suffered and sacrificed too."

"I did, but what I went through pales in comparison to what you had to endure. My point is that the Fates will either find a way for us to be together forever or die together."

"Don't talk like that. You're immortal. You must go on."

He shrugged. "I'd rather have nine hundred blissful years with my truelove mate, give or take a couple of centuries, than spend eternity alone."

67

JADE

"Nervous?" Phinas took Jade's hand.

She yanked it out of his grasp. "I'm not nervous. I'm angry that I have to wait. I want to be done with it."

They weren't alone, and their entourage included two purebloods in addition to Toven, Mia, Yamanu, Arwel, Merlin, and two Guardians whose names she didn't know.

Jade didn't mind the immortals seeing her holding hands with Phinas, but she didn't want to give the purebloods any more fuel for gossip.

By now, everyone probably knew that she and Phinas were a thing, but she hoped her people assumed that she was doing what she'd done with Igor, which was to collect information to help their cause and get more concessions from their new allies.

It might have been true in the beginning, but even then she'd felt a connection with Phinas that she hadn't felt with any male before him.

And now... well, now she was still trying to wrap her head around them being destined for each other.

Truelove mates.

A gift from the Mother of all Life, or the Fates, to compensate her for what she'd been through.

Except, as much as Jade appreciated Phinas and the new life he offered her, he could never replace her sons, their fathers, or the other males Igor had murdered.

One just did not equate to the other.

Perhaps others could be satisfied replacing the family they'd lost with a new one, but she couldn't understand how anyone could even think like that.

She would always remember those she'd lost, and she would mourn them to the day she died and then join them in the fields of the brave.

Regrettably, there were only two options for a Kra-ell's afterlife, and the valley of the shamed was not good enough for Igor, or rather not bad enough. His rotten soul should spend eternity in the deepest recesses of the humans' hell, forever tortured by fire and brimstone.

As their group stepped out of the elevator on the clinic's level, Yamanu led them to a massive steel door that she'd seen before but assumed led to a bank vault or maybe more cold storage.

Yamanu typed a code into the keypad, and when a click sounded, indicating that the lock was released, he turned the big wheel in the center of the door and yanked it open.

"It's a watertight door," he explained. "In case of a hull breach, it locks automatically. For some reason, the brig and the morgue are located behind it."

"Convenient," Phinas said.

Jade hoped he wasn't too upset about her refusing to let him hold her hand.

It was true that they'd reached a new stage in their relationship, but she was still uncomfortable about displays of physical affection in public.

Hell, she was uncomfortable about any displays of affection, physical or otherwise. She was a tough warrior and a strong leader. She couldn't afford to appear soft.

"After you." Yamanu motioned for Toven and Mia to enter first.

Jade stopped next to the Guardian. "Perhaps the rest of us should wait outside while they conduct their test? I don't want Igor to get the impression that he's so important." She looked behind her at the two young Kra-ell purebloods. "They shouldn't be anywhere near him because they don't have earpieces."

"They are going to stay outside here," Yamanu agreed. "That's the only way in or out, and I want them guarding the entrance in case one of yours decides to break Igor free."

Since the brig was secure, with the strength of the bars having been tested by Pavel, she'd wondered why Yamanu had insisted on the purebloods accompanying them.

It hadn't occurred to her that any of her people could be that stupid, but Yamanu was right not to take the risk. Igor might have left a deep-seated compulsion in some of those who were loyal to him with instructions about what to do if he ever got captured.

The guy was smart, and he didn't leave things to chance.

Toven and Mia waited for them outside the brig's outer door, and as the rest of them caught up, Yamanu didn't open it right away.

"Please check your earpieces one more time before entering."

"Is he awake?" Mia asked.

Merlin nodded. "We put him in there while still sedated, but he's had all night and morning to shake off the effects."

Igor was probably going mad with thirst, but all that was available to him was water from the faucet in the bathroom, provided that the brig had a bathroom. It had been days since he'd had blood, and water wouldn't satisfy his thirst.

Perhaps the promise of a last meal would be enough to make him talk in case Mia's enhancing powers wouldn't bolster Toven's compulsion ability enough to compel him.

68

TOVEN

*A*s everyone checked their earpieces, Jade leaned toward Merlin. "I wish you'd taken out Igor's vocal cords."

"It wouldn't have worked. He would have regrown new ones overnight."

She frowned. "That's impossible."

They hadn't told her about the experiment Merlin had done last night. Toven had decided that it could wait until after he and Mia had given compelling Igor a try. His reasoning had been that if it worked, Jade would be less anxious learning about Igor's enhanced genetics, and if it didn't, she would probably guess that Igor was not a pureblooded Kra-ell.

After all, they had speculated on the subject before, so it shouldn't come as a big surprise. But it seemed like she was going to learn about it sooner rather than later.

"Unfortunately, it is not." Toven checked the fit of Mia's earpieces. "As we've suspected, Igor must be part god. He heals incredibly fast."

"How do you know that?"

"Last night, before we brought him here, Merlin tested his healing speed. Igor heals almost as fast as I do."

Curiously, Igor hadn't required a larger dose of sedatives than the other Kra-ell. Toven wondered if a god would have needed a bigger dose to be sedated than a pureblood or an immortal, but he had no wish to experiment on himself, so it would remain a mystery.

Jade lifted her hand to get his attention. "Does that change anything?"

"In what way?" Yamanu asked.

"In any way. Do I still get to behead Igor even though he's part god?"

Toven nodded. "He's yours to do with as you please. I just hope that you can summon a little more patience and allow us enough time to get information out of him."

Her eyes flashed red. "You have twenty-four hours. Make them count."

Stubborn female.

Toven couldn't really blame her. If someone had murdered his children, he would have torn them apart with his bare fangs. Looking at it from that perspective, Jade was being more than reasonable.

"Is everyone ready?" Yamanu looked at each of them to confirm before inputting the code into the keypad.

"Phinas, you are with me." He pulled out his dart gun and motioned for the male to take his out as well.

Regrettably, the ship hadn't been equipped with any surveillance cameras yet, and if Igor somehow managed to break through the bars of the prison cell and made it to the office or reception area, or whatever the space was called, they wouldn't know that without checking in person.

Phinas pulled out a handgun and aimed it at the door. "If he heals so fast, I'd rather put a bullet in him."

Jade patted her hip as if looking for her sword and murmured something unintelligible under her breath.

"Arwel." Yamanu motioned to the Guardian. "You know your part."

"Of course."

As Yamanu pushed the door open, Phinas walked in with his gun pointing the way.

"All clear," he said from the inside before walking out into the hallway. "The butcher is behind bars."

Yamanu glanced at Arwel. "Anything?"

The Guardian shook his head. "Absolutely nothing. It's like no one is there."

Jade huffed. "He's a sociopath. What did you expect?"

"Fear," Arwel said. "Even sociopaths feel that." He looked at Toven. "He either doesn't feel fear or knows how to block his body from emitting emotions."

"I'll take it under consideration."

Yamanu motioned for Toven to go in. "Do your thing. We will wait outside until you need us, but I want the door to remain slightly open for Arwel."

"Thank you." Toven took a deep breath, walked into the room, and left the door ajar.

The prisoner was behind the iron bars, his long body sprawled on the cot they had laid him on when they'd brought him in. His arms were crossed over his chest and his feet at the ankles, and he didn't seem perturbed by his visitors.

"Hello, Igor." Toven pulled out a chair and sat facing the bars, far enough from them so Igor couldn't reach for him.

"Release me," Igor said in perfect English.

For a moment, Toven was startled by how American he sounded, but then he remembered that the earpieces translated what was being said, and the machine voice was programmed to sound like a native Californian.

"Your compulsion is not going to work on me."

That got Igor's attention. Lifting his head, he took a look at his visitor, and his eyes widened for a brief moment before going back to their blank expression.

A string of words followed.

Toven recognized it as the gods' language, or some dialect that was related to it, but he couldn't understand a single word.

He lifted a hand to stop him. "I don't understand what you are trying to say."

"Are you trying to pass for a human?"

Toven smiled. "And succeeding."

"Good for you. Were you sent to retrieve me?"

Perhaps Igor's command of English wasn't as good, and he'd used the wrong words.

"Retrieve you from where?" Toven asked in Russian.

Igor tilted his head. "You don't know what I'm talking about, do you?"

"No. I don't. But I will find out in a moment."

Mia was right outside the room, which should be enough to give him the boost he needed, but he wasn't taking any shortcuts.

Rising to his feet, he turned around, walked to the door, and opened it all the way. "Come on, my love. Let's do this together."

Mia wheeled her chair in but stopped as soon as she crossed the threshold. "It should be fine from here, right?"

"Yes." He took her hand.

"What is that?" Igor rose to his feet and approached the bars. "Who's the female?"

"I'm the one asking the questions." Toven focused his compulsion and turned it into a sharp spear. "Who was supposed to retrieve you?"

"Your relatives." Igor went back to his cot and sat down. "If you're trying to compel me, you are wasting your time. I'm immune."

69

JADE

*J*ade had heard Igor loud and clear.

"I guess there is no point in waiting twenty-four hours. I should have brought my sword with me and ended it right now." She looked at Arwel. "Anything?"

He shook his head. "He's a vault."

"Would it help if you go inside?"

"No. This is close enough."

She nodded. "Well, you tried." She turned around and strode into the room with Phinas and Yamanu on her heel.

"Jade." Igor smiled creepily.

What the hell? What was he smiling about? She couldn't remember him ever smiling at her.

"You shouldn't be so happy to see me," she said in English. "I'm here to end your miserable existence."

"I don't think so," he said in Kra-ell. "Tell the others to leave."

It was her turn to smile. "You can't compel me either." She pushed away the strand of hair covering her earpiece. "Who would have thought that a simple device like that could nullify your power. You're now at my mercy, and I have none to give. Prepare to die."

"Not so fast." He rose to his feet and approached the bars. "I have something you want," he said in Kra-ell. "Something you are desperate to find out. But I'm only going to give you the information you seek if you vow to the Mother that you will keep me alive."

The male was delusional. "There is nothing you can give me that is worth that to me. I've dreamt for twenty-three years about the day I'd avenge my sons, their fathers, and all the other males of my tribe, and that day is today." She tilted her head toward Toven. "They asked me to give them time to interrogate you, but since they can't compel you to talk, I see no reason to deny myself the pleasure of killing you right now."

His eyes darted to her hip, where her sword should have been. Toven had explicitly asked her to leave it behind, and Jade regretted agreeing to his request.

She'd accommodated him enough already.

"Then you are never going to find the royal twins," he said in Kra-ell.

Her breath caught in her throat. She'd never asked him about the twins explicitly, only in a roundabout way. How did he know that she knew they'd been on the ship? How did he know that she would do anything to find them?

"Do you want me to switch to English so they will understand?" He smiled his creepy smile again. "I can tell the god about them, and you know what he will do. He will have to kill them to protect his people."

"He wouldn't," she said in Kra-ell. "Unlike you, he's a decent person."

Igor shrugged. "Everyone thinks that they are doing the best they can and that their cause is right. Your new friend the god will have to eliminate the threat to his people."

He was bluffing, Jade knew that, but she also knew that she had to keep the twins safe, which meant not letting the immortals find out about them.

The thing was, she didn't understand why her gut was telling her to hide that information from them.

So far, Toven and his people had done everything they had promised. They had freed her and her people, captured Igor, and even invited her and her people to join their community. Decency required that she tell them about the twins, but she'd given a life-debt vow to protect the queen and her family, and telling anyone about the twins might cost them their lives. She had no doubt that the queen had a good reason to keep them veiled their entire lives and then smuggle them out on the settlers' ship.

"Why are they a threat to anyone? They are priests, not warriors. And how do you know they were on the ship? I don't even know that for sure."

"I'm not going to tell you anything more until the others leave the room and we are alone."

"They don't understand Kra-ell."

"Those are my terms. You can kill me right now and wonder about the twins' fate until the day you die. Or you can ask your companions to leave the room."

Letting out a breath, she turned to face the others. "I need you to leave. He's willing to share some information with me but only if we are alone."

"It's a trick," Phinas said. "I'm not leaving you alone with him."

She gave him a reassuring smile. "He can't bend bars with his compulsion power, and he can't use it against me as long as I have the earpieces. You can wait for me out in the hallway."

Phinas shook his head. "Whatever he promised you, it's not worth the risk."

She threw her hands in the air. "What risk? He's not omnipotent. If he were, he wouldn't be behind bars."

"Jade is right." Toven put his hand on Phinas's shoulder. "If she wants a few private minutes with him, it's her right."

Phinas pulled his gun out of his waistband. "Do you know how to use it?" She nodded.

"Let me show you anyway." He removed the safety. "Just point it at his chest and shoot. It won't kill him, but you're more likely to hit the target when you're aiming at a larger mass. It's easy to miss the head."

She chuckled. "I know how to handle firearms, and I happen to be a very good shot."

"Of course, you are." He put the handgun in her outstretched hand and leaned in to plant a quick kiss on her cheek. "Be careful."

"Always."

7 0

PHINAS

"*I* don't like it." Phinas leaned against the steel door. "There is no reason for him to want to speak with Jade alone when they can talk in Kra-ell, which none of us understand."

"He was probably concerned about me," Toven said. "I know only a little of the gods' language, and the dialect he used was so different that I couldn't understand a single word, but he can't be sure of that. He probably thinks that I know both languages, and I'm bluffing."

There was some logic to that, but not much. "What can he say to her that's not meant for us to understand?"

"Maybe he wants to appeal to her on a personal level," Mia said. "They have a daughter together, so he might use that for leverage."

They all turned to Arwel, who shrugged. "There was a little something I felt when Jade walked in, but then it winked out. The Kra-ell don't emit much to start with, and this guy must have been trained to control what he emits."

Merlin jingled the various vials he carried in his pocket, which was annoying since Phinas was trying to listen to what was being said behind the closed door.

"Can you please stop making that noise?"

The doctor looked at him as if he didn't know what Phinas was talking about, then looked down at his pocket as if he hadn't noticed it before, and the noise stopped. "Sorry about that. I didn't realize what my hand was doing. I was thinking about Igor and why he wanted Jade alone. He's probably pleading with her for his life and didn't want us to witness his humiliation."

"I don't think so." Toven leaned against the wall and crossed his arms over his chest. "I think he's bargaining with her, and whatever he's offering her is not meant for our ears. This means that Jade is hiding something from us because she seemed anxious for us to leave."

Toven was right.

Most of the exchange between Igor and Jade had been in Kra-ell, so Phinas could only gauge her reactions to what Igor was saying by her tone of voice.

At first, she'd sounded annoyed and impatient, then angry and impatient, and then her tone had turned anxious.

"I also wonder what he meant about me coming to retrieve him," Toven asked. "Was he expecting the gods to come to get him after seven thousand years?"

Phinas put his ear to the door. He didn't understand what was being said, but as long as they were talking, he knew that Jade was okay.

Yamanu snorted. "Maybe he had an accomplice among the gods on Earth. What if someone didn't want the Kra-ell to arrive and hired Igor to sabotage the ship?"

"It's not such a far-fetched idea." Toven shifted his weight to his other leg. "The settlers' ship left the gods' home world shortly after the rebel gods were exiled to Earth. Well, shortly in immortal terms. It could have been a couple of centuries later. But back then, the gods could still communicate with their home, so it's possible that some sort of a conspiracy was hatched."

As Phinas's phone vibrated in his pocket, he pulled it out and groaned. "I have to take it." He looked at Yamanu. "Can you listen at the door for me?"

Yamanu nodded. "I got her back. Don't worry."

"Thanks." Phinas accepted the call. "Hello, boss. Is it urgent?"

"Not really. I just wanted to know what you found out about Igor. Can Toven compel him?"

"He's immune."

Kalugal sighed. "I was afraid of that. What's next?"

Phinas walked to the end of the corridor. The god and the immortals could still hear him, but they might not hear Kalugal.

"Jade is inside, talking with him alone, and we suspect that he's trying to bargain with her. By the looks of him, he's confident that he has a good bargaining chip, but I doubt she'll accept any offer he can make her."

"Let me know as soon as you know. Now I'm even more curious to hear what he has to say."

"I will."

"Are you excited about your girl coming to live in the village with you?"

Phinas chuckled. "Never call her a girl to her face, and yes, I'm excited. Things are progressing well."

"I'm glad. I'm even more glad that she decided to join you in the village. I knew that you would follow her wherever she went, and I hated the idea of losing you."

"You wouldn't have lost me. The only other option was Safe Haven, and it's not that far away. Besides, you would have hardly missed me. You have Jacki, Darius, and Rufsur."

"I like to keep those I care deeply about close by, and you are just as dear to me as Rufsur. I need both my devils with me."

Something eased in Phinas's chest, a hard place that he hadn't been aware of softening. Ever since Kalugal had promoted him and Rufsur to be his second- and third-in-command, there had been an unofficial competition between them on who was closer to Kalugal, and who was officially his second. But even though Kalugal refused to name one or the other, it had always seemed to Phinas that Rufsur had been the favorite.

It was nice to hear that Kalugal considered them equally dear and useful.

"That's good to know, boss." He would have said more, but he had company. Or at least that was his excuse. What was he supposed to tell Kalugal? That it meant a lot to him?

Kalugal already knew that.

71

JADE

*J*ade sat down on the only chair in the room and put the handgun on her lap.

The chair was placed far enough from the bars, so there was no chance Igor could reach out and grab her, and the gun wasn't really necessary. If she held it pointed at him, it would look as if she was scared of him, and she wouldn't give him the satisfaction.

It was his turn to be afraid of her, and she would revel in every moment of it.

Except, the scumbag didn't look scared at all. Sitting on his cot with his thighs spread as if he owned the place, he seemed as confident and as calm and collected as ever.

When he just stared at her in silence, she asked, "What do you know about the twins?"

"First, tell me if you are under the god's compulsion."

"He's not like you. He freed us from your compulsion and set us free."

"In exchange for what?"

"Eliminating the threat you represented."

"I was no threat to them. I didn't know that any gods were still on Earth. I couldn't find any, and believe me, I looked. They must be very good at hiding."

"They are."

"Are they all still here?"

"No more questions, Igor. The twins. Where are they?"

"I want your vow first. The life-debt vow." He stared her in the eyes the same way he used to do when she was still under his control. "I want you to spend your life protecting mine."

"Not going to happen. Not even for the twins."

He tilted his head. "Really? I thought that a traditionalist like you would never break her vow. But evidently, you are not as righteous as you like everyone to believe."

Her blood chilled.

No one on the settler ship had known each other. They had been selected by a lottery that every young, childless Kra-ell had to participate in.

Neither Igor nor anyone else knew what she had done before joining the expedition. She'd told Kagra some things over the years, though, and it was possible that Igor had compelled her second to tell him what she knew and then compelled her to keep it from Jade.

Except, Toven had released Kagra from Igor's compulsion, and she would have told her that her secrets had been compromised.

Unless Kagra felt guilty and was too embarrassed to admit that.

She'd never told Kagra about the vow, but she'd told her about serving in the queen's guard, and everyone who'd served in it had to vow to protect the queen and her family.

"What vow?" She arched a brow, hoping to look nonchalant. "I didn't give you any vow."

"You owe the queen a life-debt vow, and that includes her children. You are obligated to do everything in your power to protect them. How are you going to do that if you don't know where they are?"

"And you do?"

"I know how to find them."

"If you did, you would have found them already and killed them. They are probably dead anyway, and so are the queen and her consorts. My life debt is null. Besides, I didn't even know that they were on the ship, I only suspected it, and you have somehow found out about it, and you're trying to trick me into sparing your life."

"I admit that I don't know whether they are alive or dead, but they might be still alive and in stasis, but that could change at any moment. They could be found by humans, their pod might malfunction, and if it landed in the ocean, which it probably did, the hull might get breached, and they would drown. If you do nothing to find them, you'll be breaking your vow, and after a lifetime of adherence to the Mother's ways, you will end up in the valley of the shamed." He tilted his head. "Wouldn't that be a shame?"

Damn him all to hell.

The doubt he'd put in her mind was enough to stay her hand. If she killed him, she would eliminate the only potential link she had to the twins, and if they died as a result, she would definitely find herself in the valley of the shamed when the time came to shed her mortal existence.

She needed advice, but she couldn't tell Phinas and the others about the twins.

Tilting her head back, she looked at the ceiling and offered a prayer to the Mother, asking for guidance.

"Give me the vow, Jade. You know that you have to do it, so why prolong the charade?"

"If you could find them, you would have done so already. You're just trying to manipulate me into sparing your life."

"Well, we have a conundrum. I'm not going to tell you how to find them until you vow a life debt to me, and you don't want to give me the vow before I can prove I know how to find them. But I've already proven that I can. How do you think I found you and the others?"

"We had trackers implanted in us without our knowledge."

He nodded. "I figured that you found out about them. I also figured out that the gods had somehow found the compound and taken everyone by force. I thought that I would need to save my people from slavery. It never occurred to me that you went willingly."

"They freed us from slavery." Or so she hoped.

It was still possible that what awaited them in the village was not the promised utopia but forced labor and breeding. But that was unlikely.

Phinas loved her, and he would have warned her about it.

"If you say so." Igor leaned his back against the wall.

"What about the other pods? There are still sixty-two pods missing."

"They could be found the same way as the twins' pod, and I hold the key, literally."

She assumed that their theory about the trackers not transmitting when their hosts were in stasis was correct, but that still begged the question why Igor had waited for nearly a century to find her tribe and the others. If he had the key, as he claimed, he should have found them sooner. Also, assuming that the pods would magically activate the revival sequence after a century was illogical. All the other settlers were most likely dead.

"Your claim doesn't make sense. If you had the key all along, why did it take you so long to find us? And why should I believe that the other pods are still functioning and will one day spontaneously revive the people inside them from stasis?"

As he looked at her with those piercing eyes of his, she felt as if he was reaching into her mind to read her thoughts. But since Toven couldn't do that to pureblooded Kra-ell, it was unlikely that Igor could.

"You are a smart female, Jade. That's why I chose you as my prime. You're also strong of body and mind. It's a shame you didn't give me a son."

"The Mother gave you a daughter, which all males back home would have been grateful for and proud of. But you barely paid her any attention."

No emotion crossed his eyes. "I wanted a son from you, but that's irrelevant to our discussion. You wanted to know why it took me so long to find you and the others. The answer to this is simple. The ship was gone, and with it, all the technological marvels the gods equipped us with. I had to wait for human technology to catch up, so they could build receivers strong enough to identify the signals coming from the trackers. Also, not all the pods came out of stasis at the same time. Yours did right after the landing, but it has taken some of the others decades to come out of stasis. If you don't believe me, talk with the other females. If they are no longer under my compulsion, they should be able to tell you when they woke up."

It hadn't occurred to her to ask that, but she would. "I assume the trackers were activated as soon as they got out of stasis."

"That's most likely, but since I didn't have the proper devices to locate the signals, I can't say that for sure." He tilted his head in that annoying way of his. "I found all of you and none of those who haven't come out of stasis yet, so I assume that they are still in their pods. The moment their pods activate their revival, their trackers will start transmitting, and I'm the only one who can find them."

If Igor needed to wait for human technology to advance enough to build a device, then William could build a similar one. They had dozens of those trackers, so he should be able to crack their technology and build receivers for the signal they emitted. But she had to make sure that he could before killing Igor.

Jade rose to her feet. "I need to think about it. I still think that you are trying to trick me."

"Take your time." He pulled his legs onto the cot and lay down. "I need blood. Have someone deliver it to me."

Jade snorted. "If I do, it will be for your last meal." She pivoted on her heel and walked toward the door.

"I've told you more than enough," Igor said. "I will not say anything more to you or your new friends until you give me your vow. I also expect to be properly fed and clothed."

Not deigning to answer, Jade pulled the door open, stepped out into the corridor, and slammed the door closed behind her.

7 2

PHINAS

"We need to talk," Jade said as the door slammed shut behind her.

That didn't sound good, especially since Phinas didn't know whether she meant all of them or just him.

"What did he say?" Toven asked.

"Let's go to your war room and get the others on the line." She lifted her hand. "It's not an emergency, and nothing is about to blow up, so stop looking so worried. It has to do with the missing pods and how to find them."

Phinas let out a breath. "Thanks for clarifying. For a moment there, I thought that Igor had a bomb in his stomach and threatened to detonate it and blow up along with the ship."

Yamanu chuckled. "It would have been just like him to do something like that."

Jade handed Phinas his gun. "He's way more sophisticated than that, and his plans usually don't involve him going down with the ship, so to speak."

"True." Phinas fell in step with her. "Can you tell us more on the way?"

She shook her head. "I need to organize my thoughts, and I don't want Pavel and Aleksei to hear what Igor said before we decide what to do about it."

"Makes sense."

Phinas stuck his hands in his pockets to keep from reaching for her hand.

Yamanu put in the code and opened the waterproofed door, and as they walked through, Pavel regarded Toven with a frown.

"That wasn't a success, was it?"

"He's immune," Toven admitted.

Pavel cast Jade a worried glance. "Are you going to kill him?"

"Eventually." She grimaced. "But not today. I promised Yamanu and Tom a stay of execution for twenty-four hours to interrogate him."

She didn't sound as sure as she'd sounded before, and Pavel either picked up on that or didn't understand what a stay of execution meant. "What did Igor say to you?"

Jade stopped and looked at him. "I can't tell you yet, but as soon as I have more information, I'll share it with everybody."

When they got to the war room, Jade strode to the kitchenette and opened the refrigerator. "Oh, good. There's some vodka left." She took out the bottle and poured a generous helping into a coffee mug. "Does anyone else want a shot?"

"It's not even nine in the morning," Toven said. "I would prefer some coffee."

Jade shrugged and walked over to the couch with the mug in hand.

"I'll make it," Phinas volunteered.

He was agitated, and having something to do would calm his nerves.

He filled the water in the coffeemaker tank and popped a pod into the slot. "Anyone else want coffee?"

"I do," Mia said.

Merlin raised his hand. "So do I."

Phinas turned to Yamanu. "What about you?"

"I'll pass. I want to know what Igor said before I contact Kian."

Jade put her mug on the coffee table. "He claims to know how to find the other pods the moment they activate and rouse their occupants from stasis. Our suspicions about the trackers were correct in that regard. He also said that he couldn't do that until human technology got advanced enough for him to build a receiver. I didn't ask whether he had it built or whether any store-bought device would do, but I figured that your William would be able to either build a device like that or obtain it, and then I will have no reason to keep Igor alive. But first, I need you to contact your home base and ask William if that's possible."

"So that's the bargain he offered you?" Toven asked. "His life in exchange for finding the other pods if and when they activate?"

Jade nodded. "More or less. We are talking about twelve hundred and forty people. If they wake up and get caught by humans, it will endanger all of us. We need to get to them as soon as they get out of stasis, and if possible, before that. It's a miracle that none were discovered yet."

"Perhaps some of them were," Mia said. "All those rumors about the government hiding aliens in Area 51 might be true." She chuckled. "Sometimes I think that the conspiracy theories are just the tip of the iceberg and that if we knew what was really going on, we would have laughed at them not because they were untrue but because they were so trivial compared to the real thing." She waved a hand at Toven. "I present to you exhibit number one." She smiled at Jade. "And exhibit number two. Two aliens having drinks on a ship owned by a clan of immortals. If anyone had written about that, it would have been called fiction."

Phinas was still stuck on the number Jade had thrown. Why had no one asked her how many people had been on the ship before?

It seemed like such an obvious question to ask.

"How many pods were on the ship?" Yamanu asked.

"Seventy." As Jade took a sip from her vodka, she glanced at Phinas. "You look surprised. Didn't I tell you that before?"

"You didn't." He handed Mia a mug filled with coffee and another to Toven. "How do you know that was the number of pods? Did you count them, or were you told?"

"We were told that there were fourteen hundred settlers on the ship, and since each pod could only hold twenty, that makes seventy pods." She smiled at Toven. "The gods liked to group things in multiples of seven or six. I never understood why."

"I've noticed that," he said. "Seven days in a week, twelve months, and numerous other examples. But back to the ship, that's actually fewer people than I thought were on it, but it's a good enough number to create a viable colony. It has just enough genetic variety."

73

JADE

*I*t was working.

No one was questioning her motives. They'd accepted her desire to find the rest of her people as perfectly natural, and they understood that it was vital to find the pods before humans discovered them.

The royal twins could remain her secret, and once Igor was dead, she and Kagra would be the only ones who knew about them.

If Igor told anyone it would be Valstar, and his days were numbered as well. She'd been against letting him stand trial and leaving it in the hands of the immortals' judge, but now she needed Toven and Kian's help more than ever, and if that made them more positively disposed to her, then Valstar's demise could wait a little longer.

Hopefully, she wouldn't have to keep Igor alive as well. Now that she was free of his compulsion and no longer terrified of what he might do to her people if she misbehaved, she allowed herself to feel the full extent of her hatred for him, and every moment that he still lived was a moment too long for her to tolerate.

"I'm calling Kian first." Yamanu looked at her. "He can put William on a three-way call with us and maybe get Turner on a four-way. I would like to run it by him as well."

She nodded. "Whatever works for you. I just need to get the answer before I go back to talk to that snake. It will make me really happy to see his face when I tell him that he can take what he knows to the grave because I don't need it. I can find my people without him."

"That might not be the only thing he knows," Toven said. "He asked me if I came to retrieve him. Aren't you intrigued by that question?"

She'd heard Igor ask it, but she'd forgotten about it. "Maybe he meant to ask whether you were sent to capture him. That makes more sense."

"I don't think Igor has a problem with expressing himself. He thought that I was sent to get him, and when I asked him by whom, he said my relatives. I assume he meant the gods. Why would the gods want to retrieve him? Was he working for them? I need answers for that."

Jade grimaced. "He's not going to tell you or me anything else unless I vow a life debt to him."

Phinas's eyes started glowing. "Over my dead body. You are not vowing anything to him."

"If William can't find the other trackers when they come online, I might have no choice. My vengeance is not worth the lives of over twelve hundred people."

There was no guarantee that any of them were still alive, and if they got revived, they might be able to evade detection like she and her pod members had done, as well as the other pods that had gotten activated.

Except, today's world wasn't the same one she'd woken up to over a century ago, and it wasn't as easy to go unnoticed and disappear nowadays. A group of confused newly-awakened settlers was very likely to be found, reported, and captured.

"A life debt means that you'll have to protect the life of the maggot who murdered your family." Phinas pushed to his feet and started pacing. "We can solve it. Yamanu can lock you up in one of the safes, and if you try to fight him, Merlin can put you to sleep. And while you are out, I'll kill Igor for you. I know it's not as satisfying as killing him yourself, but at least you won't be bound to him for life."

She smiled. "You know that I can't agree to that, right? It would mean breaking my vow. Let's just hope that I don't need to give it."

He stopped pacing and crouched in front of her. "I'm not asking your permission. If you give him your vow in exchange for information, I will get rid of him. It's a promise whether you like it or not."

Reaching with her hand, she cupped his cheek. "There is one problem with your solution. A life debt also means that I will have to avenge his death."

Phinas narrowed his eyes at her. "I'm really trying to be tolerant and respectful of your religion, but this is absurd. You need to re-evaluate your beliefs."

Jade had been doing that for a while, but she didn't appreciate him telling her what to do.

"This is not the time for this, Phinas. We can continue this discussion after we talk with William."

74

KIAN

*A*s Kian listened to Jade recounting her meeting with Igor and the deal he'd offered her, his heart went out to her.

She'd been placed in an impossible situation, and neither outcome would allow her to finally have peace. If she killed Igor, she would have the revenge she'd craved for so long, but she would forfeit the slim chance of finding her people. If she capitulated and offered him a life-debt vow, she might be able to find her people when they woke up from stasis, but she wouldn't get to kill Igor.

At least not with her own two hands.

Kian was more than willing to do the deed for her, but that wouldn't be nearly as satisfying to her.

Igor might be bluffing to keep his head attached to his neck, but not about his ability to find the pods. He'd proven that he knew how to track them. But the bluff might be that some of them were still alive and in stasis. Igor might know that it wasn't true, but the way he'd phrased it was that he didn't.

When she was done, Toven took over to report his impression of Igor, and when he was done, Phinas volunteered to take care of the Igor problem for Jade.

She lifted her hand. "As I said, let's explore other possibilities first. If William can find them, the rest of this discussion is irrelevant."

"I agree." Kian transferred the video call from his phone to the big screen in front of his desk and added William to the call.

"Hello, team." William smiled. "Congratulations on capturing Igor and arriving safely in Greenland."

"Thank you," Toven said. "We have a question for you." He proceeded to explain, with the others adding comments to clarify things.

"I see." William pushed his glasses up his nose. "I will need to check the other trackers, but if they all have similar transmission signatures, it's not going to be difficult to pinpoint where they are transmitting from, especially since the signal doesn't weaken with distance. I will have to calibrate two receivers to that signal's signature and triangulate the signal's location. Because they could be coming from anywhere in the world, I will have one receiver scanning for the signal from the village and the other one from our European location."

Kian had a very superficial understanding of what William was trying to explain, but he didn't need to understand the technical details to decide on a course of action.

"The bottom line is that William needs to check a few more trackers to verify that they all emit a similar signal." He trained his eyes on Jade. "Until he gets them, you can't kill Igor, but you shouldn't give him your vow either."

"What about the two hybrids you have in the keep?" Toven asked. "The ones who were following Sofia. What kind of trackers did they have?"

"Simple ones," William said. "The only alien tracker I have here is the one we removed from Sofia. But since you are bringing me many more, I can crack this one open and examine it more thoroughly."

Jade leaned forward. "So what's the plan? Do I stay in Greenland with Igor and a few Guardians until William gets the other trackers, or do we bring Igor with us to the village? "

"Good question." Kian drummed his fingers on his desk. "I don't like the idea of getting him anywhere near here, but it's going to be much more convenient to keep him contained and interrogate him in our dungeon in the keep."

Yamanu nodded. "We are keeping him in the ship's brig. There is nowhere in this town we can secure him."

"Maybe he can stay on the ship," Jade suggested. "I'll have to stay as well to guard him, and if William says that he's not needed, I'll end him." She smiled a chilling smile. "The morgue is right next to the brig."

William cleared his throat to get their attention. "We need to consider the possibility that the trackers produce very different signals, which is entirely possible since they use alien technology that I'm not familiar with. If that's the case, I won't be able to identify them among all the other signals permeating the airways. The thing that makes it less likely is that Igor would have had to memorize the signal's signature for fourteen hundred people and store it in his brain for the duration of the voyage and afterward. That's impossible unless he's a savant." He looked at Toven. "Since he has some godly genetics in him, maybe he inherited incredible memory from his godly ancestors. Have you ever heard of a god with a talent for memorizing long numbers?"

The god shook his head. "I didn't, but then I was only familiar with the talents of the small group of gods on Earth."

Kian wondered if Shai could memorize hundreds of numbers and letters combinations. Eidetic memory didn't mean that he actually remembered everything. Shai needed to form an image of what he wanted to remember or attach a story to it, and he doubted he could do that with meaningless numbers and letter sequences.

"Maybe Igor is an Odu in a Kra-ell disguise," Yamanu said. "A computer would have no trouble remembering an infinite number of combinations."

"He's not," Merlin said. "A tranquilizer dart wouldn't have worked on him." He chuckled. "Or a bullet or a grenade. The Odus are indestructible."

A chill ran down Kian's spine. Yamanu had said it as a joke, but he was onto something.

If Igor was sent by the gods to sabotage the ship or maybe even harm the gods on Earth, he might have been implanted with a computer chip in his brain. If humans were on the cusp of developing such an interface, the gods must have known how to do that for eons.

JADE

*a*fter the call ended, Jade rose to her feet. "I'll try to get Igor to tell me what he knows about the trackers."

Phinas followed her up. "He's not going to tell you anything without the vow, and you can't give it to him."

"I won't." She gave him a tight smile. "He's not getting the life-debt vow from me. But I can trick him into telling me more without promising him anything."

"How?" Toven asked.

"I'll tell him that we don't need him to find the pods. We have enough trackers to crack the technology and the knowhow to build the receiver. If what William suspects is true and the signals from the alien trackers don't share the same frequency or whatever, Igor will boast about having memorized each of the sequences. "

"I'm coming with you," Phinas said.

Jade had expected that, but she didn't want either of them inside the brig when she talked with Igor. If he threatened to tell them about the twins when she refused to give him the life-debt vow, she would kill him. Doing it with her sword would have been more satisfying, but a bullet in the eye cavity would do the job as well, and she wouldn't have to get close to him.

"I need to talk to him alone, but I will take your handgun before I go in."

He nodded.

"I'll accompany you as well." Toven pushed to his feet. "We will wait for you outside the door like we did before."

"So will I." Yamanu put his mug on the kitchenette counter and joined them by the door.

"I don't see why you all need to come, but you are welcome to accompany me."

As soon as Igor issued the threat, she would put a bullet in his head, so he wouldn't have time to shout the secret to them.

It felt bad to keep it from Toven and Kian, and even worse to keep it from Phinas, but the life-debt vow she'd sworn to the queen left her no choice. If there was even a slight chance that the clan would want to eliminate the twins, she couldn't risk it.

The queen had been the most powerful Kra-ell compeller, and her children were rumored to be even stronger. The clan had mobilized a force and traveled across the globe to eliminate Igor, who they considered a threat after he'd discovered Safe Haven. Saving her people had been a secondary goal to that.

They couldn't allow two powerful compellers to go free, and they wouldn't offer them an alliance either. If that was an option, they would have offered it to Igor. She didn't believe that Igor's actions against his own people really mattered to Kian. He'd sent a force to liberate the compound and catch Igor because Igor was a threat to the clan.

"Good luck," Mia said. "I'm going back to our cabin."

"I'll take you," Merlin volunteered and then turned to Toven. "Unless my services are needed?"

"I think we've got it covered. Thank you for escorting Mia." Toven leaned to kiss Mia's cheek.

Phinas walked up to the doctor. "I'll take the potions if you don't mind. Just in case Igor does something unexpected."

Jade wished she could use them, but Merlin's potion would surely incapacitate her, while it might not work on Igor, who had godly genes in him.

The doctor reached into his pocket and pulled out three vials. "All you need to do is break them. Tossing them on the floor next to him should do it."

"Thank you." Phinas put them in the inner pocket of his jacket.

They parted ways with Mia and Merlin at the elevators and continued down to the bowels of the ship.

The two Guardians and two purebloods guarding the door greeted them with nods, but Pavel was the only one who approached them. "What's going on? Are you going to kill him now?"

"Perhaps." She put her hand on his shoulder. "Does it bother you?"

"No. You can kill Igor. Just don't kill my father."

"I won't. I promised you that." He cast a look at Yamanu. "What about your people?"

She'd already told him that, but maybe he needed to hear it from Yamanu, who was the highest authority on the ship, even higher than Toven, who was there in an advisory position.

"We don't have a say in any of this. Your people will have to decide the future of Igor's men."

"But your judge will judge them. So you do have a say."

What had gotten into Pavel?

Had he talked with his father? Or had he heard something that had upset him and made him anxious?

She would find out later, but now was not the time for that.

"The timing of your inquiry is inappropriate." She removed her hand from his shoulder. "As I explained before, their judge will provide her special probing services and preside over the trial, but our people will determine their future."

When he opened his mouth to respond, Jade lifted her hand. "Not now, Pavel."

"Yes, mistress." He dipped his head.

Chuckling, Phinas clapped him on the back. "Smart boy. That was the correct answer."

PHINAS

*P*hinas handed Jade his gun. "When was the last time you practiced shooting?"

"Two decades ago." She let it hang down by her side. "Don't worry. I was an excellent shot, and that's a skill not easily forgotten."

As usual, Jade was fronting a tough attitude, and she was emitting next to no emotional scents, but Phinas knew her well enough by now to read the almost imperceptible signs of nervous anxiety.

She shouldn't go in there in less than perfect form, and he knew how to get her there, but she wouldn't appreciate him doing it with Toven and Yamanu present.

"You are not used to this one. Maybe we should go to the top deck so you can get a few practice shots before you go in there?"

"I'll be fine." She cast him a tight smile. "Thank you for the offer, though." Her eyes tried to communicate more than her words, but he didn't want to read too much into the softness he saw in them.

If they had no witnesses, he would have pulled her into his arms, kissed her hard, and called her his mate several times to rile her up.

Why couldn't Toven and Yamanu get the hint and make themselves scarce for a few minutes?

He turned to Yamanu and blinked three times. "I hate to bother you, but Jade is thirsty, and all she's had to drink was vodka. I don't want her going in there in less-than-perfect form. Could you and Toven get us a couple of bottles of water?" He blinked again.

Grinning, Yamanu nodded. "Of course." He clapped Toven on the back. "Let's get some water bottles for the lads guarding the entrance to this corridor as well."

Toven looked puzzled, but when Yamanu nudged his arm, he shrugged and followed.

Phinas waited until the door closed behind them and pulled Jade into his arms.

Sighing, she rested her cheek on his shoulder. "Thank you. I needed that."

"I will always be there for you. When you go in there, remember that your people chose you willingly as their leader, while the maggot inside had to compel their compliance. He's nothing compared to you, and when he tries to put you down and undermine your confidence, put him in his place." He patted the gun she was holding by her side. "With this, if needed."

"They didn't choose me. There just wasn't anyone else to take the lead, so I was the default."

"It's the same thing as choosing you. If they didn't want you as their leader, they would have objected and selected someone else. You didn't threaten anyone with retribution or negative consequences if they rejected your leadership, and you didn't make false promises to coerce them into accepting you as their leader. You didn't use compulsion to force them to answer to you, either. Your people just know that you are the best among them, and there is no one better to look after their interests."

She lifted her head off his shoulder and cupped his cheek with the hand that wasn't holding a loaded gun. "That was the best pep talk I've ever gotten. Thank you." She leaned in and kissed him softly, then leaned away and looked into his eyes. "I'll tell you a secret if you vow not to tell anyone."

Chuckling, he lifted a hand and put it over his chest. "I promise to take it to my grave."

Jade frowned. "That's too much. Just promise me you won't tell anyone until I say it's okay."

He was about to tease her about how serious she was, but the sound of the door opening at the end of the corridor announced Toven and Yamanu's return, and he realized that he was out of time. "I promise not to tell anyone until you allow it."

She leaned closer and whispered, "I love you."

77

JADE

*A*fter putting in her earpieces and checking the fit, Jade entered the ship's jail with a smile on her face and fluttering in her heart. Even Igor's despised visage couldn't spoil her good mood.

She'd finally done it.

She'd told Phinas that she loved him, and she was as sure of that as she was sure that the Earth was spinning.

The pep talk he'd given her had finally brought home what having a mate was all about, and it helped spring free the tight lock she'd had on her emotions.

She still had a lot to learn about being a mate, and perhaps Phinas didn't have it all figured out yet either, but the examples he'd given her so far were an excellent start.

"What are you so happy about?" Igor approached the bars and gripped them.

"I'm happy because I don't need you to find the other pods. We removed all the trackers from everyone, and we have plenty of those that were made by the gods. My new friends have the technological knowhow to take them apart, figure out how they work, and build receivers without your help." She leaned a little closer, but not close enough for him to grab her. "Prepare to die, Igor."

Regrettably, he didn't seem scared or even discouraged. The maggot looked smug.

"Even if they had a receiver built by the gods, it would be useless without the code. And I'm the only one who knows it. Not only that, the code changes every fifteen seconds, so even if you got it out of me somehow, it would be useless. You need me alive and awake to decipher where the signal is coming from."

Jade frowned. "Do you have a computer chip installed in your brain?"

Perhaps Merlin could remove it after she killed Igor, and William could use it to decipher the code.

Igor laughed, a chilling sound she'd never heard him emit. "I can see the wheels in your head spinning, but I'm glad to disappoint you. I don't have a computer chip in my brain. Part of my brain was designed to work like the computer chip you were thinking of, and you can't cut it out and decipher it. As soon as my brain is dead, the deciphering ability dies with it. I'm not even consciously aware of it. As soon as I identify the right signal, my mind unravels the encryption."

"How is that even possible?"

He shrugged. "The wonders of genetic manipulation."

"You were made by the gods."

"In a manner of speaking. But I think you get the picture now. If you want to find the twins and the rest of the settlers, you have to keep me alive and well, and you have to protect me from your new friends. I'll have your vow now."

Jade shook her head. "How do I know any of this is true? You could have fabricated the story to manipulate me into sparing your life."

"It's easy to prove. Have your new friends build a couple of receivers, send a couple of people with embedded trackers to undisclosed locations without recording the signal's signature ahead of time, and try to identify the signals. Without the code, they will fail. But if I'm there, equipped with your vow and well-nourished and cared for, I'll decode it for them, and they will be able to pinpoint the location."

"There is one problem with your offer. You want me to make a vow to you before you prove your utility, and I won't do that."

"As long as you don't kill me before the proof is obtained, I can wait. Perhaps I can sweeten the deal for you, but I need to think it through so I leave no loopholes. I want to guarantee my survival even after the pods are found."

Jade turned the chair around, straddled it, and put the gun on top of her thigh. "Take your time. I have all day."

"Let's start with a simple vow that you shouldn't have a problem with. I want to find out more about your new friends and what they want to do with me, but I need you to answer truthfully. Can you vow to do it?"

"I vow not to lie to you. But I don't vow to tell you everything you want to know. If I don't want to answer, I won't."

Igor regarded her with pride in his cold eyes. "So clever. I taught you well."

"You ruined my life."

"And yet, you emerged anew, better than you were before. Like a phoenix, you were forged in fire and reborn."

Jade grimaced. "How poetic. What do you want to know?"

"It seems that they left my fate in your hands. Is that true?"

"It is."

"If we reach an agreement and you vow not to kill me, will they want my death?"

"Probably. You are too dangerous to leave alive. On the other hand, the gods don't believe in capital punishment, so they won't execute you. They'll probably entomb you, and since you are part god, you'll go into stasis."

She might have said too much, but the surprised look on his face was worth it, even if it lasted only a split second.

"How do you know that?"

"You heal as fast as a god, but you look Kra-ell, so I assume you are a hybrid. Your compulsion ability is also a giveaway. No Kra-ell is as strong a compeller."

"That's not true. The queen was a very powerful compeller."

"As powerful as you?"

"I don't know. I was never pitted against her. I also don't think I can go into stasis without a pod. I don't know which parts of my genetics are Kra-ell and which are god."

It was impossible to tell whether Igor was being truthful or deceitful, and with the earpieces in, she didn't even have the benefit of identifying slight fluctuations in his tone.

"You will have to negotiate something with them. All I can promise is not to kill you until you prove that what you told me about the signal is true, and if it is, I will vow to never take your life. But I will not give you a life-debt vow. I will not protect you."

"That's not good enough. You can vow that, and once you find the twins, you could send Kagra or someone else to kill me."

That hadn't occurred to her, but she wasn't a devious bastard like Igor.

"I will add to my vow that I will not command anyone to kill you or even knowingly allow it. Besides, my new friends, as you call them, are very curious about you, and they want to interrogate you. You can strike a deal with them and have them protect you, just not from me. I was promised your and Valstar's heads."

"Did you kill Valstar?"

Jade smiled coldly. "Do you care?"

"No. I'm just curious. So, do we have a deal?"

Reluctantly, Jade nodded. "With one caveat. If you tell anyone aside from me about the twins, the vow is nullified."

He tilted his head. "Vows don't work like that. They are absolute, and they have no caveats."

"Mine do." She stared him in the eyes. "I'm not as traditional as you think. I'm adapting to my new environment."

"I see that you don't trust your new friends with that information."

"I can't. If I hadn't given the queen a life-debt vow to protect her and her family, I might have shared the information with them."

"I doubt that."

He wasn't wrong.

She would have protected the royal twins even without the vow. But she would have told Phinas about them and asked him to keep it a secret from his people.

"Think what you will. I don't care."

He nodded. "It doesn't matter to me. You can include the caveat in the vow."

Jade took a moment to think of the exact phrasing. "I vow not to kill you until you prove that you are the only one who can decipher the signals the gods' trackers emit, and if you prove it beyond a shadow of a doubt, I vow not to kill you and not allow anyone under my control to kill you as long as you fulfill your part of the bargain and decipher every signal until we find all the pods. If you falter on your promise or try to negotiate for more things in exchange for locating the pods, the vow will be nullified. But if you fulfill your obligation and all the pods are found, my vow not to kill you by my hand, or that of anyone I control will extend indefinitely. However, all my vows to you will be nullified if anyone else finds out about the twins from you."

"We have a deal." He extended his hand through the bars.

She looked at it with disgust. "Do you think I'm stupid?"

He retracted his hand and smiled. "Not at all. I think you're brilliant."

If he thought his compliment meant anything to her, he was dead wrong. Just not dead, and that was one of the greatest disappointments of her life.

Perhaps William would come through and crack the code somehow, and she would still get to kill Igor, but she had a feeling that he had told her the truth. She also suspected that Toven and Kian could learn a lot from him, and if she cared to admit it, she was curious to find out who had sent him and why.

Rising to her feet, Jade turned around without another look at the monster behind bars and walked over to the door.

Phinas was waiting for her on the other side, and with him, a future better than she could have ever imagined. She would always carry the pain of what she'd lost and keep the memory of her sons and their fathers in her heart, but she was ready to embrace the next chapter of her life, and Jade had no doubt that it would be the best one yet.

COMING UP NEXT
DARK HEALING TRILOGY
Children of the Gods Series books 71-73

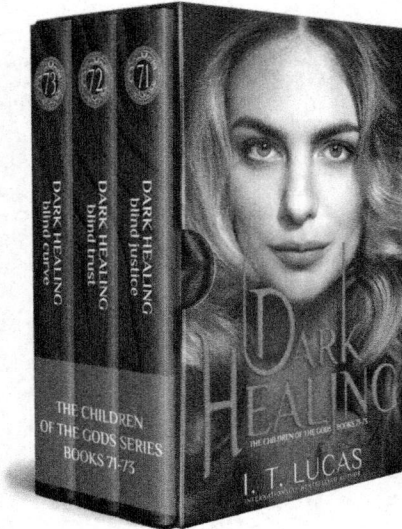

Read the enclosed excerpt

The sanctuary is Vanessa's life project. The monumental task of rehabilitating the traumatized victims of trafficking doesn't leave much time for personal life, let alone dating or finding her one and only.

When Kian asks her to help the Kra-ell, she's torn between her duty to the sanctuary and a group of emotionally wounded aliens who no other psychologist can treat.

She's the only immortal with the necessary training to get it done.

The Kra-ell culture and the purebloods' nearly androgynous alien looks shouldn't appeal to her, and yet, she finds one of them disturbingly attractive.

Is it the dangerous vibe he emits?

Does it speak to her on a subconscious level?

Or is it her need to put the broken pieces of him back together?

And why is he interested in her?

She cannot offer him a fight for dominance like a Kra-ell female would, but some strange and unfamiliar part of her wishes she could.

Also coming soon:
A NEW PERFECT MATCH!
The Thief Who Loved Me
A FULL-LENGTH STANDALONE *007*
VIRTUAL FANTASY ROMANCE ADVENTURE

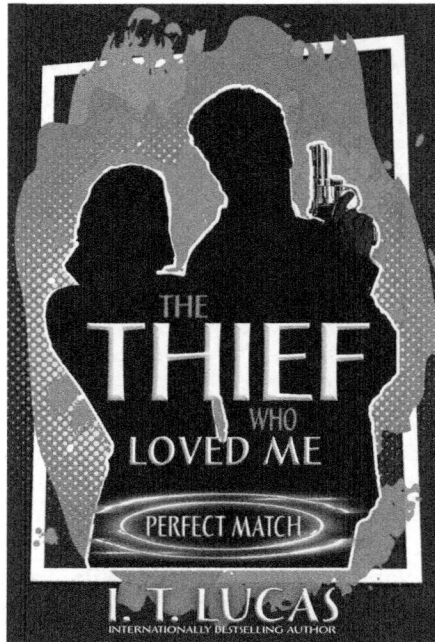

When Marian splurges on a Perfect Match Virtual adventure as a world infamous jewel thief, she expects high-wire fun with a hot partner who she will never have to see again in real life.

A virtual encounter seems like the perfect answer to Marcus's string of dating disasters. No strings attached, no drama, and definitely no love. As a die-hard James Bond fan, he chooses as his avatar a dashing MI6 operative, and to complement his adventure, a dangerously seductive partner.

Neither expects to find their forever Perfect Match.

Dear reader,

Thank you for reading the Children of the Gods.

As an independent author, I rely on your support to spread the word. So if you enjoyed the story, please share your experience with others, and if it isn't too much trouble, I would greatly appreciate a brief review on Amazon.

Love & happy reading,

Isabell

DARK HEALING EXCERPT

Mo-red

*M*o-red shivered as the brutal wind whipped through the thin jacket the immortals had given him. He was a Kra-ell warrior, and the cold should be the least of his worries as he was led to the plane that would bring him one step closer to his death, but he'd been born on a warm planet and had never gotten used to the northern latitude Igor had chosen to settle them in.

Still, as cold as Karelia was, it had nothing on Greenland, and as he dragged his chained feet toward the boarding staircase, he was chilled to the bone.

Somehow, the cold didn't seem to affect the immortals, and he wondered if the gods had altered their genetics so they wouldn't be susceptible to extreme weather.

"Wait." The soldier escorting him put a hand on his shoulder. "Let the other guy finish climbing first."

Mo-red lifted his eyes to Madbar, who was struggling up the boarding stairs with the short chain around his ankles forcing him to go super slow.

With an inward sigh, he braced for the same awkward experience.

743

As soon as Madbar was done, the immortal soldier gave Mo-red a slight shove. "Your turn."

He had to climb the steps to the plane one at a time. The damn chain was just long enough for him to lift his foot and put it at the edge of the step, and as he teetered on that edge, he had to lift the other foot and bring it over before repeating the laborious process.

In the grand scheme of things, it was a minor inconvenience, but it was humiliating, especially with Pavel watching him from below.

Standing next to a group of immortals, his son was chatting with one of them as if they had known each other for years. He'd always been a clever boy, and he'd smartly joined Jade's rebellion right from the start, making himself indispensable to her and her new friends.

When Jade had finally admitted that their so-called liberators were not human, Mo-red hadn't been surprised. Humans, no matter how well equipped, couldn't have stormed the Kra-ell compound and emerged victorious against the superior physical strength and training of the Kra-ell defenders.

Besides, the powerful compeller who had been instrumental to their success and freed the Kra-ell from Igor's compulsion was so obviously not human that trying to pass him off as one was ridiculous. The guy called himself Tom, a mundane human name, but his powerful compulsion ability and physical perfection gave his godly genetics away.

Still, Mo-red hadn't said anything, not even hinting at knowing who the invaders were until he'd been told that they were the immortal descendants of the gods.

After serving under Igor for over a century, he'd learned that self-preservation meant keeping his mouth shut and not asking too many questions. He'd been a victim just the same as all the other Kra-ell settlers in the compound, and like the rest of Igor's pod members, helpless to rebel against the compeller's rule and forced to be the sociopath's henchmen, but the others didn't see it that way, and they wanted him dead.

He was probably alive only thanks to the god and his army of immortals. The gods didn't condone executions, and neither did their descendants. They must have insisted that Igor's surviving pod members stand trial first.

"Let me give you a hand." Pavel came up from behind him and threaded his arm through his.

"Don't," Mo-red murmured under his breath. "This is humiliating enough."

"As you wish." His son pulled out his arm but stayed beside him, ready to catch him if he fell.

"Do you know where we are going?" Mo-red asked as he climbed the last step.

"The United States of America. That's all I am allowed to tell you."

That was better than nothing. "I'm glad. I've always wanted to visit there."

The immortal standing in the middle of the aisle pointed to a window seat. "Over here. Pavel, you sit next to him."

"That's my father," Pavel said. "Are you okay with me guarding him?"

The immortal shrugged. "He has nowhere to go and is under Tom's compulsion to behave. But if you want to sit with Drova, I can assign someone else to guard him."

Mo-red frowned. Had his son lost his mind?

Drova was only sixteen, but even if she were an adult, the girl was Igor's daughter and shared many of her father's characteristics. Those were some-what mitigated by Jade's influence, but Pavel should stay away from her nonetheless.

"I'll stay here." Pavel slid into the seat. "I want to make sure that my father is not mistreated."

His son had only visited him once throughout the sea voyage, so concern for his well-being wasn't why he wanted to sit next to him.

The immortal cast him an incredulous look. "Did he complain?"

"He couldn't even if he wanted to," Pavel said. "Tom put such a strong compulsion on the remaining members of Igor's clique that they can't go to the bathroom without asking permission. I wouldn't be surprised if he forbade them to complain too."

Mo-red tensed. Why was Pavel aggravating the immortals? He should cooperate with them so they wouldn't turn against him and also put him in chains.

The soldier laughed. "I wish. They complained nonstop about every-thing. I thought the Kra-ell purebloods were tough, but your dad and his buddies behaved like a bunch of spoiled princesses." He made a face. "It's uncomfortable sleeping with chains on," he mimicked Madbar's voice. "It's uncomfortable to drink blood from a goat or a sheep while chained. Etcetera."

It had been uncomfortable, but they wouldn't have complained if the reason for the discomfort was of their own choosing.

As prisoners bound by physical and mental chains, complaining was the only way for them to assert some power over their hopeless situation and feel less like victims.

Were they indeed victims, though?

It was a question that Mo-red had struggled with for over a century.

When he'd first awoken from stasis and found himself at Igor's mercy, he'd made several futile attempts to resist, to run off, but when it had become clear that there was no way to escape Igor's compulsion, Mo-red had resigned himself to his new life and had tried to make the best of it.

The Kra-ell were militant people, so attacking other tribes for resources wasn't anything new, but Igor's compulsion ability had turned them from warriors into butchers. If they had fought the other males and killed them in battle, Mo-red wouldn't have felt guilty, but that wasn't what they had done. They'd slaughtered males who'd been frozen by Igor's command and couldn't fight back.

After a while, though, the guilt had subsided.

Mo-red could not have opposed Igor, and speaking against his methods had resulted in being compelled to do even worse things. Keeping his head down and his mouth shut had been the best way Mo-red could protect himself and others.

Nevertheless, he was guilty of enjoying the fruits of Igor's cruelty.

As a young, fatherless male, he'd convinced himself that having plenty of females at his disposal was the flip side of being a tool in Igor's hands.

After fathering Pavel and his two half-brothers, though, Mo-red had started to worry about the future of his sons. The ratio of males to females had been nearly equal after they had slaughtered the other tribes' males and taken their females. But Igor couldn't control biology, and the next generation born in the compound was split along the normal Kra-ell gender birth ratio of four males to one female.

The realization of Igor's vision of a Kra-ell society that was run by males with plenty of females to serve them required the elimination of excess males. Mo-red had lived in constant fear of Igor deciding to do away with the young males.

Now that the danger was over and Igor was about to meet his end, Mo-red could finally breathe more easily even though his own end was also imminent.

If he had to die to secure the futures of his sons, so be it.

After all, wasn't that a father's duty?

To give life to the next generation and ensure its survival?

Vanessa

"Compassion is not a weakness, Nancy." Vanessa leaned over and patted the hand of the young woman sitting across from her. "It takes a brave soul to take on the pain of others."

There goes another volunteer.

Since the sanctuary had opened its doors to the rescued victims of trafficking, many had volunteered to help. Some were professional psychologists like Vanessa, while others were kind souls who wanted to lend a hand, like Vivian with her sewing class, Karen with Krav Maga training, and many others. But even though everyone knew what to expect when they signed up, at least half didn't make it past the two-week mark.

Were they expecting a walk in the park?

The Ojai location was beautiful, and maybe that was part of the draw, but the stories of suffering that were told within the walls of the restored monastery were too difficult for many to stomach.

"I'm supposed to be a professional." Nancy pulled a tissue out of the box Vanessa kept on her desk and wiped the tears from her eyes. "I chose to study psychology to help people, but maybe I made a mistake. I'm not strong enough for this." She looked at Vanessa with red-rimmed eyes. "I'm not as strong as you."

Affecting a neutral expression, she said the same thing she'd said many times before to other volunteers who couldn't handle the job. "Give it some time. It gets easier."

Was Nancy right? Was she really strong?

She had to be to run the sanctuary, but perhaps she'd become inured to the stories of pain.

No, that wasn't true.

The stories no longer shocked Vanessa, but they still pained her. She'd just changed her perspective, and instead of fixating on stories of the women's pasts, she focused on the inspiring stories of the courageous survivors who had gone through the program and ventured out into the world ready to live the best life they could.

In moments of weakness, when she wished she was still practicing her craft in the village and dealing with the occasional phobia or disorder her clan members needed help with, Vanessa would open her drawer and pull out the letters she'd gotten from survivors, thanking her and the charity foundation for helping them restore their faith in humanity, achieve independence, and live a productive and fulfilling life.

"I don't know if I can do that." Nancy blew her nose into the tissue.

Years of experience had taught Vanessa to keep her professional expression compassionate but not pitying, thoughtful but not judgmental, and to keep her feelings to herself even when talking with a fellow psychologist.

Pulling out another tissue, she handed it to the volunteer. "When you feel discouraged, read through the success stories. Sometimes it takes everything I have not to cry with the victims, but then I read the thank-you letters from the survivors, and the satisfaction I get from that is worth every heart-wrenching moment." She looked into the woman's eyes. "They need your help. The sanctuary needs every volunteer it can get."

"I know." Nancy sniffled. "That's why I came. I knew that it was going to be hard, but I was tired of listening to spoiled rich brats complaining about their terrible parents who didn't understand them while having the parents pay for my time and everything else in their entitled lives. I had to continue doing that to make a living, but I wanted to do something meaningful, at least part-time." She looked down at the crumpled tissues in her hand. "But I don't want to go home to my family in the evening and force myself to smile for my kids." She lifted her eyes to Vanessa's. "I haven't made love to my husband even once since I started volunteering here." Her chin wobbled. "Poor guy doesn't deserve the dirty looks I give him, but after hearing the victims' stories, it's hard not to see every male as the enemy."

Vanessa smiled. "As I said, it takes time. You never get used to it, but you can learn how to compartmentalize and leave the horror stories behind when you go home."

"Can you do that?"

"To a certain degree." Vanessa rose to her feet. "A stroll in nature helps center me. In fact, I was planning to do that when you came into my office. Do you want to join me on a walk around the sanctuary? We can continue talking in the fresh air."

She often did that with the girls. Sometimes it was easier to talk outside than in the therapist's office.

"Oh, I can't." Nancy glanced at her watch and pushed her chair back. "I need to head home. When are you leaving?"

"I'm staying here tonight. I don't commute every day. I live far away." Vanessa opened the door to her office and waited for Nancy to step out.

The sanctuary was only an hour's drive away from the village, but someone needed to be there at night for the girls, and more often than not, Vanessa couldn't get any of the volunteers to take the night shift.

Perhaps it was time to hire more permanent staff.

Between the clan's and Kalugal's monthly donations and the fundraising effort Ella had started for the sanctuary, there was no shortage of funds, and Vanessa could afford more full-time help. The problem was finding the time and energy to start interviewing suitable candidates.

Besides, every penny she saved on running the sanctuary went to helping the victims get back on their feet, and she preferred the money to go there instead of spending it on more salaries just so she could take it easy.

Nancy gave her a pitying look. "I've heard that you often do that. Is your family okay with you staying here overnight?"

"No one is waiting for me at home," she admitted.

Jackson was happily mated and had his own house, but even if he was still living with her, it wasn't as if she could tell Nancy that she had a twenty-three-year-old son.

Vanessa was over three centuries old but looked to be in her late twenties or early thirties. The only way to explain how she could have an adult child was to claim that she'd acquired him through marriage.

Being immortal meant a lot of lying, but she did her best to minimize it.

Nancy nodded sagely and whispered, "It's this job. That's the only reason a gorgeous woman like you is alone. It makes us regard all men as the enemy."

The woman would have never said those things to anyone other than a fellow psychologist, but that was why psychologists needed each other's help. To function at their jobs, they needed to dump their negative feelings on someone who understood and wouldn't judge them.

"I don't think of men as the enemy." Vanessa smiled. "I happen to know many good men, and I definitely don't judge their entire gender based on a few rotten apples."

Jackson was an amazing male, one of the best people she knew, but he was her son, so she wasn't objective. Still, the fact that he was mated to a former victim of trafficking and had helped Tessa heal her deep emotional wounds spoke volumes about his character.

There were also plenty of other males she loved and admired. Other than a handful of exceptions, all the males of her clan were great.

In fact, most men were good people, just like most women were good.

Well, the scale might be tilted slightly in favor of females in the goodness department, but that wasn't what Nancy needed to hear right now.

"I know." The woman sighed. "I don't think that either. Not really. My Kevin is a sweetheart, and he deserves better than a grumpy wife who gives him dirty looks when she comes home, especially after he's picked up the kids from my mother's and cooked dinner for us."

Vanessa put her arm around the shorter woman's shoulders. "You need to change the script playing in your head. Just think of all the heroes, like the men who save babies from burning buildings and jump into rushing rapids to save drowning victims. And who do you think rescues these girls from the sex slavers?"

The Guardians of her clan did that, but it was a secret that neither Nancy nor anyone else in the sanctuary was privy to, including the rescued victims themselves.

"I wondered about that." Nancy looked up at her. "The girls I asked about it couldn't remember whether their saviors had worn uniforms or identified themselves as the police. I assumed they belonged to a special task force assigned to taking out traffickers and saving the victims. I'm sure they flashed some kind of badges when they arrested the scumbags, but the girls were too traumatized to notice."

Vanessa nodded without verbally confirming or denying. "When you're tempted to bundle all men together as evil, you need to remember that the people serving in those special units are mostly men, and they are the good guys. They are the heroes who save these victims from a horrible fate and give them another chance at life."

The war on trafficking wasn't waged by some government agency. The victims didn't remember their rescuers because the Guardians thralled them to forget specific details about the operation, but they were primarily males.

Kri was the only female Guardian, and she didn't participate in the attacks. She was responsible for collecting the traumatized trafficking victims, calming them down, and driving them to the sanctuary. The reason she wasn't part of the assault team wasn't that she didn't measure up, she did, and then some, but because her paranormal talent was instilling calm, which was best utilized in getting the victims to safety.

The Guardian also volunteered in the sanctuary, teaching self-defense. Her class was in high demand, and once a week wasn't enough, but that was all the time Kri could spare. Thankfully, a human teacher Tessa had recommended had agreed to teach Krav Maga twice weekly.

Jackson's mate attributed the Krav Maga class and its fierce teacher with getting her to feel stronger and less fearful even before her transition into immortality.

When the no-nonsense former military fitness instructor started teaching her special brand of self-defense in the sanctuary, she did the same for its residents. The girls loved Karen and her take-no-prisoners attitude, and Vanessa suspected that the woman was doing more for their self-confidence than all the therapy sessions provided by the slew of volunteer psychologists combined.

"That's a good image to hold in my head." Nancy let out a breath. "Thank you for sharing it with me."

"You're welcome." Vanessa stopped in front of the woman's car. "So, will I see you tomorrow?"

"Of course." Nancy used the crumpled tissue to dab at her nose. "I'm not a quitter. I just needed to vent to someone." She smiled. "I'm going to be really nice to Kevin tonight. If nasty thoughts interfere with my plans, I'll chase them away by imagining a hunky firefighter saving a baby from a burning building."

"That's an excellent plan." Vanessa waited until Nancy opened the door and got in. "Have a great evening. I'll see you tomorrow."

"Can I ask you a personal question?" Nancy pulled the seatbelt down and buckled it.

Not really. "Sure."

"Are you recently divorced or separated?"

"I've never been married."

"Oh." Nancy eyed her with curiosity. "So you like men, but you don't like-like them."

Vanessa laughed. "I very much like-like men. I just haven't found my one and only yet."

Kian

"I brought you a cup of tea," Syssi said as she walked into Kian's office with a cup in each hand. "By the way, have you spoken with Vanessa about the Kra-ell?" She sat on the couch and put the cups on the coffee table.

It had completely slipped his mind.

Getting the village ready for the Kra-ell refugees and Safe Haven for the humans who had chosen not to accompany their former overseers was a clan-wide effort, and everyone was hustling to get it done in time.

"I forgot. I'll call her tomorrow."

Syssi shook her head. "You should have called her as soon as the decision was made to bring the Kra-ell to the village. She needs someone to take over for her in the sanctuary or she won't be able to do this. Last I've spoken with her, she told me that she had trouble keeping volunteers from leaving. Did you know that she stays there during the week? Sometimes she doesn't come home even during the weekend."

"I didn't know that," he admitted. "Why doesn't she hire more people?"

Syssi shrugged. "I guess it's not easy to find professionals willing to commute to the remote location. Besides, it takes special people to work in a place like that." She shivered. "I'm ashamed to admit it, but I wouldn't be able to handle it. The horrors would follow me even in sleep."

Kian rose to his feet and walked over to sit next to his wife. "You are a gentle soul, my love." He wrapped his arm around her shoulders. "You are also a mother of a baby girl and can't afford to let yourself get depressed. It would affect Allegra, and Fates only know what damage it could do to a young child."

Syssi nodded. "She's very attuned to me. Sometimes I think that she can read my mind."

"I get that feeling too." He kissed her temple. "She is the daughter of a seer, and she communicated with you even in the womb."

"We have an extraordinary girl." She lifted her face to him and smiled. "I bet every parent thinks that."

"Yeah, but we are right. We really do have an extraordinary child."

"Indeed." Syssi leaned her head on his arm. "Nevertheless, I wouldn't be able to work in the sanctuary even if I didn't have a baby daughter at home. I'm not strong enough, and it makes me feel ashamed."

"Don't. Each of us has different things to contribute to our community. You're helping Amanda research paranormal phenomena, which might help us find more dormant carriers of godly genes, and you are creating fascinating virtual environments for Perfect Match, which helps countless people enjoy things they could never have enjoyed in the real world."

Syssi was also helping keep him calm, which everyone in the village was thankful to her for, but she wouldn't like him saying that.

She sighed. "I guess my work is important too, but what Vanessa is doing is so difficult, and we have only one of her. The Kra-ell will need an army of psychologists, and the one we have has her plate full. I doubt she will be able to find a replacement in time."

"There is no urgency." He smoothed his hand over her bare arm. "The Kra-ell psychological assessment can wait. First, they will be probed by Edna, and only if she can't determine their intentions, Vanessa will have to step in and psychoanalyze them."

"Your mother might be able to get into their heads. You tend to underestimate what Annani can do."

Did he?

Not really.

Annani was a force of nature, and Kian suspected she was a much more powerful god than Toven. But where he had no problem using Toven in the Kra-ell operation, he was reluctant to involve his mother.

Annani was impulsive and too kind for her own good. She needed him to protect and shield her, or maybe Kian just needed to do that for her. He had to keep her in the loop but could spare her the details.

Given his mother's positive and optimistic outlook, it was easy to forget how much suffering she'd experienced and witnessed. It was Kian and his sisters' turn to shoulder the burden and let Annani enjoy the large family she'd created or whatever else gave her pleasure.

At this stage of her life, she should be enjoying the fruits of her efforts that were thousands of years in the making.

"I would be a fool to underestimate my mother's abilities. I just don't want her to have to deal with Igor and what has been done to the people under his rule. Like you, she's too delicate and compassionate to be exposed to all that evil."

Syssi laughed. "Are we talking about the same goddess? The one who has singlehandedly kept humanity from falling prey to Navuh's grand subjugation plan?"

Kian frowned at his wife. "Not singlehandedly. She had lots of help from Alena, Sari, me, and the rest of the clan."

"True, but to think of Annani as fragile is a fallacy. Your mother is the strongest person I know." Syssi smiled and patted his knee. "Except for you, of course. But since you are not nearly as powerful a thraller as your mother, and your capacity for empathy is not that great either, she's much better suited to deal with the emotionally damaged Kra-ell."

"We don't know how badly damaged they are, or if at all. Their society is militant in nature, and they are the farthest from fragile you can imagine.

These people are raised as warriors whose ultimate goal in life is to die honorably in battle."

Syssi sighed. "Those born in Igor's compound were not raised on the Kra-ell traditions, and all of them are either the children or grandchildren of Igor's pod buddies. Nearly half of those males were recently killed, and the others are imprisoned and about to stand trial. I suspect that many of those young Kra-ell need Vanessa's help, and since they are about to become part of our community, it's in our best interest to ensure their mental stability. But that's the easy part compared to healing the emotional wounds of the women who had their families murdered before them and were then compelled to have sex with the killers. They will probably need years of therapy."

Syssi had the unique ability to distill problems to their very essence and present them in a way that spoke to him.

"You are right." Kian pulled out his phone. "I'll text Vanessa and ask her to call me."

Smiling, Syssi glanced at her watch. "I love how you are always so quick to implement my suggestions, but it's eleven-thirty at night."

"I'm sure Vanessa is still awake, and if she's not, she'll see my text when she wakes up and call me first thing in the morning."

THE CHILDREN OF THE GODS SERIES

THE CHILDREN OF THE GODS ORIGINS

1: GODDESS'S CHOICE

When gods and immortals still ruled the ancient world, one young goddess risked everything for love.

2: GODDESS'S HOPE

Hungry for power and infatuated with the beautiful Areana, Navuh plots his father's demise. After all, by getting rid of the insane god he would be doing the world a favor. Except, when gods and immortals conspire against each other, humanity pays the price.

But things are not what they seem, and prophecies should not to be trusted...

THE CHILDREN OF THE GODS

1: DARK STRANGER THE DREAM

Syssi's paranormal foresight lands her a job at Dr. Amanda Dokani's neuroscience lab, but it fails to predict the thrilling yet terrifying turn her life will take. Syssi has no clue that her boss is an immortal who'll drag her into a secret, millennia-old battle over humanity's future. Nor does she realize that the professor's imposing brother is the mysterious stranger who's been starring in her dreams.

Since the dawn of human civilization, two warring factions of immortals—the descendants of the gods of old—have been secretly shaping its destiny. Leading the clandestine battle from his luxurious Los Angeles high-rise, Kian is surrounded by his clan, yet alone. Descending from a single goddess, clan members are forbidden to each other. And as the only other immortals are their hated enemies, Kian and his kin have been long resigned to a lonely existence of fleeting trysts with human partners. That is, until his sister makes a game-changing discovery—a mortal seeress who she believes is a dormant carrier of their genes. Ever the realist, Kian is skeptical and refuses Amanda's plea to attempt Syssi's activation. But when his enemies learn of the Dormant's existence, he's forced to rush her to the safety of his keep. Inexorably drawn to Syssi, Kian wrestles with his conscience as he is tempted to explore her budding interest in the darker shades of sensuality.

2: DARK STRANGER REVEALED

While sheltered in the clan's stronghold, Syssi is unaware that Kian and Amanda are not human, and neither are the supposedly religious fanatics that are after her. She feels a powerful connection to Kian, and as he introduces her to a world of pleasure she never dared imagine, his dominant sexuality is a revelation. Considering that she's completely out of her element, Syssi feels comfortable and safe letting go with him. That is, until she begins to suspect that all is not as it seems. Piecing the puzzle together, she draws a scary, yet wrong conclusion...

3: DARK STRANGER IMMORTAL

When Kian confesses his true nature, Syssi is not as much shocked by the revelation as she is wounded by what she perceives as his callous plans for her.

If she doesn't turn, he'll be forced to erase her memories and let her go. His family's safety demands secrecy – no one in the mortal world is allowed to know that immortals exist.

Resigned to the cruel reality that even if she stays on to never again leave the keep, she'll get old while Kian won't, Syssi is determined to enjoy what little time she has with him, one day at a time.

Can Kian let go of the mortal woman he loves? Will Syssi turn? And if she does, will she survive the dangerous transition?

4: DARK ENEMY TAKEN

Dalhu can't believe his luck when he stumbles upon the beautiful immortal professor. Presented with a once in a lifetime opportunity to grab an immortal female for himself, he kidnaps her and runs. If he ever gets caught, either by her people or his, his life is forfeit. But for a chance of a loving mate and a family of his own, Dalhu is prepared to do everything in his power to win Amanda's heart, and that includes leaving the Doom brotherhood and his old life behind.

Amanda soon discovers that there is more to the handsome Doomer than his dark past and a hulking, sexy body. But succumbing to her enemy's seduction, or worse, developing feelings for a ruthless killer is out of the question. No man is worth life on the run, not even the one and only immortal male she could claim as her own…

Her clan and her research must come first…

5: DARK ENEMY CAPTIVE

When the rescue team returns with Amanda and the chained Dalhu to the keep, Amanda is not as thrilled to be back as she thought she'd be. Between Kian's contempt for her and Dalhu's imprisonment, Amanda's budding relationship with Dalhu seems doomed. Things start to look up when Annani offers her help, and together with Syssi they resolve to find a way for Amanda to be with Dalhu. But will she still want him when she realizes that he is responsible for her nephew's murder? Could she? Will she take the easy way out and choose Andrew instead?

6: Dark Enemy Redeemed

Amanda suspects that something fishy is going on onboard the Anna. But when her investigation of the peculiar all-female Russian crew fails to uncover anything other than more speculation, she decides it's time to stop playing detective and face her real problem—a man she shouldn't want but can't live without.

6.5: My Dark Amazon

When Michael and Kri fight off a gang of humans, Michael gets stabbed. The injury to his immortal body recovers fast, but the one to his ego takes longer, putting a strain on his relationship with Kri.

7: Dark Warrior Mine

When Andrew is forced to retire from active duty, he believes that all he has to look forward to is a boring desk job. His glory days in special ops are over. But as it turns out, his thrill ride has just begun. Andrew discovers not only that immortals exist and have been manipulating global affairs since antiquity, but that he and his sister are rare possessors of the immortal genes.

Problem is, Andrew might be too old to attempt the activation process. His sister, who is fourteen years his junior, barely made it through the transition, so the odds of him coming out of it alive, let alone immortal, are slim.

But fate may force his hand.

Helping a friend find his long-lost daughter, Andrew finds a woman who's worth taking the risk for. Nathalie might be a Dormant, but the only way to find out for sure requires fangs and venom.

8: Dark Warrior's Promise

Andrew and Nathalie's love flourishes, but the secrets they keep from each other taint their relationship with doubts and suspicions. In the meantime, Sebastian and his men are getting bolder, and the storm that's brewing will shift the balance of power in the millennia-old conflict between Annani's clan and its enemies.

9: Dark Warrior's Destiny

The new ghost in Nathalie's head remembers who he was in life, providing Andrew and her with indisputable proof that he is real and not a figment of her imagination.

Convinced that she is a Dormant, Andrew decides to go forward with his transition immediately after the rescue mission at the Doomers' HQ.

Fearing for his life, Nathalie pleads with him to reconsider. She'd rather spend the rest of her mortal days with Andrew than risk what they have for the fickle promise of immortality.

While the clan gets ready for battle, Carol gets help from an unlikely ally. Sebastian's second-in-command can no longer ignore the torment she suffers at the hands of his commander and offers to help her, but only if she agrees to his terms.

10: Dark Warrior's Legacy

Andrew's acclimation to his post-transition body isn't easy. His senses are sharper, he's bigger, stronger, and hungrier. Nathalie fears that the changes in the man she loves are more than physical. Measuring up to this new version of him is going to be a challenge.

Carol and Robert are disillusioned with each other. They are not destined mates, and love is not on the horizon. When Robert's three months are up, he might be left with nothing to show for his sacrifice.

Lana contacts Anandur with disturbing news; the yacht and its human cargo are in Mexico. Kian must find a way to apprehend Alex and rescue the women on board without causing an international incident.

11: Dark Guardian Found

What would you do if you stopped aging?

Eva runs. The ex-DEA agent doesn't know what caused her strange mutation, only that if discovered, she'll be dissected like a lab rat. What Eva doesn't know, though, is that she's a descendant of the gods, and that she is not alone. The man who rocked her world in one life-changing encounter over thirty years ago is an immortal as well.

To keep his people's existence secret, Bhathian was forced to turn his back on the only woman who ever captured his heart, but he's never forgotten and never stopped looking for her.

12: Dark Guardian Craved

Cautious after a lifetime of disappointments, Eva is mistrustful of Bhathian's professed feelings of love. She accepts him as a lover and a confidant but not as a life partner.

Jackson suspects that Tessa is his true love mate, but unless she overcomes her fears, he might never find out.

Carol gets an offer she can't refuse—a chance to prove that there is more to her than meets the eye. Robert believes she's about to commit a deadly mistake, but when he tries to dissuade her, she tells him to leave.

13: Dark Guardian's Mate

Prepare for the heart-warming culmination of Eva and Bhathian's story!

14: Dark Angel's Obsession

The cold and stoic warrior is an enigma even to those closest to him. His secrets are about to unravel...

15: Dark Angel's Seduction

Brundar is fighting a losing battle. Calypso is slowly chipping away his icy armor from the outside, while his need for her is melting it from the inside.

He can't allow it to happen. Calypso is a human with none of the Dormant indicators. There is no way he can keep her for more than a few weeks.

16: Dark Angel's Surrender

Get ready for the heart pounding conclusion to Brundar and Calypso's story.

Callie still couldn't wrap her head around it, nor could she summon even a smidgen of sorrow or regret. After all, she had some memories with him that weren't horrible. She should've felt something. But there was nothing, not even shock. Not even horror at what had transpired over the last couple of hours.

Maybe it was a typical response for survivors--feeling euphoric for the simple reason that they were alive. Especially when that survival was nothing short of miraculous.

Brundar's cold hand closed around hers, reminding her that they weren't out of the woods yet. Her injuries were superficial, and the most she had to worry about was some scarring. But, despite his and Anandur's reassurances, Brundar might never walk again.

If he ended up crippled because of her, she would never forgive herself for getting him involved in her crap.

"Are you okay, sweetling? Are you in pain?" Brundar asked.

Her injuries were nothing compared to his, and yet he was concerned about her. God, she loved this man. The thing was, if she told him that, he would run off, or crawl away as was the case.

Hey, maybe this was the perfect opportunity to spring it on him.

17: Dark Operative: A Shadow of Death

As a brilliant strategist and the only human entrusted with the secret of immortals' existence, Turner is both an asset and a liability to the clan. His request to attempt transition into immortality as an alternative to cancer treatments cannot be denied without risking the clan's exposure. On the other hand, approving it means risking his premature death. In both scenarios, the clan will lose a valuable ally.

When the decision is left to the clan's physician, Turner makes plans to manipulate her by taking advantage of her interest in him.

Will Bridget fall for the cold, calculated operative? Or will Turner fall into his own trap?

18: DARK OPERATIVE: A GLIMMER OF HOPE

As Turner and Bridget's relationship deepens, living together seems like the right move, but to make it work both need to make concessions.

Bridget is realistic and keeps her expectations low. Turner could never be the truelove mate she yearns for, but he is as good as she's going to get. Other than his emotional limitations, he's perfect in every way.

Turner's hard shell is starting to show cracks. He wants immortality, he wants to be part of the clan, and he wants Bridget, but he doesn't want to cause her pain.

His options are either abandon his quest for immortality and give Bridget his few remaining decades, or abandon Bridget by going for the transition and most likely dying. His rational mind dictates that he chooses the former, but his gut pulls him toward the latter. Which one is he going to trust?

19: DARK OPERATIVE: THE DAWN OF LOVE

Get ready for the exciting finale of Bridget and Turner's story!

20: DARK SURVIVOR AWAKENED

This was a strange new world she had awakened to.

Her memory loss must have been catastrophic because almost nothing was familiar. The language was foreign to her, with only a few words bearing some similarity to the language she thought in. Still, a full moon cycle had passed since her awakening, and little by little she was gaining basic understanding of it--only a few words and phrases, but she was learning more each day.

A week or so ago, a little girl on the street had tugged on her mother's sleeve and pointed at her. "Look, Mama, Wonder Woman!"

The mother smiled apologetically, saying something in the language these people spoke, then scurried away with the child looking behind her shoulder and grinning.

When it happened again with another child on the same day, it was settled.

Wonder Woman must have been the name of someone important in this strange world she had awoken to, and since both times it had been said with a smile it must have been a good one.

Wonder had a nice ring to it.

She just wished she knew what it meant.

21: DARK SURVIVOR ECHOES OF LOVE

Wonder's journey continues in *Dark Survivor Echoes of Love*.

22: DARK SURVIVOR REUNITED

The exciting finale of Wonder and Anandur's story.

23: DARK WIDOW'S SECRET

Vivian and her daughter share a powerful telepathic connection, so when Ella can't be reached by conventional or psychic means, her mother fears the worst.

Help arrives from an unexpected source when Vivian gets a call from the young doctor she met at a psychic convention. Turns out Julian belongs to a private organization specializing in retrieving missing girls.

As Julian's clan mobilizes its considerable resources to rescue the daughter, Magnus is charged with keeping the gorgeous young mother safe.

Worry for Ella and the secrets Vivian and Magnus keep from each other should be enough to prevent the sparks of attraction from kindling a blaze of desire. Except, these pesky sparks have a mind of their own.

24: DARK WIDOW'S CURSE

A simple rescue operation turns into mission impossible when the Russian mafia gets involved. Bad things are supposed to come in threes, but in Vivian's case, it seems like there is no limit to bad luck. Her family and everyone who gets close to her is affected by her curse.

Will Magnus and his people prove her wrong?

25: DARK WIDOW'S BLESSING

The thrilling finale of the Dark Widow trilogy!

26: DARK DREAM'S TEMPTATION

Julian has known Ella is the one for him from the moment he saw her picture, but when he finally frees her from captivity, she seems indifferent to him. Could he have been mistaken?

Ella's rescue should've ended that chapter in her life, but it seems like the road back to normalcy has just begun and it's full of obstacles. Between the pitying looks she gets and her mother's attempts to get her into therapy, Ella feels like she's typecast as a victim, when nothing could be further from the truth. She's a tough survivor, and she's going to prove it.

Strangely, the only one who seems to understand is Logan, who keeps popping up in her dreams. But then, he's a figment of her imagination—or is he?

27: Dark Dream's Unraveling

While trying to figure out a way around Logan's silencing compulsion, Ella concocts an ambitious plan. What if instead of trying to keep him out of her dreams, she could pretend to like him and lure him into a trap?

Catching Navuh's son would be a major boon for the clan, as well as for Ella. She will have her revenge, turning the tables on another scumbag out to get her.

28: Dark Dream's Trap

The trap is set, but who is the hunter and who is the prey? Find out in this heart-pounding conclusion to the *Dark Dream* trilogy.

29: Dark Prince's Enigma

As the son of the most dangerous male on the planet, Lokan lives by three rules:

Don't trust a soul.

Don't show emotions.

And don't get attached.

Will one extraordinary woman make him break all three?

30: Dark Prince's Dilemma

Will Kian decide that the benefits of trusting Lokan outweigh the risks?

Will Lokan betray his father and brothers for the greater good of his people?

Are Carol and Lokan true-love mates, or is one of them playing the other?

So many questions, the path ahead is anything but clear.

31: Dark Prince's Agenda

While Turner and Kian work out the details of Areana's rescue plan, Carol and Lokan's tumultuous relationship hits another snag. Is it a sign of things to come?

32 : Dark Queen's Quest

A former beauty queen, a retired undercover agent, and a successful model, Mey is not the typical damsel in distress. But when her sister drops off the radar and then someone starts following her around, she panics.

Following a vague clue that Kalugal might be in New York, Kian sends a team headed by Yamanu to search for him.

As Mey and Yamanu's paths cross, he offers her his help and protection, but will that be all?

33: Dark Queen's Knight

As the only member of his clan with a godlike power over human minds, Yamanu has been shielding his people for centuries, but that power comes at a steep price. When Mey enters his life, he's faced with the most difficult choice.

The safety of his clan or a future with his fated mate.

34: Dark Queen's Army

As Mey anxiously waits for her transition to begin and for Yamanu to test whether his godlike powers are gone, the clan sets out to solve two mysteries:

Where is Jin, and is she there voluntarily?

Where is Kalugal, and what is he up to?

35: Dark Spy Conscripted

Jin possesses a unique paranormal ability. Just by touching someone, she can insert a mental hook into their psyche and tie a string of her consciousness to it, creating a tether. That doesn't make her a spy, though, not unless her talent is discovered by those seeking to exploit it.

36: Dark Spy's Mission

Jin's first spying mission is supposed to be easy. Walk into the club, touch Kalugal to tether her consciousness to him, and walk out.

Except, they should have known better.

37: Dark Spy's Resolution

The best-laid plans often go awry...

38: Dark Overlord New Horizon

Jacki has two talents that set her apart from the rest of the human race.

She has unpredictable glimpses of other people's futures, and she is immune to mind manipulation.

Unfortunately, both talents are pretty useless for finding a job other than the one she had in the government's paranormal division.

It seemed like a sweet deal, until she found out that the director planned on producing super babies by compelling the recruits into pairing up. When an opportunity to escape the program presented itself, she took it, only to find out that humans are not at the top of the food chain.

Immortals are real, and at the very top of the hierarchy is Kalugal, the most powerful, arrogant, and sexiest male she has ever met.

With one look, he sets her blood on fire, but Jacki is not a fool. A man like him will never think of her as anything more than a tasty snack, while she will never settle for anything less than his heart.

39: Dark Overlord's Wife

Jacki is still clinging to her all-or-nothing policy, but Kalugal is chipping away at her resistance. Perhaps it's time to ease up on her convictions. A little less than all is still much better than nothing, and a couple of decades with a demigod is probably worth more than a lifetime with a mere mortal.

40: Dark Overlord's Clan

As Jacki and Kalugal prepare to celebrate their union, Kian takes every precaution to safeguard his people. Except, Kalugal and his men are not his only potential adversaries, and compulsion is not the only power he should fear.

41: Dark Choices The Quandary

When Rufsur and Edna meet, the attraction is as unexpected as it is undeniable. Except, she's the clan's judge and councilwoman, and he's Kalugal's second-in-command. Will loyalty and duty to their people keep them apart?

42: Dark Choices Paradigm Shift

Edna and Rufsur are miserable without each other, and their two-week separation seems like an eternity. Long-distance relationships are difficult, but for immortal couples they are impossible. Unless one of them is willing to leave everything behind for the other, things are just going to get worse. Except, the cost of compromise is far greater than giving up their comfortable lives and hard-earned positions. The future of their people is on the line.

43: Dark Choices The Accord

The winds of change blowing over the village demand hard choices. For better or worse, Kian's decisions will alter the trajectory of the clan's future, and he is not ready to take the plunge. But as Edna and Rufsur's plight gains widespread support, his resistance slowly begins to erode.

44: Dark Secrets Resurgence

On a sabbatical from his Stanford teaching position, Professor David Levinson finally has time to write the sci-fi novel he's been thinking about for years.

The phenomena of past life memories and near-death experiences are too controversial to include in his formal psychiatric research, while fiction is the perfect outlet for his esoteric ideas.

Hoping that a change of pace will provide the inspiration he needs, David accepts a friend's invitation to an old Scottish castle.

45: Dark Secrets Unveiled

When Professor David Levinson accepts a friend's invitation to an old Scottish castle, what he finds there is more fantastical than his most outlandish theories. The castle is home to a clan of immortals, their leader is a stunning demigoddess, and even more shockingly, it might be precisely where he belongs.

Except, the clan founder is hiding a secret that might cast a dark shadow on David's relationship with her daughter.

Nevertheless, when offered a chance at immortality, he agrees to undergo the dangerous induction process.

Will David survive his transition into immortality? And if he does, will his relationship with Sari survive the unveiling of her mother's secret?

46: Dark Secrets Absolved

Absolution.

David had given and received it.

The few short hours since he'd emerged from the coma had felt incredible. He'd finally been free of the guilt and pain, and for the first time since Jonah's death, he had felt truly happy and optimistic about the future.

He'd survived the transition into immortality, had been accepted into the clan, and was about to marry the best woman on the face of the planet, his true love mate, his salvation, his everything.

What could have possibly gone wrong?

Just about everything.

47: Dark haven Illusion

Welcome to Safe Haven, where not everything is what it seems.

On a quest to process personal pain, Anastasia joins the Safe Haven Spiritual Retreat.

Through meditation, self-reflection, and hard work, she hopes to make peace with the voices in her head.

This is where she belongs.

Except, membership comes with a hefty price, doubts are sacrilege, and leaving is not as easy as walking out the front gate.

Is living in utopia worth the sacrifice?

Anastasia believes so until the arrival of a new acolyte changes everything.

Apparently, the gods of old were not a myth, their immortal descendants share the planet with humans, and she might be a carrier of their genes.

48: Dark Haven Unmasked

As Anastasia leaves Safe Haven for a week-long romantic vacation with Leon, she hopes to explore her newly discovered passionate side, their budding relationship, and perhaps also solve the mystery of the voices in her head. What she discovers exceeds her wildest expectations.

In the meantime, Eleanor and Peter hope to solve another mystery. Who is Emmett Haderech, and what is he up to?

49: Dark Haven Found

Anastasia is growing suspicious, and Leon is running out of excuses.

Risking death for a chance at immortality should've been her choice to make. Will she ever forgive him for taking it away from her?

50: Dark Power Untamed

Attending a charity gala as the clan's figurehead, Onegus is ready for the pesky socialites he'll have a hard time keeping away. Instead, he encounters an intriguing beauty who won't give him the time of day.

Bad things happen when Cassandra gets all worked up, and given her fiery temper, the destructive power is difficult to tame. When she meets a gorgeous, cocky billionaire at a charity event, things just might start blowing up again.

51: Dark Power Unleashed

Cassandra's power is unpredictable, uncontrollable, and destructive. If she doesn't learn to harness it, people might get hurt.

Onegus's self-control is legendary. Even his fangs and venom glands obey his commands.

They say that opposites attract, and perhaps it's true, but are they any good for each other?

52: Dark Power Convergence

The threads of fate converge, mysteries unfold, and the clan's future is forever altered in the least expected way.

53: Dark Memories Submerged

Geraldine's memories are spotty at best, and many of them are pure fiction. While her family attempts to solve the puzzle with far too many pieces missing, she's forced to confront a past life that she can't remember, a present that's more fantastic than her wildest made-up stories, and a future that might be better than her most heartfelt fantasies. But as more clues are uncovered, the picture starting to emerge is beyond anything she or her family could have ever imagined.

54: DARK MEMORIES EMERGE

The more clues emerge about Geraldine's past, the more questions arise.

Did she really have a twin sister who drowned?

Who is the mysterious benefactor in her hazy recollections?

Did he have anything to do with her becoming immortal?

Thankfully, she doesn't have to find the answers alone.

Cassandra and Onegus are there for her, and so is Shai, the immortal who sets her body on fire.

As they work together to solve the mystery, the four of them stumble upon a millennia-old secret that could tip the balance of power between the clan and its enemies.

55: DARK MEMORIES RESTORED

As the past collides with the present, a new future emerges.

56: DARK HUNTER'S QUERY

For most of his five centuries of existence, Orion has walked the earth alone, searching for answers.

Why is he immortal?

Where did his powers come from?

Is he the only one of his kind?

When fate puts Orion face to face with the god who sired him, he learns the secret behind his immortality and that he might not be the only one.

As the goddess's eldest daughter and a mother of thirteen, Alena deserves the title of Clan Mother just as much as Annani, but she's not interested in honorifics. Being her mother's companion and keeping the mischievous goddess out of trouble is a rewarding, full-time job. Lately, though, Alena's love for her mother and the clan's gratitude is not enough.

She craves adventure, excitement, and perhaps a true-love mate of her own.

When Alena and Orion meet, sparks fly, but they both resist the pull. Alena could never bring herself to trust the powerful compeller, and Orion could never allow himself to fall in love again.

57: Dark Hunter's Prey

When Alena and Orion join Kalugal and Jacki on a romantic vacation to the enchanting Lake Lugu in China, they anticipate a couple of visits to Kalugal's archeological dig, some sightseeing, and a lot of lovemaking.

Their excursion takes an unexpected turn when Jacki's vision sends them on a perilous hunt for the elusive Kra-ell.

As things progress from bad to worse, Alena beseeches the Fates to keep everyone in their group alive. She can't fathom losing any of them, but most of all, Orion.

For over two thousand years, she walked the earth alone, but after mere days with him at her side, she can't imagine life without him.

58: Dark Hunter's Boon

As Orion and Alena's relationship blooms and solidifies, the two investigative teams combine their recent discoveries to piece together more of the Kra-ell mystery.

Attacking the puzzle from another angle, Eleanor works on gaining access to Echelon's powerful AI spy network.

Together, they are getting dangerously close to finding the elusive Kra-ell.

59: Dark God's Avatar

Unaware of the time bomb ticking inside her, Mia had lived the perfect life until it all came to a screeching halt, but despite the difficulties she faces, she doggedly pursues her dreams.

Once known as the god of knowledge and wisdom, Toven has grown cold and indifferent. Disillusioned with humanity, he travels the world and pens novels about the love he can no longer feel.

Seeking to escape his ever-present ennui, Toven gives a cutting-edge virtual experience a try. When his avatar meets Mia's, their sizzling virtual romance unexpectedly turns into something deeper and more meaningful.

Will it endure in the real world?

60: Dark God's Reviviscence

Toven might have failed in his attempts to improve humanity's condition, but he isn't going to fail to improve Mia's life, making it the best it can be despite her fragile health, and he can do that not as a god, but as a man who possesses the means, the smarts, and the determination to do it.

No effort is enough to repay Mia for reviving his deadened heart and making him excited for the next day, but the flip side of his reviviscence is the fear of losing its catalyst.

Given Mia's condition, Toven doesn't dare to over excite her. His venom is a powerful aphrodisiac, euphoric, and an all-around health booster, but it's also extremely potent. It might kill her instead of making her better.

61: Dark God Destinies Converge

Destinies converge, and secrets are revealed in part three of Mia and Toven's story.

62: Dark Whispers From The Past

A brilliant scientist and programmer, William lives for his work, but when he recruits a young bioinformatician to help him decipher the gods' genetic blueprints, he find himself smitten with more than just her brain.

A Ph.d at nineteen, Kaia is considered a prodigy and expects a bright future in academia. But when William invites her to join his secret research team, she accepts for reasons that have nothing to do with her career objectives. Wiliam's promise to look into her best friend's disappearance is an offer she just can't refuse.

63: Dark Whispers From Afar

William knows that his budding relationship with the nineteen-year-old Kaia will be frowned upon, but he's unprepared for her family's vehement opposition.

Family means everything to Kaia, so when she finds herself in the impossible position of having to choose between them and William, she resorts to unconventional means to resolve the conflict.

64: Dark Whispers From Beyond

The sacrifices Kaia and her family have to make for a chance of gaining immortality might tear them apart, and success is not guaranteed.

Is the dubious promise of eternal life worth the risk of losing everything?

65: Dark Gambit The Pawn

Temporarily assigned to supervise a team of bioinformaticians, Marcel expects to spend a couple of weeks in the peaceful retreat of Safe Haven, enjoying Oregon Coast's cool weather and rugged beauty.

Things quickly turn chaotic when the retreat's director receives an email with an encoded message about a potential new threat to the clan.

While those in charge of security debate what to do next, Safe Haven's first ever paranormal retreat is about to begin, and one of the attendees is a mysterious woman who makes Marcel's heart beat faster whenever she's near.

Is the beautiful mortal his one truelove?

Or is she the harbinger of more bad news?

66: Dark Gambit The Play

To get to Safe Haven's inner circle, the Kra-ell leader sacrifices a pawn. He does not expect her to reach the final rank and promote to a queen.

67: Dark Gambit Reliance

Marcel takes a big risk by telling Sofia his greatest sin. Can he trust her to keep it a secret? Or maybe it's time to confess his crime and submit to whatever punishment Edna deems appropriate?

Three miserable centuries of living with guilt and remorse are long enough.

Once the dust settles on the Kra-ell crisis, he will gather the courage to put himself at the court's mercy.

68: Dark Alliance Kindred Souls

A daring operation half a world away devolves into a full-scale crisis that escalates rapidly, requiring the clan's full might and technological wizardry to manage and survive.

Hardened by duty and tragedy, Jade is driven by a burning desire for revenge. When Phinas saves her second-in-command, Jade's gratitude quickly becomes something more.

69: Dark Alliance Turbulent Waters

When a dangerous foe turns the tables on the clan, complicating the Kra-ell rescue operation in unforeseeable ways, Kian and his crew bet all on a brilliant misdirection.

On board the Aurora, Phinas and Jade brace for battle while enjoying a few stolen moments of passion.

Drawn to the woman he sees behind the aloof leader, Phinas realizes that what has started as a calculated political move has evolved into a deepening sense of companionship.

Jade finds reprieve in Phinas's arms, but duty and tradition make it difficult for her to accept that what she feels for him is more than just gratitude and desire.

After all, the Kra-ell don't believe in love.

70: Dark Alliance Perfect Storm

After two decades in captivity, Jade is finally free, her quest for revenge within grasp, but danger still looms large. A storm is brewing on the horizon, gathering momentum and threatening to obliterate Jade's tenuous hold on hope for a better future.

71: Dark Healing Blind Justice

The sanctuary is Vanessa's life project. The monumental task of rehabilitating the traumatized victims of trafficking doesn't leave much time for personal life, let alone dating or finding her one and only.

When Kian asks her to help the Kra-ell, she's torn between her duty to the sanctuary and a group of emotionally wounded aliens who no other psychologist can treat.

She's the only immortal with the necessary training to get it done.

The Kra-ell culture and the purebloods' nearly androgynous alien looks shouldn't appeal to her, and yet, she finds one of them disturbingly attractive.

Is it the dangerous vibe he emits?

Does it speak to her on a subconscious level?

Or is it her need to put the broken pieces of him back together?

And why is he interested in her?

She cannot offer him a fight for dominance like a Kra-ell female would, but some strange and unfamiliar part of her wishes she could.

72: Dark Healing Blind Trust

Riddled with guilt over the crimes he was forced to commit, Mo-red is ready to stand trial and accept the death sentence he believes he deserves, but when the clan's alluring psychologist offers a new perspective on his past and hope for a better future, he resolves to fight for his life.

73: Dark healing Blind Curve

Kian is still reeling from the shocking revelations about the twins when a new threat manifests, eclipsing everything he's had to deal with up until now. In light of the new developments, Igor, the other Kra-ell prisoners, and the pending trial are no longer at the forefront of his mind, but the opposite is true for Vanessa. As her relationship with Mo-red solidifies, she is determined to save the male she loves, even if it means breaking him free and living on the run.

74: Dark Encounters of the Close Kind

Convinced that her family is hiding a terrible secret from her, Gabi decides to pay them a surprise visit.

Something is very fishy about the stories her brothers have been telling her lately. Her niece, a nineteen-year-old prodigy with a Ph.D. in bioinformatics, has gotten engaged to a much older guy she met while working on some top-secret project, and if Gabi's older, overprotective brother's approval of the engagement wasn't suspicious enough, he also uprooted his family and moved to be closer to the couple.

What Gabi discovers when she gets to L.A. is wilder than anything she could have imagined. Her entire family possesses godly genes, her brothers and her niece have already turned immortal, and she could transition as soon as she finds an immortal male to induce her. Finding a suitable candidate in a village full of handsome immortals shouldn't be a problem, but Gabi's thoughts keep wandering to the gorgeous guy she met on her flight over.

Could Uriel be a lost descendant of the gods?

He certainly looks like them, but that doesn't mean that he's a good guy or that he's even immortal. He could be a descendant of a different god—a member of an enemy faction of immortals who seek to eradicate her family's adoptive clan, or what is more likely, he's just an extraordinarily good-looking human.

75: Dark Encounters of the Unexpected Kind

Who is Uriel?

Is he a lost descendant of the gods or just a gorgeous and charming human who has rocked Gabi's world?

THE PERFECT MATCH SERIES

PERFECT MATCH: VAMPIRE'S CONSORT

When Gabriel's company is ready to start beta testing, he invites his old crush to inspect its medical safety protocol.

Curious about the revolutionary technology of the *Perfect Match Virtual Fantasy-Fulfillment studios*, Brenna agrees.

Neither expects to end up partnering for its first fully immersive test run.

PERFECT MATCH: KING'S CHOSEN

When Lisa's nutty friends get her a gift certificate to *Perfect Match Virtual Fantasy Studios*, she has no intentions of using it. But since the only way to get a refund is if no partner can be found for her, she makes sure to request a fantasy so girly and over the top that no sane guy will pick it up.

Except, someone does.

Warning: This fantasy contains a hot, domineering crown prince, sweet insta-love, steamy love scenes painted with light shades of gray, a wedding, and a HEA in both the virtual and real worlds.

Intended for mature audience.

Perfect Match: Captain's Conquest

Working as a Starbucks barista, Alicia fends off flirting all day long, but none of the guys are as charming and sexy as Gregg. His frequent visits are the highlight of her day, but since he's never asked her out, she assumes he's taken. Besides, between a day job and a budding music career, she has no time to start a new relationship.

That is until Gregg makes her an offer she can't refuse—a gift certificate to the virtual fantasy fulfillment service everyone is talking about. As a huge Star Trek fan, Alicia has a perfect match in mind—the captain of the Starship Enterprise.

The Thief Who Loved Me

When Marian splurges on a Perfect Match Virtual adventure as a world infamous jewel thief, she expects high-wire fun with a hot partner who she will never have to see again in real life.

A virtual encounter seems like the perfect answer to Marcus's string of dating disasters. No strings attached, no drama, and definitely no love. As a die-hard James Bond fan, he chooses as his avatar a dashing MI6 operative, and to complement his adventure, a dangerously seductive partner.

Neither expects to find their forever Perfect Match.

My Merman Prince

The beautiful architect working late on the twelfth floor of my building thinks that I'm just the maintenance guy. She's also under the impression that I'm not interested.

Nothing could be further from the truth.

I want her like I've never wanted a woman before, but I don't play where I work.

I don't need the complications.

When she tells me about living out her mermaid fantasy with a stranger in a Perfect Match virtual adventure, I decide to do everything possible to ensure that the stranger is me.

The Dragon King

To save his beloved kingdom from a devastating war, the Crown Prince of Trieste makes a deal with a witch that costs him half of his humanity and dooms him to an eternity of loneliness.

Now king, he's a fearsome cobalt-winged dragon by day and a short-tempered monarch by night. Not many are brave enough to serve in the palace of the brooding and volatile ruler, but Charlotte ignores the rumors and accepts a scribe position in court.

As the young scribe reawakens Bruce's frozen heart, all that stands in the way of their happiness is the witch's bargain. Outsmarting the evil hag will take cunning and courage, and Charlotte is just the right woman for the job.

My Werewolf Romeo

The father of my star student is a big-shot screenwriter and the patron of the drama department who thinks he can dictate what production I should put on. The principal makes it very clear that I need to cooperate with the opinionated asshat or walk away from my dream job at the exclusive private high school.

It doesn't help matters that the guy is single, hot, charming, creative, and seems to like me despite my thinly-veiled hostility.

When he invites me to a custom-tailored Perfect Match virtual adventure to prove that his screenplay is perfect for my production, I accept, intending to have fun while proving that messing with the classics is a foolish idea.

I don't expect to be wowed by his werewolf adaptation of Red Riding Hood mesh-up with Romeo and Juliet, and I certainly don't expect to fall in love with the virtual fantasy's leading man.

The Channeler's Companion

A treat for fans of *The Wheel of Time*.

When Erika hires Rand to assist in her pediatric clinic, she does so despite his good looks and irresistible charm, not because of them.

He's empathic, adores children, and has the patience of a saint.

He's also all she can think about, but he's off limits.

What's a doctor to do to scratch that irresistible itch without risking workplace complications?

A shared adventure in the Perfect Match Virtual Studios seems like the solution, but instead of letting the algorithm choose a partner for her, Erika can try to influence it to select the one she wants. Awarding Rand a gift certificate to the service will get him into their database, but unless Erika can tip the odds in her favor, getting paired with him is a long shot.

Hopefully, a virtual adventure based on her and Rand's favorite series will do the trick.

FOR EXCLUSIVE PEEKS AT UPCOMING RELEASES & A FREE COMPANION BOOK

JOIN MY *VIP CLUB* AND GAIN ACCESS TO THE VIP PORTAL AT ITLUCAS.COM

INCLUDED IN YOUR FREE MEMBERSHIP:

YOUR VIP PORTAL

- READ PREVIEW CHAPTERS OF UPCOMING RELEASES.
- LISTEN TO GODDESS'S CHOICE NARRATION BY CHARLES LAWRENCE
- EXCLUSIVE CONTENT OFFERED ONLY TO MY VIPs.

FREE I.T. LUCAS COMPANION INCLUDES:

- GODDESS'S CHOICE PART 1
- PERFECT MATCH: VAMPIRE'S CONSORT (A STANDALONE NOVELLA)
- INTERVIEW Q & A
- CHARACTER CHARTS

IF YOU'RE ALREADY A SUBSCRIBER, YOU'LL RECEIVE A DOWNLOAD LINK FOR MY NEXT BOOK'S PREVIEW CHAPTERS IN THE NEW RELEASE ANNOUNCEMENT EMAIL. IF YOU ARE NOT GETTING MY EMAILS, YOUR PROVIDER IS SENDING THEM TO YOUR JUNK FOLDER, AND YOU ARE MISSING OUT ON **IMPORTANT UPDATES, SIDE CHARACTERS' PORTRAITS, ADDITIONAL CONTENT, AND OTHER GOODIES.** TO FIX THAT, ADD isabell@itlucas.com TO YOUR EMAIL CONTACTS OR YOUR EMAIL VIP LIST.

Published by Evening Star Press

EveningStarPress.com

ISBN-13: 978-1-957139-98-2

Printed in Great Britain
by Amazon